ABOUT THE BOOK

Maui Murders takes place on the North Shore of Maui in the city of Paia. The area is known as the windsurfing capital of the world. The main characters are two "youthful" senior couples; a brilliant man in his midtwenties trying to escape the daunting responsibility of heading up a leading video game company; a lonely, beautiful woman in her midtwenties mourning the loss of her baby and living through an unhappy marriage; a charming ninety-something Chinese gentleman who walks daily throughout the city, greeting his many friends and having his coveted daily fi x of fried foods; the sheriff, a retired lawman from Alaska who yearns to be warm and return to his chosen field. Plus an array of memorable characters all shattered by the devastation of Maui Murders.

Maui Murders

A Novel

Kathy Callahan

Library of Congress Control Number:		2017913847
ISBN:	Hardcover	978-1-5434-5023-1
	Softcover	978-1-5434-5022-4
	eBook	978-1-5434-5021-7

Print information available on the last page.

Rev. date: 03/19/2018

To order additional copies of this book, contact:
Xlibris
1-888-795-4274
www.Xlibris.com
Orders@Xlibris.com
763306

AUTHOR'S NOTE

With full intent, the government structure for the City of Paia and the County of Maui was changed. Also knowingly altered was the makeup of the police force for the City of Paia, the County of Maui, and the State of Hawaii. (Actually, there is no State of Hawaii Police Force. Five O is fictional, like this book.)

CHAPTER 1

Donald Munson and Warren Knudson made an agreement one bitter cold Milwaukee morning as they rolled papers for their daily paper routes. They would work hard, do all types of odd jobs, save their money, and as soon as they graduated from high school, before college, they would spend two weeks in the warmth of a tropical island. It was a dream not many thirteen-year-olds would keep, but Donald and Warren were stubborn. In January of their senior year, Donald was a weekly customer at Robert's Travel Agency to see if any new brochures on summer bargains had arrived.

In March, Robert told them about a two-island special to Oahu and Maui, Hawaii, but they would have to book and pay half the down payment by the end of the month. Donald was speechless; he figured they would be headed to the Caribbean, but Hawaii—such a marvelous, faraway place! He hurried to Warren's home with brochures and details. Both boys rushed to withdraw the required amount from their savings accounts, and then they headed to Roberts Travel; their boyhood dream was headed toward reality.

In Maui, the day before their vacation ended, they took a drive to Paia (Pah-ee-ah) because a local told them it was worth a visit to see the windsurfers. He told them, once there, to ask where Ho'okipa Beach was so they can see the surfers. They figured it wouldn't cost them anything but gas money; besides, windsurfing sounded like fun. They found themselves in the funky old-fashioned town of Paia. They got directions to

Ho'okipa Beach, and what they saw awed them; out in the ocean, behind huge breaking waves, were surfers on surfboards fitted with some type of metalwork and sails. Riding the waves, their sails caught the wind and soared into the air, as a bird would catch an updraft. Donald and Warren knew this was not a sport for them, but they stayed on the beach most of the day, watching the bird people in flight.

Back at their motel, Donald announced he was not going back with Warren. He would find a summer job and stay in Maui until it was time for him to return to the mainland and start college. Warren reluctantly returned to Milwaukee; his summer job was in his father's hardware store, and there was no escape for him.

For the first time in Donald's life, he felt warm; although his pale pinkish complexion seemed to have a permanent slightly red, sunburned hue, he didn't care. When it was time to return for college, he couldn't leave; instead, he enrolled at the University of Hawaii, majoring in business. He shared a two-bedroom apartment in the low-rent part of Oahu and worked weekends and after school as a desk clerk at a motel. Becoming more experienced, he was able to upgrade to better motels/hotels and, in his junior year of college, was promoted to the billing and collections section of a high-end hotel. His cherub face, liquid blue eyes, and gentle manner served him well in a job that could leave customers with a hostel impression of their expensive vacation lodgings.

After graduating, Donald began looking for work that would pay him enough to have his own apartment, buy a couple of proper suits, and make a down payment on a good used car. One day, while checking the want ads, he saw an opening in Maui, in Paia of all places. Donald had never forgotten his fascination with that city and decided to phone and request an interview. He spoke directly with the bank manager who said he didn't want to have him pay for a flight to Maui, so he would mail him an application, and they would go from there. When

Mr. Newhouse, the bank manager, received the application and saw Donald's impressive background, he phoned him, and they arranged an interview. No other applicant's resume was as impressive as Donald's; Mr. Newhouse had found his new assistant bank manager.

When Donald saw the tiny bank, his heart sank. Nevertheless, he entered and greeted Mr. Newhouse in his usual courteous manner. Mr. Newhouse explained there was one full-time teller and a part-time teller. The assistant manager would handle all new accounts, fill in breaks and lunch at the window, and assist wherever needed. Mr. Newhouse was in charge of all loans and would train Donald in that aspect. Mr. Newhouse told Donald that he planned on retiring in the next three years, and he felt Donald would be an excellent replacement choice with the proper training. The salary was less than what he expected, but rents were lower than in Oahu, and Donald liked the old-fashioned feel of Paia.

Three weeks later, Donald arrived at his new job. Mr. Newhouse found a reasonable apartment for him to look at during his lunch break. It was a small furnished bachelor pad, just what Donald wanted. Plus, it was only three blocks to the bank and close to a market. Donald shipped everything except his clothes and personal items and, luckily, found a couple of cheap places to eat until his pots and pans arrived. After his first week on the job, Donald knew he had found the perfect home. The people were friendly, introducing themselves to Donald and welcoming him to their city.

The Monday of Donald's second week, he heard a happy laugh at the teller's window and looked up to see a beautiful Hawaiian girl. Donald walked over and introduced himself to MayLee; he was in love. There stood this lovely girl with huge brown eyes, a ready smile, and a laugh that made you want to join in on the joke. They were married six months later.

Chapter 2

The county sheriff had a substation located in Paia, the last town on the road to Hana. The station had two full-time employees: Deputy Danny Kino, a local Paia man, and nonsworn dispatcher/secretary, Charlene Griffin. Deputy Kino was well-liked by everyone and intolerant of illegal marijuana growing and its trafficking that was becoming too frequent in the area. Charlene ran the substation with an iron fist. Truant youngsters were often sent to assist Charlene with filing and answering the phones; one day with "Officer" Charlene and they decided never to miss school again. She ran a tight ship; raised by a military family and a young widow of a Vietnam officer, order was her way of life.

Donald Munson made his way to the substation; it was an important day for Donnie, one that would hopefully see his plan to fruition. Since coming to Paia, he and MayLee had three children, and he served in the city council and was now in his second term as mayor. As usual, Donnie gave the job his all; in particular, he was concerned about some of the unsavory elements coming into Paia, and he was afraid there might be more drug trafficking than Deputy Kino could keep up with. He had spoken with the county sheriff on numerous occasions about adding another deputy, but the economy being what it was, that was impossible.

Donnie talked to area merchants, and they too had concerns and were afraid of losing tourist dollars. Donnie had a plan; if he could get thirty to thirty-five of the local merchants to come up with $50 a month, they could hire a retired law enforcement officer to help. First, he would have to convince the sheriff to cover workman's compensation and provide the officer with an official vehicle. The city owned a small but well-kept trailer that sat on a beautiful spot overlooking the ocean, originally used to house a lifeguard that kept an eye on wayward swimmers. Budget shortfalls eliminated that position. They would offer the new hire a free place to live and a salary between $1,500 and $1,750 per month, which would still enable him to draw his retirement pension, as he would not be working as a sworn law enforcement officer but in a contract position.

After four months of working things out with county officials and plowing through a sea of red tape, Donnie placed an ad in a law enforcement magazine popular with retirees. To his surprise, he received over twenty replies; all, except for the ninety-year-old retiree from Texas who swore he could whip anyone's ass with or without his teeth in, were carefully considered by the city council and a merchant's committee. Three applicants were contacted via e-mail and asked several questions the council and committee had put together. Donnie was partial to one applicant, Lester Phillips, who stated one of the reasons he would like to be considered was he wanted to feel warm again.

Donnie understood that sentiment from his own experience. Lester lived in Alaska where he and his late wife retired after he left law enforcement in Nevada. His wife had family in Sitka, and since she and Lester had no children, she longed to be near the grandchildren of her brother. A freak avalanche had taken her life six months ago, and Lester was ready to leave for somewhere he could thaw out, never adjusting to the cold of Alaska.

Donnie e-mailed Lester's references, and all came back with high regard for his work ethic, his dogged pursuit to the end of a case, and his humanitarian approach to victims. Today Donnie had arranged a personal phone call to Lester's last superior in Nevada. They had agreed on a specific date and time, so Donnie sat down at the desk behind Charlene and told her, "Let's make the call, please."

Charlene dialed the number and connected Donnie to chief of police, Michael Burton.

"Hello, Mayor Munson, how are things in the land of hula dancers?" Chief Burton's voice boomed over the phone, forcing Donnie to hold it away from his ear.

"Fine, thank you, sir."

"You want to know what I can tell you about Detective Lester Phillips," Chief Burton asked.

"Yes, sir, any information will help in our selection."

Chief Burton cleared his throat and began, "You could hire no one finer. He's a real hero in this area. Lester Phillips captured that pervert serial killer, Bailey Frye. Did you know that?"

"Really!" Donnie answered, amazed that he had been so lucky to recruit such a renowned candidate. "Please continue," Donnie said.

"Frye had slain over sixteen people in the tristate area, six in Nevada alone. Two of those six were close personal friends of Lester and his wife. Lester never told me. I heard it after he retired, but he always felt Frye would someday come after him and his missus.

"Lester spent almost three years gathering clues, tracking, and backtracking, trying to get some small inkling who was committing these unthinkable crimes. One day, he stumbled upon a reference made by a recent victim to her neighbor the day before she was slain. She said she ran into this nice man who lived in a trailer park behind one of the casinos, said they had a long conversation at a local Laundromat and he seemed quite surprised that she was a happily married woman. Lester found two trailer parks that were located behind a casino, one in particular was near the Laundromat. He began staking out the location, almost twenty-four hours a day, taking photos of the cars going in and out. Lester found two residents that did not check out well. One, a teenage druggie, who was lucky he was able to make it home one night a week. The other, a man in his late fifties with no visible means of support who came and went all hours of the day and night. But the most telling aspect of this suspect was the name he used at the trailer park, F. R. Bailey. The name Bailey had come up in three of the other slayings. Lester got a warrant to search his car and trailer. The next day, while his suspect was at the supermarket, Lester opened the trunk of Frye's car and, under the spare tire, found a roll of masking tape, a long blade knife with what looked like dried blood on it, and a box of latex surgical gloves. Bailey Frye was arrested coming out of the market. The blood on the knife proved to be that of the last victim, and the slayings stopped."

"I remember that case. It went nationwide, but I don't remember the name Lester Phillips."

"Nope," Chief Burton said. "Lester shunned all publicity, and he asked me to fill in for him whenever possible. I was happy to oblige, naturally, for Lester's sake."

"Chief, whatever happened to Bailey Frye?"

"Some damned liberal judge sentenced him to the local mental hospital," Chief Burton said with disgust. "But Frye finally got what was due him, courtesy of another inmate. About four months after Frye's arrival, a delivery was being made of laughing gas to the dentistry when the deliveryman was attacked near the kitchen. This other crazy pushed the deliveryman into the kitchen area, where several kettles were on the stove, boiling hot water for the evening's pasta. One of the tanks got too close to the stove, and everything blew to high heaven. Frye had been egging the attacker on when the explosion occurred. Not much left of the deliveryman, the other crazy, and Frye. All they had to identify Frye was a tooth. Better than the other two, they were powder."

"That's some story. How did Lester take the news?"

"That's kind of funny," Chief Burton replied. "Right after he heard about the explosion, Lester said he was relieved and it was time he retired. He was gone in about a month. Real sorry to hear about his missus. She was a good woman."

Donnie was anxious to report the good news about Lester Phillips. He thanked Chief Burton and ended the call as quickly and politely as he could.

"Charlene, can you please phone two members of the city council and the merchant's committee? I need to get with them about the excellent recommendation I've received on Mr. Phillips. It sounds like he's just what Paia needs," Donnie said enthusiastically.

The meeting was scheduled for noon the next day. The two city council members and the committee agreed with Donnie that once everything was cleared through the county sheriff, he should make an offer to Lester Phillips. Four weeks later, he got approval from the county sheriff's office.

Donnie e-mailed Lester Phillips, telling him the job was his if he still wanted it and to reply back, giving Donnie a convenient date so he could make arrangements for him to fly to Maui and see Paia for himself at the city's expense.

Six hours later, he received a reply from Phillips, saying he thought the deal was off the table because of the length of time since he last heard from Mayor Munson. He had packed up his things, had sold his home with furnishings, and was in the process of moving to a warmer climate. He said he would take the job as described and was available to be on any flight Mayor Munson could arrange, the sooner, the better.

Donnie e-mailed Phillips right back that he would put Charlene Griffin in charge of getting him and his things to Maui and arrange for him to be picked up at the airport. He told him he could depend on her to get him to a warmer climate as soon as possible.

Donnie phoned Charlene and explained what he needed her to do and arrange a meeting for tomorrow between the two council members and the committee so he could announce the good news. Relief swept over Donnie, now feeling he would be able to look back on his tenure with pride, knowing he had made a difference to his beloved Paia.

CHAPTER 3

Layla Madison Morgan Richfield had never experience such excruciating pain before and welcomed every breathtakingly painful moment. This was motherhood; the sweet, devastating pain that was necessary to bring new life into the world. Layla and Kyle's beautiful baby daughter was about to make an entrance. Layla was glad to accept this burden of pain because her little girl would be the start of a real family for her and Kyle, something Layla had always dreamed of, a real family. She would see to it that theirs was a good family with lots of love, hugs, kisses, and words of encouragement; things Layla had never gotten from the globe-trotting Morgans, things Layla had missed growing up in the huge penthouse in Manhattan or the sprawling mansion in the Hamptons. Layla knew nannies and servants and people whose job it was to tend to her every need and whim, but she wanted her parents to love her and let her know they were grateful she had been born.

Most thought Layla had a charmed life, born into one of the old-money families of America. Fair-skinned with light soft curly hair and haunting deep blue eyes, she had excelled in everything she did; she knew she was only trying to please and get the attention of her parents. To everyone else, she seemed too perfect. To Layla, it was her cry for parental love. In college and graduate school, she was at the top of her class in grades, as was expected. Her degree in art history led her into art restoration, a field she loved, being surrounded by beautiful art her whole life.

Layla had known Kyle Jeffers Richfield her whole life; from the same background, they always saw each other at various functions. One day, she ran into him on a trip to Washington, DC. He was at Georgetown Medical Center getting his doctor's degree. They grabbed a quick coffee and made plans for dinner the following evening. Their dinner turned into a discussion that lasted into the early morning hours, each sharing their dreams and ambitions. Layla left Washington with a new feeling for Kyle Richfield. She and Kyle both wanted a family; he too was an only child and wanted to give his doting parents a grandchild. She envied Kyle's childhood, so different from her own; he had loving parents that encouraged him to be his own person. Although the family wealth was in banking, they were proud their son had entered the field of medicine. She hoped she would be seeing Kyle again during the holiday season and imagined she would; their paths always crossed at various parties and events that time of year. A week before one of the big parties, Kyle phoned, asking her if he could escort her to the party. She immediately said yes; the Morgan-Richfield romance began, and two years later, theirs was the ultimate in lavish weddings.

The honeymoon had been a quick five-day trip to a high-end Caribbean resort catering to newlyweds. Layla wasn't a virgin, and her times with Kyle left her feeling lovemaking was not one of his strong points. She thought he had other things on his mind and decided it was the stress of obtaining a medical degree. Kyle was doing his internship at Georgetown Medical and decided he would stay on staff there. Aside from a medical school and renowned hospital, it was also an outstanding research facility. Kyle had gone into the field of anesthesiology, following his good friend from the beginning of medical school, Kim Okamoto. Kim, from the island of Maui in Hawaii, had chosen anesthesiology because so few doctors were doing research in the field, and he believed there were large strides to be made, along with large sums of money. Kim's parents ran a small grocery store in the city of Paia on the north shore of the island. They worked many long hours to afford Kim the opportunity at Georgetown Medical, and Kim wanted to repay them. He hoped within the next five years to be able to make enough money through research and development for his parents to sell their grocery store and enjoy their remaining years work free.

Kim came into Layla's room and squeezed her hand to assure her he was there when she needed him. Kim was her anesthesiologist; Kyle, the husband/father-to-be, was not allowed to administer to Layla. Layla smiled at Kim as another contraction assaulted her body. Immediately thereafter, Kim received a page to report to his office stat. Kim told her there was plenty of time for him to run to his office and be back before the baby was ready to make an appearance. He told her Kyle should be finishing up in emergency and would be with her shortly.

Layla felt alone and scared, but she knew soon her daughter would be there for her to love, and the loneliness of a doctor's wife would be replaced with the joys of motherhood.

Kyle left Kim's office going to the nurses' station, requesting Kim be paged to come to his office stat. When Kim arrived, he asked Kyle why the hurry, and Kyle told him Mr. Tashika had phoned to change their teleconference meeting time to 3:00 p.m., which only gave them fifteen minutes to get their notes together, fresh ties and lab coats on, and ready their pitch to Mr. Tashika of Pollack Pharmaceuticals. Both Kyle and Kim had plans for research using Pollack Pharmaceutical grant funding, which would be coming their way if they could convince Mr. Tashika of their research goals. Kyle asked Kim how Layla was doing and was told she had a good hour of labor and not to worry. Kim stepped out to the nurses' station, saying he and Kyle would be on an overseas consultation and no calls or pages, as the consultation was regarding a high-level government official of a foreign country, a tale he and Kyle had devised to avoid interruptions.

Layla knew something was wrong; there had been no contractions in nearly five minutes, and she felt terrible pain in her abdomen. She rang for the nurse, and when she arrived, Layla relayed her concerns. After checking the monitor, the nurse left, saying she was going to get the doctor. Layla knew her baby was in trouble. She prayed for Kyle to come into the room, to hold her hand, to console her, to show concern about their child. Once again, she was alone and needing someone who never seemed to be there, and an old familiar loneliness crept into Layla's heart.

When the doctor arrived and looked at the monitor, he told Layla her baby was in distress, and they would be taking her in for a C-section immediately. Layla begged him to find Kyle; she needed him with her and their baby. The doctor instructed the nurse to have both Kyle and Kim paged stat. As Layla was wheeled into surgery, she prayed to God to save her baby girl and to bring Kyle to her side. Kim, she needed Kim too; where was everybody? Layla could not understand what was happening and felt panic growing by the second as she neared the massive doors to surgery.

When she awoke, Layla was assailed by the cold of the recovery room. She reached to pull the covers up and found tubes running into her veins. She felt her stomach; her baby was gone, replaced by a huge bandage, and a sudden fear jumped into her heart. *Where is my baby? Where is my husband? Is the world gone, and am I all that is left?*

Silently, Kyle walked into the recovery room and stroked her forehead. He smiled down at her and asked how she felt. The only thing Layla wanted to know was "Where's our daughter? Is she all right?"

Kyle took her hand gently into his and cast his eyes downward. He explained to her, they did not get to the baby in time, and she had died in surgery. The umbilical cord had been twisted around her neck, and she had been too long without oxygen. Layla could not grasp what Kyle was saying; she only wanted her baby. Slowly, Kyle's words penetrated her mind, and Layla realized her dream of a family was not to be; her daughter would never know the love Layla had to give. Kyle said he would leave her to rest and be back later; he was going to console Kim who had become distraught at not getting the page sooner. Kyle squeezed her hand and walked out of the recovery room. Layla knew he blamed her for losing their daughter and did not want to be in the room with the woman who could not delivery their daughter into the world.

Kyle and Kim felt terrible about the loss, but they were elated that the Pollack Pharmaceutical deal had gone through. Their future as leaders in the field of anesthesiology would be assured, and other babies could be made at a more opportune time.

Eight months had passed since the loss of the baby. Kyle and Kim had done important research and published a paper on a new drug-injection technique using a drug Pollack Pharmaceutical was already producing. This new drug-delivery technique would bring in millions to Pollack and sealed the success of Kyle and Kim in the field of anesthesiology research. In a week, they were to be honored in Honolulu, Hawaii, at a pharmaceutical convention that would bring acclaim to both them and Pollack. Kyle had insisted that Layla attend with him, saying the sun and warmth would do her good. She was still on leave from her job and had grown reclusive. Her stunning youthful appearance had now become bleak and severe. She wore her once fluffy hair pulled back tightly in a bun, and her lively blue eyes were dull and lifeless. Her complexion was pale, and she had lost fifteen pounds, making all her clothes hang on her like ill-fitting hand-me-downs. Still not venturing outside their apartment, Layla had shops deliver clothing for her to try on and selected suitable items for the Hawaiian climate.

Kim had talked Kyle into spending a week in Maui in the city of Paia where they could all relax. He thought his mom would be good for Layla to help her through her mourning period. They boarded a jet to Los Angeles, then onto Oahu and their hotel in Honolulu.

After their second day in Honolulu, there was a possible hurricane watch issued for the islands. The first chance it would hit the islands was six days away, giving them plenty of time to make the big dinner where both Kyle and Kim would be introduced and another day to get to Maui to ride out the storm.

CHAPTER 4

Wind blew through the open hotel lobby as the three made their way into the convention dining room; Layla walked between Kyle and Kim with her arm through Kyle's for support. She looked chic in a strapless pale blue silk sheath. She wore low-heeled silver sandals, carried a small silver designer purse, and her only jewelry, diamond stud earrings. Her makeup was a hint of blush, mascara, and pink lip gloss. She looked model thin, New York sophisticated, and unapproachable. Both men looked handsome in their tuxedos and walked with strides of self-assurance.

Kim had invited his mother and father who were already seated when the trio arrived at the table. Introductions were made, and Kim sat next to his father, Layla sat next to Kim's mother, and Kyle next to Layla. Layla knew she was supposed to keep a conversation going with Kim's mother, but she didn't feel up to the rigors of talk with a total stranger.

Mitsu Okamoto smiled at Layla and grabbed her hand as she was placing her napkin in her lap. Mitsu said, "I know what you have been through. Kim told me about the loss of your daughter. I too lost my first child. I was only four months along, so my loss was different from yours, but I still have the ache in my heart for that child. My husband and I were just starting our market, and we were working so hard. We were doing all the manual labor ourselves, along with tending to our customers. I was very sick the first three months and was not taking proper care of myself. I began to feel better in the fourth month, and then a terrible pain seized me as I was reaching to place something on an upper shelf. That is when I lost our baby."

Mitsu's grip tightened on Layla's hand, and she looked sadly into her eyes.

"Two years later, I became pregnant with Kim. My husband would not let me work in the market. I rested, ate well, and had a healthy baby boy. What I want to say to you is that you will have another baby, and things will be different. Get your body and mind healthy, and you and your husband can try again to bring a baby into your family."

Layla squeezed Mitsu's hand and smiled a sad knowing smile. "Thank you for sharing your loss with me. I hope, in a few years, Kyle and I can try again for a baby. You're right, I have to get both my body and mind healthy first."

Mitsu's phone gave a gentle ring; she answered, speaking Japanese, and looked at her husband with a worried grimace on her face. She related something to her husband, then turned to Layla, saying, "That was my cousin's son, who works at the airport in Maui. Because of crosswinds, it is anticipated the airport will close down at 1:00 a.m. This means unless we catch the 11:00 p.m. to Maui, we will be stranded in Oahu until the winds have quieted. We have to open the market tomorrow. We have customers depending on us to open before the storm gets worse. My husband and I will leave as soon as the speech honoring your husband and our son is finished. You and Kyle should also leave. I would feel safer if you were in Maui, and I could look in on you both."

Layla grabbed Kyle's arm and told him she was going up to their room to pack and change their plane reservations and they would leave on the 11:00 p.m. flight with Mr. and Mrs. Okamoto. Kyle was surprised; he wasn't used to Layla being so firm, and he planned to celebrate with Kim and some of his doctor friends. However, he realized Layla asked for so little, and things had been so hard for her these last months, he agreed to her request.

The flight from Oahu to Maui qualified as a theme park adventure ride. Everyone was grateful to place their feet on the solid ground of Maui. A light rain was falling and gusts of wind made the rain whirl in all directions. Kyle insisted the Okamotos ride with them to Paia instead of waiting for their relative to get off work. Gratefully, his offer was accepted. Kyle got their SUV rental, loaded everyone and their luggage inside, and drove the few miles to Paia.

On the ride to the market, Mrs. Okamoto commented on Kyle and Layla's luck to rent Joe Wong's home. It was one of the nicest rentals in the area and had a beautiful ocean view. Although she conceded, it might be a little frightening if the storm made it to hurricane proportions. At the market, Kyle helped the Okamotos with their luggage as the rain came down harder and the wind picked up steadily.

While Kyle assisted the Okamotos, Layla noticed what appeared to be a drunk homeless man asleep under a side awning of a local bar. How anyone could sleep through the noise of the wind, she could not fathom; besides, it appeared he was getting wet from the rain. Poor soul, she wondered what sadness he had endured to be in such a state.

When Kyle got back in the car, he said the Okamotos had given him simple directions to the Wong home: down the hill to their right, last house on the left. Kyle parked under an open connected carport and got their luggage upstairs and inside.

Kyle sat on a kitchen barstool with a towel, drying his hair and face. Layla looked closely at him and commented he looked a tad green. He said he felt green between the rich dinner, the roller-coaster ride to Maui, toting luggage upstairs in two homes, combined with the wind and rain; he felt queasy. He suggested they leave things packed for the night and go to bed. Layla said she wanted to clean her face and find a long T-shirt to wear to bed. Kyle went to the bedroom, undressed, and crawled into bed with a slight moan.

Layla liked the sound of the wind and roar of the surf as it crashed onto the shore below. She walked out onto the lanai and decided that it was too close to the crashing surf. She went back inside, leaving the slider open to the sound and smell of the ocean. The night air was warm; she curled up on the sofa to take in the fury of the storm.

Nighttime, when she felt so lonely, so vulnerable, when an arm around her shoulder would save her from all the emptiness she felt, an arm that never seemed to be there.

CHAPTER 5

Annie Boone stood at the kitchen sink, cutting stalks of celery into pieces and placing them in a storage bag which, when the electricity went out because of the storm, would be placed in one of five ice chests. Annie was at her best when planning things, and she made quite a few contingent plans when she heard a tropical storm or hurricane might hit the islands: one container for fruit and vegetables, one for dairy products, one for bottled water, one for condiments, and the biggest one for meat. Two weeks ago, she purchased $400 worth of meat, an excellent purchase—prime steaks, chops, hamburgers, and free-range chickens—except now it would have to withstand ice-chest storage or be grilled once power is lost. George teased her, saying her great bargain just might have caused the hurricane. Annie did not find much humor in his joke.

Thinking of George, she wondered where he was; he was supposed to begin nailing plywood sheets up to the windows that looked out on the ocean. He had gone down the beach over an hour ago, and she knew he was checking on any windsurfers he could spot farther down the shore. George always worried about the windsurfers, such a scary sport but a beautiful sight to see them soar into the air. When they first saw the windsurfers, George confessed he was not up to the sport; although still in his twenties, he felt it took skill you learned at an early age.

Annie stopped chopping, dried her hands, and walked out to their front lanai. She wore shorts and a loose-fitting T-shirt, figuring she would have to be dressed for any emergency after today; she purposely left off her bra, giving "the girls" a day of rest. She looked up the beach but no George. She wished he would come home; there was so much to do. The sky was overcast, and the large waves crashed with such force on the beach.

Annie needed George and was proud that as they had grown older together, they had grown closer, more loving, and needier of each other's touch. She had loved George for so long, she was surprised that once they retired and both their children and grandchildren were on the mainland, their love seemed to bloom once again.

She had met George in her third year at Stanford; he was in his second year, being a year younger than her. She left her last class of the afternoon and was hurrying to get back to her sorority house. Her head was down as she moved quickly around other students and teachers. That was when she ran into George literally, head first right into his chest. Although Annie was five-foot-seven, she hit six-foot-four George in the chest. He was looking into a textbook with one hand and holding a Starbucks cup in the other. Both went flying, and George grabbed Annie around the waist to keep her from falling and began apologizing for his lack of attention. Annie looked up into laughing blue eyes and heard the soft, clear, melodious tone of his voice; she caught her breath. After assuring him she was all right, he insisted she accompany him back to Starbucks, and he would buy coffee or anything she wanted. She thanked him but explained she was not one of those gals who were into the jock thing. George admitted he was an athlete, but he was an alternate on the Stanford volleyball team and wondered if that counted in her "jock" book. He looked so distressed, and those blue eyes began to sway her, and then he grinned the cutest lopsided grin that grabbed at Annie's heart. He introduced himself as George Boone, and she replied, "Annie Miller." Neither one of them ever dated anyone else after that coffee; it seemed their meeting was fated. Neither looked back, only forward with their dreams and the deep love that developed between them.

Annie went to Stanford because her father had graduated from there and insisted his daughter and only child should also attend his alma mater. Annie's father had a degree in engineering and worked for Boeing in Long Beach where the family lived since before Annie was born. Annie would have been just as happy going to Long Beach State for her teaching credentials, but her father insisted and her mother had gone back to work when Annie was thirteen, with her salary going into a "send Annie to Stanford" fund. Annie's graduation was a big thing for her parents, and she was proud to have made them so happy.

They were thrilled with George; aside from getting an engineering degree, he had developed into a much heralded volleyball player, pleasing her father tremendously. George told them a year before Annie graduated that they were in love and would marry once he graduated and had a substantial job.

Annie began teaching in the Santa Barbara Unified School District and loved helping young minds develop and learn; it was her calling, and she was an excellent teacher. Her students liked her, parents were thrilled by the way she was able to get through to their kids, and school management thought she was an excellent addition to their staff. Annie was not too well-liked by her fellow teachers. Jealousy could be one factor, but in reality, Annie was not the friendliest of people. She was the first to admit she was horrible at small talk and was often lacking in people skills; students and parents were fine, but her peers often found her standoffish. Around George, she was open in all things and never felt pressed into conversation. She felt a sense of relaxation and peacefulness around him she never felt around any other person, not even her parents.

George had gone to several recruitment days prior to graduation, where interested companies were seeking Stanford engineer graduates. One recruiter had gotten his attention because it was a work source George had never envisioned. A representative from United Airlines was there looking for a graduate who would be part of a two-man team developing long runways for the island of Maui in Hawaii to handle the new larger jets that would be dropping off tourists to the island; along with the runways, adjustments in the entire system of baggage delivery, tourist delivery, and the biggest of all obstacles, the daily deliveries of necessities that everyone on the island depended upon. The representative assured the recruits he spoke with it would probably be a lifelong position, if they so desired.

Both parents had helped plan a big wedding, which neither Annie nor George really wanted but made their parents happy. They were not so sure the news that George had accepted a position with United Airlines in Hawaii would make them happy. Annie was sorry to leave her school but knew kids in Hawaii would be as open to learning as kids in Santa Barbara with the right teacher, and Annie knew she was that teacher.

After they were married, United Airlines shipped all their possessions to Maui. George had gone ahead and found a pleasant but small apartment for them in the city of Paia because it was close to the airport and had a homey feel. Annie liked the quaint town and started putting in her application for teaching. Although the first few years she did not teach directly in Paia, she was close enough to their apartment and the commute was easy.

They decided to purchase a home as soon as possible; it would make a good investment, and besides, someday they wanted to start a family. George came home one Saturday afternoon after jogging and told Annie he had found the perfect home, right on the beach. Annie knew the prices and told him he was dreaming; they could not afford anything as expensive as beach property. George would not be deterred and phoned the agent to set up a viewing for the next day. Annie decided she wouldn't fight it; besides, it would be fun to see what a luxury beach home looked like inside. Sadly, the former owner had let the home run down terribly. The inside was dirty, the appliances needed replacing, and all the walls needed Spackle and painting. The floors, beautiful hardwood, had been damaged possibly beyond repair. The front had a sweeping lanai that was too rotten to even walk on, and the back slider dropped off steeply to a driveway that ran behind the beachfront homes. They were appalled, not understanding how someone could let such a once lovely home turn into such a dump. The agent explained the owners lived on the mainland, and their two children, out of high school for two years, had lived there, partying and bumming around.

There was a silver lining; there had been no offers on the house, and the owner was anxious to sell the home and not spend any money on repairs. The agent told George and Annie she thought she could get them into the home for about $155,000. Annie teetered; George did his lopsided grin and told the agent if she could get it down to $150,000, they would have a deal. They scrimped and saved for several years, and as both their salaries escalated, they saw their way to remodeling and, best of all, adding children to their home. Now that good deal George had gotten for $150,000 was worth over a million dollars, and to Annie, it was her dream home.

She walked to the end of the lanai that gave her the best view farther up the beach. She spotted a tall, lean, shirtless man half-jogging, half-walking headed her way. As he got closer, she waved; he stopped, looked up, waved back, and gave her his lopsided grin. Damn, she loved that man. He really hadn't changed that much, still lean and, for his age, still solid. That curly brown hair was now silver with curls at the back, and there was far less of it then when they first met. He seemed to always be a soft tan color, which only highlighted his silver hair. And those laughing blue eyes, although still laughing, found themselves behind glasses. George's large hands had made him an outstanding volleyball star at Stanford; Annie called them his bear paws. She loved the gentleness of their caress and how safe she felt when she was in their grip. Annie sighed and drew herself away from the lanai and back into the kitchen to her vegetables and her list of to-dos before the storm hit.

George was enjoying jogging with the surf crashing on the shore and the strong wind blowing; it was invigorating and stimulating. The storm clouds were intermixed with white cotton-ball clouds that hung low above the waves. He looked up and saw his Annie waving from their lanai; he grinned and waved back at her, admiring the trim, sexy grandmother that was his wife.

He recalled the first time he laid eyes on her; she was engaged in a conversation with a girl his best friend at Stanford was dating. He turned to his friend and declared that was the woman he was going to marry. His friend reminded him there were several brothers at the house that were psychiatry majors, and perhaps he should make an appointment with one of them. George asked his friend to find out who she was, what house she was affiliated with, and anything and everything he could about his wife-to-be. The next afternoon he got a report that her name was Annie Miller, and she was a year ahead of them. She was a real brain, on the dean's list. She was at their sister sorority, the one associated with their own fraternity. George could not believe he had never seen her before until he was told she was not social. She was truly into her studies, she dated a few times but nothing serious, and no rumors had ever gone around about Annie Miller.

George secretly began to follow her around and devised a plan to accidentally bump into her; today he would be a stalker. He had the exact day planned a week in advance. Two hours before they would accidentally bump into each other, he purchased a large cup of coffee from Starbucks and drank about three-fourths of it. As he approached Annie, he held the lidless coffee outward in one hand as he appeared to be reading a book in his other hand. The moment arrived and his plan worked perfectly. They had coffee together and agreed to a date the following weekend. Three weekends after that and quite a few sensual kisses later, George asked Annie if she would go away with him for a weekend. She agreed, and he raided his savings account to pay for a weekend at one of the many romantic inns in the area. George knew Annie was a reserved, somewhat shy person, and he would have to tread carefully when it came to their romantic liaison. When they arrived at their cabin, George confessed that the moment he saw her, he had decided he was going to marry her. Annie said that was great, walked up to George much to his dismay and pleasure, and began unbuttoning his shirt. George learned that weekend that shy, reserved Annie was anything but that in bed. She was shy and reserved and told him the only two places she excelled were the classroom and the bedroom.

George bounded up the lanai stairs, through the backdoor to the kitchen. Annie turned from the sink and, with one hand on her hip, said, "George, you've got to begin nailing plywood up to the windows."

George grinned and grabbed her around the waist, saying, "The only thing I want to nail at the moment is you!"

"George!" Annie exclaimed. "What's gotten into you?"

"It's the storm, the surf, it's exhilarating, brings out the animal in me, which, of course, led me directly to you," George said, drawing her even closer as he cupped her head in his hand and kissed her lustfully. With his other hand, he reached up under her T-shirt and pulled back, saying, "Honey, you're not wearing a bra."

"I figured I would have one on straight for the next few days, in case we have to evacuate, so I'm taking a little breather."

George grunted, "Huh," as he began lifting her T-shirt.

"George, what are you doing?" Annie exclaimed, pushing his hands and T-shirt back down.

"I wanted to feel those lovely breasts next to my bare chest," George said, looking innocently into Annie's eyes.

"In front of the kitchen window? I don't think so."

"Oh," George replied, crestfallen. Looking over Annie's shoulder, he said, "Do you ever get the urge to make love someplace wild and exciting?"

Annie turned and followed George's gaze, then exclaimed, "George, are you looking at our dining room table? My god, this storm has made you crazy! That's open to the world through the back lanai windows."

George grinned, asking, "We could close the curtains."

Annie shook her head, turned, and grabbed George's hand, leading him through the kitchen and dining room to the bedroom.

George gladly followed his wife.

CHAPTER 6

A clap of thunder woke George; he rolled over to find Annie sitting up on her side of the bed, her hands hugging herself.

"Honey, what's the matter?" he asked.

"I have this horrible feeling of foreboding."

George felt sure it was storm-related and put his arms around her, pulling her into him. "Sweetheart, don't worry about this storm. We've secured things as best as we can. This is just a house. It has many memories, and we've packed a lot of those memories into the Jeep, ready to go if we have to leave quickly. The main thing we have to worry about is us. This house and most everything in it can be replaced, we can't."

George held Annie until she went back to sleep, but now it was his turn to feel uneasy. He recalled the first time she had one of her feelings; she was cleaning the breakfast dishes and putting them in the dishwasher. He was rounding up the kids to drop them off at school on his way to work when Annie spotted Sally Rogers riding her bike on the street. A car turned onto the street, and Sally ran into the side of the car. One broken arm and two distraught parents later, Annie confessed to George that the night before, she had woken up with this terrible feeling of dread and had carried it with her all morning. Now she knew why. There were several other occasions where Annie had those feeling, and usually, something had happened that bore her feelings out.

The next morning George was up before Annie; he thought her anxiety from the previous night had worn her out and she was sleeping late. He could feel the change in the air, much heavier than the night before. He decided to get the plywood sheets up to the lanai windows right away. Going to their closet, he got his work shorts, T-shirt, heavy socks, an old pair of high-top hiking boots now used for working around the house and went into the bathroom to change.

A year after retiring, they couldn't decide whether to go on a cruise through the Panama Canal or have central air-conditioning installed. Each had both pros and cons, and it was truly a toss-up which one they would decide upon. So they did the only thing two well-educated people could do: they wrote "Canal" on a three-by-five card and "Air" on another. Folded them, placed them in a coffee can, and asked their neighbor, Mr. Soo, to draw for them. He picked the "Air" card, and air-conditioning was installed and used often; with Mr. Soo a frequent visitor when muggy weather arrived. George shut the bathroom window and the windows in the other two bedrooms. He quietly walked back into their bedroom and closed the slider, then walked over to the bed and threw a sheet over his wife and quietly walked out of the bedroom.

In the hallway, he turned the air-conditioning on, went to the kitchen, and started the coffee, a chore Annie usually handled. He walked down the back lanai stairs to the garage and got a coffee can of long nails and a hammer. Back inside the house, he felt the cool air coming out of the vents and knew it would be short-lived; the storm would soon take its toll on everyone's electricity, but they could enjoy it while it lasted. George wouldn't start nailing until Annie was up; he didn't want to wake her. He had coffee, fruit, and yogurt, hoping Annie would fix him a big breakfast after he finished nailing the plywood sheets up to the lanai windows. He was putting his things in the dishwasher when Annie sleepily walked into the dining room.

"George, how long have you been up?"

"About forty-five minutes," he replied, pouring a cup of coffee, handing it to her as she sat at the counter.

Annie accepted the coffee and reached her arms up to George's neck, pulling him down for their good morning kiss.

"Yum," Annie said. "You look sexy in your work clothes. All ready to start pounding?"

"Yup," George said, "I was waiting until you got up. Didn't want to wake you, thought you needed the sleep after last night."

"I'm sorry about that, honey. I hate it when I get those feelings. I hope I didn't keep you from getting back to sleep."

"No problem," he said, smiling down at her. "Well, off to the dreaded nailing task."

"Honey, I left a message on Mitsu's phone that I would come and pick up a big can of Yuban early this morning. I told her to put it on the counter, and I would leave the money under her money rock. She could put any change in the charity jar. After I finish my coffee, I'm going to get dressed and walk up to the market, then come right back home. I thought they might be sleeping as I'm sure they got in late last night or early this morning. By the way, thanks for turning the air on. It looks hot and humid out there."

"Damn, Annie!" George exclaimed. "Why didn't you think of this sooner? I hate that you are going to walk up those slippery stairs in this wind. Don't wait much longer. It will be raining soon. I get upset when you do things like this. I worry about you so much."

Annie got up and grabbed George around the middle, hugging him to her. "I'm sorry. I'm scared I'll run out of coffee. No telling how many people we'll end up feeding. and I don't dare run out of coffee. George, you know you do not want to be around me when I don't have coffee." She kissed him again, hoping to smooth things over.

Twenty minutes later, Annie, dressed in shorts, T-shirt, and an old pair of running shoes with a rain parka thrown over her, went to the lanai to tell George she was leaving and check on his progress. He had raised and secured the retractable stairs to the beach and had three windows covered. He stopped and came inside. "Annie, where's your cell phone?"

Annie went to her purse and took out her cell, handing it to George. He went to a kitchen cabinet took out a baggie, put the cell phone in the baggie, and asked her for the $20 she was taking with her, adding that to the baggie.

George handed the baggie to Annie, saying, "Carry this in your pocket, and call me if anything happens or if you need help. I have my cell phone with both the ringer and vibrator on, so I won't miss your call."

"Oh, George, you worry so. I can take care of myself."

"Damn right, I worry. I love you, got it?"

Annie felt bad at the tone she had used and reached up, pulled him down to her, giving him a loving kiss. "I'm sorry, George, sometimes I get too independent. I love you like crazy, you big lug."

George hugged her to him, then turned her around and headed her out the back slider toward the stairs leading up to the main highway. "Now be careful, watch for low-flying birds blown off course."

"My god, George, can you think of any other weird thing that could happen?" Annie asked, laughing.

George watched Annie head up the stairs as the rain began to come down; he went back to his nailing duties. He couldn't get Annie's feeling of foreboding out of his mind; he wanted his Annie back home safely.

George was right; the stairs were slippery, and the wind did not help. More than once, Annie grabbed the rail to keep from slipping. At the top of the stairs, she looked up and down the deserted Hana Highway, bolted across the street, up the stairs to the market's veranda, and around the side to the store entrance. She opened the screen door and walked inside; there sitting on the counter was her coveted Yuban. She put her money under the money rock and was ready to leave when she heard noise from the Okamotos' living quarters; the entrance was directly behind a tropical drape. Annie quietly pulled back the curtain and looked into the living room. She saw the Okamotos sitting in their recliners, Mr. Okamoto's hand holding his wife's, while the television gave current storm updates. Annie imagined they had been quite tired, to have gone to sleep in their recliners.

Annie never figured out what made her walk into the living room, around the outside of Mr. Okamoto's recliner to the television and turn the set off. She turned around to tiptoe out when she let out a silent scream and backed up into the television for support, hugging her Yuban like it was her life support.

In front of her sat the Okamotos, their heads hung loosely, both their throats were slit, and blood covered their bodies. Annie propelled herself around the recliners, out the draped doorway, through the market, and outside to the veranda. She made it as far as the front steps and hung on to the stair column for support. After several deep breaths, she backed up and sank into one of the rattan chairs on the veranda. She kept taking deep breaths and reached inside her slicker to retrieve her cell phone. She dialed the sheriff's office, and Charlene answered.

"Charlene, this is Annie Boone. Is the sheriff or Danny there?"

"No, Danny is checking flooded areas and the sheriff is on patrol. Is there a problem?"

"Yes, something terrible has happened. Have one of them get to Okamoto's Market immediately." Annie hung up and called George.

"What's happened, honey? Do you need help?"

Annie replied with a stern, serious tone. "I'm fine, but something horrible has happened, and I'll be with the sheriff for a while. Listen to me, George, and I want you to do exactly as I ask. Lock the house up, all the entrances. Get your gun from the safe, and keep it with you at all times. Someone will bring me to you, but do not leave the house. There is a crazy person out there who has committed a horrendous crime."

George could not believe what Annie was telling him but knew by the sound of her voice she wasn't kidding. "You don't want me to come for you, just stay here?"

"Yes, please, honey. You can keep our home safe, and we know there won't be anyone waiting for us while we're away." Annie saw the sheriff pull up in front of the market. "I have to go now, the sheriff is here. I'll be home just as soon as I can. I love you," Annie said and disconnected the call.

CHAPTER 7

The sheriff looked up the walkway and saw Annie Boone sitting in a wicker chair on the wraparound veranda, elbows on her knees and head between her knees.

"Christ," he muttered, rushing up on the veranda. Softly, he said, "Annie, it's the sheriff. You called the office and told Charlene you needed me here right away. How can I help you?"

Annie raised her head; her eyes were red and her voice was shaky. "Go into the Okamotos' living quarters and see for yourself. I found them."

A couple of minutes passed until the sheriff returned to Annie's side. "Annie, I'm so sorry you had to be the one to find the Okamotos. This is horrible. No civilian should have this vision in their memory."

The sheriff called Charlene. "Call Danny and have him bring two cups of hot coffee to Okamoto's Market. Then contact the county coroner. We need him here right away."

"Forget the county coroner, the roads are washed out on their side. I'll get Danny on his way immediately."

The sheriff sat with Annie, rubbing her hands; in ten minutes, Danny Kino arrived, walked up to the veranda, and handed the coffee to the sheriff, who passed a cup to Annie.

The sheriff turned and addressed Danny, "Tape off the area from the street to include the entire market area."

"What's the problem, Chief?"

"So you understand the gravity of this situation, go in the market and look into the Okamotos' living quarters, but don't touch anything."

Less than a minute later, Danny came running out, his hand to his mouth.

The sheriff yelled at him, "Don't puke on my crime scene! Go down to the curb if you're going to be sick." The sheriff turned to Annie. "I'll have Danny walk you down to your home as soon as he has this area taped off. In the meantime, go sit in my truck. It'll be more comfortable."

Annie nodded in agreement, got up, and began walking down the stairs, when she let out a shriek. "My god," she cried, "another body!" She pointed to a man slumped against the brick wall of Otis's Diner.

"Christ!" the sheriff exclaimed. "I'll check it out, but first, I want you safely in the truck."

He escorted Annie down the veranda steps, blocking her view of the wall. The sheriff walked to the body and heard snoring coming from the recognizable figure asleep against the wall.

"Damn it, Dewey. What the hell are you doing passed out here?" the sheriff asked, nudging him in the thigh.

The man moved, smiled, and said, "I went to Joey's bachelor party last night, had too much to drink, walked to Otis's for a hamburger and fries. He was ready to close but fixed me something to eat and told me I would have to eat it out here." Dewey gestured to a table and four chairs in a small covered area next to the diner. "I ate my food and just dropped off to sleep. I woke up when someone brought the Okamotos home."

The sheriff interrupted, "What time was that? Do you have any idea?"

Dewey sighed, trying to make his brain come up with the correct answer, "Oh, I remember, when I went into the market, the clock over the cooler said 3:30."

"You were inside the market?"

"Yep, I was so thirsty. Too much booze can do that to you, you know, cotton mouth?" Dewey asked, smiling up at the sheriff.

"Dewey, go on with what happened when you were in the market. Did anyone come in while you were there?"

"Sheriff," Annie yelled, "is everything OK?"

"Everything is fine. It's Dewey. He was sleeping. He had too much to drink. I'll have Danny get you home just as soon as he can," the sheriff replied.

"No, just Mrs. Okamoto and me. I told her I needed something for a fuzzy tongue, and she got me an orange soda. She said they had just gotten back from Oahu. They attended a dinner and program where her son and his coworker were honored. She said his friend and his wife brought them from the airport. They had flown together, getting the last flight from Oahu to Maui." Dewey related his story as well as his memory would serve him. "She also said they were staying in Joe Wong's rental, the one at the end of the street, on the left."

"Go on," the sheriff said, offering the other coffee to Dewey.

"Thanks, I really need this," Dewey said, accepting the coffee. "I tried to pay Mrs. Okamoto for the soda, but she said she was too tired to turn on the cash register and I should put the money in the charity jar. I put two dollars in the jar, thanked Mrs. Okamoto, left, and came back here under the awning to drink my soda. I figured I would stay here until the rain stopped. It was too windy and rainy to get home right then."

"So you just fell asleep, on the ground, with all the rain and wind?" the sheriff asked Dewey, sounding like he didn't quite believe his story.

"Well, while sitting, drinking the soda, and feeling miserable, I remembered a favor given out at the bachelor party," Dewey said with a wince on his face. "So I lit up and smoked half and sort of slipped off to sleep."

"Dewey, are you telling me that marijuana cigarettes were given out as party favors at a bachelor party, and you sat here, smoked one, and passed out?" The sheriff could not believe what he was hearing.

"Yes, sir, I'll pay a fine."

The sheriff told Dewey that Annie Boone had come into the store and found the Okamotos murdered in front of their television.

"I feel really bad. I might have been able to help the Okamotos, had I not passed out."

"Son, I doubt you could have done anything. It appears someone snuck in and committed the murders while it was raining and the wind was blowing. You probably wouldn't have been able to hear anything."

"But, Sheriff, if I heard a gunshot, I would have helped them," Dewey said with agony in his voice.

The sheriff looked at Dewey, sighed, and said, "They weren't killed by a gunshot. Dewey, I need your help now. Annie Boone found the bodies. She needs to get back home. She's in my truck. Can you please get her down the steps to her home and wait for me there?"

Dewey got to his feet and went toward the sheriff's truck with the sheriff right behind him. The sheriff said as he opened the passenger's side door, "Annie, Dewey is going to walk you down the stairs and wait at your house until I get there. It could be a while. Will that be OK with you?"

"Yes, thank you. I'll call George to let him know we're on our way. Dewey, you're soaking wet," she said, shaking her head. "I'll tell George to get you in the shower, and we'll find some of my son's clothes that he leaves behind for you to wear, and you look like you could use breakfast."

Annie was in a motherly mode, helping to distract her from the horrible vision earlier that morning.

Annie called George, "Honey, Dewey is bringing me home. Just wait for us on the back lanai. Dewey will need a shower and some clean clothes—use some of Charlie's—then he needs breakfast."

"I'll be here waiting for you both. Take extra care coming down those steps, OK, honey?"

"We'll be fine, dear. We're leaving now."

"Sheriff, you and Danny come and get breakfast when you can."

"Thank you, Annie. We surely will do that, but it will take us sometime to finish here." The sheriff herded Annie and Dewey across the street to begin their trek down the stairs.

Dewey tapped Annie on the arm and asked her, "May I carry that can of coffee for you in case you need to grip the handrail?"

Annie handed over her can of Yuban. "Thank you, Dewey. That's very thoughtful of you."

They began slowly going down the wet stairs.

The sheriff went back to his truck where it was dry and contacted Charlene. "Charlene, Mr. and Mrs. Okamoto have been murdered in their living quarters. This is a terrible situation, but we need to keep a lid on it as long as possible. Since we can't get the coroner here, can you have Dr. Tan come to Okamoto's Market?"

"Sorry, Sheriff," Charlene replied, "I got a call from Dr. Tan about five hours ago. He went to Hana to help a tourist that was having a heart attack. Only, it was indigestion, but he's stuck there until the washed-out road is repaired, which will be sometime."

"Damn," the sheriff replied, "I'll let you know what we are going to do once Danny and I talk it over. I'll contact the county sheriff and update him on the situation and see how he wants me to handle things. Call me on my cell if anything else happens. Danny and I will be at Okamoto's Market until we let you know differently."

"Sheriff," Charlene said hesitantly, "Mrs. Okamoto told me about going to Honolulu. What about Kim Okamoto? Should I try and reach him?"

"Not yet. He can't get to the island because of the weather. No sense telling him the bad news without him being able to

get over here. I'll get back to you on that one. We'll keep each
other informed."

Dewey and Annie started down the stairs, more precarious
now as a gusty wind was blowing off the ocean into their path,
along with a steady rain. They gripped the rail to avoid slipping
and finally finished their journey.

"Annie!" George exclaimed. He rushed up and grabbed his
wife as she stepped onto their covered back lanai; he hugged
her and felt her slump in his arms. "I've been so worried. What
happened?"

Dewey walked over to the large table and sat down. He also
wanted to know what exactly had happened.

George led Annie to a chair, pulled it out for her, and sat
by her side. He put his arm around her and drew her into his
shoulder. "Whenever you're ready, honey."

Annie related the horrors of her discovery, trying to
remember the terrible details so both George and Dewey could
fathom what some monster had done. She cried softly into
George's shoulder when she finished, then Dewey told them
what he knew and how bad he felt that he did not help the
Okamotos and would carry that guilt with him forever.

Dewey did not relate to either of them that he would have to
change his life as events seemed to be bringing him back to a
former life he had managed to escape from for a while. Dewey
sighed, realizing it was time he returned to adulthood.

The tension drained from Annie, so George suggested she
get out of her wet clothes. He would get Dewey into a shower
and locate clean clothes then fix him breakfast.

"George, don't leave the lanai doors unlocked. There is a
psycho out there, and I don't want us to be his next victims."

"I took your suggestion and got the gun out of the safe. I'll
carry it with me for now. Come on. Let's get everyone clean
and into dry clothes. Annie, are you going to be OK using the
shower? Will you need help?"

"No, I'll be fine. Get Dewey into the shower and find him some clothes. Oh, Dewey, give George the Yuban."

Dewey handed over the large can of Yuban. George took the coffee and frowned. "This damn coffee has caused more trouble than any of us could have imagined."

"George, I told the sheriff that he and Danny should come by for breakfast when they finished at the market."

"Sweetheart, that was very thoughtful of you. I'll fix them breakfast when they get here."

Twenty minutes later, a clean and dry Dewey appeared on the lanai. His hair was combed, and although he couldn't be sure, George thought he might have trimmed his beard some.

"How do you want your steak and eggs?"

"Medium on the steak and scrambled for the eggs, if you please. It's really kind of you and Annie to get me cleaned up and feed me breakfast."

"Dewey," George said, looking intently at him, "I've always felt there were more layers to you than any of us see. Your speech is more educated, and when we discuss windsurfing, you use terms that definitely are from someone with a knowledge of engineering."

Annie stepped onto the lanai; she wore shorts and a faded Stanford T-shirt. "Honey, what would you like to eat?"

"Scrambled eggs with grated cheddar and toast."

"No problem, coffee?"

"Lord, yes, I need another cup right now," Annie said, going to the plate on the griddle, holding an old-fashioned percolator coffeepot. She poured herself a cup of dark coffee, took a sip, and sighed. "Dewey, would like some coffee?"

"Yes, that would be great. Thank you."

"I smell food cooking" came the voice of Mr. Soo as he ascended the lanai stairs.

Mr. Soo, George and Annie's neighbor for many years, was a frequent visitor whenever grilling took place. He was certain Mrs. Soo had been trying to kill him since the day they married many years ago in China. She fed him nothing but fish, rice, and vegetables, all cooked Chinese style. The thought of fried food sent Mrs. Soo into a shrill Chinese lecture that had kept the mention of such foods out of the house for her children and Mr. Soo. Mr. Soo ate a small bowl of rice for breakfast then went to Otis's Diner for an American breakfast. He would stay away from home most of the day, greeting old friends, talking, and back to Otis's for lunch, usually a cheeseburger, fries, and malt. Although he ate a fattening breakfast and lunch, walking throughout Paia kept him slim.

Mr. Soo had the franchise for cheap trinkets from China on all the islands for many years and kept the franchise for his sons, who now ran the business. He enjoyed his retirement, except for living with Mrs. Soo; their marriage had been arranged by both sets of parents. Mr. Soo had loved another and resented from the beginning the woman he was forced to marry. Once they came to the islands, he settled her in Paia and spent most of his time in Oahu. Although he was a millionaire many times over, he never took another woman, his passion being American fast food.

Mr. Soo carried a large covered bowl of steamed rice. "Annie, Mrs. Soo thought you might be able to use this since you would probably be feeding a lot of folks, so she prepared this before the power went out."

"Mr. Soo, this is a very appreciated gift from Mrs. Soo. Please thank her and ask her to come over and join us for a meal."

Annie knew Mrs. Soo would not join the group on the lanai, but it was proper to extend the invitation.

"What's for breakfast, George?" Mr. Soo asked.

"Well, how about bacon, scrambled eggs, and toast?"

"Sounds great, lots of bacon!" Mr. Soo exclaimed.

"Be right with you, Mr. Soo, as soon as I finish getting Annie's breakfast."

"Dewey, what got you here so early this morning?" Mr. Soo asked.

George, Annie, and Dewey all looked at each other and realized they would have to bring Mr. Soo up-to-date on the tragedy that Annie had discovered.

"Mr. Soo, we have some horribly sad news," Dewey said, feeling he would be the one retelling the story. As Dewey related the gruesome details of the murders of Mr. and Mrs. Okamoto, Mr. Soo sat and looked from Dewey to Annie to George, hoping one of them would tell him this was a miserable joke. He realized by the look on everyone's faces, the tragedy was real: the Okamotos had been murdered.

Mr. Soo got up from his chair and walked to the end of the lanai and stared out toward the market. His shoulders heaved, and he offered a prayer for the safe journey of the souls of the Okamotos. Never an emotional man, tears ran down his cheeks. He and Mr. Okamoto had shared time almost every afternoon sitting on the market's veranda, talking, often venturing into the Chinese-Japanese War. They were old friends, and Mr. Soo would miss him greatly.

Turning back to the group on the lanai, he said, "I'm so saddened by the loss of my friends. They were good, hardworking people. Does the sheriff have any idea who might have committed this crime?"

"Annie and I came here as Danny was taping off the crime scene. The sheriff questioned us both and made notes of the time when I went into the market and talked with Mrs. Okamoto. The sheriff will be here and let us know the latest," Dewey said.

"I invited him and Danny to come and have breakfast," Annie said. "Mr. Soo, I think you should go home and invite Mrs. Soo to come over here where she is safe among us or at least be sure she is securely locked in your home."

"Yes, I'll do that. She will not join us but will secure herself in our home."

When Mr. Soo finished eating, he left the group, assuring them he would be back shortly.

Annie, George, and Dewey were sitting around the table, George finally eating breakfast, when a gust of wet wind came roaring into the west side of the lanai.

"Quick, Dewey," George said, jumping up and running to the bamboo curtains rolled up under the overhanging lanai awning. "We'll get these down, and that will keep the wind and rain out. Didn't expect it to change direction. I thought it would continue to come in off the ocean."

George and Dewey unrolled the bamboo shields, both of them getting soaked. Annie went inside and brought out towels.

"This is going to be one of those times when we all will end up wet no matter how hard we try to stay dry."

CHAPTER 8

The sheriff motioned to Danny, as he was finishing up taping off the market area, to come up to the veranda. "Danny, we're pretty much on our own here. Doc Tan is stuck in Hana, and the road is out. The county sheriff and coroner can't get here either because of the roads being flooded. I see the Okamotos' refrigerator section is working. Guess their generator kicked in, so we will want to keep that fueled. You and I need to get the bodies into that unit," the sheriff said.

"Sheriff, I'm not sure we should move the bodies. What about any potential evidence?"

"Son, in this humidity, those bodies will be in pretty bad shape before long. We have to take some type of action."

"I'll go check on the fuel for the generator, and I guess you're right, we'll have to move the bodies. Sure hope I'm up to the task, Sheriff," Danny admitted reluctantly.

"First, I'll take lots of crime-scene photos. The county sheriff was really specific we do that. Then we get the bodies inside the refrigeration unit, we dust for fingerprints, and we get elimination prints from Annie and Dewey. Worse, we need to get prints from the Okamotos. Lord, Danny, I wish we had ourselves a doctor. I'm not sure I can properly print a dead person. I've never done that before," the sheriff admitted.

"Damn it!" the sheriff exclaimed. "That's what I've been trying to remember. Dewey said Mrs. Okamoto told him the young man that dropped them off had shared the spotlight with their son at the event on Oahu. He must be a doctor too. He and his wife are staying at Joe Wong's rental. I'm going down to get George, and I'll bring the doctor here. George can take the wife over to his place."

"OK, boss," Danny said, feeling better, knowing he would not have to help in moving the Okamotos. "I'll fuel up the generator and lock the market. We never know when some fool might cross the tape and wander in to satisfy his curiosity."

"Great. Danny, also call Charlene and keep her updated on what we both are doing. She needs to know everything that is going on in case anyone from the county calls. I'm headed to George's."

Before crossing the street, the sheriff stopped at his truck and laid his Stetson on the back seat and grabbed a baseball cap from the glove compartment. Between the wind and the rain, keeping his Stetson dry would not be possible. He went down the slick stairs, turning a shoulder against the wind and rain. Climbing up the lanai steps, the sheriff was assaulted by the smells of breakfast; his stomach growled.

"Sheriff, ready for some breakfast?"

"No, George, I'm here to ask for your help. I've got to go to Joe Wong's rental and take the young man back to the market with me, and I would like you to bring his wife over here with you folks. Dewey, you mentioned that he and Kim had been honored together so that must mean he's a doctor. If so, he's the only one left in Paia. The county coroner can't get here 'cause the roads are flooded. George, get your rain gear on. We're going to get rained on making our way to the Wong place."

"OK, Sheriff. Annie, get the sheriff some coffee while I get ready. Dewey, come give me a hand," George said, nodding at Dewey and motioning him into the house.

Dewey looked puzzled but followed George. "Glad to help, but what can I do?"

"I want you to take this gun to protect Annie. You never know what might happen. I'll be safe with the sheriff." George undid the cargo pocket on his shorts and passed the handgun to Dewey. "Do you know how to use one of these?"

"My mom shot skeet, and she taught me."

"Skeet shooting? That seems an odd sport for a Mom."

"Mom was a tad neurotic. She said she either shot skeet or Dad. Sadly enough, she meant it." Dewey took the gun, checking to be sure the safety was on, and slipped it in the pocket of his shorts. "Don't worry. I'll take good care of Annie. Be careful. It's rough out there."

George went to the kitchen for his rain gear, and Dewey went back to the lanai.

Annie made sure the sheriff drank a glass of orange juice before he got his coffee. "All that's happening and in this weather, you need to keep up your blood sugar. We all need you, Sheriff."

The sheriff drank his orange juice and sipped hot coffee, waiting for George to reappear. The orange juice helped to stop his growling stomach. "Danny and I will be back for breakfast as soon as we can. We'll bring the young doctor too. I know you'll take care of his wife."

George came back onto the lanai dressed in rain gear. The sheriff ushered him away from Annie and Dewey. "George, time is crucial. Things are getting a bit gamy back at the market, if you get my meaning. I've got to get the doctor there right away and get the Okamotos in the refrigeration unit. We can go over to the Wong house by the rock walkway. There are rope rails on each side, and even though the slabs will be slick, we're both pretty strong and should be able to withstand the wind and water. I'll take the doc up by the road and you bring his wife to your house by the driveway. How does that sound? Are you OK with that plan?"

George thought for a second and replied, "Well, not exactly OK, but it's the fastest option. Let's go before the weather gets any worse."

George turned to Annie. "Honey, don't worry. The sheriff and I will be careful, and we'll back as soon as possible. Dewey has every means for your protection, understand?"

"Yes, I understand." Annie hugged George tightly and said quietly, "Be careful. One scare today was plenty!"

"I'll be careful, sweetheart," George said, giving Annie a peck on her forehead.

George and the sheriff went down the lanai steps and up the small slope to the rock walkway leading to the Wong house. Annie said a silent prayer for their safety.

The rain made the rock steps slicker than either man had anticipated; both gripped the rope rails tightly and looked down at every step. When the weather was good, the steps carved out of the lava rock cliff were easily accessible, especially when using the set of ropes, one on the inside wall and the other along the outside walkway. The view from the walk up to the Wong residence was spectacular and far enough away from the ocean that water from breaking waves did not hit the walkway. This, however, was navigation of the walkway during a storm, and the sheriff and George were having trouble keeping their balance while moving upward.

The sheriff realized too late he was wearing the wrong type of shoes. Cowboy boots on the slick lava rocks were making him slip even more than George was experiencing in his hiking boots, giving him traction, and yet in the wind, he too slipped occasionally.

"Damn!" the sheriff exclaimed as he slipped backward. George placed a hand between his shoulder blades and caught him before he fell.

They were almost to the lanai steps when the toe of the sheriff's boot hit an upraised slab of rock; his heel slipped, and the sheriff quickly went down and under the outside rope rail. Dangling precariously by one hand gripping the rope rail, he found himself swaying on the cliff and looking at a drop to the beach, bouncing him off a high wall of lava rock. George quickly swung around and pulled some slack in the inside rope, twisting it around his wrist, holding it tightly in his hand. With his other hand, he grabbed the sheriff's arm and began hauling him upward. The sheriff looked up and saw George motion with his head to try and turn around to face the cliff. The dead weight mixed with the wind and water was hindering George in bringing the sheriff back upon the walkway.

The sheriff reached with his right boot for some type of rock outcropping without luck. He did the same with his left boot and found a small ledge; he placed his boot on the ledge, looked up at George, nodded, and swung his body around to face the lava wall. As he did this, a jutting piece of lava rock cut through his trousers and gashed his upper thigh, sending blood down his pant leg. With the change in leverage, George pulled the sheriff upward and brought him back up under the rope rail. George saw the blood on the sheriff's pant leg but said nothing. There was no time to stop; they had to get to the lanai.

They reached the lanai without further incident; George held the sheriff around his midsection and helped him up the stairs. The sheriff turned to George and said, "You saved my life, George, and I owe you big time."

"Forget it. You would have done the same for me."

The sheriff sat down on a patio chair, and George looked inside. He saw a young woman asleep on the sofa and yelled for her to wake up. With a start, Layla woke to find a rain-soaked man pounding at her lanai door. She let out a small whimper and cowered into the sofa.

George yelled at her to be heard over the wind. "My name is George Boone! I live next door. Sitting on your patio chair with a bad cut on his leg is the sheriff. We need your husband right away."

Layla hesitantly got up from the sofa and looked on the lanai. She saw a man sitting there with a bloody pant leg, a smile on his face, and a badge in his hand.

"I'll get my husband. He's asleep in the bedroom."

Layla ran from the living room to the bedroom.

She shook Kyle. "Wake up. The sheriff is on the lanai, and he's injured. Get your bag."

Kyle sat up, got out of bed, put on the shorts Layla tossed at him, and grabbed his medical bag. He ran to the lanai and saw the sheriff and George, both rain soaked.

"What the heck happened to you two?"

"We came up the outside walkway," George said. "I live in the house across the road from yours. At the time, it seemed like the best and quickest way to get to you, but on reflection, it doesn't seem to have been a very good idea. Can you fix the sheriff up? We need to get your wife over to my house and the sheriff has to take you up the road to Okamoto's Market."

"I'm Kyle Richfield, and this is my wife Layla," Kyle said as he took out scissors and cut away the top part of the sheriff's trousers.

"Whew, looks like I'm going to be showing a little leg here," the sheriff said, grinning.

George was taking off his rain gear and wet shoes, and he turned to Layla and said, "You need to get a bag of things for both you and your husband. You'll be staying at our place until the storm blows over."

"Oh, that won't be necessary. We'll be fine here."

"No, Mrs. Richfield," the sheriff said firmly. "Someone will brief you once you get to George's."

Layla and George went into the house. Kyle cleaned the wound on the sheriff's thigh and told him he was going to put in some butterfly stitches. "I'll give you a shot so you won't feel the stitching, but you are going to have one sore leg for a couple of days."

In the bedroom, Layla lifted an expensive piece of Hartman luggage onto the bed. "We haven't actually unpacked yet, so I'll just put some of our things together and I'll be ready."

George eyed the luggage and said, "We are going outside, across the back driveway to my house in the midst of a possible hurricane. I really don't think that is the proper luggage for the trip. Do you have a duffel bag?"

"Of course not. We don't travel with duffel bags," Layla said, somewhat indignantly.

"Lord!" George exclaimed and walked out of the bedroom to the kitchen. He looked under the sink and grabbed a roll of thirteen-gallon trash bags then went back to the bedroom. "Put your things in one or two of these bags, then we'll place that bag inside another one. Tie it tightly, and it should make the trip without getting wet." He offered the roll to Layla, who took it begrudgingly.

She began sorting through the items of clothing, selecting things for a couple of days. She asked George to leave the room, and she would change into something more appropriate.

George exited the bedroom, commenting under his breath about snooty rich Easterners. He went to the lanai to check on Kyle's progress.

"How's it going out here, guys?"

"Just about finished," Kyle said. "I'll help the sheriff up the road to the market. I'm saddened and shocked at what happened to Mr. and Mrs. Okamoto. We just met them yesterday evening. They were the parents of our good friend, Kim. I realize you haven't been able to notify Kim yet, but when you can, I would like to be the one to break the news."

"Son, I have no problem with that, but we all need to get going. Things are getting worse," the sheriff said as a gust of wet wind blew onto the lanai.

George went back inside and found Layla sitting on the bed dressed in cutoffs, T-shirt, and sneakers; he had to admit he was impressed she had used such good judgment in her clothes. "What type of rain gear do you have?"

"We did not expect to run into this kind of weather. The only thing either one of us has is an umbrella."

"I can understand why this is not the type of weather expected on a trip to paradise, but your umbrella wouldn't last five seconds in this wind. Let's see what we can come up with using trash bags. You'll probably get your legs and shorts wet." George looked at Layla, hoping she would not go into hysterics or something.

Layla stepped into a bag, making a hole for both of her legs, tying it at her waist. She put the other one over her head, tying it loosely around her neck, and made openings for her arms. She put on a souvenir baseball hat that said Oahu, turned to George, and asked, "Will this work?"

"You won't receive a nod from the fashion police, but it's an excellent choice. Let's get your clothes double packed and outside. I'll put my gear back on for as little good as it did," George said, looking down at his rain-soaked clothes.

George and Layla went back to the lanai; the wind was howling even louder, the rain was coming down in a solid sheet, and the waves were huge and pounding high on the lava rocks beneath the lanai.

"We've got to leave now, folks," the sheriff said.

"Take care, you guys, and come to the house when you're done. Breakfast will be waiting."

George led Layla down the lanai steps, trying to balance the two garbage bags full of clothes. "Layla, you're going to have to help me here. I want to keep an arm on you, and I can't carry two bags and do that too."

Layla took the lightest bag that George offered, pulled her cap down, and headed toward the driveway. George noticed that neither she nor Kyle had said a word to one another, and he thought that was strange.

George walked to the left side of Layla to shield her from the brunt of the wind and rain, although staying dry would not be an option for her. It seemed like it took them forever to make it to the lanai stairs. Once at the top of the lanai, Annie handed Layla a large bath towel and helped her out of her trash bags. She then went over and began toweling George off.

"George!" she exclaimed. "What happened to your wrist? Are you hurt anyplace else?"

"I hadn't noticed the rope burn with everything else that was happening. Maybe some ointment on it when I change into dry clothes, then I'll tell you all about our adventure."

Dewey approached Layla to introduce himself and reassure her she was safe. Layla saw him coming, backed up to a corner of the lanai, and screamed.

"What's wrong?"

"You're that bum I saw passed out by the tavern wall. Stay away from me."

Gently, Dewey said, "Yes, I was passed out by the tavern, which is not my usual state. Secondly, I'm not a bum. I'm a windsurfer, and I have independent means."

"Sounds like a bum to me," Layla said, looking up gratefully as Annie came back outside.

"I can't believe you've let this person onto your lanai," Layla said, looking at Dewey.

"That's Dewey. He's like family to us. I'm Annie Boone, George's wife. Let's go inside and get you into some dry clothes. When we get back, I'll fix you some breakfast and fill you in on what has happened."

Annie picked up one of the bags and Layla the other, then they went into the house.

CHAPTER 9

Kyle used garbage bags to fashion rain protection for himself, then double-wrapped his medical bag, giving it to the sheriff to carry so he could concentrate on getting the sheriff down the lanai stairs and up the roadway; not an easy task in normal weather, made much more difficult under the current conditions. They decided the sheriff would sit and scoot down the stairs, and Kyle would hold him around the midsection to get him up the road. Very slowly, they made their way up the roadway, Kyle stopping a couple of times to adjust his grip and catch his breath. Finally at the curb, the sheriff saw Danny sitting on the veranda and motioned him to come across the road and relieve Kyle of his burden.

"My god, Sheriff, were you attacked?"

"No, Danny, I slipped and got cut on some lava rock. The doc stitched me up before we left the Wong house. I want you to go tell Joe Wong I know he doesn't have the lanai windows covered on his rental. And if he doesn't get plywood on them within a couple of hours, the fine I impose will cost him half a year's rental. I don't want all that glass on my beach when waves begin to crash into that house. I know what I'm talking about. We just left that lanai, and it's getting really bad."

"Impossible to phone Mr. Wong, but I can go over there and be back in twenty minutes, if that will help?" Danny asked, hoping that would keep him from going back into the market.

"That will have to do. Get me inside and you can leave, but be back as soon as you can. We need you here."

Danny and Kyle helped the sheriff into the market. Danny left for Joe Wong's, while the sheriff and Kyle handled things inside. Leading Kyle to the scene of the crime, he handed him rubber gloves and put on his own pair.

Kyle gasped, not realizing the extent of the crime until he saw the gruesome slashing of the Okamotos. "Jesus, Sheriff, how could someone do something like this? It takes a very sick individual to commit this type of crime."

"Not going to argue with you there, Doc. I've not moved the bodies, but I have taken plenty of photos. What I need you to do, if possible, is to determine the time of death and to take fingerprints of the victims."

"I don't have the proper probe a coroner would use, but I'll do my best to give you a rough time of death within a couple of hours. Do you have a fingerprinting kit?"

"Yes, left the kit by the counter. I'll hop out and get it while you work on the time of death."

"That was easy. Mr. Okamoto's watch broke, probably struggling, at exactly 4:11 a.m."

The sheriff nodded. "That would match with what Dewey said. It was 3:30 a.m. when he was in the market. Then Annie got here at about 6:10 a.m., which means our killer actually had a short window between the time Dewey left the market and the Okamotos were murdered. Could be he didn't realize Dewey was even here or passed out over by the diner wall. Dewey might just be lucky he's alive."

Kyle looked questionably at the sheriff. "Are you sure this Dewey person didn't commit this crime?"

"Quite sure. He passed out after smoking a joint given out at a bachelor party. He'll never forgive himself now that he found out the Okamotos were murdered while he was sleeping it off."

"Sheriff, let's get these bodies into the cooler. You aren't going to be of much help with that leg. How soon will your deputy be back?"

The sheriff looked at his watch. "About fifteen minutes, but I'm sure I can help."

"I'm the doctor, and I'm sure you can't. We can't run the risk of dropping them or doing any more damage to the corpses. We need to find something we can put the bodies on to haul them into the cooler."

"I saw a dolly back in the cooler. Do you think we could somehow use that?"

"Take me where you saw the dolly."

The sheriff hopped to the cooler and pointed to a corner area where two dollies were kept.

Kyle got the dollies out of the cooler, saying, "First off, I'm going to give you a shot for the pain. You're wincing with every step you take. Secondly, we'll wait for your deputy to get here, and he can help me get the Okamotos onto the dollies. I don't want you opening those stitches and getting your blood all over the place."

"Reckon I'm not going to argue with you. Damn leg is hurting like a son-of-a-bitch. I'm worried about Danny's ability to help. He got sick when I sent him in here initially."

"Tell him that's his damn job. This is the last thing he can do for the Okamotos, and they deserve his best."

The sheriff was impressed with Kyle's sternness, and he was right; it was Danny's duty.

Kyle found rubbing alcohol and cotton gauze on a shelf. He wiped the dollies down as best he could while they waited for Danny. He got several kitchen towels and took them along with a roll of duct tape. "I'm going to use the towels to secure the heads of the Okamotos and tape the towels on with duct tape. I don't want the heads rolling around when we move them."

Ten minutes later, Danny returned. "Joe Wong didn't want to go out in this storm, then I explained there had been a double murder, not mentioning any names and he wouldn't want the murderer to hole up in his place since the doc and his missus were staying at the Boone's. That did it. He got his sons, and when I left, they were loading plywood and getting ready to go do some nailing."

"Good work, Danny," the sheriff said. "Now put some gloves on. You are going to help the doc load Mr. and Mrs. Okamoto onto these dollies and get them into the cooler."

Danny paled as the sheriff gave him the instructions. "Sheriff, I don't know if I can do that. I got real queasy when I was in there the last time."

"Damn right you can do it, Deputy. It's your duty." Kyle snapped the sentence out and then apologized. "I'm sorry, they are the parents of a dear friend, and we need to get them into the cooler right away. Because of the damage to the sheriff's leg, it is impossible for him to assist. We owe it to these folks to make this final effort for them."

"Right, Doc, sorry for acting this way, but I've never seen this type of thing. I've witnessed horrible auto accidents, surfing deaths, but this is so cruel and inhuman, I can't understand something like this."

"You're not alone there, Danny. I don't think any of us can understand this. I've secured the neck areas, which might make it easier for you to view the corpses. We need to take them out of their lounge chairs, put each of them on a separate dolly, and get them in the cooler. Once there, I will need your help in getting their fingerprints. Are you OK with this so far?"

"Sounds good, Doc."

In under an hour, Kyle and Danny had both bodies in the cooler and fingerprinted. Danny added more fuel to the generator, and the sheriff placed a "Crime Scene" sticker on the outside doorframe of the market. The sheriff let Charlene know what was accomplished, and that all were going to the Boone's for breakfast.

CHAPTER 10

Annie led Layla to a guest bedroom to select something dry to wear. Layla took her wet clothes off and looked in a bag for dry clothes; she found bra, panties, white clamdiggers, and a white T-shirt that fell just above her waist. She slipped into the bra and panties, then turned to Annie and said, "If you will tell me where to put these wet things, I'll hang them up."

Annie looked at Layla, letting out a small gasp as her eyes fell on the reddish C-section scar. "I didn't know you had a baby."

Layla cast her eyes downward. "She didn't survive. The C-section wasn't in time, and the umbilical cord was wrapped too long around her little neck."

Annie saw the tears welling in Layla's eyes; she went over and gave her a hug. "I'm so sorry. Losing a child is an experience that must be unbearable. God was gracious to us. Both our children were born without any problems. I'm sure you will try again and have beautiful children."

"I feel that everyone blames me for my baby's death. Everything was normal until almost time for me to deliver."

"You carried her to full term?"

"Yes, there was confusion because Kim Okamoto, my anesthesiologist, thought I had another hour before delivery, so he went back to his office. While there, he was called to an emergency. Kyle, being my husband, was not permitted to be my attending anesthesiologist. I felt a terrible pain and called the nurse who got my doctor. My doctor determined there was such distress to my baby, they would have to do an emergency

C-section, and I was rushed into surgery. However, there was no anesthesiologist available. About eight minutes later, Dr. Hammond, who had been finishing up in another surgery, came and administered the anesthetic, and then they began the C-section. But it was too late. She was gone. It should not have happened. This was Georgetown University Hospital, one of the best in the nation. I was the wife of a noted doctor, but my baby was gone."

The pain in Layla's voice told Annie that she blamed herself for something that clearly wasn't her fault. She reached for Layla's hand, squeezed it, and said, "You wash your face, then come back to the lanai. I'll have coffee waiting for you, then you can decide what you want for breakfast while I fix George something to eat."

Annie got up and walked back outside. "Listen, guys, please don't say anything to Layla about the deaths of Mr. and Mrs. Okamoto. That poor girl recently lost a full-term baby in childbirth, and she's in a delicate state of mind. Kyle should tell her what had happened."

Annie walked over and scooted next to George, who was stretched out on a chaise lounge. Annie put her head on his chest and whispered, "Honey, this has been a bad day for each of us, but I listened to that poor child and I realize how lucky we are. We have two great kids, and best of all, we have each other. I don't think Layla and Kyle are getting along too well, and Layla is really suffering."

"Funny you sensed that, I got the same vibe over at the Wong place. Something was off, almost like he was ignoring her presence."

Layla walked out onto the lanai, looking pale and gaunt. Annie got up and poured her coffee. She walked back to George and asked him what she could fix him to eat.

"You probably won't believe this," he said, grinning, "but I feel for pancakes."

"George, you never eat pancakes."

"I know, must be the weather. I'm just craving pancakes."

"Coming right up. Honey, how's the wrist?"

"I put ointment on it, and that took the sting out."

Dewey sat in his chair, mesmerized by Layla. She was so pale, her hair white blond, and she wore white pants and a white T-shirt. She reminded him of a delicate china angel that his parents put on top of the family Christmas tree. Delicate, fragile, like a whisper of a person; Dewey was aware he was looking way too intently at her. Annie had whispered to them about the loss of her daughter. He couldn't believe she had lost a baby; how horrible that must be for her and Kyle. He was glad Annie had warned them not to say anything about the Okamotos.

George was at the table digging into his pancakes; Annie served scrambled eggs and toast to Layla, then sat down with a fresh cup of coffee, and Dewey continued gawking at Layla. The wind and rain were hammering the well-protected lanai.

Everyone gave a start as Mr. Soo thumped up the steps onto the lanai. "Hi, all. Yum, I smell food. Are we eating again so soon?"

"No," Annie said emphatically, "I just served George his breakfast, and this is Layla. She and her husband, Kyle, are staying at Joe Wong's rental. The sheriff asked for Kyle's assistance because Kyle is a doctor, and instead of being alone in this weather, we had Layla come stay here." Annie was hoping Mr. Soo would not blurt out anything about the Okamotos, but she feared he would not be able to contain himself.

"I have Mrs. Soo safely secured in our house and warned her not to open any of the sliders or doors unless she was sure who was out there. I feel certain she is safe. She will be sensible in this situation."

Dewey had gotten to his feet and was hoping to get to Mr. Soo before he said anything more on the subject. "Mr. Soo, come over here and sit a spell. Do you think Otis will open the diner today?"

"He might considering all that is going on at Okamoto's Market, but he will probably stay home because of the storm. Annie, good thing you and George can be counted on to feed us strays."

Layla began looking at the various faces, but no one was returning her inquisitive stares. "What happened at the Okamoto's Market?"

"You don't know?" Mr. Soo began. "Someone came in the early morning and killed them both by slitting their throats."

Layla quickly rose from her chair, tipping it over. She grabbed at her neck; what little color she had completely drained from her face. "What are you saying? Kyle and I dropped them off at their market last night after riding over with them on the airplane. My god, those are Kim's parents you're talking about."

Annie rushed to Layla's side and got her to sit back down. "I'm sorry. I thought it best to wait and have Kyle tell you, but what Mr. Soo said is true. They were murdered last night, and Kyle is helping our sheriff with the investigation. Our local doctor can't get back from Hana, and the county coroner can't get here because the roads are washed out."

Layla grabbed Annie's arm and looked at her beseechingly. "I really liked Mrs. Okamoto. She was so kind and a very good-hearted person. Does Kim know about any of this yet?"

"No, it's impossible to reach Kim, and if that was possible, there is no way for him to get here in this weather. The sheriff decided to wait and contact Kim when he's able to get to Maui. Kyle has requested he be the one to speak with Kim," George added.

"Of course, Kyle should be the one to speak with Kim," Layla said a slight edge in her voice. "I'm sorry, Annie, I'm unable to eat any more. Thank you. It was delicious." Layla got up and sat in a chaise lounge away from the group. She tucked her feet under her, turning her back on everyone, lost in her own world of thought.

Except for the noise of wind and rain, lanai activity had settled down. Annie was tucked into George on another chaise;

Dewey sat facing Layla's back, so he could jump at a moment's notice in case she needed anything; Mr. Soo sat at the table, happily munching on Fritos, enhancing each with bean dip.

The calm was broken when the sheriff's voice broke through. "Damn it, Danny, I can make it up the stairs on my own. Don't even think of carrying me! I'll hop up one stair at a time and lift my bad leg up with my hand. You stand in front and the doc will stand behind in case I slip."

"George, fire the grill up. You've three hungry men here," Danny called.

Startled, George woke up and realized with the comfort of Annie next to him, he had fallen asleep. She too had dozed off. He gently kissed her cheek and whispered into her ear, "Honey, the next wave of hungry people are here. Time for us to get back to our soup kitchen chores."

Annie hugged George to her, saying, "I would rather stay right here and have you whisper in my ear, kiss my cheek, and forget this day ever happened."

"That would be much better than reality. Unfortunately, my love, that isn't going to happen. Let's get up and take care of these guys before they decided to start cooking on their own."

"Good to have you all here safely. Sheriff, sit here." George pulled out a chair. "And the rest of you, find a seat at the table. We have steak, bacon, eggs, pancakes, and even hamburgers if you like. What will it be?"

"Steak and eggs for me, I'm starved," the sheriff said, stretching his leg out and rubbing his straining calf muscle.

"Sounds good, me too," Danny agreed.

"Bacon and eggs will do for me, George," said Kyle.

"Best I can do is scramble the eggs and grill some toast. Let me know if you want cheese in those eggs," George said to the group.

They all agreed on cheese in their eggs and toast. Annie and George began getting food on the grill when Mr. Soo chimed in, "As long as you're at it, I'll take a hamburger, please."

George and Annie grinned at each other, both knowing Mr. Soo never missed an opportunity to have a hamburger.

Dewey walked over to the group and was introduced to Kyle. He asked if there were any new developments and was told what they had accomplished at the market, and there was nothing new to report. Danny mentioned he would need to get fingerprints from Dewey and Annie once things had settled down for elimination purposes, orders from the county sheriff.

"Mine are on file with the state. As a teacher, I had to be fingerprinted," Annie said.

"No problem," Dewey said and added, "Sheriff, I will need to talk to you about something very personal shortly, after this storm blows over."

"Fine, son, but let's do wait until this storm settles down. Worst should be over in a day or two. When Danny and I are finished eating, I'm heading back to the office and sending Danny back on patrol. Annie and George, with your approval, I would like to have Charlene come stay with everyone else on your lanai. She lives alone, and I would feel safer."

"We would be happy to have Charlene join us. We have plenty of food," Annie said.

Dewey went over to Kyle and said quietly, "Your wife got very upset when she heard about what happened to the Okamotos. Maybe you could talk to her. Looks like this hit her hard."

"She'll be fine. She needs to rest and let it all soak in," Kyle said, almost ignoring Dewey.

Annie looked at George and shook her head. Neither could believe the indifference Kyle was showing to Layla.

Everyone was fed; Dewey helped Annie and George with cleanup while the three men rested briefly. Danny and the sheriff got back into their rain garb and slowly headed back up the walkway. Kyle stretched out on a chaise lounge and went to sleep.

Layla walked over to Annie and softly asked if she could have another cup of coffee. Annie poured each of them a cup, and they sat at the table. Annie told her about her teaching career and what she had been doing since her retirement. They talked quietly for almost an hour, each enjoying the other's company. Dewey sat close by, not missing a word as he became more and more enraptured with Layla, his angel. George noticed the look on Dewey's face and shook his head; he was going to have a fatherly talk with that boy.

Mr. Soo, finally full, rested his head on his arms, fast asleep. Even though the wind and rain were hard to live with, the heavy humidity was making everyone lethargic.

Late that afternoon, Mr. Soo went back to his home to check on Mrs. Soo. Dewey went with him to help carry a couple more chaise lounges back to George and Annie's as their growing guest list would need more space to stretch out during the night hours.

The next twenty-four hours, people came and went, ate and slept. The storm began to wane late the following afternoon. Danny came by to tell everyone that power would be back up for most of the city within three hours and telephone service should be up by the next morning. Kyle asked about the flights to Maui, and Danny said Maui runways had to be visually gone over very carefully and the wind had to die down more, but interisland flights were expect to resume in twenty-four to thirty hours. The sheriff would let him know when he should contact Kim. He also mentioned he should not tell Kim the extent of what happened only that there had been an accident at the market and Kyle could pick Kim up at the airport and explain the details at that time.

Kyle agreed that was the best plan and said he would be waiting anxiously to contact his friend.

CHAPTER 11

Kyle sat in the sheriff's office, ready to make the call to Kim at his hotel in Oahu.

"Anytime you're ready, Doc," the sheriff said.

Kyle dialed the hotel's phone number and extension for Kim's room. The phone rang a couple of times, and Kim answered in a sleepy voice, "Kim here."

"Kim, it's Kyle."

"Kyle, buddy, how did you weather the storm?"

"We did just fine. A group of us ended up on George and Annie Boone's lanai and spent a couple of nights and days there. They had tons of food. We ate like royalty."

"Wow, that's great. No damage to Mr. Wong's place?"

"No, it came through the storm just fine. Had a lot of wind, rain, and high surf but no damage."

"Who was in your lanai group?"

"Layla and I, Mr. Soo, Dewey the windsurfer guy, and Charlene from the sheriff's office spent the nights."

"Mr. Soo, I bet he ate all the junk food he could. Probably had George cooking hamburgers a couple times a day."

Kyle laughed. "Sounds like you know Mr. Soo. What a character."

"Annie and George are terrific people. Annie was one of my teachers in school, neat lady. George worked wonders with a bunch of us uncoordinated kids teaching us volleyball. He was a big star at Stanford."

"I didn't know that. They are great people, very generous with their hospitality. Kim, why I called was to let you know there has been an accident at the market, and I think you had better get here on the next flight."

"Are Mom and Dad all right?" Kim asked anxiously.

"Get the first plane to Maui, call me with that information, and I'll explain when I pick you up at the airport."

"I'll make the reservation right away, and I'll let you know when to meet the plane. Tell my folks I'll be there just as soon as I can."

"Fine, I'm going to hang up now so you can make that reservation." Kyle disconnected the line. He looked at the sheriff and said, "Kim wants me to tell his folks he'll be here as soon as possible. It's going to be very difficult to tell him what happened."

"After you pick up Kim, both of you come back here, and we all will go to the county coroner together. Not a pleasant task but something that has to be done. I assume that Kim will be staying with you and Layla. We can't have him staying at the market residence. The forensic unit is still going over things."

"Of course," Kyle said. Although he had not discussed it with Layla, he was sure she was able to figure out that Kim could not stay at the market and would stay with them in the spare room at Mr. Wong's.

Annie was carrying an armful of freshly washed and dried clothes to Layla for her to pack up and take back with her. As she entered the spare room, Layla was sitting on the side of the bed, her head in her hands, sobbing. Annie dropped the clothes on the dresser and sat next to Layla, putting her arm around her shoulder.

"Layla, what's the matter?" Are you feeling OK? What can I do to help?"

"Annie, I'm sorry to be such a burden. I just don't know how I'm going to handle this situation. I realized that Kim would being staying with us. I'm sure it isn't possible for him to stay at the market residence, and besides, he probably wouldn't want to do that anyway."

Annie looked at Layla, so thin and pale, and Annie's heart ached for her. She hugged her a little tighter and said, "Let me go talk to George. I think we can work something out."

Annie walked out to the back lanai where George was cleaning up after so many guests and so many meals. He was working on getting the barbecue back to ready. "Honey, we need to help Layla. She is distraught, and I don't blame her."

"What's the matter?" George asked.

"She can't face going back to that house and have Kim there once he finds out what has happened to his parents. Her grief is so great, I don't think she can take any more. Honey, can we suggest that she stay here with us for a while? You and she can go over there before Kyle and Kim arrive and get the rest of her things and leave Kyle's clean clothes along with a note telling him she will be staying with us for a few more days. She and Kyle can work things out later, but right now, she needs our help." Annie reached out and touched George's arm.

George put his arm around Annie and drew her into him. "If she agrees, she and I can get started right away."

"Thank you, I know she needs us right now. I'll go tell her what we've agreed on."

Annie returned to Layla's side. "I spoke with George, and we've come up with an idea that I think you will like. We'll pack all of Kyle's clean things in a bag, and you and George go to Mr. Wong's. Once there, pack up all your things, leave Kyle a note saying you will be staying with us for a while, and leave all his clean clothes. You and George can bring your things back here. This room is yours for as long as you like. How does that sound?"

Layla sniffed, took the sleeve of her T-shirt, and wiped her eyes. "Annie, do you and George really mean it? You would do this for me?"

"Of course, George and I are pleased that we can do this. I like having you here."

Fresh tears came to Layla's eyes as she hugged Annie. "Thank you both so much."

Annie separated Layla's clean clothes from Kyle's and placed his in a fresh plastic bag. Layla placed her things in the dresser drawer and hung a few things back in the closet. She felt a calm coming over her as she performed these simple tasks. Now she just wanted to get over to Mr. Wong's, get her things, and get back to George and Annie's.

"Annie, tell George I'm ready to go."

"George will be glad to get a break from his cleanup duties."

Annie and Layla went to the lanai. George saw them coming and put his T-shirt back on and smiled. "Ladies, at your service."

"Honey, Layla is ready to get her things from Mr. Wong's. I don't think it will take too long. She said she hadn't unpacked much, so you can be back in no time working on your grill," Annie said in a teasing tone.

"Oh, I can't think of anything I would rather be doing. I love cleaning the grill. Come on, Layla, we'll get this done, then you and Annie can fix me lunch. I need a reward after all my hard work."

Layla quickly gathered up her bags, placed Kyle's clean clothes on the bed, and left him a brief note where she would be staying. She decided she would not explain her reason. If he wanted to know more he could ask her, but she knew he wouldn't bother.

In less than half an hour, Layla was back in her room at George and Annie's, putting away her things. She would join Annie in the kitchen shortly and help her prepare lunch. She was looking forward to the warmth of this house and of the two loving people that called it home.

CHAPTER 12

Kyle waited at the arrival area for Kim's plane. He dreaded telling Kim what happened but knew it was the least he could do for his good friend. He saw the plane land and, within fifteen minutes, saw Kim walking toward him.

Kim approached with a big grin and grabbed Kyle by the shoulders, saying, "Hi, buddy, good to see you. That storm was quite an experience. Knocked out some of the ocean-facing windows at the hotel, scary. Let's get my luggage. I'm anxious to see Mom and Dad. I hope things aren't too bad at the store. There must have been serious damage. That's why they needed me here so quickly."

They retrieved the luggage and went to Kyle's rental. They loaded the luggage and got in. Kyle locked the doors, started the car, and turned on the air conditioner. He placed his arms on the steering wheel and bowed into his arms. "Kim, I have terrible news for you. I'm afraid it is much more serious than you ever could imagine."

"What the hell happened?"

Kyle explained that between the time they dropped his parents off and when Annie Boone had come at 6:30 a.m. to pick up a can of Yuban, someone had murdered his parents. He left out the manner they were murdered, deciding the sheriff could provide that detail.

Kim looked at Kyle, grabbing his arm. "Is this some type of sick joke? This can't be happening. I was ready to tell my parents they could retire. I would be able to take care of them. They could now enjoy life as they had always dreamed."

"Kim, I'm so sorry, this is no joke."

"Who did this to my parents?"

"The sheriff and a team from the county are investigating, but because of the storm, a lot of the forensic evidence were washed away. Because of the power outage, the best we could do with the bodies was to get them in the market cooler, which was kept going by the generator. So unofficially, anything the coroner might find would probably be compromised. Kim, I'm so sorry. I'll help you through this any way I can. Right now, we need to go to the sheriff's office. Then the three of us will drive to the county coroner's office and the county sheriff's office. Are you able to do this now?"

"I have no choice. I'm numb right now. I can't believe anyone could do this to Mom and Dad. They were good, kind people. They always gave people credit and never pushed anyone to pay if they couldn't. Why, Kyle?"

"I don't know. I think the theory is that someone was high on dope and did it as a thrill kill, but no one knows right now. There was money in the charity jar and money under the rock, so they don't think robbery was the motive, and it didn't appear anything was taken from the store. You'll have to speak with the sheriff for more theories and details."

"How did you get involved, Kyle?"

"I was the only medical person available, and the sheriff recruited me to help him with your parents' bodies and try to determine the time of death. That turned out easy. Your father had broken his watch, no doubt, in the struggle with his assailant. I was glad I could do this for your folks. I treated them well, Kim, with respect, believe me."

"I know you did. That is the kind of person you are, and I thank you on behalf of my parents."

Kyle backed the SUV out of the parking lot and began the short drive to the sheriff's office.

Dewey decided it was time to call on the sheriff, something he was dreading. He walked into the office and smiled at Charlene. "Charlene, I'm here to see the sheriff."

"He's in his office, waiting for Kyle to pick up Kim Okamoto at the airport. Then they are coming here, and the three of them will go to the county coroner's office. I don't think anyone is looking forward to this afternoon."

"Maybe I should come back at a better time."

"No, this is good. It will get his mind off things for a while. Let me buzz him."

"Sheriff, Dewey is here and would like a brief word with you. Is now a good time?"

"Sure, send him in."

"Remember, Dewey, a *brief* word. Don't draw out whatever you have to say."

"Yes, I understand and thank you."

Dewey walked to the sheriff's office, went in, and closed the door. "Sheriff, it's time I came clean and told you who I really am. Although I've enjoyed being Dewey the windsurfer for these past months, I'm afraid once you run my fingerprints, the truth will come out."

The sheriff sat up a little straighter, placed his arms on his desk, and folded his hands into each other, anxious to hear Dewey's confession. "Go ahead, son, I'm all ears."

Dewey cleared his throat and said, "My real name is Dewey McMaster, also known as the DewMaster to some. I'm the founder and owner of McMaster Enterprises in Salt Lake City, Utah. I'm sort of the Bill Gates of the video gaming world, and now, we are involved in digital work for the movies, hoping to give those California boys a run for their money. I'm worth millions, and I have two doctorate degrees from MIT, one in engineering and one in computer science. I graduated with both degrees when I was twenty-one and had actually made my first million by the time I was twenty. I'm now thirty. I was burned out, my brain felt numb, and I just wanted to escape for a while, get lost where no one knew me. I grew a beard, came here after seeing a special on windsurfing, and had been enjoying life as a nobody windsurfer. Once Danny said you would need to get my fingerprints, I knew it was time to get back to the real world."

"Holy shit! Even I've heard of you. Who knew you were *that* Dewey. Well, son, I'm glad you've let me know who you are. How about we get those fingerprints?"

The sheriff led Dewey out of his office and proceeded to fingerprint him, still amazed that the well-known millionaire had managed to hide his identity in Paia. Good for him, the sheriff decided. He was glad the city had made it possible for him to rest his brain for a bit.

After cleaning up, Dewey shook the sheriff's hand. "Thank you, Sheriff, I know I can count on you to keep my secret. I'll tell George and Annie. They've been so kind. I owe them, but that's it until I'm ready to leave. I'll stick around until after the services for the Okamotos. I want to pay my respects. I feel like I owe them."

"Don't blame yourself for what happened to the Okamotos. Whoever did this terrible thing would probably have killed you too without hesitation. Your secret is safe with me for as long as you like."

Dewey left the sheriff's office and walked to the local florist, buying a large bouquet for Annie Boone. She and George had invited him to dinner, and best of all, he learned Layla would be joining them. Dewey dressed in a pair of khaki trousers and a pale blue oxford shirt; he trimmed his beard and cut his sun-bleached hair a little. He used some very expensive cologne and bathed in a soap of the same fragrance. He still wasn't back to his DewMaster style but much closer.

CHAPTER 13

The sheriff, Kyle, and Kim were on their way to the county coroner's, all three dreading the moment when Kim had to identify the bodies of his parents. When the time came, Kyle had to grab Kim quickly, as he appeared to wilt when he saw the ashen bodies. The coroner kept the sheets pulled above the slit in their throats, although the sheriff had filled him in on the exact cause of the murders. After seeing the bodies, Kim reconciled himself to the devastating loss and began to sob. The sheriff left him and Kyle in the hallway on a bench, while he went to discuss things with the coroner, in particular if he had found any new evidence on the bodies.

"The killer was right-handed, telling from the way the knife was drawn across their throats. These were not young people, and both were overweight. Those two factors would make the actual slicing harder. The cartilage would be tougher, and excess fat around the neck area of each victim added to the needed strength of the murderer. The CSI team took the recliners to the lab for testing to try and determine the height of the assailant and other pertinent facts. I've sent tissue samples to the lab for analysis, but frankly, I'm not expecting to find anything out of the ordinary. The one thing I did find on the upper neck of each victim was what appears to be a mark from a Taser. I've sent samples of those areas also to the lab. If it can be determined they were Tasered, then it would make it easier for their throats to be cut. The county sheriff will fill you in on all the aspects of the case. He has my report."

"When do you think the bodies will be released to Kim? You know he lives in Washington, DC, and is on staff at Georgetown Hospital. I don't how know long he will be able to stay on the island."

"I'll speak with the county sheriff. The lab has tissue and blood samples, and as far as I'm concerned, I could release the bodies as early as tomorrow."

"I'll run that by him. We're going there next. Thank you for the information and your help."

The sheriff left the lab area and went out to where Kyle and Kim were sitting. Kim looked a little less shocked but still under a cloud of sadness that the sheriff knew would not lift for some time. "Gentlemen, we have an appointment in forty-five minutes with the county sheriff, and I thought we might stop and get a cup of coffee first. We could use some before the next meeting."

The three men left the county coroner's and walked a half block to a café and had coffee. The sheriff filled them both in on the information he learned, including the possible release of the bodies as early as tomorrow.

"I didn't learn too much from the coroner. However, he did speculate that your parents had been Tasered, prior to the actual murder because of marks he found on each of their necks. I realize this is harsh, but what I wanted you to take from this information is that it's likely they felt no pain."

"Thank you, Sheriff. It would make it easier for me to know that Mom and Dad did not feel the horrible death that was happening to them."

After coffee, they walked to the county sheriff's office. He filled them in on the latest information and speculation. As originally thought, someone or more persons were high on dope, went into the market, and committed the brutal murders as a thrill kill. Because of the storm, there were no clues, sightings, or any evidence except what the coroner believed were Taser marks on Mr. and Mrs. Okamoto's neck. This in itself was the only thing that made the thrill kill theory off base, as dopers would not likely have a Taser gun, but the theories were just that because of the lack of evidence. Tests, canvassing, questioning, etc., was still being done, but so far, there was nothing to report.

Kim asked about the release of the bodies, and the county sheriff said he had just gotten off the phone with the coroner, and he was fine with the release tomorrow. Kim expressed his gratefulness and thanked the county sheriff for his assistance; he also asked that he be kept informed if any new information surfaced. He left his cell phone number and his Washington, DC, address. Silently, all three headed to the sheriff's vehicle.

Driving back to Paia, the sheriff spoke with Kim about an idea he had regarding the services and the market.

"Kim, you know Donald Munson, right? He has contacts throughout the islands and he is a 'get things done' type of guy. Here's my idea. Let him handle getting your folks back to Paia. Let him take care of the services, and he will do this with the highest respect for you and your family. He can arrange to have people come in and clean up the market area, and I don't imagine you want to keep the market running. He can arrange to dispose of the nonperishables, and the perishables that are still good, he can give to one of the island's local shelters. He can have the market cleaned up. It's now full of fingerprint dust. He will hire all the help needed to do a good and swift job. I don't know what you want to do with the residence area. Perhaps you and Kyle should discuss that, but let Donald help with everything."

"Sheriff, thank you. Donald is exactly the person I want and trust to handle the things you outlined. It is our custom to have the dead cremated. I imagine he can arrange with the local agency to do that, and there should be some type of service. I know Donald, his heart is good. I'm not able to make these plans, and I trust him."

"I'll phone him as soon as we get back to the office. You could speak with him at that time if you like."

"Yes, I want him to understand the arrangements I envision for my parents and that money is no object. They would want their ashes scattered into the Pacific." Kim broke down and began to sob once again. No one said any more until they reached the sheriff's office.

CHAPTER 14

Dewey knocked on the back lanai screen door and heard Annie yell, "Come on in, Dewey!"

He slid the screen open and went to the kitchen where Annie was preparing dinner. He held out the huge bouquet of flowers, saying, "This is for the best hostess in all of Maui."

"Dewey, thank you. You shouldn't have gone to all that expense on my account."

George walked into the kitchen, stopping short when he saw the huge mass of flowers. "Dewey, did you bring those? That's a couple of hundred dollars' worth of flowers."

"It's one way I could express my appreciation for taking me in during the hurricane. It meant a lot to me, how generous you both were to a wet and stinky windsurfer."

"Dewey, you know I've always thought you were something other than just a windsurfer, and looking at you now, I'm almost sure of my original estimation," George said.

"George, let's go out front and have a little talk."

They walked to the lanai where ocean waves could be seen breaking onto the shore. Annie was getting vases from her breakfront to handle the massive bouquet of flowers. Layla came out to the kitchen and, seeing the huge amount of flowers, lent Annie a hand in arranging them. Annie explained they were a thank-you gift from Dewey.

"Heavens, he might just as well have bought you the whole flower shop."

"George, you were right from the start. I'm a fugitive from the corporate world. I burned out at the ripe old age of thirty. I needed to escape where no one knew me, where I could rest my brain. The death of the Okamotos and knowing I would have to be fingerprinted brought me back to reality. You were right about my engineering references. I just couldn't control myself. I have a doctorate from MIT in both engineering and computer science. My real name is Dewey McMaster."

"I knew it, but I never dreamed you were *the* Dewey McMaster. You're famous, a genius, a legend in the computer-gaming world. Who else knows?"

"Only the sheriff and now you. You can tell Annie but no one else, especially not Layla. I want to get cleaned up more. I've contacted my secretary, and she'll be sending clothes with my jet when it comes over to take me back to Utah. I need a couple of more days to say goodbye to my fellow windsurfers, thank them for accepting me as one of their own and teaching me to be one of the bird people, and attend the funeral.

"By the way, George, we are doing something different at our studios. We're working on a new digital process to be used in movies, television, music videos, etc. I've got a great crew working on the new programs, and we are very close to finishing the final process. I'm anxious to get back to this aspect of my business."

Annie and Layla stepped out onto the lanai.

"What are you two being so secretive about?" Annie asked.

"Just guy talk. How's dinner coming along? I'm starved."

"That's what we came to tell you. Let's eat!"

Everyone went back inside, sat at the dining room table, well adorned with flowers, and enjoyed their meal. After dinner, Layla and Annie cleared the table and loaded the dishwasher. Dewey and George went back on the front lanai and discussed windsurfing from the viewpoint of two engineers.

Annie brought mugs of coffee for everyone; they sat down around the table to watch the orange ball of sun slide into the ocean.

There was not much conversation, everyone in his or her own thoughts, enjoying the sunset.

"George, do you and Annie have cable?"

"Sure, Dewey, why something on you want to see?"

"In about ten minutes, there's a movie I would like to watch. The technical work is excellent for its time. I've seen the movie. It's a comedy, so it will be fun."

"OK, let's go watch Dewey's comedy." George got up and herded the others into the living room. George and Annie sat in stylish recliners, and Dewey and Layla sat on the sofa, each on separate ends. "What is it we are going to be watching?"

"It's called *G-Force*, and it's part animation, but I think you'll get a kick out of it."

By the middle of the movie, everyone was laughing, Layla was caught up in the fun with the hamsters in the movie. Afterward, Dewey thanked everyone for a great evening, especially Annie for such a wonderful dinner. George accompanied him down the back lanai steps and asked him if he could give him a ride.

"No, thanks, George. I left my Escalade parked a couple of blocks up. I make sure no one sees me getting out or in. I would hate to blow my cover. The windows are tinted, and no one has caught me yet. Not too much longer hiding, which, in all honesty, was becoming a little old. Thanks again, George. I enjoyed our talk. Take care."

Dewey turned and walked up to the main street, his mind on Layla. He recalled her soft laughter as she watched the movie. He wanted to slide over to her, put his arm around her, and hold her tight, but holding an angel can be so difficult.

George strolled back to the house, closing and locking the lanai door. He turned on the air conditioner, asking Annie and Layla if all other windows and doors were locked securely. No one in Paia was leaving their doors or windows open; everyone was living under air conditioner or fans while they slept.

Layla turned to George and Annie and said, "I want to thank you both for a great evening, a terrific dinner, and I have to admit I enjoyed the movie."

"You're quite welcome." George smiled at Layla. "Dewey is like an onion, not just any onion, but a Maui onion. There are many layers but a very sweet core."

Both ladies looked at each other, shook their heads, and smiled walking to their respective bedrooms. George followed Annie who had sat down and began removing her makeup. George sat next to her on the bench, and putting his arm around her, he said, "Well, I was right. I knew it. He couldn't fool me."

"George, first your Maui onion speech, now this little tidbit. What's going on?"

"Dewey has a doctorate from MIT in engineering and computer science. You might know him by his full name, Dewey McMaster."

"That name is familiar. Where do I know it from?"

"Perhaps when your grandkids visited and you had to pull them away from their McMaster video games. He told me he had a burnout and just dropped out for six months. Now he's ready to get back to work. How about that onion?" George was beaming at the news he relayed to Annie.

"Annie, you can't tell anybody, especially Layla. Dewey said he's only told the sheriff and us and isn't ready for Layla to know yet. I told him his secret was safe with us."

"Your intuition was right, and my lips are sealed."

"Sealing your lips is my job." George reached around Annie's waist and drew her into him, kissing her lovingly.

CHAPTER 15

Donald Munson was using every resource he had to ensure the Okamotos had the best funeral possible. He was meeting this afternoon with Kim and Kyle to go over the plans. He had pulled the proverbial strings and had the bodies cremated directly instead of the usual wait, as only a few number of bodies were cremated per day, pollution the culprit in this instance.

Friends from his church had gone to the market and threw out what was old, cleaned the shelves, and took the good perishables to a shelter. A pickup truck full of usable items was taken to the local food bank and donated in the name of Mr. and Mrs. Okamoto. Donald saw to it that a notice was in the local papers, making sure the date and time of the funeral was made public in a half-page article on the contributions the Okamotos had made to Paia. Donald Munson was planning a huge turnout for the funeral, which was one reason he had scheduled it at 10:00 a.m. on Saturday.

Donald knocked on the door of the Wong rental and was met by Kyle. They introduced themselves; Kyle thanked Donald for his work on Kim's behalf and motioned Donald to a seat on one of the facing sofas. Kyle sat on the sofa opposite Donald next to Kim.

"Donald, no words can express my appreciation for what you have done for my parents and for me. I wanted to explain something to you so that you do not think harshly of my decision. When I saw my parents at the county coroner's, I did not want to see them again in that condition, no matter how much they were made-up. I wanted my last memories of them to be in Oahu the night I received recognition for my work. They were smiling and laughing, so happy and proud. It made my years of hard work and being away from home seem so worthwhile, to see the joy it brought to their faces, and that is how I wanted to remember them."

"I applaud your decision. I too believe that the last memories of our loved ones should be when they are alive, not when they have been claimed by death."

"Thank you, Donald. I know you are responsible for the wonderful newspaper article. I have several copies which I will cherish always."

"Everything I said about them was true. They were loved by many here in Paia. Let me tell you what I have planned for the services. It is open to your approval, and please do not hesitate to make any changes.

"I have secured the use of the lookout above Ho'okipa Beach Park. There will be windsurfers below, but somehow I think your parents would enjoy that. I found a beautiful portrait they had painted on their fortieth wedding anniversary. I had it blown up, and it will be displayed with the two urns containing your parents' remains on a table in front. I will host the ceremonies, and if you choose to speak, that would be wonderful. However, I realize that will be difficult. There will be several speakers, and after everyone has spoken, you will be taken directly to a boat that will go out to sea with both urns. You will release the ashes and throw leis in the ocean. Those on shore will be watching this ceremony from high above on the lookout. After that, I have arranged for a buffet to be served on the beach. Upon your return, you can thank folks, shake hands, etc. How is all this sounding?"

"Donald, it's masterful. Your plans seem flawless. Yes, I wish to speak at the service, to honor my parents before all those in attendance. I'm not sure it will be the best speech, but it will be from my heart. Thank you, Donald," Kim said as he rose from the sofa and offered his hand to Donald.

Donald could see the strain on Kim's face and took his leave.

*　　*　　*

Layla joined Annie at the counter after pouring herself a cup of coffee. "Where's George this morning?"

"He's on the beach, enjoying his morning walk or jog or whatever he calls it. He likes the freedom of his thoughts. He says his mind works wonders when he's out on the sand."

"Annie, last night was the best time I've had since I came home from the hospital, and I made a decision while I lay in bed. You all are so good to me, and Dewey truly is a gentleman. It made me realize life could get better if I just let it. I must go over and pay my condolences to Kim and have a talk with Kyle. Before I go, however, I'm going to call my booking agent in New York and see if there is any restoration work available. I need to get back to work and back to New York. I still have the family brownstone. All I have to do is move a few things back from Washington and I'm home once more. I think it's time Kyle and I went our separate ways. We hardly speak, and I believe what once was between us is now lost forever."

"I usually don't agree when someone wants to get a divorce. However, in your case, it's a wise decision. To stay would only lead you into a deeper depression, and I think you realize things can get better. I hope there is work for you, but even if there isn't, you should go back to New York. I'm sure you have many friends who would welcome you."

"You're right, Annie, I need to get back to a life of the living. I'll make my New York call right away. It doesn't matter though. I'm still going to speak with Kyle, and I'm going back to New York."

With purpose, Layla made the journey to the Wong rental. She found Kyle sitting in a lounge chair, his eyes closed. "Kyle, I've come to see Kim."

"Layla, I've been meaning to come over and see you. Things have been so hectic around here. I'm sorry. I should have made more of an effort."

"Don't worry. Annie and George have been looking after me. Do you think it is OK if I see Kim?"

"I'm sure he would welcome your visit. He's working on what he wants to say at the memorial, which will be Saturday at 10:00 a.m., all the details are in the paper. Of course, you, George, and Annie will attend."

"Certainly, we'll attend," Layla said forcefully as she opened the screen door and walked into the living room. "Kim, I've been wanting to come over and pay my respects and tell you how sorry I am at the loss of your parents. I enjoyed that evening with your mom. She was a very sweet lady. I'm sorry I didn't get the opportunity to visit with her more and to get to know your father. Please accept my heartfelt sympathy."

Kim got up and hugged Layla, saying, "Now I understand profound loss much better, and I somewhat know what you must have gone through when you lost your baby. Forgive me, Layla, for not showing more kindness toward you. I simply did not understand."

"Thank you. I'm sorry you had to lose both your parents in such a horrible manner."

They talked for almost thirty minutes, then Layla decided Kim was looking weary and told him she would be attending the memorial with the Boones and left. Outside, she asked Kyle to walk her halfway back to the Boone home.

"Kyle, earlier today, I phoned my booking agent in New York to see if he had any restoration work available. He had just received a commission to restore the entrance to a three-story art deco vestibule that had been damaged by smoke. I agreed to take on the assignment. After the memorial, I'm flying back to

Washington, packing up my things, and returning to New York. I'm smart enough to know our marriage is over. I don't blame myself anymore or you for that matter. I hope you won't object to any of my decisions."

"Layla, I'm sorry about so many things that happened between us, and I will not stand in your way with anything you decide. It's probably best we divorce, and it is best for you to go back to New York. You have lots of friends and a good career there. I only want you to be happy again." Kyle reached for Layla and held her in his arms. Tears streamed down their cheeks.

CHAPTER 16

George closed his cell phone and walked to the front lanai where Annie and Layla were sitting. "We've received an invitation from Dewey to join him tomorrow for his swan song to windsurfing. How about it, ladies?"

"I guess I should see the fabled windsurfers before leaving the island. Count me in."

"Honey, I have some things I must attend to before the services. You and Layla go ahead and tell Dewey I'm sorry to have missed his farewell."

"Layla, you won't believe the bird people. They are a wonder."

"Why is Dewey leaving?" Layla questioned.

"He'll have to tell you that himself, and I think you will be quite surprised."

*　　*　　*

George drove to the cliff overlooking the beach, parked the Jeep, and told Layla if she wanted to, she could leave her blouse and shorts in the car. Layla took them off as George pulled off his T-shirt. She walked over to George's side of the car, where the path to the beach began.

"Damn, Layla, you really are too thin. Is that a New York thing?"

"No, I'm just now beginning to eat again and coming out of my mourning period, which is probably weird, considering what happened to Mr. and Mrs. Okamoto, but I can't help the way things have affected my life."

They walked down the steep path to the beach. When Layla finally looked up, the sight took her breath away. "My god, are they crazy? What the hell are they thinking? Someone must get hurt or die on a daily basis."

"No, they are very disciplined. If the wind gets too rough and takes them toward the rocks, they come back to shore and police the water for any novice that thinks he or she can just get on a board and windsurf. Dewey told me it took him three months and quite a few one-on-one lessons before they would allow him on a board by himself."

"George, I don't know if I can watch this. It scares me. Oh, there's Dewey. Look at the goofy grin on his face. This maybe selfish, but I'm glad this is Dewey's last day. He's been so nice to me. I would hate to have anything happen to him. Do you think he knows we're here?"

"He's spotted us. Wave at him."

Layla and George waved at Dewey. Layla was hoping he would come back in to the beach and be safe. Dewey was headed back out to catch his final wave. He waited until he felt just the right swell, then took off and caught one of the best of the day. He adjusted his sail and soared up off the wave, and for a split second, he was airborne, a feeling he would never be able to equal no matter what his accomplishments. *Well*, he thought, *making love to Layla would definitely be better. Imagine making love to an angel.* He smiled to himself and headed to shore.

George and Layla met him, Layla with a frown on her face. "Dewey, I hope that is truly your swan song because I think it's silly to tempt fate so often." Gesturing to the windsurfers in the water, she continued, "Any of you could be killed or seriously injured. Just look at how young some of those kids are out there. Frankly, I'm appalled."

"I'm done, and yes, it is a dangerous sport but no more dangerous than driving on a freeway or skiing or I don't know."

Dewey grinned at both of them, then asked George if he would try and get Kemo Munson's attention and get him to come into shore. Kemo was Donald Munson's eldest son, an avid windsurfer and a future champion of the sport.

"Sure, it may take a bit. He seems very intent on the waves."

"No problem. I want to talk to Layla a minute." Dewey grabbed Layla's elbow and directed her to an outcropping of rocks. She rested against one and looked at him questionably.

"Layla, I imagine you think I'm a goofball or surf bum, but that's a long way from the truth. I'm thirty years old and have been working intently for most of those years. First, two doctorate degrees, then my own company where I employ over two hundred people—that in itself is a big responsibility, plus continuing to try and be one jump ahead of my competition. It all exacted a price. I burned out, and I've spent the last six months escaping reality. It's been quite an experience. I've done things I should have done when I was a kid, but there was always so much to accomplish when I was young. I don't know if you ever play video games, but my company is in the business of developing them, and now we are developing a new digital process aimed at movies, television, music videos, etc. I'm Dewey McMaster, and I live in Salt Lake City, Utah, where my company is located."

"Are you the DewMaster?"

"Yep, but just call me Dewey."

"That old saying, 'You can't judge a book by its cover,' certainly holds true. The first time I saw you I thought you were a homeless person. George told me you were special, referred you to a Maui onion."

"He what?" Dewey asked wide eyes.

"He said you had many layers but a sweet core."

"That's a hell of a compliment, I think."

George came toward them with Kemo Munson in tow. "Kemo, my man, I have a proposition for you."

Kemo shook Dewey's hand, knowing this was his last day windsurfing. News had spread fast about Dewey's real identity. "Hey, DewMaster, what can I do for you?"

"Kemo, I want you to have my board. Everyone knows one day you will be a champion, and I want you to have the advantage of this board. It's one of the finest made, and I think you deserve to use it to its fullest potential."

"Wow, Dewey, that's so cool. Thank you. Wait till Dad hears about this. He'll be thrilled."

Kemo gathered his new board and walked off toward the surf. Dewey looked back at Layla who stood there, hands on hips, frowning.

"Dewey, how could you give a mere child that board?"

"He's more capable of using it than I was. He'll be fine."

Layla turned sharply and tromped off toward the upward path to the Jeep.

"What did I do?"

"Layla doesn't get windsurfing. She thinks it's too dangerous, especially for someone as young as Kemo."

"My poor angel, maybe you or Annie could enlighten her. Doesn't she look adorable when she's mad?"

Again, George shook his head at Dewey's infatuation with Layla. "We'll see what we can do. You keep referring to her as your angel. That's the scrawniest angel I've ever seen. She needs about ten or twenty more pounds to be a proper angel."

"You're right. She needs someone to care for her, a job which I would like to handle."

"You have to give her more time. She's decided to fly back to Washington, DC, pack her things up, and head back to New York. She even has a job waiting for her. Plus, she has decided to end her marriage to Kyle."

Dewey grabbed George's arm, stopping him cold. "You've got to be kidding. That's terrific news! I want to invite you, Annie, and Layla to Bird's tonight. I'm throwing an all-you-can-eat farewell party for my windsurfing friends and their families.

Let me know within a couple of hours, and I'll let Byrd know to expect you. Please talk the ladies into joining the fun."

"I'll do my best. No problem with Annie, but Layla might be a hard sell."

"You can do it, George. I have faith in your powers of persuasion."

Layla was anxious to tell Annie about the youngsters in peril. Annie laughed. "Paia is considered a windsurfing capital. Some of these kids are probably safer on a board than a bike. Sure, there have been broken legs and arms, but that's about all, and everyone watches out for everyone else. Our kids didn't want to attempt it. They were satisfied with surfing, so it was something we didn't have to face, but with the proper training, I would have been OK if one of them had wanted to take up the sport."

"I guess I'm being overly protective, probably because of my recent loss. I was pretty rude to Dewey."

George overheard what Layla said. "You can make it up to him by joining Annie and me at Bird's tonight. Dewey has invited us to a dinner for the windsurfers and their families. He wanted to do something to thank everyone for their hospitality. This will be fun. We can use some fun before the funeral."

"George, you shouldn't talk like that."

"Maybe not, but it's true. That funeral is going to be a sad time for everyone. Can I call Dewey and tell him all three of us will be there tonight?"

"Yes, include me in. That's the least I can do after my earlier behavior."

George phoned Dewey and told him the good news. Dewey let out a long sigh of relief.

"Thanks, George. I knew you could do it, and I need another favor. Mr. Soo will be attending tonight, and he would like a ride. Is that OK?"

"Sure, I'll call him, and let me know what time we're leaving."

"Thanks, I really like Mr. Soo. We became good friends over these last six months. He's kind of a lonely man. Even though he has sons, they are busy on Oahu and don't get over too often. Mrs. Soo, she seems to live in a world eighty years ago in China, sad lady. I think he's cool. He gave me an idea for a video game. Pretty good for a man his age."

As the sun began its evening journey to the sea, everyone piled into the Jeep and headed to Bird's. On the way, George noticed a light in the sheriff's office and pulled into a parking spot.

"I'm just going to be a minute. I want to see how the sheriff is feeling and if there are any new developments in the case. Mr. Soo, do you want to stay with the ladies or come with me?"

"I'm staying with these lovely ladies. It's getting dark. They may need my protection."

"Good thinking, Mr. Soo."

George walked into the sheriff's substation, calling out, "Sheriff, it's George Boone. I came to see how you were feeling."

"Come on back, George, I'm all propped up and don't want to get up and have to get repositioned."

"Jeez, you don't look very comfortable," George said as he came into the office and saw the sheriff setting behind his desk with one leg slung over an opened desk drawer. He also noticed the sheriff sitting on a pillow. "What's with the pillow?"

"Saw Dr. Tan when he got back from Hana. He said Kyle had done a great job disinfecting the wound and stitching it up. However, he gave me a shitload of antibiotics in the ass for infection. I don't know what hurts worse, my leg or my ass. Hell of a look for a sheriff!"

"Sorry you're feeling so rotten. It could be worse. You could have broken a leg."

"Or be dead if you hadn't grabbed a hold of me. Thanks again, George, I've thought about that moment a lot. Damn, we were dumb to try going over those rocks in that weather, even though it seemed like a good idea at the time."

"Yeah, it wasn't our brightest moment. Any new developments on the murders?"

"It's been confirmed a stun gun was used on both the Okamotos prior to their actual murder. The good thing about that is they felt no pain."

"I'm glad they didn't suffer. Any clue on the stun gun?"

"The police have checked, and none of their Tasers have been lost or stolen. Can't ship them here, it's illegal. I thought maybe some retired cop lost one or had it stolen and either failed to report it or doesn't know it's missing."

"I had better be going, got a car full of hungry folks."

"Who all you feeding this time?"

"You know Layla is staying with us and Mr. Soo couldn't miss going out for an evening meal. We've all been invited to Bird's for a bash Dewey is throwing."

"Oh yeah, that's tonight. He phoned and invited me, but I didn't feel up to being seen by so many in this pitiful condition. Carrying a pillow is pretty pathetic."

*   *   *

Back at the Jeep, George told everyone about the sheriff and his pillow and the news about the stun-gun marks on the Okamotos. Within a few minutes, they were parked and on their way into Bird's.

Jim Byrd and his wife Jessie purchased the bar after his return from Vietnam. An entryway partitioned off the bar with stained-glass bird of paradise, waves, and sunset panels. Past the entryway, a long polished wooden bar ran almost the length of the room with booths on the right. At the end of the room were a jukebox and a medium-sized dance floor. Past the bar and through an arch were restrooms on the right and a kitchen on the left. A door led to the outside and the grill room as everyone called it. This is where Jim Byrd did his magic; he grilled steaks, chicken, available fresh seafood, and vegetables each night for those who called in advanced orders. Picnic tables under a pergola accommodated overflow for those not eating in the bar.

When Byrd purchased the bar, he had a neon sign made by a local who gave him a terrific price; unfortunately, he spelled the name Bird's and not Byrd's. Jim left it that way, and Bird's was born. Something about the name drew the windsurfers, often called the bird people, and Bird's had been their place for years.

Then there was Bird's bird. Gene, the local veterinarian, had aided the state police with a group of injured exotic birds that were seized being shipped illegally from Central and South American. A beautiful young parrot's wings had been so damaged in shipment that Gene had to clip the wings and the parrot could never fly again. Jessie volunteered at Gene's hospital and said she would give the parrot a home. She had gone to Bird's to show Jim, and once there, the parrot hopped off Jessie's shoulder and onto Jim's shoulder, and he became Bird's bird. From then on, he was known as Bird and became a fixture as you entered the bar. He perched on a hat tree just inside the door and was the official greeter. The funny thing was the amorous way Bird greeted certain ladies as they entered the bar. If he liked a man, he would say a crisp "Hi, bud." The ladies were often subject to loving endearments and coos. If he didn't like you, Bird turned his back, totally ignoring the incoming patron.

Annie and George had filled Layla in on Bird's history, making her anxious to see what her greeting would be from the parrot. When she entered, Bird threw his head back and sized her up and said, "Pretty little thing." Then he spied Annie and cooed, "Hot mama, give us a kiss!" Annie walked over and placed her face close to Bird, and he rubbed his beak against her cheek, the highest compliment he paid a lady. Bird noticed the two men and gave them a "Hi, bud" greeting.

They continued into the bar and out the door to the eating area. Byrd had set up long tables and hung lanterns over the back area. The aroma from two huge grills filled the air. There were probably thirty men, women, and children enjoying the feast and about ten or twelve inside eating. Dewey hired a bartender

for the inside and outside bars. Byrd was busy grilling, Jessie
was serving plates she received from her husband, and Dewey
was greeting all those that were arriving. When he saw George
and his group, his face lit up, and he hurried over to them. He
shook hands with George and Mr. Soo, kissed Annie on the
cheek, and hugged Layla.

"I'm happy all of you decided to attend tonight. Tell Jessie
your order. I have a table for us right over here." Dewey nodded
to a table where a "reserved" sign was placed. "Jessie will serve
your meat order and grilled vegetables, but you will have to
select your salads, bread, dessert, etc., from that long table to
your right. What can I get you to drink?"

All but Mr. Soo agreed on beers; he ordered a Coke, and then
he was off to the table with the food. As Dewey was bringing
back drinks, Mr. Soo returned with a dinner-size plate loaded
with salads and breads, along with a dessert plate with two kinds
of dessert.

"Lord, Mr. Soo, are you going to eat all that and your meat
and vegetables too?" Annie asked.

"Have hollow leg, eat it all," Mr. Soo said as he began to dig
into his salads.

"Well, I've got to try some of those salads. Layla, come on
and try a couple with me. George, how about you?"

"Right behind you. It looks terrific. I'm starved."

Annie, Layla, George, and Dewey returned with salad plates
and dessert plates all respectfully full, but none came close to
Mr. Soo's plates loaded with food. Jessie brought their orders;
when everyone was full, even Mr. Soo, they drank coffee or tea
and enjoyed the crowd of happily eating and sociable people.

At ten o'clock, cooking stopped, and Dewey's cleanup crew
began to disassemble the backyard. Those staying went into the
bar where music played; the majority thanked Dewey, told him
how much he would be missed, and went on their way home.
Mr. Soo said it was past his bedtime and hitched a ride with a
couple that was going his way. George, Annie, Layla, and Dewey

went inside and found an empty table. After a round of beer was served, the jukebox played "Always," and George and Annie were off to the dance floor.

"George said you would be going back to Washington, DC, right after the funeral. Have you made your airline reservations yet?

"I must do that tomorrow. I've been so forgetful, enjoying my time in Paia."

"May I offer you a lift?"

"I'm not going just down the street. I'm going clear to the nations' capital. I'll need to take an airplane."

"I know, I'm offering you my airplane. My plane and crew will get into Maui in about an hour. If you let me know when you want to leave, I'll get you home."

"Are you kidding? That would be great. Could we leave Sunday morning?"

"Perfect, although I'm afraid I will have to leave the plane in Salt Lake City. I have a big meeting upcoming, and I need to get up-to-speed. The plane has a bedroom, and you will be able to sleep and be rested when you get to Washington."

"Dewey, I can't believe you are willing to withstand the expense of flying me all the way from Salt Lake City to Washington. I'll catch a commercial flight."

"I found out this morning I'm no longer a millionaire after talking to my head accountant. I've now made it into the billionaire category. I think I can afford to give you a lift to Washington," Dewey said.

"I guess you can. I accept with gratitude."

Annie and George returned to the table, and George said, "Annie and I will be on our way home. Layla, are you going to stay? Dewey will drive you back, and Annie can give you her key to the door next to the kitchen window."

"Stay awhile, Layla. I'll even try a dance if you'll stay," Dewey pleaded.

"Oh, all right, but just a while longer."

Dewey walked behind George and Annie as they were leaving. "Thank you both for coming tonight, and guess what? Layla is flying back with me on Sunday. Isn't that terrific?"

"Dewey, I must admit you are moving in the right direction, but go slow."

"Unfortunately, I have to leave the plane in Salt Lake City, but the crew will fly her on to Washington. Between Maui and Salt Lake, I will do my best to endear myself to her."

Dewey got up enough courage to ask his angel to dance a couple of slow songs. He saw Layla back to the Boone's and made sure she was safely locked inside their home. He wasn't sure if he had walked back to his car or floated, he was so happy.

CHAPTER 17

The next day Layla went to talk with Kyle and let him know she was leaving on Sunday but decided there wasn't any need to tell him she would be traveling on Dewey's jet.

Kyle had seen Layla approaching and slid the screen open for her.

"Layla!" boomed Donald Munson. "Good seeing you again. Lovely evening last night. I think everyone had a good time."

Layla was caught off guard by the sight of Donald and his reference to last night at Bird's. "Yes, I think everything went well. Kemo must be thrilled with his new board?"

"My goodness, yes, very kind of Dewey to make him the benefactor of such an expensive board. Well, folks, I must be leaving, still plenty of work to be done before the services. You will be there, Layla?"

"Yes, I'll be attending with George, Annie, Mr. Soo, and Dewey. Then I'll be going back to Washington the next day." Layla stepped aside from the screen in what she hoped was an obvious gesture for Donald to leave.

Donald left, and Kyle looked at Layla with a quizzical expression on his face, which she decided to ignore. "Kim, how are you doing?"

"Thank you for asking. I'm doing better. I spoke with Donald about the market, and he has a wonderful idea for a memorial to my parents that will benefit the entire city. I don't need the large sum of money the sale of the property would generate. My main concern is to honor my parents' memory. Donald understood and suggested I deed the property to the city, and with fund-raising, the market would be turned into the Okamoto Visitors Center. Donald said the city had been trying for years to find a suitable property for such a center, but none ever came on the market the city could afford."

Kim continued, "He suggested, once the center is completed, a grand opening be held with notice going to all the islands. He anticipates everything can be completed in eighteen to twenty-four months, depending how fast donations needed for an architect, contractor, etc., are forthcoming. But once completed, he would like all of us back here for the dedication. Isn't that a wonderful idea?"

Layla could not help herself; her eyes got moist, and she went over and hugged Kim. "Kim, that's a wonderful memorial to your parents. What do you think, Kyle?"

"Frankly, I was overwhelmed. I think it's great and would make Mr. and Mrs. Okamoto proud to know their market will live on and be visited by so many."

"I'll be leaving now. I'll see you both on Saturday." Layla hugged Kim again and nodded at Kyle who walked her out to the lanai.

"Layla, are you mad or angry at me?"

"No, Kyle, but over these last few days, I realized that I have to live again. I'm not sure exactly what I want out of life, only that I won't find it in Washington, DC. I don't want to sound harsh, but I'm moving on." Layla went down the lanai steps back to the Boone home.

Layla told George and Annie about the proposal for the market.

Annie asked George, "Honey, can we afford to donate $500 to the fund? I feel very connected to this whole situation. Plus, I adored those two."

"No problem. Take our checkbook with you to the services tomorrow. I'll see if Donald has a fund set up yet for checks, and knowing Donald, he will have one ready."

"George, can we call the bank and see if Donald is there to be sure he has a fund set up by tomorrow, then he can make an announcement about the proposed plans for the Visitors Center and show that he has already received donations. I will also write a check, and I'm sure Dewey will." Layla was excited and wanted to be sure the project got off successfully.

George placed the call and explained the donation idea. Donnie thought it was a wise plan, and he immediately deemed it the Okamoto Visitors Center Fund, saying he would set up the account right away and make provisions to receive checks tomorrow.

Layla, raised among the rich, had no problem asking for donations; she asked George for Mr. Soo's and Dewey's phone number. Once she had them on the line, she explained the memorial fund and asked if she could count on them to bring a check tomorrow. Both agreed to bring a sizable check. Since Mr. Soo would be riding with their group, they would present Donald with all the checks at once. Layla knew it would be a good start for the memorial fund.

Dewey pulled into the driveway behind the Boone home, and his group of riders assembled on the lanai. His good clothes arrived with his jet, and he had gotten a proper haircut. His beige gabardine trousers, pale blue cotton shirt, medium brown Italian loafers, and matching trouser belt portrayed a sleek and successful businessman. Adding an air of casualness, he had rolled up his sleeves to the elbow, exposing a gold Rolex watch.

"My god!" exclaimed Annie. She was the first to see Dewey as he came up the stairs. "Who's that great-looking guy that resembles our Dewey?"

"Holy cow, you are one handsome dude. Looks like lots of money too." Only Mr. Soo could state the obvious in such a charming manner.

Layla had her mouth halfway open. "Dewey, is that really you?"

A big grin spread over Dewey's face. "Yes, it's me. This is what the right clothes, a haircut, and shave can do for you."

Dewey looked at Layla, and once again, he was in awe of his angel. She wore a simple pale yellow gauze sundress with a short jacket that would keep her shoulders and arms from the burn of the sun. Her shoes were gold sandals, and she carried a matching small purse. She wore her hair pulled back in a ponytail. He had no idea what anyone else wore.

"We should be going. There will be lots of people attending the services, and parking will be at a premium. I'll drop everyone off at the entrance, find a place to park, then walk back. Layla, here's my check. I imagine you want to give Donnie the checks prior to the services, and if I don't get back in time, hand him mine with the others and save me a seat."

CHAPTER 18

Layla, Mr. Soo, Annie, and George got in line with those going to the services. Approaching the entrance, they noticed the sheriff sitting on a folding chair, greeting everyone that entered. He had given up trying to hide his pillow. Word had gotten around quickly, and he took the good-natured ribbing.

When he saw the group heading his way, he got up from the chair and shook hands with Mr. Soo, George, and Layla. He held Annie by the arm and said, "Annie, I've been worried about you. How are you doing? You had a terrible shock, and I should have called, but between the investigation and my injury, I'm sorry to say I neglected checking on you."

"Layla staying with us has been a godsent. It has kept my mind off the discovery. I'm worried that it will hit me hard today. I'm just hoping I don't fall apart at the services."

"Hell, Annie, no one could blame you. You made a gruesome discovery that would haunt anybody."

"Thank you, Sheriff," Annie said, patting his hand.

Making their way into the seating area, Layla pulled Annie aside. "Annie, I'm about to do something not very nice. Want to join me?"

"I can't imagine you doing anything like that, and yes, I'll join you. George, hold it a minute. Layla and I have to talk about something."

Everyone stopped, and Layla turned her back to George and Mr. Soo, talking to Annie, "This is a terrible breach of etiquette, but I've just got to see the amount of Dewey's check. Look with me, OK?"

Layla unfolded the check, and both women caught their breath. "My god, it's for $50,000! With all our checks and this one, that means the fund will start with $100,500. Isn't that wonderful? We've got to get Donald's attention and let him announce how much is already in the fund. That ought to spur more donations."

"Honey, will you please get Donnie's attention? You're taller than most, and you should be able to spot him and get him over here."

George spotted Donnie in front talking with a local minister; he caught his attention and motioned to him. Donnie waved the group forward, indicating they would be sitting in the front row.

"Oh great, now if I get hysterical, I can do it in the front row for everyone to see," Annie quipped.

"Sweetie, after all the publicity in the papers, everyone knows that you found the bodies, and no one is going to deny that you might break down at the services, so don't worry."

"Thanks, I think."

The group made their way down to the front-row seats. Donnie came up to them and, in a somber tone, asked how he could help.

Layla offered the four checks to him, saying, "Donnie, these four checks represent $100,500, making a good start to the fund. I hope you will announce this amount, and maybe it will inspire others to make a donation today."

"Layla, thank you for getting the center off the ground. I know you are responsible for getting these beginning donations."

Layla smiled and let Donnie lead her and the others to their seats. Donnie had the seating set up in rows of folding chairs on the left and right of a wide aisle in the middle. He told them Kim would be sitting on the end and Kyle next to him, followed by Layla and the rest of the group. Donnie, his wife, and Kemo would take the three remaining chairs on the end. The other front side would sit those speaking, City of Paia officials, etc.

"Mr. Soo, when Dewey gets here, be sure you scoot over next to George and let him sit next to Layla," Annie said, winking at Mr. Soo.

A long table was in front covered in a white cloth. On it sat a tabletop dais equipped with a microphone. To the right sat two urns holding the ashes surrounded by an arrangement of orchids. Behind the table was a large projection screen. At five minutes before ten, Donnie and Kemo got up from their chairs, and each went to one side of the screen, pulling a hidden cord. Unfolding from the top of the screen was a large blown-up copy of the Okamotos' anniversary portrait. Donnie and Kemo secured the portrait at the bottom of the screen and took their seats.

When the portrait was unfolded, there was an audible gasp from the crowd. Tears streamed down Kim's cheeks. Annie removed her sunglasses and lowered her head. George put his arm around her, drawing her into his shoulder.

Dewey found his seat next to Layla a minute before the services began. "Hard to find a parking space. I believe the entire island has turned out for the services." He looked at Layla. "Are you feeling all right?"

"Yes, but I think Annie is in trouble. We've all been afraid the services would hit her hard. I'm glad she has George to hold on to."

The services got under way, and one by one, the speakers came forward, some offering prayers, some told stories of the warmhearted Okamotos, some speaking about the loss to the city, and then Kyle came to the microphone. He began telling how he and Kim had become friends going through medical school together, their specialized training in anesthesiology, their internship at Georgetown Hospital, and as he continued on, Dewey noted Layla's shoulders become tense; she sat forward, gripping the chair seat tightly.

Dewey grabbed her hand, releasing it from the chair, and whispered into her ear, "What's the matter? You look upset."

"That bastard, he's said more at this service than he did at the service for our baby. In fact, I believe he has said more here than he's said to me in the last six months."

Dewey heard the anger in her voice, and he put her hand in both of his. "Mad is good. It helps to heal."

Layla slowly turned her head and looked at Dewey, the beginnings of a smile on her face. "You're right. Sometimes, mad can be good."

Kim was next to speak; he was shaky and wiped his eyes more than once. When Kim finished, Kemo and Kyle walked up and removed the urns, carrying them to Donnie's car parked nearby. When the car was out of sight, Donnie walked to the microphone and began telling everyone about Kim's donation of the Okamoto's market and the large sum already received to the Okamoto Paia Visitors Center Fund. He hoped everyone would give what he or she was able to in memory of this wonderful couple.

Donnie and his wife went to the screen and pulled the portrait up, then brought the screen down, giving everyone a clear view of the ocean. Soft music played in the background as everyone waited for the boat to be visible.

Within ten minutes, the boat came into view; visible from the hill perch, everyone could see a bevy of leis filled a large section of the boat. As everyone followed the progress of the boat, a large Norwegian cruise ship went by on its journey to a neighboring island. The small boat slowed down and circled a particular area several times before dropping anchor. Once done, Kim went to the side of the vessel and began releasing the ashes of his parents into the waters of the Pacific. Kyle and one of the deckhands began tossing the leis into the water. When everything was complete, the boat slowly left the area, and as it did, several hundred leis lay floating in the water; it was an impressive sight. Donnie had made sure all floral shops on the island knew only to send leis to the services, resulting in the floating flower garden.

Donnie went back to the microphone, thanking everyone for attending on behalf of Kim and reminding them of the donations needed to open the Visitors Center. He motioned to a back-area setup with buffet tables full of food.

Donnie stayed at the dais, accepting donations; there was a line of people waiting to present checks and bills. George leaned into the group, saying, "Annie needs to get out of here. You folks ready to leave, or do you want to stay and have something to eat?"

"No, let's leave," Layla said.

"Lunch will be my treat at Mama's Fish House," Mr. Soo insisted.

"Now we just have to get out with as little fuss as possible. I'll leave and bring the car to the front. You folks can make your way to the exit."

"OK, Dewey, you go," said George. "We'll sit here for a bit and give you time, then figure out the best way to get away from all the well-meaning people. I'm afraid too many of them will try and approach Annie and say how sorry they are she had to make the discovery. That's just the kind of thing she doesn't need right now."

Dewey left the group, and in less than fifteen minutes, he was back with the car. The group had made their way through the throng, and because most were interested in the buffet table, few noticed them. A couple of Annie's teacher friends hugged her and said anything she needed just call, but they were the only ones to approach. All jumped in the Escalade, and Dewey drove away.

At the restaurant, Annie asked Layla if she too had been upset at the services.

"You're damn right. I was upset. That bastard Kyle spoke for about six minutes, which was three more minutes than he gave to our baby when she was buried. His six minutes was about five minutes more than he has spoken to me at one time since we lost her. I can't wait to get back to Washington to get the hell out of there before he returns."

"Oh," Annie said quietly.

Their waiter came to the table, asking if anyone would like a cocktail.

"Yes, I need one," replied Annie. "I'll have a vodka martini with olives."

"That sounds good. I'll have the same," Layla said.

Both men ordered Heinekens.

The waiter looked at Mr. Soo, who was looking pensive.

"I'll have a Shirley Temple."

Everyone at the table looked at each other and burst out laughing. Suddenly, the gloomy and angry moods were gone.

"Mr. Soo, why a Shirley Temple and not a Roy Rogers?" asked Dewey.

"Shirley Temple, cute little curly-headed tot, happy, singing, and dancing. Roy Rogers is a gun-toting, rough-riding cowboy. Happy little girl much better."

Everyone enjoyed their lunch; realizing that Dewey and Layla would be gone by this time tomorrow seemed to bring the group of five even closer.

On the way back to the Boone's, George said to meet back at their place close to seven, and he would grill something for a light dinner. Although everyone currently felt stuffed, he said they would be hungry again by then. All agreed to enjoy one final meal together on the Boone's lanai.

Annie brought beers for Dewey and George and iced tea for everyone else. They were seated on the front lanai, eating veggies, chips, and dip, watching the sunset.

Dewey sighed. "Seems hard to believe by this time tomorrow, I'll probably be wearing a parka. Lots of snow in Utah this time of year."

"I think it's snowing in Washington, DC, too. I'm not going to miss all the bad things that have happened here, but I'm going to miss the warm sunny weather. Most of all, I'm going to miss all of you," Layla's voice trailed off in sadness.

"Here's the great thing, Layla. Just pick up the phone call Dewey and tell him you need a lift to Maui, and he'll send the plane, then tell him he has to come along because we miss you both," George said, trying to lighten the mood.

"Layla, anytime, call me, and we'll be off to Maui."

The sun made its nightly dip into the Pacific, and George herded the group to the back lanai where he was set up to grill fresh fish. Annie had prepared a couple of simple salads and fresh fruit for dessert. At eleven, Dewey and Mr. Soo said their good nights. Dewey said he would be back at nine thirty the next morning.

Annie went back inside to help Layla finish packing as George was cleaning up the lanai. She sat down on the bed next to Layla and noticed she was sitting there, looking sad. "Layla, what's the matter? You look like you are about to break out in tears."

"That's what I feel like doing because I'm going to miss you so much and George too. But I'm really going to miss you, Annie. You have treated me more like a daughter than my own mother. That's wonderful and hurtful at the same time. I know I'm so much stronger than when we came to Maui, and I feel terrible that it took a horrible event to make this transition. I'm leaving here determined to start a new beginning for myself on what seems like the other side of the world, and I'm going to miss the closeness we've developed."

"You are stronger now, and I'm only a phone call away. If you need to come over for a quick visit, call Dewey Airways and he'll send the plane," Annie said.

"Believe me, I'll be calling you, and I really am starting a new life, not just spouting wishes. I'll pack up my SUV and be headed to New York within four days, and then I'll be in my job and rejoining my old friends. I know everything will not work out as easily as it sounds, but I'll get through it all. I especially hope the divorce from Kyle will be easy. He can have the townhouse in Washington—it's close to Georgetown—and all the furniture too. I brought a couple of small pieces from New York, but I'll either ship them or perhaps load them in my SUV. I don't think Kyle will fight me on anything about the divorce, do you?"

"I don't think you will have any problem in that respect. George and I have talked about something we both felt. I'm going to ask you point-blank: did you ever suspect there might be a relationship between Kyle and Kim, let's say, more on a very personal level?"

"Oh, you're kidding, my god, maybe that is the problem. Now that you mention it, in the past months, they do seem closer than normal. Damn, how stupid am I? You would think I could have detected something like that."

"Often, when we are as close to a situation as you were and going through your pregnancy and the loss of your daughter, something like that is so far on the periphery, you would have no way of noticing."

"Well, they can have each other. I want away from both of them, the quicker, the better."

Dewey pulled his Escalade to the back lanai steps where George helped with Layla's luggage.

Everyone got in, and they left for the private airstrip at the Maui Airport.

"I sort of expected Mr. Soo might come along," Layla said.

"It was hard enough for him to say goodbye last night. He couldn't face saying goodbye again today. Remember, he lost a close pal in Mr. Okamoto. Speaking of the Okamotos, I got a call from the sheriff this morning to report on some action taken by the state police. They raided a home in the high country and found a budding chemistry student setup, cooking a meth lab. He had three helpers: a fifty-year-old biker, a black militant in his midthirties, and a twenty-something white supremacist. Is that not the strangest assembly you ever heard of? Anyway, they are investigating very thoroughly, thinking maybe one or more of those crazies had something to do with the Okamotos' murders."

"What a weird mix of people. I wonder how they all got together," Layla asked.

"The sheriff said they were paid off in drugs. The case is going to take a lot of investigation by several branches. The sheriff said he heard the DEA might be getting involved. No telling how long it will take or what the final outcome will be, but we'll keep you both informed."

"Looks like we're here," Dewey said as he pulled into the private section of the airport, driving toward a large Gulfstream. He stopped, and everyone got out as the two pilots came down the plane's stairs and approached. They began unloading the luggage and stowing it in the cargo section.

"Dewey, I'm impressed with the size of this airplane," Annie said, wide-eyed.

"My company uses this one when either myself or staff have to fly across country or out of the States. My staff makes a lot of trips to Asia, and this is much more comfortable for them, less stress, and they are rested when they arrive.

"George, Annie, anytime you want to visit me in Salt Lake City, just call and I'll send a plane. There is nothing that would make me happier than to have you two come for a visit, and, George, with your engineering background, you would have a ball touring McMaster Enterprises."

"Dewey, we'll take you up on that offer in the future. I would love to see the new digital process you're working on."

When everything was loaded, Dewey pulled George aside, handing him the keys to the Escalade. "George, you can't take this back to the dealer."

"What do you mean? Where am I supposed to take it?"

"You can put it in the empty spot in your garage next to your Jeep. I've purchased the car in your names, and there is also three days' insurance in your names. You'll find the paperwork and an extra set of keys in the glove compartment."

"Dewey, I can't accept this. My god, it's a fabulous car!"

"Too late, it's already yours. You're stuck with it, and I happen to think Annie will look quite smart behind the wheel."

George thanked Dewey for his overly generous gift.

"George, both of you have been my friends and treated me with respect, letting me live on your lanai during the storm. Heck, if not for that, I would never have met my angel," Dewey said with a grin.

Dewey hugged and kissed Annie goodbye on the cheek, thanking her without telling her about his gift. He led Layla onto the plane. When they both were inside the door, they turned and waved their final goodbyes.

"Gosh, I'm going to miss those two," Annie said with a catch in her voice.

"Honey, we have to leave this area before they can take off. Get in the car, and let's clear the field so they can be on their way."

Once outside the field, Annie asked George to park for a while so they could see the plane off into the air. Back in the car, George asked her to open the glove compartment.

"I would, if I knew where it was," Annie said, looking in several obvious places.

George began to laugh. "Just my luck, owning a high-end car like this, and I can't find the ownership papers."

"George Boone, what are you talking about?"

"Dewey bought the car in our names and said it was a gift. The papers and an extra set of car keys are in the glove compartment. He even purchased three days of insurance for us. Do you believe it?"

"Honey, are you sure you heard him correctly? Oh, I think I found the glove compartment, and there are papers and extra keys in here." Annie opened the papers and read, "This is our car. Wow, I can't wait to drive it!"

CHAPTER 19

When the captain turned off the Fasten Seat Belt sign, Dewey got up and asked Layla to join him on the sofa; he would be back with drinks.

Dewey explained when they boarded, there were seafood salads in the galley and a special chocolate cake dessert for lunch. They also had a fully stocked bar. Everything was at her disposal; the galley would be restocked for dinner once they were in Salt Lake City. Everyone heats their own meals; a steward was seldom used, saying that was too pretentious for his taste.

He returned from the galley with two champagne flutes of mimosas; handing one to Layla, he proposed a toast, "To new beginnings."

"I'll drink to that." Layla clinked her glass to Dewey's.

"Are you apprehensive about leaving Washington, getting a divorce, and restarting your career?"

"I'm more determined and more sure of myself every day. Funny because I haven't felt this positive in months."

"Your appearance has changed. You walk straighter. You have color in your cheeks and life back in your eyes."

"Thank you, Dewey. I can't wait to get back to New York. What about you? You've made this fabulous transition to a successful-looking businessman, which, of course, you are, but I can't help wonder if you won't miss the freedom you had in Paia."

"All my life, I've sought to reach goals and be the best. It was expected with my abilities. I never had the opportunity to explore a haunted house on Halloween, play Little League baseball, and have my first date with someone who didn't have her eyes glued to a computer screen like me. I missed a lot of fun kid things. However, I created a dream world for myself, and I created work for a group of highly skilled and intelligent people, making myself very rich in the process. Yes, I'll miss the freedom I had in Paia, but most of all, I'll miss the people. I never had the time to get to know people like I have these past months. I met some great people. The windsurfers are generous, athletic, and very close-knit. They made me one of them with no questions asked. I don't need to tell you how I feel about George, Annie, and Mr. Soo."

"I feel that Annie might have saved my life. I was just filling space. Most of the time my mind was blank. I lost the ability to feel, to think. Kyle made me get up, get dressed, eat, but I would have been just as happy to stay in bed in a daze. This is embarrassing to admit, but when George brought me to their home and Annie saw my scar, she knew right away I had a child, and then I told her what happened. She hugged me, Dewey. It was the first time anyone had done that since I lost the baby. Not Kyle, not Kim, my parents still in Europe or wherever the hell they are. That simple human contact made me feel again. Does that sound crazy?"

"Nope, I know exactly what you're saying. My dad and I were real close. He was a retired postal inspector. He helped me build my home, which is huge. We got carried away. Then we built a smaller but similar home for him and Mom, got it all furnished, and they went back to Huntington Beach to sell their home. And—boom!—he dropped dead of a heart attack. Mom could not think of moving here without Dad. She still lives in their home. She has a lot of friends and is involved in several charities. She is active, and I guess she's happy. She blames me for Dad's heart attack, that I put too much stress on him. He loved everything he was doing. He bossed the crews and got things done on time. I miss my dad, and Mom hasn't come around since we lost Dad. I keep her informed where I am. She knew about Paia, but she doesn't keep in touch. I have no brothers or sisters, and both my parents were only children, so like you, I miss the human touch."

"Well, aren't we a sad pair? Both of us have all the money we need, great careers, excellent educations, and here we are, confessing to each other how miserable we are. Dewey, promise you will always be my friend?"

Dewey felt like someone put a knife through his heart. *Friend, did she say* friend? He sighed. "Layla count on me, friend for life."

"OK, friend," Layla continued, "I have something very personal to ask your opinion about. Do see Kyle and Kim as a couple?"

"What?" Dewey stammered. "I never thought about it, and I'm not a good person to ask. I'm not very good with insight like that, too sheltered, I guess. What makes you ask?"

"Annie said she and George suspected that might be the case, and with all that happened to me in the last six months, I was too close to the situation to suspect. I don't see how that could be. My god, we were married, we made love, he was the father of our daughter, and the bastard is gay? I don't know how that could happen overnight. Perhaps, if it's true, the tendency was always there and was suppressed. I'm pretty dumb about such things, like I said. I think we could use another drink."

He took her glass and went back to the galley to make them another round. When he returned with the drinks, they agreed to keep the conversation light. They told of humorous incidents in their childhood, and Dewey told stories of his friendships in Paia. In no time, they realized they were hungry, and Layla helped him retrieve their lunch from the galley. After lunch, Layla curled up on one end of the sofa and dozed off, feeling relaxed and at ease with her good friend Dewey.

Dewey went to a desk area and began work on a letter he would be sending to his staff, explaining his return and why he had been absent for six months. A little more than an hour out from Salt Lake City, Layla woke and asked where she could freshen up. Dewey sent her to the guest bathroom that was part of the bedroom.

"What a bathroom, even a shower. A gal could get used to this pampered lifestyle."

"I was serious. Anytime you want to go anywhere, call me, I'll send a plane. It might not be this one, but I have two other ones without bedrooms. They carry a nice small group."

"Dewey, you are too good to me."

"Heck, what are rich friends for? We'll be in Salt Lake City shortly, and there will be about a couple hours layover while we refuel and get food and a new crew on board. What would you like to do, or what can I show you about the city?"

"How about you show me your home?"

"To be clear, it was my dad's idea. It's huge, way too big for me, and sort of over-the-top. I have a wonderful live-in couple, Agnes and Ted, who takes care of the place and me for that matter. The surrounding land requires a full-time maintenance staff of three. The home my father built for him and Mom is kept closed, but Ted checks on it frequently. I offered to let them live there, but they knew my dad and couldn't bring themselves to live in his home. I would love to show you the place as long as you understand I'm not trying to show off."

"Dewey, I know you well enough to know that. Remember, I'm from a very wealthy old-money family. Our home in the Hamptons is probably as big as yours or bigger."

When they landed, Dewey and Layla thanked the pilots for a smooth flight. A McMaster employee drove a Range Rover to pick them up, load Dewey's luggage, and bring him a parka. Layla had the heavy coat she wore from Washington to Oahu; it was cold, and a sharp wind blew across the tarmac. In the car, a heater warmed the interior, and Dewey gave instructions to drive to his residence.

A large wrought-iron gate with DM in the center opened, and a winding driveway meandered through snow-covered trees, ending at a large brick mansion with a circular driveway. Steps from the driveway led to a massive double wooden door opened by a smiling couple that greeted Dewey with hugs. Dewey introduced Layla to Agnes and Ted and told them she came by to see the house before continuing onto Washington, DC. Agnes said she would make some coffee, and Ted toted Dewey's luggage inside.

"Dewey, this is grand, and what I like is the homey feel. All this wood and cozy furniture makes it feel warm. Of course, that roaring fire helps," Layla said as she walked over to a huge fireplace, rubbing her hands together.

Dewey showed Layla his home, and she was impressed with the indoor swimming pool.

"OK, you got me here," she said as she walked around the steaming pool. "Even we don't have an indoor pool. This is terrific. Just what I need in my brownstone so I wouldn't have to go to the gym to swim. I'm very faithful. I exercise every other day and that includes laps. That is, when I'm in good health." As she said this, she looked down at her thinness and was embarrassed for a moment. Then she spread her arms and shrugged.

"You'll be back to your normal self. I hear nothing keeps those New York society gals down."

"That's not me, although I am obligated to attend some events because of my family name. I like wandering through the various neighborhoods and visiting antique stores and especially pawnshops. I've found some of the most amazing items in neighborhood pawnshops."

"Great, I didn't really see you as the snooty high-society type."

"No, that would be my parents," Layla said, laughing.

"We better get our coffee, then get back to the plane. Got to keep on schedule. You never can tell about the weather this time of year."

They returned to the kitchen and joined Agnes and Ted for coffee and some of Agnes's home-baked treats, Layla claiming she had never tasted anything so good. Agnes wrapped up a batch of her baked goods and gave it to Layla for the trip home. When it was time to leave, Layla shook hands with Agnes and Ted, thanking them for their hospitality, especially the baked goods.

Dewey drove the car back to the airfield, never feeling too comfortable with a driver. Like he said to Layla, it made him feel like a damned rock star instead of a businessman.

Dewey was beginning to get a sick feeling in his stomach, or was it his heart? He wasn't sure. He looked over at Layla as she gazed out the window and smiled at his angel, wondering how long it would be before he saw her again.

"Here we are," Dewey said as he drove up to the plane. Seeing their arrival, the gangway was let down, and both he and Layla entered the plane. He asked the pilot if everything was ready to go and was told they would be taking off in twenty minutes.

Layla got her coat hung up and stashed her package in the galley. She returned to the main cabin to say farewell to Dewey. Walking up to him, she threw her arms around his waist and drew him to her. Hugging him closely, she said, "Dewey, I'm so grateful we met and I got to know you. You have been so kind and generous to me, and I know in you, I have a friend for life, someone I can count on, and I will always be there for you too."

Dewey was lost in her embrace, her smell, and the sound of her voice; finally, he found his voice. "I'll always be here for you. Call me when you get home to let me know everything is fine and you arrived safely. Call me anytime you want to talk, need a long-distance shoulder to cry on, or need someone to laugh with."

He handed her a card with his private cell number and told her there were very few people that had that number, and he carried that cell with him no matter where he was or what he was doing.

"I'll call you when I get home, and I'll call you often."

Dewey bent down and planted a lingering kiss on her cheek. Again, they said goodbye as Dewey departed. He got in the Range Rover and drove off the tarmac but stopped, got out, and stood beside the car, waving toward the plane. Layla waved from the window and hoped Dewey could see her toss a kiss in his direction.

Shortly, the plane roared to life, taxied out onto the runway, and was soon a blur in the sky. Dewey stood and looked in the direction of the departing plane, long after it was out of sight, his heart leaving with the flight.

CHAPTER 20

George approached Annie who was in the kitchen, spotting one of his grilling T-shirts prior to putting it in the washer. "I'm going to take Pearl to the car wash."

"You're going to take who to the car wash?" Annie asked, thinking she could not possibly have heard correctly.

"Pearl. Now I know we used to laugh at people who named their cars, but honestly, I feel silly saying I'm going to take the Escalade here or there, and if I say car, you'll never know if I mean the Jeep or what. So since she's pearly white, I decided I'd just call her Pearl."

"George Boone, did I hear you correctly? First, it's she, now it's Pearl. I think you are in love with that car."

George walked up behind Annie and nuzzled the left side of her neck. "Yum, essence of Tide." Then he nuzzled the right side of her neck. "Ah, the scent of Downy." He turned her around and placed a couple of fingers on her lips, smiling. "And the best part of all, a taste of Annie." He bent down and kissed her.

"Go take Pearl to the car wash. You two have a good time. Named the car, I wouldn't have believed it a week ago. You're always surprising me."

George went out the back lanai steps to the garage. As he was raising the garage door, Mr. Soo walked up and asked where he was going. George told him the car wash and asked if he would like to ride along. Mr. Soo agreed, and they were off to the local car wash.

After the car wash, George suggested they stop by the sheriff's office to check on any developments in the case. Mr. Soo was happy to stop, noting that there were usually doughnuts available, and he enjoyed talking to Charlene.

"Mr. Soo and George, how nice to see you both. What brings you gentlemen here?" Charlene asked.

"Mr. Soo was anxious to see you Charlene, and I wanted to ask the sheriff if there was anything new in the Okamoto case."

"Let me see if the Sheriff is available. Mr. Soo, behind me on Danny's desk is a box of doughnuts, and there are some yummy ones in there."

Charlene was used to Mr. Soo on a doughnut hunt and did not keep him waiting. She rang the sheriff, who said to have George come right back.

"George, want a doughnut? Oh, look one of my favorites, a raspberry-filled, healthy fruit inside."

"No, thanks, I'll skip it this time."

Both greeted each other cordially, and George sat down in a chair facing the sheriff, causally stretching his long legs out in front of him. He asked if there was any further information on the case.

"I just came back from a meeting with the state police and the local Maui law enforcement. So far, they have learned that the biker had a great alibi for the time of the murders. He was jailed in Hilo on a drunk and disorderly charge. Believe it or not, the other two jerks have declined to give any alibi. They believe one or both are either covering up the murders or covering up some drug activity. That's about all we know, which isn't a whole hell of a lot."

"Yesterday, two state police came and interviewed Annie. They didn't call ahead, just came to the door. It really pissed me off, but Annie answered all their questions politely and to the best of her ability. After they left, she was a mess, and it took her the rest of the day to recover. Reliving those events isn't easy for her. She may not show it, but this has affected her more than she may even know. Sometimes, I'll find her just staring out into space, and I know she is reliving something from that morning. I hate this happened to her."

"I do too, George."

"They also asked about Dewey and our opinion of him. We told them we thought he was a good person, a brilliant person who escaped for a few months from the pressures of his life. They wished he were here in person to speak with them. I suggested they set up a telecommunication conversation. I told them if they needed his help, Dewey would be glad to assist. They were a bit lofty in their attitude."

"They tend to get full of themselves sometimes, but they are pretty sharp and have excellent backgrounds and training. Have you spoken with Dewey and let him know the latest?"

"No, we'll call him this evening. Thought he would know how Layla was doing by then. She's determined to be moved back into her New York brownstone in four days."

"What do you mean, leaving Washington and moving back to New York?"

"While here, with everything going on, she decided her relationship to Kyle had deteriorated beyond the point of saving. You know about them losing the baby. Once she decided to leave Kyle, there was no need for her to stay in Washington. She has the family brownstone in New York and has an art restoration job lined up. Annie and I couldn't see her and Kyle making it together. I'm glad for her. She could do a lot better."

"I think you might have Dewey in mind as someone she could do better with."

"He sure fell for her. Well, Sheriff, I'll be going before Mr. Soo eats all your doughnuts. Before I go, do you have any new theory of what happened?"

"That's an interesting question because I have changed my original idea on what happened. I now think it was a local that had a grudge against the Okamotos. Maybe they were jealous of Kim's success, maybe the Okamotos did something at the market they took offense to, but I feel it was personal. I was going over and over the crime-scene photos because I always felt I was missing something and finally saw it." The sheriff pulled a photo from under his desk plotter, turned it around, and motioned George to come forward and look.

George jerked up in his chair. "I'm not good with the gore stuff."

"Nothing like that, but I want you to see why I think it was personal."

George leaned forward and peered at the photo, which showed the back of the two large chairs that sat in front of the Okamotos' television. All you could see of the bodies was each of their arms with Mr. Okamoto's hand clasping his wife's. "Notice, it's a light clasp, like their fingers were placed together. This was staged. That's why I think it was personal."

"Damn, Sheriff, I hate to hear that because that would mean the killer is still around, and that's a scary thought. But after looking at this photo, I see what you mean. Did you tell the state police your theory?"

"Yep, but to them, I'm some old cowboy who's not up on all the new forensics, and unlike several of them, I've never been to Quantico to learn profiling. Had I been schooled in the art of profiling, I would see that my theory is invalid. Frankly, I think they want an easy answer that won't taint tourist trade. Don't go telling this around, it's just between us, but keep things locked up for a while longer. I'm not sure it's safe yet."

George rose to leave and shook the sheriff's hand. "Thanks again. Annie and I appreciate your concern."

George went to gather Mr. Soo and say goodbye to Charlene. On the way home, Mr. Soo asked if there were any developments, and George told him everything except for the sheriff's new theory and suggested Mr. Soo still keep the house secure because there hadn't been an official arrest.

George put Pearl in the garage, and Mr. Soo went home for a nap, saying he might have eaten one too many doughnuts.

George opened the screen to the back lanai and realized they had indeed become lax in security; the screen had been unlocked all the while he was gone, and Annie was washing and drying clothes, causing quite a noise.

Annie was sitting at the kitchen bar doing a crossword and having coffee. She looked up when George came in. "Glad to see you and your lady friend made it back safely."

"Yep, me, Mr. Soo, and Pearl are all home safe. Honey, we have to talk about something, and I'm not happy about having to do this."

George went to the counter and swiveled her chair around so that she was facing him.

"Annie, we stopped by the sheriff's office, and he has been in meetings with the state police and local law enforcement. They are no further along in finding who murdered the Okamotos. However, the sheriff has changed his theory. He now believes that it was someone local with possibly a grudge against them or even jealous of Kim's success. This new line of thinking was based upon a crime-scene photo, which he showed me, and it looks like the killer took the time to stage them holding hands. No crazed doper would ever do that. The sheriff wanted you and me to know of his new theory so that we stay diligent on our security. We haven't done that, and we need to get back in the habit."

As George related all this information to Annie, she became pale and grasped her throat with her hand. She slowly slid off the chair and stumbled into George's grasp.

George hugged her to him and patted her back, saying, "We'll be OK, honey. We'll be OK."

CHAPTER 21

Layla took advantage of the bedroom and slept for two hours; she woke hungry, went to the galley, and heated the dinner Dewey provided. After taking her dishes back to the galley, she called the captain and inquired how long before they landed, and he told her in a little over one hour. Layla went to Dewey's desk and found a yellow tablet and pen. She sat about making a to-do list in priority to meet her goal of leaving Washington within four days. The list turned out to be more daunting once everything was on paper, and Layla realized she would need help. She would ask their housekeeper Zenzi for assistance. Zenzi had a sister, Magda, that Layla would gladly pay to aid in the packing. She would call Zenzi and ask her to arrange for Magda's help. Then she would call Dewey, to thank him for everything.

Hearing the ding of the Fasten Seat Belts sign, she took a seat, buckling up for the landing. After landing, she went to the front of the plane to thank the pilots for a safe journey. She also wanted to ask where she could call for a taxi to take her into the city.

"That won't be necessary. Mr. McMaster has arranged a car for you. He always provides transportation for his guests and for us. He's very considerate."

The stairs were lowered, and two limos were there to pick up their passengers. The driver assisted the crew in getting Layla's luggage into the trunk as she sat in the car and kept warm. Layla placed a call to Zenzi and told her she was leaving

Kyle and moving back to New York. Layla told her about all the packing, sorting, getting boxes, and straightening up that would need to be done and asked if she thought Magda would like to earn some extra money and assist. Zenzi said Magda would be glad to help; she rung off to call her, arranging to be at Layla's at nine the next morning.

Probably because Layla was dreading going back to the home she had known while she was pregnant, it seemed like she was there in no time. She reached into her wallet and pulled out $50 for the tip. Once the driver had her bags inside, she handed him the money.

"No, thank you, my tip has already been taken care of. You have a nice evening now." The driver tipped his hat, closed the door, and was gone.

Layla secured the lock, sighed, and looked around the cold apartment. Suddenly, a sense of loss and loneliness came over her, and she began to cry. She moved to the stairs that led to the upper level, threw her arms around her knees, and cried for the loss of her daughter, the years wasted with Kyle, and for almost losing herself. She had to move on, but she felt so alone, and then she remembered she must phone Dewey.

Layla dialed Dewey's number.

"Hello, Layla, is that you?"

"Yes, I'm home and on a crying jag. It's so empty and lonely here, I wish you were here."

"I can get a plane and be there in several hours. Will that help?"

"Dewey, you are such a good friend. No, you stay in Salt Lake City. I just have to get past this moment. I need to thank you for so much. The waiting limo was a surprise. You are so thoughtful, and it was a fabulous plane trip. I made myself a list of all the things I have to get done before I go back to New York. There is much more than I anticipated so I phoned my housekeeper. She and her sister will be here at nine in the morning to help me begin the move. Tonight, though, I felt down when I got inside, and now I feel much better. I'm going to take a nice hot shower and go to bed. There's a lot to begin doing tomorrow."

"Anytime you want to talk, remember, just call. There is nothing I'm doing that can't be interrupted to help a friend."

"Thanks again, Dewey. I'll call you before I leave for New York so you can keep tabs on me. I know you'll worry about how things are going, and I'm glad you are there to worry. It's nice to have someone who cares. Good night."

"Good night, Layla."

Dewey was in bed, reading technical papers, when Layla called, but after talking with her, he was unable to concentrate. He kept thinking of Layla in the shower, tucked in bed all alone, and he began to fantasize.

"Shit," he said out loud, turned the bedside light off, fluffed his pillow, and tried to sleep. He spent a fitful night dreaming of angels on top of Christmas trees, all with Layla's face.

Dewey's phone rang the following evening. "Hello, Layla?"

"Sorry, Dewey, it's George. Haven't you heard from Layla?"

"She called last night. I thought she was calling again."

"She got back safely, and is everything all right?"

"Yes, she made it safely home, but she got very emotional once inside, told me she had a crying jag. That must be a female thing. I wasn't quite sure what it meant."

"Yea, it's a female thing. When their emotions overwhelm them, a crying jag relieves the pressure. We guy cuss, kick things, have a beer, I go and pound things with a hammer. It's a pressure relief valve. Get used to it, son, if you want to have a successful marriage."

"Thanks, I never thought of that."

"One of the other reasons I called is to let you know you will probably be contacted by the Hawaii State Police to set up some type of video questioning. I suggested it since I knew your equipment and theirs would accommodate such a process. They came to the house yesterday, a Sunday no less, unannounced, to questioned Annie. She retold her story in vivid detail to their satisfaction. I felt so bad for her. The rest of the day she was so upset, and she had a crying jag, which did seem to help."

"I'm sorry Annie had to go through all that again. Any progress with those guys they arrested?"

"No, nothing. The biker was in jail in Hilo, and the college guy had a solid alibi. The other two aren't talking, and no one knows if one or both are involved or if they are keeping quiet because of their drug connections."

"I wonder if this thing will ever get solved."

"The sheriff told me confidentially, he has changed his theory about the murders. He now believes it was someone with a grudge against the Okamotos or against Kim for his success. He warned that we should maintain tight security. I'm letting you know, but don't tell Layla. He showed me a crime-scene photo, where the Okamotos were holding hands, and you could tell it was staged. The sheriff doesn't feel anyone high on dope would take the time to do such a thing, and I agree."

"That's horrible. What do the state police think?"

"They don't agree and laughed his theory off. But, Dewey, damned if I don't see his point."

"What about Mr. Soo? Did you say something to him?"

"I told him no arrest had been made, and he should continue to secure his home."

"George, give me the phone. I want to say hello. Hi, Dewey, I wanted to say hello personally and tell you that we miss you and Layla."

"I miss you both too, and I'm serious, I expect to see you both here this summer. Call me and I'll send a plane. In fact, I'll plan something special while you're here."

"We will come for a visit. Think you can get Layla to join us?"

"When you give me an exact date, I'll try. I know she'll want to see you both again."

George was back on the line again. "We'll say our goodbyes now, Dewey. Take care. We'll talk again soon, and see you this summer."

After George and Annie rang off, Dewey smiled. Having them visit would be a perfect way to get his angel back to Salt Lake City. He would plan something special for their visit.

CHAPTER 22

By mid-Thursday afternoon, three tired ladies sat at the kitchen counter, eating delivered pizza. They finished all the packing and tagging, Zenzi and Layla had loaded the SUV, and Zenzi was going to take the extra clothing and toiletry articles over to a women's shelter after lunch. The movers would be there tomorrow to pick up the thirty-some boxes and the three pieces of furniture going to New York.

When Zenzi returned, Layla told her she had sent Magda home in a taxi. Zenzi said she would return tomorrow, and when everyone was gone, she would clean up, making sure things were in order when Kyle got home.

The next morning the three-man team of movers arrived; in no time, the van was loaded, and the movers left.

Layla gave Zenzi an envelope that contained double the amount she had originally offered, along with a letter thanking her for her many kindnesses. She handed Zenzi various keys and drove off in her SUV.

Layla was happy to be on the road so early, although darkening skies did not thrill her, and she experienced intermittent showers the whole way to New York. Exhausted after what seemed like an eternity, she pulled into her garage, a half block from her brownstone, parked the SUV, unloaded one suitcase and toiletry case, locked up securely, and made her way to what was now home. Inside, she sat her luggage at the bottom of the stairs and headed for the kitchen, hoping Mrs. Pete, her old housekeeper, had left something to eat.

Mrs. Pete had worked for Layla and her family for many years, but when Layla moved to Washington, she went to work three days a week for another family. Layla had phoned and told her she would be moving back to New York and wondered if she were available. Mrs. Pete said she could only work Tuesdays and Thursdays for her, and Layla said that would be perfect. She told her of her plans to arrive late Friday night and asked if her son Jeff would be interested in earning some extra money by helping her unload her SUV on Saturday. Ms. Pete said he would be delighted to help, and they arranged for him to meet Layla on Saturday afternoon.

Layla found a small pot roast in the refrigerator, some fresh bread, and made herself a sandwich along with a bottle of beer. Sitting at the counter, eating the sandwich, and drinking the beer, she took stock of what she had accomplished and realized she couldn't have done it two months ago.

Feeling tired, she took her dishes to the sink, turned out the lights, and headed for the stairs. It took all her energy to get her bags upstairs and into the bedroom. Too tired to take a shower, she stripped down to her underwear, turned down the bed, and was asleep within seconds.

At ten the next morning, the ringing phone woke Layla, and she noted it was Mrs. Pete. "Hello, Mrs. Pete, I made it home late last night, and thank you for the food."

"You will find fresh coffee, along with yogurt and croissants. I didn't want you to come home and have to go out for food. I thought you might be quite tired after your drive. Do you still want Jeff this afternoon?"

"Definitely. I have a lot to get in order before I start work Tuesday. I'll meet Jeff here at one o'clock."

Downstairs, she made coffee and ate the food Mrs. Pete had laid in. At one sharp, her doorbell rang, and there stood Jeff. Layla wasn't even sure it was Jeff; it had been two years since she had seen him. He was a scrawny kid then, now she was looking into the face of a handsome young man.

"Jeff, is that you?"

"It's me, Ms. Layla. Guess you can say I grew up since we last saw each other. I'm sure sorry about the loss of your baby. Is Mr. Kyle back with you?"

"No, Jeff, we are ending our marriage. Losing our daughter was too much for us. We both are moving on. Come on in, and I'll get the keys. We'll go to the garage and start getting things back here."

In less than an hour, Jeff had carried everything upstairs, leaving only a few items in the foyer. Layla paid him as agreed, included a tip, and thanked him for his swift work.

Upstairs, she unpacked the clothing items and decided to go through her custom closets to see if there were any items she no longer wanted. To her dismay, over half the items in the closet were no longer stylish, including several with price tags still attached.

"Lord, this is going to be another project I had not anticipated," Layla said out loud.

Layla cleaned out old items and hung things she brought with her; she boxed some of the discarded clothing but would wait until the movers arrived and unpacked the other boxes before finishing up. She had pot roast for dinner and straightened up the kitchen, then she realized it was after eight and she was in need of a shower. After a steaming hot shower that relieved her sore muscles, she crawled into bed, got her cell phone, and feeling relaxed and happy, she called Dewey.

Dewey's cell was lying on his desk when it rang, and he grabbed it immediately.

"Hi, Dewey, I'm back in New York, in my home, and in somewhat a semblance of order, which will change when the movers bring the boxes."

"I thought you said you didn't have that much."

"Well, it didn't look like much, but once packed, I had over thirty boxes, plus several big items. Worse yet, when I got home and went to hang my clothes in the closet, I found that over half the things hanging there had to go. I've turned into a folding and packing fool," Layla said, laughing. "Are you at home enjoying that nice roaring fireplace?"

"I'm at work. We have a big presentation for the new digital format tomorrow. It's to a rapper who wants to use it in one of his videos, not my first choice, but it will get the product name known because he's a big name in rap music."

"Dewey, you need to go home and get some rest so you'll be bright and alert when you make your presentation."

"I'm about through here. I'll sleep at the office. Hidden behind a wall, I have a bedroom, bath, and closet full of clothes. Actually, it's quite comfortable. I've spent many nights sleeping here, don't mind it at all. Plus, it will save time getting here in the morning, making it easier to get our group to the airport, then to Los Angeles for our presentation."

"Sometimes, your life sounds exciting, but it also sounds lonely. You need somebody to share your life."

"One day, hopefully, some woman will fall in love with me, and we can raise a houseful of little DewMasters."

"You would be a fabulous catch for any woman, but you have to be careful to avoid the fortune hunters of this world. I've certainly dated my share in the past, easy to spot."

"I wouldn't know a fortune hunter unless they wore a sign. I don't date much. I don't have the time."

"My poor Dewey, what am I going to do with you?"

The only answer Dewey could think of would cause his angel to slam the phone down and never speak to him again. He mumbled, "Don't know, maybe you'll think of something."

They talked for a while longer before ending the call.

CHAPTER 23

George and Annie were on their front lanai, watching the sunset, snacking on clam dip, chips, and beer. They enjoyed this together time, usually an hour before dinner. George had Annie tucked across him, his left arm under her neck. The orange-red orb was getting bigger and bigger and reflecting off the blue ocean; it was a marvelous sight, one that never ceased to awe them.

"Honey, I've been thinking about visiting Dewey. We should go in May because during June and July, you and I both will be busy. You have your kids' volleyball clinic on Tuesday and Thursday, and I have my Tuesday and Thursday project at the senior center. Those folks enjoy learning how to commit their histories to a meaningful story for the heirs. We should look at a calendar and pick out a couple of weeks in May, then let Dewey know as soon as possible."

"A couple of weeks, that's a little long to impose on Dewey's hospitality, isn't it?"

"We could spend a week with Dewey, then go and visit Jennie and Charlie, spending a week between them. That way, our wonderful, adorable grandchildren will not wear us down to a couple of blithering idiots, like they do when they visit here."

"Let's go over our calendars and plan which weeks in May we should go. Call Jennie and Charlie tomorrow and see how those dates work with their schedules. Once we have that in place, we can call Dewey."

"I can't wait to see the kids and Dewey too. I sure hope he can get Layla to visit at the same time. I'm really excited about flying on a private jet. I can't imagine what that will be like. Best of all, no security hassle to contend with."

They started reviewing their calendars. The second and third weeks in May would work best for their schedules. They would call their children tomorrow then let Dewey know their plans.

The next afternoon they phoned Jennie and Charlie, deciding it would be wise to tell them they would be flying to Los Angeles the third week in May to eliminate any dispute between brother and sister which week was the most convenient for them. They would spend four days with Charlie and family and three days with Jennie and her family. They left it up to Jennie to decide if she would take the first three days to visit or the last. After three phone calls to Jennie, it was finally decided they would visit her the first three days, and everyone would drive to Charlie's for a cookout and drop George and Annie there for the remainder of their visit.

"George, will you please tell me how we could have possibly had such a well-educated airhead daughter. Can you believe she actually said she would run the options by Chad and the girls? The girls are two and five. What the hell do they have to do with the decision of when we should visit? Being a school counselor and married to a school administrator has made her too politically correct or something. Just talking to her, I've popped at least three more gray hairs," Annie said, scratching her head.

"Honey, I hate to admit it, but they are a tad ditzy, maybe too well educated. Both she and Chad are always taking some advanced class. They have advanced themselves out of reality. Now, good old Charlie, he has the clear-thinking mind of an engineer," George said with a grin.

"He has your easygoing manner, and he's sensible. Please don't tell me Jennie takes after me."

"Lord no, you are the most levelheaded person I know. I don't know where she gets it from, like I said, overeducated. Think we should phone Dewey now?"

"It's pretty late in Utah. We should wait until tomorrow. Right now, I'm too peeved at Jennie to sound happy when we speak to Dewey. Is that OK with you?"

"That's fine."

The following afternoon, George and Annie called Dewey's personal line. He answered right away. "Hi, folks, everything OK?"

"Fine. We called to take you up on your offer to come for a visit, if you still want us."

"Are you kidding? I've even planned in advance things to do and places for us to visit. When can I send the plane?"

George hesitated, feeling awkward having Dewey send a plane for them. "If it isn't too much trouble, we thought we would visit the second week in May. Then we will catch a regular flight out of Salt Lake City and spend the third week in the Los Angeles area, visiting our kids and grandkids. We'll head home from Los Angeles."

"I'm checking and I have nothing happening then, so I'm blocking that week off. Do not even consider getting any commercial flights. My plane will take you two anywhere you want to go. I won't have it any other way."

Annie got on the line. "Dewey, you are so good to us. We really appreciate you flying us around. Do you think you can get Layla out for a visit too? I miss her. Let her know I asked you to coax her into a visit."

"I'll call her this evening, and by things she's said in our weekly conversations, she's anxious to see you both. Hope she wants to see me too."

"Dewey, you had better do something about that situation between you and her before someone else grabs her up. She is a prime catch, and once word gets out she's getting divorced, she'll have a lot of guys chasing her," George cautioned.

"I know, I'm afraid of that. I'm so stupid when I'm around her. She's so precious to me, and I don't want to say or do anything to screw up what we have."

"Maybe when we all get together, George and I can steer her in your direction. Do you know how her divorce is coming along?"

"She told me she and Kyle have talked things out, and to make things easier for him because of his schedule, he will be filing, and she will not contest anything, provided things are spelled out as they agreed. When we last talked about it, she wasn't sure how long that would take. When would you folks like to leave Maui, on a Sunday or a Monday?"

"Dewey, that's your choice. Let us know a little in advance, and we'll be ready to leave when the plane arrives."

Dewey rang Layla's number. "Hi, Layla, it's Dewey."

"Dewey, what's new in Utah?"

"I have great news. Spoke with George and Annie, and they're coming for a visit the second week in May. They asked me to talk with you and let you know how much they would love for all of us to get together. Is it possible for you to come and visit for a week? I'll send a plane."

"There should be no problem. If I'm not finished with the vestibule restoration, I'm certain Judy won't mind if I take a week off. She can go to the spa she keeps talking about."

"Great, I'm working on plans for us. We'll have a wonderful visit, and I know Annie and George will be happy you can join us. Who's Judy?"

"She's the lady that owns the brownstone where I'm doing the restoration, and she is one of my two friends, you being the other."

"What are you talking about? I thought you had a large New York group of friends."

"I did when I left, but now that I'm back, things have changed. I should have told you sooner, but I was embarrassed to admit that I don't fit in here anymore. About three-fourths of my old friends are married and have or are expecting children. I visited two of them for dinner, and because they knew of my circumstances, it was a touchy situation for all. The other group of my friends are still out there on the nightclub and party circuit, and that's not my scene, frankly, never felt very comfortable at those clubs."

"I wish you had told me sooner. I could have come for a visit and cheered you up."

"That's where Judy's comes in. When I first went to see the vestibule, Judy greeted me with a Bloody Mary in hand, and it was only ten in the morning. She was brassy looking and pretty looped. I was impressed with the work the cleaners had already done and anxious to have something to do or else I would have walked out right then. Every morning, Judy would open the door with her Bloody Mary and coffee for me. She expected that we talk before I started work. I felt sorry for her, and I knew from experience how much having someone to talk with means to a person. I listened to her story, and darn if I didn't begin to feel sorry for her, so I told her what had happened to me, even including the Maui events. Before long, I was looking forward to our morning discussions, and Judy now met me with coffee for both of us. Judy married her husband when she was twenty-one and he was thirty. They agreed not to have children until they were in better financial shape. Judy is now forty-three, with no kids because they never got around to it. His secretary took a month off to be with her daughter who was undergoing cancer treatment and a cute young blonde temp came to replace her. Six months later, Bernard is filing for divorce. A year later, he and the temp are getting married, and two weeks ago, Judy found out the happy couple are expecting."

"That's horrible. I hope she got a good settlement."

"Yes, she did very well in the divorce. He could well afford the money, and from what she told me, he had more than a little guilt. We have become friends. She had me take her shopping for a new wardrobe, new hairdo, in fact, a complete makeover.

She looks great, certainly a far cry from that boozy divorcee I first met. I took her shopping with me last Saturday to various consignment stores. We seem to connect in a manner in which my old friends and I cannot. So you see. I have two great friends. You are my best friend, Dewey, and then Judy is my other friend. Pretty sad for someone my age, only two friends."

"I remember reading a paper when I was in school that said as we get older, our circle of friends naturally diminish. As people age, their likes and dislikes change, their perspectives on life changes, thus, their friendships usually narrow down to one or two people they can trust and speak with freely. Seems to me you're right on track."

"I knew it, Dewey, I should have told you this all along. As usual, you have made me feel better. Thank you, my friend," Layla said, a catch in her voice.

"If you're sure you can be here the second week in May, I'll phone George and Annie and give them the good news. Let me know when you want me to send the plane, Friday, Saturday, or Sunday, and I'll make the arrangements. They will either be coming on a Sunday or Monday. Everyone can stay here before we head out on our journey."

"What journey?"

"That's my surprise, but be sure you bring a camera, plenty of film, hiking boots, and that's all I'm telling you."

"Now I'm really excited. I'll call you tomorrow night to hear what George and Annie said. Thank you again, Dewey. Talk with you tomorrow."

George answered the phone, "Aloha."

"Aloha yourself, it's Dewey. Just spoke with Layla and I had to call and let you know she'll be here and can't wait to see you both."

"Dewey, that's terrific. Annie, come here, it's Dewey," George called out to Annie, putting the phone on speaker. "He just spoke with Layla, and she'll be joining us this May."

"Dewey, that's wonderful. I'm so excited to see you both. Thank you for asking her, and I'm sure she is anxious to see you just as much as she is to see George and me."

"I hope that's the case. We talked quite a long time tonight, and whatever happens, I know I'll have a friend for life. Maybe we can become more than friends."

"Annie and I are best friends. Believe me, friendship is a wonderful start on the road to love. Of course, lust isn't bad either," George said, laughing.

"George Boone, watch what you say. You'll give him ideas."

"As if he hasn't already had those ideas."

"Got to admit, Annie, my imagination has run a wide range of possibilities where Layla is concerned."

"Men, you all are alike," Annie said, laughing.

"I'll tell you what I told Layla. I'm planning a surprise, bring a camera, plenty of film, and hiking boots. We're going to have a fun adventure."

"What's that mean, adventure?" Annie asked.

"You'll have to wait and see."

Chapter 24

Layla watched as the plane Dewey sent approached the hangar area. She turned to gather Pullman cases and a tote; there was a lot of luggage, but Dewey had been so vague on their "adventure" she decided to pack for anything he had arranged. She turned back and began to maneuver her luggage to the plane; the stairs were lowered, and bounding down them came Dewey. Layla let go of the luggage handles, rushing to him.

"Dewey, what a wonderful surprise." Saying this, she pressed herself to him, giving him a big hug.

Taken by surprise, Dewey gripped her tightly, returning the embrace. As a certain part of his body began to respond to Layla, he grabbed her waist with both hands, holding her away from his body. "I can't believe you. What a difference these months have made! You look even more beautiful than I remember. Your hair is adorable, short, and bouncy, makes you look happier. You've put on some weight. You look wonderful!"

"Dewey, always saying just the right thing. I'm so happy you're here. When will Annie and George be arriving?"

"They come in Sunday afternoon. I'm glad you were able to leave on a Friday. You can help me with my surprise tomorrow."

"I don't suppose you are going to tell me or give me any hint as to what that might be?"

"Nope."

*   *   *

Saturday morning, Dewey and Layla sat at the large kitchen counter eating breakfast prepared by Agnes. Layla ate a three-egg, sausage, cheese, onion, and salsa omelet, along with fried potatoes, and was on her third homemade biscuit with butter and honey.

"I'm amazed at the amount of food you're eating," Dewey said.

"Me too. I don't get this type of cooking back home, and these biscuits are sheer heaven," she said to Agnes. "Dewey, you must enjoy all this excellent cooking. No junk food served here, I'm sure."

"When I was in Paia, I ate enough junk food to last a lifetime. Mr. Soo was my mentor in that respect."

"I can't imagine he has an artery in his body that isn't clogged."

"That's the funny part because he is chairman of the board of his company. It is required he take a yearly physical. He passes with flying colors each year. I guess it's because he spends his days walking all over the place. He's quite a guy. Wish he had a happier home life."

"Me too. Annie explained his situation to me. Guess all of us have parts of our lives that cause pain and anxiety. I hope when I'm his age, I will be with someone and be as happy as Annie and George."

"You and me both," Dewey said, looking longingly at Layla as she enjoyed the remains of her breakfast. "I'll go and bring a car around to the front, and you can get ready for today's little trip. This is really to check up on what we'll need for our big adventure. Agnes, everything ready on your end?"

"All set here, Dewey," Agnes said.

Dewey turned the Jeep into an industrial section of Salt Lake City. He drove into a garage where Layla saw a huge motor home befitting a rock star sitting front and center.

"Dewey McMaster, welcome."

"Orin, good to be here. She's a beauty," Dewey said, nodding at the motor home. Orin, I would like you to meet my friend, Layla Richfield. Layla, this is Orin Johnson. He runs this establishment, and he provides custom-made cars, motor homes, and trailers. He's the best in the business, and a lot of people come to him for custom jobs."

Layla extended her hand to Orin. "A pleasure to meet you, Mr. Johnson. Are you responsible for this big I'm not sure what one calls it?"

"Yes, I am. It's made to Dewey's specifications. He's a whiz at specifications. Guess it comes with his background. It's a mobile home and comes with two bedrooms, two bathrooms, living room, dining room, a nice-sized kitchen, and a built-in outdoor grilling area. I had a blueprint from Dewey for everything he wanted."

"No place to land a helicopter?" Layla asked, laughing.

"Now why didn't I think of that?" Dewey said. "Let's look inside. We've just got today to get everything right before we take off."

"Ready to share with me any of our travel plans?"

A short time later, Dewey and Layla said their goodbyes and were on their way back to Dewey's, Layla following Dewey in the Jeep.

"Not yet. You just focus on what Agnes could be fixing for lunch."

"Yummy, can't wait."

George and Annie watched the plane taxi toward them. "Wow, he sent the big one. This is exciting. All those years working in the airline industry, and I've never flown on a private jet until now. I feel like a kid on his first trip to Disneyland. We are so going to enjoy this experience."

Making their way toward the plane, George rolled the large suitcases while Annie handled the totes. Down the steps came the pilot extending his hand, introducing himself. "I'm Neil Russell, your pilot. You must be George and Annie Boone.

Dewey has instructed us to take good care of you both." He then introduced his copilot. "This is Leslie Garcia, your copilot."

George and Annie shook hands with both pilots. Leslie told them she was in charge of refueling and getting food on board. Leaving the group, she headed for the hangar.

"Honey, why don't you go on inside and I'll help Mr. Russell stow our luggage. Mr. Russell, I'm thrilled to be flying on a private jet. I've worked at this airport all my life and have always wanted to fly on one of these babies, I just never got the opportunity. I'm a retired engineer for United. My specialty was baggage configuration, and I did all types of engineering studies involving passengers, security, check-in, etc. Pretty much know my way around the whole place."

"It will be my pleasure to show you around this beauty inside and out."

"Terrific, I would love to know all I can," George said, assisting in loading the luggage.

Half an hour later, George and Neil made their way inside the cabin.

"Good to see you. I was wondering what happened to you guys."

"Mr. Boone was eager to see the workings on the outside of the plane, and I was happy to show her off to someone that could appreciate what this plane is capable of. Now, let me show you the cockpit."

Annie smiled and nodded at George to go ahead; she could see he was having a grand time familiarizing himself with the plane. Several minutes later, Leslie returned to the cabin and said they would be leaving in forty-five minutes, and soon she and Neil would begin preflight procedures. Following Leslie were caterers bringing food for their trip.

When George returned to Annie's side, he was all smiles, and Annie was in a mellow mood, enjoying a large mug of Kona coffee. "George, you have to look around. The bathroom is fabulous. It even has a shower, off the bedroom."

"What did you say?"

"I said the bathroom is fabulous. The lotions are really first class."

"No, I mean about the bedroom."

"Beyond the bathroom is a bedroom with a king-sized bed."

George shot out of his seat and headed toward the rear of the plane. He came back. "Annie, this trip just keeps getting better and better."

Neil's voice came over the PA system, announcing they would be taking off and to buckle their seat belts. Annie quickly took her empty cup back to the galley, eyed the coffeepot, and promised herself another cup once in the air. George traded seats with her so he could check things out during takeoff. Annie squeezed his arm, thinking he was so cute when he got excited about mechanical things.

After they were clear of the island, Leslie came into the cabin and said, "I know it's early for you folks, but Neil and I are hungry. It's been a long time since we last ate. I'm going to sit the meat and cheese platters out, along with several salads, and you can help yourselves or I can put things away and you can eat later. But first, I'm making fresh coffee."

"All that walking around outside and the excitement of seeing everything has made me hungry. How about you, Annie?"

"Yes, I could eat."

Neil and Leslie ate their lunch, Neil joining George and Annie at a table in the lounge. He and George enjoyed technical talk while Annie enjoyed more Kona coffee.

George and Annie moved to the sofa, and Annie admitted, "I'm so mellow. That was a great lunch and with the easy movement of the plane, I bet I could take a nap."

"Annie, you know all the years working for the airlines, the guys often teased me about my status in the mile-high club. I hate to admit this, but I would just wink and smile. Which, of course, led them to believe we were members. Well, sweetheart, here is our chance to become legitimate members. There's a great big bed just beyond those doors, and it would be natural for us to take a nap after that big lunch. What do ya say?" George asked, pulling Annie to his side and stroking her cheek.

Annie reached her arm around George's neck, pulling his face close to her. "Far be it for me not to fulfill our membership qualifications. Frankly, I think it will be sort of fun, with the plane's motion and all." She kissed him lightly on the lips; they got up from the sofa, walking down the aisle toward the bedroom.

"Damn, honey, that was amazing. You were right. The motion of the plane made it even more intense. Let me officially thank you for my membership in the mile-high club."

"I believe that qualifies both of us for membership. Do we have time for a little nap? I'm actually sleepy."

George checked his watch. "We have another three hours until we get into Salt Lake City. I can set the alarm for an hour and a half from now, and we both can get a quick nap. How does that sound?"

Yawning, Annie replied, "Perfect, honey, and make sure you set it right. I don't want Leslie or Neil coming back here, finding us like this."

"Just make them jealous," George said with a grin.

When the plane landed, George and Annie thanked Neil and Leslie for a great flight and their wonderful hospitality. Walking down the stairway, they looked up, and to their surprise, there stood Dewey and Layla.

"Oh gosh!" Annie exclaimed as she gave them big hugs. "I didn't expect to see both of you. This has been such a fantastic day, and now both of you are here." Annie teared up and hugged Layla again as Dewey headed toward George and the luggage.

Before they returned to the company of the ladies, George turned to Dewey and said, "I've just got to thank you for sending the big plane. Neil and Leslie were amazing, but somehow I think you had another motive in mind, which we took full advantage of."

George's grin was all Dewey needed to know that his actual motive in sending the big plane had paid off.

Luggage was loaded in Dewey's SUV, and everyone settled in. Annie asked where the adventure was taking them.

"Wait until you see what Dewey has gotten for our trip. You simply won't believe it. I was amazed."

"George, you're going to love this," Dewey said, knowing George's penchant for anything mechanical.

As they entered the gates to Dewey's estate, George immediately spied the large mobile home. "Wow, she's beautiful. I can't wait to hear where we're going."

"Let's get the luggage in the house, then Layla and I will give you a tour. Afterward, we'll go inside for drinks, and I'll show you our itinerary," Dewey announced proudly.

After George and Annie went on their jaw-dropping tour, Dewey ushered everyone inside to the family room and offered drinks. They all opted for beer as they sat around a table, eagerly awaiting the promised itinerary.

Dewey gave everyone a printed copy of the adventure and watched as they read through the listed points.

"I went to the Grand Canyon when I was young, to the South Rim. I've always heard the North Rim was much nicer and that there are hardly any people. My dad wanted to go on to Zion, but he had promised Mom he would take her to Laughlin, so we only saw the Grand Canyon. But what a sight! Being raised around Los Angeles, the first thing that came to my mind when I saw it was it looked like a movie backdrop. It just couldn't possibly be real."

"George, did you really think that? How cute," Annie said. "My family went to the South Rim too, but I didn't like it. Too many people, gas fumes, and there was smog."

"They have controlled the South Rim much better over the last years, keeping cars away and taking green buses. Visibility has almost gotten back to normal, and I understand there is now a daily limit on visitors. For all the years I've lived in Utah,

I've never seen the Grand Canyon, Bryce Canyon, or Zion, so this will be a real treat for me. Layla, have you ever visited any of these areas before?"

"You have to be kidding. My parents would consider a trip like this so beneath them. I'm so excited, but, Dewey, are you sure you can maneuver through those mountains with that big tank out there?"

"Sure, I came home every summer from MIT for eight weeks' vacation. Dad would rent a big mobile home and take it to Pismo Beach. He let me drive it the first time when I was sixteen. He said if I was genius enough to be at MIT, I was genius enough to drive a mobile home to Pismo Beach. Mom hated going, so it was just Dad and me. If she had known I was driving a mobile home, she would have killed Dad. It was always our secret. Those times hold special memories for me. We were a great team."

Everyone was quite for a minute after Dewey spoke. Layla patted his hand. "With your early experience, I think you will be the perfect driver."

"Dewey, maybe if there is a stretch of straight land, you can give me a few driving lessons. I've always wanted to try my hand at one of these big babies."

"George, I had that exact thing in mind, and I know just the spot."

"Good lord, George, first you were goofy about that airplane, now you're wanting to drive a mobile home."

"Just want to expand my realm of knowledge."

"He'll be fine, Annie, I'm a great teacher."

The group continued to discuss the trip until Agnes came in to announce dinner was ready.

"Good, I'm starving," announced Layla.

"Ever since Layla has gotten here, she has emulated Mr. Soo's appetite," Dewey said, laughing.

"Agnes's cooking is so much better than New York take-out. I'm enjoying it while I can. By the way, Agnes, what's your hand in all this?"

"I prepared frozen dishes for you to take along. In case there aren't any good places for dinner or lunch, you can enjoy a nice meal. Take it from me. Sometimes, a good place to eat along that route is hard to come by. We've been to Bryce Canyon several times. I love that place. I find it very feminine. When the shadows fall on the spires, they turn pink and look like fine lace. Well, anyway, that's what it reminds me of," she said, laughing. "Come on, folks, while everything is still warm."

Everyone adjourned to the informal dining room for their evening meal while excitedly discussing their upcoming adventure.

CHAPTER 25

The next morning they were up early, had breakfast, loaded up the mobile home with the remaining luggage, and were on the road to Bryce Canyon by nine. Dewey and George were pilot and navigator; Annie and Layla were in the lounge, discussing their plans for the night. Dewey had pulled off at a mile-marker exit and told George it was his turn to be pilot. After explaining the workings of the mobile home, George turned back onto the interstate.

Annie knew what was going on when they stopped.

"George is now driving. I would love to go up front and see how he's doing, but I'm afraid I'll make him nervous. Could you go and check things out?" Annie asked Layla.

"Sure, glad to. I'll ask what time we should be at the Bryce Canyon Lodge."

Layla made her way to the front; she pulled the separation curtain back and acted surprised to see George driving. Layla posed her questions to Dewey.

"We'll be there around three or four, and we're staying at the lodge. We also have dinner reservations. My secretary called early this morning and has arranged for one of the touring limousines with a guide to take us through Bryce Canyon tomorrow morning."

"That sounds great," Layla said. "I brought my sketchpad and charcoals. I was hoping to get some sketching done. I'll take a lot of photos. I can sketch from those too."

"I didn't know you sketched," George said.

"Originally, I wanted to be an artist, and I started out sketching. I enjoyed doing landscapes. Those sell in some parts of the country but not in New York City. While taking a particular art course, I had a teacher who taught me how to mix paints to give them an older patina. I got started on researching paints and mixtures used in old art. The result of that was doing restoration work, which I truly love. Recapturing lost artwork or restoring something beautiful makes me feel very gratified."

"I'm impressed. I didn't realize you had such an artistic background. I don't actually know what restoration entails. You'll have to explain it more to me. Maybe we can develop a computer program that can assist restoration artists in making paint choices."

"Don't you just love this man?" Layla said, hugging Dewey from behind. "Such a curious, genius mind. It's a thrill for me just to be in your company."

"Sounds like a mutual lovefest," George said teasingly, his eyes never leaving the road.

"You might find this hard to believe," Layla said, "but I'm getting hungry. Is there a picnic ground somewhere we can pull into?"

Dewey looked at the detailed map and found one about eight miles farther up the highway. "George, I'll tell you when we're coming up on the exit, and you can head off the road. If you have any trouble parking, I'll take over. Layla, you and Annie start getting something ready for lunch that doesn't take long so we don't lose too much time off the road."

"You don't have to ask me twice to start getting the food out." Layla went back to the kitchen area, telling Annie they needed to get a start on lunch because they were pulling into a nearby rest stop. "Don't worry, George is doing a great job. He is very intent on the road and appears quite competent."

After a quick lunch stop, Dewey took the driver's seat, and they were back on the road to Bryce Canyon. Annie and Layla cleaned up the kitchen and settled in the lounge to look at the passing scenery through the large picture windows. They fell asleep, only waking as Dewey pulled off the highway, following the map given them at the canyon entrance.

The rustic look of the lodge and its dramatic setting blended right into the park's natural appearance. They gathered their luggage, locked up the mobile home, and went to register at the lodge. All three rooms were on the second floor close to one another. Annie and Layla decided to take a tour of the lodge's gift shop; George and Dewey went to the lobby to make sure all was set for the tour tomorrow. At sunset, everyone was outside, marveling at the beautiful sight that the shadows created at Bryce Canyon, awed by the color displayed on the rock formations. That evening, they went to bed, smelling fresh pine-scented mountain air.

The next morning they met for breakfast in the restaurant. Their two-hour tour in the vintage classic English touring limousine began at ten, Layla and Annie making sure they had plenty of film for their cameras. When George and Dewey saw the limousine, they had questions for their driver who was excited to have two engineers asking about the workings of the limousine. He gave them a tour under the bonnet, explaining how everything worked. The actual tour took them to major vistas and points of interest throughout the park. Resting for an hour after lunch, everyone was in hiking boots, ready to explore the Queen's Garden Trail; they watched their time closely so they would be at Sunset Point in time to see the setting sun.

It had been a spectacular day, and they decided to take advantage of Agnes's cooking for dinner, no one wanting to dress for dinner. Later, they sat outside, enjoying the night air in the shadow towers of Bryce Canyon.

The next morning luggage went back in the mobile home, and they were on to Zion National Park. There was a mobile home/campground close to a park entrance. Dewey pulled in, confirmed their reservation, and found the allotted space. For the next two nights, they would be sleeping in the mobile home and using the Jeep, which was hooked up in the back of the mobile home on a tow bar, to explore Zion.

Once in Zion, they went to the Visitors Center to collect available brochures and literature. In bold contrast to the lace-like delicate shapes of Bryce Canon, Zion's rugged canyon walls and rock formations looked formidable. They elected to take the Zion Canyon scenic drive to figure out where they would begin their hike. They stopped at a roadside rest area and ate the lunch Layla had insisted on packing. The scenic drive took most of the day, but they did manage to decide on a hike site for the following day that would afford them the most temple views. They turned in early, looking forward to a day of hiking.

After a big breakfast, each loaded their backpacks with protein bars and water and headed off in the Jeep to their hiking destination. Their hike brought them to sandstone wonders, unique plants, and some unsuspected wildlife sightings. By three that afternoon, four tired hikers piled back into the Jeep and headed for the campgrounds.

Layla declared, "I'm starving, I could eat a horse!"

Dewey suggested they grill burgers, which would provide the quickest meal for a weakening Layla who was munching on a bag of potato chips. Dewey deferred the actual grilling to George, and by four that afternoon, everyone was eating cheeseburgers with all the trimmings. After enjoying another beautiful sunset amid the mountains, they went to bed to get an early start toward the Grand Canyon.

Inside Grand Canyon National Park, Layla expected to see the canyon right away.

"Dewey, are you sure you went the correct way? There's nothing here but forests."

"Yes, you have to wait for the tree line to break and the canyon to be visible."

It wasn't long before an excited "Yikes!" came from Layla. "There it is! My god, it's huge. I thought it would be narrow, but it's mammoth. Oops, it's hiding behind trees again."

"Once we're at the Grand Canyon Lodge, you'll be able to see a great deal of the canyon."

"I can't wait. This is so exciting. New York is beginning to lose any appeal it once held for me. I love the smell of green freshness and the sights are so fabulous," Layla said with such enthusiasm, it took everyone by surprise.

"I thought you were a true New Yorker?" George asked.

"I thought I was too, but after seeing all this wonder in only four days, the skyscrapers and concrete have lost a lot of their charm."

As they continued to the lodge, views of the canyon became more and more frequent until it took up the entire panorama.

Dewey let everyone and their luggage out in front of the lodge and parked where he was directed. It was a lovely rock and timber lodge, richly appointed with a charming staff. Everyone met in the lounge after settling in, deciding how to spend the remainder of the day. Reading through brochures, Layla and Annie decided they would take a one-day mule trip into the canyon the next day with George and Dewey declining. George said he was too tall for a mule and Dewey admitted he had a vertigo issue. They walked around outside the lodge, amazed at the colors and vistas of the Grand Canyon. After lunch, they went on a small hike close to the area. After dinner, they had coffee around a huge outside fire pit with lights from the lodge aimed at a distant canyon wall. There was little conversation, the sights and night sounds making human noise seem irreverent.

The next morning Annie and Layla set out on their mule trip. George was not happy about Annie venturing on a mule that would be traversing narrow trails leading endlessly downward, but he knew better than to voice his objection. Stopping Annie from an adventure of this type would only cause regret, and he would not do anything to lessen her joy of life. Dewey was just as worried about Layla, but like George, he knew it would be unwise to voice such worry. After goodbyes, the ladies were off on their mule trip, leaving Dewey and George to spend an uneasy afternoon. They ate lunch outside on the patio, and even after a couple of beers, both still harbored fear that something bad might have happened to the ladies.

Layla and Annie were having a wonderful time; each took several rolls of film, having other tour participants take their photo and returning the favor. They ate a large catered lunch and began the return trip up the canyon wall. Late that afternoon, two giggling, happy women ended their journey and were greeted by two worried-looking men. George and Dewey went to get hugs and were immediately stopped.

"You do not want to come close to either of us. We smell like sweaty mules. Plus, we are a bit stinky ourselves," Annie said, laughing. "We both need a shower. Why don't we meet you two in the bar in a bit, and we'll tell you all about our mule safari."

George and Dewey were glad to see both ladies had made it back safely, they celebrated with more beers. By the time Annie and Layla appeared, they were in high spirits, and the ladies decided they had better go into dinner before anyone drank any more.

They left the Grand Canyon at the crack of dawn, hoping to reach Salt Lake City early enough to not keep the pilots waiting to take Annie and George onto Los Angeles. They had breakfast in the mobile home, Dewey eating once out of the canyon while George was driving on a straight stretch of highway. After breakfast, Layla began drawing with her charcoals, and Annie began addressing postcards to friends back in Maui. In no time, they were past the turnoffs to both Zion and Bryce Canyons, everyone knowing that their journey together would soon be coming to an end. Layla was working with great intent on her drawing, not even mentioning it was getting close to lunch. Annie ventured up front and suggested they pull into a rest stop and have lunch. About ten miles up the road, Dewey pulled off, while Annie prepared their final meal together.

Layla moved her work off the table and into her bedroom. She came out shortly before lunch was served and announced,

"Annie, George, I hope you will accept the liberties taken by the artist. I've combined Bryce Canyon scenery with you two at the Zion campsite, and I wanted to give you this charcoal as a memento of this wonderful week and how much it has meant to me to have shared it with you both."

George gasped and, not realizing it, grabbed his throat with his hand.

"My god, Layla. It so beautiful," Annie said. "George is speechless."

George was speechless because Layla's drawing depicted a beautiful view of Bryce Canyon at sunset, highlighting the pinks and purples; however, what caused him to gasp was that she had drawn Annie and him sitting in lawn chairs, holding hands. All that showed was their heads leaning into each other, George's long fingers entwined around Annie's hand. It was almost an exact replica of the photo the sheriff had shown him of the Okamoto crime scene without the scenery. George would not say a word to anyone, especially Annie, but the sketch troubled him. He thanked Layla, saying he knew Annie would have it framed and hung where they would see it daily.

They ate lunch quickly and were back on the road in less than an hour. There was a long stretch of road, and George was happy to drive, taking his mind off the charcoal Layla had drawn. Dewey relaxed and took a short nap. Annie and Layla talked about their trip and promised to exchange the many photos they had taken.

Annie decided it was time she broached the subject of Dewey to Layla. "Layla, I do hope you realize Dewey is in love with you."

"He's my best friend and I know he loves me as his friend, and right now, that's all I'm interested about. Having a man in my life other than a friend is not in my current plans."

Shortly before takeoff time, they were at the private field, and the luggage was loaded on Dewey's plane. George and Annie thanked and hugged both Dewey and Layla, making them promise to visit Maui soon.

As the plane lifted off, Layla grabbed Dewey's arm, with a catch in her voice. "Gosh, I'm going to miss them so much."

Dewey put his around Layla's shoulder, heading her back to the mobile home. "Stay a few more days, rest, and enjoy the clear Utah air a little longer, not to mention Agnes's cooking."

"That does it. Agnes's cooking is a deal maker. If it's OK with you, I'll stay a couple more days. Frankly, I'm pooped."

Dewey smiled and hugged her closer; that was just fine by him—in fact, that was great.

CHAPTER 26

George and Annie wearily trod up the stairway where Leslie greeted them. "You two look exhausted. You must have had quite a vacation," Leslie said, stowing their carry-on luggage.

They took their seats. Annie explained, "We had a wonderful week with Dewey and Layla. We toured Bryce, Zion, and the North Rim of the Grand Canyon. Then we visited our children and grandkids, and all hell broke loose. First, Disneyland for twelve hours. The next day, LEGOLAND. The next day, a waterslide park, then to our son's house for a family barbecue. Mercifully, the next day we stayed at Charlie's and rested. What a treat! By then, we were numb.

"The next day it was Universal Studios, and the following afternoon, Charlie and his wife thought we would enjoy going with them on a Hollywood bus tour. At least we got to sit, but I don't think either of us could tell you anything we saw. Our minds had shut down by then. We lead a slower life in Paia. This go-go-go attitude is something we aren't used to, and that freeway driving scared us like crazy. Guess we're showing our age."

"With that schedule, I wouldn't have fared much better, and I'm only thirty-six," Leslie said, laughing. "Do you want some coffee, Annie, and what can I get for you, George?"

"I would love a cup of your good coffee, thank you."

"Just a water for me. The air here has made me dry."

"I can understand that. The Santa Anas have been blowing, and they can make your throat and nose feel like a dust bowl.

I'll bring your drinks right away. Sit back, strap in, and relax. You can nap all the way to Maui."

"I hope we recover enough to handle our classes on Tuesday."

"Don't remind me. I've been trying to forget, but this nagging little voice keeps telling me volleyball camp is in two days."

"Once we get home, let's forget about unpacking and just sleep."

Leslie brought coffee and water, telling them, "We have a nice lunch ready whenever you feel like eating. Today we have a pasta dish you can heat up in the microwave, along with some garlic bread. There is green salad that just needs dressing. If you need any help, let me know. Otherwise, I'll leave you on your own."

"Thank you. When we feel like lunch, we'll help ourselves."

After takeoff, both Annie and George slept for about three hours. They woke up hungry, prepared lunch, ate, and cleaned up afterward. Taking their seats with full stomachs, they dozed until Leslie came and told them they would be landing shortly.

George and Annie followed Neil down the stairway and helped load their luggage into a waiting taxi. Annie thanked Leslie and gave her their phone number, making her promise to call if she or Neil decided to spend some time on Maui.

As the taxi pulled up to their home, Annie turned to George. "I had a great time, but I'm so glad we're home."

"Me too, honey, me too."

They got luggage from the taxi up the stairs into a stuffy house and turned on the air so they could lock the house and nap. George was taking the last piece of luggage into the bedroom when someone knocked on the lanai slider.

"George, is that someone at the door?"

"It's Ned Keller from across the driveway. Hi, Ned, come on in. We're just back from a couple of weeks on the mainland. What can I do for you?" George said, letting Ned in, Annie joining them.

"Folks, I wanted you to hear the news as soon as you got back because I didn't want you to face any awkward moments with Mr. Soo. Thursday after you left, Mrs. Soo passed away from a massive stroke."

"What! I can't believe it. Was she alone when it happened?"

"Annie, sorry to report, it happened midmorning, and Mr. Soo doesn't return from his walks until late afternoon. The coroner said she died immediately and did not suffer."

"What about services?" George asked.

"There were no services. Her remains were cremated, and after paying a large sum to the Chinese government, her sons took her remains back to China for burial next to her parents. She would have wanted that. She missed her beloved China so much."

"How is Mr. Soo doing? Is he on the island, or did he go with one of his sons in Oahu?"

"No, he's here, although not in their home. It's now for sale. Mr. Soo bought that little bungalow across the street from his former home, the one that had been on the market for over six months with owners anxious to sell. It wasn't moving because it was a two-bedroom, one-bath home. I helped him get quick occupancy, and Fiona helped him with furnishing. Mr. Soo spent about four hours in his old home, gathering things that mattered to him, then left and never went back. After getting rid of Mrs. Soo's personal items, the property is up for sale as it was left."

"Ned, we're shocked. Do you think we should go visit Mr. Soo?" George asked.

"He would love to see you both. He's back at his daily routine, except he has both breakfast and dinner at Otis's and gets home around sunset. He appears to be fine, but I do think he missed you folks. He has asked me twice when you were getting back. I'm going to go now. I know you are just getting back home and have a lot to attend to. I'm sorry I had to hit you with the news, but I felt you would want to know right away."

"Thank you, Ned. We'll go see Mr. Soo later this evening. We're so shocked all this happened and feel bad we weren't here to assist him when he might have needed us."

"Well, Annie, you never know when tragedy will strike. We can't sit around waiting for bad things to happen," Ned left Annie and George, going back to his home.

George pulled Annie into him, holding her tightly. "Honey, we should call Dewey and let him know, then he can phone Layla. I imagine she has left for New York by now."

"I hate to tell him. He was quite close to Mr. Soo. They enjoyed each other's company," Annie said.

Dewey was at his desk when his private cell rang. He saw the call was from George and Annie and assumed they were going to tell him they were back home. "Hi, folks, guess this means you made it home safely. Glad you called."

"Dewey, we're fine, but we have bad news." Annie got that much out before her voice broke, and she handed the phone to George.

"My god, what's happened?"

"Ned, our neighbor from across the street just left after telling us that Mrs. Soo passed away instantly, suffering a stroke Thursday after we left. Besides that, Mr. Soo has purchased the little bungalow across the street from his former home. He's moved in, and his beachfront home is now for sale. Mrs. Soo's remains were cremated and sent to China for burial beside her parents."

"I can't believe all this has happened so quickly. Was there or is there going to be some type of memorial service for Mrs. Soo?"

"Ned said there was no service, and nothing is planned. Mrs. Soo was a very private person and basically had no friends in Paia, except maybe Annie and me. The family felt by sending her remains back to be with her parents, they were making her spirit happy."

"Have you made plans to see Mr. Soo?"

"We're going over this evening. Ned said he now eats dinner at Otis's but is home by sunset. We'll watch for him and then go over. We'll get his phone number, and you can give him a call."

"Thanks, George, that would be great. I can get away later this month. I'll fly over and visit him. I think a lot of Mr. Soo. He's one of a kind."

"I'm sure he would appreciate seeing you. We won't mention anything about you visiting. You can discuss that with him. We'll phone you later this evening."

Annie motioned for George to hand her the phone, which was set on speaker mode. "Dewey, it would be wonderful if you could visit. I think that would help Mr. Soo. No matter how it may appear, this has to be a difficult time for him. They were married many years. Can you please phone Layla and tell her what has transpired?"

Dewey checked his watch, saying, "I'll phone her the minute we hang up. She'll be upset. She has experienced so much death lately. I'll be as gentle as possible."

"Thank you. We'll get back to you after our visit."

Hanging up from his call with Annie and George, he phoned Layla. She answered, sounding sleepy.

"Layla, it's Dewey. I'm sorry. Did I wake you?"

"I fell asleep on the sofa. I had a difficult day with my restoration work. I had to redo half of what I did yesterday. The paint did not dry correctly. Had to remix my paints. What's new?"

"I hate to tell you this, but I just received a call from Annie and George with bad news. Mrs. Soo passed away from a stroke. She did not suffer. Mr. Soo discovered her body after returning from his afternoon outing."

"Oh no, not another death. How is Mr. Soo doing? Should we go over there? Can you get away? Is there going to be a service?"

Layla had many questions for Dewey, and he addressed them all. After he told her he would be going to Maui for a few days at the end of the month, she told him she would be finished with her restoration project by then and would go with him if that would be possible.

"That would be great. I know Mr. Soo would be happy we both came to visit him. Oh, I forgot to tell you. He has his beachfront home up for sale. He bought that little blue-and-white bungalow across the street from his old home and lives there now."

"So much has happened so quickly. Have you spoken with him?"

"No, Annie and George are going to visit him this evening after he returns from dinner at Otis's, then call with his phone number. I'll call and tell him we'll come over at the end of the month. I'll send the plane to pick you up, and we can fly onto Maui together. Does that work for you?"

"Great. Let me know the specific dates. I'll be through here in about a week."

"I'll call you tomorrow with exact dates and Mr. Soo's new phone number. I'm sure he would like to hear your voice too."

CHAPTER 27

Mr. Soo's doorbell rang. He looked out and saw George and Annie; opening the door, he welcomed them inside.

Annie hugged him, saying, "Mr. Soo, I'm sorry we were not here when you lost Mrs. Soo. We're back now, and if there is anything we can do, please let us know."

George went up to the small man, putting his large hands on Mr. Soo's small shoulders, looking him in the eyes. "Mr. Soo, I'm sorry for your loss. We are here for you in any way you may need."

"Thank you. Invite me over when you grill. Everything else has been finalized. Let me show you my new home. It is filled with sunlight, modern furniture, and best of all, I have a bed to put these old bones on, no more sleeping on a mat." He ushered them around his new home; after the tour, they sat on his lanai, which provided a peekaboo view of the ocean.

"It's quite lovely here, Mr. Soo. Your view isn't as dynamic as your previous home, but I like the cozy feel," Annie said.

"Thank you, Annie. I feel good here, more freedom. May I offer you something to drink? I have iced tea and beer."

"Thanks, I'll take a beer."

"Annie, what about you? Sorry, don't have any coffee."

"I would love a glass of iced tea."

Mr. Soo went inside to fetch the drinks.

Annie turned to George. "Honey, Mr. Soo looks younger. This is horrible to say, but Mrs. Soo's death has freed him up, so to speak."

"Got to agree with you. He actually looks happy, no more complaining about his wife trying to kill him."

"George, if I go first, you had better not look that happy."

"If you go before me, I don't think I would last long. I can't imagine my life without you," George said seriously.

"Thank you, my love. I feel the same about you." Annie got up and planted a kiss on her husband's forehead.

Mr. Soo returned with the drinks. "What are you two doing? Smooching the minute my back is turned?" he said jokingly.

"You know us, Mr. Soo. We can't keep our hands off each other even after all these years," George said.

"By the way, have you kept the same phone number so we can let you know when to come over for a cookout?" Annie questioned.

"No, I got a cell phone, and I've learned to text. Been texting my grandkids like crazy, they love it," he said, laughing. "I'll write the number down for you. I don't want to miss any good meals!" He wrote the number down, saying, "Be sure to give the number to Dewey and Layla. I can text them too."

They spent another hour chatting about their recent vacation, then Annie and George excused themselves, saying they had to go home and get some sleep.

At home, George phoned Dewey with the latest information on Mr. Soo, including his new texting ability. Dewey said he would phone Mr. Soo directly; he thought it was just like him to discover texting. George finished his conversation and went into the bedroom.

"I'm going to take a shower. I've unpacked all our toiletry items and put them back where they belong. If I'm not out of the shower soon, come get me. I've fallen asleep."

"Thanks for unpacking the stuff, and don't fall asleep."

Annie finished her shower, George followed, and soon both were sound asleep.

Layla answered on the first ring. "Dewey, I was waiting for your call."

"First off, here's Mr. Soo's new phone number. It's a cell phone, and he's found the joy of texting, so be ready to receive some text messages. I just got a call from Alice Copeland, head of our research and development department. They have made a terrific breakthrough in the digital process. A meeting with a Japanese auto dealer, scheduled for this week, has been postponed until the end of the month so the new process can be incorporated into the presentation in Tokyo, and I'm doing the presentation. It's a multimillion-dollar proposal. Plus, it's excellent exposure for our digital process. I've e-mailed my staff that beginning the second Friday of next month, for ten days, I'll be unavailable. Can you change your schedule, and I'll fly to New York get you on that Friday, and we'll fly to Maui from New York?"

"Like I said, I have nothing on my agenda, no work assignments, and certainly, no social plans. Remember, my friend Judy? I told you she was going to a spa while we were on our trip. She went to one that tries to get you into a healthy lifestyle with proper diet and exercise. She met this terrific man. They have been dating full time, and I think it's serious. He lost his wife to cancer two years ago, and he has a nine-year-old son. She told me he actually wants to remarry and have another child. She's silly happy and I'm happy for her, but once again, I'm the old third wheel. I don't begrudge her any happiness, but damn it, I'm lonely. Now you're my only close friend, and you're so far away."

"I'll send the plane early, and you spend time here with Agnes and her cooking."

"I'll have to finish my restoration project, but it's almost done now. Then I'll close up the house and arrange everything to be handled by the trust while I'm gone. I can visit before we leave for Maui, if that is doable with both you and Agnes."

"Agnes is looking forward to your next visit. She has a couple of new dishes she wants to try. Layla, I'm sorry you're so lonely. I wish I were there right now to give you a big hug. Honey, you have been through so much in such a short time, you've lost a child, been involved in a gruesome double murder, and lost a husband to another man. Look how much stronger you are now than when you first arrived on Maui. You've come so far. Hurry and get things finished up and call me. I'll send the plane."

"Dewey, you always make me feel better," Layla said, crying.

"Then why, for heaven's sakes, are you crying?"

"Because you've made me feel good about myself again."

"Is this one of those times when men say they'll never understand women?"

"Yep, I do believe it is."

"I'm going to phone Mr. Soo now and tell him of our plans. I won't talk too long, then you can call. He'll be happy we called and that we're coming for a visit. I'll call George and Annie too and let them know we'll be seeing them soon."

"Great. I'm feeling good again. See how happy you make me. Give George and Annie my love."

Mr. Soo answered his ringing phone. "Soo here."

"Hi, Mr. Soo, it's Dewey. Good to hear your voice. I want to extend to you my sympathy on Mrs. Soo's death. I know sometimes your life together was difficult, but you were married a long time and she was the mother of your children."

"You're right, Dewey. I often said bad things, but she was a good woman. I never told you, but when we married, she was only thirteen. My parents paid her parents to marry me, and it was only two years later when we came to Hawaii. She was pregnant, alone in a foreign country, didn't speak the language, and was married to a man who worked eighteen- to twenty-hour days. It was difficult on her. Hawaii was making great strides forward, but she was still a child in China at heart. She had every luxury money could buy, but she never wanted them."

"That's some story, Mr. Soo. Did she learn English?"

"Yes, our sons insisted, but she would seldom speak it, except when the sons and grandchildren came to visit. She spoke Chinese to me and English to Annie and George. She liked

Annie's no-nonsense nature coupled with her gentle manner, and she liked George's grin. She felt safe around them. I wish for both of us, our lives had been different. She was a good soul but a scared child at heart. I would have liked to fall in love on my own, which is what I let our children do, against Mrs. Soo's wishes."

"Mr. Soo, you are a wise and good man. I called to ask if you would like some visitors. Layla and I are able to come for a visit starting the second Friday of next month. Layla can probably stay with George and Annie, but I thought I could hang out with you."

"Dewey, I would welcome your visit. It would be my honor to have you in my new home. You understand, I don't cook, but Otis's is right up the hill, and his cooking is getting even better, now that I'm a regular at dinner."

"No problem, and I imagine George and Annie will be grilling for us, don't you?"

"Yes, I imagine they will. I'm anxious for you and Layla to see my new home. I'm a texter now, so I'll be texting you often, if that meets with your approval?"

"My schedule and workload doesn't allow me much time for texting, but you go ahead and send your messages, and I'll get back to you when I can," Dewey said, hoping that would deter some of Mr. Soo's texting. "I'll call Annie and George now and let them know our plans and get back to you with the exact date. We're testing a new video game. I'll bring it for you to try out. I would value your opinion."

"How exciting! I can now play my video games as much as I want to. Mrs. Soo only allowed me so much time each evening. I like them, keeps my mind alert. I'll be waiting to hear your scheduled arrival time. Goodbye, Dewey, thank you for calling, and I would wait until tomorrow to call George and Annie. When they left here, they were going to get some much needed sleep."

"Thanks for reminding me. Layla and I got involved with our plans to visit, we forgot how tired Annie and George must be. I'll phone them tomorrow. Take care, Mr. Soo."

Mr. Soo was putting Dewey's personal cell number into his contact list and jumped as his phone rang again. "Soo here."

"Hello, Mr. Soo, it's Layla. I know Dewey phoned you to let you know we would be coming for a visit, but I'm calling to extend my condolences on the loss of your wife."

"Thank you, Layla. It was sudden and unexpected. She did not suffer, a blessing for the family. I was so pleased to hear you and Dewey would be visiting. I miss you both. I got to know Dewey, and for some reason, he likes this old man."

"He sure does, Mr. Soo. He thinks the world of you. We are both anxious to visit with you and see Annie and George again. We had such a fabulous vacation together."

"They left not long ago and were kind enough to tell me about your vacation adventures. You and Annie took a mule to the bottom of the Grand Canyon. That sounds frightening."

"We never would admit it to George or Dewey, but it was frightening. We were on very narrow paths with nothing on one side but a drop-off into the canyon. Those mules were great. They went along like it was nothing to them. I guess they don't have a sense of falling like Annie and I did. We were glad to get back at the lodge, but like I said, you can't ever tell George or Dewey. If they had known how scary it was, we would have never been allowed to take the tour."

"You are mistaken. If you or Annie wanted to do something, neither George nor Dewey would stop you for fear it would make you unhappy. Those two are very concerned about keeping you both happy. You know, Dewey has been goofy over you since he first saw you during the storm."

"That's what Annie told me, but currently, all I want from Dewey is his wonderful friendship. I'm not able to envision any type of relationship with a man at this point in time, except friendship. I do believe Dewey understands that."

"It's wise of him to realize this, and one day, you will see what a relationship other than friendship you two could have."

"Who knows what one day will bring? Only time will tell."

They discussed various things about his new home, the upcoming visit, and her work in New York. Layla made sure he had her cell phone number and told Mr. Soo to text her whenever he wanted. She ended the conversation, saying she was going to call George and Annie, asking if it was OK if she stayed with them during her visit.

Mr. Soo told her what he told Dewey: call them tomorrow; they had left his house to go home and get some sleep.

Layla thanked him, saying she had forgotten they had just returned from Los Angeles. She ended their call with the promise to see him soon.

The next day Layla called Dewey and said she would like to call Annie and George, asking to stay with them during their visit. Dewey was glad she had offered, feeling it would be awkward for him to ask if Layla could stay at their home.

Layla waited until late afternoon to make her call. "Hello, Annie, it's Layla. Are you folks getting rested? How was your week with your family?"

"Layla, good to hear your voice. We are getting rested. Only neither of us is looking forward to starting our classes tomorrow. Let me tell you about the family visit. It wore us both down to blithering fools." Annie went on to relate the particulars of their visit with the children and grandkids.

"I'm not sure I could have survived all those excursions on top of our week in Utah. You guys are tough."

"It's beyond us why every time we visit the kids, they think we have to go to theme parks, water parks, or whatever. We would simply enjoying visiting with our family."

"Let me make a wild guess. When you visit these places, you and George pay all the expense, right?"

"Yes, that could be the reason we are always treated to those excursions. Maybe we will have to put a stop to that in order for us to survive any future visits."

"Annie, I called to ask if you could stand to have me for a house guest for seven to ten days next month."

"Are you kidding? That would be terrific. You're actually visiting Maui next month?"

"Not only am I visiting but so is Dewey. We decided we would come and pay our respects to Mr. Soo. We both spoke with him, and he was delighted. Dewey will be staying at Mr. Soo's home, and if it's all right with you and George, I'll stay with you folks."

"Goodness, you don't need to ask. You're always welcome in our home. I can't wait to tell George. He's jog-walking on the beach right now, and I know he will be excited when he hears. Do you have an exact date and time?"

"No, not exactly. I'm going to stay at Dewey's a few days before we leave. He has a big project in Tokyo, and once he returns, we will figure out when we can come to Maui. In the meantime, I'll probably gain a ton eating Agnes's cooking. Yum, I can't wait for that."

"Be sure and bring the pictures you took on our trip and I'll have ours back. I'm having extra sets made for you and Dewey."

"I also had extra sets made."

A few minutes after Annie hung up, George walked in.

"You look pooped," Annie said, handing him a bottle of water.

"I'm still far from recovered from visiting with the kids." George sighed. "I think this is the first time in a long time I'm feeling my age."

"We were put through too much, and I assure you I will not allow those kids to do that again. I'm little pissed that they treated us like a free ticket to where they wanted to go."

"Yikes, Mrs. Boone is mad. You're right. We were just a plastic card, and we shouldn't let ourselves be used like that, worse of all, by our own kids."

"Now for some good news, Layla called. She and Dewey are heading to Maui next month to pay their respects to Mr. Soo. Dewey is staying with Mr. Soo, and Layla is going to be staying with us."

"What? I was looking forward to a long spell of alone time with you, with no one around, so I can grab your cute little ass anytime I feel like it," George said, grabbing Annie's butt.

"They'll be here ten days at the most, then you can grab my ass anytime your heart desires. Do you mind so much having Layla here?"

"Yes, but I will be charming and gracious and make you proud."

"I'm always proud of you, my love."

CHAPTER 28

Rays of morning sun streamed into the kitchen through glass windows as Layla sat at the island counter, waiting for a batch of Agnes's cookies to come from one of two ovens loaded with sheets of cookies. "How much longer, Agnes? My mouth is watering."

"Won't be much longer. Get yourself some milk or coffee, better yet, get yourself a beer."

"A beer while I'm eating cookies? Agnes, that's goofy."

"I make these when Dewey is home, and he and Ted can watch a sports event together to add to the goodies I set out for them to munch. For some reason, these go great with beer. Don't tell them the main ingredient is mincemeat. They'll never eat another one."

"Mincemeat is funny. I love mincemeat pie, but some people won't even try a bite. It's like buttermilk. You either love it or hate it."

"Neither man would ever consider eating a piece of mincemeat pie. I bake one at Thanksgiving and Christmas just for me. I tell them the cookies contain my secret ingredient, and I can't divulge it," Agnes said with a chuckle.

Layla watched Agnes take the cookies out of the oven and lay them on a cooling rack. She reached for the first cookie from the rack, jostling it back and forth in her hands to cool. Layla blew on the side, then took a bite, sucking in air as she chewed. "Oh, these are so good. You're right. I need a beer. How weird."

Layla went to the refrigerator and got a bottle, asking Agnes if she wanted one.

"I'll wait until all the cookies are baked. Then I'll have a beer and cookies. There will be some left, right?"

"I'll save you a couple. After all, you're only making four dozen so."

"There will be some for Dewey when he gets back from Tokyo, hopefully tomorrow or the next day. He feels bad he can't be here with you now, but this is a big deal for his company and it's his duty to make sure he handles it personally."

"I know, Agnes. As long as he leaves me in your good hands, I'm happy. He's always there when I feel down, and he never complains. He just listens to me while I whine."

Agnes took off her oven mitt and leaned over the counter, looking directly at Layla. "He's in love with you. It's was love at first sight, and he keeps hoping you will feel the same way. He's brilliant enough to understand it will be a long-term thing. He will never rush you, and frankly, you'll have to make the first move. I know him. He would never jeopardize your friendship with a romantic overture. He's a wonderful man. Aside from the fact he's a genius, he's generous and kind. He's lonely, although he would never admit it. Staying absorbed in his work is not the same thing as being in a loving relationship."

"You're not the first person to tell me that. Annie and Mr. Soo said the same thing. I value Dewey's friendship more than you can imagine, and I love him in a fashion. However, I'm not ready for anything else right now. It's too soon. My feelings about love and marriage are still healing. Maybe that sounds silly with a good man like Dewey out there more or less for the taking, but I owe him more. If I'm going to ever be in love with him, I owe him my total self. Does that make any sense?"

"It does, and that makes me know if you two end up together, it will be right. Anytime you want to talk about anything, I'm here to listen and I give damn good advice," Agnes said, nodding.

"Thanks, Agnes, I'll probably take you up on that. I seem to need directional help with my life currently. I feel so out of place in New York. I feel nomadic, like I'm searching for something, some type of inner peace. I think it's the loss of my daughter and maybe my marriage too. I've always been a person with specific goals, and I worked hard to attain those goals. Now I have no goal, no direction, just go from one event to another, looking for I have no idea what."

Agnes patted her hand, saying, "Don't rush into anything that doesn't feel right. You'll know where you're supposed to be when the time is right. Like Dewey, you are very intelligent. You got thrown for a hell of a loop, and you have to get your bearings back. I saw Dewey like that when his father died. He was at a loss for over a year. He was just going to work and filling space, then he finally took time-out and went to Maui while his team developed the digital process he had started about a year before he lost his father. When he got back, he was renewed and had direction."

"I was thinking about doing a charcoal of Dewey. Would he like something like that?"

"He would love it. I'll have Ted put canvas down so you won't have to worry about getting anything dirty. If you want good light, the greenhouse windows on the other side of the indoor pool would be an excellent place to sketch."

"Perfect. If I start now, maybe I can finish before Dewey gets back from Tokyo. Of course, I need to take some of the cookies with me to keep up my strength until dinner."

Layla put six cookies in a stack and wrapped them in a napkin.

"I'll call Ted and have him bring a canvas for the tile. Did you bury those jars of mincemeat in the trash outside like I asked?"

"Yes, Ted will never find them. Your secret is safe."

Layla sat on a stool with her sketchpad resting on a podium Ted had in storage, pleased with the bright sunlight coming through the windows and hoping she would be finished before Dewey returned home. She missed him and wanted to give him her gift as a way of letting him know how much she appreciated their friendship.

When the large DewMaster jet landed, a group of exhausted executives and technicians made their way to a waiting fleet of SUVs. They shook hands and congratulated each other on a job well done. Luggage was unloaded, and Dewey felt a tinge of disappointment that Layla hadn't joined Ted in meeting the plane.

"I thought Layla might accompany you," he mentioned to Ted, trying to sound casual.

"She's been working on a project for a couple of days, something to surprise you with, and she's finishing up or she would have met your plane. How did your trip go? Did they buy your digital program?"

"They were very happy, asking for more than originally proposed. This is going to be a very big money project, and it will put our digital base on the map. I can't believe what a remarkable team I've assembled over the years. They had all the right answers and helped me seal the deal, truly a team effort."

They pulled into the driveway and stopped in front of the steps. Layla and Agnes both came out as Ted and Dewey unloaded luggage.

Layla threw her arms around Dewey's neck and hugged him close. "I'm so glad you're home, and I hope everything went well for you and your staff in Tokyo."

Dewey hugged her back, thinking this is what he wanted out of life, Layla hugging him, saying she was glad he was home. Although he would have liked a passionate kiss to go along with everything else, he was thrilled with the greeting he received.

"Everything went better than anticipated. We got a bigger contract than planned. It will mean our digital program is now able to compete with the top runners in the market. Has Agnes kept you fed?"

"I weighed myself this morning, I've gained three pounds since I got here, and what a pleasure it has been. Agnes's cooking is so great, and Ted watches over me like a doting parent."

"I hear you have a project you've been working on," Dewey said, enjoying the fact Layla was still in his arms.

"Yes, but it's not quite finished yet, and I'm not telling you about it until it's done. It's a surprise."

"Great. Now you've got my curiosity piqued. Any hints?"

"Nope, you'll just have to wait." Layla turned and put her arm around his waist, walking with him inside.

Agnes smiled at Ted, nodding approvingly at the sight of Dewey and Layla. "Someday, we'll be attending their wedding."

"Yep, but not right away. Dewey would marry her in a minute, but she's not ready yet."

"Ted, you are sometimes wiser than I give you credit for," Agnes said, smiling at her husband.

After dinner, everyone drifted into the den where the fire roared. Dewey explained a little more about the digital process between yawns. Finally, he excused himself, saying he was being hit with jet lag and had to get to bed.

Layla went to her bedroom, spending the night and a few early morning hours finishing her charcoal portrait. Before she presented him with it, she was going to ask Agnes's opinion, wanting to be sure she had captured everything about his face. Drawing him, she realized he was a very handsome man with fine, strong features. She stepped back and looked at the face staring back at her and felt she was seeing Dewey for the first time and she liked what she saw.

"You are a sexy man, great eyes, charming smile with a touch of mischief in your eyes," she said to the portrait.

Layla asked Agnes for an appraisal of the portrait. Agnes gasped when she saw what Layla created.

"My god, you have captured all the facets of Dewey in one drawing."

"Does that mean you like it and I should give it to him?"

"He'll love it and be overwhelmed."

No one saw Dewey until late in the afternoon when he came into the kitchen still looking tired. Everyone was sitting around the counter, eating cookies and having a beer.

"Dewey," Agnes said, "I'll fix you something to eat. You must be starving."

"I am. I'll have a couple of cookies to tide me over. Fix me leftovers from last night's great dinner."

"You look like you could use more sleep," Layla said.

"I need more sleep and would still be sleeping, but hunger got the best of me. Sorry, Layla, I'm not being a very good host, but between the jet lag and all the worry about the presentation, I'm drained."

"Heavens, don't worry about me. I'm enjoying myself."

After Dewey ate and started back to his bedroom, he asked Layla if she was ready with her surprise.

"Yes, but it can wait until you're rested."

"No, no, no, now that your surprise is ready, I would never be able to get any sleep. You had better show me."

"All right, it's still up in my bedroom."

"My god, Layla, that's me!" Dewey exclaimed as he slowly approached his portrait. "You did this? It's remarkable. I don't look like this. This guy is handsome. I'm the computer geek, remember?"

"Maybe that's how you see yourself, but this is how the world sees you, and to verify my mind's eye, Agnes agrees with the outcome of my labors."

"I'm truly touched. No one has ever done anything like this for me before. You've seen me as I didn't even know I existed. How can I ever thank you?"

"This is my thank you for all the times you've flown me here and there. You've opened your home to me, and I can talk to you like I talk to no one else. This is my thank you for being my dearest friend."

CHAPTER 29

George looked closer in the mirror above his sink, ran his hand over his forehead, and sighed. He strode to where Annie sat at the counter, making a to-do list of his errands.

"Honey, my forehead seems to be expanding."

"Is that all? The other day, while walking by the closet mirrors, I noticed I too was losing something, my ass! I'm getting a flat bottom and my boobs sag. This getting-old stuff is losing its glamour. It was fun getting the senior discounts, but now I'm seeing the results of aging and the fun is waning."

"You're still sexy to me, but will you still find me desirable when I'm bald and have to wear Coke-bottle bottoms for glasses?"

"George," Annie said seriously, "you've always been the most desirable man I've ever known. To this day, you turn me on. I'll see you reading the morning paper or watching television, and I simply lust for you. Maybe that sounds strange after all these years, but it's the way I feel about you, and that feeling is never going to change. Enough lustful thoughts, I've got to get you going on these errands. First off, the bank. I figure we should draw out $500 in cash. Here is a list of what denominations to request."

"Don't you trust me to do anything by myself?"

"Of course. It's just that, if I don't write things down, I forget what the hell I want you to do. Like I said, this getting old is maddening."

"Next stop?" George asked Annie, nuzzling her neck.

"Ooh, that's nice. George, be good or I'll get distracted, and you'll be running errands at midnight."

"And who brought up the lust subject?" George asked with a grin as he nibbled her earlobe.

"OK, now your next stop is the vitamin store. Here's a list of what we need. Next, the dry cleaners. Here is the receipt for what's there, and over on the table is what needs to be taken in. And last, your favorite place, the grocery store."

"I hate going to the grocery store because no matter how good we do it week after week, we are back there doing the same thing the next week, and then we usually go midweek because we've run out of something or need something. Do you have a list for the store?"

"Pick up a half gallon of 2 percent milk, a box of raspberry oat bars, and some fresh fish for dinner, anything you feel like grilling. I'll nuke some potatoes and do a salad with our fish for dinner. Does that meet with your approval? Since you are doing all the running around, I'll clean the grill."

"Now you're talking. That meets with my approval. Guess I had better be on my way," George said, gathering his lists along with the clothes for the dry cleaners. "Lock the slider after me," he called back to Annie.

He was getting the cash from the bank teller when he looked up and saw Donnie motioning him to come back to his office. George finished his transaction and swung the gate inward, walking toward Donnie's office.

Donnie Munson came out and greeted George warmly. "George, glad to see you folks are back from vacation. Hope all went well."

"We spent a wonderful week visiting National Parks in Utah with Dewey and Layla. You've got to take the wife and kids to see the Grand Canyon. It's truly unbelievable, and go to the North Rim, not many people. The second week we split between both our kids in the Los Angeles area, they ran us ragged. Made us appreciate the quiet pace of Paia even more."

"How is Layla doing?"

"You know, she and Kyle are divorcing? I believe he and Kim are now a couple. That and the loss of her baby would not be easy on anyone, but she's involved in her art restoration work and looks a lot better than when you saw her last. She's still in the healing process. I'm sure that will take some time. How are things going on the Visitors Center?"

Donnie grimaced. "Had I known what I was getting myself into, I'm not sure I would have proposed the project or at least not volunteered to head the makeover. The permit process and environmental aspects are daunting. I've lost weight. A miracle! I never lose weight over anything," Donnie said, shaking his head.

"When I worked for the airlines, I would occasionally be sent to the mainland for engineering conferences. It was always a laughing topic about the environmental restrictions put on projects in Hawaii and in California. So I imagine getting permits is a major task."

Donnie asked, "Have you noticed how we leveled the right side of the front yard? We were going to put in gravel and use that area and the area farther up at the entrance to the Visitors Center for parking. We anticipate special events usage, so we want plenty of space to ease street parking. Anyway, the gravel came and was disbursed as planned. However, it was not correct according to the environmental code. It would create too much dust when used by numerous cars at once. The contractor said he had been using that particular gravel for several years, and it had always passed code. We found out it was fine for private residences, but for multi-car use, it was not acceptable. So all those tons of gravel had to be shoveled and put in piles, then a front-end loader came in and loaded it back into trucks to be hauled away. Since there was dirt in with the gravel, it was not salvageable and had to be dumped. The contractor is a terrific guy and agreed to eat half the cost, but the other half came out of the foundation funds. I'm just sick about the whole thing and feel responsible."

"Donnie it's not your fault. If I told you the number of times projects at the airport had to be redone for similar reasons, you would be amazed. Has you contractor determined what type of gravel you need to use?"

"He's still working with the powers that be, but it's another reason the project has slowed. Stop by this coming Friday afternoon. I'll show you around, and you can see what has been accomplished so far. You'll be surprised at how large the old market is, and you might come up with some ideas with your keen engineer's eye."

George grinned, knowing he was being flattered but was anxious to see how things were evolving, so he agreed to meet Donnie on Friday. Donnie suggested he bring Annie if she was up to being inside the old market again.

George said he would ask but didn't think she was ready to revisit the site yet.

They exchanged goodbyes, then George headed to his next stop. At the vitamin store, he got the items on Annie's list, then on to the dry cleaners.

"Hi, Maria, good to see you," George said as he greeted the owner, Maria Lopez, handing her the batch of clothes he was bringing in and his receipt for what needed picking up.

"Mr. Boone, did you have a nice vacation visiting your children and grandchildren?"

"Well, they certainly kept us busy, and we had a great week before we got to Los Angeles, visiting the National Parks of Utah. When Annie and I got back to Paia, we were two very grateful people that we lived in such a peaceful place with such good friends."

"You are right, Mr. Boone. Our family loves it here. We feel blessed that fate led my father here many years ago and started this business for the family. We have wonderful friends, and our customers are so kind." Marie wrote up his next slip and brought the carousel around to match the slip number for pickup.

George paid for his cleaning and left the store. He wasn't too far from the sheriff's office and decided to check to see if there were any new developments in the Okamoto murders.

After exchanging a vacation update with Charlene, he was directed back to the sheriff's office. Both men greeted each other warmly, and once again, George went into detail about their vacation experiences. "Why I really stopped by was to find out if there had been any news regarding the Okamoto case."

"Wish I could give you some positive information, George, but still nothing. In fact, I'm not too happy with the way things are going. Seems like the murders have fallen on the back burner. I still want you and Annie to keep things locked up and give Mr. Soo a heads-up too. I was sorry to hear about the loss of his wife and surprised he moved so quickly into his new home. Don't think I've been here long enough to understand the dynamics of everyone yet, and Mr. Soo is one I can't quite figure out."

"Someday, I'll fill you in on the Soo history, but I'm on an errand run for Annie, and I have to get to the market. I just wanted to stop by and see how things were going. Good talking with you, Sheriff. When we get back into the swing of things, we'll have you over for a cookout." George got up, shook the sheriff's hand, and left.

As he was opening Pearl's door, he heard Mr. Soo's voice call him.

"Hi, Mr. Soo, I was just going to the grocery store to get a few items, including some fish to grill for dinner. Would you like to join us?"

"Fish, you say? Ah no, thanks. Otis is expecting me." He said Otis had a special he was making so did not want to disappoint him. "But I would appreciate a ride to the grocery, then you can drop me off at my new home."

"Glad to have your company. How are things going in your new place?"

"I am most happy. I feel like a bird let out of a cage. Now don't repeat that, but you know how things were for all those years."

"Good for you, Mr. Soo. I just came from the sheriff's office, and I told him we will be grilling soon and will have him over and you too."

Both men finished their shopping, Mr. Soo's shopping cart full but George's just those items on his list. George stopped in front of Mr. Soo's home and helped him get his groceries into the house. "The sheriff wanted me to remind you there has been no arrests in the Okamoto case and to keep your doors and screens secure."

"Thank you, George. I am ever mindful that the person or persons that attacked my friends has not been caught, and I am very careful to keep my house secure. I want to enjoy this newfound freedom. I do not want some crazy person taking it from me."

"I'm glad to hear you are taking precautions. We are too. The sheriff still thinks it was a local, which scares the hell out of me."

Mr. Soo shook his head and waved goodbye to George as he drove the short distance to his home.

"I saw you helping Mr. Soo unload. Did you invite him for dinner?" Annie asked, taking the cleaning while George tried to carry groceries and the vitamins and close the garage without spilling anything.

"Funny, once he found out we were having fish, he said Otis was fixing something special for him tonight. Mr. Soo isn't a fish eater."

"Mrs. Soo told me she grilled fish for them almost every night. If I had to eat fish for all those years, I would probably be on the outs with fish too."

"I told him we would have him over for steaks soon. I stopped by the sheriff's office today to see if there were any new developments and also invited him over the next time we grilled steaks."

"Maybe weekend after next when I've shed a couple of pounds. We'll stick with fish and chicken for a bit."

"We had better stick mostly with chicken. Annie, two medium pieces of fish cost $25 and we live on the ocean. I couldn't believe it."

"What kind of fish did you pick out?"

"Halibut," George said, grinning.

"Sweetie, that comes from the Atlantic. Guess we paid for the fuel to get it here."

"Yikes, shopping for fish is not my strong point. You had better do that if we're going to be eating more than usual."

Annie asked if there was anything new on the case since they had been gone.

"No, and the sheriff again warned us to be sure and keep the house secure. He feels uneasy about the situation. I sure hope he's wrong about this being someone local."

George then told Annie about his visit with Donnie Munson and the troubles he was having. He told her they were meeting this coming Friday afternoon at the site and Donnie had also included her in his invitation.

"No, I'm not ready to go back there yet. I'll probably wait until the official grand opening."

"That's what I told Donnie, I'll go and have a look. I think he wanted my opinion as an engineer. He seems depressed at how slow the project is coming along."

"I'm sure he'll value your visit and anything you can add will be taken seriously."

"Thank you, honey, my best fan has spoken," George said, patting her bottom as he headed into the bedroom to change clothes.

George walked up the steps to the main street, crossed, and paused on the sidewalk in front of the old market, seeing only a slight change in the facade. His long stride carried him up the slight slope of the new driveway, and he immediately liked the planned parking for the center. He looked over at the porch that surrounded the center and saw Donnie standing just inside the doorway. "Hi, I like the driveway and the way parking has been planned. Good thinking on the architect's part."

"Thanks, George. It will be good if we ever get it finished."

George went inside. "This place is so much larger than I thought it would be. It was so chopped up before, with the market, backroom storage, freezer, coolers, and living quarters. I had no idea it would turn out to be such a large open space."

"It is pretty amazing. We were thrilled at the space and have a few ideas I would like to run by you for your opinion. First off, let me ask if you have any ideas for all this open space?"

George walked around the entire empty space, then asked, "What about the roof? Are you putting a new roof on or will the current one stay in place?"

"It's close to twenty years old, and the architect strongly suggests we put a new one on."

"I think that's a wise suggestion. Have you considered putting in skylights to help defray the cost of electricity?"

"No, I didn't see that in any plans, but that's a terrific idea."

"Also, you might consider some small side windows high up on the southwest side of the building to catch the afternoon sun, which will also help the lighting. I would put in disappearing sliders on the porch that faces the street. That way you could take advantage of the sea breeze. It usually is cooler at this elevation than it is right on the beach. You could put tables and chairs out there, and maybe in one corner of this huge area, have a snack shop with shaved ice, specialty coffees, sodas, snacks, etc. It would be a moneymaker and could be manned by volunteers or you could contract out the entire enterprise, which would probably be the wisest idea. Still, it would bring money into the center, and in the contract, the center would be guaranteed a percentage of the net take. You know all about those type of deals, right, Donnie?"

"I knew you were the one to come in and take a look around. That's a great idea. That would mean more permits and hook-ups for water and more electricity, but it would be profitable. I like your sunlight ideas. I'll speak with the architect on Monday and see if he concurs."

"You know, you will still have a lot of empty space. How about setting up a small gift shop featuring local arts and craft items, along with some tourist junk, maybe magnets, pens, pencils with Paia and a windsurfer on them. That would work well with volunteers and help the local artists too."

"George, I'm surprised the airlines let you retire. You have great ideas. Those two will certainly help fill this huge space and help the local economy. We will probably need another permit to sell things," Donnie said with a sigh.

"Sometimes, when someone not involved in the initial work sees the plans or space available, they picture possibilities that someone working close to a project doesn't see."

"You sometimes need an outsider to see a possibility you've missed because you have worked so close to the project."

"Exactly. Let me know what your architect has to say, I'm eager to hear his thoughts on my proposals."

Donnie and George walked the area for almost half an hour, Donnie pointing out the proposed layout for the center and the materials to be used along with various other proposals made by the architect.

"Thank you, Donnie, for asking me here today. I've enjoyed seeing the old market gutted, and I'm can't wait to see it evolve into the Visitors Center."

When George got back home, he found Annie sitting on the front lanai, reading. "Honey, you would be amazed at the size of the old market without all the rooms and equipment, it's huge. I gave Donnie a couple of pretty good ideas, and he's going to pass them along to his architect. Want to hear them?" George asked with a grin.

"Well, of course, and I know they had to be pretty good ideas. After all, I'm married to a genius engineer."

"I wouldn't say that, but I came up with some things that will please everyone." George proceeded to tell Annie his ideas, and she was excited about the gift shop displaying local artist works and crafts. She even thought she might like to volunteer to work in the shop a few hours each week.

"Honey, that would be terrific. We both could volunteer the same day. I could work the front desk and direct them to the lovely, sexy lady selling her wares in the gift shop."

"George, you're silly. I'll keep you to what you said about volunteering to work the front desk. A handsome man like yourself would surely bring in a flood of ladies."

"Sweetheart, I think you're piling it on a little thick. I'm hungry. I need a snack. I worked my brain too hard!"

CHAPTER 30

Dewey and Layla stood at the top of the DewMaster jet stairs, enjoying the kiss of tropical air on their skin.

George pulled Pearl up to greet Layla and Dewey and collect the luggage. Annie jumped out, walked to the end of the stairs, and hugged Layla. Annie was surprised at a rush of tears coming from her friend. "Honey, what's the matter?"

"I'm so glad to see you both. I really miss you both." Saying that, she rushed over to George and hugged him too, tears still streaming down her cheeks.

George looked over helplessly at Annie, who shrugged as if saying she had no idea what was going on. "Layla, it's good to see you too. Let me go over with Dewey and help with the luggage. Then let's get you both to Paia," George said as he extricated himself from her grasp.

He walked over to Dewey, helping unload the luggage, asking, "What's with Layla? She's in tears. Anything happen on the flight over?"

They began loading luggage into Pearl. "Everything was fine until she saw you two. I think I know what's wrong. I'll tell you later when I'm sure she can't overhear."

On the short drive to Paia, Dewey and George sat silently in the front; Layla and Annie chatted in the back. Layla asked how Mr. Soo was doing adjusting to his new home.

"He's doing great. He's back to his daily walks, has dinner at Otis's each night and back home by sunset. His home is lovely. Fiona did a wonderful job decorating."

"Oh lord, that woman."

"George, say what you want about Fiona. She has a wonderful eye for decorating for her clientele. I've never heard anyone complain about the final outcome of her projects. She simply knows how to bring the client's personality into their home."

"She's a real—"

"George, stop right there. I know what you're going to say, but that's just your opinion."

"Annie, I didn't think she ranked very high on your close friends' list. In fact, I seem to remember at one time you were in a snit over something she did to you."

"She didn't do anything to me. Later, she realized what she had done and brought me a lovely bouquet of flowers to make up for her insensitivity."

"What did she say?" Layla asked.

"I had just started my morning jog, and I always start slow, then speed up. She flew by me, saying, 'Got to pick it up if you want to stay in shape.'"

"Wow, she sounds like a piece of work," said Layla.

"She's quite a looker too. She's married to Ned Keller, the realtor. Mr. Soo said she was a member of the Italian Olympic shooting team when she was young" was Dewey's contribution to the topic of Fiona.

"Good, we're here at Mr. Soo's. No more Fiona talk," George said, pulling over to the curb next to Mr. Soo's steps.

Mr. Soo came down the steps, sporting a huge smile. Layla opened her door, rushed out, and hugged him, again, tears streaming down her cheeks.

"Layla, you make an old man feel good shedding tears for me. But please don't. I feel good, and I'm most happy in my new home. Dewey, I'll let you get your luggage. I want to show Layla my home." Mr. Soo led Layla up the stairs to his lanai and inside.

"OK, Dewey, what's going on with her?"

"She's finished her restoration project, and her best friend in New York, Judy, has met someone and it's very serious. Layla said once again she was the third wheel. She told Agnes she didn't feel like she belonged anywhere. She was always so goal oriented, and now she has no goals. Said she feels like a nomad. I think seeing you two just brought back her sense of not knowing where she belongs. Of course, I told her she was welcome to stay with me for as long as she wanted. For me, that would be forever. She's still at loose ends. Maybe you two can figure something out." Dewey took the last of his luggage and proceeded up the stairs.

"Everyone at seven for cocktails, then dinner," George said.

"Right, we'll see you then."

Layla, Dewey, and Mr. Soo made their way up the front lanai stairs to where Annie and George sat.

"Hi folks, we're here," they all chimed in.

"Welcome. Who wants what to drink?" George asked, greeting his friends and directing them to chairs.

When everyone had drinks and small plates of snacks, Layla jumped up, saying, "Photos, Annie, we have photos to share."

"You're right. Let's get our sets and beguile Mr. Soo with our journey into the depths of the Grand Canyon."

Both got up and went inside to get their photos. George looked at Mr. Soo. "Afraid you will have to go through two sets of snapshots. Hope you don't mind too much."

"Oh no, I'm most anxious to see them. Maybe someday, Dewey would take me to see the Grand Canyon. I have always heard it was a most wonderful hole in the earth."

Laughing, Dewey said, "Well, that's one way of putting it, and I would be honored to show it to you. We'll set that up for some time in the near future. You will be amazed at the largeness, colors, and beauty of that hole."

Annie and Layla brought their photos out. Annie exchanged hers with Layla and Dewey, and Layla with George and Annie. Dewey and Layla explained their photos to Mr. Soo, who seemed amazed at the beauty of all the national parks. Then George and Annie went through their photos with Mr. Soo as the sun began its setting journey.

"Annie, Dewey said he would take me to see the Grand Canyon sometime in the near future, but now I think I would also like to see both Zion and Bryce Canyon."

"They all three are beautiful and so very different, I'm sure you guys would have a good time. And you could even take a mule trip to the bottom of the Grand Canyon, like Layla and I did."

"No, this old man does not have that many years left and don't intend to trust any of that time to some mule walking on a narrow trail. Mr. Soo no fool!"

Everyone laughed, George and Dewey thinking Mr. Soo's resolve was well stated, although neither said anything out loud. After the sun set, they made their way to the back lanai and enjoyed grilled steaks, salad, and baked potatoes. Afterward, varied conversations were carried on until Mr. Soo said it was getting past his bedtime, and he graciously thanked everyone and began to leave. "Oh, wait, Dewey, I forgot you are staying at my home. Walk with me and you can let me in and keep my key."

"Actually, Mr. Soo, I'm tired too. It was a long day for Layla and me. I'm still on Salt Lake time, and frankly, now that I'm full, I'm getting really sleepy. I think I will join you."

Dewey thanked George and Annie for an excellent evening, kissed Layla on the cheek, and joined Mr. Soo on the short walk to his house.

Layla smiled after them; turning to George and Annie, she said, "I'm so happy now that I'm among friends and I'm also feeling sleepy. I should unpack tonight, but I'm so tired. If it's OK, I'll just go to bed."

"Of course, honey, you go on. Like Dewey said, you both are on Salt Lake time, and it was a long trip here. Plus, talking with Mr. Soo about the loss of Mrs. Soo and his new home was probably a bit stressful for you. Go to bed. I'll help you unpack in the morning."

"Thank you both." Layla kissed them each on the cheek and went to her bedroom and to bed.

"That was a nice evening. I enjoyed seeing Layla's pictures. She had some like yours and then some very different."

Earlier, George explained to Annie why Dewey thought Layla had broken down at the airport. They decided to be extra gentle with Layla and let her know she was welcome to stay with them; even George conceded she could stay without his complaining.

Dishwasher loaded, back lanai cleaned and secure, Annie and George went to the front lanai and sat on the glider together. Annie snuggled under George's arm and wrapped her arm around his waist. "Honey, you were pretty charming yourself tonight."

"I was," George said, smiling. "I enjoy being around Dewey, Layla, and Mr. Soo. Seems like we have developed some type of bond from the storm and murders. I realize that may sound strange, but I can't help but feel that way."

Annie tilted her head, looking up at George. "Sweetheart, I believe you've hit the nail on the head. I never thought of it that way before, but I think you're right."

CHAPTER 31

Layla woke early, not used to the time zone she was now in, and needed a cup of coffee. She went to the kitchen, and she started the coffee maker, enjoying its delicious aroma. After the coffee was brewed, she poured a cup, took a sip, and sighed happily, then walked to the front lanai slider. Unlocking the door and removing the pole George had inserted on the bottom inside of the slider after the Okamoto murders, she pulled the slider open and stepped onto the lanai. The sun was slowly rising from the water, and the air was fresh and warm. She stood at the rail, looking at the surf as it rolled onto the beach. Turning her head, she peered over at the home Mr. and Mrs. Soo had shared.

"What a sad house," Layla said softly to no one. She walked to the far end of the lanai, passing the slider to Annie and George's bedroom where the curtains were slightly open; she glanced into the bedroom. Annie was curled into George, her arm slung over his chest, his arm draped down her back. Her heart caught in her throat, and she gulped back tears, never knowing love like that and wondering if she ever would.

She looked appraisingly at the house. Draining her coffee cup, Layla decided she had to have another. She went back into the house, closing and securing the lanai door, and got another cup of coffee. Looking out the kitchen window, she saw someone on Mr. Soo's lanai. Walking to the back lanai, she went to the far end and waved at the figure, realizing it was Dewey.

Finally, he looked up and waved back at her, toasting her with his cup of coffee.

He took a long look and reasoned she had no idea that with the morning light behind her, you could see right through her thin cotton nightgown. Dewey leaned over the railing for a better look and saw beneath the gown that she only wore a pair of bikini underpants. He thought his angel looked magnificent, and he was transfixed for a few more moments. Realizing he was gawking, he raised his arm, motioning to his wristwatch and holding up seven fingers, pointing up toward Otis's, hoping Layla would get the message to join him and Mr. Soo at Otis's for breakfast at seven o'clock.

Layla gave Dewey a thumbs-up accompanied by a huge smile.

Dewey returned her thumbs-up, smiled, and watched her walk back inside. "God help me," he mumbled, "I'm so in love with that woman. I hope one day she'll see how much she means to me because this is taking a physical toll." He turned and walked inside to tell Mr. Soo that Layla would be joining them for breakfast.

A couple of minutes before seven, Layla walked out the kitchen door, locking it behind her. George and Annie would be up soon, so she left a note by a fresh pot of coffee, telling them of her plans.

Dewey and Mr. Soo were at the end of the street and watched her come out of the house.

"Oh lord, she just looks too damn good. I've got to get these romantic thoughts under control."

Mr. Soo chuckled. "Yes, Dewey, you must learn to control your ardor until she is ready."

Layla wore white hip-huggers, a pale blue halter top, and a pair of tennis shoes, thinking she might join them on their morning constitutional.

"Gentlemen, you both look charming this morning," Layla said, walking between them and hooking her arm through theirs.

Dewey found his arm next to Layla's bosom, and he was again feeling himself in physical distress. He really did have to control himself better. He realized Layla was talking to him.

"I'm sorry, I was daydreaming. What did you say, Layla?"

"Nothing important, just asked if you had slept well."

"Went out like a light. I don't think I moved the whole night."

"Same with me. I think it's the warm weather, the great meal we had, and best of all, seeing our friends again."

"I agree with you. Funny, though, I'm starving this morning. Can't wait to eat one of Otis's greasy breakfasts."

"Otis prepares wonderful breakfast feasts. I've eaten almost everything on his menu, except for his lite breakfast selections. All is excellent, he uses real butter in his preparation. It gives everything an excellent taste," Mr. Soo said, smiling.

"That's why I'm wearing tennis shoes. After enjoying one of Otis's buttery meals, I thought I'd join you gentlemen for your morning walk."

"Excellent. We will enjoy your lovely company," said Mr. Soo.

All three ate a cholesterol-clogging meal and spent the next several hours walking about the town, greeting shop owners and friends, finally making their way back to their original starting point. Layla went to say good morning to George and Annie; even though it was getting close to the afternoon, she felt the urge for another cup of coffee, knowing Annie would have the pot brewing. Walking up the stairs to the back lanai, she found both watching them as they trooped down the slope from the main street.

"Did you have a good breakfast and a nice walk with the boys?"

"I had a most fattening breakfast. It was terrific! Then we walked for over two hours and greeted shop owners. Dewey is so charming. He got and gave plenty of hugs and high fives."

"He's a charmer," Annie said, nudging George under the table.

"Layla, I'm telling you, don't let him get away. He's a prime catch for some lady, and I think you are that lady."

"George!" Annie said, faking a shocked look.

"I know Dewey is wonderful and would make any woman an excellent husband. I can't or maybe won't let myself think in that direction until I get my life on track again. I know my health has improved, but emotionally, I still have healing to do, and I feel like I'm drifting. I haven't got my bearings yet."

Annie arose and put her arm around Layla's shoulders. "You hang in there. George and I are here for you, Dewey and Mr. Soo too. We all want you 100 percent better."

"Thank you both for being so kind and understanding. With friends like all of you, how can I not get better?"

Later that afternoon, George, Annie, and Layla walked over to Mr. Soo's after seeing him and Dewey sitting on the lanai, having a beer, their legs raised on the lanai railing. George said they both were no doubt solving the problems of the world.

Both men rose and made sure everyone was seated and had drinks.

George said, "I have an idea for this evening. How about I call Byrd and tell him we will be coming for dinner and he can grill something for us? How does that sound?"

"Terrific," said Dewey. "I'll be able to meet up with a lot of my old windsurfing buddies. I'll take one of his steaks, and the evening is on me. This will be fun."

"George, you and I can have the chicken. We had steak last night," Annie said, smiling sweetly at George.

"I suppose you're right, and I'll ask him to grill some of his good veggies too. Layla and Mr. Soo, what about your dinner order?"

"I'll take fish if he has any available. If not, chicken will be fine."

"If it is permissible, I will pass on this evening. I will eat at Otis's, then come back home. I have a lot of texting to my grandchildren to catch up on. Dewey, I found an extra key for you to use."

"We'll miss you, Mr. Soo, but we can understand you wanting to keep up on your texting," Dewey said, smiling fondly at Mr. Soo.

Annie and George sat in a booth at Bird's, watching the younger crowd dancing to '70s rock music. Everyone had eaten a hearty dinner of grilled chicken or steak, vegetables, and baked potatoes.

"George, we should be out there working off our meal off instead of sitting here drinking beer."

"I'll get out there for a slow number." Just then, a slow song came up on the jukebox. "See, a slow song. Come on, my lady."

"Look, Dewey, George and Annie are dancing."

Annie had her arms around George at his waist, and George's arms were pressing her into him as he nuzzled her neck. Whatever he said elected a smile and soft chuckle from Annie, and she placed her head on his chest.

"Makes my heart feel good to see them like that," said Layla. "I just hope when I get that age, there is someone in love with me, like George is with Annie."

Dewey had decided he was physically unable to dance another slow dance with Layla, but she refused to walk off the dance floor when the music started. He had positioned her in such a manner that he could keep the lower portion of his body from hers, but he felt himself weakening, and if this damn song didn't end soon, he would just draw her into him and be done with it. Now she was talking about Annie and George, and he would have to answer and lose his concentration. Damn, just look at them. They certainly were dancing pretty sexily.

"Dewey, are you feeling all right? Did you eat too much?"

"No, not much air in here. And you'll never have to worry about finding someone to fall in love with you."

The music ended, and both couples slid back in the booth they shared.

"Dewey, are feeling ill?" Annie asked.

"Fine, fine, just the lack of air in here."

"Right, you did get a little close," George said, grinning at Dewey, knowing exactly what his problem was.

Dewey grinned back at George, shook his head, and rolled his eyes.

CHAPTER 32

Layla knew a small seed of her current idea planted itself the first morning she was in Maui, gazing at Mr. Soo's former home, thinking how sad and forlorn it looked. Yesterday, the idea materialized, and she phoned Ned Keller, the realtor listed on the posting at Mr. Soo's. She had met both Ned and Fiona Keller at the Okamotos' funeral and was glad they lived across the road from George and Annie. She explained to Ned she wanted to view the property at a specific time on Tuesday, when George was teaching his volleyball clinic and Annie was volunteering at the senior center because if her plan matured, she wanted to surprise them.

Ned suggested he bring Fiona on the tour and warned her she would be sadly shocked at the inside of the house; it would need a lot of remodeling. They arranged to meet on Tuesday afternoon. Layla greeted them as they came down the front stairs, and all three walked to Mr. Soo's former home.

Ned explained he would normally open a house up and let it air out, but because she wanted to keep the viewing private, he decided not to. He warned her there would be an odor from years of Mrs. Soo's inside grilling. Once again, he alerted Layla she would be shocked at what she saw inside.

Fiona added, "But don't let Ned scare you. It can be made into a show place. Mr. Soo's price is quite reasonable for this beachfront property. He is a wise businessman to realize it will take a considerable sum of money to make the home livable again. Everything you see in the house stays with the purchase price. There are some valuable Chinese rugs that simply need cleaning to restore them to their original beauty."

Layla looked at Fiona and said quietly, "Money is not a consideration. I'm not worried about spending money. In my field, art restoration, we are trained to see a vision of what something can be returned to with care and time."

Fiona gave Layla a big smile. "I do believe you are the perfect person for this property. You will be able to see the potential, and you and I can work together to make it into your dream home."

They walked to the back lanai. Ned unlocked and opened the door, and immediately, Layla was assailed with the dank musty odor of a home where old people lived, along with a lingering smoky smell mixed with various spices and perhaps incense.

"This does have a peculiar smell, and my god, what has happened to this floor plan?" Layla said, stopping short, as she was halfway into what should have been a large kitchen.

"Like I warned you, this is a mess. Mrs. Soo had Shoji dividers placed everywhere to divide the home into a myriad of small rooms. After all the years of grilling done inside, the original white screens are now a dingy yellow or sickening orange. Look at the once-beautiful wood, now so discolored. I believe a lot of this wood is now illegal to harvest, but at the time, I suppose you were able to purchase it or Mr. Soo just got it with his export/ import expertise."

Layla began examining the wood. "This wood is magnificent and will need refinishing, but it looks like it's still in good shape. Even the wood on the Shoji screen dividers looks exotic. Perhaps the wood could be salvaged and used elsewhere in the home."

As Layla talked, Fiona nudged Ned's arm and smiled. "Layla, with your artistic eye, you truly do see the potential in this property and wait till you see the view from the front lanai."

Saying that, they walked to the living room, and Fiona pushed the Shoji screens open so they could access the slider to the front lanai.

"You're right, Fiona. It's lovely. This is nicer than the Boones' view. It gives you a wider panorama. And I assume there is a master bedroom that also shares this view?"

"In a manner of speaking, although it is now partitioned off into three rooms, it would make a lovely large master bedroom. It's different from the Boones' home in that it has a new modern master bathroom directly off the master bedroom. Mr. Soo wanted a new bathroom and had one put in about three years ago. It even includes a steam room. He had some space taken off the master bedroom, but this entire house is larger than the Boones', so I believe the master bedroom is now about the same size as they have in their home. All that was done against Mrs. Soo's wishes. She was not one to enjoy the world of modern conveniences."

Fiona and Ned guided Layla through the many dividers until she had seen the entire house. Wisely, they kept their comments to themselves, sensing Layla's artistic eye was doing the remodeling and selling for them.

Finally, she asked, "How much is Mr. Soo asking?"

"He understands it will take a considerable sum to refurbish the home, and currently, this is not a seller's market. I believe you can purchase the home for $1,250,000, and for this location, that is an excellent price," Ned said, knowing Layla was sold on the property.

"I agree with you, the location is great. Fiona, roughly, how much do you think it will take to refurbish, and I'm talking here completely, making it truly livable?"

"Honestly, I believe it will be between $500,000 to $750,000, depending if there is any remodeling done to the core floor plan once all the dividers and screens are removed. That sum does not include furnishings, which would be an additional large sum, as almost everything has to be imported."

"So to make this livable, it will cost about $3 million at a minimum."

"Yes," Fiona said, quickly realizing Layla was not a person to backpedal on price.

"Ned, do you believe Mr. Soo would take the $1,250,000 offer?"

"No doubt, he is anxious to be rid of the property, and once he finds out you're buying the property, it will be a quick sell."

"No, I don't want Mr. Soo to know I'm the one interested in the property until the last minute. I don't want him to compromise his price based on our friendship. Would you folks mind if we went back to your home and discussed this more? The smell is beginning to make me slightly dizzy."

"No, dear," Fiona said, guiding her outside, "that's an excellent idea. I'll fix us something cold to drink to take the taste out of our mouths. I agree this stench really penetrates your senses."

Back at the Keller residence, Fiona brought fresh pineapple punch for everyone that included a hint of rum.

"This is delicious. Thank you, Fiona. So where do we go from here, Ned?"

"I can draw up the papers without listing you specifically and tell him the buyer wishes to remain anonymous until the final signing but that I know the person and vouch for them."

"That will be perfect, Ned. As soon as I hear he has accepted my offer, I can phone my trust officer in New York and get the funds wired to Donnie's bank, into Mr. Soo's account, or however you want to handle that end of the transaction. I would prefer if you and my trust officer work out those details between you two."

"Ladies, you stay here and discuss remodeling. I'm going into my office and printing up the papers for Mr. Soo to look over and for your approval, Layla."

Ned proceeded to his office, leaving Fiona and Layla sitting at their dining room table.

"Fiona, where should we begin on this project?"

"Take all those damn dividers and screens down and see what wood is salvageable. We might be surprised at what can be saved once it is cleaned up and restained—perhaps make end tables, shelves, or whatever your artistic eye can imagine. Once that is done, the next step is the ceiling. Thanks goodness, only the living and dining rooms have the wood ceilings. However, once cleaned and restained, a dark ceiling with stark white walls would be stunning, don't you think?"

"Yes, we must do all we can to save the beautiful wood. Also, I insist that central air-conditioning be put in. I want to lock up at night and will need that for cool air during that time. I imagine that can be installed while work on the wood is being done. What I would like is for the master bedroom and kitchen to be the first rooms completely finished. That will enable me to move from the Boones' and give them their privacy back."

"That's a good idea. However, to keep all the flooring one color, refinishing all the wood floors should be done at the same time. The other individual rooms can be painted later after the rooms you requested are finished. While the work is being completed, you and I will need to find furniture and appliances. Many times, what you want is a catalogue item and can take several months to make it here from the mainland. Believe me, Layla, this is no simple project. It could take a year or more before it is finished to your satisfaction."

"Great, a project I can work on that will end up being my new home, something I can build from the ground up, just as I want it to be. I'm excited about the prospect."

Ned returned with the paperwork for Layla's inspection. She read it carefully, gave her approval, and said she had to be getting back to the Boones'.

Ned and Fiona sat on their front lanai and lay in wait for Mr. Soo and Dewey to catch them returning from their afternoon sojourn.

Back at the Boones', Layla felt happy, and a calm began to settle inside her. She found a place to belong, one she could make her own.

Layla had returned to the Boones' swiftly, not wanting Dewey or Mr. Soo to spot her, afraid that if she saw either of them before dinner, she might say something about her meeting with Ned and Fiona. She didn't want to do that until she found out if Ned was successful in his meeting with Mr. Soo. If he was, she intended to surprise them at dinner tonight. Mr. Soo was treating everyone to dinner at Mama's Fish House.

She made herself a sandwich, got a glass of iced tea, and went out to the front lanai. She ate her lunch at the end railing, looking at the Soo home, hoping she would be able to make it hers and stay close to her friends. All except Dewey, and he was as close to Maui as he was to New York. Annie, George, Mr. Soo, and all his windsurfing friends were here, much better than traveling to New York. Layla felt assured Dewey would visit often.

Last night had been such fun. Everyone had gone to Spreckles Beach at high tide to watch the windsurfers. Mr. Soo had not seen them up close, and he was thrilled. Afterward, they went to a beach fish shack and had baskets of fish and chips; they sat at a beachside table, ate dinner, and talked well after sunset.

Layla spent the next couple of hours killing time, hoping she would hear from Ned before the Boones returned home. Her cell rang, and she jumped, grabbing it out of her shorts pocket.

"Hello, Layla speaking."

"Layla, it's Ned. I just finished talking with Mr. Soo, and he is thrilled at the deal. I'll draw the papers up tonight, talk with your trust officer tomorrow, and this should be in the works in a couple of days. Be sure you call your trust officer. Tell him what is going on and to expect my call."

"Ned, that's terrific news. You made sure not to mention my name?"

"I told Mr. Soo once he was presented with the final papers to sign, he would know the name of the buyer, but currently, the buyer wished to remain anonymous. Just between us, I think he believes it's a celebrity."

"That's so cute. I'm having dinner with him, George, Annie, and Dewey tonight, and I'll break the news to ~~him~~ them. Hope he won't be too disappointed. And I'll be sure and phone my trust officer tomorrow morning. Thank you, Ned. Both you and Fiona have been very professional and swift with this transaction. Please tell Fiona she and I will have to start working on the remodeling project immediately after all the paperwork is completed."

"No problem. She is already lining up people to do the work. Fiona is a person who makes plans ahead of time."

"That's great. I'll talk to you tomorrow, and thanks again." Layla was thrilled and excited; she could hardly wait for dinner this evening.

Everyone was seated, drinks had been served, and Mr. Soo had ordered appetizers. Mr. Soo cleared his throat to get everyone's attention, then said, "I have some good news. My former home has been sold. I do not know yet who the buyer is and won't until the final papers are signed. However, I believe it might be some big celebrity."

Appetizers arrived, and everyone began eating, forgetting about the possible celebrity who bought Mr. Soo's former home.

Enjoying either tea or coffee after dessert, Layla saw her opportunity and said, "I know who's buying your home, Mr. Soo."

"You do?" Mr. Soo questioned.

"I bought it."

"What?" Dewey exclaimed.

"Excellent," said Mr. Soo. "I'll have a lovely lady to take to Otis's."

George grabbed Annie's thigh under the table, too startled to utter a word.

"Oomph," Annie said in reaction to George's pressure on her thigh.

"I realize some of you may think I've lost my mind, but I feel like I belong here and I want to live here permanently. Fiona has already begun lining up workers to help restore Mr. Soo's home. Annie and George, I can assure you I will be out of your hair just as soon as possible. We will finish first with the kitchen, the master bedroom, and then I can move in and finish up with everything else. That should take no more than three months according to Fiona."

George's squeeze on Annie's thigh became even more intense.

"I'm glad you have decided to stay here with your friends," said Dewey. "Will you have much work to do on your new home?"

"I can answer that," said Mr. Soo. "She will have a great deal of restoring to do. Mrs. Soo never remodeled, and she divided rooms off with those silly Shoji screens. It drove me crazy, opening and closing them all the time. Layla has undertaken a costly project, but with her restoration background, she is more than up to the task."

"Thank you, Mr. Soo. It is a large task, but the wood in your home is wonderful, and bringing it back to its original state will be a joy."

"It will be nicer to come to Maui to visit than to New York. Sure you don't want to move to Salt Lake City?" Dewey asked with a grin.

Layla was the only one at the table not knowing he was asking a serious question. "Nope, I'm setting down my roots here, and, Dewey, I expect to have you as a regular guest."

Annie found her voice after forcing George's hand from her thigh. "Layla, I'm so happy for you, and I think you have made a wise decision to stay here where all of us can be your extended family."

"Thank you, Annie. I hope you and George can put up with me until the house is semicompleted. I'm sorry for the inconvenience. You know, I could always get a hotel room. I wouldn't mind."

"Heavens no, you're staying with us, right, George?"

"Huh," George said.

Annie could tell George was still in a state of shock and suggested they leave the restaurant.

They walked to Pearl where everyone piled in, and George drove back home. He stopped at Mr. Soo's and let Dewey and Mr. Soo out; Layla said she would go with them as Dewey said he would show her the video game he and his team were working on, the one he had brought for Mr. Soo's approval.

Annie gave Layla her key to the back door and said to be sure it was securely locked when she came in if she and George were already in bed.

Once inside, George made sure everything was locked, set the air on low, and went into the bedroom. He undressed, brushed his teeth, took off his glasses, and laid them on his nightstand, then crawled into bed. Having trouble sleeping, he realized he was mad at Layla for asking or assuming something, like being able to stay with them, and putting them on the spot by asking in front of Mr. Soo and Dewey. Most of all, he was mad at Annie for giving approval without even asking him, not even considering the lack of privacy and intimacy her living with them for months would mean. George felt they had renewed their close and often playful relationship that waned during the years the kids were growing up and both of them were working so hard. Now they were enjoying this renewed closeness, but obviously, his wife did not share his feelings. George felt hurt, sad, and betrayed.

Annie needed a cup of coffee, and instead of starting the pot, she made a cup of instant. She needed to talk to George about Layla staying several months while Mr. Soo's former home was being made livable. She sat at the counter and finally walked into the bedroom, looking for George. Finding him in bed, asleep, surprised her because he didn't even say good night. She hoped he wasn't feeling ill.

Annie walked back to the kitchen, got her coffee, and went to the living room to read a couple of chapters in her current book. Finally feeling tired, she went into the bathroom and got ready for bed. Getting into bed, she kissed George softly on his back. He hadn't said or kissed her good night; she knew he was angry. They would talk in the morning and get everything straightened out.

CHAPTER 33

Early the next morning, George got out of bed, trying not to wake Annie. He was awake when Annie came to bed and kissed him on the back; he thought about confronting her then, but he wanted his comments to be concise and clear. He put on his running shorts, shoes, and slipped on an old T-shirt, then went out to the kitchen to start the coffee. He sat at the counter with his coffee and cereal, doing the morning crossword when Annie came out.

"That coffee smells great. I need a cup of the good stuff. Made myself a cup of instant last night, but it doesn't hit the spot like this brew." She poured herself a cup.

George finished his breakfast, took his dishes, rinsed them off, and placed them in the dishwasher.

"I'm going for a run," he said and headed out the back door.

Annie watched him as he ran down the sand and knew he was still mad. She began to surmise that Layla, whether she realized it or not, had placed them in a bad spot last night by asking in front of Dewey and Mr. Soo about extending her stay for several months. Invited for a week or so was one thing, but two or three months was something else. Annie felt antsy and thought a run might be best for her too; she needed to clear her head in order to talk with George about the situation. She made herself some toast, had another cup of coffee, then went back into the bedroom, and changed into her running attire. Returning to the kitchen, she found Layla pouring herself a cup of coffee.

"I'm going for a run. You can keep the key I gave you last night. I found another one and put it on my key ring. Be sure and lock up if you leave. George is also running, and he always carries his key."

Without waiting for a reply, Annie was out the door.

"Wow," Layla said quietly, "someone must have gotten up on the wrong side of the bed."

She wasn't going to let Annie's shortness diminish the joy she was feeling. The only thing she felt bad about was this was Dewey's last evening on Maui. She was glad Annie and George was having everyone over for grilled steaks. George had also invited the sheriff to join them; the whole group would be together for Dewey's final evening. It was not quite eight o'clock, maybe Dewey and Mr. Soo hadn't gone to Otis' yet, and she could join them for a final breakfast. She got her cell and dialed Dewey. He told her they had just got coffee and were trying to decide what to order, they would wait for her but to hurry; they were hungry.

George finished his run; the strenuous pace he maintained did nothing to diminish his anger. He unlocked the door, then went to take a shower.

Annie came back and heard the shower running. She decided maybe if she joined George in the shower, they could kiss and make up and work through this dilemma. She went into the bathroom, undressed, and opened the shower door about to step in when George turned off the water, grabbed a towel, and stepped out, saying, "I'm done, it's all yours."

Annie walked into the shower and turned on the water, putting her face up to the spray. She wanted to hide her tears. She knew George was very mad at her, and all she wanted to do was grab him, hug and kiss him, and find out what she could do to rectify the situation. As soon as she was out of the shower, they must talk.

George finished dressing and went out to the kitchen for lunch. He found some tuna salad and made a sandwich, along with a glass of iced tea. He opened up the lanai sliders and walked out, sat down at the table, and began to eat.

He had just finished and was drinking the last of his iced tea when Annie came out on the lanai. She sat down at the table and looked at him, a worried frown on her face.

"Honey, I know you're mad at me, and I realize it has to do with Layla staying with us for several months. What can I do to fix things?"

"It appears you did it all. You gave your consent for both of us. I don't seem to have a say in the matter." That said, George got up took his dishes inside and put them in the dishwasher.

"George, I felt trapped. It wasn't right that she asked us in front of others. I didn't know what to say."

"Well, why did you have to say anything, or at least say 'George and I will discuss it'? No, you happily agreed right away. I know many times you think you run our marriage, and I go along because most of the time I agree with you. However, this time you were wrong. Well, on second thought, maybe you're not into our newfound relationship as much as I am. Maybe I'm just seeing things for the first time."

Annie gasped, but before she could say anything, Layla unlocked the door and came into the kitchen. "Hi, folks, had a final breakfast with Dewey and Mr. Soo, then joined them on their constitutional."

"Lovely, I'm going to the grocery to get beer for tonight. Do you need anything while I'm there?" George asked.

"Yes, I'll make you a list," Annie said, walking inside and taking a small memo pad and pencil out of a drawer.

"I'm capable of making a list. What do you need?" George took the pad and pencil from her hand.

Annie walked to the refrigerator and opened the door, peering inside. "We need a dozen eggs, another big can of Yuban, a couple of Maui onions if you can find them. If not, don't get any." She shut the door and scratched her forehead, trying to remember if she needed anything else. Her mind was so muddled with what George had said, and not being able to respond was only making things worse.

"Be sure that is all you need. I'm not going back out once I get home," George said sharply.

Layla stood at the door, dumbfounded, watching the exchange between them.

Finally, she realized they both were looking at her, and she said she was going to make a sandwich and have a glass of tea. She opened the breadbox and Annie said to add bread to the list and a pound of soft butter.

George got his wallet out and checked the bills, knowing he did not have enough for his expanding list. He slammed the wallet down on the counter and went to their bedroom, getting into the closet safe, retrieving a couple of fifties. He went back to the kitchen, opened his wallet, and placed the bills inside. He tore the list off the memo pad, grabbed his car keys, and left.

After he was gone, Annie could hardly hold back the tears. She opened the refrigerator door and took out the big bowl of potato salad she had prepared yesterday and gave it a good stirring. She then got the filet steaks she had laid out to thaw and prepared them for grilling. She rubbed salt, pepper, and garlic powder on them; wrapped a strip of bacon around each; placed them in a glass dish; covered it with aluminum foil; and put everything back in the refrigerator. Going to both bathrooms, she picked up the dirty towels and brought them to the washer. She got the washer going and went back into the kitchen to fix herself a sandwich and glass of tea.

"Annie, I can only assume you and George are having a disagreement. I'm sorry, is there anything I can do to help? Get out of your way or anything?"

Annie had poured her iced tea and was beginning to prepare her sandwich. That was all she could take; she sat things down, rushed off to the bedroom, slammed the door, and cried. After about ten minutes, she got control of herself and went back out to the kitchen. Layla had finished making Annie a sandwich and placed it and the tea back in the refrigerator.

"Here, let me get your sandwich and tea. Sit at the counter," she instructed Annie. "Do you want to talk about anything?"

"No."

"OK, just eat then. You had a good run. You need the protein."

Layla left Annie at the counter and went to her bedroom where she placed a call to her trust officer. She explained everything and gave him Ned's phone number. He told her he would call Ned and have him fax a copy of the signed documents, and they would then be able to work out all the details. Layla felt buoyed, then remembered the drama going on between Annie and George and just shook her head in disbelief. She returned to the kitchen, just as Annie finished her lunch and George drove back into the garage with the groceries. He brought the groceries into the kitchen, and Annie put things away. He grabbed a cold beer from the refrigerator and went out on the front lanai. Instead of sitting in the glider, where he and Annie usually sat, he sat in the lounge chair with his beer and the rest of the day's paper to finish reading.

Annie came out, and seeing him in the lounge chair, she sighed and sat in the glider. "George, we really must talk. This thing between us is driving me crazy. Honey, I love you so much, I never want anything I do to come between us, especially something I do without thinking. I'm sorry, and you are right, I should have talked things over with you."

Just then, Layla came out on the lanai with a glass of tea, bringing one for Annie. She sat down on the glider and commented on the beauty of the sea and how much she was going to enjoy the view from her own lanai. She talked on for several minutes, then realized no one else was saying anything and thought maybe she had interrupted their conversation.

"Gosh, I'm sorry. Did I interrupt something?"

"Nope, I'm going inside for a nap. You ladies enjoy the rest of the afternoon," George said as he got up and went inside.

Annie felt trapped; she wanted to get away from Layla, but she didn't want to disturb George, and within several hours, people would be coming for the evening. She sat in the glider sipping her tea, looking out at the sea as waves rolled softly on the sand. This was something she and George enjoyed doing. This belonged to them; now here she was, sitting with Layla.

CHAPTER 34

Layla was setting on the back lanai, waiting for Dewey and Mr. Soo to make their way over to the Boones'. Seeing Mr. Soo locking his front door, she ran down the stairs to walk back with them.

"Hi, gentlemen, I thought I would walk with you and warn you about something. George and Annie are having quite a disagreement. They're hardly speaking, and when they're in a room together, it feels like the Artic."

"I'm so sorry to hear that. When did this start?" Mr. Soo asked.

"I noticed it this morning. I guess something must have happened last night while we were playing Dewey's new video game."

Mr. Soo shook his head. Dewey looked at Mr. Soo, a glum expression on his face.

Layla escorted them to the front lanai, George made sure everyone had a drink, and Annie sat out vegetables, chips, and dips.

The sheriff rapped on the back lanai screen, and hearing him, George walked from the front lanai to let him in to join the rest of the group. Everyone was settling in with drinks and plates of snacks, ready for the sun to take its evening dip.

Dewey noticed neither George nor Annie had spoken to each other; although both had been gracious to their guests, it was obvious to those who knew them something was definitely wrong. He glanced at Mr. Soo, raising his eyebrows. Mr. Soo looked down, nodding.

The sheriff told them that, unfortunately, there was nothing new to report on the Okamoto murders from any of the agencies involved.

"Sheriff, I have some news for you," Layla said, smiling. "Paia has a new resident. I've purchased Mr. Soo's former home. I will be refurbishing it, and I intend to make this my new home."

"Layla, I'm happily surprised. After your first visit here, I was afraid we would never get you back, let alone become a resident. I'm happy for all of us."

"I have wonderful friends here. Plus, who can beat this weather? Believe me, much better than New York. I grew weary of New York and the pace. Paia is more peaceful, and people really care here. They take the time to know one another."

"Let me make this official. Welcome to Paia, and if the sheriff's office can be of any service, do not hesitate to contact me personally. Wait until I tell Charlene. She always knows everything first. This time I'll beat her with the latest!"

The sun had set, and everyone went to the back lanai, eager for George to work his magic on the grill. Easy conversation flowed. Layla walked over to Dewey, asking if he was ready to leave tomorrow.

"No, I would rather stay here, but I have to get back and run my business. A lot of people are depending upon this new video game release and on me to keep on top of the digital process. We tycoons have our empire to run," he said, laughing. "After dinner, let's you and I go for a walk. There's something I need to discuss with you."

"Great, I look forward to that. For me, I'm sad to see you go. I wish you were going to stay and help me put my new home in order. It would be such fun to have your input."

"You'll do great on your own. I'll be anxious to visit once it's all finished."

"I'm going to keep you to that. I'll expect a visit when all the finishing touches are completed. I can assure you Fiona will do her utmost to hasten the completion to earn her commission," Layla said, laughing.

"From what I've heard, I'm sure you're right. Just give me as much warning as you can, and I'll be here," Dewey said, putting an arm around her shoulder and hugging her.

Everyone enjoyed dinner, the evening drawing too soon to a close. Mr. Soo said it was past his bedtime, and the sheriff said he would walk him back to his home. He thanked George and Annie for a wonderful dinner, wished Dewey a safe journey, then he and Mr. Soo proceeded down the steps.

Dewey said he and Layla were going for a walk. Annie asked if she had her key, in case they weren't up when she returned. Layla said it was in her pocket.

George came over to Dewey and patted him on the shoulder. "We'll be at Mr. Soo's at 8:30 a.m. tomorrow to get you and your luggage. This time I know you'll be back."

Dewey looked at George and smiled fondly. "I'll see you and Annie tomorrow morning. Thanks for a great last night in Paia. Being here with everyone makes it harder for me to go home, but I must." He grabbed Layla's hand, and they headed out for their walk, leaving George and Annie alone on the lanai.

"George, we've got to talk. There is no one here to interrupt us. There is no reason we can't talk this through. I'm so broken up inside, I could hardly handle my hostess duties this evening. Every time I looked over at you, it seemed you actually avoided looking at me, and it's breaking my heart. Please, honey, help us through this," Annie said, walking over to George, throwing her arms around him.

He sighed and grabbed her arms, gently prying her loose so he could look into her eyes. "Annie, what exactly do you expect I can do or we can do for that matter?"

"I don't know about the Layla situation, but what I do know is that I cherish what we had and I want it back. I never meant to diminish our relationship. I did something stupid without thinking, and I want you to know how sorry I am and how much I want you to forgive me. Do you still love me?" Annie whispered.

"Don't be silly. Of course, I still love you. I'll always be in love with you. I'm hurt, and I think you want to be a mother figure to Layla and help her through this rough period. We don't know how much time we have left, and I was enjoying this special time with the lady I've loved for so many years, and I thought she was enjoying it as much as I was."

Annie reached up and took George's face in her hands. "Believe me, with all my heart, I enjoy it very much. I'm proud that after all these years, you still find me desirable, still want me, and still love me. I've seen so many couples that reach our age divorce, and the man goes out and gets a much younger wife. I thank my lucky stars you still love me." Annie drew George's face down and kissed him passionately.

George returned her kiss, drawing her into him. "Let's get things inside, then go to bed. I've missed you."

"Thank you, darling, for forgiving me. I don't know what we can do about this Layla thing, but damn it, we'll do something."

"Yes, but we'll worry about it in the morning."

CHAPTER 35

Dewey and Layla walked down the street that ran behind George and Annie's home and in front of Mr. Soo's, a three-block walk between entranceways to the street.

Whispering because of the late hour, Dewey turned Layla to face him, saying, "Layla, I'm your friend, and good friends sometimes have to point things out that might be hurtful, but I'm doing this because I am your friend, and I don't want to see things get any further out of hand."

"Dewey, you're frightening me."

"You made an error last night at dinner. You sprang the purchase of Mr. Soo's home on everyone, plus the fact you wanted to stay with George and Annie a few months until it was ready for you to move in. You did that in front of Mr. Soo and me. You should have done that in private. You put the Boones in a very awkward position. I'm afraid George is mad at Annie because she gave her approval without discussing it with him. See, honey, George and Annie have a renewed relationship, something few seniors are able to recapture. A big part of that relationship is based on privacy, which they enjoyed when they were first married before the kids started arriving. Interrupting that privacy for a week or two is fine, but you're talking months. That wasn't fair, Layla. Now I know you come from a very different environment from any of us. I'm sure you have houseguests for months at a time, which is no problem in your circle. You have a huge estate in the Hamptons and a large brownstone in New York, but Annie and George's home is small compared to those, and privacy is an issue. Mr. Soo and I discussed it last night. We were afraid something like this might happen. What I'm trying to say, in a way, it's not your fault. Your lifestyle is so different.

"There's something else you probably won't be thrilled to hear, but I got to be your friend and tell you. Let's face it, Mr. Soo and I are rich. Money is no problem for us. However, the Boones live on retirement income. Their house has great value, but it's not liquid cash. It cost them a bundle the week they were in Los Angeles. I tried to pay for everything during our week together. That's why I booked so much in advance. You're talking added groceries, electricity, etc., and how about when you need to go somewhere other than walking? You will have to ask one of them to drive you. Have you noticed the price of gasoline here?"

Layla lowered her head and said, "I feel like such a fool. I've wished many times that George and Annie were my parents, and yet I have treated them so badly. What must they think of me? Do you have any ideas how I can make it up to them?"

"Mr. Soo and I have talked it over, and we have come up with something for you to consider."

"Anything. I want to straighten this mess out. Annie and George angry with each other breaks my heart, and to think I caused it makes me appear uncaring and insensitive."

"Talk with Annie and George, apologize to them, and let them know you now realize what you did was done out of excitement. Tell them Mr. Soo has offered to have you stay with him during the remodeling. He thought having you join him for meals would dazzle Otis."

Layla had to laugh, knowing Mr. Soo did enjoy having her join them at Otis's for breakfast.

"I'll talk with Mr. Soo tomorrow and make sure it is fine with him. I certainly don't want to cause any more problems."

They continued their walk, talking about a variety of things, then returned to the Boones' after nearly two hours. Layla was already missing Dewey and told him how much she depended on his friendship. Dewey smiled and sighed. They noticed there was only a faint light in the kitchen and on the back porch; both hoped that meant George and Annie had gone to bed early, back to being a loving couple.

Layla sat her alarm clock so she could meet Mr. Soo and Dewey for breakfast. She dressed, went to the kitchen, started a pot of coffee for George and Annie, then quietly made her way out the back door. She waited for Dewey and Mr. Soo at the end of the block; soon they came out and joined her for the walk up to Otis's.

"Mr. Soo, I'm sure by now, Dewey has told you that he had a heart-to-heart talk with me last night, thank God. I feel so bad about all the trouble I've caused between Annie and George, and I want to make sure you really want me to stay at your new home."

"Yes, Layla, it was my idea in the first place. It will be my honor to have you stay in my new home while you remodel my former home. We will have many things to discuss during the remodeling. It will be fun for both of us, and we will be able to take at least one meal a day with Otis. Your company pleases him so very much," Mr. Soo said, beaming.

"Great, then I'm the one that is honored to be staying with you, and eating at Otis's is always a calorie-laden joy. I guess it must be this uphill walk, but by the time we get here for breakfast, I'm always starving."

Everyone agreed, ordering one of Otis's big breakfasts.

George heard Layla's alarm go off and figured she would join the boys for one last breakfast together at Otis's. He decided he would just lay in bed until she left, enjoying the feel of Annie tucked into him.

When he heard the door close, he began rubbing Annie's arm that lay across his chest and kissed her on top of the nose. "Wake up, honey, we've got to get up, get ready, eat breakfast, and get Dewey to the airport."

Annie stretched. "So soon? It seems like I just closed my eyes. Why is it so hard to get up when you have to get up early and, at other times, you wake up early anyway?"

"That's a question for greater minds that are ours to answer. Sleep well?"

Annie smiled up at George, stretched up, and gave him a kiss. "I slept satisfied and peaceful once again next to my sexy husband."

George put his arms around her and gave her a kiss of his own. "Honey, we have to get going."

"You're right. I'll shower, put my face on, then you can follow me."

Dressed and out to the kitchen, both were grateful Layla had made a pot of coffee; they each got a cup and grabbed a banana. Layla came in the back door as they were finishing their bananas.

"Well, ladies, guess I had better get Pearl out, and we should pick up Dewey. Sure hate to see him go. I know Mr. Soo enjoyed his company. No matter what he says, it's still a rough time for him, readjusting to life without Mrs. Soo. Having Dewey around helped fill some of his empty time."

"George, how wise of you. I never considered that," Layla said thoughtfully.

As George pulled Pearl up in front of Mr. Soo's, he saw Dewey and Mr. Soo embracing, saying their farewells. George helped Dewey load his luggage, then they were off to the airfield. It was a short drive, but before they pulled into the hangar area, Layla asked George if he could stop outside the fence, she had something she wanted to say.

"Last night on our walk, my dear friend, Dewey, was kind enough to help me tumble out of my ivory tower."

George and Annie looked over at one another a puzzled look on their faces, then turned toward the back seat to focus their attention on what Layla was saying.

"George, Annie, I must apologize to both of you. It was so thoughtless of me not to tell you first about my extended plans. I just got caught up in the whole thing, and honestly, in my circle, staying with someone for months at a time is no big deal. Dewey told me that is not normal. Also, I didn't consider the added expense. I am so sorry. I have often said to Dewey that I wish I could exchange parents. I would pick you both. And yet I treated you so badly. I hope you can forgive me and will let me try and make amends.

"Mr. Soo has offered to let me stay with him. In fact, he says we can work together on the remodeling, and he and I can eat at least one meal a day at Otis's. This is very important to him."

Annie and George both grinned, hearing that Mr. Soo would parade Layla to Otis's on a daily basis for a meal.

"After we have Dewey in the air, George, if you will drive me to the regular airport, I would like to go to one of the car rental agencies and rent a car. Mr. Soo told me I could keep it in his garage, and we can go on marketing trips together. I think he will enjoy having me around with a car. Has this made things better?"

"Annie and I reconciled last night when we were alone and could talk things out, and yes, this works fine for both of us. We both still think the world of you, Layla, and want nothing more than your happiness. I think staying with Mr. Soo will do wonders to get him through this period of adjustment. For a man his age, he has had some pretty big changes in his life. First, Dewey and now you. It will help him over the hurdles he encounters on his own."

Annie didn't say a word, but a smile never left her face, and she thought things were working out just fine, thanks to Dewey.

George put Pearl into gear and headed toward the DewMaster jet waiting on the tarmac. Luggage was unloaded and placed in the plane. Annie hugged Dewey and whispered her sincere thank-you in his ear. George shook hands and told him he was welcome back anytime. George and Annie got back into Pearl and drove farther toward the hangar, leaving Layla and Dewey to say goodbye privately.

Layla went up to Dewey, reached toward his face, and kissed him sweetly on the lips.

Dewey was dumbfounded. "Thank you. What was that for? Don't get me wrong, it was terrific," Dewey said, smiling broadly.

"That's a small-time thank you to my best friend and to a man that hopefully will wait for me to get back to being someone that can give love. I know you are the best man in the world I could ever hope to be with. I'm just not quite ready to go there yet. I hope I still have more time to find myself."

"I'll be waiting for you. Take as long as you need." Dewey didn't realize what he was doing, but he reached down and grabbed the back of Layla's head, tipping her upward and kissed her lovingly on the lips.

"Wow, this may not take as long as I thought," Layla said, shaking her head in dismay.

"Got to go, honey. I'll call you when I get home."

Dewey boarded the plane, and Layla began to make her way to where Pearl was parked.

"George, did I just see what I think I saw?" Annie asked.

"Wouldn't believe it if I hadn't seen it myself. He finally kissed his angel. I don't think she minded too much either."

All three stood on the tarmac, waving to Dewey as his plane left Maui.

Layla sighed. "Gosh, I miss him already."

Layla drove her newly rented Ford Taurus wagon of out the rental yard and back to Paia, enjoying the freedom of being on her own. She rented a station wagon, thinking she would be toting things needed for her remodeling, plus grocery items. That gave her an idea, and she pulled into the parking lot of the supermarket where George and Annie shopped.

Inside, she bought a case of Heinekens, then went to the greeting card display to find a thank-you card. She selected one she could add a few words to, then proceeded to the manager's booth.

"May I help you?"

"Yes, sir, I would like to purchase a gift certificate for groceries. What is the largest dollar amount you carry?"

"We carry $10, $25, $50, and $100 gift certificates."

"Great, I'll take five of the $100 gift certificates." Layla pulled out a book of traveler's checks and began signing them.

At Mr. Soo's, she got out and asked him if she could put her car in his garage, as he had offered.

"Yes, let me see what you have rented," he said with excitement as he grabbed his garage door opener. "A station wagon. How clever of you. We will get a lot of use out of that on our shopping trips."

"My thoughts exactly. Plus, I imagine it will come in handy during the remodeling. I've gotten some beer to take to the Boones along with a thank-you card and $500 worth of grocery-store gift certificates. Do you think that will help smooth things over?"

"Most excellent idea," Mr. Soo said, beaming as he opened the garage door.

A case of Heinekens turned out to be heavier than Layla realized as she toted it and her purse up the stairs to the Boones' back door. She banged her knee on the back door as a way of knocking.

George opened the door with a surprised look on his face. "Let me get that. You shouldn't be carrying such a heavy load up the stairs. After all, you're still recovering from surgery."

"I forgot all about that. I think it will be fine. I did a lot of crawling around and stretching when I was doing my restoration project without any complications."

"Are we having a celebration?"

"Well, of sorts, a farewell party for me and a thank-you party from me to you and Annie. I'll let you handle the beer, and I'll take my purse to the bedroom."

In the bedroom, Layla added a personal message to the thank-you card, then placed the $500 worth of gift certificates inside. Back in the kitchen, Annie and George were relaying bottles of beer into the refrigerator.

"Is it too early for us to share a beer?"

"It's close to noon. We'll call it a pre-lunch cocktail," said George.

Beers were opened, and then Layla handed Annie the thank-you card, saying, "This in no way can make up for my thoughtlessness or the deep thanks I owe you both, but I wanted to give you some token of my appreciation for your kindness and understanding."

Annie opened the card, read the brief note, then looked at the gift cards. "George, look what this girl has done."

George looked at the five $100 gift certificates Annie fanned out for him. "Layla, thank you so much. What a thoughtful gift and something we can always use. I envision you and Mr. Soo joining us for some prime grilling in the very near future."

"I must admit, I did hope you might invite us over for a meal."

"Honey, this is very generous. We really appreciate you doing this for us," Annie said, giving her a hug.

Chapter 36

Bags packed, Layla sat on the lanai with George and Annie, enjoying a cup of coffee. "The first thing I'm doing today is purchase a coffee maker and coffee. Mr. Soo is a tea drinker."

"Don't blame you. You're a coffee drinker like me," Annie said.

"Layla, don't push Mr. Soo about visiting his former home. I doubt he will go back until all those screens and dividers are down. That way, things will look more like the home he originally purchased before Mrs. Soo made her changes."

"I agree with you that once the screens and dividers are down, he might be more comfortable visiting. I will keep him updated and will let him make his own decision when to visit."

After coffee, George helped take the bags over to Mr. Soo's. Annie promised they would be having them over for dinner soon.

Mr. Soo was out on his walk, which Layla was grateful for; it would give her free time to get her errands done. First, purchase a coffee maker and coffee, then go to the bank and meet with Mr. Munson as her trust officer advised.

Layla stopped by the coffee shop first. Browsing to find several different types of brew, she discovered a section of coffeepots and purchased coffee and coffee maker without looking any further.

At the bank, she asked a teller if she could speak with Donald Munson. When Donnie heard who was wanting to see him, he hurriedly went out front. "Layla, I've been in touch with your trust officer, and we've set up a sizable checking account for you. All I need is your signature and, if I may suggest, a cosigner as well," Donnie said, directing her to his office.

"I never thought of something like that. Who would you suggest?"

"George Boone would make a good choice. He's an honest man, and if his signature is needed, he would easily come in to accommodate. You can just ask George to sign this signature card and then return it to me. I will also need your signature." Donnie pushed the card toward Layla, who read it, then signed.

"Donnie, do you know how the sale of Mr. Soo's property is coming along? Is your bank handling the transfer of funds?"

"Hopefully, it should be ready for all signatures by the end of next week, and yes, our bank will receive the funds, then immediately transfer into Mr. Soo's account, which he keeps with us. These things often take longer than anticipated, and I know you are anxious to begin remodeling. To take up some of your time, come by the Visitors Center. I'm there every Friday afternoon. I'll give you a tour of where we are currently and where we hope to be when everything is finished. I'm sure you will enjoy seeing how things have developed."

"What a kind offer. I would like to see how the project is progressing and report back to Kim."

"Thank you. That would be nice if you let Kim know, and I'll look forward to seeing you this coming Friday."

Layla's next stop was the grocery store. Although she agreed to eat at Otis's, it would be no more than one meal a day. She would prepare dinner for Mr. Soo each night, being sure not to cook any fish. During the time she was married to Kyle, she had become quite a casserole queen, never knowing for sure when he would come home. She would ply Mr. Soo with her wide variety of casseroles.

At the store, she stocked up on enough for several meals and also the ingredients to Agnes's "beer" cookies. She knew George and Annie would enjoy them. On her way back to Mr.

Soo's, she spotted him chatting with the owner of a local tourist shop. She pulled over to the curb and asked him if he would like a ride home.

"Yes, that would be nice. It has turned warmer than usual today. My goodness!" Mr. Soo exclaimed when he opened the car door. "You have air conditioning. This is lovely."

On the way, Layla explained about her plans to prepare dinner for both of them. She assured Mr. Soo he would enjoy her cooking, and he said he would give it a try.

Late the next morning, Layla watched for Annie to return from her jog. Seeing her coming down the driveway, she waved and told her she would be coming over soon, bearing cookies.

"That's just what I need after jogging, some cookies," Annie said.

"They're Agnes's special beer cookies, best eaten when drinking beer. No kidding."

"George will love them. See you shortly."

Layla packed a bag of mincemeat cookies; grabbed her keys, signature card, and cell phone; made sure all was secure, and walked over to the Boones'.

Layla handed Annie the bag of cookies. "I wasn't kidding. These go great with beer. Agnes bakes them for Dewey and Don to snack on while watching sporting events and drinking beer. Weird, right?"

"I think I'll try one with a beer now. It's so miserably hot, we've lost our trade winds. I hope George gets back soon. He'll end up with a good sunburn in this heat."

As Annie finished her sentence, George came dragging through the front kitchen door. His face and chest were red, he was dripping sweat, and he was actually panting.

"Honey, are you having a heart attack?"

"No, need cold air," George said, opening the side door to the freezer section of the refrigerator and standing in front of it.

"George, what's happened? Annie asked, dampening paper towels and handing them to George. "Do you want water?"

"Yes, very cold water, please," George said in short bursts.

Annie went to refrigerator door and depressed the ice dispenser, filling a large glass with ice. She took it to the sink, added water, then handed it to George, who was still sucking in the cold air from the freezer section. He drank the whole glass down and handed it back to her, indicating more.

"Here's another glass, but get yourself out of the freezer before you catch something. What the hell happened to you?"

George closed the door to the freezer and finished his second glass of water. "Hi, Layla, didn't notice you before, eyes were seeing stars."

"George, tell me right this minute what's going on?" Annie demanded, her hands on her hips, a stern tone to her voice.

"Hell, Annie, I came down with a case of male ego," George said, plopping down on a counter stool, wiping his face with paper towels.

"What are you talking about?"

"I was making my way along the beach, you know, in my jog-walk routine. Then, wham, out of nowhere, Fiona comes tearing by, saying, 'Better pick it up, old boy.' Well, that really pissed me off, so I took off after her and that was back before the jetty. I hauled ass all the way home. I never did catch her, but I liked to kill myself."

Annie eyed George disapprovingly. "Was she wearing her four-inch heels or was she in tennis shoes?"

"Very funny. I swear that woman is a ball buster, and I don't care if you don't like me saying that. I almost died defending the males of Paia."

"I brought some of my special cookies that go great with beer. Want to try one?"

"Only if my lovely wife will permit me a beer to go with them."

"I shouldn't after that stunt you just pulled. That was so juvenile," Annie said, passing beers around.

"Thank you, honey. You know we guys sometimes do these type of things, must be in the genes. Layla, these cookies are good. Funny, they do go great with beer."

"Thanks, George, the more I hear about Fiona, I'm getting leery about working with her. What I really came over to tell you folks about was the dinner I fixed for Mr. Soo last night. I decided we could eat breakfast or even dinner at Otis's but not more than one meal a day for me, just too much fat and cholesterol. Last night, I fixed a green salad, macaroni and cheese, and pork chops. I served the salad first, making sure Mr. Soo ate some greens. Then the pork chops and macaroni, they were big center-cut chops. He put a pork chop on his plate, then eyed the macaroni, and looked at me and said he had never eaten macaroni and cheese before and wasn't sure he would like it. Can you tell me how he could have eaten all those years at Otis's and not eaten macaroni and cheese? Anyway, I suggested he try a small portion, and if he didn't like it, I would know not to serve it again. He ate a couple of bites, smiled, and loaded up his plate with more. After that, he had two more helpings and made me swear to make it again real soon. Where does that little man put all that food?"

"We've wondered that for years," said Annie, laughing.

"George, I need a favor. Would you be the cosigner on my newly opened checking account? Donnie suggested you, and all you'll have to do is sign this signature card and I'll drop it back to Donnie."

"Sure, glad to. Leave the card here, and I'll sign it and give it to Donnie tomorrow. I have errands to do in the area, so no problem. Let's sit on the front lanai and have beer and cookies. It should be cooler there," said George, still sweaty from his workout courtesy of Fiona.

Passing the charcoal Layla had done of George and Annie, Annie commented, "Layla, both Donnie and the sheriff thought your work was terrific. Neither knew you were such a talented artist."

"That's nice to hear. I must thank each of them."

Although the sheriff had told Annie he thought Layla's charcoal was terrific, when he first saw it as George was taking him to the front lanai on Dewey's last night in Maui, he grabbed George's arm, saying, "My god, George, who did this? Surely someone who saw the Okamoto murder scene or photos and has a sick sense of humor."

"This was done by Layla on our trip to the national parks in Utah. She never saw the murder scene or any of the photos. Eerie, isn't it?"

"What did Annie say when she saw it?"

"Annie made no connection to the Okamotos, which tells me she has blocked that memory out of her mind. If she was able to recall it, she would have been as shocked as I was at the resemblance of the position and placement of her and me to the Okamotos."

"Jesus, this is scary," said the sheriff, taking one last look at the charcoal.

CHAPTER 37

Friday afternoon, Donnie was sweeping off the veranda at the Visitors Center when he looked up and saw Layla walking across Baldwin headed toward the center. He was glad she was going to visit and update Kim on the progress, which he would explain to her was slower than he imagined because of various regulations and environmental requirements.

He walked down the steps and greeted Layla as she walked up the driveway. "I'm so pleased you've come to see our progress or lack of it." Donnie then explained all the trouble there had been with the driveway and the other items that had slowed things down. He told her that the anticipated opening date was now out of the picture but assured her that the center would be open as soon as possible. They had ample funding, and crews were working as fast as possible; the holdup was with the numerous inspections that were required.

"The driveway and veranda are lovely. It looks like you've planned to open up the veranda to the inside."

"Yes, that was George's idea. We will serve cold drinks, coffee, salads, and sandwiches. It will be a welcoming center where folks can browse inside, then come outside and relax. George also suggested we have an area on the inside that sells local artwork. I saw the wonderful charcoal you did for George and Annie, and I was hoping you would contribute some that we could sell, maybe even some of our windsurfers. That would be a real attribute to the center."

"Thank you, Donnie. I'm always flattered when someone compliments my charcoal work. I originally planned to be an artist, but in New York, artists doing charcoals, especially landscapes, were a dime a dozen. That's the reason I got serious about doing restoration work, which I dearly love. I would be flattered to do some charcoals for the center, and catching the windsurfers in flight will be a wonderful challenge."

They continued inside with Donnie explaining all that had been done and all that was still to be done. He was very complimentary of the ideas he had received from George and how he hoped he and Annie would lead a docent team once the center opened.

Time passed quickly, and Layla said she had to be leaving, explaining her new cooking duties in lieu of eating nightly dinner at Otis's. She assured Donnie she would tell Kim what a wonderful job was being done on the Visitors Center and let him know the opening date would be pushed back. She assured Donnie that Kim would understand as he was honored to have the Okamoto Visitors Center opening in the home and business that had belonged to his parents for so many years.

"By the way, Donnie, where do you think the best place for me to pick up some art supplies would be?"

"Well, I'm not sure. I'm afraid my knowledge of art supplies is quite lacking. We don't have an art store, per se, here in Paia. Your best bet would be to check with Fiona. She would know where the best store in all the islands is located and can assist you with what you would need."

"Thanks, I'll check with her." Layla left the center and headed back down the hill to Mr. Soo's. She hated to ask Fiona. Maybe she would be out on her lanai, and she could get it over with quickly. Layla had to admit she was beginning to feel about her the way George did. Although she did have to grin, thinking about her breezing by George and making that comment which would piss any man off.

Not finding Fiona on their front lanai, Layla decided what the hell and walked up and rang the doorbell.

Fiona opened the door in a terry-cloth sarong and a towel wrapped around her head. "You caught me hitting the bottle. The roots were beginning to show."

Caught completely off guard by her frank statement, Layla uttered, "Never thought about it. I came by to avail myself of some of your shopping wisdom."

"My favorite subject, how can I help you?"

"I do landscapes in charcoal, and I need an entire set of supplies, charcoals, easel, drawing pad, etc., Donnie Munson said you would be the person to ask where I could find the best on the islands."

"As surprising as this may sound, the best art supplies are handled by a dealer in Hilo. I deal with him frequently when refurbishing supplies or cleaners are required. In fact, that is where I've ordered the supplies for cleaning the wood in your new home. If you can give me a list of the brand and exactly what you need, I can e-mail it to Mr. Lee."

"I'll e-mail my needs, then you can send them to Mr. Lee."

"I'll phone Mr. Lee and tell him the information will be e-mailed to him. Do you want him to send it express mail, and do you want to wait until he has everything, in case he doesn't have it all in stock?"

"Yes, express mail by all means, and send what he's got and anything that remains as soon as he receives it. How will he get reimbursed?"

"I'll have him charge everything to my account, then I'll bill you. No charge for my services, one friend to another."

"How sweet of you, Fiona." Layla knew Fiona would be making a killing on her decorating, so she wasn't surprised at this gesture. "Well, I'll let you get back to your elimination of the color gray, and thanks for your help."

Within four days, Layla was sitting on the cliff where the services for the Okamotos had been held. She sketched the rolling waves as they made their way below the cliffs. Cotton-ball clouds drifted lazily on an azure sky. She felt relaxed and peaceful, the restlessness leaving her once she started her sketching. Soon she knew she would be involved in the remodeling of her new home, but at this particular moment in time, she felt a peacefulness she had not felt in such a long time. Maybe this meant she was healed, no, she decided she still wasn't ready to commit herself to a relationship with Dewey. Not commit in a way that he wanted, but she knew she was in love with him and hoped he would continue to be patient with her.

They had talked for almost an hour last Sunday; she had told him about her plans to start working in charcoal again, he telling her about the latest in the digital process.

When Dewey returned from Maui, Agnes could not believe the change that had come over him. He seemed happier than she had seen him in years. His first night home, he sat down with Agnes and Don and told them all the latest on Layla, Mr. Soo, George, and Annie. They were surprised that Layla had purchased a home on the island but happy she was with George and Annie. They didn't personally know Mr. Soo but knew he had captured Dewey's heart in a grandfatherly way.

Agnes recalled the silly grin on Dewey's face when he told them about giving Layla a big romantic smooch just before he left. Then he smiled broadly, saying, "And she liked it!" He predicted that within a year, they would be married. Dewey told them Layla was finding herself again.

He said he wasn't going back for a visit until he was invited to see her remodeled home, then explained all she was going to have to do in order to make it livable. He said, "She is experiencing the new freedom of being totally on her own, away from her kind and in a totally new environment. She asked me to wait for her, to give her time to heal totally, to be able to return my love, which she knows she already has. I told her I would be there when she was ready. I believe once her home is finished, once she moves in and realizes what she can do on her own, she will be able to let love again into her heart."

Agnes and Don looked at one another, not knowing what to say. Finally Agnes told Dewey she was amazed at his patience, proving he must be truly in love. He assured them he was from the moment he laid eyes on her.

Then he said he was going to work hard in the next few months, and he was also going to be taking a close look at his staff in order to find who could ultimately be in charge of the digital process and be more involved in the development of the video games. He told them he knew he was still young in years, but he wanted a future of more freedom once he and Layla were married.

Layla had done two charcoals since her last meeting with Donnie. It was the next Friday afternoon, and she went to the Visitors Center to show him what she had done and see if this was what he had in mind.

When she showed him the first drawing on the bluff, Donnie looked at it for a long moment, then turned away. She noticed he pulled out his handkerchief, dabbed at his eyes, and blew his nose.

"I'm sorry for this display of emotion, but it seems like the view from that bluff is etched in my mind from the terrible day of the funeral. Your drawing has brought back the beauty of that bluff."

"Donnie, may I give this drawing to you in appreciation for you getting me started again on my sketching?"

"Oh, I couldn't accept it, although it's so beautiful."

"I thought it was a Hawaiian tradition about not turning down a gift given from the heart. Therefore, you must let me give this to you."

"Thank you, Layla, this will hang in a prominent area in our home. Now this place can be remembered for its beauty."

"What do you think of this one? I tried to capture the windsurfers as they caught air? One of the reasons I do landscapes is that I'm not good at faces, so mostly, I'm just showing body language."

Donnie studied the sketch for some time, finally saying, "You have made me think I can hear the surf and feel the wind. This is amazing work, and if we put works like this for sale in the store, the center will realize a terrific profit. Plus, the purchaser will have a prize possession."

"Thank you, Donnie, for your kind words of encouragement. I hope I will be able to have five or six more before I have to start work on the remodeling. Any word yet?"

"It seems like the title search is taking longer than anticipated. Now I'm hoping for closure by the end of next week. I'm sure sorry for the delay. Mr. Soo stopped by the bank the other day also checking on the sale, and he said thanks to you, he is eating like a king."

"I cook dinner for us each night, and we've been over to Annie and George's once for some of George's magic grill work. He never had exposure to casseroles, and I'm an expert on making many different ones, so he's experiencing a new eating dimension. You know Mr. Soo and his love of food. Having had Dewey there for a while and now I'm staying with him, it's helping him recover from the loss of Mrs. Soo. A couple of evenings after dinner when we sat on the lanai, he told me stories about their marriage in the early years. I told him he should record them for his children and grandchildren, but I don't know if he wants to share all he told me with them."

"Yes, sometimes it's easier to tell something to a relative stranger than to your family," Donnie said, laughing.

They discussed the work that had been done on the center during the past week, and Donnie promised he would be in touch as soon as he got a date for the final signing. Layla made her way back to Mr. Soo's, trying to think of a different casserole to prepare for their evening meal.

CHAPTER 38

As Layla and Mr. Soo set foot on the back lanai, George popped the cork on a bottle of fine champagne, and Annie stood ready with flutes. She passed a flute to Mr. Soo and Layla, and then George raised his glass in a toast. "To Layla, officially our new neighbor."

They raised their glasses and drank, with Mr. Soo saying, "We welcome you as a permanent resident of Paia and hope you will find peace and happiness here as we have."

"Thank you, everyone. You've been so kind and understanding. How could I not be happy?" With that said, Layla burst into tears.

George and Mr. Soo looked at each other in surprise. Annie rushed to Layla's side. "Honey, what wrong?"

"Nothing. It's been so long since I've felt this happy, and I had begun to doubt I ever would again. I was so excited to sign the final papers today."

Annie put her arm around Layla. "That's OK, dear. Crying for happiness is always a good thing."

"Mr. Soo, what do you say we get the grill fired up and start the steaks? Tonight is a special meal. We have filet mignon steaks wrapped with a strip of bacon, twice-baked potatoes, fresh broccoli, and a special Annie dessert treat."

Layla composed herself, and then she and Annie started setting the table and getting potatoes and vegetables ready to serve. Everyone enjoyed an excellent meal topped off by Annie's chocolate cream pie.

It was Friday, and Layla would have a couple of days before Fiona and her team of workers began work on the remodeling. "George and Annie, I thought maybe you would like a 'before' tour. You're welcome too, Mr. Soo."

"No, thank you, I'm not ready to visit my former home yet."

"I would love to see the 'before.' How about you, George?" Annie asked.

"Count me in. We'll see the 'before,' then 'after' old Fiona does her magic."

The next day Layla met George and Annie at the agreed time and welcomed them into her new home. They entered through the kitchen door off the back lanai, exactly like their back entryway. Annie caught her breath as she made her way through the kitchen so chopped up with the Shoji screens. They continued on through the front of the house into the bedrooms.

"Layla, I hope you've left a trail of bread crumbs or we'll never find our way out of this maze. What in the world was Mrs. Soo thinking when she partitioned off this beautiful space?" George asked.

"Mr. Soo said in the China of Mrs. Soo's youth, their house, although large, was partitioned off into small rooms. Every room had some purpose: a sleeping space, an eating space, a prayer place, a place to meditate, and so on. She could not leave these old ways behind and made this house into her own China world. I find it so sad. She must have been a very lonely lady."

"I knew her, sort of. She was very shy and gently pleasant. I brought her some flowers once to thank her and Mr. Soo for something. She was so surprised, and her small face lit up with a glorious smile. I don't think anyone called on her. She was like a forgotten woman. I know Mr. Soo made every effort to bring her forward, but she just couldn't move forward."

When they got to the master bedroom, Annie spied the new bathroom Mr. Soo had put in. "George can we do this? Honey, look at that shower."

"What a great shower. I would love to be able to stand straight up and take a shower, not possible in our old bathtub shower. I don't think we could do this without losing a lot of bedroom space, although we could take out that linen closet. What do you think?"

"Take the linen closet. For a bathroom like this, you can have it!"

"I'll have to ask Mr. Soo who his contractor was because I'm serious about having a shower like this. I do believe there's room enough for two."

"Oh, George," Annie said with a blushing smile.

They finished their tour, and both told Layla she was undertaking a big job, but they had to admit, if anyone could do it, it was Fiona.

Monday morning, Layla went over to open up her home and let the fresh air in through the sliders, hoping to dispel some of the lingering cooking odors.

At eight, Fiona arrived in denim shorts, T-shirt, and tennis shoes. She sniffed the air, saying, "I know why Mr. Soo was always outside. Having to be inside this place, one would want all the fresh air they could get. Let me tell you about the crew I have coming.

"When we worked on Oahu, my main focus was on decorating. It wasn't long before I needed an expert carpenter, and the owner of the paint store I bought from recommended Martin Elwood. I met with Marty, and we hit it off right away. He was only seventeen and was stationed in Italy in World War II. He knew the town I'm from, and we both had even frequented some of the same pastarias. He's a charming man, and he turned out to be a master carpenter. After using him on several jobs, I actually had a three-year waiting list of people willing to pay considerably for his craftsmanship. When he retired, I never found anyone that compared to the work he crafted.

"Imagine my surprise about two years ago when I ran into him at the local market. He was here visiting his son who had just had his second child, and Marty was thinking of moving to the area to be near his family. About the same time, his son, Chris, found himself out of a job. He had worked for years making some of the best surfboards on the islands. He was well sought after for surfboards and made an excellent living. Then one day, making surfboards on the islands was no longer possible because of environmental issues, and they are now being made in Thailand. Chris did not want to move the family to Thailand.

"A couple of weeks later, he found himself restaining lanais, and he built a reputation for excellent and swift work. You can imagine in this tropical weather, lanais and decks need restaining frequently. Ned and I used him a couple of years ago, and about that time, I had a client who needed some work done inside her home, restaining the floors and shelving in her library/office. I contacted Chris, and once again, his work proved outstanding. He does both inside and outside work and has an assistant, a local Hawaiian girl, Josie, who has lovely petite hands that are excellent for getting to small areas for staining. They are a great team, and I'm sure they will do excellent work on your home once you have trained them on the proper wood restoration procedures."

CHAPTER 39

Marty, Chris, and Josie made their way up the stairs where they were greeted by Fiona.

"I'm so happy you could meet with us today. Let me introduce you to Layla Richfield, who has purchased Mr. Soo's former home. As you will see, it will need a great deal of restoration to bring it back to what it once was."

Layla greeted everyone. "I work in art restoration, and I will train you in the restoration process. The supplies will be costly, and it will take some time, but I'm ready to spend the time and money because I believe, when finished, this will be a fabulous home. Why don't we all go inside, and you can see what I'm talking about?"

Slowly, they made their way through the home. Several times, Marty, Chris, or Josie commented about the damage done to the home.

"I've seen my share of Shoji screens but never anything like this. What a shame to put those runners into this wood floor," declared Marty.

They walked back into the kitchen where Chris and Marty began making notes, while Josie discussed cleaning the wood frames of the Shoji screens with Layla.

"Fiona, because of our long friendship and because you are the loveliest lady on Maui, I will be working with Chris and Josie on this restoration. I will make the dowels necessary to repair the holes left by the removal of the Shoji screens. Josie will clean the wood we salvage from the screen frames, which I believe should be quite ample. Chris will work on the remaining wood restoration. Of course, all restoration and cleaning will need Mrs. Richfield's supervision at first. But Chris and Josie are good learners."

"We can start tomorrow. First off, we'll get rid of all the screens and dividers. We will carefully remove the screens from their wood frames and try to save as much of that fabulous wood as possible. Then we'll start to clean the wood on the walls and ceiling. That will be a real chore, smoke rises, and we will have to be very careful not to do any damage. Finally, we'll refinish all the floors. I don't think they've ever been refinished in all these years, if they have, only certain sections. Most of this wood is no longer legal to harvest, so you will have a fabulous home."

"If that meets with everyone's approval, we'll see you at 7:00 a.m. tomorrow. Fiona, here is a very rough estimate of our fee. We will leave the purchase of the restoration supplies to you or Layla," said Chris.

"That will be perfect. I'll come over early and open up so we can get some fresh air in here, and I'll work on getting the restoration supplies right away. I imagine the first few days will be taken up removing the screens.

"Marty, Chris, everything you proposed sounds right. Of course, we realize a lot of different things can and probably will happen, so we realize your estimate is flexible. I'm so glad you will be able to start tomorrow," said Fiona.

The crew left, and Fiona suggested Layla lock up and they go over to her place and work on the restoration supplies, a possible timetable, and review cost figures.

Over fresh coffee, Fiona laid out an updated cost estimate along with an estimated timetable for completion of each phase. "Layla, I will need a check from you for $25,000, and I will give you a complete itemized breakdown of all expenses."

"Let me give you a check for $50,000. That way, I won't have to write another one so soon. I see the timetable, but how does that work with getting appliances and furniture?"

"I would say no later than two weeks from now, we will have to start shopping for appliances and furniture. I'm not too worried about the appliances. I think we can find all those at the Pacific Sales Store inside Best Buy in Honolulu. In case you find some furniture you want that has to come from the mainland, we need to get that order placed right away, sometimes it takes three or four months to get here. I once had a client that ordered a specific fabric from Italy to go on a sofa made in South Carolina. Twenty months later, the sofa finally arrived, and we were thrilled it got here that soon. So you can understand my insistence on finding things right away."

"Lord, I had no idea it was going to be so complicated. When you live in New York, shopping for furniture is a snap."

"Yes, I'm sure it is. However, you are now living on an exotic tropical island, and the rules have changed."

"Let's see how things go the rest of this week, then schedule a shopping day for late the second week. How does that sound?"

"You will need to give me several days' notice. I'll have to make round-trip airline reservations, rent a car, and set up appointments with my contacts on Oahu."

"I'm thinking Wednesday of next week. Things should be going pretty well on the remodeling, and then we both will be here on Friday to finish up the week with the crew."

"Wednesday of next week is perfect."

"Is there anything I should take or will need to have with me?"

"No, just bring your patience and rest up. It will be a busy day. Ned and I have rolled up those wonderful Oriental rugs, and I'm taking them to a trustworthy cleaning facility. They do excellent restoration work. Those rugs are worth a fortune. You will want them displayed prominently once we have all your new furniture."

"Fiona, I'm not into Oriental furniture. I lean more to contemporary or modern."

"These rugs will make a huge impact mixed with any type of furniture. Personally, I like one piece of antique furniture mixed in with ultramodern. Makes a conversation piece in the room."

Layla finished her coffee, thanked Fiona for her valuable insight, then left to go back to Mr. Soo's.

Layla phoned Dewey that night and updated him on all that had transpired during the day. He was happy to hear that Chris and Josie were doing the work; he thought they both were competent and honest people. She said she was dreading her shopping foray with Fiona, although she knew it was necessary.

She told him Fiona was going to order all the restoration supplies from her Hilo supplier. She hoped he had everything on hand and didn't have to order anything from the mainland, which would slow everything down. Fiona said he would FedEx them to her as soon as everything is available.

Dewey said he thought Fiona the perfect person to help with the project; he laughed, saying she has a source for everything.

CHAPTER 40

Layla did not join Mr. Soo at Otis's but had toast, yogurt, and coffee at six in the morning and, half an hour later, was opening up and airing out her home so things would be as fresh as possible when Chris, Josie, and Marty arrived. Promptly at 7:00 a.m., they arrived, carrying ladders and tools.

Chris told Layla to return about 2:45 p.m., and she could assess what had been done for the day and ask him any questions, then close the house up when he and his crew left at three.

Layla gave him her cell phone number and returned to Mr. Soo's. Feeling a bit lost, she grabbed her charcoals and decided she would head to nearby Spreckle Beach for some sketching. It was a nice beach and would make a good display piece for the gift shop. A couple of hours later, she had sketched a rough outline of the area and knew what colors she would use to fill in, so she packed up her gear and headed back to Mr. Soo's. Storing her sketching gear, she stood out on the front lanai, looking at her watch, counting down to her 2:45 p.m. deadline.

At the prescribed time, she walked across the street, up the stairs, and into the house. She was shocked; all the screens were down in the kitchen and dining room. Some of the runners still remained, but she was very pleased at the progress made. Chris noticed her looking around as they began finishing up for the night.

"Things went pretty fast today. It will take the majority of the week for the careful removal of all the screens. The problem will come in making and fitting the dowels to cover the holes made by the runners and the careful removal of the screens from the wood. Got to save that wood, some of it I've never even seen before, very exotic and the carving is something special. You may not have noticed, as it is so covered with soot. Let me show you a piece I cleaned slightly."

He led her to the kitchen to see a bottom part of a Shoji screen frame. "I've only cleaned it once, but look at these lotus flowers carved in the wood. I think most of the framework has hand carvings."

"I didn't see that. It's beautiful, so delicate. Chris, I appreciate your consideration for saving this beautifully carved wood. Is there anything I can do to assist any of you or make your job easier?"

"No, right now, everything is going as planned."

Chris left, and Layla began closing the house. She walked around and was surprised at the amount of room there was once a majority of the screens were down. She finished locking up the house and headed back to Mr. Soo's when the sheriff came driving by.

"Well, Layla, has work started on your remodeling?"

"Yes, Chris Elwood and crew were here bright and early this morning and did a considerable amount of work. I just finished locking up and was going back to Mr. Soo's."

"What's your procedure in unlocking and locking up?"

"I open up the house and try to get some fresh air in before the crew arrives, and before they leave, I return and start locking up."

"I think you should reconsider how you open and close your house. I wish you would wait until Chris gets here to open up and start closing while he's still here. Walk out of the house when the crew does. I'm still convinced that whoever killed the Okamotos is a local, and I don't want anyone to become complacent in their security."

"Thank you, Sheriff. I never gave it a thought, but I see your point. It's easy to forget about security when you live in a place like Paia. I will do as you suggest. Glad we have you looking out for us."

"That's what I'm here for. Give my regards to Mr. Soo."

Layla was waiting on the lanai the next morning when Chris arrived. She explained to him what the sheriff told her about security, and Chris agreed it was a wise idea; a young woman on her own can never be too cautious.

Before Mr. Soo left for his breakfast with Otis, Layla told him she would be taking him out to dinner tonight and decided to ask Annie and George to join them. It was too early to phone, and she was feeling antsy. She got her cell phone and dialed Dewey's number. He answered immediately, "Layla it's not Sunday. Is something wrong?"

"Nope, just wanted to hear your voice. Can you talk a minute?"

"For you, I can talk all day."

"I've got the crew at my house on their second day, and it's amazing how fast things are going. They are doing a great job, and Chris has discovered that the framework holding the Shoji screens has delicate carvings, absolutely beautiful."

They continued talking for some time, and finally, Layla said she had better be going; she had some chores to attend to, and she would talk to Dewey again on Sunday.

Phoning the Boones, she spoke with Annie and asked if they would like to be her guest for dinner tonight. Annie checked with George and he said that would be great, then asked where they were going. Would he need his tux?

Layla laughed. "Tell George we'll go someplace where Levi's and T-shirts are the dress of the evening, unless, of course, he feels the need to wear a tux."

"Honey, George doesn't even own a tux."

"Let me think," Layla said. "I know, how about Bird's?"

"George, how does Bird's sound?" Annie asked.

"Great, not a better steak anywhere. I assume Mr. Soo will also be joining us?" George asked, now on the extension phone.

"Yes, I told him before he left for Otis's that dinner was out tonight and my treat. I bet he would enjoy a steak at Bird's. George, could you call and order steaks for both Mr. Soo and me and whatever you and Annie want. Make it for 7:00 p.m. Does that sound all right?"

"I'll phone Byrd and place our orders, and the time is just fine. Only thing missing is Dewey. Have you talked to him lately?"

"As a matter of fact, I just hung up talking with him before I phoned you. He's fine and busy at work. We talked for quite a bit. It always makes me feel better after we talk. I'll hang up now and let you two get back to whatever you were doing, and I'll see you tonight. George, can you drive? I'm still not too good at night. It gets so dark here without bright city lights."

"No problem, I'll pick you folks up at six, and we can have a beer before dinner."

"Great, see you then."

CHAPTER 41

Tuesday before the big shopping day, Layla had given the keys to Chris and explained she and Fiona were off to Oahu to shop for appliances and furniture. Chris told Layla she was in for an experience she would never forget.

The next morning Layla dressed in lightweight olive cargo pants, a pale yellow gauze blouse, and thick-soled sandals she found locally, ready to tackle shopping with Fiona. Her one concession to New York style was a huge designer tote that held among other things a bottle of water, oat bars, and Advil. She saw Fiona's car and went down the steps to the street; taking a deep breath, she entered. "Good morning. It seems so early to be heading to the airport."

"Yes, but with all the pre–check-in regulations, getting there two hours early is always your safest bet. Once we get checked in, we can get a coffee." Casting a downward glance at Layla's outfit, Fiona continued, "I see you opted for the island casual look today."

"Well, we are on an island, and since I imagine you are going to have us running around like crazy, I decided to dress for comfort. I think the main thing is the amount of the check I write. Speaking of dressing, you look more like you're hitting the New York shops." Layla eyed Fiona's four-inch patent heels, tight black skirt, and white high-collar, long-sleeved blouse. She didn't see her purse but felt sure it was a large designer tote.

"I command more respect and attention, which, of course, is better for my client, when I enter a store dressed in non-island business-oriented attire."

"Whatever works," Layla said with a shrug, hoping Fiona would get the message that she was not impressed.

Leaving the Oahu airport in the rental car, Layla was amazed at the traffic. "I had no idea it would be so crowded this time of day, so different from Paia."

"Not everyone has gotten to work yet. We'll get on the back streets in a minute and skirt around the traffic."

Although Fiona used the word *skirt*, as far as Layla was concerned, she should have said roared through traffic. Until they got to their first stop, Layla sat with her hands pushed into the dashboard, and most of the time her eyes were closed.

Fiona smiled, noticing Layla with eyes closed. "I learned to drive in Italy. Driving is very aggressive there."

"Oh" was all Layla could manage to utter.

Entering the Pacific Sales section inside the Home Depot Store, Fiona was immediately greeted by a salesman, welcoming them both and asking how he may be of service. Fiona grabbed his arm and started walking toward the refrigerator section, leaving Layla in her wake. She spied a huge model, whipped out her measuring tape, and measured. "This will be perfect for your kitchen."

Emphatically, Layla replied, "No, this is not what I want." Layla then walked to a more industrial-looking stainless steel model. "Fiona, could you measure this and see if it would fit?" Layla said with authority.

"Certainly." After measuring, Fiona said, "This will fit just fine. Is this the one you want?"

Layla carefully looked inside, checked the various things she wanted, and told the salesman, Jim Marshall, it was what she wanted. After that, Jim and Layla went from section to section. Fiona rightly pointing out things Layla didn't realize she would need, and they were able to purchase everything at the store. Layla wrote a very large check for her purchases.

Layla was pleased to get that much done for the day and thanked Fiona for all her help. "Let me take you to lunch now."

"Heavens, we're only getting started. If we have time, we'll get something later. We have a lot of ground to cover."

"Great," Layla said, trying to sound enthusiastic.

Their next stop was a high-end designer furniture store. Fiona stormed in, high heels clicking on the tile, and waved, parade fashion, to several clerks. A woman dressed similarly to Fiona came out and buzzed her on each cheek. Fiona introduced her to Layla, and they were off in search of bedroom furniture.

After seeing several rooms of furniture that were on display, Layla spotted a taupe-colored button-tucked suede headboard. "I want this. Will it accommodate a king-sized bed?"

"Yes, either a king- or queen-sized bed will work perfectly with this," the clerk replied. "What else will you want for your bedroom?"

"Generous nightstands so I can load them with books, a good reading light, a clock, something durable and attractive."

"I have a three-piece set, but it's only three pieces, and most people want more than that. The set includes two ample nightstands and a very large dresser. It's a honey-colored lacquer imported from Italy. Beautifully made but not enough pieces for the American market. If you would be interested, we can offer you a very attractive price." The clerk led them to a back area where the three pieces were covered in padding. Uncovered, Fiona and Layla began taking stock of the lovely Italian pieces.

Layla looked at Fiona and gave a slight nod. Fiona looked at the price tags, got Layla's attention when the sales clerk wasn't looking, rolled her eyes, and smiled.

"These pieces will work fine in my home. If you think I'm getting a good price on them, Fiona, I'll take them."

Fiona turned toward the clerk and told her they would take them, priced as marked, along with her professional discount. The clerk readily agreed, wanting to get the pieces off the floor.

They continued on, and Layla spotted a dining room table and chairs she knew were meant for her home. It would seat three on each side and one at each end. It was almost identical to one her family had in an informal dining room in their Hamptons home, a set Layla always felt comfortable using. The chairs were covered in a gaudy pattern, but they looked through the catalogue and found one that was perfect.

Orders were placed, and once again, Layla wrote a large check. She wished the chairs didn't have to be special ordered, but she couldn't live with the fabric that was on the display chairs. A new table would also be arriving with the chairs, so everything would come directly from the mainland. Since Layla did not need a formal dining room to start living in her new home, she was fine with the wait.

Back in the car, Layla turned to Fiona, asking hopefully, "Lunch?"

"Not yet, I want to take you to a special store I often use. It's a consignment store. I don't know what we will find there, but I would be remiss if I didn't take you." As Fiona talked, Layla thought she was actually glowing. "This is a top-of-the-line store. They usually only deal in items submitted from million-dollar residents. So you can be sure you are going to see some spectacular pieces."

Fiona was greeted like an old friend by a lovely older lady, who was very gracious when introduced to Layla. Although there were wonderful pieces of furniture and art pieces, Layla did not see anything that she could envision in her home. Fiona suggested they check out the back area where items were kept that had not sold within the allotted time and were going back to the original owner.

That's where Fiona spotted the largest sofa Layla had ever seen. It was a huge sectional in an eggplant color, and she could not determine what the fabric was. She asked and was amazed to find out it was made of water buffalo hide. Fiona explained it would look fabulous in the living room and would eliminate the need for any other furniture, except one large chair and tables. Layla sat down on the sofa, surprised how comfortable and cozy the hide felt. She began to visualize the picture Fiona painted and agreed it would be quite a talking point.

Fiona worked her magic on the price, and since it was set to go back to the owner, a call was made, and another $500 was deducted from the price. Before leaving, Layla spotted several small items she wanted and was able to take those with her. Fiona made all the final arrangements, and Layla wrote another check.

Settling into the car, Layla asked her usual question, "Lunch?"

"No, dear, we've got to get to the airport, turn the car in, and go through security. Wonderful shopping day!"

"Want an oat bar?" Layla asked.

"No, thanks, I get so excited on these shopping trips, I'm not able to eat a thing until later in the evening."

At the airport, Layla got a latte and a sandwich. After eating, she realized how tired she was; on the short flight to Maui, she slept soundly.

Layla told Fiona to go ahead and stop at her house as one of her purchases was for Annie, and she wanted to take it to her. Layla thanked Fiona for all her help, guidance, and professional discounts. They both laughed, and then Layla remember she should find out how things were going to get to Maui.

Fiona explained she arranged with a warehouse to store items until they hear from her to send them over to Maui. She would arrange with each store for a particular delivery date then let the warehouse know. She told Layla she had used this particular warehouse and delivery system before with excellent results.

Annie saw Layla dragging up the back stairs and opened the door to let her in. "Lord, you look exhausted. Want a beer?"

"Yes, please. That woman wore me out, and she pranced around in four-inch heels, didn't eat all day, and said she was exhilarated once it was all over."

"Told you about her, was I right or what?" George asked.

"I'll never doubt your judgment of people again, George. I think every bone in my body is beginning to ache."

Annie sat a beer on the counter for Layla, then asked, "Show us what you have in the bags."

"I bought you something for your dining room chest. Sorry, Annie, I never liked that wicker basket you use for fruit, so I found this terrific chrome basket, which really looks like silver but without the problem of polishing."

"It's lovely, and it will make a perfect replacement for that old basket," Annie said, taking the basket and heading for the dining room.

"Can I have the basket?" asked George. "I can really use it in the garage. I've had my eye on it for quite a while."

"You've had your eye on it for the garage?" Annie asked puzzled. "Well, certainly, you can have it."

George walked over and took the fruit out of the basket for Annie who arranged it in her new basket. He grabbed the straw basket, uttered "Neat," and was off to the garage.

Annie shook her head and looked at Layla, saying, "Men."

After leaving the Boones', Layla made her way slowly to Mr. Soo's who was sitting on his lanai, having a cup of tea. Once she had made it up the stairs, she smiled weakly at Mr. Soo, offering him her other sack. "I bought something for your lanai."

"Thank you. You look very weak. Would you like a cup of tea?"

"No, thanks, I need food."

Mr. Soo took the bag Layla offered and looked inside, a puzzled expression coming over his face.

"This is a candle. I'm not too comfortable with candles. Too much chance for accidents and fire."

"Yes, I agree, but this is a flameless hurricane lamp candle for your lanai. You use batteries and turn it on and off with a button on the bottom. You may run low on batteries but no fire."

"What a wonderful invention! Thank you, Layla, this is just what I need. On moonless nights, it gets quite dark out here. This is a perfect gift. I think you are too tired to fix dinner. Let's walk to Otis's."

"I'm starving. I want a cheeseburger, fries, and a chocolate malt. Let's take the car. The only other way is for you to carry me."

"Taking the car is good idea," said Mr. Soo.

CHAPTER 42

On Monday morning, Layla was at Fiona's, loading up her station wagon with all the restoration supplies that had arrived. She drove them over to her house where Chris helped with the unloading.

"There's a lot here. Will we be needing it all?"

"Probably not, but I would rather have more on hand than not enough and have to wait for another shipment. I will have to do the cleaning/restoring on the kitchen cabinets, and that will take some of the supplies."

Chris and Josie spent most of the morning learning the intricate part of mixing cleaners and how to use them on wood without damage. Marty selected his wood for the dowels and began crafting the dowels using equipment he had set up on the front lanai.

The day flew by; Chris and Marty were getting ready to leave but stayed until Layla had the house closed up then were on their way.

*   *   *

Two weeks had passed since work started on Layla's home. Marty decided he would stain the frames that Josie had done such a meticulous job cleaning. Fiona had purchased from her Hilo contact the exact shade everyone decided upon.

Marty began the slow process of staining, rubbing, waiting for the coat to dry into the wood, then repeating the process several times until the correct shade was obtained. He had assembled quite a few newly stained frame pieces, and he looked at them pensively. He asked Layla, "Do you have anything in mind for the frame pieces?"

Layla led him into the living room and said maybe shelves on one of the long sidewalls.

"That would be a pity. You would be covering up so much of the carvings by putting things on the shelves. I was thinking I could make a beautiful large oval coffee table, and then a single sheet of glass could top it. That way, none of the frames would be harmed if something was spilled on the table, and yet the carvings would still be visible. What do you think?"

"That sounds wonderful, but I've purchased a huge sectional that will require a huge table. Fiona could give you the proper measurements, and you could then tell if you would be able to construct a table large enough for the sectional."

"Definitely, we will need Fiona's input. Will you contact her?"

"Consider it done, I'll call right now." Layla dialed Fiona's and told her of Marty's idea. Fiona said she would see them after lunch.

When Fiona arrived, Layla explained Marty's idea of a coffee table using the refurbished frames. Fiona thought it was a genius idea and flashed Marty an admiring smile. Layla explained she told Marty is was an unusually large sectional and would require a large coffee table. Marty said it would be possible, but he would like the measurement of the sofa.

Fiona told him she had the measurements back at her home and she could draw a fairly comprehensive diagram of the sofa, but he would have to imagine it in the exact dimensions. "Follow me home and I'll get the information for you. You can tell Ned all about your visit to my hometown during the war. He and I have visited there several times. We took our sons there several years ago."

"That will do nicely. I've never met your husband, lucky man that he is," Marty said as he followed Fiona out of the house.

"She's a hoot," said Chris. "I have to admire a woman that uses her charm on Gramps to get him to do things without complaint. He can be an old devil when he decides to get testy."

"Fiona sure works her magic on him. I think most men are a tad afraid of her. She can be fierce, but she also is a charmer, and as her client, I can tell you she will do anything to please. I've learned to appreciate Fiona."

As they were closing up for the night, Marty was returning from Fiona's. He had several papers in his hand. "That Ned is a swell guy. He sat down with the drawing and specs Fiona gave him, and he measured everything out then made an excellent diagram. The table I envision will now fit perfectly in front of that sofa. It will be an outstanding addition to your home, Ms. Layla."

When Layla got to Mr. Soo's, she spent about half an hour preparing a casserole, deciding she could not take one more night eating out. She would toss a salad before they were ready to sit down. First, she wanted to call Dewey and report on the great coffee table caper that Marty was planning. Layla was finding it important she phone Dewey and report on progress more than once a week. So whenever something out of the ordinary occurred, she made a call.

Layla anxiously told Dewey about the massive coffee table Marty was designing using the beautifully restored frames. Dewey suggested she take photos with her cell, saying they might be a nice keepsake for a "before" and "after" of her new home.

"Dewey, your thought process is ahead of mine. I would have wished I had done that once everything was completed. What would I do without you?"

"Well, at this point in our relationship, I'm more curious what you would do to me," Dewey said with a chuckle.

"I can't wait for my place to be finished, and you'll see what I'll do to you," Layla promised.

"Huh, please tell me I heard you right."

"You did, since you've been gone, I've realized now very much I miss you, and after that kiss at the airport, I realized we have a future as a couple. I can hardly wait for that future to begin."

"We don't have to wait for your new home to be completed. The Four Seasons is just on the other side of the island, and they have wonderful, romantic accommodations."

"That would be lovely, except I want so much to show you the finished product. For us to begin our future together in that house, guess I want your approval on what I've accomplished."

"Honey, you'll always have my approval. You don't need to prove anything to me."

"I know that. I suppose I really want to prove something to myself. That I can take on a project of this proportion on my own and complete it successfully, a personal project, not just something for business. I've always had so many personal things done for me. Doing this on my own is very important to my own self-esteem."

"The minute it's complete, I'll be there."

"I knew you of all people would understand what I'm talking about."

They spoke for a bit longer then hung up, promising to call within a few days.

Charlene looked up as Donnie Munson walked into the sheriff's office, bearing doughnuts. "Yummy, a special occasion?"

"Just stopped by say hello and thought you folks might enjoy some of these great doughnuts. I used to eat a couple a day, but lately, things have been so hectic, I've sort of lost my appetite."

"Thanks, Donnie. I can assure you these will be enjoyed. You do look like you've lost weight. I don't think I've ever seen you thinner."

"I don't remember when I've ever been this thin. Stress can be a weird thing. Some people eat and gain weight. I've lost all desire to eat. MayLee said I'm going to have to buy all new clothes 'cause she can't take them in anymore," Donnie said, shaking his head.

"Let me see if the sheriff is available." After speaking with the sheriff, Charlene told Donnie to go back to his office.

"Donnie, you're wasting away. Are you feeling poorly?"

"No, it's stress. That Visitors Center has turned out to be more daunting that I dreamed. That, plus we're having to foreclose on some good people lately, and I'm sick about that." Donnie slumped down in the chair across from the sheriff's desk.

"Donnie, you need to get away for a few days, something to relieve that stress. You don't want to find yourself in the hospital."

They chatted a bit longer, then Donnie checked his watch, saying, "Sheriff, I've got to get to the bank."

"Do you have any idea when the Visitors Center will have its official opening?"

"I'm hopeful in about three or four months, only about a half year off schedule, but damned, it will be up to code," Donnie said, raising his voice slightly.

"Are you lining up your docents?"

"Not yet. I'm going to enlist the help of the Boones. Between the two of them, they will have a pretty good idea who in Paia would do a good job on a weekly basis. I've already hinted that they could help out by training the docents. I think they will be glad to do the training."

"We've gotten a wonderful, unexpected donation. Hilo Hattie's in Lahaina is donating all the shirts for the docents and will keep a particular pattern in stock. I just have to get down there and pick out a fabric, then they will make some them up for the volunteer docents. Of course, they will be listed on the donor wall and rightly so."

"Why don't you have MayLee go and have her take Ms. Layla with her? After all, she's a very capable artist."

"I'll speak with MayLee tonight. She'll enjoy doing that, and I'll have her ask Annie also. That might help cement her docent involvement."

"Are you doing OK on cash funding?"

"Yes, a benefactor called about a week ago asking the same question. I told him I was keeping a very detailed expenditure record, and we are holding our own as long as nothing else comes to light. The very next day, he wired $50,000 into the donation account."

"Well, that's got to be Dewey. He's very generous. You know, he's pretty sweet on Ms. Layla."

"Really, I didn't know that. I knew she divorced Kyle, but I didn't know about her and Dewey. Good, he's a great guy. I've really got to be on my way."

With that, Donnie went to open the bank.

CHAPTER 43

Annie and George sat on the back lanai, enjoying coffee, when they saw Donnie Munson walking their way.

George said quietly to Annie, "What could Donnie want this early in the morning?"

"Sorry, folks, to intrude so early, but, Annie, I wanted to speak with you and thought this might be my only spare time before the bank opens. I wanted to ask you and Layla if you would accompany MayLee to Hilo Hattie's in Lahaina on Friday to select the material for the docents' shirts. They're donating the material and are going to make up shirts for the docents. Isn't that wonderful?"

"What a lovely donation, very thoughtful. I would be honored to join MayLee and Layla," Annie said. "Did you say this coming Friday?"

"Yes. Will that day be suitable for you?"

"That will be great. Have you spoken with Layla?"

"No. I'm headed to her house next. I see the Elwood's truck, so I thought she might be over there."

"That's correct. She works with Chris and crew every day."

"I'll have MayLee give you a call this evening, and you can arrange a time for her to pick you and Layla up. I feel confident you ladies will make a much better selection than I would."

Donnie left the Boones and walked the short distance to Layla's. He knocked on the back lanai screen; Chris Elwood came over and opened the screen so Donnie could enter. Donnie said he was looking for Layla, and Chris pointed to the front lanai where she and Marty were looking over pieces of Shoji screen frames.

With a surprised look on her face, Layla noticed Donnie and worried she might have some type of money problem. "Donnie, how nice to see you. Come for a tour?"

"No, thank you, Layla. I was wondering if you would be available this coming Friday to go with MayLee and Annie into Lahaina to Hilo Hattie's. They are donating shirts for the Visitors Center docents and want us to select the fabric. I felt you ladies were more adept at selecting a proper design than I would be, especially you, Layla, with your artistic background."

Layla walked back inside and asked Chris if he thought they could get along without her this coming Friday. Chris assured her they would be fine, so she agreed to the outing. She told Donnie she would check with Annie for the time and saw Donnie out and on his way to the bank. She noticed Fiona and Ned having morning coffee on their lanai and walked over to talk with them.

"Good morning, folks. I've been thinking I should begin to have the air conditioner installed, and, Fiona, we need to talk about the two guest bathrooms. The more I look at them, I will need to have some work done. The work could be done while we work on the wood restoration, don't you think?"

"Absolutely, it would save time. I'll go back with you, and we can figure out what to do with those other two bathrooms. I've forgotten if they need a lot of work or just a cosmetic touch-up. Ned, can you get in touch with the air-conditioning people and have them come out to give Layla an estimate of cost and time?"

"Will call this morning. Any time fine with you, Layla?"

"Yes, just not this Friday, I'll be away for the day."

"I'll get back with you ladies once I've set something up. Are you going over to the house now, Fiona?"

"I'll follow Layla back and take notes on what we decide she'll need for the bathrooms."

"Fiona, I've made a list of other furniture pieces I'll be needing. Seems it would be cheaper for me to get everything to the warehouse and shipped all at once instead of just a few pieces at a time."

"We'll have to plan another trip to Oahu."

"Can't wait," Layla said with a broad grin.

Back at Layla's, Fiona began her appraisal of the guest bathrooms. The first bathroom was one shared by two of the bedrooms. "The toilet needs to be replaced, along with the sink and surrounding tiles. Layla, do you realize this floor is linoleum? This has to be original, gads! The shower looks fine, small, but it really is quite nicely retro. The tub is never going to come clean. I think whoever used this facility soaked for hours and never cleaned it properly. Naturally, the room will have to be repainted."

"Yikes," said Layla with a sigh, "well, on to the next one."

"This is a smaller bathroom, probably because it wasn't a shared facility. This too will need a new toilet, tub, floor, sink, and surrounding tiles or whatever type of top you want, new flooring and painting. I think work should begin now. Once Chris is done with the ceilings and starts on the floors, I expect things will go swiftly. It would be wise to have the bathrooms as finished as possible prior to that."

"Hi, ladies," Ned said as he entered the doorway of the small bathroom, "I spoke with the air-conditioning people. They will be out tomorrow at ten to give you an estimate, and I'll be here to go with them through the house."

"Thank you, Ned, that's terrific. Fiona and I have finished going through both the guest baths. A lot of work has to be done to them, and I want to get things started right away."

"You'll need to have the building inspector people sign off on the installation of toilet or tub replacements, and that can add time to any project. Although building has gone dead because of the economy, the wait has gotten much shorter.

That is, if Donnie isn't having all the inspectors at the Visitors Center," Ned said with a laugh.

"Oh no, not the dreaded building inspectors. Poor Donnie, he's looking quite stressed. He dropped by this morning to ask for a favor, and I believe he has lost about thirty or forty pounds."

"You know, I should go over and see if I can help him out with the Visitors Center. This is probably his first time with a contractor, let alone building inspectors."

"How thoughtful of you," Fiona said, kissing Ned on the cheek.

"Well, ladies, if you don't need me for anything, I'll head over to the bank and talk to Donnie while I'm still in the mood to relinquish some golf time."

"No, you go on. Layla and I have more things to work out. Layla, I will call my contractor that does bathroom work for my clients. I'll see if I can get him here tomorrow afternoon. You and I will have to go over what you want as far as tile and countertops. I would recommend just standard toilets and tubs, nothing fancy that might mean a special time-consuming order."

They made their way out to the kitchen area, where Layla had a card table and folding chairs set up. "I'm beginning to get that overwhelmed feeling again, Fiona."

"Don't think that way. This house is going to be full of men working their butts off to give you a beautiful new home. Think of it that way, and you will feel better. Now, I would like to make a suggestion, something I've been wanting to talk to you about. Chris is doing great work on the ceilings, in fact, he's further along than I thought he would be. You should let him finish, and you should begin cleaning the wood on the kitchen cabinets. That way, you can begin to fill them up with eating and cooking items. It will take a couple of weeks of cleaning to get them in pristine condition. What do you think?"

"Fiona, what would I do without you? I was so engrossed in working with Chris on the ceilings, I never thought about the kitchen cabinets. You're right. I will start on those tomorrow. I also wanted to go over with you the other furniture I will need to purchase.

"First off, I want three or four kitchen island bar stools and some type of small kitchen table and chairs for the wall opposite the counter island. For the living room, I thought I was going to use Shoji screen frame pieces to make shelves, but Marty is using those pieces to make the coffee table. I want some type of shelving for books, CDs, photo albums, small art objects, and in the middle of the shelving, a big-screen LCD television. I bought a new Bose music system I'm using at Mr. Soo's and I'll bring it here. Next, I need a large chair for the area across from the shelves and next to the front lanai window. I think Marty can make a side table for the chair, so I won't need that."

"Whew," Fiona said, writing like crazy, "are you going to need televisions for any of the other rooms?"

"Yes, a medium to large for the master bedroom, medium for the guest bedrooms and kitchen."

"With that many, you will get a great deal from Pacific Sales, and we can get them all shipped at once."

"I'll need furniture for two guest bedrooms: one queen bed and two twin beds and nightstands, a chest of drawers, and for the larger of the two guest bedrooms, I would like a small secretary desk and chair."

"What about your fourth bedroom?"

"I'm going to leave that empty for now. I'm pondering a combination art room and workout room, but right now, that's the last thing I want to put much thought into."

"I also want you to think about some type of breakfront for the dining room wall. You will need something there. Your table and chairs will not take up enough space, and the room will look empty. Also, there is the matter of lamps and wall pieces to consider."

"Let's get through the contractor for the air-conditioning and bathrooms first. Then we'll work on the furniture. How will I pick out the flooring and other items needed for the bathrooms? Will the contractor bring samples?"

"You and I can go to a home store and select what you want, get a sample, and then the contractor will make the purchase. I'll make it easy for you. Don't worry, dear. This will go smoother than you think," Fiona said with a reassuring smile. "I'm free on Saturdays, Ned always has an early morning golf game and lunch, so if you want to shop on Saturday mornings here in Maui, that will work out quite well."

"Maybe this coming Saturday, we can start at some of the home stores. Are there any lamp stores or places where I can purchase quality lighting items here on Maui? I really hate the idea of shipping lamps and shades from Oahu."

"There are several stores I can take you to. I don't know if we can cover everything in one day, but we sure can get a good start. I'm glad you are thinking about all these things now because the time will come when everything will be finished and you will be ready to move in and it will come upon you in a flash. Being prepared will make it all go so much easier."

"Thanks, Fiona. I'm sure you're correct. My initial idea of having several rooms finished first is not going to work. It will all have to be finished at once before I can make the move. I'm glad Mr. Soo and I get along so well, he'll be putting up with me longer than I anticipated."

"Having you around is just what he needs at this time in his life. Losing Mrs. Soo, no matter what he says or how he seems, has to have left a big emptiness in his life. You are doing him a lovely service by filling that empty house with your presence."

"That's kind of you to put it that way. We both are filling an empty space for each other."

Fiona and Layla agreed to meet early the following Saturday morning and shop for bathroom items and possibly lamps.

Fiona went back home, and Layla sat about making a list of all the appointments she had made in the past couple of hours.

Ned walked to the bank and spotted Donnie in his office. Donnie waved him back. "Ned, good to see you. How can we be of assistance?"

"Actually, Donnie, I came here to see if I can be of assistance to you. Damn, you've lost a lot of weight," Ned said, eyeing Donnie as he came from behind his desk to shake Ned's hand.

"I'm afraid it's not something I've worked at. It's been the stress of working on the Visitors Center, plus the strain of seeing people foreclosed on, and in too many cases, their loans can't be readjusted. Breaks my heart. We've never had this happen to this degree before."

"I came to see if I can lend an experienced hand in working with the building inspectors and contractor at the Visitors Center. Layla told me you seemed so stressed, and I've done this type of thing for years being in the real estate business, so if you think I can be of assistance, I'm willing to help."

Donnie's mouth fell open. "Ned, if you could help, it would be a godsent. I'm so lost and over my head working on this project. I sure could use your experienced guidance."

"Just let me know when we can go and look things over."

"Let me check out front and we can go now. I have nothing on my calendar for the remainder of the day." Donnie checked with the head cashier, and she told him to go ahead; she would call him on his cell phone if anything came up that needed his attention.

Donnie and Ned walked the few blocks to the Visitors Center. Ned greeted his old contractor friend and then spied another old friend who was doing an inspection on recently installed plumbing. The three men chatted about old times, and the inspector signed off on everything and was on his way, quicker than anticipated.

"Ned, how can I ever thank you? You made a difference today, and I feel like a ton of bricks has been lifted from my shoulders."

"I can be here any day an inspection is due or any day your contractor needs me. I'll give him my cell number, and he can call me if there is a problem. Is there a set of plans I can take home with me and familiarize myself with?"

Donnie went inside the center and got an extra set of plans for Ned while Ned and the contactor conferred on various upcoming details. Donnie kept thanking Ned, and finally, Ned was able to leave and head back down the hill to his home.

Ned rapped on the front screen, and Fiona came and unlocked the screen, letting him in. "Well, how did it go with Donnie? You were gone a long time."

"Went to the bank, talked to him, and then we went to the Visitors Center. I knew both the contractor and the inspector that was inspecting the latest plumbing installation. We caught up on what is happening in the real estate market, the inspector signed off without looking too closely, and I thought Donnie was going to faint. He thanked me several times, and I told him I can be there any day and also got a set of plans from him that I intend to review to see if I can catch anything that maybe a future problem."

"Ned, you are so sweet. I wish one of us had thought of you helping out before this, don't you?"

"Yep, but at least now I can help. By the way, my dear, you look particularly fetching, actually, you look almost naked."

Fiona looked down at herself; she was wearing a pair of very short shorts and a small tube top, her hair in a ponytail. "I was going out on the lanai and repot some plants and thought I would get some sun while there. You don't like the way I look?" she said with a pout.

Ned put his arms round her and pulled her into him, saying, "Actually, you look very sexy, and I'm thinking we need to do a little potting ourselves."

"Ned, are you suggesting what I think you are suggesting?" Fiona said in a quiet husky voice.

"Yes, I can't resist you. You're still the hottest thing on the island. Hell, if you don't believe me, just ask Marty!"

"Ned, is that a backhanded compliment?"

Ned locked the door and then headed her toward the bedroom. "Come on, you lusty Italian."

Layla had given Chris an extra set of keys at the end of last week and asked him if he would lock up today; she had a killer headache. She headed to Mr. Soo's, took a quick shower, then lay down, falling asleep for almost an hour.

She woke up when Mr. Soo arrived. "Ms. Layla, are you here?"

"Yes, Mr. Soo, I came home early today. I had a headache. I took a nap, and I'm feeling a lot better now. How was your day?"

"Interesting. I met Donnie coming back from the Visitors Center, and he was whistling. I have not seen him that happy since he started plans for the Visitors Center. I asked him why he was whistling, and he told me Ned Keller offered to assist with the Visitors Center and would be helping with the contractor and inspectors. He said now he feels he has someone that is knowable that will be able oversee things and help him make sure no costly mistakes are made."

"Ned and Fiona were over at the house today, and when Ned left, he said he was going to find Donnie and offer him his assistance. I'm so glad Donnie got some help. I was getting worried about his health. Did you notice he has lost a lot of weight?"

"Although he will be healthier now that he has lost weight, but losing it because of stress is never a good diet plan."

"I spoke with Fiona about having the air-conditioning people start work and also about having the two guest bathrooms remodeled. Ned has arranged to have the air-conditioning company come out tomorrow morning for an estimate, then tomorrow afternoon, the bathroom contractor will come out and give me an estimate. Friday, I'm going to Lahaina with MayLee Munson and Annie to Hilo Hattie's to pick out material for the Visitors Center's docents' shirts, which Hilo Hattie's is donating. Saturday, Fiona and I are going to a home store to pick out flooring and countertops for the bathrooms, and if we have time, we'll look for lamps. I also discussed with Fiona other furniture I will need, and we have to make another trip to Oahu. Mr. Soo, my mind is so full, I'm not sure I should have undertaken all this remodeling by myself."

"Layla, you will do fine. You have the excellent guidance of Fiona and Ned, and you know Annie, George, and I will lend you all the support we can. I think on Sunday, you should gather your charcoals and do some sketching. That always relaxes you and you can sketch something for your new home."

"Mr. Soo, thank you for your support and your excellent idea. I will do some sketching. You're right. That always relaxes me. Let's go down to one of the beach shacks and have dinner there tonight. We can catch the sunset."

When they returned from their dinner by the shore, Layla phoned Annie to ask if she had heard from MayLee.

"MayLee phoned Hilo Hattie's, and we have an appointment at ten Friday morning, so she will pick us up at nine. We thought we would have lunch at Hamburger Heaven, that's such a fun place to people watch. How does that sound to you?"

"Great, I especially like the people watching," Layla said, laughing. "I'm going to have both my guest bathrooms remodeled. They are in pretty bad shape. Once they are finished, could you take me to a store that sells nice bathroom things? I need to furnish my master bathroom and the two others with towels, wastepaper baskets, etc. All the things we pick up here and there, I will need to get all at once."

"I would love to help you with that shopping chore. There are some great stores that sell bed and bath linens and a couple are very upscale. Have you got your mattresses and frames?"

"No, I guess Fiona and I will have to hunt them down on our next trip to Oahu, more things to ship over," Layla said with a sigh.

"Layla, don't buy them on Oahu. A good friend of ours is the brother of the man that makes most of the mattresses for the hotels here on Maui, and we've always gotten our mattresses from him. His quality is excellent, and prices are less than half of Oahu retail. Plus, if you are going to buy several, they will deliver and set up for you at no extra charge. You will also want to buy your mattress pads from his store. They are the best, and he'll sell them to you at wholesale."

"That's such good news since I don't have any idea when I'll be ready to get furniture. How soon should I give him the order?"

"We could stop by on Friday and ask him, and you might want to pick out what you want, then just phone him a couple of weeks before you'll need delivery and he can make them up at that time."

"Do you think it will be OK with MayLee if we stop by the store?"

"Yes, she wanted me to ask you if you need to do any shopping while we were on that side of the island, as we would have plenty of time to go places."

"Any chance we could shop for bed linens tomorrow?"

"Probably, but you may want to put that off a bit until you decide your colors, or have you decided on that all ready?" Annie asked, knowing Layla was beginning to get ahead of herself.

"You're right, getting too excited about all this. We will have to go back because hopefully, I can also find items for the kitchen too. I will need both cooking and eating items. I think I should call my trust officer and get more money sent my way," Layla said with a laugh.

They talked for a time longer then said their goodbyes, both excited about their upcoming excursion.

CHAPTER 44

Layla was up early the next morning to phone Dewey and tell him what all had transpired yesterday. She told him of her upcoming visit to Lahaina and the mattress store, the news of Ned helping out Donnie, and that on Sunday, she was going to do some sketching to relieve stress. Then on Monday, she would start work on restoring the kitchen cabinets.

"You're just full of news!" exclaimed Dewey. "I'm glad you are getting started on the kitchen. I can hardly wait for your whole project to be finished. I want us to be together so badly. I think of you all the time," Dewey said wistfully.

"I think of how nice it would be to feel loved and to feel someone beside me to see me through life, and, Dewey, you are the only person I want to be with," Layla said softly. "You've been there for me for close to a year now, and you have been so patient and understanding. There aren't many men, especially in your circumstance, that would stick with someone while they get their life back together."

"This may sound silly, but the minute I laid eyes on you, I saw you as my angel, and I fell in love instantly. Didn't know such a thing was possible, certainly didn't expect it would happen to me, but it did, and I will wait for our time together so that it's the absolute right time."

"Dewey, that's so beautifully romantic. I'm deeply touched, and my feelings for you have grown so that I envision us making a future with each other. I hope you don't think that's silly of me," Layla said.

"Honey, that's what I want too. We'll take it slow. We'll get to know each other intimately, to know how each of us can make the other happy. We'll each give, and we each will take, and we will make an awesome couple."

"I believe we will," Layla said softly, touched by Dewey's words.

Their conversation continued on lighter subjects, and then they said their goodbyes, with Layla promising to phone him Sunday after returning from her sketching to let him know about her shopping adventures.

The next morning Layla explained to Chris about the two estimators that would be coming and that she would be gone on Friday. She also told him that he was doing such a great job; she was going to start work on cleaning the kitchen cabinets.

Chris was pleased with her compliments and told her that Josie was almost finished cleaning the Shoji frames and would she help with the ceiling restoration.

Layla went to the cleaning supplies, found a spare bucket, put on gloves, and started to work on cabinet cleaning. After cleaning one door, she realized she had made a mistake and should have cleaned out the inside of the cabinets first. To her dismay, inside the cabinets and drawers, she found many full of assorted items. She sighed and thought, *More sorting to do.*

At ten o'clock, Ned and the first contractor arrived. Layla told Ned to handle the walkthrough; she would wait in the kitchen for the appraisal. Layla had set out the contents of four cabinets and two drawers. She was unsure if she should discuss them with Mr. Soo or Fiona first. She decided on Fiona, as the items seemed old and unused. There were only a couple of things she would want to keep for her own use and nothing of any value. After she had a cabinet cleaned out, she washed the shelves several times to get the accumulated dust and dirt out, then dried them off. The shelves inside were pure wood and had never been lined or covered in any way. After a good cleaning, they were in great shape and would not need any more work, unlike the outside of the cabinets and drawers, which had received the brunt of the cooking smoke.

Thirty minutes later, Ned and the contractor came into the kitchen and gave Layla the estimate for air-conditioning. The contractor told Layla the cost, which was a bit under what she thought it would be, and said he could order the supplies right away and start a week from this coming Monday.

Layla looked over at Ned, who gave her a nod of approval.

"Do you have a contract for me to sign, and how much of a down payment will you require?"

The contractor said he would bring by a formal contract later this afternoon and told her how much her first payment would be. They agreed on a time, and Layla thanked Ned for his time, knowing it would be on Fiona's final bill but happy that Ned's expertise was available to look out for her own interests.

After lunch, Layla had time to get two more shelves cleared out and cleaned. She had all the items lined up on the countertop and would wait for Fiona's review. When Fiona and her contractor arrived, she gave a puzzled look at the items.

After greeting the contractor, Herb, everyone preceded to the guest bathrooms. Layla let Fiona do all the talking and explaining as Herb made notes. He suggested using recessed lighting in the ceiling with decorative lighting on the sides of a new modern mirror over the sink area. In the larger of the two bathrooms, he carefully measured and said it would be a property upgrade to make the vanity cabinet a his and hers with double sinks. He showed Fiona there was plenty of room, then sketched the type of mirror and lighting he envisioned. Layla approved the plan, thinking it would make a smart-looking bathroom. They went on to the smaller bathroom, and except for recessed ceiling lights and a different light over the mirror, everything else stayed as Fiona and Layla had discussed earlier. They went back to the kitchen table, and Layla got her estimate, which turned out to be considerably more than she had planned. Herb said it did not include the price of any of the fixtures, permits, plumbing, etc. He said a lot of the labor cost was the removal of the flooring and tiles and disposal of everything. There were environmental rules on disposal for the sinks, tubs, and toilets. Layla smiled politely and said to go ahead and write the contract, and she would sign and give him a check for the start-up.

Once he left, she turned to Fiona, saying, "This has been an expensive day. Speaking of expenses, I must owe you something by now."

"I wouldn't mind a check, but I can present you a final bill, or I can bring by our expenses up till now on Monday and you can write me a check then."

"That's fair. You and Ned have been invaluable, and I want to keep it that way," Layla said, smiling.

"I found all this in the cabinets and drawers, and I don't even have them all cleaned out yet. I'm not sure what to do with this stuff, although there are a couple of pieces I'm keeping," Layla said, gesturing toward the items on the counter.

Fiona began looking at the items. "First, trash all glass items that are chipped or cracked. There is nothing here of any value. Looks like odd lots of various utensils, some of them not seen too often. Oh, can I have this?" Fiona asked, holding up something that looked like a ring of measuring spoons but with tiny metal cups of three different sizes.

"Sure, what the heck is that?" asked Layla.

"It's a three different-sized melon ball scoops. I love it. I didn't even know there was such a thing," Fiona said happily.

"Well, please take it. I'm glad you can use something like that."

Fiona picked out a couple more items then suggested Layla call Annie over and have her look through the lot and also Chris, Marty, and Josie. Anything left over, she could box up and take to the thrift store.

After Fiona left, Layla phoned Annie, asking if she and George could come over for a few minutes; she had some items she wanted them to look through to see if there was anything they might be able to use. Within ten minutes, Annie and George were surveying the items.

"Can I have this slotted spoon? I can use it in the garage," George asked.

"By all means, it's yours," Layla said with a grin, looking over at Annie who shook her head in wonder.

"I've got a couple of things I could use, so I'll be glad to take them off your hands. That's all for me. George, how about you?"

"I'm happy with my spoon. Thanks, Layla, for letting us look at these things. Any more?"

"There will be a couple more displays for you to look through. It seems I'm finding things in each kitchen cabinet and drawer I go through. I'll let you know when the next viewing will be."

When they left, Layla reminded Chris she would be gone all day tomorrow, and she invited him and his crew to look through the items in the kitchen and take anything they wanted. She would box the rest up over the weekend and take it to the local charity thrift store.

Chris said he would box the remaining items up for her because his wife's mother volunteered at the store and would be happy to take the items for her. Layla thanked him and told him there would be more coming.

Layla was glad for her late afternoon bath and then worked on a to-do list for tomorrow. She was just as excited about going on tomorrow's outing as she had been as a child when going to a friend's birthday party. She was expanding her friendships and knowledge of Maui, getting to know her new home.

CHAPTER 45

Annie rinsed her coffee cup, putting it in the dishwasher; hearing George was up, she poured him a mug of coffee.

"Here, honey," Annie said, handing him the mug, "you look tired and worried. What's wrong?"

"I know you're going to say it's silly, but I worry about you going to Lahaina. MayLee is known for her fast driving, and I'm concerned for you and Layla," George said, putting his arms around Annie and hugging her to him.

"That's so sweet, but don't think for a minute if I feel she's going too fast, I won't tell her to slow down. I have no problem speaking my mind when I'm with someone who is driving dangerously."

"I know, I still worry. Don't want anything to happen to my love."

"You kept me tucked into you all last night. I would try to turn over, but you would reach out and pull me back. You must have been trying to protect me in your sleep. You are such a darling." Annie reached up and gave George a big kiss.

"Are you sure you really have to go into Lahaina? Another kiss like that and I won't let you leave," George said with a devilish grin.

"Yes, it's my civic duty," Annie said, laughing.

Layla knocked on the kitchen door, and Annie left George's embrace, letting her in. "Hi, folks. Are you ready for our outing, Annie?"

"All set, although George is afraid of us going with MayLee. I've told him if she starts driving too fast, I'll slow her down."

"She's a fast driver?" Layla asked.

"Two speeding tickets in the last six months," George replied.

"Speaking of MayLee, here she comes now. Don't worry, George, between Annie and I, we'll keep her within the speed limit."

George followed Layla and Annie out the back and saw them into MayLee's car, waving as they drove off.

The sheriff, coming up the street in the opposite direction, stopped and said to George, "I see the ladies are on their way to Hilo Hattie's. Donnie has told half the town about the trip and the ladies picking out fabric. He's making a big deal about Hilo Hattie's generosity. I think he's angling for other donations."

"I'm worried about MayLee and her fast driving."

"I might have helped with that," the sheriff said with a big smile. "I stopped by the bank yesterday and told Donnie speed traps were being set up this weekend, starting on Friday and be sure and tell MayLee to keep within the posted limit. She didn't want another speeding ticket. It would cost a bundle."

"Donnie assured me he would lay the law down and he will. Spending more money on speeding tickets would drive him crazy."

"That was nice of you to let Donnie know so he could warn MayLee and I thank you too. It makes me feel better about Annie and Layla driving with her."

"There aren't really any speed traps being set up," the sheriff said, laughing. "I wanted to be sure they got to Lahaina and back safely."

"Sheriff, you are a good man to have in charge."

The sheriff waved and turned up the hill to go back on patrol.

On the way out of Paia, MayLee told Annie and Layla about the speed traps the sheriff warned Donnie about.

"Donnie said I was going to be in big trouble if I got another speeding ticket, so I've got to watch my speed," MayLee said, giggling. "I've driven these roads since I was a teenager, and I could drive them with my eyes closed."

"But you won't, will you, MayLee?" Annie asked sternly.

"Oh no, just kidding," MayLee said with her usual giggle.

Annie and Layla kept the conversation to a minimum, keeping an eye on MayLee's speed.

Inside Hilo Hattie's, they met with their representative, Loretta, who showed them to a table where ten bolts of material were lined up for their review. MayLee chose a black fabric with bright red hibiscus flowers and pale yellow orchids. Annie said it would look fabulous on a darker skinned person, but some of the older folks with gray hair and pale skin wouldn't look good in a shirt with a black background. MayLee agreed, and they took out each bolt, examining patterns to find one that would blend with all complexions. A small bolt of fabric near the end of the grouping caught Layla's eye.

"Look at this!" Layla exclaimed, pulling material from a bolt.

"That's it," said Annie. "This shade of blue will complement all skin tones, and, ladies, this has to be meant for us. Can you believe a windsurfer riding into the sky?"

The ladies looked at the fabric and knew it was perfect. A cascading wave propelled a windsurfer into a sky, and the blue-green color of the water melted into the horizon atop white-capped waves. The windsurfer arched his sail and board to catch the wind, and you knew that flight was his; the artist made the whole vision come alive.

They told Loretta this was the fabric and suggested the store not spend extra money making shirts up ahead of time; they would call and give her the size of the docents when they had been selected. Loretta thanked them for their consideration and said she would place an order for more fabric to make sure there was plenty when needed.

Annie, MayLee, and Layla left the store happy with their choice, amazed that such a fitting fabric had been found. It was a little past eleven, too early for lunch, so they decided to go to the mattress store.

Annie walked in and was greeted by a clerk she and George had done business with.

"Mrs. Boone, how nice to see you. How may I assist you?"

"My friend, Layla Richfield, will be needing some mattresses for her new home."

"Thank you, Mrs. Boone," the clerk said. Turning to Layla, he asked, "What will you be needing?"

"I'll need one king-sized, one queen-sized, and two twin mattresses, box frames, bed frames along with mattress covers. However, I can only pick out the items now. Once restoration on my new home is nearly completed, I would then make an official order."

Annie added, "I told Ms. Richfield she could pick out what she wanted, then phone you a couple of weeks before she needed delivery. You could make them up and deliver them to her at that time."

"Absolutely, that's how a lot of the hotels handle things during their remodeling. We are very adept at working with your scheduling."

"In that case, I'll need to look at your floor samples."

"We actually have five types to choose from." The clerk showed them to the various samples, and each lady tried out deep pillow-top mattresses, mattress without pillow tops, then Layla saw a solid mattress with no pillow top, no quilting, and asked what type of mattress it was.

"This is our high-end latex mattress. Try it, and you will be surprised at the comfort. It conforms to your body yet retains solid support."

Layla kicked off her shoes and lay down on the mattress, expecting to sink into the foam. She was surprised at how firm it felt and gave such good back support. "This is very comfortable, but won't it be hot sleeping on it?"

"Not at all, especially once you use a mattress cover and sheets. This is an excellent mattress and affords wonderful spinal support."

Layla got up, and Annie lay down next. "Wow, I can tell you right now what our next mattress will be. This is very comfortable."

She got up, and MayLee tried the mattress out. "My goodness, is this the way a good mattress is supposed to feel? The one Donnie and I sleep on we've had for twenty years, and it sags so much in the middle. If I roll too far into the center, I have to push myself out."

"Not changing your mattress for that long of a time is very hard on your back. I guarantee you a good night's sleep. Plus, you will wake up with your body feeling much better," the salesman said.

"Excuse me," MayLee said, "I'm calling Donnie."

"Donnie, it's MayLee," she said once outside.

"Lord, MayLee, you didn't get another speeding ticket?"

"No, I did not," she said indignantly. "I'm at the mattress factory with Annie and Layla, and we're getting a new mattress, not only for us but also for our daughter. I can't believe we have been sleeping on that old thing all this time and never considered getting it replaced. I'm not discussing this. I'm ordering the mattresses, and that's that."

"How much are these new mattresses going to cost?" Donnie asked, loyal to his financial background.

"It doesn't matter, we can afford it. I'm calling to tell you what I'm doing." MayLee hung up, went back to the store, and placed her order.

Layla also placed an order with the provision she would call them back with a delivery date. MayLee's order would be delivered a week from this Saturday. The ladies left the store, happy and hungry.

On the way to Hamburger Heaven, MayLee said, "Now maybe I can enjoy wickie-wickie again."

Annie turned around, looked at Layla in the back seat, and both ladies burst out laughing while MayLee giggled.

After a leisurely lunch, they visited some of the shops in the area, then decided to return to Paia before they spent any more money.

Layla thanked MayLee for the day, saying it was such fun, and they should get together again for more shopping. Annie agreed it was a terrific day. MayLee drove off, leaving Annie and Layla on their street. Annie asked Layla if she wanted to come in, but she declined and headed back to Mr. Soo's.

Inside, Annie sat down her purchases and got a big hug from George. "You're back earlier than I expected. How did it go?"

"Great. We picked out a fabric that actually had a windsurfer on it, and at the mattress store, Layla picked out her mattresses and will call a delivery date when she wants them, but, honey, I've got to tell you about MayLee. She ordered a new mattress for her and Donnie and their daughter. On the way to lunch, she said now maybe she could enjoy wickie-wickie again."

"You're kidding?" George asked with a big grin. "She actually said that?"

"Layla and I were in tears laughing, and MayLee was giggling, it was so funny. We had a great day!"

"I'm glad you had such a good time and made it home safely."

CHAPTER 46

Layla walked toward Fiona's house, knowing today would be nothing like yesterday, but it was important she and Fiona begin selecting materials for the bathroom upgrades. With a sigh, she walked up the steps and knocked on the slider screen.

Fiona opened it, saying, "Hello, I'm glad you're here. I'm ready to get started. Just let me get my tote, and we can be off to the home store. I've compiled a list of items we need to check out."

En route, Layla told Fiona about the selection of the fabric for the docent shirts and about selecting her mattresses. She left out the revelation MayLee made about wicky-wicky.

"I'm glad Annie knew about the mattress factory. That will save you both time and money. Were they easy to deal with?"

"Terrific. They understood my remodeling schedule and were used to working on that basis with local hotels when they remodeled."

Fiona looked pensive, saying, "I'll speak with Annie and get her store contact. It might be prudent for me to become acquainted with these people."

"You'll like them. They're very professional."

At the home store, Fiona went to the flooring section, discussing with Layla the pros and cons of various types of flooring for the bathrooms. When she finished, Layla found nothing that felt just right.

"What I had in mind was some type of white tile but with colored grout. I saw that somewhere, and I liked the way it looked. Is something like that possible?"

"Sure, let's look at white tiles and see what looks good. Do you have any idea what color grout you might want?"

"Frankly, no. Do you have any ideas, Fiona?"

"How about keeping an island or nautical theme with a blue-green color or even a navy blue? Either would look great with white tiles."

"I like the navy blue idea. Then I could use that same nautical theme in the bedrooms," Layla said, imagining white walls, navy blue bedspreads, with white throw pillows.

"I'm getting into the nautical idea too. I like it," Fiona said, tapping her chin with her finger.

They selected a floor-sized subway tile and dark navy blue grout. Fiona checked with the clerk to make sure all were in stock.

Next, they looked at bathtubs. Layla selected a simple style, and Fiona verified there were two in stock, then they moved to the toilet section.

"Layla, I'm going to suggest you get a toilet that is ADA approved. Those are higher in height, and since many seniors purchase the expensive beachfront homes, this will be a plus if you ever decide to sell. Mr. Soo has installed one in the master bathroom."

"You're right. I should use the same type of toilet throughout the house. Let's get two of those. If the contractor picks up all these things, will I have space for them in my garage?"

"Since you keep your car at Mr. Soo's, your double garage is empty, so there is plenty of storage space. On to vanities. This will probably be the most difficult decision, especially since you want to carry out the same theme in both a his and hers bathroom and a single-sink bathroom."

Neither Fiona nor Layla liked any of the vanities that were displayed.

"I have an idea. I'm calling the contractor to see if he's in the area and can come over and look at everything we've selected and give us his input on the vanities. I'll tell him to bring his truck, and he can take the small things with him."

Fiona stepped outside and called Herb. He said he was coming back from Kihei, would be there in about twenty minutes, and would meet the ladies outside at the snack tables.

Fiona found Layla inside, pondering different types of bathtub fixtures, and told her the contractor would meet them outside and suggested they go to the snack area and get a cup of coffee.

Layla drank her coffee while watching the locals come and go while Fiona greeted a number of people.

Herb strode toward Fiona and Layla twenty minutes later. Layla turned to Fiona, saying, "That's one great-looking man."

"You think he's good-looking, you should see his partner. He's gorgeous. Many Maui ladies think those two are a great waste of testosterone. A friend's daughter was determined to change Herb's persuasion. She failed," Fiona said, laughing.

"Aside from being such a hunk, he's so polite and charming. I can see why the ladies fall for him," Layla said.

Herb greeted them with a disarming smile, saying, "I hope I didn't keep you lovely ladies waiting too long. What can I do for you?"

"We were just people watching, having a cup of coffee," Fiona said while Layla offered a pleasant smile. "Layla has selected some items for her bathrooms, and we're stuck on the vanities. We thought you could give us your input."

"My pleasure, ladies. Let's see what you've selected."

Layla and Fiona showed Herb the selections already made and told him of the nautical theme.

"Sounds perfect with the large subway tiles and navy grout. The mirrors and light fixtures I sketched will go great with your theme. It will be subtle, and it will look very classy."

"That's what I hope to achieve, Herb. Come look at the vanities. There doesn't seem to be anything that fits into my scheme."

At the vanity section, Herb did a lot of looking at models and color palettes. "Layla, I have an idea, and, Fiona, please voice your opinion on this too. My partner, Wade, is a terrific carpenter, and he could build you matching vanities. I have in mind a weathered-gray look, like that commonly seen on Eastern Seaboard summer homes. It would go well with the gray tiles in both those retro showers."

"Herb, that's perfect," said Fiona, nodding her approval.

"I like that idea, but is Wade a good carpenter?" asked Layla.

Herb grinned broadly, saying, "He's excellent. In fact, ask Marty. He apprenticed under him, so you know he learned from the best."

"My gosh, what a small world," said Layla.

"No, just a small island," Herb said.

"I'm learning that!" Layla said, laughing.

"For the top of Wade's vanities, we could have silestone installed in a navy blue, then have deep undermount rectangle white sinks. I think that would look stunning," Fiona said.

"That would look spectacular. Let's get simple round brushed nickel knobs for the drawers and cabinets, keeping that low-key."

"Are we all in agreement then?" Herb asked. The ladies nodded their approval. "Let's pick out the faucets while we're all here. Then you are basically done making your selections for the bathrooms."

They chose simple brushed nickel hardware for the sinks and tubs. Herb loaded everything except the tubs, sinks, and toilets in his truck, telling the clerk he would be back tomorrow with helpers to pick up the remainder of the order. He arranged to meet Layla late Sunday afternoon and unload the items into her garage.

Back in the car, Fiona said, "We don't have time for more shopping, but, my dear, we've accomplished more than I imagined."

"I agree. Thanks to you and hunky Herb."

"Oh, that's cute. I will think of him now as hunky Herb."

"May I take you to lunch?" Layla asked, figuring a refusal would be forthcoming.

"How lovely. It would be my pleasure. If you like Chinese food, there is a terrific Chinese restaurant in the strip that has the best Chinese food on the island. A good tell is that it is always full of Chinese customers."

"Great. I ate a lot of Chinese in New York, and I miss the wonderful flavors."

After they finished their egg flower soup, while waiting for the main course, Layla asked a question she had wondered about. "Fiona, where were you and Ned when the storm struck Maui?"

"Ned has a sister that lives on Oahu, and when she heard Maui would be in the storm's path, she demanded we fly to Oahu to be out of harm's way. Ned's sister is wonderful. She is the family matriarch. We all acquiesce to her, and she's usually right. When she heard about the Okamoto murders, she said but for the grace of God and her, it might have been Ned and me. Well, I didn't believe that, but frankly, I was grateful we weren't here when that horrible business happened. Do you think Annie has completely gotten over her experience?"

"No, I think she has blocked it out, and George agrees. He said she seems more delicate than she used to be and cries easier at her favorite old tunes on the radio or at old movies. I love those two. They have helped me so much, I will never be able to repay what they have given to me. They have played a big part in my recovery."

"I can only imagine how horrible the loss of your child must have been. But honestly, if Kyle had been my husband and he announced he was leaving me for Kim, I would have beat him to a pulp."

"Fiona, I believe you would have. By the time it got to that point, I was so numb, I didn't feel anything. I craved the idea of being alone."

Their food arrived, and both ate a delicious Chinese lunch. On the way back, Layla said, "I really enjoyed today. We talk so much business, it was fun just to chat about other things."

"Come in, and I'll fix us a latte. I don't care if it was Chinese, I still like a latte to finish off my meal."

"Sounds great!"

Enjoying their lattes, Layla continued the conversation, "The good thing about my divorce is what Dewey has come to mean to me. I believe I've fallen in love with that man, and he's as much as told me that's how he feels. I hope, after my home is remodeled, he'll come over for a visit, and we'll take our relationship to the next level, if you know what I mean."

"That's such an exciting and fun time. I had my first sexual experience when I was fifteen with one of my shooting coaches. All my doing, I wanted to get rid of that virgin stigma. It wasn't thrilling, but at least I got that out of the way. I had a number of lovers before making my way to Hawaii. The French and Italians are very overrated. But, honey, let me tell you the Dutch are wonderful. I learned so much from two different Dutchmen that were my lovers. Frankly, they don't call them Dutch masters for their paintings!"

"Wow, you had an exciting youth."

"It sure was, and I was quite stunning in my youth. Long red-brown hair, big breasts, tiny waist, and long muscular legs, and I knew I was a knockout and used it for all it was worth."

"Fiona, you are still a stunning woman. Everyone comments on your legs and your great shape."

"Thanks, dear, but you should have seen me in my early twenties. That is when I met Ned. I was in Hawaii on a photo shoot for the Italian Olympic team. Two team members and I were having Mai Tais at an outdoor bar in a popular plaza in Oahu. I looked at a nearby table, and there was this beautiful man. About six feet, sun-bleached blond hair, bronze tan, and dressed extremely well, looked like money. The other two people he was drinking with got up and left, and he paid the bill but sat and finished his drink. That was all I needed. I had on short shorts, a halter top, and platform sandals, and I knew I looked hot. I sauntered up to him, stuck out my hand, and in my best Italian accent, introduced myself."

* * *

"It's a pleasure to meet such a stunning representative of Italy. My name is Ned Keller. The gentlemen that left before you came over are my silent partners in a new business I'm starting up, Ned Keller Real Estate."

"Well, Mr. Ned Keller, that is wonderful. I believe I can be an asset to your new business. Hawaii is the final stop on our Italian Olympic team photo shoot, and from here, we go back to Italy, if we choose. I'm a university graduate in interior design. Hire me, and I guarantee you a distinctive interior design representative for your firm."

An amusing smile crossed Ned's face. "I believe we need to discuss this further, Fiona. Right now, I have to sign a rental agreement for my office space, but let me take you to dinner tonight."

"That would be lovely, Ned." Fiona gave him her hotel information and went back to her table of fellow Olympians. "I'm having dinner tonight with my future husband," she declared.

* * *

"Fiona, you knew right then and there you were going to marry Ned?" Layla asked, not sure she believed what she was hearing.

"Yes, no doubt about it. He moved me sexually, and he also moved a part of me that had never been touched before, my heart. It was so unexpected.

"Ned and I shared a lovely dinner at an upscale restaurant and talked business throughout dinner. I, of course, was dressed in one of my most alluring outfits, but I swear he seemed unfazed. I was shocked when after dinner, he escorted me back to my hotel and said good night at the door. I had imagined us having a wildly romantic evening, burning up the sheets. Just as I was about to close the door, he asked if I would be interested in dinner tomorrow evening. I naturally said yes. He told me to wear something very comfortable, just shorts and a top would be fine.

"The next evening I wore white eyelet short shorts and a yellow blouse that I tied up on my midriff. The yellow highlighted my tan and hair color. Once again, I knew I looked hot. I brought along a large Hermes tote, a graduating gift from a former lover, which held a portfolio of my design work. When he came to the door, he had on casual shorts and a light blue Oxford shirt with the sleeves rolled up to his elbows. He was beautiful. We got into his car, not the Lincoln of last night but an open-air Jeep, and he drove out of town to the other side of the island. He turned off on a dirt road, headed toward the ocean. That damned road was so bumpy, I thought I would lose the shape of my great buns. I took a lot of pride in their shape."

Layla started laughing. "Fiona, I can't tell you how much I'm enjoying this tale. Please continue."

"He stopped the car at a small cliff overlooking the water. We got out, and he produced a large picnic basket. He gave me a blanket and towels to carry, and we went to the beach. It was very secluded, and we set things up so we could rest our backs on some lava rocks. We had sandwiches, salads, and a remarkable red wine with fresh strawberries and papaya for dessert. After dinner, I produced my portfolio and showed him my design work. He was surprised. He thought I was not what I claimed to be. Well, I showed him. I had won several university awards for my work. After he finished viewing my work, awards, and letters of accommodation, I asked him if he was ready to give me a job. He said he was seriously considering it, then smiled his melt-your-heart smile.

"I suggested we go for a swim, then began to get up and undress. He said he didn't bring any swim trunks. I told him, laughing, I didn't either and took off my bra and panties and headed toward the water. I heard him say, 'Oh shit,' and he began stripping and followed me into the water."

Layla sat entranced by Fiona's story, saying, "This is so romantic. Go on. I can't wait to hear what you did next!"

"When he got into the water, I waded up to him, put my arms around his neck, and smiled."

*   *   *

"You have a beautiful body, Fiona. Aren't you bothered by this nude swim?"

"Of course not. I'm European. I've swam and sunbathed on nude beaches for years. Is this new for you?"

"I've never swam in the nude before with a female. With the guys, yes. You're making it difficult for me to keep my hands off you."

*   *   *

Fiona smiled with the memory. "I pushed into him closer and swung my legs around his waist, knowing I was teasing him horribly. 'Then why try?' I said, kissing him passionately. Let me tell you, Layla, that was the first of several meaningful kisses, and we went back to the beach and made love. I will say, though, an afterglow moment with all that sand stuck everywhere is impossible!

"We left the beach and went back to his condo where I spent the night. The next morning he agreed to give me a chance as his design assistant in Ned Keller Real Estate. I do believe we wore each other out making love before we reached an agreement. I also agreed to move in with him. We married six months later. It's been perfect ever since. Of course, we've had our ups and downs, which means making up is especially sweet."

Fiona gently gripped Layla's arm. "Layla, Dewey is in love with you. Don't waste the opportunity to find true love. Believe me, it makes life so wonderful. Look at Annie and George, Ned and me, happy people still in love with the person they married."

CHAPTER 47

Fiona said goodbye to Layla and reminded her about Herb's delivery the following afternoon. Fiona was ready to unlock her door when she heard a scraping noise coming from the Boones'. Looking over, she saw George cleaning their large grill with Annie supervising. Fiona waved and said, "Annie, mind if I come over? I need to talk with you about something."

"Sure, come on over."

Fiona made her way to the top of the Boones' lanai. "Come on up," said Annie. "George is doing our every-three-months grill cleaning."

"Well, it's not my damn idea. This grill does not need a good cleaning once every three months. Once every six months is plenty." He was wearing an old black T-shirt, dark board shorts, and large kitchen rubber gloves.

"George, you certainly are making a fashion statement," Fiona said, chuckling.

"Very funny, Fiona. Annie insists I do this every three months to lessen the grease buildup, she says, but I think it's more a personal torture," George said, resuming his scraping.

"Fiona, sit down," Annie said, gesturing to a chair. "What can I help you with?"

"Layla and I went on a shopping trip today, and she told me about the mattress factory you took her to yesterday. She spoke very highly of their professionalism and was impressed with their prices. I've lived here for years, and I never heard about them, so I thought maybe you could give me a card or name so I could go and introduce myself."

"Sure, no problem. We found out about them because George worked with the brother of the owner, and we've been buying from them for years. They don't solicit individual business but concentrate on local hotels, hospitals, those types of clients. However, they gladly sell to the general public. We've always been happy with their quality and service. Let me go inside and get you their card."

Fiona got up and walked over to the grill; looking in at George's work, she said, "Bet you won't use that again soon?"

"Going to use it tonight. It aggravates Annie. I figure it's the least I can do if I have to clean it every three months. You better step back before I splash grease on you."

"Sorry, I didn't mean to get in your way."

Annie returned with the business card and handed it to Fiona.

"Thanks so much. When I call, I'll be sure and say you gave me their card," Fiona said, looking at her watch.

"I was going to offer you a drink, but if you have to be somewhere, I'll understand," Annie said.

"No, I'll take a drink. It's just that Ned should have been back from his golf game by now."

"When I was coming back from my Saturday honey-do run, I saw him and Donnie going into the Visitors Center. Ned had an armload of blueprints with him."

"Thank you, George. You have relieved my mind."

"Did you just say honey-do run? You're a grumpy old geezer this afternoon. Hurry up, and I'll get you a beer," Annie said, shaking her head and smiling. "What can I get for you, Fiona? I might add, I make a great Mai Tai."

"That sounds lovely. Will you join me, Annie?"

"Yep, need something to cheer me up after all the verbal abuse I've been taking from my husband."

George mumbled into his grill, neither woman able to understand what he was saying. Fiona decided she would steer clear of George while Annie went in and made their Mai Tais. As Annie was coming out with their drinks, Ned pulled into his driveway. Fiona got up and signaled him. "Ned, I'm over here. Come on over."

Ned walked onto the lanai, and Fiona went over and hugged him. "I was worried about you," she said, planting a kiss on his cheek.

"I'm sorry. I should have called and told you Donnie and I went to check out something I discovered last night while going over the plans for the Visitors Center, a small thing that could turn into difficulty later on. Now all has been taken of," Ned said, putting his arm around her and smiling. "Always good to be missed by my lovely wife."

"See, Annie, a loving couple," George said crisply.

"George, are you two fighting?" Ned asked with a grin.

"No, we're not fighting. George gets a bit testy when he scrubs the grill."

"Damned dirty job and only necessary every six months, not three," George said emphatically.

"Fiona, that's why I don't grill anymore. I hated cleaning that thing, so I bought us the Jenn-Air inside grill."

"Honey, it's not the same as food grilled over charcoals," Fiona said softly.

Anxious to change the subject, Annie asked Ned if he would like a drink, and he also decided on a Mai Tai.

When Annie came out with his drink, George said to Annie, "OK, Sarge, ready for your inspection."

"Sweetie, I don't need to inspect anything. You always do a good job. Go clean up, and I'll have a cold beer waiting for you."

When George returned, Annie handed him his beer, saying, "Thank you, honey, for cleaning the grill."

"You're welcome, and we're grilling tonight. Fiona and Ned, we're not having anything special, just hamburgers. Want to join us?"

"Well, you don't have to ask me twice. Absolutely," said Fiona. "What can I bring? I know, I make a killer lemon cream pie, and it doesn't take any time to make."

"Great," said George. "Annie has already made her terrific pea salad, and we'll do cheeseburgers. I'm getting hungry all ready."

"We should invite Layla and Mr. Soo. He'll smell the grilling and be hurt he wasn't invited."

"By all means," said George, "give them a call."

Annie called Layla, and both she and Mr. Soo eagerly accepted the invitation. Layla said she was in the process of making baked macaroni and cheese for Mr. Soo and would bring that with them.

"That sounds terrific. I haven't had macaroni and cheese for ages. We'll have drinks and snacks about seven, and George can fire up the grill at eight. See you then."

"My god, did you say Layla was bringing macaroni and cheese? Cheeseburgers and macaroni and cheese, I do believe I've died and gone to food heaven!" exclaimed Fiona.

At seven, two sets of neighbors made their way to the Boones' back lanai. Fiona told Layla she loved macaroni and cheese and was so glad she had made a large casserole.

"Me too," said Mr. Soo. "I never tried it before Layla fixed it, and now I must have it at least once a week. It is a pleasure for my palate."

"What have you got there?" Layla asked, indicating the pie case Ned was carrying.

"It's a lemon cream pie, delicious and very refreshing after a big meal. I'm sure you'll love it. Everyone is always surprised at how light it is and so sweet," Fiona said.

"That sounds yummy. I hope Annie has plenty of snacks. I'm hungry just walking over to their house."

"Me too!" said Mr. Soo.

"I had a light lunch after eighteen holes of golf today, then spent a couple of hours with Donnie at the Visitors Center. When George invited us for hamburgers, my mouth started watering, and that was hours ago," declared Ned.

They all sat around the table on the Boones' lanai. Drinks were made, snacks were laid out, and everyone was digging in, enjoying the food and company.

"Layla, I heard you and Fiona had a very successful outing today," Annie said.

"We sure did, and Fiona called hunky Herb who came to the store and helped us out with our choices. We were unhappy with the vanity choices, and he suggested his partner, an excellent carpenter who apprenticed under Marty, make what we had in mind. A great idea, so we agreed."

"Wade is a terrific carpenter. He did some excellent restoration work at the Country Club after the storm, very impressive."

"I still say those two gorgeous men are the biggest waste of testosterone on the island," said Fiona.

"What's that mean?" George asked.

All eyes turned toward George. "What, what did I say?" he asked in response to their stares.

"George, surely you knew that Herb and Wade are a couple?" Fiona asked.

"What do you mean a couple?" George asked, looking around the table as everyone looked at him in disbelief.

"Oh, for heaven's sakes, George, they're gay, didn't you know?" asked Annie, shaking her head.

"Of course, I didn't know. How would I know? Did all of you know?" George asked his fellow tablemates.

Everyone nodded, saying yes.

"How come I'm always the last to know these type of things? I just don't understand it. I'm starting the grill." George got up and went over to his grill, leaving those at the table suppressing laughter.

After dinner and dessert, everyone one made their way to lounge chairs, complaining they ate too much.

"I feel miserable, but I'm glad I overate on such terrific food. I won't be able to eat for a day or two," moaned Fiona.

At the top of the road, looking down on the terrace of houses, the sheriff watched those on the Boones' lanai. He pulled binoculars from the glove compartment and brought them into focus. There was food and laughter, neighbors enjoying themselves, being neighborly.

"Well, well," he said out loud, "the Boones and the Kellers. That's a new group, and there's Layla and Mr. Soo. This is what island life should be about. Hope the Kellers and Mr. Soo locked up before going to the Boones'."

Annie sat down on the glider with a sigh. "Honey, that was a great idea you had last night making extra burgers. They tasted great nuked, but why did we eat so much?"

"Probably because we had to finish off Fiona's pie. You've got to get the recipe from her. That was great, and I'm not that much of a pie person." George was standing on the side of the lanai looking over toward Layla's. "Honey, come here a minute."

"OK, but getting up is a chore," Annie said, making her way to the rail. "Oh, gosh, I wonder if something has happened." Annie saw Layla sitting on her porch steps, chin cupped in her hands, gazing in the distance. "I think I'll go over and see if something's wrong. She was going sketching today. That should have made her happy."

"Annie, I was thinking last night as we were talking about things in our youth, Layla hasn't any friends her age here. She pals around with you gals and lives with Mr. Soo. She has workers her age, but they work for her, and with her background, a friendship would not be possible. That might be hard on her whether she realizes it or not. I know she talks to Dewey several times weekly, but that's not like having a living, breathing person you can interact with."

"George, you have a valid point that I never considered. I don't know of anyone her age that I could get her acquainted with, especially a girlfriend. Gals like to confide to girlfriends while they're single."

"When they marry, do you share everything with their husband?"

"Lord, no!" Annie exclaimed as she left to go and check on Layla.

Approaching Layla, Annie spoke out, "You look pretty sad for someone that was going to enjoy a morning of sketching."

"No, I'm not sad, just pensive. I had a wonderful time sketching and did a darn good job of capturing a windsurfer. I'm feeling hormonal or something. I want to call Dewey, but I don't want to sound too needy. Thought I would just sit here and wait for that beautiful man to come and deliver bathroom fixtures."

Annie frowned and asked, "Layla, what exactly are you feeling?"

"Ever since Fiona told me how she met Ned, and let me tell you it was one erotic story, I've had this overwhelming desire to be with Dewey. It's like something has awakened in me."

"My god, Layla, what did Fiona tell you?"

"Did I hear someone mention my name?" Fiona said, walking up the driveway.

"What have you done to Layla?" Annie laughed, looking at Fiona.

"What did I do?" Fiona asked.

"It was that romantic, erotic story of how you and Ned got together. Don't get me wrong, ladies, I'm glad to have this feeling again. This means I'm back or almost back being female again. It's just that I'm unsure what I should do next."

"How did you and Ned meet?" Annie asked Fiona.

"I'll tell you the whole tale one day soon, but we need to be sure Layla is thinking straight first," Fiona said to Annie.

Turning into the street between the homes, the ladies saw Herb's truck, and an audible sigh was heard from Layla. "Well darn, looking at him right now is all I need."

"You are getting in a bad way," said Fiona, shaking her head.

Layla hit the remote, and the garage doors came open. Herb maneuvered his truck so that the items could be unloaded and taken into the garage. This was Layla first sighting of Wade. As he got out of the truck and came around to help Herb unload, she let out an audible gasp. Fiona and Annie looked sharply at Layla and grinned.

"Is this a welcoming committee?" Herb asked.

"Annie was keeping Layla company while she waited, and I came to talk to Wade about an idea for Layla's wall unit," Fiona said. "The unit would house shelves for books and her large flat-screen television. I was thinking maybe you could custom-make it and stain it the same color as the wood throughout the house."

"Would it be possible for me look at the wall area and the wood you referenced?" Wade asked.

"Sure, Layla, can we get inside today?" Fiona asked, looking in Layla's direction.

Layla did not answer until Annie nudged her, then she said, "Sorry, I was out sketching today, and I think I spent too much time in the sun. My brain must have gotten fried. What did you say?"

Fiona looked surprised at Layla and repeated Wade's question. "Wade asked if it would be possible to look inside to consider whether he would undertake making the shelving for your living room."

"Sure, I've got the keys with me. I'll open up, and you guys can come on up when you're done unloading."

"If everyone is all set, I'll go back home and see if George is still moaning over eating too much for lunch, and, Fiona, he's blaming you for making such a good pie that he just had to finish it all."

"How lovely," Fiona said, laughing. "Serves him right, but thank him for the compliment."

"He asked me to get your recipe, but I won't be in any rush to make the pie, for fear we both will overindulge again."

Fiona and Layla went into the house so Layla could open it up and get some fresh ocean breezes into the living room. Annie went back to tend to George.

Annie found George lying in the glider, long legs hung over the side. "Are you feeling any better?"

"My stomach is sore."

"Want me to rub your tummy? That's what I did when the kids had a tummy ache," Annie said.

"That would be very kind of you. What's wrong with Layla?"

Annie pushed George over and sat down next to him. She pulled up his T-shirt and began rubbing his stomach. "She's beginning to have adult feelings for Dewey, which surprised her. She seems a bit conflicted about, shall we say, her awakening."

"Good for Dewey, about damned time. So when does she plan to see him?"

"Well, that is where her conflict comes in. She wants to wait until her house is finished, and they can have total privacy. Even though his home is huge, there is Agnes and Ted, and Layla wants their first time to be special."

"Good lord, why doesn't she just meet him in San Francisco or San Diego or even Malibu," George said with disgust.

"Because, sweetheart, sometimes women get romantic ideas in their head. They picture their first time with someone, right out of a romance novel. Layla has been through so much in the past year, she has this romantic picture in her head, and it has to play out for her."

"Seems like things were easier when we were young."

"You and I never went through what Layla has. We fell in love, got married, had kids, and here we are today. Except for some financial hurdles and the usual child-rearing nightmares, things have been good for us. We've been lucky. Best yet, we're still in love with each other," Annie said with a smile.

"Annie, we are the new face of seniors. There are a lot of us now and more on the way. We exercise, eat healthy, are happily married to the spouse we started life with, and are enthusiastic about our future. We engage in an active sex life, and we feel alive."

"That's deep. When did you come up with this revelation?"

"It dawned on me the other afternoon when Ned came over and Fiona went over to greet him. I could see the same type of chemistry between them that you and I share. I don't think they're pouring over real estate stats or blueprints every night. They both are fit, and except for the past twenty-four hours when we all slipped off the healthy-eating wagon, they eat properly and are involved with our community. They are busy, active seniors." Saying that, George reached up, tilted Annie's chin toward him, and kissed her.

Wade and Herb stood in Layla's living room and looked around in marvel. "What a fabulous home you are turning this into. This wood is beyond description," said Wade.

"Mr. Soo had all this wood imported, and the intricate carvings are a wonder," Layla said with pride in her voice. "I feel lucky I was able to purchase it and to find the right people to restore it to what it once was."

Wade turned to Layla, saying, "I know this seems like a dumb statement at this time, but if for some reason you ever want to sell your home, please call me first. I would cherish this wood, and I think living here would be an honor."

"Wade, after what you just said, if I ever do sell, I promise I'll contact you first," Layla said, smiling.

"Wade, you do know that by the time Layla is finished, this home will be worth over two million?" Fiona asked.

"That wouldn't be a problem," Wade said with confidence.

He walked to the only wall in the living room where shelving would work and studied it for a few moments. "Yes, wood shelves in the same color as the wood throughout would be possible and add to the drama of this room. What color are you going to paint the walls?" he asked, turning to Layla.

"All walls in the house will be done in Sawyer white. I wanted something subtle that would highlight the wood," said Layla.

"Excellent choice. I could make floating shelves. Those are shelves that are secured to the wall but without the linkage of sidepieces. It eliminates the boxy feeling of the shelving. What do you think, Fiona?"

"Wonderful. It would make a stunning statement. What do you think, Layla?"

"I never imagined anything like that either, but I can picture it now, and I like what I see. Let's do it, Wade."

"Great. I feel blessed that I can have an imprint on this house," Wade said with a genuine smile. "Can I have a tour of the rest of your home?"

"Sure, let me take you around. Excuse the kitchen. I'm in the process of cleaning up the cabinets myself." Layla led Wade through to the other rooms, leaving Herb and Fiona in the living room.

Herb turned to Fiona, saying, "Don't worry about Wade having enough money to afford this home. He's very rich. No one knows this outside Donnie Munson and me, but he's a trust fund baby, and it's a huge trust fund. He came here when he graduated college to get out of the reach of his family. When they realized he was happy and successful, they released his money, but he hardly ever touches it. Money doesn't play much of a part in his happiness."

"Who knew?" Fiona said, shaking her head. "I promise you, if Layla ever decides to sell, Wade will be my first call. Frankly, I see her marrying Dewey and moving to Utah, but that's just between us, Herb."

"You're kidding. I had no idea they even knew each other."

"They met during the storm, and Dewey fell in love with her at first sight. It's a long sorted story, but Dewey has stayed by her side through all the disasters she has encountered. Bringing this house back to life is really about Layla bringing Layla back to life."

CHAPTER 48

Fiona stayed with Layla after Herb and Wade left while she closed up the house. "Fiona, if you and Ned want to come over tomorrow and browse, here's another counter of heaven-knows-what."

"I'll just rummage through things now," Fiona said, scanning the items on the counter. "There are a couple of other things I can use."

"Please take anything you like," said Layla.

"I'll call Annie and ask her and George over before Chris boxes things up and takes them to his mother-in-law."

After locking up, Layla turned to Fiona and said, "Thank you for your idea to have Wade do the shelving. I've got to call Dewey. I'm more in control now," Layla said, trying to reassure herself.

*   *   *

Dewey and Ted were outside when the phone rang, so Agnes answered, "Layla, good to hear your voice. How's the remodeling going?"

"Making progress, Agnes, but it's taking longer than I anticipated. What's new with everyone there?"

"Not much, snow is gone, and Dewey and Ted are taking down the storm windows and putting up the screens, which means more snow. I told them it was too early, but they both are anxious for spring to get here. Dewey loves the sunshine.

Growing up in Southern California and then spending time in Maui makes him miss the warm climate and sunshine even more. Utah will have to be his home for years, but at heart, he's a sunshine, warm-climate man.

"I've answered Dewey's cell, so let me take this outside to him. I know he's anxious to talk with you," Agnes said, carrying on their conversation as she went outside.

Dewey took the offered phone from Agnes and walked toward the patio for some privacy. "Layla, I was wondering if you were going to call today."

"The day got away from me, and I mentally drifted. I went sketching this morning. Mr. Soo thought it would help me relax, and of course, he was right. It has been such a hectic week, and then I had today's delivery. Remember, I told you about that? Fiona arranged with Wade, who is making the bathroom vanities, to design my living-room-wall unit. It will be stained the same color as the wood throughout the house, and the shelving will be floating shelves. I think it will have a stunning visual impact. I'm still cleaning out the kitchen drawers and shelves. I wish you were here to see some of things I've found. There are items I have no idea what they could be. If I wasn't trying to get so much done, I would enjoy all this." Layla took a deep breath, then continued, "Dewey, do you know Wade and Herb?"

"No, I haven't met them, but I've seen them around Paia. Why do you ask?"

"They are so good-looking, and do you know they have been a couple for a number of years? Fiona said quite a few of the ladies have tried to change the persuasion of each of them without any luck. She said it's a waste of testosterone. I tend to agree with her."

Dewey raised his voice slightly and asked, "Do I need to be jealous of a couple of gay men who will be working on your home?"

"No, I'm just telling you gossip among us gals. Dewey, you never have to worry about me, you're the only man in my life," Layla said softly.

"I wish I was there right now."

"I wish you were here too. I want you to hold me and kiss me, and I'm not sure I can wait until everything is finished on the house."

"Are you serious?"

"Yes," Layla whispered.

Dewey cleared this throat. "I have to be here through Thursday, but I'll have a flight crew and plane ready to leave Friday morning. I'll make arrangements for us to have a suite at the Four Seasons through Sunday night. I have to head back to Utah on Monday. I'm not talking about making love. I'm just talking about us being with each other, talking, laughing, catching up, and if something develops, fine. If not, that's fine too. Will you pick me up at the airport on Friday?"

"Yes, and about making love, I was looking forward to it. You've been patient way too long, and now I can't wait any longer."

Dewey held the phone away from his ear and looked at it for several seconds before he answered, "Honey, you've made me a happy man. I'll get back to you on with my arrival time. I'm speechless at the moment, you'll have to carry the conversation."

"I have much to accomplish before Friday. I'll have George and Annie come over and make sure everything is secure for the weekend once the crew leaves on Friday. They obviously will know we are going away together," Layla said with a laugh.

"Tell them. They've wanted us together for a long time. They'll be happy. They both know that I fell in love with you at their home. My god, that was almost a year ago. That doesn't seem possible."

"Was it that long ago? You're right, so much has happened since then. My divorce, moving to New York, going with you, Annie, and George on vacation, ending up here, buying Mr.

Soo's former home, and this remodeling. I can't believe so much good came from so much bad."

"Funny, that's how it seems, doesn't it? Kyle and Kim coming to Hawaii to get their award, a storm, and the murders. All I know is that it brought us together," Dewey said.

"I just remembered I was going shopping with Fiona on Saturday. I'm going to tell her you and I will be going away for a long weekend. She'll be very happy for us. We've become friends, and she's a hoot. She told me the story of how she snared Ned. It was very exotic. It may surprise you to know, but she is crazy in love with him and he with her. In fact, they are very touchy-feely with each other. Mr. Soo and I were at Annie and George's for a cookout yesterday evening, and Ned and Fiona were there too. I was surprised at how lovingly they treated each other."

"Wait a minute. Did you just say Ned and Fiona were at Annie and George's with you and Mr. Soo for a cookout?"

"Yes, we had a great time. Everyone talked about goofy things they did in their youth. That Fiona was a wild thing, but she had a plan and she kept her focus. Got her degree in interior design, was good enough for the Italian Olympic shooting team, and when she set her eye on Ned, he was a goner. It was a fun evening, a lot of laughter."

"Somehow I'm surprised that Annie and George enjoyed Fiona. You know what George always called her?"

"I believe he has changed his mind about Fiona. In fact, after hearing Fiona's stories and seeing how demonstrative she and Ned were toward each other is when I began to think of us being together. It seemed that everyone had someone they loved. Yet here I was, an ocean away from you. I spent most of this morning and afternoon trying to come up with a way I could entice you to visit without my home being finished, and here you came to my rescue."

Dewey shook his head, still uncertain this was his Layla. "I'm sorry we have to wait until Friday, but it's the soonest I can get away. Don't worry about telling people of our long weekend. As far as I'm concerned, you can stand in the middle of the street and tell all of Paia."

"Friday is fine. That will give me time to get myself looking feminine again. I need a haircut, a manicure, and a pedicure. I've been so busy with the house, I'm looking pretty ragged. If it's all the same with you, I'll just keep it to a few about our weekend plans," Layla said.

They ended their conversation with Dewey telling Layla he would call her back with his arrival time on Friday and she assuring him she would be waiting at the airport when his plane arrived.

Layla went into the kitchen and began to assemble a casserole when Mr. Soo returned from his walk. "Layla, have you called Dewey?"

"Yes, we just finished."

"I hope you gave him my best wishes."

"I always do, and he asked about you as well. I have some surprising news for you. Dewey is flying in on Friday, and he and I are going to spend a weekend together at the Four Seasons."

Mr. Soo went to Layla and placed her hand between both of his. "I could not be happier for both of you. I believe you two will share many wonderful years together, and this will be your beginning."

"Thank you. I think you are right." Layla smiled fondly at him.

After dinner, Layla placed a call to the Boones. "I have a couple of things I want to talk to you both about."

"Let me get Annie on the extension." George called out for Annie to pick up the extension.

"All set, what's going on?" George asked.

"First, if you can come over tomorrow, I have another counter full of stuff for you to go through."

"Great," they both said.

"Now I hope you both are sitting down," Layla said with a slight laugh. "Dewey is flying in on Friday, and we are spending a long weekend together at the Four Seasons."

"Well, about damn time," said George. "I was beginning to wonder if you two were ever going to get serious."

"I'm so happy for you both," Annie said. "I feel this will be the beginning of a relationship that will last."

"Thank you, and I agree with you. Could I ask both or one of you to make sure my house is locked on Friday and opened on Monday, if you're going to be available, that is? I'll be home sometime Monday afternoon."

"We will be glad to do that for you. We'll get keys from you tomorrow," George said.

"Hello, Fiona here," she said, answering her cell phone.

"Hi, Fiona, it's Layla, and I desperately need your help."

"What's happened?" Fiona asked, anxiety in her voice.

"I'm picking up Dewey at the airport Friday morning, and we are spending a long weekend at the Four Seasons. I took an inventory of my appearance, and I look terrible. I need a manicure, pedicure, facial, waxing, haircut, and a massage. Can you arrange some of that for both of us? And whatever you want is my treat."

"Did you say you're spending this coming weekend with Dewey?"

"Yes, finally," Layla said.

"Thank god. When a woman drools over two gay men, I begin to worry about her mental state. I can help. I'll make arrangements for us to have the works on Wednesday with the exception of the haircut. One of my best girlfriends is retired from a very high-end salon, and she is a marvel at cutting hair. I'll arrange for us to go over to her house on Thursday, and she can take care of your hair. Your color is terrific. The sun has bleached it out beautifully, but it does look like you are somewhere between a long and short style without any shaping."

"I knew I could count on your help. Thank you so much. I want to look fetching when I meet Dewey's plane."

"You shall, my dear. Maybe we should get you some lovely underwear for the upcoming occasion?"

"You're right, and a few other sexy things to wear for dinners. I'm grateful you're looking out for me, and Dewey will be too!"

"I'll get back with you tomorrow and give you all the details. Sleep well tonight and have erotic dreams," Fiona said, ringing off.

* * *

Ned looked wide-eyed at Fiona. "Did you just say Dewey and Layla were going away for a weekend?"

"Can't believe it myself. She really needs to get laid."

"Fiona!" Ned said, gawking at his wife.

"And poor Dewey. He must be horny as hell after all this time, waiting for her to come around," Fiona said, walking over to the counter stool where Ned sat.

"Fiona, there are still times when you amaze me. I never thought about the situation," Ned said, putting his arms around his wife's waist.

"That's because when it comes to sexual things, I'm quite aware. I've always been keenly aware of sexual situations."

"I know you have, and I'm just the lucky man you chose to share that keen awareness with."

* * *

Annie rushed into the kitchen just as George was hanging up the extension. "George, do you believe it?"

"I'm going to call Dewey. Get on the extension."

"Honey, do you think you should?"

"Sure," George said, grinning, "he may need some guidance."

"Oh brother," Annie said as she left to go to an extension phone.

George dialed Dewey's cell number, surprised that Dewey answered immediately. "Layla, is that you?"

"Sorry, it's me, George Boone."

"George, I thought it might be Layla calling back."

"You afraid she was going to back out on your upcoming weekend?"

"She called you guys all ready? Good, then she was serious. Honestly, I still can't believe this all happened so quickly after so long a time. She actually was the one that wanted us to get together sooner rather than wait until she had her home completed. I'm going to make it all happen this coming weekend."

"Now, Dewey, let me make a suggestion," chimed in George. "Send her a bunch of red roses so that she gets them tomorrow. She'll be at her house working in the kitchen. That'll thrill her."

"George, that's so romantic of you," Annie said admiringly.

"Honey, I'm a very romantic guy."

"I'll call the florist right after we hang up. Three or four dozen red roses should be plenty, don't you think?"

"No more than three. You want to be sure she can carry them back to Mr. Soo's," Annie said, chuckling.

"Annie, could you please hang the extension up? I want to discuss something man-to-man with Dewey."

"Oh, for heaven's sakes, I'm hanging up now," said Annie, then she quietly walked into the kitchen behind George.

"Dewey, just wanted to remind you, don't forget protection."

"When I returned from Maui after the storm, I bought a box of condoms and put a sticky note on them that said, For Layla Only. That box traveled with us on vacation and to Maui and back. Believe me, I won't forget to take it this time," said Dewey.

"If you have time before you go back to Utah, stop by and say a quick hello. Annie and I would love to see you."

"I would like to see you both and Mr. Soo too. I'll fit that into my scheduling. I really do miss all of you," Dewey said with sincerity.

When George hung up the phone, he turned and found Annie leaning against the wall behind him; he jumped, startled. "How long have you been standing there?"

"I heard everything on your end of the conversation, but I'm dying to know what Dewey said," Annie said, grinning.

"Can't we guys have any secrets?"

"Sure you can. I just want to know what Dewey said when you told him to take protection. Is that asking too much?"

"Annie, that's a man thing," George said with a frown, "but I suppose I might as well tell you or you'll bug me all night long." George repeated his entire conversation with Dewey.

"Thank you, darling, and I'm especially excited to hear Dewey will stop by to say a quick hello on his way to the airport. Let's celebrate. Fix us one of your special brandy Mai Tais," Annie said, smiling sweetly, trying to get back on George's good side.

"Can you scrape up something to munch on?"

"No problem, honey," Annie said as she began rummaging through the refrigerator.

Annie and George were sitting on the back lanai enjoying their drinks and snacks when Ned came out on his front lanai with a cup of coffee.

"Looks like Fiona has banished Ned out of the kitchen. Ask him to come over for a drink," Annie said to George.

"Ned, come on over. We're having brandy Mai Tais. We're celebrating," George called out, shielding his mouth toward Mr. Soo's direction.

"That sounds great." Ned made his way over to the Boones' as George went inside to make him a drink.

"I imagine you and Fiona have heard the good news about Layla and Dewey's weekend plans by now," asked Annie.

"Fiona is thrilled. Layla asked her for assistance in getting herself looking feminine again, and she's anxious to tackle that project. She's fixing us a healthy dinner after all we ate last night. She will have a fit when she sees I'm over here having a cocktail and eating snacks," Ned said, laughing.

George brought Ned his drink; after a long draw on the straw, Ned said, "This is terrific! I've never had a brandy Mai Tai before."

Fiona stepped out on their lanai and spotted Ned across the street. "Ned Keller, are you drinking and eating too?"

"Busted! Lock up and come on over. You've got to try one of George's special brandy Mai Tais. It's a celebration."

"Did you say a brandy Mai Tai?"

"They're excellent. Come on over," Ned coaxed.

After locking up, Fiona made her way across the street. George offered her a freshly made drink. "Yum, this is so good. Why haven't we ever had something like this before?"

"Our daughter hates rum, and a friend introduced her to using brandy in its place. Since the cost of a good brandy is considerably more than good rum, we only have brandy Mai Tais on special occasions. Naturally, the weekend plans of Layla and Dewey are cause for celebration," Annie said.

"I agree," said Fiona. "Annie, weren't you worried about Layla this afternoon the way she drooled over Wade and Herb?"

"She was admiring lovely male bodies. They are quite a pair of lookers."

"Just a minute here," George said, frowning. "Ned and I aren't exactly out-of-shape old men."

"Of course, you aren't, darling. I'm speaking from Layla's perspective. I think she got turned on."

"I'm sure it's been over two years since she had sex, and well, frankly, all things considered, how good could Kyle have been?" asked Fiona.

"Fiona!" exclaimed both Ned and Annie, while George burst out laughing.

"Fiona, I like that you come right out and say what the rest of us are thinking."

"Thank you, George. I've never been one to hold my tongue," Fiona said with a nod.

"Not to change the subject but, honey, Donnie asked if you will accompany me tomorrow when he and I meet at the Visitors Center."

"No, no, no, I'm not getting involved with any those projects of his that end up consuming so much time. One member of this family should be enough."

"He wanted to consult you on a design aspect, and like he said, the best interior designer on the island is living just a few steps from the center. The least he could do was ask for your input."

"Donnie actually said that about me?" Fiona asked pleased.

Under the table, Annie nudged George's thigh and smiled, knowing that Fiona had succumbed to Donnie's flattery.

"He certainly did, so will you join me tomorrow?" Ned asked.

"OK, dear, I've got to see what Donnie has up his sleeve."

"George, I hear you had a great input on the center. Donnie said almost all the interior design was spun from original ideas you offered. How do you think things are shaping up?"

"To tell you the truth, since the first time I offered Donnie my ideas, I haven't been back to see how things have progressed."

"Join us tomorrow. You will be surprised how well things are coming along. Annie, why don't you make it a foursome?" Ned asked.

"Thanks, Ned, but I'm just not ready yet. Of course, I will visit the center, but it will have to be on my own time. Thank you for asking."

To lighten the mood, Fiona lifted her drink. "I would like to propose a toast to Layla and Dewey."

"Fiona, keep it respectable," warned Ned.

Fiona looked at Ned and smiled. "To Layla and Dewey, may this be the start of much happiness for them both. Personally, I hope they return with wide grins on their faces."

"Hear, hear" was heard from those around the table.

CHAPTER 49

Layla was working in the kitchen when Chris interrupted her. "Layla, there's something I need to talk with you about."

"Sure, Chris, what's up?"

"By the end of Wednesday, all the wood restoration will be complete, and we'll be ready to start on the floors. Where do we begin?"

"I'll call Fiona. I don't know what she has planned with the other contractors."

Layla pulled out her cell phone and dialed Fiona. "Fiona, it's Layla. Would it be possible for you to come over? Chris and I need to discuss something with you about doing the floors."

"I'll be right there."

"Fiona is on her way, and we'll let her figure out where we go from here."

There was a knock on the screen, and Chris let Annie and George into the kitchen.

"Hi, folks. Chris, I want to tell you what's going to be happening. I'll be leaving Friday morning, and I won't be back until Monday afternoon. I'll leave you the Boones' phone number, and if there is any problem, please call them or Fiona. The air-conditioning people will start work on Monday, so there might be quite a few folks around. Remember, any problems call the Boones or Fiona."

"Glad to see you taking some time away. You've been working really hard," said Chris.

There was another knock on the door. Chris went to the door and exclaimed, "Holy cow! Who gets those?"

"Someone named Layla," came a voice hidden behind three-dozen long-stemmed red roses.

"Layla, come and get your flowers."

"My gosh!" exclaimed Layla as she lifted the huge vase of roses over to the kitchen counter. She removed the card from its holder and read, "Layla, Friday! Love, Dewey."

Annie went over to Layla. "Lovely."

"I've had flowers before but never in this abundance."

There was another knock on the door, and Fiona entered.

"My god," she said, walking directly to the flowers. "I'm assuming these are from Dewey."

"Aren't they beautiful and so many?" Layla said, beaming.

"Let's see the card," Fiona said, taking the card from Layla. After reading the greeting, she turned to Layla, saying, "Maybe we won't need to bother with the fancy underwear after all."

Layla smiled weakly at Fiona. Chris saw Fiona and said, "Fiona, we need your input on where we should start on the floors. Josie and I will be able to begin that work on Thursday."

Layla was grateful Chris drew Fiona's interest away from the flowers and her underwear purchases, so she turned to Annie and George. "Please go ahead and take anything from this counter full of stuff. I'll ask Chris to box it up and free the space for my final cleanout."

Fiona, Chris, and Josie were in the dining area discussing floors, Annie and George were going through the items on the counter, and Layla decided to go out on the lanai and phone Dewey to thank him for the fabulous roses. As she opened her cell phone, there was a knock on the screen door. George turned to see who was there and loudly announced, "Mr. Soo, welcome, welcome," as he opened the screen, ushering him inside.

"I saw so many people heading over here, I was afraid something was wrong. My goodness, what a large floral display, yours, Layla?"

"Mr. Soo!" Layla exclaimed and went over and hugged him. "I'm so happy to see you here. Dewey sent the roses. Aren't they lovely?"

"Lovely flowers for his lady love," Mr. Soo said softly.

"Thank you" was all Layla could say as tears formed in her eyes.

Fiona heard Mr. Soo's gentle voice and went to greet him. "Mr. Soo, a pleasure to see you here. Can I take you on a tour? Chris and Josie have done a wonderful job refurbishing the wood, and we were just discussing where he should start on the floors. Layla, he should start buffing, and as soon as the air-conditioning work is completed, then the floors can be stained. I don't want any stain on before that work is completed because of dust particles and who knows what else in the air. Stain the fourth bedroom first. That way, if any furniture is delivered early, it will give us a place to store it. As soon as that floor is finished, I will have the painter in to paint that room. The second room to stain should be the living room, then we'll paint so Wade can start work on the shelves. I don't think it will take him too long to design and make the bathroom cabinets. What do you think?"

"Fiona, I defer to your judgment. You are the expert."

Fiona walked toward Mr. Soo and extended her hand. "Mr. Soo, let's tour."

"Whew," said Layla, "what a morning."

Fiona, Chris, and Mr. Soo were in the living room, Mr. Soo commenting on the wonderful wood restoration.

"Fiona, is that your lovely voice I hear?" Marty asked, coming in from the front lanai.

"Marty, dear friend," said Mr. Soo, walking over to shake hands.

"Mr. Soo, I'm so proud of what Chris, my grandson, and Josie have done to restore your wonderful wood to its original beauty. Come out to the lanai and see what Josie and I have done with the Shoji screen frames."

Mr. Soo, Fiona, Chris, and Josie followed Marty to the front lanai.

"Marty, are you finished?" asked Fiona.

"Yes, I finished adding the final ridge for the glass top, and Josie stained it yesterday. I was checking to make sure everything was ready for your glass man to come and measure."

"This is wonderful!" exclaimed Mr. Soo. "I can't believe you made this remarkable table from those frame pieces. The woodcarvings have once again been restored to their original beauty. I'm so grateful this was possible."

Fiona smiled fondly at Josie. "Josie's tiny hands were able to clean the small intricate carvings on the frames and stain everything evenly. She did a very professional job. Marty's craftsmanship enabled him to design and build this table that will sit in front of Layla's large sofa. I'm having a clear glass top made that will allow all the carvings to show through."

George and Annie joined the group.

"Marty, this is so beautiful!" exclaimed Annie. "I can't imagine how you managed to shape all those straight frame pieces into this beautiful table. You are a genius."

"Thank you, Mrs. Boone," beamed Marty. "While there are two able-bodied young men here, I would like to ask if Chris and George can help me carry this into one of the rooms. I want to get it inside now that it's finished."

George laughed. "Marty, calling me a young man will get you everywhere. Come on, Chris, you and I can get this inside. Fiona, where do you want it?"

"Could you please sit it in the middle of the dining room? That will enable the glass man to measure it easily."

George and Chris toted the table into the dining room with everyone following to make sure they did a good job.

"How's that?" asked Chris.

"Perfect. Thank you, gentlemen," Fiona said.

"Well, it's time Annie and I head back home. I've just been called a young man and a gentleman, can't do any better than that," said George, grinning.

"Layla, I've got a couple of things from the counter. Oh, before I forget, do you have a key for us?"

"Thanks, Annie, I would have forgotten." Layla went to her tote bag and began rummaging through it, soon producing another spare key. She handed the key ring to Annie and George, then gave them Chris's phone number.

Fiona and Mr. Soo were on tour. Marty had returned to the lanai to clean the area, and Chris and Josie were back at work on the wood. Layla went to the back lanai and dialed Dewey's cell number.

A very professional-sounding Dewey answered, "Hello, McMaster here."

"Dewey, it's Layla, and I've caught you at a bad time. I wanted to let you know that I received your beautiful bouquet of red roses, and I'm thrilled. I can't wait for Friday, and I'll thank you properly."

"Excuse me, folks. I have to take this call," Dewey said, walking out of his meeting and closing the door behind him. "Layla, I'm glad you like the flowers. I've missed you so much, no, I've missed us so much."

"Me too, it's so crazy here right now, the house is full of people, but all I wanted to do is hear the sound of your voice and thank you. I know you have to get back. I'll be there for you at the airport on Friday, and I can't wait!"

"I'll see you then, honey, and yes, I've got to get back to the meeting. Until Friday!" Dewey closed the phone and went back to his meeting a happier man.

Fiona was finishing her tour with Mr. Soo. "Well, what do you think so far?"

"I'm amazed at how wonderful my former home looks. You, Layla, and all these talented craftspeople are turning this into a masterpiece of island living."

Layla walked over to Mr. Soo and grabbed his small arm, hugging it to her. "Thank you, Mr. Soo, we are all grateful for your glowing words of approval."

Mr. Soo went across the street back to his home, and Layla continued working on the kitchen cabinets and drawers.

Fiona went to speak with Marty. "Marty, your sofa table is breathtaking. I'm going to call my glass person when I get home, and hopefully, he'll come out tomorrow. Is there enough of the frame pieces to construct a small end table that would go next to a chair? It doesn't need to be large, no lamp will be set on it, something to hold, say a drink, and a bottom shelf for books or magazines."

"That should be no problem. How soon would you need it made? You see, this old back needs some time off," Marty said.

"Layla and I won't be able to go to Oahu until next week to find just the right chair. When we do, I'll get you measurements, and you can make the table accordingly. Take a couple of weeks off. Enjoy some playtime with your great-grandson."

"Perfect, just tell Chris when you'll need me back, and thank you, Fiona, for allowing me to work on this project. It's been a sheer delight."

Fiona gave Marty a peck on his cheek, saying, "Thank you, Marty, for lending your expertise to this home."

Fiona left Layla's and was walking in the middle of the street making notes on whom to call when the sheriff pulled up almost directly behind her. He leaned his head out the window and called, "Fiona, you shouldn't be walking in the middle of the road. You didn't even realize I was behind you."

"Huh, oh, my goodness, Sheriff, you're right. I was so absorbed in what I was doing I was oblivious to where I was walking. Thank you for looking out for me," Fiona said, walking back to the sheriff's truck.

"How's Layla's house coming along?"

"We are beginning to see the light at the end of the tunnel. Chris will start on the floors later this week, then the painters, then Herb and Wade are redoing the bathrooms. Goodness, that sounds like the light might be dimmer than I thought," Fiona said with a slight frown.

"It's exciting with Layla's home getting this major makeover and the Visitors Center, Paia is quite the construction hub," the sheriff said with a smile. "Who knows everything could be finished around the same time."

"You're right, Sheriff, I never thought of that. I consider myself lucky that I have Chris. He and Josie have done wonders on the wood restoration. I recommend him to anyone that needs that type of work."

"Good for you. We need to keep the young people here in Paia with good jobs. Well, take care and no more walking in the middle of the street," the sheriff said, tipping his hat toward Fiona and driving up the hill to Hana Highway.

CHAPTER 50

Fiona walked into her home. "Ned, where are you?"

"In the office, dear."

Walking into their third bedroom, now a shared office, Fiona said, "I have just made a fool of myself, I'm so embarrassed. I was walking back from Layla's, making a mental list of people I had to phone, and I lost track of where I was walking. The sheriff pulled in behind me and admonished me for walking in the middle of the street. I felt like an idiot. We chatted, but I couldn't wait for him to be on his way."

"Just think, honey, you might have gotten a ticket."

"That would have been humiliating." Fiona went over and sat down on Ned's lap. "Wait till you hear who showed up at Layla's."

"Elvis?"

"No, dear, he's in Kauai this week. Mr. Soo! We were all curious if he would visit his old home, and he walked right in and had compliments for the work Chris and Josie have done. Made me so proud."

"I've got to get over there and see how things are progressing. Next time you go, drag me along."

"You should see the huge bouquet of red roses Dewey sent Layla with a very seductive card. There were at least three dozen long-stemmed beauties."

"You've always been my long-stemmed beauty."

"Ned, you're such a romantic," Fiona said, planting a kiss on his forehead. "Marty finished making the coffee table from the Shoji screen frames. You cannot imagine the beauty of this table.

323

You'll be blown away when you see how it's turned out. That's one of the phone calls I've got to make. Call the glass man and see if he can come and measure for a tabletop piece of glass. Then I've got to call the Grand Wailea and make reservations for Layla and me to have the works on Wednesday. Plus, I'll call Choo Choo Bacca and get Layla in for a haircut on Thursday. Layla and I will do some shopping for her on Wednesday while we are in Wailea. Whew, I had better get going."

"That Choo Choo may cut great hair, but that name is so stupid. She had to have stolen the idea from *Star Wars*."

"Absolutely, that's exactly where she got her Choo Choo from. Her career was going nowhere, even though she was outstanding in color and cut. She decided it was her name that was hindering her. Ned, if I tell you her real name, you must make a solemn promise to God you won't tell a living soul."

"I promise," Ned said with a mock serious face.

"It's Matilda Bacca. Within a year after changing her name, she was working at the best hotel on Oahu and had top clients, and the rest is history," said Fiona with a knowing nod.

"I now have changed my whole prospective on Choo Choo. She's a very savvy businesswoman."

"Even though I hate to leave you, my love, I've got to make calls."

Within an hour, Fiona had completed her calls and had made a schedule for both Layla and herself. "I'll fix us something for lunch, then we both can go over to Layla's. I'll give her this schedule, and you can check out what all has been done and see Marty's table."

"Great, I'm hungry and I'm anxious to see that table."

After lunch, Fiona called Layla to make sure she was still at her house, saying she and Ned were on their way over.

Ned walked in and saw the roses, saying, "My god, Layla, there can't possibly be a red rose left on Maui."

"I've taken several photos with my phone for Dewey. I thought he would like to see them."

"That's a good idea. Be sure and say something sexy to go along with the photos," suggested Fiona.

"Fiona!"

"Oh, Ned, when we were young, we said outrageous things to each other, remember?"

"Yes, dear, and you're still saying them."

Layla couldn't help herself, she burst out laughing. "I love to hear you tease Ned, Fiona. George teases Annie the same way. I can tell that both Ned and Annie enjoy it, even though they pretend not to."

"I believe you have a point there, Layla," Ned said with a smile. "Where's that table Marty made that Fiona has been raving about?"

"Let me show you. It's in the dining room," Layla said, directing Ned to the table.

"My god, this is a work of art. It looks like something an old-world craftsman might have created two or three hundred years ago. The ceilings and wood trim are almost finished, I see, and they have turned out beautiful. This is going to be a true showplace. Layla, I'm glad you had the finances and the background to understand what was possible here. You will be very proud of this home's legacy once everything is completed."

"Ned, that's a lovely thing to say. A lot of the credit goes to Fiona. Without her advice and knowledge, most of this would not have been possible."

Fiona smiled and thanked Layla, then gave her Wednesday's itinerary. "We'll leave for Wailea at seven in the morning. If we get there too early, we can have a coffee. At eight, we get waxed. After that, facials, then massages, manicures, and pedicures, and then lunch. After lunch, we'll head to the shops at Wailea. I feel sure you'll be able to find everything you need, between there and the hotel shops. Not sure when we'll get home, but we'll be beautiful! Thursday, at three in the afternoon, you have an appointment with my friend Choo Choo Bacca for a haircut.

I'll drive us over there. Thank goodness she retired close. I would hate to fly to Oahu every time I wanted my hair cut."

"She's that good?" asked Layla.

"Best these islands ever saw. Quite a few women and men were mortified when she retired. We're all set then, Layla. We'll let you get back to work. Oh, I almost forgot, the glass man will be here at ten tomorrow, and I'll be here to work with him."

Fiona and Ned left Layla's and went back to their home. Fiona turned to Ned, saying, "The sheriff mentioned both the Visitors Center and Layla's house might be finished about the same time. Do you think that might happen?"

"It's possible, although I believe Layla's will be finished first. So many little odds and ends to get in place before an official opening can be scheduled. Why do you ask?"

"Once everything is finished, I would like us to go on vacation. Things have been so crazy and seem to only be getting worse. You and Donnie are going to get me involved in the center, so I can imagine life even more hectic."

"That's a good idea, honey, do you have a place in mind?" Ned asked, knowing full well Fiona had something in mind or she wouldn't have brought the subject up.

"Yes, as a matter of fact, I do. You will be surprised at where I would like to go."

"Let me guess, the Ritz in Paris or the Villa d'Este on Lake Como in Italy?"

"No, I want to take a trip to Utah in one of those big mobile homes, like Annie and George and Layla and Dewey did. I want to see those places, especially the Grand Canyon. The photos Annie and Layla showed us just didn't look real, and I want to experience that for myself. I know you can drive one of those big things because you drove one to trade shows so that should be no problem."

Ned's mouth hung open slightly, and he just stared at his wife.

"Ned, damn it, say something."

"Who are you, and what did you do with my Fiona?"

"Ned, don't be an ass. I am a naturalized citizen, and I think I should see some of the wonders of these United States, don't you?"

"Honey, you realize you will have to do a lot of the cooking. There will be no maid service or room service."

"Well, of course, I do most of the cooking here, and although we do have a cleaning crew weekly, I still do a lot of work on my own." Fiona moved into Ned and threw her arms around his neck, smiling. "And, honey, I count on you for your most excellent room service."

Ned put his arms around his wife and kissed her on the forehead. "Thank you, my dear, I do my best. I think we would have a great time, and I bet I can get the same trailer that Dewey had. It may be bigger than we need, but I like the luxury sound of all it contains."

"What a brilliant idea!"

Fiona walked into Layla's at fifteen minutes to ten and told her the glass man would be there at ten to measure the table.

"Great, I'm anxious to see that piece finished. I have one more cabinet to clear out and clean up, then my part in the kitchen is complete. I mentioned to Chris this morning that I was getting all new appliances, and he said he would buy the refrigerator, stove, and dishwasher. I told him he could have them with my blessings for taking them out. Josie chimed in and said she would take the microwave."

"Wonderful," said Fiona, "that will save hiring someone for removal and disposal."

"I told Chris and Josie they could take them anytime they wanted, but the replacements wouldn't be here for a while. They decided to take the stove and dishwasher this weekend but leave the rest until closer to a delivery date for the new appliances. We all use the fridge and microwave."

"Everything in the kitchen seems to be falling into place quite nicely," said Fiona, looking out the kitchen window. "Here comes our glass man. I'll flag him so he doesn't waste time being lost." Fiona went out on the back lanai and waved.

Once inside, Fiona made the introductions and directed him to the dining room where the table sat. "My, this is beautiful. You wouldn't want to sell it, would you?"

"No, this stays with the house," said Layla. "Can you make a glass top that will fit into the grooves?"

"Should be an easy job. Let me get the exact measurements." He got out his tape measure and began measuring. Shortly, he gave Fiona an estimate that she approved, then she asked how long it would take to complete. He told her he had several projects for the Visitors Center but could have this completed and ready to install by next Tuesday. They all agreed that would do, and he left to go to the Visitors Center.

"That was easy," said Layla.

"He's very agreeable, easy to work with, and I find his prices quite reasonable," said Fiona. "All set for tomorrow?"

"I guess so. I'll leave here early and fix dinner, take a long soak, and relax some. I'm looking forward to a day of pampering and shopping. If you and Ned are available, come back in an hour or so and check out the final display of stuff."

"We will and won't it be good to have everything cleaned out?"

"It will, but then, I'll have to fill the shelves with my own dishes, glasses, pot, and pans. I'm not looking forward to shopping for all that on top of linens and towels."

"We'll get Annie and make a day of it. Between the three of us, we'll be able to get quite a bit accomplished and have fun doing it too."

"Terrific, we'll plan that in the near future."

"I'm going. Ned and I will see you in a couple of hours."

The drive to the Grand Wailea took about forty-five minutes by the time they parked and went inside. They went directly to the spa to wait for their first appointment. Layla made arrangements at the front desk to pay for everything, adding a nice tip for each procedure. They were directed to changing rooms where they disrobed and went into individual waxing rooms.

Less than thirty minutes later, Layla joined Fiona in the spa lounge for a cup of herbal tea. Layla said, "I do not consider this a lounge, I consider this a recovery room. I'm so sore from that bikini wax, I think this weekend maybe a disaster before it even begins. There were certain areas I told her not to touch with wax. I have my zipper, where I had my cesarean section, and that's still tender. She was very cautious, but farther down, yikes. It had been years since I had a bikini wax, and that area was quite tender."

"Don't worry, dear, you'll recover fine before you put that area to use," Fiona said in a casual manner.

Layla shook her head and smiled. "Fiona, have you heard of a Brazilian V wax? I hadn't, and when the attendant told me what it was, I couldn't believe someone would have such a painful procedure. She could tell by the look on my face I didn't want that type of a wax job."

"It's called a Brazilian V because those gorgeous Brazilian women with great bodies roam the beach with tiny bits of material they call a bikini. The ones with the string that goes up the crack, hence the Brazilian V. I wouldn't want one of those wax jobs if I were dead."

Layla had no idea what that last statement meant and simply said, "My gosh."

An attendant came out and directed the ladies to their facial appointment.

Afterward, they met again in the lounge, their faces feeling marvelous, Fiona saying, "Like a new baby's butt."

"Fiona, being around you is such fun. None of my New York friends ever come up with such fun sayings."

Next, they had hot rock massages done outside where they could hear the sound of the waves and smell the freshness of the ocean. Following that, they each had a manicure and pedicure, then lunch.

"I need a couple of cups of strong coffee because right now, I'm so mellow I would prefer a nice nap instead of food," said Layla.

"Glad you said that. I thought I was just getting old. I guess we got overrelaxed, but it probably does one good once in a while. Of course, not too often or we wouldn't get anything done. Let's start with a mimosa, then lunch, and finish off with coffee and dessert. Then we hit the shops!"

They visited the shops at the Grand Wailea, then the upscale shops in Wailea. Layla was pleased that she found everything she had hope to find and more. She bought a pair of bronze wedge sandals for both of them that were expensive but simply too fabulous to pass up. It was her gift to Fiona for helping with her pre-Dewey beautification. On the way back to Paia, Layla asked Fiona if she would mind turning the car's air-conditioning on, even though a nice breeze blew through the windows. Fiona closed the windows and turned on the air conditioner. Once cold air was blowing out, Layla directed all her vents to a downward angle, scooted down in her seat, and lifted her skirt, exposing her newly waxed bikini area to the cold air.

Fiona looked over and started laughing so hard she had to wipe away the tears. "Layla, that's so funny but clever. Trust me, it will cool down overnight, and you'll be fine by Friday."

Fiona pulled into Mr. Soo's driveway and helped Layla take her packages inside. They hugged, and Layla thanked her for all her help; Fiona thanked Layla for treating her to a spa day and for the new sandals. Layla told her Mr. Soo was taking them out to dinner tonight, then she was going home to bed; she was pooped.

When Fiona got home, she called out, "Ned, let's have Annie and George over for cocktails and dinner. I'll nuke some of my spaghetti sauce, boil pasta, and make a green salad. You handle drinks."

"What's the occasion?"

"I've got a funny story to tell, and I might as well tell it once instead of me telling you and Annie and then Annie telling George. Is that OK with you?" Fiona asked, already getting salad fixings out of the refrigerator.

"Great, I'll phone them right now."

George and Annie said they would love to come to dinner and would be over in about fifteen minutes. Fiona got her salad ready, prepared garlic bread for the oven, and was heating her sauce when George and Annie arrived.

"Set at the counter and have cocktails while I work on dinner. I've got to share with you the funny moment of the day." Fiona went ahead and told them about the spa day, then tore into the living room to retrieve her sandals that wowed everyone. Then she said, "Here's what I really want to tell you. This is so funny." She told them about the air-conditioning adventure.

Fiona began laughing and tearing up; George tickled at the story, but even more affected by Fiona's laughter, he began laughing so hard he gulped to catch his breath. Annie and Ned sat stunned.

Fiona looked over at them, saying, "You two, if I had told you separately, you know you would be laughing, but because I'm telling this in mixed company, you're holding back."

Ned and Annie looked at each other; they broke out in wide grins, then laughed.

CHAPTER 51

"Dewey, sit down and eat breakfast. Your plane doesn't leave until tomorrow, and you're running around like a kid at Christmas," said Agnes sternly.

"Agnes, I just want to get to Maui and see Layla. You know, I'm going to ask her to marry me."

"Well, I imagined you might, and you know she'll say yes, so why are you such a mess?"

"I just want it decided, I want it finalized. There are so many things that can go wrong. Maybe she won't want to leave Maui and George and Annie and Mr. Soo. Now she's gotten real friendly with Fiona Keller. Maybe she won't want to come here to Salt Lake City 'cause it's a far cry from the balmy weather of Hawaii. Maybe she's just lonely for male companionship, maybe she doesn't really feel for me like I feel for her. You know, Agnes, I fell in love with her the moment I saw her."

"Yes, dear, so you've told us numerous times. Here's an egg-and-cheese omelet, toast, and coffee. Sit, eat, and quit whining."

"Yes, Agnes," Dewey said, smiling weakly at her.

Layla was standing outside on Mr. Soo's front lanai, enjoying her morning coffee, and spotted Annie leaving her house on her morning run. Layla walked down the steps to the street and asked Annie if she had a minute.

"I've finished cleaning the kitchen and have the last of the items on the counter if you and George want to go over sometime today and look through them. I'll have Chris box everything up tomorrow. I also wanted to tell you that he and some of his friends are taking the stove and dishwasher over the weekend. I'm glad they could use them. It saves me having to hire someone to remove and dispose of them."

"George and I will go over sometime today. How did things go yesterday?" Annie asked, not letting on she had heard everything from Fiona last night.

"The shopping was terrific. The spa experience was very relaxing, except for the waxing. That was painful. All is healing nicely. The redness and swelling has gone down, thank goodness. I was afraid my romantic getaway was going to be over before it began."

"I'm certainly glad everything is getting back to normal, and that it turned out to be such an otherwise great day. I can't wait to see your new haircut."

"I'm hesitant to have someone named Choo Choo Bacca cut my hair. She sounds like a stripper," Layla said with a concerned look.

"Choo Choo is excellent. My daughter and daughter-in-law took me to Oahu for Mother's Day one year for a haircut by Choo Choo. It took them three months to get an appointment with her, and it was the best haircut I ever had. It cost $250! The next day I went to my local lady and showed her what Choo Choo had done, and she was able to emulate the cut for a number of years until I decided to let my hair grow longer."

"Well, I guess I'll trust her. You know I want to look good for Dewey. It's been too long since I've seen him, and I still had my New York style. Now I've gone native."

"Honey, you could probably shave your head and Dewey wouldn't care. That man is in love with you."

"I know, but he deserves someone that looks their best."

"I've got to get back to my jogging. I'll see you later."

"Hi, Chris, Josie," Layla said, announcing herself.

"Good morning. How was your spa day?" asked Josie.

"It was great, very relaxing. Now all I need is some shape to this hair, and I'll look a bit more feminine. I wanted to let you and Chris know that after George and Annie come over today and look at the items on the counter, they are ready to box up for Chris's mother-in-law. Speaking of Chris, where is he?"

"He's over at Fiona's. She is going with him to rent a sander. She can get him a discount price on a rental."

"Josie, I don't like you being here alone. He should have waited until I got here before he left."

"I'm fine. I know everyone is still being careful, but I think it was some dopers, just random madness."

"I hope you're right."

As Layla and Fiona were in the car driving to Choo Choo's, Layla told Fiona she had found Josie alone while Chris was at her house. Layla said the sheriff felt the murders were not random but committed by someone local.

"Funny you say that, Ned always felt the same way. I find it hard to believe some local could have any animosity for that lovely couple. They were kind to everyone and extended credit to anyone, especially the kids. From the bottom of my heart, I hope the sheriff is wrong. We're here," said Fiona, driving into Choo Choo's driveway.

Two hours, three cups of coffee, and way too many delicious homemade cookies later, Fiona and Layla were on their way back. Layla's hair was a soft fluffy cap of sun-bleached blond hair, making her look younger than her age. Layla said she felt cute and sexy at the same time. Fiona assured her Dewey would love the way her haircut had turned out.

When they returned, Annie and George were on the back lanai. Annie yelled as Layla got out of the car, "Come on over, ladies! We've got to see how this turned out."

When Layla got to the top of the stairs, both George and Annie uttered "Wow" in unison.

"Dewey will adore the way you look," George said.

"Perfect for your face, and the color your hair has bleached out to adds to the effect. Choo Choo has done her magic!" exclaimed Annie.

"Any man would be thrilled to have her meeting his plane. By the time she has on one of the outfits we purchased yesterday and a bit of makeup, she'll knock Dewey over at first sight."

"Hi, everyone," said Ned, ascending the stairs. "Layla, that's a terrific haircut. It's just adorable."

"Thanks, Ned. I guess I have everyone's approval. Oops, I forgot Mr. Soo. I hope he likes it."

"I imagine he's like Dewey. You could be bald and he would say it's lovely," said Annie, creating laughter from everyone.

Annie and George invited everyone for a beer, and they all stayed except Layla. She had things to attend to and went on home. She wanted to fix Mr. Soo his favorite meal tonight since she wouldn't be there to make sure he ate a good dinner for several evenings. George said they would invite him over for a barbecue one night.

Fiona and Ned had finished breakfast; Ned sat at the kitchen counter with his second cup of coffee doing the morning crossword. Fiona walked into the kitchen and poured herself another coffee.

"Fiona, why are you dressed so early? Are you going out?"

"Well, I thought I would just pop over to Layla's to make sure she has everything for the weekend and put herself together just right."

"Honey, Layla will be fine. Are you sure you just don't want to know if all is working?"

"No, I checked on that yesterday. She's fine in that regard."

"I believe your motherly side is showing. Maybe you see Layla as the daughter we never had. Layla looks to both you and Annie as mother figures. I remember you told me her parental background, and God only knows she could use some good mothering. Go, my love, check on Layla."

"I hate it when you analyze me so perfectly. Am I that transparent?"

"Yes, dear, and I find your concern adorable."

Fiona kissed Ned tenderly on his cheek. "I love you," she said softly into his ear.

Layla was looking at herself in the mirror, amazed at how different she appeared from yesterday. She smiled, pleased at the transformation. She put pink blush on her cheeks, applied mascara, and was ready to put on lipstick when the doorbell rang.

"Damn!" she said out loud. She threw her robe on and went to the door, surprised to see Fiona standing there, "Fiona, did something happen?"

"No, everything is fine. Honestly, I just came over to be sure you put everything together properly and had everything packed. Ned said you awakened my mothering instinct, and as usual, he's correct."

"Come back to my room and see what you think of the outfit I've chosen to wear."

Laid out on the bed was a short, strapless, tropical hibiscus print sundress with a soft coral background along with her bronze sandals.

"Perfect, have you got the right undergarments on?"

Layla opened her robe to show off a very sexy strapless bra and matching bikini panties.

"Excellent."

"So how's the makeup and did I fluff my hair enough?"

Fiona scanned Layla's face. "Except for lipstick, coral, I presume, you've done a great job. How about earrings?"

"I forgot. Good thing you're checking on me. I'm wearing diamond studs," Layla said, reaching to a drawer and pulling out a box holding large diamond stud earrings.

"Amazing, my dear," Fiona said, going over to Layla and hugging her gently. "Tell Dewey I said hello. Of course, he probably doesn't even remember me, but I feel like I know him through you."

"Thank you, Fiona, for caring, and Dewey knows who you are. He says you are indomitable. I'm going to tell him different. You are a lovely, sweet lady."

After Fiona left, Layla did a final check to make sure she had packed everything and that all was locked up. She went to her car, stowed her luggage, and went to claim her Dewey.

CHAPTER 52

Layla arrived at the private airfield thirty minutes early; she didn't want Dewey's plane to land and for him to not find her waiting. Driving onto the tarmac as far as vehicles were permitted, she checked her makeup and hair in the car's vanity mirror. She tried getting out of the car, but it was too windy and sat back inside to wait. Making herself a nervous wreck, she turned on the radio to try and relax.

A jet the size of Dewey's smaller one landed and taxied toward the hangars, but it was too far to make out any insignia. As Layla watched, the plane turned off toward one of the other private hangars. She slumped down in the car seat and continued to wait.

"Dewey, we'll have to start circling if you don't sit down and fasten your seat belt," the captain said from the cockpit.

"Sorry, doing it right now. Don't circle, just land."

The captain shook his head and began landing procedures.

Layla saw another plane land and begin taxiing in her direction. This was Dewey, she knew it; she opened the car door and stood as close as permitted. The jet turned in toward the hangar and stopped. Layla began walking toward the plane with a sure stride. She saw the hatch open and the stairway come down, and then Dewey appeared at the top of the stairs. Layla smiled as she walked hurriedly toward him.

Dewey saw her as the plane halted on the tarmac. The minute the pilot had the engine off, he was out of his seat and aiding in opening the door.

OK, he thought, *"take it easy, or you'll fall flat on your face racing down the stairs.*

When he got to the bottom step, he looked up and arched his neck, not sure it was Layla walking toward him. "Layla, is that you?"

"Yes, Dewey, it's me!" Layla exclaimed, walking forward, extending her arms.

"My god, you look more beautiful than I remember," Dewey said as he reached her and drew her to him.

"You feel so good. Now kiss me. I've been waiting way too long for this kiss," Layla said, looking up into his face.

"Not half as long as I have," Dewey said, kissing his angel. After a long, passionate kiss, Dewey pulled back and said, "Layla, you look so good, tan, healthy, cute, and sexy as hell. I need another kiss."

"Fine with me. I could use another one too."

Breaking the spell, one of the pilots came with Dewey's luggage. "Want me to load this for you?"

"Thank you," Layla said as she used her remote, unlocking the car. She held on to Dewey and smiled. "I don't think you're in any condition to load luggage." Saying that, she wiggled herself into him. "Think we could hop back in that plane for a bit?"

"No, once the pilots leave, they secure it, and besides, I want us to be comfortable. That plane only has a couch."

"Then let's get to the hotel," said Layla.

Dewey put his arm around Layla and, with his other hand, fluffed her hair. "Sorry, had to do that. You want me to drive?"

"Sure, and touch me anytime, anywhere," Layla said wickedly.

"Oh god," Dewey said as he opened the door, ushered Layla inside, then raced around to the driver's side, got in, and tore out of the airport. Dewey swore it was the longest drive in his life. Layla told him the latest about her home, the Boones, the Kellers, and Mr. Soo. Several times, she reached over and rubbed his arm as he was steering, saying she wanted to touch him to assure herself he was real.

At the Four Seasons, they checked in and were ushered to their suite, along with their luggage. They waited while their escort explained the amenities, and finally, Dewey handed him fifty dollars and told him they were fine. He had opened the drapes in the living room, exposing a wide expanse of white-sand beach. Opening the patio doors, they could hear the sound of the waves and smell the ocean.

Their luggage sat on luggage racks in the large bedroom. Dewey pulled the drapes back and opened the door, then he closed one of the drape panels, dulling the light but allowing the ocean sound to filter into the room. Layla threw the comforter back on the bed and turned the sheet down; she fluffed the pillows.

"Well, we've finished our housekeeping, now what?" Her wicked grin returned.

Dewey sat down on the bed and took off his tennis shoes and socks. Layla came up behind him, reached around him, and began unbuttoning his shirt. She tugged and pulled it from his Levi's.

"Damn, honey, did you wear enough clothes? A T-shirt too?"

"I came from Utah, not so warm there," he said, shrugging out of his shirt and turning slightly to pull her into his lap. "And how about you? Are you now running around Paia almost naked?"

"Nope, I bought this outfit to drive you crazy. How's it doing?"

"You are definitely driving me crazy," Dewey said, drawing her around, cradling her in his arms, then kissing her deeply. He drew away, asking, "Just how does one get this sexy little number off?"

Layla stood up and pulled him up with her. She turned to her side and pointed to a zipper hidden in the side of her dress. "Just pull down and tug downward," she said, smiling.

Dewey did as he was told, her dress dropping to her feet. In one deft kick, Layla tossed it behind Dewey, who was standing there looking at his angel.

"You are magnificent!"

"Thank you, but there is this zipper on my stomach that certainly isn't very magnificent," Layla said, gesturing to her stomach.

Dewey bent down on his knees, drew her to him, and placed several gentle kisses on her zipper. "It's all part of you. That means I love everything."

"Oh, honey." Layla pulled him up, kissing him.

Dewey reached behind her and undid her bra; he removed the straps from her shoulders and cupped her breasts in his hands. She grabbed at the sides of his T-shirt, moving his hands away from her breasts and pulled it up so he could pull it over his head.

"Hmm, your skin feels good on mine," Layla murmured as they hugged, feeling the warmth of each other's body.

As she held on to him, he slipped his thumbs beneath each side of her brief panties and slid them down her thighs. Layla pushed them farther down and stepped out of them, then undid the button of Dewey's Levi's and pulled down the zipper. She slid her fingers beneath both his Levi's and briefs and tugged them down over his slim hips. They fell to his feet, and Dewey stepped out of them.

"My goodness, it appears brains was not the only thing God was generous with you about," Layla said, appraising Dewey's manhood.

Layla lay down on the bed and pulled Dewey with her, their desire for each other becoming intense.

"Wait, I almost forgot," said Dewey, pulling away from her. "I've got an entire box of protection, a large box I might add, especially for the occasion."

"Dewey," Layla said softly, "would it be bad if I did get pregnant?"

Dewey tilted his head, thought for a couple of seconds, then beamed. "No, sweetheart, that would be wonderful!"

"Then just leave the protection in the box it came in."

"Terrific!" Dewey said as he continued his caresses and kisses. In much less time than either of them anticipated, they reached the pinnacle of their lovemaking.

"Gosh, that was quick," Layla said breathlessly. "I guess it has been quite a long time for both of us."

Dewey rolled over on his side, grabbing Layla's back, bringing her with him. "I had no desire to be with another woman since I saw you," Dewey said. "I can feel your heart beating with mine. It might have been quick for both of us, but, honey, it was great!"

"Oh yes, and we'll take a little longer next time."

Dewey planted soft kisses on her cheeks and eyelids and then kissed her lovingly on the lips. He began softly caressing her breasts, pushing himself deeper into her.

"Dewey, are you doing what I think you're doing?"

"Can't help myself. I can't get enough of you."

Layla reached up and pulled his lips to hers; she kissed him, saying, "I'll never get enough of you either. I knew how deeply I felt about you, and now that we have been together, I know you feel that way about me. I'm such a lucky woman."

"I have felt that way about you forever it seems. I want us to love each other and enjoy being in love."

Later in the afternoon, they ordered a room service lunch, both wanting the privacy of their suite. They ate on the patio. They talked and made love and napped, then once again ordered room service for dinner, vowing the next day to go outside their suite for meals.

Layla lay on her side, arm thrown over Dewey's chest, sleep closing in on them when Dewey said, "Layla, I want to make sure of something, so I'm going to make this formal, well, if you can consider lying in bed naked, formal."

Layla yawned. "Sure, ask me anything, but I'm not getting out of bed."

"Layla, will you marry me?"

Layla jerked up and rested her head on one elbow. "Well, of course, and I had decided if you hadn't asked me by tomorrow afternoon, I was going to ask you."

They kissed to seal their commitment, one thing leading to another, but finally, they got to sleep with the promise of making marriage plans later in the day.

CHAPTER 53

Ned, Fiona, and George began walking up to the Hanna Highway to meet with Donnie at the Visitors Center. From behind, they heard a voice calling, "Wait up, I'll walk with you folks."

They turned to see Mr. Soo scurrying to catch up.

"Good afternoon, are you going to Otis's for a late lunch?" asked Fiona.

"Yes, my morning walk took longer than usual. Had to answer queries about Layla and Dewey. This town certainly does not miss anything. I need one of Otis's jumbo cheeseburgers and fries to regain my strength. Where are you folks going?"

"We're meeting Donnie at the Visitors Center. George hasn't been there in a while, and he's anxious to see how his original ideas have been incorporated into the final concept. Ned works closely with Donnie and the contractor. I'm unfortunately being roped into something as yet unknown by Donnie," said Fiona with a grimace.

"Now, honey, don't be that way," said Ned. "I'm sure Donnie just wants your valuable opinion on furnishings or decorations."

"That better be all he wants. I don't have time to put up with all the things you tell me go on with the various factions putting their noses into this project."

"Ms. Fiona, I am sure whatever Donnie has in mind for your services will be of the utmost value to the center," said Mr. Soo.

"Mr. Soo, you're so charming," said Fiona.

After crossing the street, Fiona and Ned walked up the driveway to the Visitors Center, and George hung back, saying to Mr. Soo, "I'll be over to Otis's in a bit. I've got to have one of his chocolate malts. Annie would have a fit if she found out I was having something so fattening and high in cholesterol, but she'll never suspect that I would detour over to Otis's after the Visitors Center."

"Ah, a conspiracy. Your secret is safe with me."

George strode up the embankment to the Visitors Center, and Mr. Soo made his way to Otis's. George took a couple of steps inside, removed his sunglasses, and gazed around the large open space in amazement.

"George, good to see you," said Donnie, walking toward him.

"I can't believe you have turned my ideas into reality. I'm speechless."

"When I mentioned your ideas to the architect, he saw their value and incorporated almost all of them into our design. He was especially fond of the upper windows and reflective pole mirrors that bring light into the facility—very green and, best of all, saves on the electric bill. The large greeting desk, which our docents will man, was also your idea, along with the food and the gift areas. The rest remains open so tourists and guests can walk around, looking at these wonderful photos we have blown up of old Paia."

Under the small high windows were large sepia photos of old Paia, some of them going back over 105 years to the historic days when Paia was a plantation town during the height of the sugarcane industry. George walked around, fascinated at the old pictures of his town.

"Donnie, where did you find these? They are wonderful and certainly paint a historic picture of Paia."

"This was our architect's idea. I spent time with some of the city's old-timers to find photos we could use. I believe these will make the center very appealing to residents as well as tourists."

"I'm very impressed with all I've seen, especially these pictures, they are a treasure. You did really well, Donnie," Fiona said.

"Thank you, Fiona, that compliment coming from someone of your design caliber means a great deal to me."

"And, George, Ned was telling me how much of this design was your idea. I didn't realize you were so darn clever. It's wonderful."

"Thanks, but you know we engineers are a clever lot," George said with his usual grin.

As they were chatting, from behind the gift counter, Wade popped up, saying, "Hi, everybody. Donnie, I finished the gift counter. I still have some finishing touches to make on the food counter, then I'm all done."

"Wade, did you design and build these counters and desks?" asked Fiona.

"I made them, but I believe this is about half the design concept of George and the architect. Turned out wonderful. The wrapped teak wood is just right to offset the original dark wood of the market."

"Absolutely, the contrast is perfect, and I especially like how you set in a glass viewing space in the gift counter. Very classy looking," said Ned.

George and Wade walked over to the food counter and were discussing finishing details. Ned spotted the contractor outside and went to talk with him, leaving Fiona with Donnie.

Donnie guided Fiona over to the gift counter. "Fiona, this is where I would like to solicit your expertise and good taste. George and I thought this would be an excellent place to display and sell the work of local artists. No cheap tourist items like magnets, pens with windsurfers in liquid gel, you know the type of items I'm referencing. I'll place an ad in the area papers asking those interested to submit a letter describing what they would sell, the prices, and send photos. They would also have to work one day a week at the center, behind the gift counter, manning the cash register. I wonder if you would be willing to go through the candidates and select those that you feel would be proper to represent the real art work of Paia."

"That would be a very interesting task. I would enjoy working with our many talented local artists. How many should we consider?"

"I know there are enough quality craftspeople or artists in Paia for us to select a minimum of seven candidates."

"I imagine we will have a large number of applicants to screen. I'm sure I'll be offending some folks, but I understand what type of items you are interested in displaying."

"See those shelves?" Donnie asked, pointing to two sets of shelves above the display area. "Those will hold the six charcoals that Layla has done. They are of the beach area and the windsurfers. Magnificent works of art, and I have no idea what price to put on them. I'll need your help there too."

"Where are you storing them?" Fiona asked.

"I have them in the safe at the bank. I thought that would keep them out of the moist air for as long as possible. Let me know when you would like to come by and look at them."

"First, you need to get your ad in the local paper. Do you have a script for the ad?"

"No, I'm sorry to say. I tried writing something a couple of times, but it sounded stuffy, or so my wife says."

"I'll take care of that for you. We won't want to offend anybody, but we'll want to make it clear from the beginning we are only interested in true artists."

"Excellent, Fiona, I truly appreciate your help," said Donnie.

"I had no idea what you were going to ask of me, but I'm going to enjoy this project. Something different, and I have always been an exponent of our local artists."

"Wade, I like what has been done with the food area. The way you've set up the entrance to the ordering counter once you are in, the only exit with your food is to the outside patio. That's a good way to keep food from inside the center. It's obvious, but the way the wood is wrapped around so softly, it's non-obtrusive," said George, gliding his hand along the wood.

"I thought the flow was good, and it will get folks outside to eat or drink and be on their way."

George shook Wade's hand, saying, "I've got to go and meet a friend, but we'll be seeing you at Layla's."

George found Donnie and Fiona, and Fiona told him about her new assignment. "You are the perfect person for the job. You have such good taste. I'm sure everything sold here will be the best Paia has to offer."

"Thank you, George. There's Ned. I can't wait to tell him," Fiona said and hurried to tell Ned of her involvement in the Visitors Center.

"Well, Donnie, I'm going to be going. I appreciate the tour. Great idea having Fiona handling the artists. That way, you won't lose any bank customers if they aren't chosen to place their work in the center."

Donnie blushed. "George, you are too clever. That's one of the reasons I chose Fiona. People seldom get mad at her. They just say that's Fiona and forget about being slighted. I want you to know that on the bronze plaque that will go beside the main entrance door to the center, both the architect and I wanted your name there listed as a design consultant."

"I'm grateful. That's a cool tribute. Annie will be so proud. My appreciation to both you and the architect." George said goodbye and walked next door to join Mr. Soo at Otis's.

George entered Otis's and spotted Mr. Soo sitting at the counter with the sheriff; he sat down on the other side of the sheriff.

"Hi, guys," he said, slouching down on the counter stool. "I don't want anyone reporting to Annie I'm in here having a malt. She wouldn't say anything, but I would get that 'if looks could kill' stare for a day or two, and that's a terrible thing to go through."

"Well, hello, George," Otis said, coming up to the counter, "I take it you're here for one of your chocolate malt fixes."

"I've been dying for one for several weeks now. I just had to time it right," George said, grinning, knowing Otis was aware of Annie not wanting him to imbibe in something like a malt.

"Coming right up," Otis said, walking away to his malt-making duties.

"Good to see you again, Sheriff. Anything exciting happening in our little city?"

"Not much, arrested a couple of kids selling pot to tourists last weekend. Arrested five for being drunk in public last week. And I'm sorry to say arrested a spouse on domestic violence."

"Damn, I hate to hear that a man has beat up on his wife. Hope she leaves him," George said.

"Well, actually, she was arrested for beating the bejesus out of him with a frying pan. Said she couldn't stand him watching another soccer game, and he didn't take her seriously. Think he understands now. The poor guy is still recovering from head injuries."

"My goodness, and I thought the late Mrs. Soo was the only spouse trying to kill her husband," Mr. Soo said in all seriousness.

George and the sheriff looked at each other, both suppressing grins.

"Anything new on the Okamoto murders?" George asked.

"Tell you what, once you get your malt, let's go and sit in a booth where there is more privacy and I'll tell you the latest."

Otis brought a large malt glass, oozing with richness, to George along with a regular-sized water glass also filled with chocolate malt. George took a long draw on the straw.

"Ah, like manna from heaven. No one makes chocolate malts like you do, Otis. We're going to take our drinks over to a booth," George said, laying five dollars on the counter. He, the sheriff, and Mr. Soo walked to a booth and sat down. "Can I offer either of you gentlemen this other glass of malt?"

"Not me," said the sheriff, "I'm not a chocolate malt fan, but a strawberry malt, that's another story."

"I have to admit I'm full," said Mr. Soo. "I had the jumbo bacon cheeseburger and a large order of fries, most satisfying."

"I don't think I could handle all that in one sitting," said George.

"What latest developments do you have to share with us on the murder of my dear friends, the Okamotos?" asked Mr. Soo.

"There was a meeting about two weeks ago, all the bigwigs involved. The case is being put in the unsolved files. They all felt it was just someone passing through, and since they have no leads, they have chosen not to continue any investigation. I told them I disagreed with their assessment, but when they asked me what I based my assumption on and I said it was my gut instinct, they laughed and teased me about being the old guy and that ended that."

"This is very disturbing news, Sheriff," Mr. Soo said, shaking his head, his brow furrowed.

"Doesn't seem right to me either," said George.

"Funds have been cut back everywhere, so they didn't feel they could waste any more man-hours working on a case with absolutely no clues. They did tell me, in my spare time, I could pursue my own investigation. Which I thought was damn considerate of them since it happened on my watch," the sheriff said heatedly.

"Anything we can do to help, Sheriff, just let us know. I'm sincere about that. Mr. Soo and I are out and about daily. We see all sorts of things, and we would be good at asking questions informally."

"I make many stops daily and speak with many people. Perhaps I will begin asking them if they have heard any news on the murders," offered Mr. Soo.

"That's a good idea, Mr. Soo, and get back with me right away if anyone offers anything. The same goes for you, George. I'm still in the belief that these murders were committed by someone local. I have felt that from the beginning, and I've told you both that before. Gentlemen, I got to be going. It was a pleasure speaking with you both," the sheriff smiled, leaving the booth.

"George, can you speak with some of the young windsurfers to see if they have any ideas? I will causally talk with the many friends I encounter daily. Who knows we may be able to learn something accidentally that these people don't even realize they know."

"I will talk with the young folks. This is a good idea of yours, Mr. Soo. I hope we can find something that will help the sheriff. In the meantime, we'll still lock up."

"I'm very cautious, and I've been sure Layla is also. I wonder how she and Dewey are getting along."

"I have a feeling they are doing just fine," George said with a knowing grin.

Annie stood at the kitchen sink, dicing tomatoes for the evening's salad when she saw George come toward home. She met him at the back lanai screen. "How was your tour of the Visitors Center?"

George walked into the dining room, pulled a chair out, grabbed Annie around the waist, and sat her down on his lap. "Honey, wait till I tell you what's happened. Most of those off-the-cuff ideas I threw out to Donnie have been incorporated into the final design. I couldn't believe my eyes. You know, my engineering background has been more in the mechanics of things. How to get luggage from plane to passenger sooner, how to route planes safely, but this time I gave Donnie some design ideas more in the architectural vein and, damn, if he and the architect didn't use them. There's more. On the usual bronze plaque by the entrance door, they are listing my name as a design consultant."

"I'm so proud of you! What an honor and well deserved, I might add." Annie reached up to give him a kiss. As she placed her lips on his, she suddenly pulled back, saying, "I smell chocolate malt."

"You certainly do. I knew Mr. Soo was next door at Otis's, and when I left the Visitors Center, I decided to celebrate, so I went next door and had a chocolate malt. It was so damn good."

"You deserved it, my brilliant engineer," Annie said, continuing with the kiss she had previously started.

After their kiss ended, George proceeded to tell her about the center. He emphasized the wonderful large photographs that hung below the windows, telling her she would be awed at the old photos of their town.

"That does it. I want to go next Friday. Will you go with me? I've really got to see it now. With your contributions and those old photos, it's time I got myself acquainted with our new Visitors Center."

George hugged Annie to him and said softly into her ear, "Sweetheart, I'm so glad you're ready to make this move, and you'll be fine. I'll be there for you."

"I knew I could count on your support," Annie said softly.

George went on to mention that the sheriff was sitting with Mr. Soo when he arrived at Otis's and that they all had moved to a booth to discuss privately the Okamoto murders.

"Is there a suspect?" Annie asked hopefully.

"No, actually, it's the opposite. The other agencies have declared it a closed case and filed it away. The sheriff said he believed it was a local, but they ignored his theory as that of an old-timer."

"That's terrible news," said Annie, dismay in her voice. "How can they dismiss the murders so easily?"

"I guess because there were no clues or suspects, just nothing to go on. The sheriff suggested to Mr. Soo and me that we keep vigilant on our home security. I told him it had become habit for us to lock up even when we are home. Mr. Soo and I offered to, very casually, when talking to various people, start up a conversation on the murders. We would start things out by our dismay at it being a closed case and then see if we can find out anything. Someone may know something but have no idea that they know something. Know what I mean?"

"That's a terrific idea. I'll apply the same approach when I go to the retirement centers. Although I'm sure none of those folks were at the scene, the gossip mill works overtime at those places and no telling what I might hear. Let's hope between the three of us, we can pick up a little clue somewhere."

CHAPTER 54

Layla and Dewey were having breakfast on their patio, opting to discuss their marriage plans in private. They agreed to the ceremony in Salt Lake City in deference to the many employees at DewMaster and others in the area that would want to attend. Layla said she realized it was his first marriage, and it should be a big event, considering who he was and his company representation. She did insist they use one of his company planes to fly Mr. Soo, Annie, George, Fiona, and Ned over and thought maybe they could be housed in the empty house that Dewey's father had built.

"Splendid idea. Now what about a date or some estimate?"

"Dewey, you've got to understand that I must finish the restoration of my home, which will be our home-away-from-home when we're married. In fact, I hope we can fly back with everyone and spend our honeymoon in Paia. I do love this place, the people are friendly, and the pace is easy. I can't quite put my finger on why I feel so at home there, but I just do, and I know you also have good feelings for the town and people."

"Absolutely, the six months I spent hiding out there were terrific. I made many friends. No one knew who I was or how much I was worth. It didn't matter. I was just Dewey, and they accepted me. The windsurfers are extra special people, and of course, George and Annie and Mr. Soo are a very important part of my life now. I imagine you will help me get to know Fiona and Ned. I guess my initial opinion of Fiona was off the mark."

"Definitely, she's been a spark of life for me. She is a moving force, and yet she is caring, kind, and extremely fair and honest. She and Ned share a loving relationship, actually much like Annie and George. She and George are more alike, more ornery, and Annie and Ned are akin, more reserved. Those four are fun together, and Fiona has some great stories. They had a rich and active life in Oahu but chose to come to Paia when their children were ready for high school and raise them in a slower atmosphere. Fiona told me it was a hard decision at the time. They were used to a fast-paced life with high-profile clients and million-dollar deals, but it was the best choice they ever made for their family. She firmly believes that it has extended Ned's life by reducing his stress level. She sees that, most of the time, they eat well and exercise almost daily. She does work for locals occasionally, and believe me, she has great contacts and works hard, but she handles no more than two projects a year. She said her main focus is Ned."

"Honey, I have a feeling I'm going to learn to like Fiona, and she might be responsible for that wicked sexy grin you've come by."

Layla laughed. "You're probably right. Do you like it?"

"I love it," Dewey said, leaning across and kissing her.

"That was yummy," said Layla. "Now getting back to our marriage, I know we will be living in Salt Lake City, that's where your business is, and you have a lot of people depending on you for their livelihood. As long as we can keep the Paia house for vacations and relaxing time, I think it will take between four and five months to have everything finished. Fiona thinks it will be sooner, but when I go inside, I see so many things to be accomplished. I get scared of a faster time frame. Do you think it might be possible for you to take a quick look before you have to get back?"

"I would like that since it will be our vacation home and where we spend our honeymoon, the least I can do is see how things are coming along. Do you want to start making wedding plans now or wait a bit? There are a lot of plans we will have to make well in advance."

"When I married Kyle, our marriage was one of the big events in the Hamptons that season. My parents had a lot of European friends in for the event and Kyle's family had big-time politicians and Wall Street types in attendance. It wasn't a wedding, it was a production. It was horrible. Do you think we could hire a wedding planner to work with you and make it what you had in mind? I have a couple of friends from New York and our Paia friends. Other than that, I don't want to invite anyone else. I will ask my parents, but I'm sure they will have other plans."

"If you're serious, then I would love to ask Agnes to plan things, and my secretary can assist her. She would love planning our wedding. She feels very close to you, did you know that?"

"No, I didn't. And it would make me extremely happy for Agnes to plan our wedding. Perhaps we could have it in your fabulous backyard, providing it's late summer or early fall."

"That would be terrific. Ted can get the yard fixed up like a something out of nurseryman's dream. We can have a large tent for the reception with a dance floor and make it warm with space heaters."

"Great, see how much we've gotten decided. We work well together. We do a lot of things well together," Layla teased.

After breakfast, they decided to put on swim gear and go out to the pool/beach area. After some sun time, they stopped by the shops, and Layla picked up gifts for Annie, Fiona, and Mr. Soo. She also picked out something for Agnes and Ted from both of them, then insisted Dewey select something for his secretary. They enjoyed a leisurely lunch outdoors, then went back to their suite.

The rest of Saturday and Sunday seemed to fly by, and when Sunday evening rolled around, they decided to dine in their suite, enjoying the intimacy of being alone with each other. They made love often, and each spoke of their past, the happy times and sad times and how much they were looking forward to married life together.

"Layla, tomorrow before I leave Maui, let's find a jewelry store and at least look in the window so you can give me some idea what type of engagement ring you would like."

"Oh dear."

"What's the matter, honey? I can afford anything, so don't worry if you want something outrageous."

"Please don't take this the wrong way, but I don't want an engagement ring. I had a bad experience with my last one, and I would simply prefer a gold band for each of us. If you want to add diamonds, that's fine, but no big, gaudy engagement ring."

With a surprised look on his face, Dewey asked, "What could possibly have happened to make you feel this way about an engagement ring?"

"When Kyle and I became engaged, he gave me a fabulous ring from his mother's side of the family. It had been her grandmother's. Lord, it was something to see, a huge blue-white diamond surrounded by deep blue sapphires and set in platinum. Everyone always was commenting about its beauty. Heck, most of the time I was afraid to wear it, easy picking for a thief.

"When Kyle and I divorced, I didn't want to return it to him, damned if I wanted to see Kim wearing it as a pinky ring. Kyle's mother and I were always close, and I drove up to their Hamptons estate one day and returned it to her. She understood why I brought it back and thanked me, saying it would stay in her direct family. She would pass it on to her sister for her to give to her eldest daughter when she became engaged. That's my story and why I'm not into engagement rings."

Dewey smiled. "Gold bands for both of us."

CHAPTER 55

Annie and George invited Ned, Fiona, and Mr. Soo over at ten Monday morning. Annie provided coffee, tea, and made a coffee cake. At twenty minutes past ten, Dewey made the turn off the Hana Highway, and all on the Boones' lanai stood up and waved.

"Look, Dewey, we have a welcoming committee," Layla said, waving from her side window.

"They want to know how our weekend went."

"I'll tell them we made love so much, walking is a chore. That ought to appease them."

"Layla, you wouldn't! That Fiona has really changed you."

"No, sweetheart, I wouldn't say that, but I know I'm glowing."

Dewey held the car door for Layla, and then they made their way where all were assembled.

"I'm so glad to see you both," said Annie, hugging Layla and giving Dewey a hug and a kiss on the cheek.

George went over and gave Dewey a manly hug, saying quietly, "Hope that special box is now empty."

"Nope, not even opened."

"What?" George said, stepping back wide-eyed.

"Layla said not to bother, as long as I didn't mind if she got pregnant. I said fine with me, so the contents of the box never saw the light of day," Dewey said with a broad grin.

"Just the best, isn't it?" George said knowingly.

"First time I had not used protection, it was wonderful."

"What are you two chatting about?" asked Mr. Soo, coming over to greet Dewey.

"Mr. Soo, I'm so glad to see you," Dewey said, giving the little man a hug.

"I'm most happy to see you too, Dewey. I've missed you, but I've been happy to have Layla staying with me. I will be sorry to lose her once her home is completed."

"Dewey, let me officially introduce you to Fiona and Ned Keller," Layla said, making the introductions.

They shook hands, and then Dewey said to Fiona, "I believe I have you to thank for spicing Layla up. She has been slightly wicked, and I love it."

"I'm guilty and proud of it," Fiona said, laughing.

"Folks, we have an official announcement to make," said Dewey, slipping his arm around Layla. "Layla and I are engaged and will be married as soon as her home is finished to her liking. We will use it as our vacation home, and we also plan to honeymoon there. We will be married in Salt Lake City. However, I will send a plane for all of you to bring you to the festivities. I have a second home on my compound. In fact, my father built it for him and Mom to live in, but he died before they could move in, and you folks can stay there. It is a lovely home, and I will have a housekeeper assigned to it while you're there."

"It sounds like you two have really planned things out. All of us would be honored to attend your wedding, something we have been anticipating," said Fiona.

"In my heart, you are my family, and I couldn't be married without you in attendance," Layla said, tears coming to her eyes.

Annie went and placed her arm around Layla. "Honey, you and Dewey are so special to us, and I'm going to miss you terribly, but I'm so happy for you both."

"I knew the minute I saw my angel, she was the only woman I would ever love, and I feel so lucky she now feels the same way," Dewey said, beaming.

"This is supposed to be a happy occasion, but here I am crying," said Fiona, motioning Ned for his handkerchief.

"We have some Dom at home, saving it for something special, and this qualifies," said Ned, going down the stairs toward their home.

"Afterward, Fiona, will you join Layla and me as we tour her home? She's anxious for me to see what's been done."

"Make that our home, honey," Layla said, smiling.

"Wonderful, perhaps you can get a sense when it will be ready. Layla and I differ about two months, but I believe we can get a great deal done quickly. Things are now moving along rapidly. The air-conditioning folks started today, Wade is there taking measurements, and Chris and Josie are working on the floors. Has Layla told you what all we purchased so far and what all is purposed?"

"Yes, she explained in detail where everything stands and what has to be done. I think she is more overwhelmed with her part than with what the contractors have to accomplish," said Dewey.

"Honey, I have a whole house to outfit, so many things to buy. It's not the big purchases, so much as the small items that worry me," said Layla, concern in her voice.

"Fiona and I will be here to help you with everything, from linens to toilet paper," said Annie.

"Do not underestimate a couple of senior women shopping. We are experienced shoppers, and we know how to outfit a kitchen, bathroom, laundry room. We've had lots of personal experience, right, Annie?"

"Absolutely, we'll have things done very quickly!"

"I wouldn't think of tackling these purchases without your guidance. I have to be honest. That type of buying is a new experience. You know the poor little rich girl cliché, well, it's certainly true in my case."

"Here we are, folks," said Ned, producing a couple of chilled bottles of champagne.

George brought flutes, Ned uncorked and poured, and Mr. Soo made the first toast. "Two people truly in love, may your years together be long, may your happiness be forever, and may your union be blessed with children."

Everyone clicked their glasses and drank to Mr. Soo's toast.

They continued discussing various subjects when Dewey looked at his watch. "Where has the time gone? Ladies, we have to go and look at the house now."

Dewey said farewell to everyone on the lanai, then he, Fiona, and Layla proceeded over to the house. Walking up the back lanai steps, they could hear the buzz of workmen. Fiona opened the screen and walked into the kitchen, followed by Dewey and Layla. She explained how hard Layla had worked on clearing out the cabinets and cleaning the wood. She then walked to the dining room and took the protective mover's blanket off Marty's coffee table.

"This is amazing. Layla described it to me, but until you see it for yourself, you have no idea of how wonderful this is. I'm overwhelmed."

"Marty did a wonderful job. He's an artist," said Fiona.

They moved to the living room where Fiona and Layla explained Wade's concept of floating shelves. Dewey marveled at the expansive ocean view from the front windows, even better than that afforded from the Boones'. They found Wade measuring in the large bathroom that connected to the larger of the spare bedrooms.

"Wade, let me introduce Dewey McMaster. He and Layla are engaged and will make this their vacation home, and they also plan to honeymoon here."

Wade and Dewey shook hands, and Wade proceeded to explain what he and Herb would be doing in both bathrooms. When he finished, Dewey thanked him and turned to Fiona. "The people you have assembled to work on this place seem so professional and artistic. Layla said you were amazing. Now I see what she means."

"Thank you, Dewey, and flattery will get you everywhere."

They moved to the master bedroom where Chris and Josie were sanding the floors. Chris turned off the sander the minute he saw Dewey. They embraced, then Josie came over and gave Dewey a big hug. "Bro, how you been?"

"Fine, Josie, glad to see you and Chris have found something that you enjoy doing."

"I love this type of work. Restoring this beautiful wood is gratifying for Chris and me both. How about joining us for the next high tide?"

"Thanks, but I have a plane to catch in less than an hour. I just came by to see how things were coming along. Layla and I are engaged, and we will be making this our vacation home, and believe me, we will be vacationing a lot."

"Cool, bro," said Josie, "we'll be seeing you back on the waves."

"I imagine so, providing the missus will let me."

"Of course, dear, as long as your will is in order," said Layla.

"Ouch, that hurts," said Dewey, putting his arm around Layla and kissing her on the cheek.

They toured the remainder of the house; Dewey lingered in the master bedroom, once again admiring the view. He looked at his watch and hustled Layla out. Fiona stayed on, Wade saying he needed to speak with her about an opportunity she might want to avail herself and Layla of.

As Layla and Dewey walked to the car, they waved to those left on the Boones' lanai, Dewey shouting he would be back soon.

Back in the car, Layla turned to Dewey and asked, "What did you think of our Paia home?"

"Honey, I'm overwhelmed. I never imagined such magnificent wood. I know what you told me, but it is much better than I thought. And that ocean view is fabulous. We will have the most beautiful home in Paia, maybe all of Maui, no, all of Hawaii."

"I take it you approve," Layla asked, laughing. "I can't wait for us to honeymoon there. We'll be so happy. I just know it."

As they continued to the airport, a quiet sadness seemed to envelop both of them. Their happiness would become memories, and the torment of missing one another would begin.

"Layla, I'm returning in two or three weeks, hopefully for three or four days. How about we stay locally? I can check that out and make reservations as soon as I get back and review my schedule."

"That would make me very happy. I loved the Four Seasons, but I like being near our friends. Just promise me it won't be longer than three weeks. I've never been so happy as when I'm with you."

"I promise."

They arrived at the airfield where the pilots loaded his luggage. Dewey and Layla kissed for the last time. Layla waved as the plane taxied toward the runway.

"Fiona, I want to run something by you that might be of interest to both you and Layla," said Wade. "Do you know Rebecca Steinmetz? She's the widow of the former manager of the cattle ranch on the big island. They lived a semiprivate life off one of the side roads from the Hana Highway. Mr. Steinmetz spend ten years building their home, and when he retired about twelve years ago, it was ready for him and Rebecca to move into along with their eldest daughter, who was going to college at that time. All their children are now married, one lives in Texas and one in Oahu. Mr. Steinmetz died about three years ago, and Rebecca now wants to move to Oahu to be near her daughter and grandchildren. She needed some work done on her home about a year ago, and I went to see her. Fiona, have you heard anything about that home?"

"Sort of, I heard it was built of imported stone and filled with beautiful European pieces and furniture made on the islands specifically for that home. I have never met anyone that has seen the inside of the home. I can only go on speculation."

"Well, you have now, and it is quite an array of European style and hand-carved Hawaiian furniture. Rebecca and I have become good friends, and she has let me select several items to purchase before she puts her home up for sale. I was out there last week and told her about the work I was doing for Layla, and she suggested she come out and see if there is anything she could use in her home since it's being restored. I told her Layla was working with you, and she said that was fine. She had always wanted to meet the notorious Fiona."

"Did she say notorious?"

"Yes, but she meant it in a kindly way. She really is a sweetheart."

"She can call me anything she wants as long as I get to see what's inside that home. When can we go?"

"How about Wednesday? Will that work for you and Layla?"

"It certainly will. We have no other projects planned for that day. Thank you, Wade. This will be quite exciting!"

Fiona walked back to the Boone's lanai and told everyone about the upcoming trip to see Mrs. Steinmetz's home and furniture. She and Ned left so he could get to his tee time, and Fiona wanted to work on the list of things Layla still needed.

Mr. Soo got up from the lounge chair, moving to the table with George and Annie. "I wanted to tell you both about a conversation I had yesterday. I was at an outdoor table enjoying a cup of tea when one of my old friends sat down. I told him about the close cased tag on the Okamoto murders and how sad I was about that. He then said the thing he could never understand was how neither of the Okamotos didn't hear an intruder enter because, as he put it, that damned bell always clanged loudly when the screen door was opened."

"My god, I just realized something," said Annie with a startled look on her face. "The bell did not clang when I entered that morning. I noticed it at the time and decided the Okamotos had not put it back in place since returning from Oahu. Do you think this important?"

Mr. Soo said, "I think we should ask Dewey if he can remember if the bell was there when he went into the shop when the Okamotos returned from Oahu. If it was there, it meant someone took it down after they left the store. That could be a clue for the sheriff. I'm pretty certain Dewey will phone Layla when he gets to Salt Lake City. I will ask to speak to him at that time. This is something we must definitely determine. Who knows this might be one of those things everyone overlooked that will provide an insight to the authorities. I'm going to go to Otis's now for lunch, then take a short walk. I don't want to miss Dewey's call. I will advise you both of the outcome of our conversation."

"George, I feel stupid that I didn't think about that bell before now. Had I thought about it sooner, it might have had an impact on finding out who committed the murders."

"Honey, you sustained a horrible shock. I'm in awe at how you cope," said George, putting his arm around Annie and kissing her gently on the forehead.

Layla returned from the airport and lugged her suitcase upstairs. Beginning to unpack, she noticed she hadn't given Annie or Fiona the items she had purchased for them. She decided to wait until another day, her mood not being good enough to want to be around anyone. She got her clothes unpacked, hung up, and sorted. She sat her cell phone on the nightstand and lay down on her bed. Startled, she woke about an hour later when she heard the front door open and called out, "Mr. Soo, is that you?"

"Yes, back from lunch and my walk. May I come into your room and speak with you about something?"

"Certainly, I'm was just resting and thinking of Dewey. I miss him. Why does life have to be so complicated sometimes?"

"Perhaps complications arise to make us appreciate those times when everything goes perfectly."

"You make an excellent point. What did you want to speak with me about?"

"I'm assuming Dewey will be calling you when he arrives in Salt Lake City to let you know he is home safely. When he does, would it be possible for me to speak with him a moment? I must ask him an important question regarding the Okamoto murders."

"Of course, I'm sure he will help you in any way possible."

"Excellent, and I want you to know I'm happy for you both, but it's nice to have you back. I missed your company and your cooking."

"Thank you. Maybe I should teach you how to make some of your favorite dishes."

Mr. Soo looked astonished. "Me cook, oh no, that's way beyond my abilities. Making tea is the extent of my cooking accomplishments, and that's just the way I want to keep it. Thank you anyway."

Several more hours passed, but finally, Layla received her call from Dewey. He told her of an uneventful flight and of his thoughts of their time together.

"Dewey, Mr. Soo wants to speak with you. He needs to ask you something about the Okamoto murders."

"Sure, but I can't imagine how he thinks I can help."

Layla walked into the living room and handed the phone to Mr. Soo. "Dewey, I am pleased you have arrived safely at your home. I must ask you something that has come up in my discussions with Annie and George. When you went into the market upon the Okamotos' return that fateful evening, do you remember if the screen bell rang?"

"Funny because I distinctly remember that darn bell clanging. I was in the beginning of a hangover, and it vibrated inside my head. Why do you ask?"

"Annie recalls when she went into the store that terrible morning, there was no bell on the screen door. This leads one to believe someone took the bell down, perhaps the intruder, perhaps someone knowing in advance the bell would make its usual loud sound."

"Annie is sure there was no bell?"

"Yes, she's emphatic about that recollection."

"Has anyone said anything to the sheriff?" asked Dewey.

"No, we decided to wait until I spoke with you to see if you had a recollection of the bell being there, and now that you do, we will meet with the sheriff and advise him of our findings. Thank you, Dewey, and don't be surprised if the sheriff calls you to confirm your memory."

"I will be glad to help in any manner possible."

Dewey and Layla spoke a bit longer. After she hung up, she asked Mr. Soo if he were going over to speak with Annie and George.

"Yes, I think I will after dinner. Do you want to go with me?"

"I have a small gift I picked out for Annie while we were at the Four Seasons, so I'll go with you and give that to her."

CHAPTER 56

Mr. Soo and Layla made their way to the Boones later that evening. Layla presented her gift to Annie, who assured her it wasn't necessary but loved what she had selected.

"I spoke with Dewey when he called Layla. He distinctly remembers the bell ringing when he went into the store. He was beginning to suffer the effects of overindulging and said the bell rang inside his head. I believe we should tell the sheriff of our findings right away. What do you think?"

"George, why don't you get in touch with the sheriff tomorrow morning and invite him for lunch, nothing fancy, just cold cuts and salad? Mr. Soo, you'll join us? How about you, Layla?"

"Yes, an excellent idea," Mr. Soo said, smiling, always being available for a meal at the Boones'.

"Count me out. I've got too much going on over at the house," said Layla.

"I'll call the sheriff first thing tomorrow morning. Then we can get together here at noon for lunch. If there is any problem, I'll let you know, Mr. Soo," said George.

"Excellent, excellent," said Mr. Soo.

Dewey helped the pilot load his luggage into his SUV, then drove out of the DewMaster hangar, and headed home. He was anxious to tell Agnes and Ted about the wedding plans. He wanted to get back to her as soon as possible; now that she was officially his, as he thought of it, he couldn't stand not having her by his side.

He opened the front door, yelling, "Agnes, Ted, it's me, and Layla and I are officially engaged!"

They came out of the kitchen. "Honey, I'm so happy for you both. Ted and I were just talking about you two, hoping all had gone well."

"It went perfectly, and I know we will be a happily married couple forever. I do have some what I think will be good news. I just hope you both feel the same way," Dewey said hesitantly.

"Oh," said Agnes, giving Dewey a quizzical look, "let's hear your news."

"Layla understands our wedding will be here to accommodate the people at work and others that will want to attend. We will be sending a company plane to Maui to pick up Annie and George, Mr. Soo, and Ned and Fiona Keller. I proposed they stay in the other house. Agnes, perhaps you can find a housekeeper/cook that can stay there and provide for them. We will all fly back to Maui together where Layla and I will spend our honeymoon in our new refurbished home, formerly Mr. Soo's old home. How is this sounding so far?"

"So far, sounds great, only why do I feel there is more to come?" said Agnes.

"I don't know if Layla told you about her parents. They are a piece of work. But they are her parents, and she feels obligated to invite them. If they are able to attend, they will stay here in the main house."

"Why in the world would they not want to attend?" asked Ted.

"If we have the ceremony between Memorial Day and Labor Day, they will be busy entertaining their usual European guests at their Hamptons estate. After that, they are off to Europe to be guests at the homes of their European friends."

"Ye gods!" exclaimed Agnes. "Frankly, I hope they don't show up. Can't imagine they would fit in too well around here."

"Honestly, I can't either, but we will invite them. When I discussed the wedding plans with Layla, she told me her marriage

to Kyle had been the event of the year in the Hamptons, and
it was very trying and stressful. She said she would provide a
small list of people she wanted to invite. Other than that, she
said hire a wedding planner to handle everything. She thought
it would be fun to have Annie and Fiona as her attendants, and
she will take care of dresses for them and her. She would leave
everything else to the planner."

"Go on," Agnes said.

"I would like the ceremony and reception to be held here
on the property. Depending on the weather, we can use a big
tent, have it outside, or whatever will work best." Dewey looked
at Agnes and Ted for any type of disagreement. Seeing none,
he continued, "I told Layla that a wedding planner would work,
but I first wanted to give the opportunity to you folks and see
if you wanted to handle things, with the help of my secretary,
caterers, and florists, of course." Dewey took a deep breath and
looked expectedly at the couple for an answer.

"My, my," said Agnes, tearing up, "I'm honored you would
consider us for such an important event in your life. Honestly,
I think I can speak for Ted when I say it would be our pleasure
to plan this event for you and Layla. Right, dear?" Agnes said,
looking at her husband.

"Yes, and I hope it's in late summer, early fall, before it
gets too cold. We'll have the back property looking stunning.
I'll draw up plans, and we can go over the details and add or
subtract as you see fit. This will be quite a celebration!" said Ted
with pride.

"One other thing I just thought of," said Dewey. "My Mom,
I'll phone her and tell her I'm engaged. Sure hope she takes it
well. She can be so picky sometimes. It will probably upset her
that Layla is divorced."

"Just tell your mom her social background. That ought to
keep her quiet and let her know you aren't marrying a gold
digger, something she has always worried about," said Agnes
with authority.

"What, my mom actually told you that?"

"Many times, my dear, many times. It always annoyed me that she shortchanged your ability to judge women, but I guess you being her only child and so darn rich so young, she naturally worried. I told her you were very well grounded in that aspect, but she never really believed me."

"That would be a hoot if Layla's parents show up with your mom here," said Ted with a grin.

Agnes banged him on the shoulder. "Now, Ted, none of that. Where do we stand on a date, Dewey?"

"Well, unfortunately, I can't give you much of a clue yet. Fiona says one thing, she's the designer on the house, and Layla says another. I'll be going back over there in two or three weeks, and I should be able to get a handle on things better at that time."

"Going back so soon?" asked Ted.

"Got too, can't stay away from my angel for long. I miss her like crazy, and it's only been a few hours," said Dewey, shaking his head. "I guess while I'm at it, I should call Mom and break the news to her. Wish me luck."

Dewey phoned his mom, and after a lengthy explanation, she seemed to understand that Layla was definitely not marrying her Dewey for his money or status and that they were truly in love. She asked Dewey to send her a photo of Layla, which Dewey did from his cell phone to her. Seeing the photo, she returned to the line and told him Layla was very lovely. Dewey also felt obligated to tell her about Layla's first marriage, the horrible loss of her baby, and of the tragic circumstances of her divorce.

Surprisingly, his mother said that he had found himself a very strong woman, someone that would hold up well under the pressure of being married to her genius billionaire son. Dewey hung up the phone, feeling the happiest he had in a long time after talking with his mom.

He smiled then called his angel.

CHAPTER 57

Layla woke Tuesday morning with a sigh, not looking forward to going to the house with all the noise and dust. After a quick breakfast, she sat off across the street, wanting to arrive before Fiona and delivery of the glass tabletop. Upon entering, she saw Chris and Josie wearing white masks. Chris came over and told her the air-conditioning people were providing these to everyone that came into the house because of the high level of dust and particles in the air. He handed her a mask, which she put it on.

A short while later, Fiona arrived to find Layla in the kitchen.

"You look weird with that mask on," Fiona said.

"I may look weird, but you have to put one on too," Layla said, handing Fiona a mask.

"This is going to mess up my hair."

"Too bad, air conditioner's rule. Your hair will snap back. It always looks great."

"Thank you, dear," Fiona said, slipping on her mask. "Once we get the tabletop on, let's go over to my place. We're going someplace very special tomorrow, a furniture shopping expedition with Wade."

"With Wade, really?"

"Really, I'll tell you all about our adventure."

"Can't wait," Layla said, looking at her watch. "Where is that man with the glass top? I want to get out of here. All this noise and dirt is making me antsy."

"He should be here soon. It's not quite ten yet. I'm going to take a look around and see how the air-conditioning work is coming along. You go out on the lanai and wait for him."

"Gladly, I'm curious for your opinion on the air-conditioning work."

Layla, glad to get outside, removed her mask, took a breath of clean air, and shook off the dust. Fiona spoke with the air-conditioning foreman and learned that things were going as planned with no problems so far. She went outside to report to Layla.

"Everything is going along fine with the air-conditioning. It isn't the fastest process in the world, so be patient. Look," Fiona said, motioning toward the street, "there comes the glass man."

The ladies watched as two men carried the large heavy piece of glass up the lanai stairs and into the house. Fiona took the blanket off the table, and the glass top was carefully lowered into place.

"Wow," said Layla, "that's amazing. The glass has managed to enhance the overall beauty of the table. Terrific job, gentlemen."

Fiona showed them out, received the bill, and went back inside to join Layla and Chris. Chris had his cell phone out, taking shots of the table to show Marty. Fiona securely reblanketed the table, then she and Layla left.

Layla sat at Fiona's kitchen counter, waiting for her to fix something to drink, and could not contain herself any longer, "Fiona, I'm dying to know about this shopping trip we are going on with Wade."

Fiona related Wade's story about Rebecca Steinmetz and of the furniture they were likely to encounter, emphasizing the Hawaiian-made pieces, feeling they would add to the restoration value of Layla's home. She told Layla they were to meet Wade at ten tomorrow morning at her home, and he would drive them in his truck. He said sometimes if there had been rain, the going could be tricky, and he wanted to be sure they had the weight of the truck in case they hit any large puddles. He said that Rebecca had insisted they all join her for lunch after their tour, saying she enjoyed hostess duties.

George placed a call to the sheriff's office and spoke with Charlene, who connected the call to the sheriff.

"Sheriff, I would like to invite you to lunch tomorrow. It will be Mr. Soo, Annie, and me. We have some interesting information for you. Nothing special, just cold cuts and salads. Will noon do?"

"Sounds great to me. I'll see you folks tomorrow at noon."

Charlene stepped into the sheriff's office after he had hung up, asking if anything was wrong.

"No, having lunch at the Boones'. They're being neighborly. I enjoy their company, good people."

Charlene left and went back to her desk, satisfied with the sheriff's answer.

The sheriff had no intention of telling Charlene about any detective work being done by the Boones' or Mr. Soo; he would keep that information to himself.

Ned walked into their bedroom, wondering what Fiona had been doing in there for such a long time.

"What are you looking for?" he asked as she sorted through her generous wardrobe.

"I want to find the proper outfit for tomorrow to meet Rebecca Steinmetz. I want to look professional, nonthreatening, and sweet."

"Honey, did you say sweet?" Ned asked with a slight laugh.

"Damn it, I can be pretty sweet if I want to. Need I remind you?"

"Nope, you're my sweetheart, but I never thought you were too anxious to portray that image to other people."

"Mrs. Steinmetz thinks I'm notorious. I want to change her perspective and let her know I'm a lovely, sweet, lady. Also, give me several of your business cards. She is going to be putting her home on the market, and that would be fun for you to sell."

"Oh, Fiona, now I see your cunning self come shining through. That's my girl."

"Thank you, dear. You always know when to say the right thing," Fiona said with a wicked smile.

Dewey had worked like he was possessed Tuesday morning, and by late afternoon, he had made a big dent in items for the rest of the week. Now all he needed was to work on the following week's schedule and try to shorten things so he could get out on Friday and not be back until Wednesday of the following week.

He had spoken with all his department heads and told them he would be traveling more often to Maui and expected them to begin making more decisions and assuming more responsibility for the everyday running of the company and also for the long-range projects. He and his secretary worked out a tentative schedule for the department heads to follow, and he would review that at a meeting tomorrow morning. As soon as he was sure he would be able to leave a week from Friday, he would have her make reservations and notify the pilots, then he would call Layla.

He wondered what his angel was doing right now; how he missed her.

Layla had one more thing on her list of things to do for the day; she pulled out her computer and e-mailed her parents, telling them about her engagement to Dewey and that it had not been announced to the public yet. Considering who he was, she wanted to advise them prior to a public announcement. Feeling like she had gotten ahead of any problem, she began thinking about her next meeting with Dewey and wishing it was sooner than they had planned.

CHAPTER 58

Layla and Fiona were waiting in Layla's lanai when Wade drove up.

"Well, ladies, it appears you're anxious to meet Mrs. Steinmetz." Wade got out of his truck, walked to the passenger's side, and opened the door for them.

They were glad to have taken Wade's truck because of some late-evening showers, and as Wade had predicted, the road close to the Steinmetz's home was pitted with water holes.

"I wouldn't want to live so isolated. I imagine Mrs. Steinmetz must have been terrified during that tropical storm," said Fiona.

"Things are pretty self-sustaining. The house has its own generators, and there is a large supply of food on hand. However, I agree with you. It would have been scary for an older lady all alone," said Wade. He pulled into the circular stone driveway and stopped in front of the Steinmetz's door. Fiona and Layla were impressed at the size and beauty of the stone façade.

"I'm surprised to find such a beautiful home hidden up here off the Hana Highway. It's quite European," said Layla.

"I'm amazed," said Fiona. "I didn't know this home even existed."

Wade smiled, knowing Fiona was in tune to everything that went on, in, and around Paia. "You have to understand, after their daughter left, the Steinmetzes were happy being alone. They truly enjoyed their home and each other's company. Years of living on the big ranch, with so many people always around, made them cherish their privacy."

He came around to assist the ladies from his truck. The front door opened, and Mrs. Steinmetz came out to greet them, smiling. "I'm so glad to see all of you. Please come in, and welcome to my home." She stepped aside, and Fiona, Layla, and Wade entered.

"My god in heaven, this is unbelievable!" exclaimed Fiona.

"I've never seen anything like this," said Layla, eyes wide, taking in what was before her in the foyer.

Wade had deliberately not told them about the spectacular view once you entered the home. He wanted to see the initial shock that would register on their faces. He was not disappointed.

Before them was a two-story glass atrium open to the outside from the top and backside; it sat behind five large two-story sheets of glass. The atrium was filled with exotic tropical plants that continued into the backyard. In the center of the atrium was a beautiful three-tiered fountain, with water gently flowing into each tier. The colorful flowers in the atrium radiated both brilliant and soft hues. The various green shades of the plants and trees added to the overall beauty. On either side of the atrium were winding staircases leading to the second-floor balcony.

"How is this possible? It appears inside, yet I do believe it is totally separate from the outside," asked Fiona.

"You're right. My husband worked with several architects before one young man saw my husband's vision and the house was built. I'm glad you like it."

Rebecca Steinmetz walked toward Fiona and extended her hand. "I'm Rebecca Steinmetz, and you're, Fiona Keller, right?"

"Yes, I'm sorry not to have introduced myself sooner, but I was so taken back by this amazing atrium, I forgot the introductions. Let me introduce Layla Richmond, the lady who is restoring the beachfront property Wade has told you about. Thank you so much for inviting us into your wonderful home."

"It's my pleasure to have you both here, and of course, having Wade or Herb here is always a pleasure. Terrific young men."

"They are and wonderful craftsmen too," said Layla, shaking hands with Rebecca.

"You must have a large gardening staff to work on this amazing atrium," asked Fiona.

"When my husband was alive, it was our passion, working with the plants and flowers. I'm afraid we extended it out farther than we intended, but it was all working so well we just kept on going. Now I have one gardener who comes two days a week. He and I do all the work, and it is a chore, however, for me, a labor of love. I hate to sell my home, but I miss my daughter and grandchildren so much that I've decided to move to Oahu to be near them. I realize I'm slowing down, and continued upkeep of this property will be more than one gardener and I can do. Except for the backyard, all the rest of the property we let grow wild."

"How much more property is there?" asked Fiona, her real-estate sense taking charge.

"Approximately eight acres, I would have to look at the property deed to know the exact amount."

"You will receive a very handsome price for this house with that much land."

"Do you think so, Fiona?"

"Definitely, my husband, Ned Keller, owned the most prominent, high-end real estate company in Oahu up until our retirement. I was his decorator, and I got to know property and prices pretty well over the years. Your wonderful home and all the acreage will probably garner between four or five million, and that might be conservative. Ned is much better than I am at pricing."

"Heavens," said Rebecca, her hand going to her throat, "I never dreamed that much. I thought maybe a million or a million and a half. Let me show you the rest of the house so you can look at furniture."

Fiona felt she had just secured Ned as the realtor to sell the Steinmetz house. She would ingrain herself a bit more to Mrs. Steinmetz.

Rebecca led them up a staircase to the master bedroom. She wanted them to see the view from the balcony but told them none of the rooms' furniture was for sale, it would be going with her to Oahu. Next she showed them her daughter's room and adjoining bath. Here again, she told them none of that furniture was for sale; her daughter wanted it for her own home, except for a small secretary desk and chair. Fiona and Layla immediately said they would take it. It was a replica of an old European secretary and just what Layla envisioned for the larger spare bedroom.

Rebecca then led everyone to the bedrooms on the other side. "These are the rooms I thought you might find something. Everything in these rooms is for sale."

The larger of the two rooms was furnished in Hawaiian carved furniture, featuring simple lines but carved in a beautiful dark brown almost black wood. The simplicity of design was stunning. The furniture consisted of a triple dresser, two nightstands, and a large headboard and footboard. Fiona got her tape measure out to ensure a queen-sized bed would fit and found out that was the mattress size already on the bed. Fiona and Layla decided immediately, they would take all the pieces; all was perfect for the larger guestroom.

The next bedroom consisted of twin beds with one nightstand between them and a double dresser. What made this furniture stand out was that it was intricately carved with pineapples and various Hawaiian flowers. A bit outrageous and gaudy but Layla fell in love with it immediately.

"I'll take it all, and please tell me that pineapple lamp on the nightstand is included."

"Heavens, yes, you can have that thing without charge. Never did like it," Rebecca said.

On the way out the door, Wade nudged Fiona, who seemed in semishock. He grinned at her and said, "Too much for your taste?"

"Actually, it's very authentic, just a lot to take in at once."

Downstairs, Rebecca showed them the den where nothing was for sale and the living room, but they didn't find anything there that was on the list, lastly, the dining room. Both Fiona and Layla let out ohs when they saw a beautiful three-section beveled glass buffet table.

Fiona walked over to the table. "Please tell us, Rebecca, that this beauty is for sale. Layla has the perfect spot for it in her dining room."

"It's for sale, but once you buy it, I can't make any guarantees about getting it into your home safely. It's quite delicate. It was a major project to get it here from Austria. It took us over two years."

"I have the utmost faith in Three Brothers Movers. They are very careful. I've used them for a number of years, and as long as your delivery date is flexible, you can be sure it will arrive safely."

"Who are Three Brothers Movers?" asked Layla.

"They are three very large Hawaiian brothers who look like big bears but are extremely careful with furniture moving. They are known for their care in moving delicate items. Their only shortcoming is their timetable and your timetable may not coincide. They often get sidetracked with family obligations, like roasting a pig for a luau or cheering a family member in an outrigger race. Everyone who hires them is aware of this, but because of their excellent record, folks are grateful they are moving them," said Wade.

"Sounds like they are the ones we'll need to hire. I can picture this marvelous buffet table in my dining room now," said Layla.

"It will be perfect," said Wade.

"The only item you haven't seen is a silly little table I have in the kitchen that my husband just had to have. I never liked the thing as the color was a little too bright for me, but he saw it in Norway and I couldn't talk him out of it." Rebecca led the way through to the kitchen where they saw a very bright leaf green table with three matching chairs made from a heavy-duty wood.

"This is perfect for the small kitchen table you wanted, Layla, and I like this green. It will brighten up that side of the kitchen, don't you think?" asked Fiona.

"Another item sold. We've done extremely well today," said Layla.

"We certainly have. This is an amazing home you have, Rebecca, and some extremely wonderful furniture."

"It is my pleasure to have you here, and I can tell I am selling my things to someone who will appreciate and enjoy them. I have set a table on a side lanai, so let's proceed there and have some lunch."

After lunch, they discussed when it would be possible to get the furniture, Layla explaining where the restoration was on her home. Rebecca said she still had much packing and sorting to do and did not anticipate any type of move for the next three months. Layla and Rebecca discussed pricing of the items selected and agreed that Rebecca would make a list with what she felt was a fair price. Layla, Fiona, and Rebecca would review the list later on.

Before leaving, Fiona gave Rebecca one of Ned's business cards and told her she could check with anyone in real estate to verify his ability and even suggested the local or Oahu real estate board. She emphasized his background with high-end clientele; he would have knowledge of potential buyers for her estate, as Fiona now referred to the Steinmetz home. She asked Rebecca if she could set up an appointment with her for Ned to come and see her estate sometime within the next couple of weeks. Whether she used Ned or not, he would be able to give her an honest estimate of the property's worth. Rebecca said that would be fine, and Fiona said she would get back to her as soon as she could verify a time with Ned.

Wade held the truck door for the ladies, and Layla reached up and gave him a kiss on the cheek. "That's for thinking of us. I'm so grateful you brought us here. I love everything I've selected, and it will look terrific once here."

"Thank you, ladies. I know this will help Rebecca too. Fiona, I think you've sold her on Ned handling the property. I'm happy about that. She is a lovely lady, and I know Ned will make an honest sale for her, where some others might take advantage of her lack of real estate knowledge."

"I'm anxious for Ned to see this property, and he'll probably know someone, somewhere that will buy it right away. He's uncanny that way."

They drove back toward the Hana Highway, trying to beat an afternoon shower that was looming.

CHAPTER 59

After his morning walk, Mr. Soo showered and put on fresh clothes. He checked his watch and left for the Boones at exactly 11:45 a.m. When he arrived, George told him they were eating on the front lanai and went outside where Annie had the table set and ready to begin bringing food out once the sheriff arrived.

The sheriff didn't arrive until 12:15 p.m., making apologies for being late. "A couple of Canadian students thought, with the assistance of some Maui Wowie, it was perfectly legal to go topless on our public beach. They managed to draw a large crowd. It took Danny and me several minutes to get them to put their tops back on, disperse the crowd, and take them to the station. We put them in a cell until their high could wear off and find out where they bought the weed."

"Got to love our tourists," said George with a grin.

"Sheriff, you and George go out front, and I'll bring the food."

"Thanks, Annie, I appreciate the invitation."

George and the sheriff went outside where Mr. Soo greeted the sheriff. "So glad you were able to have lunch with us today, Sheriff. I feel certain we all will enjoy one of Annie's meals."

Lunch consisted of three different types of lunchmeats, two salads, deviled eggs, two types of cheese, a table of full of condiments, and was topped off with fresh strawberry shortcake. After dessert, Annie cleared the table, and Mr. Soo began with the discussion he had with his friend who brought up the subject of the screen doorbell. Annie confirmed that it was not there when she walked into the store. Mr. Soo told the sheriff that he had spoken with Dewey and ascertained that the bell was there when he went into the store when the Okamotos first got home from Oahu.

"We summarized that the murderer was familiar enough with the store to make sure the bell was silenced when they entered the store. What do you think of our detective work, Sheriff?" asked George.

"Very commendable, folks, very commendable. However, I'm going to do my own follow-up on this information and not share with the other authorities until I can get a better handle on it. Damn shame that old door has been replaced. I would like to have checked it out, maybe even get some fingerprints."

"Sheriff, I feel terrible that I waited so long to remember the absence of that bell. You might have been able to find the murderer if I had my wits about me that terrible night," said Annie, almost in tears.

"Annie, no one could fault you for not remembering something so trivial. You had a horrible shock. Frankly, I was worried sick about you that night. You might not remember this, but you hugged that big old can of coffee like it was a sack of gold. I tried to help you with it, and if looks would have killed, I would have been dead."

"Sheriff, I don't remember that happening, I'm so sorry."

"Don't be. I think it represented some type of safety net for you." The sheriff stayed a while longer, thanked Annie for a wonderful lunch, and told George and Mr. Soo to continue their subtle inquiries.

Back in his truck, the sheriff shook his head. He marveled at how sincere these people were but wondered where the hell they thought this new revolution would lead. He laughed softly to himself.

Wade dropped Fiona off at her house, then parked in Layla's driveway. He and Layla went to speak with Herb.

"How was your shopping trip?"

"Herb, Rebecca Steinmetz is a remarkable lady, and I bought a ton of her items. Remember that beautiful beveled glass buffet table? I'm getting that for the dining room. Won't it be spectacular?"

"Sure thing, Fiona will arrange to have the Three Brothers move things for you. They are probably the only ones that could get it here in one piece."

"Wade filled me in on the brothers, and Fiona has a great working relationship with them. Do you need me for anything, Herb?"

"No, just adding to the dust bowl by tearing things up here."

"I want to call Dewey and tell him about our visit to Rebecca's. I'm curious if he even knew about the home." Layla said goodbye to Herb and thanked Wade again for taking them to meet Rebecca Steinmetz.

After she left, Herb turned to Wade, smiling at his handsome partner. "That lady is going to have your home furnished just perfectly. I'll give her and Dewey three years or until the kids start coming, then it's yours or should I say ours."

Fiona rushed into her home, calling out, "Ned, where are you?"

"In the den, honey, what's the matter?"

"Ned, did you know about the Steinmetz home? I didn't, and it's wonderful. I mean, you won't believe it until you see it. Plus, there are almost eight acres included. I think I have the listing sewed up for you. I thought I would call her next week and arrange for us to take her to brunch at the country club a week from this Sunday, then she can show you the place at that time. I'm telling you, sweetie, you won't believe your eyes."

"Slow down, Fiona, you're rattling. I've heard of the property, but there aren't too many folks around anymore that actually worked on the building of the home, and the Steinmetzes were not that social."

Fiona went to where Ned was sitting at his desk and plopped down on his lap. "You won't believe this home inside, and I'm not telling you about it because you must see it yourself to understand the uniqueness of what Mr. Steinmetz and the architect accomplished."

Ned put his arms around Fiona's waist and gave her a kiss on the forehead. "Now you have me intrigued, so make the arrangements with Mrs. Steinmetz for a week from this Sunday. I'll prepare myself to be shocked," Ned said, laughing.

"You will be shocked, trust me. If I was speechless, then you know, it must really be something."

"Good god, Fiona Keller speechless, I've got to see this home!"

CHAPTER 60

When Mr. Soo returned home, Layla told him all about her visit with Mrs. Steinmetz and the items she purchased. He told her about the meeting with the sheriff and asked when she phoned Dewey later in the evening, tell him they had spoken with the sheriff and he was now aware of the missing bell.

An hour later, Layla phoned Dewey, wanting to be sure he was home and able to talk. She told him all about the Steinmetz home and the items she had agreed to purchase. He knew of the Three Brother movers and assured her they were the best on any of the islands. He told her things were going well, and he should be on his way a week from this coming Friday, and the way it looked now, he would be able to stay through Tuesday.

Layla was overjoyed and told him how much she missed him. She also relayed Mr. Soo's message. They talked for about an hour, and then he said he would call her Saturday when he had everything firmed up for the following week.

Friday afternoon and Paia was overcast and humid. Ned, Fiona, Annie, and George made their way up the hill to the Visitors Center. Annie had assured everyone she would be fine. George had called Donnie Munson earlier in the week and told them he and Annie would be accompanying Ned on Friday, knowing Donnie wanted to speak with them about recruiting docents. Fiona had developed several ad copies for the recruitment of local artists, and she wanted to run them by Donnie.

Everyone walked up the driveway to the Visitors Center where Donnie greeted and ushered them inside to the welcome air-conditioning.

"If we don't get a thunderstorm by tonight, I'll be surprised."

"Got to agree with you there, Ned," said Donnie. "You can cut the air with a knife. Well, Annie, what do you think of our Visitors Center?"

"I'm so impressed. I was apprehensive about coming here, afraid I would be reminded of the old market. This no way resembles the market. Your architect has done a wonderful job."

"You know, your husband made suggestions that were incorporated into the final product. You should be very proud of George."

"I've always been proud of George, but when he told me you were going to put his name on the plaque outside the door, I realized what an impact he must have had on the center," Annie said, lacing her arm through George's and smiling up at him.

"George, why don't you show Annie around, and I'll talk with you folks later. I need a few minutes with Fiona."

"Sure, Donnie," George said, and he and Annie went about touring the center.

Donnie spoke with Ned who told him he and the contractor were meeting with yet another inspector in about thirty minutes; there were a few plans to go over, but nothing that he couldn't handle.

"Well, Fiona, let's see how the ad looks," Donnie said, walking over to the craft sales area.

Fiona showed Donnie two ads she had put together, and they combined phrases from both to make one ad. They agreed it said everything intended, and Donnie said he would take the script back to the bank, have it retyped, and get it off to the local papers. Fiona said to let her know when the product packets began to arrive at the bank so she could start screening them. She showed him two letters she had drafted: one rejection letter and one setting up an appointment for further consideration. Donnie thought the letters were well done.

Fiona thanked him and decided she would go back home, accomplishing all she had intended.

Annie and George completed their tour, meeting Donnie at the large counter where the docents would greet the visitors.

"Well, folks, I'm sure you know what I'm going to ask of you, especially you, Annie, with your knowledge and contacts in the senior community."

"You want us to recruit and train the docents. I hope you plan on intergrading age groups. I think it is important we have all ages involved in the center. Somehow, with the impressive photos of the past, I don't think we'll have any problems getting recruits," said Annie.

"I was thinking of having a younger person working alongside a senior when possible. What do you folks think of that?"

"I like that idea," said Annie. "A number of our seniors miss their grandchildren, and this will give them an opportunity to connect with teens and those in their early twenties."

"I like the pairing too. It's a good way to educate the younger folks of Paia about the city's heritage," said George.

"George, I thought you might be able to recruit some of the younger windsurfers."

"I'll try. Those with Paia roots will be glad to assist a couple of hours a week. Are there going to be brochures or some type of handouts visitors to the center can take with them?"

"I hired a company that specializes in brochures and maps that focus on a specific town and the surrounding area. They are in the process of getting their draft ready, and I'm hoping to run it by you both and the Kellers to see what you think about the work they have done."

"Let us know, and we'll be glad to give our opinion. It's vital for the docents to have good literature to hand to tourists," said Annie.

"The draft will be ready in a couple of weeks. All is coming together nicely. Fiona and I are working on getting craftspeople, and I've gotten a bid written up for the food concession. I'll be placing that in the local papers in a week or two. Right now, we are waiting for toilet fixtures to arrive, then we'll need to have that work signed off once it is completed, but I know Ned is on top of that. He's been my savior. Without him, we wouldn't be anywhere near where we are now."

"You know, Donnie, Annie and I have become good friends with Ned and Fiona. They both are intelligent, hardworking, and caring people. Fiona is a hoot too," said George laughing.

"She still scares me," said Donnie quietly.

"George and I will get working on the docent recruits and get back with you when we have a good list. MayLee said she wanted to be counted as a docent. Do you think she still feels that way?"

"Most definitely, I'll tell her you are putting her on your list."

Annie and George went back to their home after hearing a distant clap of thunder.

Saturday morning, George and Annie were having coffee on the lanai when George suggested they go to Bird's for dinner. It would give him a chance to speak with some of the windsurfers about docent work, and Byrd might be able to suggest others he could recruit. Annie thought she would be able to get Jessie, Byrd's wife, as a docent.

"Let's ask Ned and Fiona if they want to join us. I think a place like Bird's will fascinate Fiona, and Ned will have a good time."

"George, you're just trying to see how Fiona will react to Bird's. That's ornery, but let's ask them anyway," Annie said, grinning.

Ten minutes later, Ned walked out on their lanai with coffee and the morning paper. He waved across at Annie and George.

"OK if I come over for a second?" George yelled across to Ned.

"Sure thing," Ned replied.

George refilled his mug and walked over to the Kellers' lanai. He greeted Ned, and they chatted about his and Annie trip to the Visitors Center yesterday. Ned was curious how Annie reacted to the center, if she handled everything without a problem. George said he was proud of how Annie had done and said it didn't seem to have caused her any added anxiety.

"Annie and I are going to Bird's for dinner tonight. I need to talk with some of the windsurfers and do some recruiting among them for docents. Donnie wants to pair a senior with a younger person. Maybe you and Fiona might enjoy going along," George asked.

"I've always wanted to go there, so count me in. Fiona can be a bit snobbish at times, but I'll talk her into going."

"I heard that, Ned Keller, I had to be snobbish to work with some of the clientele you stuck me with," said Fiona, opening the screen door and joining them on the lanai with her own mug of coffee. "Where have you always wanted to go?"

"Annie and I are going to Bird's for dinner. I want to do some docent recruiting, and we thought you and Ned might care to come along with us. Ned said he always wanted to go there."

"They serve food?" Fiona asked with a slightly huffy tone.

"See what I mean?" asked Ned with a smug grin.

"Great meals, Fiona, the only catch is you have to place you order before noon. Byrd buys his meat fresh daily and only buys enough for orders already placed. You either can have steak, chicken, or fish. What would you folks like me to order?"

"Steak for me," Ned said.

"Does he serve prime cuts of meat?" asked Fiona.

"He serves terrific steaks, usually T-bone, porterhouse, or filet mignon, and they are prime."

"Well, in that case, I'll try a steak too. What does one wear?"

"Annie and I usually wear Levi's, T-shirts, and comfortable shoes. Nothing fancy, it isn't that type of place. We'll leave here at seven, have a couple of drinks before dinner, and plan on eating at eight. Does that suit you, folks?"

"We'll be ready. Looking forward to the evening, George," said Ned sincerely.

George left and went back home. He felt sure Ned was going to get an earful from Fiona.

"How come you never told me you wanted to go to Bird's?"

"Because I knew you wouldn't want to go, and I like to defer to my lovely wife."

"Then how come we're going tonight?"

"Because our good neighbors asked us to join them, and they are doing work for the Visitors Center," said Ned sharply.

"Oh, right, I forgot about that. Who knows, it might be a fun night, and I promise I won't be snooty." Fiona reached over and gave Ned a kiss on the cheek.

"Annie," George called out, "Ned and Fiona are joining us. I don't think Fiona is too thrilled about it, but Ned said he always wanted to go to Bird's."

George called Bird's and ordered steaks for four; when he told Byrd who they would be bringing, he sounded about as happy to have Fiona in his place as she was to be there. George hung up, saying they would see him around seven for drinks, then dinner at eight.

CHAPTER 61

Dewey phoned Layla Saturday morning telling her everything was set for him to arrive next Friday. They had reservations at an inn at Mama's through Tuesday of the next week. He would return to Salt Lake City late Wednesday morning.

"Honey, you've made me so happy. I miss you so much and feel so safe when we're together."

"Safe, that's a funny word to use. Is someone bothering you? Is something wrong?"

"No, it's just that—oh, I don't know, sometimes I wonder if everything is truly real here."

"Layla, what are you talking about?" Dewey asked, deep concern in his voice.

"Everything is going so well, the work on our house, finding furniture, the Visitors Center is really coming along, you and I are going to be married, and yet none of this would have happened if it hadn't been for those horrible murders. Thinking of that scares me."

"I need you too. Sometimes I get too nerdy for my own good. That's why I ended up in Paia, hiding out for half a year. I was afraid if I kept on at the pace I was going, I would end up with a breakdown or worse. We'll take care of each other. OK with you?"

"I'll love you like crazy, and we will always take care of each other. Thank you for telling me what you just shared. Now I don't feel so needy," Layla said.

"That's just it, honey. We are needy, we need each other."

"On a lighter note, I'm going out sketching tomorrow to finish a couple more charcoals for the house and one more for the Visitors Center to sell."

"What plans do you have for the rest of the week?"

"I'll check with Fiona later today, no telling what she has in store. We still have to make a trip to Oahu, which I would like to get out of the way. I've got to get the dimensions to Wade for the large flat-screen television for the living room so he can begin to make the shelves. The air-conditioning people will be finished by the end of next week or first of the following week. Then things will really start to move fast."

"I can't wait to see where things stand. That's going to be our home-away-from-home for many years."

Thirty minutes after she finished talking with Dewey, Layla was sitting on Mr. Soo's lanai when she saw Fiona returning from a run. Fiona looked like she had run a marathon, sweaty, slightly panting, hair flying all over, and red faced.

"How about coming up for a cold glass of either iced tea or lemonade?" Layla called out.

"I could use the lemonade, I'm thirsty."

Fiona made her way up to Mr. Soo's lanai and sat down weakly in a chair. Layla came out with a cold pitcher of fresh lemonade and poured a glass for Fiona who drank the cold sugar-boost and held out her glass for a refill.

"Are you in training for some type of marathon or something?"

"No, I'm in training for eating a fattening dinner this evening. If I do this now, I can enjoy the meal without feeling guilty."

"Fiona, your logic is amazing," said Layla, laughing. "I need your sage advice on a couple of items. First off, let me tell you Dewey is coming for five days, beginning this coming Friday."

"You're not staying with Mr. Soo, are you? I imagine you will be spending the first couple of days in bed, and that could be awkward."

"Funny, a month ago, I would have been shocked by that remark. Now I think it's thoughtful of you to ask. Dewey has arranged for a bungalow at Mama's. That way, we will ensure our privacy. Anyway, I noticed while I was sitting here this morning, my legs are getting fuzzy, and I need another manicure and pedicure. I hate to have to go all the way to the Four Seasons for the upkeep. Is there any local place you can recommend, and do you think my hair needs a little clipping?"

"Glad you've made other sleeping arrangements," Fiona said, smiling. She reached into her pocket and pulled out her cell phone. "Get a paper and pencil, and I'll give you the name and phone number of local places that do great work. I use them. Be sure and tell them I recommended you. They will treat you right or they will hear from me, and they know it. Your hair is fine for a couple of more weeks, then you will need to get it cut again."

Layla got a paper and pencil and copied names and phone numbers from Fiona's contact list, including Choo Choo's. "Do you need another refill on the lemonade?"

"No, another one, and I'll have to run that off too. I need to go home and get a good hot shower. If Ned is home, he can give me a rubdown. I'm sure I'll have sore thighs."

"My, that sounds romantic, a nice warm shower and a rubdown."

"Well, it might if Ned was a few years younger, but after last night, I don't think he'll be, shall we say, up for anything else this afternoon. Enjoy it frequently for as long as you can. Poor boys, their testosterone level really starts falling off once they hit there sixties, and they are only good for maybe a couple of times a week. Pity, I'm just as ready and able as ever."

"I think Dewey and I have quite a few good years left, but I'll keep that in the back of my mind. Have you ever considered that Viagra pill?"

"There is no way I would even consider letting Ned take one of those, and he knows it. Here's my thinking: they do not have radar, and they enlarge muscle. The heart is a muscle, and I don't give a damn what the doctors say, I don't think they're safe. Besides, if I can't take care of getting my Ned excited enough for sex, I better turn in my Italian heritage."

"Fiona, you need to write a book," Layla said, laughing.

"Actually, I once said that to Ned, and he said it would have to wait until he was dead because if not, he would probably die of embarrassment. I can't imagine why he feels that way. Everything I say would be truthful."

"Well, you know some men like to keep their love life, especially with their wife, private."

"Perhaps you're right, but he should be proud. He was and is a real stud."

CHAPTER 62

At seven Saturday evening, the Boones and Kellers were on their way to Bird's. George pulled into the gravel lot of Bird's, which looked better after dark than in daylight.

"Well, folks, here we are," George said. He aided Annie out of the car as Ned helped Fiona. Fiona gave a faint audible sigh as they went up the ramp to the foyer of Bird's.

Annie walked into the bar, followed by Fiona, Ned, and George. When Bird saw Annie, he let out one of his whistles, and she went over and placed her cheek close for him to nudge.

Next, Bird saw Fiona and let out a loud shrieking whistle. Fiona smiled fondly at him, went to his perch, and stroked the soft feathers on his head, something no one dared attempt. She cooed to him, and he bent down and nuzzled her cheek as she continued petting him.

"My name is Fiona," she told him softly.

Bird yelled "Fiona!" at the top of his bird voice, silencing those in the bar and causing Bird to come from behind the bar into the foyer.

"What the heck? My god, you're petting him!"

"Goodness, yes, he's the sweetest little darling I've ever seen," Fiona said softly.

Byrd shook his head and went back behind the bar.

"Let's get a table and a drink," said George.

"You folks go ahead, and, Ned, order me a vodka martini. I'm just going to stay here a minute and talk to this baby."

Making their way to a booth midway inside the bar, Ned said, "Mark my words, the minute she gets over here, she'll want a parrot. Then I'll have to talk her out of it, which will make her pout." Ned shook his head and ginned at the Boones.

Byrd came over to take their drink order.

"What's with your namesake there, Byrd?" asked George.

"Apparently, he's found his soul mate, or better yet, with the color of her hair and the way she's talking to him, he probably thinks she's his mommy."

"Don't tell Fiona that. She'll want to take her baby home."

"I've never seen him so smitten before. I guess Fiona Keller has lived up to her reputation."

"My wife, in some way or another, is always living up to her reputation." Ned said with a laugh. "She's instructed me to order her a vodka martini with olives, and I'll have a Heineken Light."

"I'll try one of Fiona's martinis too," said Annie.

"I'll take the same as Ned," said George.

Byrd brought drinks, and Fiona tore herself away from her new pal, sitting down at their booth. "Ned, we should seriously look into owning an exotic bird."

"Absolutely not, they spit seeds, and their toilet habits take a great deal of tending to. Whenever you feel a need to fluff some exotic bird feathers, we'll come here."

"Ned, you're being unreasonable. Think how much fun we could have teaching a bird to talk."

"Dearest, we are on the go too much to tend to any animal."

"Oh, perhaps you have a point there," said Fiona, tasting her drink. "My goodness, this is lovely. How's yours, Annie?"

"I like this. I never tried a vodka martini before, much better than gin. I had an aunt that if she ran out of perfume, she would put gin behind her ears and on her wrists, said it smelled so much like perfume no one never knew."

"Tastes like it too," declared Fiona.

"Hi, folks," greeted Jessie Byrd, who came in the nights Byrd cooked to tend bar in his place. "Good to see you, George, Annie, and who are our new customers?"

"Ned and Fiona Keller," said Ned, extending his hand to Jessie.

"I love your beautiful bird. Do you take him home at night, or does he stay here and act as a guard bird?"

"Pleased to meet you, folks. Bird comes home with us each night. We screened in a section of our lanai, then added lots of plants and bushes. We let him roam around at night. He's not able to fly, but he likes to hop around and perch wherever he wants. He's family to us. We never had children, and I guess, he's our child substitute. Funniest thing is him riding in the car. He gets in the back seat and bobs around looking out the rear window. We get a lot of stares. I better get behind the bar so Byrd can get to his grill."

"Jessie, when you have time, I need to talk with you," said Annie.

"Fine, let's make it after Byrd is through cooking."

Byrd brought their dinners. Porterhouse steaks were served with garlic mashed potatoes, grilled asparagus, and Maui onions.

After several bites, Fiona declared, "This is superb. I don't believe I've ever eaten a finer piece of meat. These potatoes and grilled vegetables are excellent. Ned, why haven't you brought us here before?"

"Well, guess I never thought of it. I'm glad you're enjoying dinner."

Annie and George looked at each other, smiling.

After dinner, everyone sat and moaned about how they had overeaten but enjoyed every morsel. Annie saw Byrd relieve Jessie from behind the bar and went over to speak with her.

"Jessie, I'm signing up Paia residents to work a two-hour shift at the Visitors Center as docents. George and I will be doing the training, and Hilo Hatties is providing custom-fitted Hawaiian shirts. I hope I can add your name to our list. We'll have a meeting where those volunteering can select their desired shift."

"Annie, it would be my honor to be a docent at the center. I am so pleased that you have asked me. Have you scheduled a meeting date yet?"

"No, I'm still recruiting and so is George. The plan is to have an older person work with a younger Paia person at the reception desk. George is hoping to recruit some of the windsurfers here tonight."

"There are a lot of the young Paia folks that have deep ties to this area, and I believe he will find them anxious to contribute their time, keeping in mind they have pretty heavy schedules. Many of them go to college and work, plus windsurfing, but I know they will try their best to work this into their schedule."

Annie went back to their table and added Jessie to her list. She told George what Jessie said about the windsurfers' willingness to volunteer. The band was busy setting up for the evening, and soon sixties, seventies, and eighties rock music filled the bar.

"Ned, let's get out there. That's what we need to work off some of this dinner," said Fiona, nudging Ned toward the end of his seat.

"Lord, Fiona, look out there. There's nothing but young folks on the dance floor."

"Excellent, we can show them how to dance."

With that, Fiona and Ned headed toward the dance floor. George and Annie scooted around, George saying, "I can't want to see what Fiona does. No doubt she feels free to abandon restraint."

"Honey, I don't believe the words *restraint* and *Fiona* are compatible."

Amazingly, Ned and Fiona danced very well to "Honky Tonk Woman." It seemed like they had a silent routine; several of the younger crowd paused to admire the older couple. That was followed by a slower "Always" with George and Annie joining in on the dance floor. After the number ended, George and Annie went back to the booth as "Jumpin' Jack Flash" boomed from the jukebox. Fiona and Ned stayed dancing. Ned came back to the booth, but Fiona continued dancing with one of the younger men.

"Whew, I'm worn out and need a beer," Ned declared, dropping into the booth.

"Where does she get all the stamina?" asked Annie.

"Beats the hell out of me," said Ned. "She's always had this higher than normal energy level. I'll tell you this, though, when she goes to sleep, she's dead to the world. We once were in Southern California when they had a 5.0 earthquake. I jumped out of the hotel bed and figured she was behind me, but nope, she never stirred, slept through the whole thing."

George gazed at the dance floor and spotted Fiona with arms high in the air, wiggling away.

"She's having a ball," he said, laughing. "I'm going to guess that between that bird, the food, and dancing, she'll have you bringing her back here before long."

"No doubt," said Ned with a smile.

"If you folks will excuse me, I see a couple of windsurfers I want to speak to about doing docent work. These are Paia-born kids, and they knew the Okamotos, so I think I'll have no trouble recruiting them for a couple of hours per week. Annie, give me your pad and pencil. That way, I can get names and phone numbers."

George went to his recruitment duties, and Fiona made her way back to the booth. "I need something cold to drink, catch my breath, then I'm back out there. This is so much fun!"

Fiona drank half a beer, and Ned got Annie out on the dance floor for a milder oldie. When they got back, George was sitting at the booth with a big smile. "You looked great out there, honey."

"You don't dance?" asked Ned.

"Only the slow ones, I always felt uncomfortable dancing fast with my height. Annie, not only did I get six windsurfers to sign up, but two of them said their moms wanted to be docents also. I've got their names and phone numbers for you. They also gave me names of other windsurfers not here tonight because of their age whom I should ask. We're doing quite well. Is Fiona still out on the dance floor?" George asked, looking into the crowd on the dance floor.

"I expect so, said she was having a ball, then headed back out," said Ned.

Close to one o'clock, the group made their way out of Bird's, Fiona cooing goodbye to Bird with a promise she would be back to see him soon. She thanked George and Annie several times for the great evening.

CHAPTER 63

Layla and Mr. Soo were coming back from the grocery store when Layla spotted Fiona on her lanai.

"After we get things inside, I'm going to talk to Fiona about making a trip to Oahu this coming week. I need to finish up buying the big-ticket items for the house."

"You go on over. I'll put things away for us."

"Thanks." Layla walked next door and asked Fiona if she had a minute.

"Sure, Ned's out for a round of golf, and I was sitting here thinking about how much fun we had last night. Have you ever been to Bird's?"

"Love it, great place, and food is terrific too."

"George and Annie took us there last night. They both wanted to do some docent recruiting. I fell madly in love with Bird, the parrot, that is," Fiona added quickly. "The food was outstanding. Then we danced the night away. Well, I actually danced a lot more than Ned. Those young folks really know how to have fun," Fiona said, smiling fondly.

"Sounds like you did have a good time. Can we schedule a trip to Oahu for next Wednesday? It seems there is nothing for me to do at the house, you have everyone working so well, and I'm feeling lost, just waiting for Dewey to get here on Friday."

"Definitely, I'll make the plans tomorrow. Layla, I had a thought about you and Dewey. I've done remodels for years, and over half the time, the owner hasn't been present. Why don't you return to Salt Lake City with Dewey, and then you two can come back to Maui in a couple of weeks when a lot more work will be completed? You won't just be sitting around waiting and driving yourself crazy."

Layla looked at Fiona, her mouth slightly open. "Fiona, you're a genius. That never crossed my mind. You set up our Oahu trip. I've got to go home and phone Dewey." Layla got up and went over and gave Fiona a kiss on the cheek. "Thank you so much!"

Layla raced back to Mr. Soo's and dialed Dewey. When he answered, she said, "Dewey, Fiona had the most marvelous idea. Since there is hardly anything for me to do here, once we finish our shopping in Oahu, she suggested I go back with you to Salt Lake City for a couple of weeks. Then we can return here and see how things are coming along. What do you think?"

"Wonderful. I can come home to you every night! Why didn't we think of that? I'm sending Fiona a big bouquet of flowers."

"She'll love that. I'm glad you approve of her idea. The rest of this week will be busy. I'll need to pack for our stay here, then pack for Utah. Hopefully on Wednesday, Fiona and I are going to Oahu to finish our shopping, and Thursday is a beautification day for me."

"What's a beautification day?"

"That's a day when I get a manicure and pedicure, among other things to get ready for you on Friday."

"Honey, you don't have to do anything special for me."

"Oh, but I do. Angels should always look their best."

"Guess you have a point. Are you still going to go sketching today?"

"Heading out to the bluff after we hang up. Mr. Soo and I went grocery shopping, then I spotted Fiona on her lanai on the way home, and you know the rest. Annie and George took them to Bird's last night, and Fiona loved it. She thought the food was excellent, fell in love with Bird's bird, and said she danced the night away."

"Bird's is the last place I would imagine she would like. We should go there with them and Annie and George this weekend. I could use one of Bird's steaks. Can you make the arrangements?"

"That will be so much fun. Yes, I'll talk with everyone and then speak with Byrd. Can't wait for this weekend. I'm going to let you go now and leave so I can get some good light. Love you, darling."

"Love you too. See you on Friday."

Fiona needed some fresh coffee and didn't want to brew another pot. She locked up and, with coffee cup in hand, went over to the Boones'. At the lanai screen, she noticed Annie drawing something at her dining room table.

"Hi, neighbor, got a fresh pot brewing?"

"Heavens yes, come on in." Annie got up, unlocked the screen, and let Fiona inside.

"I knew you would have fresh coffee. What are you working on?"

"I'm making a rough draft of a chart I'm going to have George duplicate on the computer. It will list the open docent slots and then the filled docent slots. I'm surprised at how many people are asking to be on the list before I've done much recruiting. George is out at the beach with the windsurfers. He's in charge of recruiting the young folks. The center will be open seven days a week, from nine to five daily. Each docent will work a two-hour shift, which means we will need a total of fifty-six docents, hopefully one older person and one younger person. I also would like four alternates to fill in during vacation, illness, etc. I want everyone in place as soon as possible because we have to get measurements for the shirts, then have them made. How's your task of recruiting artists coming along?"

"Donnie and I have an ad ready to place in the local papers. When he starts receiving packets with the type of wares the artists will be offering, I will review each one and send either a no-thank-you letter or make arrangements to meet in person and review their art. I expect quite a few packets arriving the first week the ad appears."

"Sounds very interesting, but when it comes to final choices, it could be agonizing."

"Not for me. I'll have no problem telling someone thank you but it just won't work for the center. I'm really excited about next Sunday. Ned and I are meeting with Rebecca Steinmetz at her estate. She will give Ned a tour of her home and some of the property so he can give her an estimate of its worth. Then we're going to take her to brunch at the country club. When we put the estate on the market, I insist you and George come with me one day and see this home. You will not believe your eyes. It's simply fabulous."

"Actually, I've already seen her marvelous home. Her daughter was in my class, and late one afternoon, she got really sick. She had about a half-mile walk from where the school bus let her off to her home, so I volunteered to drive her. Mrs. Steinmetz insisted I come in and have a cool drink. When I saw the foyer, you could have knocked me over with a feather. It was so beautiful, beyond anything I've ever seen. I would love to have George see that atrium and staircase. With his engineering background, he would be fascinated."

"Yes, I imagine he would be. Thanks for the coffee. I've got to go home and make a list of shops for Layla and me to go to Oahu on Wednesday. She wants to get the rest of her furniture shopping out of the way. I suggested she take a couple of weeks away from here and go back to Salt Lake City with Dewey. There isn't much she can do till things are further along, and until then, I'll handle the workers. Staying here will just make her a nervous wreck."

"Fiona, that was a grand idea."

"Thank you, it was one of my better ones."

CHAPTER 64

Fiona was finishing up her Monday morning confirmation calls for Wednesday when there was a knock at the front lanai. "Ned, can you get that, please?"

"Got it," Ned said, going to the screen and finding Archie from the florist with a beautiful array of pink and white roses.

"Hi, Mr. Keller, is Mrs. Keller in? These are for her."

"Fiona, get out here. Your secret admirer is getting bolder."

"Ned, what the hell are you talking about?" Fiona asked, making her way to the living room. "My goodness, are those for me?"

"Good morning, Mrs. Keller, these are most certainly for you," said Archie, pushing the bouquet toward Fiona.

"Are you going to read that card in front of me?" asked Ned.

"Don't be silly. I have no idea who sent these." Fiona opened the small envelope and read out loud, "Thank you, Fiona. You're terrific. Signed, Dewey."

"Bless his heart. This is for my suggestion that Layla return with Dewey for a couple of weeks. He's so thoughtful."

"Here I was worried those might be from a lovelorn parrot."

"I'm sure, if he had the funds, he would have sent flowers too."

"Probably," said Ned, laughing.

"I'm going to call Layla and get her over here," said Fiona.

Fiona phoned Layla, who said she would be over shortly. When she arrived, she told Fiona that Dewey said he was sending flowers, but as usual, he had outdone himself; her bouquet was lovely.

"Dewey suggested we all get together Saturday evening for dinner at Bird's. I told him how much you enjoyed yourself last weekend, and he said he would like to take everyone there. He thought it would be a fun evening."

"Wonderful, I'm in. How about you, Ned?"

"Sounds like a nice evening, and you can see your baby again."

"Yes, I bet he misses me. We should stop by one evening before Saturday, just to have a drink, so he doesn't forget me."

"I'm going to call Byrd and make the dinner arrangements. Do you want steak, chicken, or fish?"

"Steak, medium," they both said in unison.

"Layla, I've got our trip to Oahu all set for Wednesday. We leave at 9:00 a.m. I received a flyer from this wonderful high-end linen shop and they're having a big sale, so I want both of us to carry an empty suitcase. That way, if we find things to buy, and I'm sure we will, we can bring them on the airplane in our luggage instead of having to pay to ship them."

"Fiona, you are one clever lady," said Layla admiringly.

"Thank you. Always looking out for the interest of my clients."

Ned, standing out of Layla's range of vision, rolled his eyes.

"I'm going over to see George and Annie and make sure they can go on Saturday. I guess I should make a list of things I'll need from the linen store. Just bedding items, correct?" asked Layla.

"Exactly, and remember, you have three bedrooms to supply. Plus, they carry comforters, spreads, and pillows. We should find a lot of good buys. This is a once-a-year blow-out sale."

"Sounds exciting, well, I'm off to George and Annie's."

Layla left the Kellers and went across the street. She found George and Annie bent over their docent list. "Sorry to bother, but I would like to invite you to be Dewey's guest, along with the Kellers, this coming Saturday night for dinner at Bird's."

"Terrific," said George. "That'll be fun."

"What can I order you folks for dinner?" asked Layla.

"I've got to have another steak, medium well," said George.

"If possible, I'll have fish with Bird's mango salsa. An excellent flavoring with the fish," said Annie.

"That does sound good. I'll try that too. I'll get back to you on the time once Dewey gets here. Did Fiona tell you I'm going back to Salt Lake City with him?"

"She did. I know Agnes will enjoy your input on the wedding," said Annie.

"I'll enjoy working with Agnes. I won't feel so bad about putting so much on her shoulders."

Layla left and returned to Mr. Soo's. She waited until late afternoon to call Byrd to let him know of the group coming in for dinner on Saturday, telling him she'd get back on the time but wanted to give him their menu orders.

Wednesday morning, Layla and Fiona were hurling through the streets from the airport, Layla holding on and Fiona oblivious to the fact she was maneuvering their rental like an Italian racecar driver. Layla took a deep breath as they pulled into their first stop.

"Do you have an idea of what size televisions you want?"

"Not the slightest, do you?"

"Yes, I've taken measurements and several other things into consideration. You'll want all LCD-HD models, and for the living room, you should get a sixty-inch, the master bedroom a forty-six-inch, and the two guest bedrooms a forty-inch. I will take exact measurements for Wade so that he can begin designing your shelving."

"I'll leave everything in your capable hands," said Layla, making her way to their salesman's desk and sitting in the guest chair, checkbook at the ready.

Fiona phoned Wade and continued to get precise measurements on the large television. Finally, all was finished, and she and Layla left the store. In the car, they discussed where their next stop should be. They decided to try the design store first.

Fiona found her favorite salesperson and explained they were looking for a large chair to fit in with an eggplant-colored sectional sofa and also three barstools. Layla and Fiona had previously decided on three barstools since they had the table and accompanying chairs for the kitchen. They wandered around the store, looking at various items.

"Fiona, look at the large pistachio-colored chair. It certainly looks comfortable, and it's large enough, but what's this fabric?"

"That color will go great with the sofa, but the fabric eludes me."

"This new high-quality process is coated linen, much like the designer fabric used in expensive handbags, a water-resistant and stain-resistant process," offered their salesperson.

"Do you have experience with this type of product?" asked Fiona.

"I've sold a dining room table with eight chairs that had the same coating. I have not heard anything negative back from the buyer, and this is a lady I've dealt with for a number of years who is quite critical."

"I like that lady. Sounds like me," said Fiona with a slight chuckle.

Layla sat in the chair. "This is comfortable, and I do like this color. What do you think, Fiona?"

"If you're satisfied with the comfort, I'm very happy with the design and the color. We'll take it," she said to the salesperson. "Now let's concentrate on barstools."

They revisited all the barstools available and didn't find anything either of them liked. They paid the bill and made delivery arrangements to the warehouse. Fiona suggested they try the consignment store. At that store, they didn't find anything and decided to go onto the big sale.

"This is some store. What elegant linens and the prices are great. I want all white linens and towels. Bed toppings can be colorful, but I like the look of crisp white sheets and towels," said Layla. "I especially like tuxedo-striped sheets. Let's get two sets for all the beds, except the master, and three sets for that bed. I also want two sets of pillowcases per sheet set. Do you think we can get them all in our luggage?"

"They are folded very tightly, and we should be able to get them all back. I'm just not sure about the weight. We might have to pay something, but it would be less than shipping them."

They found all the sheets and pillowcases, and although the bill was high, Layla realized she had saved a great deal with the sale. She was also surprised how compact it all appeared. They continued their tour. Layla grabbed Fiona's arm and pointed to a store display highlighting place mats, napkins, and napkin rings on a replica of a kitchen eating counter. What Layla wanted Fiona to see were the three barstools displayed with the counter.

"Those are just what we're looking for," uttered Fiona.

"Perfect," said Layla, "but will they sell them to us?"

"They'll sell them. This is a seasonal display. I'm sure they will be happy to rid themselves of those barstools in lieu of storing them. Now all that's left is to negotiate a good price."

After twenty minutes negotiating with the salesperson and the store manager, Fiona returned to Layla, saying, "We have an excellent price. These were originally bought at wholesale for $250 each, and they are selling them to us for $100 each. I've checked each one over, and there's not a scratch or mar on them. What a lucky fine! This also opens up a whole new avenue of thought. Since these will have to go to the warehouse for shipment to Maui, we can shop for more items that are on sale and add them to the items going to the warehouse. If I recall correctly, we need pillows and toppings for all the beds, do you agree?"

"Yes, those are the items left on my list. I want eiderdown pillows, two for each twin bed, four for the main guest room, and six for the master bedroom. I'm curious if any of those are on sale."

At the pillow section, all pillows displayed were on sale. Their salesperson explained the only thing different from last year's model and this year's was the outside covering, which, of course, a pillowcase would cover. Because they were purchasing such a large quantity of pillows, Fiona got an added price reduction, plus her usual discount. Next stop, comforters and bedspreads.

Layla immediately spotted a comforter she knew she was meant to have. It had a two-inch dark-chocolate stripe, next the same-sized tan strip, and lastly, a vivid white stripe, then the sequence repeated. The dust ruffle was tan, and Layla thought it would contrast perfectly with the dark wood floors of the master bedroom. She loved the elegant beauty of the comforter that neither was feminine or masculine but perfect for a couple's master bedroom. Layla didn't want any shams, preferring the comforter cover the pillows. After Fiona did her pricing miracle, they moved on to look at toppings for the other beds.

Layla found bedspreads with a light green background covered in yellow pineapples with darker green pineapple crowns. "Oh, just what I had in mind for the twin beds. What do you think, Fiona?"

"Layla, this would not be my first choice, probably not my second either." Fiona looked inquiringly at Layla, saying, "Layla, do you have some type of plan for that small bedroom?"

"Possibly," said Layla with a wink. "Fiona, I'm at a loss for what type of covering to get for the bed in the main guest room. I simply can't get a handle on anything."

"I would go with a stark-white comforter, some dark-chocolate throw pillows, and a couple of sky-blue pillows for accents. With the dark furniture, dark floors, and white walls, that combination will keep it simple and elegant. I also noticed rectangle white shag throw rugs that would be perfect for each side of the bed. What do you think?"

"It sounds just right, and I especially like the throw rugs. Let's get four of them. I would like them in the master bedroom as well."

"That takes care of everything. Half a block down on our right is a nice outdoors restaurant. Why don't you go and get something cool to drink, and I'll be along after I get everything set here. We'll still take the sheets on the plane, but everything else will go to the warehouse."

"I could use a cold drink, and I hope we have time for lunch. Should I write a blank check and leave it with you?"

"Yes, the store knows me, and I can vouch for your credit. If there's a problem, I'll charge it and add it to your bill."

When Fiona arrived at the restaurant, she gave Layla a receipt for the amount of the check. "This is a lot of money, but with all I purchased and the high quality of the items, I'm getting an excellent deal. You need to get me a current bill so I can write you a check before I leave for Utah."

"I'll work on that tomorrow. Once we get home, we both will be exhausted. Amazing how shopping and spending gobs of money can wear a person out."

The ladies enjoyed a hearty lunch, then caught their return flight to Maui.

CHAPTER 65

Layla returned to Mr. Soo's a little after one Thursday afternoon. She admired the pinkish salmon color on her nails and toes, but best of all, she was thrilled that her second bikini wax was hardly painful. Her first task was to go to Fiona's and pay her current bill. She also wanted Fiona to accompany her as she told the workers of her upcoming plans. Once all that was accomplished, she would begin her packing and make a couple of casseroles of macaroni and cheese for Mr. Soo.

Fiona and Layla sat at Fiona's counter as she explained her bill, emphasizing that she did not charge for her time at Mrs. Steinmetz's, fully expecting that visit would lead to a large commission for Ned. Layla knew Fiona would not forget the charges unless she wanted to forget. She paid the bill as presented, adding a large sum, which was Fiona's estimate for the final payment for the air-condition installation.

Fiona felt sure by the time Layla returned from Salt Lake City, all floors would be done, walls painted, bathrooms close to complete, if not totally completed, and the living room shelving finished. If things got done earlier, she would make arrangements to have the furniture shipped over from Oahu. Layla could not believe her ears. It was just like Fiona had predicted: when everything began to be completed, it would all be done at once.

At Layla's, they spoke with Wade and Herb about Layla's plans and were told that would be fine, and if needed, they would contact Fiona; the same response was echoed by Chris and Josie. Satisfied all was taken care of, Layla and Fiona headed back to their respective homes. Layla began making macaroni-and-cheese casseroles, and Fiona went to the bank to deposit her large check.

By six o'clock Friday morning, Layla was up and in the shower. She was not able to sleep any longer and decided to have breakfast with Mr. Soo at Otis's. Dewey told her the earliest he would arrive would be ten o'clock but would call about thirty minutes before their estimated landing time. Mr. Soo and Layla enjoyed their breakfast together. He let her know he would be fine while she was in Utah and reminded her that she would be getting married before too long and moving away permanently, so he had to get used to being without her pleasant company.

Layla reached across the table and laid her hand on top of his. "I will miss you so very much. We've had great fun together. You are very dear to me."

"Thank you, Layla, you are dear to me also. Mrs. Soo and I only had sons, but if we would have had a daughter, I could not have wished for any better one than you. For that matter, if I had a granddaughter, I would want her to be like you. It seems the Soo family can only produce males, and they are too much like their father. It has not been until I've gotten to be an old man that I realize I missed so much of my sons as children, teens, and young men. Now they are all on Oahu keeping the business going, and I don't even get to see my grandchildren that often."

"Have you ever thought of moving to back to Oahu?"

"No, too hectic. I lived that fast-paced life too long. I'm used to the tranquility of Paia, and I have all my wonderful friends here. No, I'll stay here. Besides, you and Dewey will come to your home often, and we will visit then."

"We will be here as often as we can. Dewey has begun to reassign his workload. He's putting more responsibility on others and freeing up his time."

They finished their breakfast, said goodbye to Otis, and walked back to Mr. Soo's. Layla loaded her first set of luggage in the car and went back inside to get another cup of coffee. After several hours of puttering, she decided to go and speak with Donnie, get a latte, and wait for Dewey's call.

When she got to the bank, she asked Donnie if he would be going to the Visitors Center this afternoon and wondered if she and Dewey could drop by for a brief look around. Donnie, aware of the contribution Dewey had made to the project, readily agreed.

Layla was coming out of the coffee shop when her cell phone rang. It was Dewey telling her he would be landing in twenty minutes and couldn't wait to see her. Layla got in her car and made the short drive to the airport.

Dewey peered out the window as his plane taxied toward the hangar. He thought he spotted Layla's car and saw a figure standing near. As the plane grew closer, he could see it was his Layla, and he felt silly with anticipation, reminding himself he was a grown man and this was the woman he was going to marry. What the heck, he couldn't wait to hold her and kiss her, too long without her near.

When the plane's engines shut down, Layla drove on the tarmac to pick up Dewey and his luggage. The stair ramp was lowered, and Dewey came bounding toward her. They kissed and embraced, enjoying their togetherness. Dewey transferred his luggage to her car, and they left the airport.

"Dewey, it's too early to check in, but I've arranged with Donnie to drop by the Visitors Center so you can see how the work is progressing. I also thought we could drop by our home so you can see how things are coming along. After the Visitors Center, lunch, and by the time we've finished, we can check in at Mama's."

"Sound good to me, and you look beautiful. I've missed you so much. I'm so happy you're coming back with me. Agnes and Ted are thrilled you'll be visiting. The way things are going here, it won't be long before you'll be moving in permanently to our Salt Lake City home. I'm assuming that it's suitable for you."

"Dewey, are you kidding? Your home is fabulous or, should I say, your compound. It has everything one could imagine."

"Three-fourths of the house is closed most of the time, and we've never utilized the stable or tennis court areas. When it's necessary to open up some of the rooms, we'll hire more staff. I imagine once we're married, we'll open up more rooms. I've always hoped that home would be full of people, especially kids," Dewey said, winking at Layla.

Layla grabbed Dewey's hand and squeezed. "That would suit me just fine."

Back in Paia, Layla pulled into her driveway, and they went in so Dewey could see all that had been accomplished since his last visit.

"I don't see any of the air-conditioning people. Have they finished?" asked Dewey.

"Yes, they finished up yesterday. Chris and Josie are about finished sanding the floors. However, before they begin staining them, Fiona is having a crew in to wash walls and clean up the dust particles. As you can see, there is a layer of film everywhere. Until the air-conditioning people left, everyone coming in had to wear a mask."

"I'm impressed with the ceilings, they are beautiful, and once dust is cleaned, they will shine. After the staining is done, will they paint?"

"Yes, and then basically, all will be done. I think Herb is close to having the larger of the two bathrooms finished, and he's also working on the smaller one. Wade has the measurements for the shelves, and he'll do the staining on them. As soon as the floors are done, Fiona will start moving the furniture in. Items coming from Mrs. Steinmetz may be delayed in arriving until she leaves the island."

They went to the various rooms and greeted Chris, Josie, and Herb, commenting on their great work. Dewey imagined how peaceful it was going to be sitting out on the front lanai and watching the surf, Layla by his side.

Layla looked at her watch. "Let's drop by the Boones so you can say hello to George and Annie. It's too early to meet Donnie at the Visitors Center."

They walked next door to the Boones'. George and Annie invited them in and explained the large docent chart that lay on the dining room table.

"I'm impressed how many people you've recruited," said Dewey.

"It's been easy. Many sought us out and asked to be on the list. We're having a meeting a week from this coming Sunday at the Visitors Center to acquaint them with the inside, and the Hilo Hattie lady is coming to take measurements for shirts. Everyone will sign up for a shift time that will work into his or her schedules. Donnie is having brochures and city maps made, and hopefully, those will be ready for the meeting so each docent can take one home and become familiar with what's inside. Annie is preparing a program she and I can work from to instruct the docents on information and procedures that will need to be followed in this type of an endeavor. Should be a busy and interesting few weeks."

"Sounds to me like you guys have planned everything out. Of course, I realize one can never plan for the unexpected, but with you and Annie heading up this project, you'll keep it all under control," said Dewey, smiling at his friends.

Layla noticed Ned come outside to begin his Friday walk to the Visitors Center. She opened the lanai screen and yelled, "Ned, wait up! Dewey and I will go with you. We are going to meet Donnie there for a tour. I'm so anxious for Dewey to see how much progress has been made."

Ned turned back and headed for the Boones'. George and Annie were on the back lanai, saying goodbye to Layla and Dewey.

"Layla and I will meet everyone at eight tomorrow evening at Bird's. I'm sure looking forward to one of his good steaks."

"Me too. It should be a fun evening. You and Layla will get to see Fiona and that parrot. Darnest thing I've ever seen," said George.

"So I've heard. That Fiona, only she could charm that old Bird," said Dewey with a laugh.

"What was that I heard about my Fiona?" Ned asked, smiling.

"George was commenting on how only Fiona could charm that parrot."

"Lord, don't remind me. Almost every evening, she wants to drive over there so she can coo to that bird. Frankly, I think it's a little weird, but it makes her happy and a heck of a lot better than us getting our own parrot."

"Dewey, let's drive up to the center because we'll have to leave around one for lunch. Come on, we'll give you a lift," said Layla, making her way down the stairs.

"Great, I've already played eighteen holes today, and it's quite humid this afternoon. I will enjoy the ride up the hill."

Dewey parked in the parking lot at the center and was impressed with the broad veranda that would serve as the eating area. Once inside, his jaw dropped in amazement. He could not believe this was the former Okamoto Market. There was no resemblance whatsoever to a market or store format. He was delighted with the openness and marveled at the old photos of Paia.

"Honey, are you all right?" asked Layla.

"I'm fine. This is a fabulous transformation. The residents of Paia can take pride in this facility. It's beautiful."

Ned went on to explain the architect's vision and filled Dewey in on the immense contribution George had made to the final plans. He explained the area that Fiona would have charge of that would sell items made by local artists. He told him how the food line would work, ushering those purchasing food outside to eat on the veranda.

Dewey liked the welcoming feel of the docent's area and imagined docents dressed in colorful Hawaiian shirts greeting visitors. Donnie came into the center and greeted everyone, then took Dewey and Layla around to specific areas, explaining the function of each in more detail.

"Donnie, it appears the Visitors Center and Mr. Soo's former home will be completed about the same time. Funny how those two projects coincide."

Layla looked at Dewey and tapped her watch. They told Donnie they had to be on their way, thanked him for the tour, and praised him for his dedication to the center. On the way out, they confirmed with Ned their eight o'clock dinnertime tomorrow night at Bird's. They got in the car and went to Mama's for lunch before check-in.

After lunch, they had about forty-five minutes before check-in. Dewey went to the check-in office and found out their room was ready and went ahead and checked-in. They spent the rest of the afternoon making love, discussing their future plans, and more than once laughing about Fiona and her Bird.

Chapter 66

Ned and Fiona arrived first. Ned sat at a large table as directed by Byrd. When Fiona walked in, Bird shrieked at the top of his bird lungs, temporarily silencing the bar. Fiona cooed and chatted with him, then joined Ned for a predinner cocktail.

George came into the living room as Annie secured the front lanai slider. "George, I don't recall that shirt. You look very handsome this evening."

"It's one I used to wear to work, remember, with the dark-blue tie you liked? You look pretty darn hot yourself. You don't wear a dress too often, but when you do, it makes me crazy," George said, drawing Annie into him.

"George, you are the—"

George quickly placed his finger on her lips, saying, "Don't say what you were going to say, just call me lustful. You, my love, make me lustful. I have a great idea. Let's go back to the bedroom and be a bit late for dinner." George bent down and kissed Annie longingly.

Annie pulled back and placed her hand on George's cheek, smiling up into his face she said, "Honey, we shouldn't be late for dinner, especially since it's Dewey's treat."

"He and Layla won't care if we're late. After all, they have been at it for about twenty-four hours. They'll probably be a bit late themselves."

Annie smiled up at her husband. "Well, since you put it that way."

Annie and George walked into Bird's only twenty minutes late. They sat down in the booth, Annie saying, "Please excuse us for being late, but something came up."

"No problem," said Dewey, "we were a few minutes late ourselves."

George beamed at his wife.

Later in the evening, when Dewey and Layla were on the dance floor, Dewey said, "George and Annie were late because they had a quickie before dinner. I could tell, George had a goofy grin on his face when Annie explained they were late because something came up."

"Now that you mention it, he did look like the cat that swallowed the canary."

Everyone enjoyed the evening with great food, dancing, and easy companionship. It was after one when they all left Bird's.

Sunday morning, Ned backed the car out into the driveway, then closed and secured the garage door. He stood by the car door, looking up at the lanai, waiting for Fiona to appear.

George was on his third cup of coffee when he spotted Ned. "Wow, you have more pep than Annie and I. We even missed church this morning. Guess we overdid it a bit last night."

"No, I'm just a tired as everyone else, but we have an appointment with Mrs. Steinmetz to see her estate, then we're taking her to brunch at the club. Now, if Fiona will just hurry up, she's a bit pooped herself but would never admit it."

"What would I never admit to?" asked Fiona, coming out onto their front lanai.

"That you're pooped like the rest of us," said Ned, curious to hear her reply.

"Damned right I'll admit to it. It took me three layers of makeup to hide the dark circles under my eyes. Geez, I hate getting older," moaned Fiona. "Hello, George, you and Annie dragging like we are?"

"Oh yeah, we even missed church this morning. Annie hardly ever lets us miss church. Maybe our trouble is we don't party enough instead of being too old. We're just not used to all that late-night drinking and dancing."

"George, I like your thinking. We'll have to try it again soon."

"Fiona, we've got to get going. Being late to Mrs. Steinmetz's would not be suitable."

"Yes, dear," Fiona said, getting into their car.

As was her custom, Rebecca Steinmetz walked outside under the porte cochere to greet her guests. She extended her hand to Ned. "You're Ned Keller. I'm so pleased you could inspect my home. I'm Rebecca Steinmetz."

"I'm honored. Fiona has raved about your home ever since she returned from her initial visit."

"Thank you, my late husband and I took such joy in living here. Ned, may I call you Ned?"

"Yes, Mrs. Steinmetz, please do."

"And call me Rebecca. I'm anxious for your advice on the property. Fiona believes it will fetch much more than I imagined."

"Let's go inside, and I'll look around. I would also like to see your deed to get the exact amount of property we are talking about."

"I have that ready for you."

"My god," uttered Ned, "Fiona said I would be amazed, and frankly, that's putting it mildly. In all my years in real estate, I've never seen anything as breathtaking as this entrance."

Rebecca gave the same details to Ned as previously given to Fiona and Layla. She then took him on a tour of the home and into the backyard. "Ned, I have to be honest. There might be a problem with the back acreage, although I don't know for sure. I have been told by several law enforcement people that there is a good likelihood marijuana is being grown illegally on the back side of the property, where no one ever goes. It's the perfect type of area, great cover and no traffic. That could be a problem in selling. What do you think?"

"Honestly, Rebecca, that's a situation I've never encountered before. However, I will check into it for you. Don't worry too much. I can always call in some favors and get the area raided."

"You could do that? My goodness, it appears I've certainly met the best real estate agent for this property."

"I'll do my best for you, Rebecca, to see that you get the highest price possible for this estate. It will make a nice legacy for your children and grandchildren."

"I never thought about getting enough money to leave a legacy, but that would be wonderful," Rebecca said a smile on her face.

"Let's be off for lunch. I'm starving," said Fiona, trying to move everyone along.

They enjoyed a long lunch at the country club with Rebecca relating tales of their experiences at the big ranch on Hawaii, how her husband came to purchase the property on Maui and build their home. Ned and Fiona listened raptly to Rebecca; her vivid stories came alive as she spoke.

Driving back to their home after returning Rebecca to hers, Fiona said, "Funny, isn't it? Just when you think you're going to endure something boring, it turns out you have a wonderful time."

"She's a charming lady and can she ever tell a story. I'm going to make an extreme effort to get top dollar for her estate. When we get home, I'm going to place a call to an old friend on Oahu, who has a handle on potential high-end buyers."

"That's good, honey. When I get home, I'm getting this ton of makeup off, get undressed, and take a nap. I'm so sleepy."

Fiona woke up several hours later, feeling greatly refreshed. She threw her legs over the side of the bed and tried to rise without making nose so she wouldn't wake Ned.

"Don't worry. I'm not asleep. I woke up about ten minutes ago. Just lying here, resting and thinking."

"I can tell you're in business mode. Your mind works overtime."

Ned turned and reached his arm around Fiona, drawing her back into bed. "Let me tell you about my call to Oahu. It was to Larry Tomoko, he's the realtor that handles all the extremely expensive estates and property on the islands. I told him about Rebecca's to get a feel for what type of buyer I might solicit. Guess what, he thinks he has someone that might be interested. However, this party must be able to build a helicopter landing pad within close walking distance to the residence. I told him about the possibility of marijuana being grown somewhere on the property, and he actually said, for this buyer, that would be worth upping the price a million or so. Turns out the person he has in mind is a producer of action films and could only dream of hanging out of his own helicopter, rifle slung through his arm, hunting illegal pot farmers. He was slated to purchases a large property in Hana, but when he found out his neighbor would be a Saudi prince, he backed out. He felt there were be too many security concerns. This property would take him away from any town, is isolated, and he could do all sorts of outlandish action things. He wants to fly over Wednesday or Thursday of this week to view the property before calling the potential buyer. I'll call Rebecca a little later and see what time would be suitable for her, and, honey, I want you to join us on this trip to Rebecca's. Having you with us will make her feel more at ease."

"That's a lot of information to absorb after just waking up, but I think I got it all. It would be my pleasure to accompany you and Larry. He's a very natty dresser. We should wear something Armani."

"Fiona, I leave it to you to think of what we should wear," Ned said, giving his wife a kiss on the forehead. "I'll need to work up an overview between now and Tomoko's arrival, not my favorite way to spend time."

"Sweetheart, just think of the huge commission from the sale, and the words will flow."

CHAPTER 67

Layla got out of bed, went to the kitchenette, and started a pot of coffee. Dewey woke up, the rich smell of Kona coffee wafting into the bedroom; he got a cup and joined Layla on their enclosed patio. He gave her a morning kiss, sitting down next to her. "I have to admit I'm hungover and I'm tired. We sure had a great time last night though. I imagine everyone else must be feeling worse than we do. Poor Ned and Fiona, they have to meet with your friend, Mrs. Steinmetz, and take her to brunch."

"Sweetheart, remember, we're taking Mr. Soo to lunch today?"

"Great. Who thought that one up? Right, I did before we overdid last night. After a long shower, I should feel better. I would feel even better if I had someone to shower with," Dewey said, smiling at Layla.

Layla reached over and cupped Dewey's face in her hand. "Oh, I think that can be arranged. Everyone on the island is committed to water conservation, and I should do my part."

Mr. Soo's soft chuckle brought grins to both Dewey and Layla. She had just told him the story of Fiona and Bird, the parrot. After Layla told him and their brief encounters, he had changed his opinion of Fiona and said he planned on developing a better friendship with her once Layla left the island.

"Better to know all the lovely ladies that surround you," Mr. Soo said in earnest.

"Right you are, Mr. Soo, especially ones that are great cooks."

"That is a factor too," said Mr. Soo seriously.

Their luncheon was longer than planned, but after several sidelong glances from the wait staff, they decided it was time to leave.

Monday morning, Ned called Rebecca, making an appointment to show her estate on Wednesday, saying he would get back with her on the time. He also mentioned it would be necessary for her to sign a contract to sell her estate but only if she felt comfortable with his representation. He didn't tell her about the potential buyer but said he would be showing the estate to another real estate professional.

Rebecca said she had no hesitation in signing a contract with him and felt secure that he had her best interest at heart. Her only concern was that if things went too quickly, she didn't know how she would get packed up and ready to move.

Ned said that should be the least of her worries but suggested she begin to sort through her belongings.

"Fiona is an expert at helping people get ready to move, and she will assist in every way possible. She'll be joining us on Wednesday."

"Oh, that's lovely. I do so enjoy her company," said Rebecca.

After speaking with Rebecca, Ned phoned Larry Tomoko and told him he had set up a meeting Wednesday with Rebecca Steinmetz. Larry said he would fly over in the company jet and be there around nine. He also asked Ned if he could secure the services of an engineer to survey a possible helicopter landing area, saying his firm would pay the usual $500 fee for services.

Hanging up from talking to Mr. Tomoko, he shook his head and uttered a resounding "Damn."

"What's the problem, honey?"

"Tomoko wants an engineer to join us on Wednesday to make sure a helicopter landing pad is possible. Does he think I can just magically pull an engineer out of the woodwork, especially one familiar with helicopter sites?"

Fiona shook her head and walked toward her husband, smiling. "Well, why not, dear? After all, you live right across the street from a highly qualified airline engineer."

"George, he might just be perfect. Fiona, you're a genius!"

"Yes, dear."

"Call and see if we can pop over. I may need your enthusiasm to talk him into going with us."

"Ned, George and Annie are not wealthy like some of us. I'm quite sure he will be happy to earn $500. I'll call and see if we can drop in for a few minutes."

Fiona placed the call, then they walked across the street to the Boones'.

George opened the back lanai slider, ushering them inside. Ned reached up and put his hand on George's shoulder, saying, "George, I have a deal for you, if you're interested and know anything about helicopters." He then went on to explain why he needed an engineer qualified to handle specs for a possible helicopter-landing site and the $500 fee involved.

"Great, it should be interesting. Frankly, I'm perfect for the job. A couple of years before I retired, I did all the initial engineering work for the new helicopter handing sites at the airport. I'll check out the FAA website to ascertain if there are any new regulations, and I'll get to see the Steinmetz's property, plus earn $500, which we can always use, right, sugar?" he said, turning toward Annie who was in the kitchen making a fresh pot of coffee.

"That's great, Ned. Thanks for thinking of George."

Fiona was standing in front of the charcoal of the Boones that Layla had done on their trip to Arizona. "Every time I see this, I'm so taken by the blend of colors and shading. I'm going to purchase one of the charcoals she's done for the center. I hope once she and Dewey are married and settled, she'll continue to draw. I'm actually quite impressed with her talent."

"I agree with you. The way she blends in the various hues is so subtle but has such an impact," said Annie.

Monday afternoon, Dewey and Layla strolled through Paia, stopping for a coffee. "I'm going to walk over to the sheriff's office and see if there's anything new on the Okamotos' case."

"Go ahead, I'll sit here and read. I've got a paperback with me."

"OK, honey, I'll be right back," Dewey said and walked the several blocks to the sheriff's office.

Charlene greeted him warmly; the sheriff was in and pleased Dewey dropped by to visit. They exchanged pleasantries, then Dewey asked, "Anything new on the Okamoto murders?"

"That's a real sore subject with me, son. It's now officially a cold case with everyone but me. They assume it's someone from out of town that could never be found, but you know from the beginning, I never succumbed to that theory, I always felt it was local."

They talked for a bit longer; Dewey excused himself and rejoined Layla, updating her on the status of the case.

Tuesday snuck up on Dewey and Layla. After breakfast, Layla packed everything she would be leaving in Paia, and they loaded it into the car and drove to Mr. Soo's. She left that luggage there and put her Salt Lake City luggage in the car. They said their farewells to Mr. Soo, then went to say goodbye to Annie and George.

George told them he would be earning extra money, helping Ned with an engineering project at Mrs. Steinmetz's tomorrow, which would go into Annie's Panama Canal Cruise fund.

Next, they stopped at Ned and Fiona's; Layla got Fiona's promise to call if anything major happened at her home. Fiona felt all would be fine and not to worry.

They had a quiet supper, went back to their room, and got as much packed as possible for their departure early Wednesday morning. At nine on Wednesday, they drove to the private jet area and were surprised to find Ned, Fiona, and George waiting in Ned's car for the arrival of the realtor from Oahu. Again, they bid farewell to everyone, loaded luggage, drove the car into the DewMaster hangar, boarded the jet, and left for Utah.

Within minutes after the DewMaster departed, Mr. Tomoko's jet landed, and Ned drove his SUV onto the tarmac. The stairs lowered, and Mr. Tomoko strode out and walked toward the SUV. Ned, Fiona, and George stood outside the car, ready to great him.

George said softly under his breath, "You all are dressed really well. I feel like the country bumpkin."

"No, George, you are dressed perfectly for an engineer hired to do surveying work. Ned and I are dressed like this because Larry is always dressed like he just stepped out of a fashion shoot. His wardrobe must cost a fortune," Fiona lamented.

Ned walked toward Larry, hand extended. "Larry, so good to see you again. It's been a year since we met at the realtor's luncheon in Oahu. You're looking well."

"So are you, my friend. Ah, the life of a retiree who only dabbles in real estate when he chooses. Soon I hope to join those ranks. Fiona, a pleasure as always to see you and lovely as ever," Larry said, planting air kisses on the side of each of her cheeks.

"Thank you, Larry, I'm so glad you might be involved in this transaction. Trust me, you will be amazed at this property."

"I'm looking forward to it. From Ned's outline on this property, it's what my client is looking for. Almost sounds too good to be true."

"Larry, I would like to introduce you to George Boone. He's a retired engineer from the airlines and did the initial engineering work for the new helicopter facility here at the airport," said Ned.

George stepped forward, extending his hand to Mr. Tomoko. "A pleasure to make your acquaintance, sir. I'm glad to be of service."

"Mr. Boone, it's my pleasure. Shall we get to the property? I'm anxious to view this estate."

"Larry, you sit up front with Ned. That way, you can see exactly the route from the airport to Mrs. Steinmetz's property. I'll sit back here with George," said Fiona.

In less than twenty minutes, they were at Rebecca's, and she was out front greeting them. After introductions were made, she ushered them inside; George and Larry gawked.

"My god," said George, "this is an engineering marvel."

"Dear lady, I never imagined anything this spectacular. These plants, trees, bushes, and flowers are all real?"

"Yes, Mr. Tomoko, my late husband and I started this as a small project, and it kept getting bigger and bigger. I work two days a week with my gardener to keep it up to this level. I'm glad you can appreciate the beauty," said Rebecca, pride showing in her voice.

"Rebecca, why don't you and Fiona show Mr. Tomoko the inside of your home, and I'll take George outside so he can start his surveying work," said Ned.

George and Ned collected the surveying gear, then went to the back area that Ned felt might be turned into a helicopter landing pad.

"Ned, I can't begin to explain, from an engineering standpoint, the complicated and imaginative design work necessary to create that atrium. Whoever came up with the design was a genius."

"Believe it or not, Mr. Steinmetz had the vision, and it was actually a university student that made the design work. Like you, I am in awe of the design. So what do you think, is a helicopter pad doable?"

"Offhand, yes, it's possible but with costly modifications."

George and Ned set up the surveying equipment, and George took a series of measurements, then moved the equipment to different areas for more measurements.

When Mr. Tomoko joined them, he asked George what his opinion was of the possibility of a helicopter site. "Yes, it's possible, and building the pad with the required lighting and water should not be a problem. The problem is the FAA requires more open space than what we have here. Trees would have to be removed all around the site, and that will be costly. I have measurements of how much clearing would be required, and I will write everything up and e-mail you my report. To get an estimate of the cost, you will need the exact measurements."

"Thank you, George. I'm pleased that it will be possible with modifications. I have a feeling once my client hears about this property, he will want to fly over and see it for himself, and I imagine the price of putting in the landing pad will not be a hindrance to him purchasing the property. I have your business card, and as soon as I get your report, I'll mail you the fee agreed upon."

"I should get the report to you by tomorrow afternoon, and I'll need your card for an e-mail address."

While the men were outside, Fiona had Ned's contract with her, and she and Rebecca went over the details, with Rebecca gladly signing the contract for Ned's representation. Fiona then told her about Mr. Tomoko's client, and she thought Ned would start the price out at twenty-two million, causing Rebecca to pull out a chair and sit down quickly. Fiona told her not to discuss the price in front of the guys or with anyone else; it was just between "us girls."

When the DewMaster jet landed in Salt Lake City, Ted and Agnes greeted Dewey and Layla. Agnes hugged Layla, and both ladies went to the SUV as the men unloaded the luggage.

"I had to come and meet the plane. I've been so anxious for you to visit. We have so many things to discuss about your wedding. I'm so excited for both of you, a perfect match!" exclaimed Agnes.

CHAPTER 68

Annie and George were going over final preparations for the docents' meeting before they went to the Visitors Center. There had been no cancellations, and the Hilo Hattie lady was on schedule to begin her measurements one hour after the start of the meeting; at which time, George and Annie felt confident they would have the docents indoctrinated. While measurements were being taken, the docents would be scheduling their time slots and asking any questions. Donnie made arrangements for a light lunch to be eaten on the patio.

"Today at church, during our silent prayer, I prayed to God for guidance in the task before us," said Annie, smiling up at George.

"Me too. I asked him not to let us screw up."

Annie looked up at George, shook her head, and began to gather their props for the presentation.

After their presentation, Annie and George received hearty applause from the docents. The Hilo Hattie lady was ready to take measurements, and Annie and George set up their scheduling. As measurements were taken and scheduling was finished, the docents were ushered to the vending area where there was a selection of sandwiches and hot or cold drinks, then directed to the patio area. Donnie was there, helping move things along, greeting everyone with his usual charm.

When there were only a handful of docents left for scheduling and measurements, Fiona walked in and motioned to Donnie. "Donnie, I need some of George's engineering skills. I've got to find out exactly how much space I can allot to each vendor. I met with a wonderful vendor on Friday who does metal sculpturing, especially of windsurfers. He brought samples, and they are outstanding, but I'm concerned about how much space would be available for him. I've brought along a measuring tape and yardstick."

Donnie went and spoke with George about Fiona's dilemma, then returned to Fiona, telling her, "He will be glad to help and should be finished in about ten minutes. Let's get a cold drink and go out on the patio to wait for him."

Fifteen minutes later, George and Annie came out each with a sandwich and something to drink.

"That took longer than anticipated, and we've got to eat, we're starving!" said Annie.

"Please go ahead. I'll be grateful for any help I can get. We've done a lot of advertising, and I'm still short two vendors. Seems like things are too klutzy or too expensive. Anybody got an idea?"

"Fiona, have you ever noticed those place mats I use?"

"Yes, where did you get those? I would like a set in red."

"A lady and her daughter who live here in Paia make them. They are hand woven, some are painted and some are left natural, then lacquered and they just last forever. She charges $20 for a set of four, which I believe is way too reasonable. Would you be interested in having her contact you about selling them?"

"Heavens, yes, see if she can come to the bank next Friday at 2:00 p.m. and ask her to bring a set of red place mats and anything else they weave besides the mats. Great, only one to go!"

When George finished his sandwich, he and Fiona went to the gift counter, and he began measuring. Annie and Donnie stayed on the patio, Annie graciously answering questions any docent may yet have.

Dewey and Ted were in the den, relaxing in recliners, drinking beers, eating snacks, and enjoying a day of football.

Layla and Agnes were at the kitchen counter, going over wedding plans.

"Honey," Agnes said, "I know you're not thrilled about having your parents attend, but they'll be coming, so just accept the fact."

"The only reason they're attending is because Dewey is so rich and known worldwide. They can brag to all their friends who their daughter snagged."

"Oh, dear, that's no way to talk."

"Wait till they've been here a few days, you will see exactly what I mean, trust me."

"I'm worried about Dewey's mom. She has a tendency to be a bit negative," said Agnes.

"She's probably concerned that her son is marrying a divorced woman who already lost one child at birth. Actually, I can't say that I blame her," said Layla with a sadness in her voice.

"Once she gets to know you, she will be as happy for you and Dewey as Ted and I are. Let's put Mr. Soo in the bedroom between your parents and Dewey's mom. If what Dewey has told me about him is true, maybe his gentleness will seep through. The Kellers and Boones can share the other house. I think that will work out well, don't you?"

"Sounds great, you're a wise planner. Do you think there is room for my girl friend and her new husband from New York?"

"Sure, we have several spare bedrooms. Invite anyone you want."

"I don't want this to be a huge affair, like my last wedding. Do you know of any place here where I can find a designer wedding gown?"

"No, I don't, but our wedding planner will. When we meet with her on Tuesday, that should be on our list."

They added finding a wedding gown to their ever-growing list.

"I've been meaning to ask you, who will be your maid or matron of honor?"

"I've talked with Dewey, and we would like to have George and Annie stand up with us. Without them, Dewey and I would never have met or gotten to know each other, and their encouragement has helped bring us to this point. We haven't asked them yet, but we intend to when we return to Paia. If I get good measurements, we should be able to fit Annie to a gown, then make adjustments when they arrive for the wedding."

"They are the perfect people to stand up with you, they are a loving couple. You can sense the affection they have for each other when you're around them."

CHAPTER 69

Wade called to Fiona as she was returning home from her morning run. "Fiona, I need a minute of your time."

"Be right there. I need some water first."

"Got bottled water right here, and it's ice-cold."

"Sold," said Fiona and went up the stairs to where Wade waited. "How can I help you?"

"You have Chris and Josie working elsewhere, but I think you should see what they have accomplished so far. The floors look terrific."

Fiona and Wade went into the bedrooms where the floors were finished. The rooms were shut off from the rest of the house because of dust coming from the work on the bathrooms.

"When I first saw these floors, I never thought they could be restored to this level, but these floors look new and the stain is wonderful. Won't it be grand to see the entire house finished?"

Wade smiled, feeling the house would be his one day. "I'm anxious to see it totally completed, furniture, wall hangings, and all. I believe you and Layla have exquisite taste."

"Thank you, my dear. I have to agree with you on that point."

Fiona looked into the small bathroom. "My god, this bathroom is complete except for the countertop. Wade, your vanity cabinets are perfect. How's the other bathroom coming along?"

"In here, Fiona," Herb called from the larger bathroom, "just finishing up the tile work. The plumbing is all in, and I'll start the installation of Wade's cabinets tomorrow. All will be finished by Friday. The silestone man comes on Monday to measure both countertops. Then we just have to wait for the counters to be made and installed. That should be about two to two and a half weeks. In the meantime, Chris and Josie might as well finish up on their staining. The countertop installation won't be messy."

"Perfect timing. Their other job finishes up on Friday, and they can start staining on Monday. Thanks, guys, for an outstanding job."

Fiona went home to call Chris to make sure he and Josie would be able to start on Monday and get an estimate how long it would take to complete the staining. Once she had that, she phoned the team that would wash the walls down, scheduling them, and then the painter. She wanted to be sure there was no lag time when there wasn't any work being done. She also phoned the moving brothers and alerted them to a large shipment of furniture and appliances that would be coming over from Oahu in less than two weeks. Giving them as much advanced notice as possible was always preferable.

Early that afternoon, Ned came in from his golf game and told Fiona he had received a call from Mr. Tomoko and he and the prospective buyer would fly in on Tuesday of next week to view Mrs. Steinmetz's property. He also wanted to hire George again to go along, in case there were more questions. "I'll get in touch with both Mrs. Steinmetz and George, but I wanted to forewarn you because I think Mrs. Steinmetz might need your help on packing and sorting."

"This is bad timing. By next week, things will really be happening at Layla's. Do you think the prospective buyer would be interested in keeping any furniture that Rebecca isn't taking with her or selling?"

"I'll pose that question to Mr. Tomoko when I confirm all is set for next Tuesday. Maybe you should go through tagging those items that are available to go with the house, and that should be done prior to the Tuesday visit. You know how that works."

"I'm going to speak with Rebecca and see how things are coming along. I'll tell her I'm going to bring someone with me to assist in all that has to be done. I'll be upfront with her and tell her it will be added to our commission. It might be wise to go over this weekend and begin things. Do you think it would be out of line if I ask Annie if she wants to help? Rebecca knows her, and I'll offer Annie $200 a day for her assistance."

"That's a great idea, honey. Let me call Rebecca now and set up the Tuesday appointment, then you can talk with her about you and Annie coming this weekend."

Rebecca was thrilled about the Tuesday visit, grateful Fiona would be coming to assist and delighted to hear that Annie Boone might be joining them, and agreed to the added expense. Ned called and invited Annie and George to be their guests for dinner at a local restaurant, telling them he had a business proposition for them both.

The restaurant was not known for great food but for ocean views and spectacular sunsets that tourists imagined when they conjured up visions of Hawaii. The orange-red sun was dipping into the horizon as the two couples enjoyed the brilliant display that played out most evenings on the islands.

"Ned, your invitation was intriguing with the mention of a business proposition for us both," said George.

"Got a call from Mr. Tomoko today. He and his prospective buyer from LA will be flying in on Tuesday to inspect Rebecca's property, and he has asked that you join the group, at the same fee."

"Great, I have no problem about earning another $500," said George with his usual grin.

"What about me?" asked Annie.

"That's my idea," chimed in Fiona, "I'm going to be helping Rebecca get things sorted, tagged what goes and what stays, and begin her packing. I told her I wanted to hire someone to assist me, and I thought that since you two knew each other, you might want the job. It pays $200 a day, and it could go on for a week or more."

"Are you kidding? Count me in. Besides earning the money, I truly like Rebecca and would love to sort through that place," Annie said.

"Wonderful! It's all settled. The Keller-Boone team will be on the job," exclaimed Fiona.

CHAPTER 70

On Friday morning, Annie was on the lanai waiting for Fiona to return from her morning run. Seeing her coming down the hill, she got up and went across the street to meet her.

"You didn't run today?" Fiona asked, panting.

"No, I only run every other day, and I ran early Thursday before it got too warm. Do you run every day?"

"No, just when I overeat, and I seem to be doing a lot of that lately. Let's go inside. I need water."

"Fine," Annie said, looking at Fiona quizzically.

"Can I get you something to drink?"

"No, I'm still drinking my coffee," Annie said, holding up her mug. "Fiona, I hope you won't be insulted, but there's something out of kilter with your left breast."

"Oh good lord!" Fiona reached into the left cup of her sports bra and pulled a Derringer cradled in a small leather holster. "I just got this new hideout holster, and I haven't softened it up properly. Can't have everyone know I'm carrying. That negates the purpose."

Annie, looking shocked, said, "You carry a gun when you jog?"

"No, I carry a hideout Derringer with me wherever I or we go. I got into the habit after the Okamoto murders. You see, I happen to agree with the sheriff. I believe it was a crazy local, and God only knows we have our share. Until or if that individual is apprehended, I will be, as they say, packing."

Fiona went to the refrigerator, dropped some ice into a glass, and added water. She then drank almost the whole glass, turned, and saw Annie sitting on the arm of the sofa, looking at her wide-eyed. "Annie, you must remember I was on the Italian Olympic shooting team. I know my way around guns, and once a week, I go into the hills to a friend's place for target practice."

"But isn't it illegal to carry a concealed weapon?"

"Yes, but who's going to look in my bra or the back of my pants?"

"When we were out to dinner last night, did you have your gun?"

"Sure, I had it strapped on my thigh."

"Does Ned know?"

"Honey, we've been married for years. Believe me, he knows I have a gun hidden on me," Fiona said, smiling.

Annie took a deep breath, then said, "I spoke with Dee, the lady that makes the place mats. She and her daughter, DeeAnn, will meet you at the bank at two this afternoon. She will bring a set of red place mats and was flattered you wanted to review their work."

"Terrific, she will make an excellent addition. Have you ever heard of Scarves by Sasha?"

"Yes, in fact, over the years, I've purchased a dozen or more of her wonderful creations. She does great lightweight painted island-themed scarves but also ones depicting holidays, like Christmas, Thanksgiving, July 4, Valentines, etc. I wore those to class and the kids loved them. When I retired, I sent a lot of them to my daughter, who also teaches, and she's gotten the same reaction from her classroom. There were quite a few teachers who wore Sasha's scarves."

"How come I never saw her scarves?"

"I can only surmise that the stores you purchase your clothes from are too high-end for her scarves."

"Oh, you have a point there," said Fiona. "Anyway, she's coming at three this afternoon, and she will make the final addition to the team. What a relief to have all the craft vendors in place. Now I'll have an orientation and scheduling meeting, like you and George had. I was hoping I could use your outline."

"No problem. Come over, talk with George, tell him what type of scheduling table you will need, and he can set up one for you easily. We can write an orientation program also. It won't need to be as complicated as the one we presented. Are you going to use a cash register or a cash drawer and give receipts?"

"I never thought of that. I'll talk with Donnie and get that settled. These damn little things are such a pain," said Fiona with a frown.

"Well, I better get back home and let you clean up. I know everything will go great today, and you'll have all your crafters."

"I hope so, and please don't tell anyone about my Derringer."

"No, I won't even tell George. He would be staring at your bosom, backside, or thighs trying to figure out where it was hidden. He would make an ass out of himself."

Shortly after one, Fiona went to the bank and saw Donnie and the sheriff talking in Donnie's office. She walked in and said, "If this is business, I don't want to interrupt, but if it's just boy talk, I have a problem at the Visitors Center and I need Donnie's assistance."

"No, no, Fiona, the sheriff and we were just shooting the breeze. Please come in, sit down, and let me see how I can tackle your problem," Donnie said with a smile.

"Fiona, take my chair. I have to get back out on patrol. Hope all is well with you and Ned?"

"Yes, everything is fine, Sheriff. I'm busy with the craft counter at the center and work is beginning to finish up at Layla's. Ned and I are involved in the sale of Rebecca Steinmetz's estate, and everything is coming together at once."

"I heard she might be selling her estate. Frankly, I'm glad. A lady her age should not be alone that far away from town. Hope she's got a buyer with deep pockets. I heard she has a great deal of land," the sheriff said inquiringly.

"This buyer's pockets are very deep. If he does purchase the estate, he will even be upgrading the property."

"More big money in the area always helps the economy," said Donnie, smiling.

"Will Mrs. Steinmetz be staying in Paia?"

"No, Sheriff, she will move to Oahu to be close to her family."

"Good luck, Fiona, with all you have on your plate. See you around, Donnie." The sheriff smiled and left Donnie's office.

"Don't get me wrong, Donnie, the sheriff is doing a wonderful job, but for some reason, he just hits me the wrong way."

"Maybe he's too folksy or something. What can I help you with?"

"How are we going to handle the craft sales? Will we use a cash register or a cash drawer with receipts? I never thought of this until this morning."

"We will use a cash drawer and handwritten receipts. My past experience with people that are artsy gives me pause to even consider a cash register. They do not have the patience to learn the mechanical workings but are good receipt writers. We will also have a phone line installed so credit cards are usable. I put in orders for the phone lines. In fact, they will be installed next week. I'll take care of getting receipt books, a proper cash drawer, bags, and popcorn paper for protective wrapping. The center will fund the cash drawer with $200 in working cash for making change, etc. How does that sound?"

"Donnie, I'm so embarrassed. These are things I never thought of. Thank you for being on top of all this."

"I always planned to handle the business end of the crafts counter. All I wanted you to worry about was the selection of qualified crafters. I knew I could count on your good taste to bring the right crafters to the center."

"Thank you. How will we handle the daily cash proceeds?"

"The last crafter of the day should close out the drawer and leave $200 for the start of the next day. They will put the proceeds in a cash envelope, which I've already ordered, and give it to the night manager at the concession stand who will put it in the safe. The next morning someone from the bank, probably me, will stop by, pick up the cash receipts from both the crafters and the concession stand, take it to the bank, have it tallied up, and deposited. At the end of the month, a check will be written to each crafter for the sale of their products, with 12 percent going to the center. I hope you've explained about the 12 percent fee when you spoke with each individual crafter?"

"Yes, and all were fine with the 12 percent. They thought it was quite reasonable, considering what some of them pay for display space in the local stores or at craft fairs."

Ned and Fiona were eating leftover lasagna and green salad, Fiona was jubilant that she had secured the final crafters and was pleased Donnie was taking care of the business end of the craft counter.

"I'm glad everyone is lined up and that George and Annie are going to help with your scheduling and orientation. What time are you and Annie leaving for Mrs. Steinmetz's tomorrow morning?"

"We talked it over earlier today and decided we would leave here at eight tomorrow morning. That should give us a full day working with Rebecca. I hope she isn't one of those sentimental types who have to tell a story about every piece she examines, no time for that."

"Well, honey, if anyone can get her going on the right path, I have faith in your ability," Ned said with a knowing smile.

*   *   *

At four thirty Saturday afternoon, Fiona and Annie left the Steinmetz estate. Fiona hit a small rut in the road. "Damn, that hurt! Every muscle and bone in my body is sore. I haven't done that much manual labor since Ned and I moved from Oahu to Maui. How do you feel?"

Annie turned her head slowly toward Fiona and said softly, "I feel like shit."

"If Annie Boone said shit, then I shall assume you are hurting as bad as I am."

"When I get home, I want a hot shower, and then I'm going to have George rub my back, arms, and legs with rubbing alcohol and pray my body will be able to move again. I'm glad we're not getting there until noon tomorrow. It will give us more time to heal."

When Fiona pulled into her driveway, George and Ned were on the Kellers' lanai, enjoying a cold beer. They took one look at their ladies and rushed to assist them up the stairs or across the street.

"Ladies, you look like you put in a day of hard labor," said Ned.

"Just get this tired butt of mine up these stairs and into a hot shower before I pass out from pain," said Fiona.

"George, after a shower, I want an alcohol rubdown, and get that silly grin off your face because believe me, buster, a rubdown is all I have in mind."

"Yes, dear," said George duly chastised.

Annie opened Fiona's car door, got in, and found a large manila folder and Scotch tape on the dash. "What's this?"

"Here's the plan for today," Fiona said. Driving to Rebecca's, Fiona explained, "As you know, Mr. Tomoko and the prospective buyer arrive on Tuesday. By the way, you get the day off. Anyway, at that time, Ned will discuss the possibility of selling the estate with any furniture, etc. not being sold or taken by Mrs. Steinmetz. To determine what is available, today we are going to mark items either with a Sold or Goes sign. Everything that is unmarked is available to stay with the estate. Yesterday, Ned went to the print store and had fifty of each made for us. I phoned Rebecca and told her what had to be done today. Hopefully, she has gone through and decided on some of the furnishings."

"Well, that sounds easier than all we did yesterday."

"I'm sure it will be, as long as Rebecca is focused. Annie, I hope you won't be mad at me, but you are going to be on your own with Rebecca from now on. Things are really happening at Layla's, and I don't feel comfortable being so far away in case I'm needed. Plus, everything is getting critical with the crafters at the Visitors Center."

"That will be fine. We'll be packing and sorting, like we did yesterday. If you don't mind, I would like to bring George with me. He can do the heavy lifting, no charge. I think that's what did us both in."

"That will be great, and he will be paid the same $200 a day as you. After all, Rebecca will be getting millions, and she can afford the cost. Do you think he will agree to assisting?"

"I'll see to it. There should be no problem."

Dewey, Layla, Agnes, and Ted were planning a luncheon Dewey decided on for the following Saturday. He would be inviting his right-hand people and department heads, along with their spouses or girl- or boyfriends. He and Layla had made an invitation on the computer, which Dewey would send to his staff via e-mail on Monday. Dewey told them to make arrangements for any extra staff they would need.

"It's important for these people to meet Layla and feel comfortable around her before the wedding. We can make a formal announcement to reach the papers next Sunday, but I want this gathering before the public announcement. I want to keep the family atmosphere that has worked so well for DewMaster."

"It's a wonderful idea, and I'm anxious to meet everyone. Dewey has been updating me on some of the individuals, and they all sound so brilliant. I hope, since I'm not genius caliber, I'll fit in."

"Layla, you needn't worry about that. As brilliant as they may be, some of them are a bit lax in the personality department. You will dazzle them, believe me," said Agnes proudly.

"I agree 100 percent," said Dewey, giving Layla a hug.

"Agnes, when we see the wedding planner on Tuesday, let's ask her to point out places where I can shop for something suitable to wear. I would like to purchase something here. Plus, it will give me an opportunity to visit the local stores. You'll come with me, won't you?"

"Wouldn't miss it for anything!"

"Today went extremely well," said Annie. "We accomplished a lot promptly. Rebecca pretty much decided what went, what was sold, and what stayed. Rebecca and I discussed it, and next, we will work on the kitchen. This is one of her biggest concerns. She knows she has pushed things into the rear of shelves and cabinets, ignoring them for years. I told her what she doesn't want to keep for the new buyer but doesn't want to take with her, we'll pack up, and George and I will take it to the Goodwill Center for her. She has boxes of Mr. Steinmetz's clothes that we'll also take. After she gets the kitchen in order, I think she will feel a lot better. Even if this prospective sale doesn't go through, she will have things cleaned out."

"We're all guilty of that. I keep telling Ned we have to go through the house and clean things out, but we never get around to doing it. Something always comes up."

"When we retired, I got the kitchen in order, and George got the garage in order. However, since then, he's added more than he got rid of, and I have no idea what he plans on doing with all that junk."

"Men are such cute little pack rats. Ned does that too, but if it hasn't moved into some type of storage within three months, I trash it. I think he just brings stuff in to keep me on my toes," said Fiona.

"I've learned a lesson from Rebecca's situation. When we're done at Rebecca's, I'm finishing the rest of our home. I know there are things in drawers, closets, and cabinets that I can trash, and I'm packing all the children's things they don't want me to throw away and sending it unannounced to them. That will clean out about 75 percent of their old bedrooms," said Annie.

"What time are you and George getting there tomorrow?"

"We'll leave our place at nine. That should give Rebecca time to get up, eat, and get ready."

"I hope George is agreeable to helping."

"He is. I told him how we needed a strong man, and the extra $200 a day sealed the deal."

"I'm so glad. I was trying to figure out how I could make sure all was going well at Layla's, handle the crafters, and still get out to Rebecca's. Now you have George, and he'll be more help than I could ever be."

Chapter 71

Fiona went over to Layla's early Monday morning to open up the house for Chris and Josie. She opened the slider on the front lanai and immediately remembered what had been nagging at her for some time. *Damn,* she thought, *I forgot about having Marty make the side table.*

When they arrived, she said, "Chris, while opening up the front lanai, I discovered that I neglected to have Marty make the small side table from the remaining Shoji screens. I don't want to have him start now when you're staining the floors because dust might fly in. Do you have any suggestions?"

Chris walked to the lanai and looked at the covered framework. "Let me put these in my truck, and I'll take them over to Granddad's after work, give him a call and ask if he can build the table at his home, which, of course, he can, then arrange to stop by and give him the proper measurements. He will be happy to have you visit. Here's my cell phone. He's under Gramps," said Chris.

She phoned Marty, and as Chris predicted, he was thrilled to work at home and even happier Fiona would be coming by with the measurements. They arranged to meet Wednesday, with Marty insisting Fiona come for an Italian lunch.

Fiona thanked Chris and told him she would be seeing Marty on Wednesday, and he was going to fix an Italian lunch for her.

"If he said he was going to fix an Italian lunch, be ready for a nine-course meal. His Italian lunches last for about three hours, and everyone leaves the table stuffed but happy."

"I'll probably be jogging like crazy for several days afterward."

Herb came at nine to meet the silestone man that would be measuring the countertops. He took measurements, Fiona made the approval on the color, and he left. She told Herb the cabinets in the large bathroom were wonderful and let Wade know how pleased she was. Fiona walked Herb out and went back home, wondering how Annie and George were doing at Rebecca's.

Focusing on the kitchen and because George was so tall, he got ladder duty for work on the top shelves. He reached into the cabinets and brought things down for the ladies to inspect and sort. When he had the top two shelves of all cleared out, they started work on packing, with George toting boxes to the garage for storage or to their car for drop-off.

While in the garage, George noticed Rebecca's Jeep and asked if that was going with the house too.

"Yes, if I'm going to have lots of money, I want a luxury car for a change. I'm so tired of bumping along and shifting, I could scream. These old bones need a softer ride. That's the only car for this area, however. When it rains, you really need the four-wheel drive to maneuver the access road."

"Be sure and let Ned or Fiona know the Jeep is part of the package. That will be an added incentive," said George.

"I will, and thank you for reminding me."

They continued packing and sorting throughout the day, calling it quits at five. Annie told Rebecca she would see her on Wednesday and that George would be with the group arriving tomorrow.

When they were ready to leave, George turned to Annie and asked, "Honey, could you drive us home? If I needed to brake hard, I'm not sure I would have the strength in my legs to hit the brake."

"I didn't realize we were working you so hard. Why didn't you say something?"

"I didn't want to sound like a wimp, at least not until we were alone. I need a hot shower, and it's my turn for a rubdown and don't ply your feminine wiles on me. I'm not able to do any more tonight than sleep."

"I wouldn't think it. Give me the keys and let me get you home."

At seven Tuesday morning, Annie walked into their bedroom and sat down next to George, who was sprawled out on his stomach. She kissed him on the cheek, saying, "Honey, it's time to get up. I'm fixing you a hardy breakfast. Then you need to shower and get ready to meet the Hollywood producer."

"I hear you. That means I'm still alive and survived yesterday."

"You did and you worked so hard." Annie frowned, looking at George, still not moving, "Dear, can you move?"

"Probably, I'm just not sure I want to try." He turned over and threw his long legs over the side of the bed, sighing. "Yep, I can move and I'm starved. You're right, I want a big breakfast."

"I'm on my way back to the kitchen. Now you're sure you're up, you won't fall back in bed once I'm gone, will you?"

"Nope, need to get up and get alert. Want to sound like an engineer who knows what he's talking about."

Agnes drove as she and Layla went to their appointment with the wedding planner. Layla sat quietly. Agnes asked, "Is something wrong?"

"No, it's just my previous experiences with these types, for my own wedding and being in my friends' weddings, I find them pretentious and they think they are some sort of wondrous all-knowing wedding sage. If I wasn't in Maui most of the time, we would not be needing this person."

"I spoke to several of my friends that run households like we do, they all say this lady is excellent, humble, and attends to every detail with dignity and charm."

"I find that description for a wedding planner incredible. I'm anxious to meet her."

After discussing the details with the wedding planner, she insisted they stay for lunch to sample some items she would like to serve for the reception dinner.

"Agnes, she's terrific. She could make millions in New York."

"She's a devoted Mormon, an active family woman that only takes on three or four weddings a year. Working for Dewey is a star on her resume."

"I feel lucky, and wasn't that lovely of her to call ahead to the dress shop to let them know we will be arriving this afternoon. I'm looking forward to working with her at the bridal salon on Friday. Thank your friends for me. She's terrific."

*   *   *

Ned phoned George, asking him to drive his car, because they didn't know how many would be coming and wanted to make sure there was ample transportation.

When the plane arrived, Mr. Tomoko introduced them to the producer and his eldest son, aged twenty-five. As they were getting in the cars, the producer opted to ride with George, saying, "I want to get an educated opinion on the helicopter pad and see just how far it is from the airport to the estate."

He and George sat off in the Escalade, the others following. George pointed out initial facts that might be of interest regarding the Maui airport. He told the producer it would be more reasonable to lease a helicopter when he was going to be on the island, that way he wouldn't have to pay a hangar fee or salary for pilots on standby. George said there were excellent helo pilots from the Desert Storm era that were familiar with the Maui interior. He easily kept up a tourist guide conversation, displaying his pride of the island and Paia. Before they reached Rebecca's, he said, "I don't know what you've been told about this foyer, but from an engineering standpoint, it's fabulous. I can't wait to hear your opinion."

George was taken back when he saw who followed Mr. Tomoko off the plane. Then surprised at the easy rapport that quickly developed between him and the producer and was anxious to tell Annie whom he was spending the day with.

Rebecca made her usual gracious greeting, then led the newcomers into the foyer with the others following.

The producer looked at George, who had a big grin on his face, and asked, "Is this for real?"

"Young man," said Rebecca a slight edge to her voice, "I can assure you this is real. My late husband and I worked quite a few years to create the visual beauty, and a very talented engineer and my husband designed this atrium."

"It's like nothing I've ever seen before or, for that matter, even imagined and I'm supposed to be damned good at imagining things. What do you think, son?"

"Buy the estate for this alone, it's worth it. You will knock your friends dead with this atrium. Plus, you should be able to feature it in a movie or two."

"Brilliant, son, this would make an outstanding location. Rebecca, show us more, please."

Mr. Tomoko, Fiona, and Ned followed the lead group around, but the estate seemed to be selling itself without their input. Once outside, George pointed out the degree of clearing necessary, required for FAA approval for the helicopter pad, and the producer and his son quietly talked among themselves.

"George, can we take a helicopter ride over the property?"

"I don't see why not. I can get in touch with a couple of pilots I know and see if they are available for this afternoon. Perhaps we all could have lunch in town?"

On the way back to their autos, Fiona said to Ned, "I don't believe any of us were needed for the sale. Between George and Rebecca, I think it's a done deal."

"I agree with you, dear. I'm giving George a bonus, I think he has that man's man image the producer is partial to. He probably sees us realtors as necessary evils."

During lunch at Mama's, George received a call from a pilot friend, saying he and his helicopter could be ready in an hour for three to tour the property. The producer, his son, and George were the chosen three. George relayed the coordinates of Rebecca's property to the pilot. He also checked with Mr. Tomoko on who was going to pay the tab for the flight. Mr. Tomoko said his company would pay.

Speaking into the headphone to the pilot, the producer said, "I heard there are pot growers down there somewhere, is that true?"

"Oh sure, so we will not be flying too close. They have been at it for a numbers of years and have gotten quite high-tech with their monitoring devices. The post-Vietnam era brought a lot of those guys, who got hooked over there, back to Hawaii where they had done their R&R. Some moved into the interior of Maui and started growing for themselves and later for illegal sales. A few oversee million-dollar businesses."

"Seriously, I had no idea my future property was being used for such a high-profit enterprise. Very interesting," he said, grinning at his son, who just shook his head.

En route back to the airfield, George mentioned that the four-wheel Jeep came with the property, and it was vital to have a four-wheel drive for the road to the estate during wet weather.

"Maybe we should think of fixing the road," his son said.

"I don't think so," said the producer, "that would lose the wild-outback feeling."

"Oh lord," said his son.

"Looks like you've decided on buying the property," said George.

"I was hooked the minute we walked into the foyer," said the producer. "Now it's down to the negotiating, and I wish them luck with my wife. She handles all our financial dealings, and frankly, she scares the hell out of me when it comes to money. I'm crazy in love with the woman. We've been married since our first year of college. I could never think of a divorce, I would be homeless in a flash."

"Mom's a whiz with money. Without her, Dad could never have done the type of movies he's done. He financed his last three films, thanks to her diligence in investments, and now we're all worth a disgusting amount. Don't get me wrong, I love what it provides, but it isn't easy following in either of their footsteps. I'm a techie, I'm into the special effects side of the movie business."

"In that case, you should meet my next-door neighbor and her fiancé. Layla is engaged to Dewey McMaster, the DewMaster."

"Your next-door neighbor? I thought you lived in Paia."

"We do. She's remodeling the house next door, and that will be their home-away-from-home once they're married. They are in Salt Lake City now but will be back in Paia in a couple of weeks."

"Well, son, this place just keeps getting better and better."

George and Annie rose early on Wednesday, anxious to see Rebecca and tell her what George had learned yesterday. George had regaled Annie about his time with the producer and his son and told her Ned hinted if the property sold like they thought, he would be in for a bonus since both Ned and Mr. Tomoko felt George had practically sold the estate without their help.

When George came into the kitchen, he found Annie going through her stack of Panama Canal cruise brochures.

"This time we're finally going to take that cruise," George said as he swung her into him and waltzed her around the kitchen to an oldie on the radio.

When they arrived at Rebecca's, she was outside, waiting anxiously for news about yesterday. George filled her in on everything, including their exciting ride over her property. He told her he was sure they were going to buy the estate but that the producer's wife was handling the financial end and she made killer deals. Rebecca told them anything over a couple of million was fine with her.

Annie said she had dropped the donations off at the Goodwill yesterday and received a donation slip for tax records, which she handed to Rebecca. "They were happy to receive the items, especially all the men's clothing. I told them there is more coming."

"After everyone left yesterday, I was antsy, so the gardener and I worked like crazy in the yard. I've also hired him to work an extra day for the next couple of weeks to clean out the storage and garage areas. I told him to sort through things and take what he wanted, then we could see what would be left for a new buyer. Any odds and ends we can give the Goodwill, if you think they might want them. George, you sort through too and take what you like."

"I'm sure Ned will be happy you've started on those areas," said Annie. Then she whispered to Rebecca, "We don't want to work George as hard as we did Monday. Poor dear could hardly get out of bed yesterday."

The phone rang; it was Ned who explained to Rebecca that everyone was in negotiations with the producer's wife on the sale of the estate. He told Rebecca he would not consider selling the estate for less than fifteen million and had started at twenty-three million. She told him she was leaving the decision in his hands, as she trusted him totally, then told him about the garage and shed cleanout that she and the gardener were working on and asked his opinion.

He said that was a splendid idea and told her that the negotiations also included all unmarked furniture and her Jeep. After ending her call, she told Annie and George about her conversation and how happy she was that things were moving along so swiftly.

Fiona knocked on Marty's door, and when he answered, she presented him with an expensive bottle of Italian wine.

"My lovely Fiona, how happy I am to see you. Welcome to my home." He stepped back from the door and motioned her inside.

She felt the warmth of an Italian home, simple furnishings, mostly handmade, with fresh flowers and fruit in bowls. The smells coming from the kitchen were making her mouth water.

"I hope this wine will go with our meal. I picked this up the last time we were in Italy and was saving it for a special occasion."

"Fiona, this is perfect. Thank you. I love this variety but cannot find it in the islands."

Chris was correct; after three hours, Fiona pulled back from the table, totally sated but happy. She didn't know how she had finished off the last bite of tiramisu, but she had managed. She had given Marty all the measurements prior to eating, so after lunch, they chatted. Much to Fiona's dismay, she found herself speaking in Italian. She had started rusty, but by the time she was ready to leave, her native tongue had returned to her with ease.

When she returned home, Fiona lay on the couch and moaned softly. Ned came out from his office and asked her what was wrong.

"I ate too much. God, it was wonderful. I'm miserable but happy. How's the sale going?"

"On our second round of negotiations. George did a damn good job. He mentioned that Rebecca was including the Jeep, something we didn't know. He would have made a good real estate agent. The wife is doing the negotiations. She's a real bear. You should be dealing with her. She's overwhelming Mr. Tomoko. He's not used to high-powered women like you two."

"It would be my pleasure, dear, if you two need my help. Anytime you want me to jump in, just let me know."

"I'm thinking about it. Believe me."

Annie and Rebecca spent the morning finishing up the kitchen, then moved onto the guest bedrooms. They checked out drawers and closets and packed small items Rebecca was keeping and other items going to the Goodwill. George spent most of his morning happily in the garage and shed with the gardener, going through all types of tools. By day's end, he had a good-sized box of things he was keeping. The ladies told George he could take Thursday off, Annie afraid he would simply add to the items he was bringing into their garage. Rebecca said she and Annie would leave boxes for him to tote on Friday, but a great deal of the heavy lifting was complete.

Thursday morning, the phone rang; Annie answered and was surprised to hear Layla's voice. She was told she was being put on speakerphone and wondered if George was available. Annie called George to the phone, then put their phone on speaker.

"We called early so we could catch you both before you went off on errands or jogging. We have something to ask of you."

"Sure, how can we help?" said George.

"We are planning our wedding, and although a date won't be set until our Paia home is finished, we wanted everything finalized in advance. What we wanted to ask if you would be our wedding party. We each want one attendant, and Layla and I said it could only be George and Annie."

Annie caught her breath and said it would mean so much to her since she felt like both of them were family.

"I don't have to wear a tux, do I?" asked George.

Dewey laughed. "No way, just a dark suit for both of us. If you don't have a dark suit, I'll order you one."

"I have a great black suit, perfect for weddings and funerals."

"That's no way to talk, George," scolded Annie.

"Dewey knows what I mean, honey. We guys understand."

"I do. I have one of those myself. That's what I'll be wearing."

"Dewey!" exclaimed Layla.

"What should I wear?" asked Annie, trying to change the subject.

"I'm going to the bridal salon tomorrow, and hopefully, I'll find something simple for both of us. Send me your measurements, and I can have your dress prefitted. When you get here a couple of days before the wedding, we can have a final fitting."

"I'm a size 6, but I'll take exact measurements for you and give you a call. Don't forget the shoes. I'm a size 7, medium, and I'm no good in those real high heels."

"Don't worry about high heels. I'll be too nervous to even attempt them. I want to be comfortable and enjoy the day."

They talked a while longer, then Annie said she had to leave for Rebecca's and left George to bring them up-to-date on the producer and the events of the last few days.

Fiona went over to Layla's to let Chris know what a wonderful afternoon she had with Marty and the feast he had served. When she walked into Layla's, she could hardly believe her eyes. Over half of the unstained area was stained and shining. It looked beautiful.

"Chris, are you here?" she called out.

Chris came out from the hallway, smiling.

"Is it OK to walk on the kitchen floor? It looks so shiny."

"Fine, it's dry. We finished the living room and kitchen yesterday. Everything went quickly and dried easily. We've had a nice sea breeze blowing through the house, and the humidity has been low. The floor seemed to dry in an instant."

"I'm so impressed, it's amazing. I knew it was going to look great, and this dark color is so impressive. You and Josie have done a marvelous job."

"Thank you. We have the dining room and the hallway left, then we're done. Josie is finishing her cleaning of the hallway, then we stain it and we should actually finish the dining room this afternoon."

"You are three or four days ahead of the schedule I had planned. I must get other things in motion. Be sure you come and see me with your final bill. I don't want to keep either of you waiting for your payment. I owe it to you both for this excellent work."

"We'll see you later this afternoon."

At home, Fiona phoned the warehouse in Oahu, which was storing all of Layla's purchases, making arrangements to have them ship the items as soon as possible. They would let her know the arrival time. She then phoned the brothers and arranged to treat them to lunch tomorrow, then show them Layla's home. This was what Fiona was afraid of, everything hitting at once. Layla's home being finished, the Visitors Center needing her attention, Rebecca's property being sold, and Layla and Dewey's upcoming wedding.

CHAPTER 72

Layla and Agnes arrived at the bridal salon and were greeted by the wedding planner and the shop's owner. The planner had selected three gowns she felt might be suitable. Layla and Agnes followed the ladies to a viewing area where the gowns were displayed.

One was an ankle-length pale blue sheath, strapless with a matching shrug covered in small seed pearls. Another was a light sea-green, also ankle length with a tight bodice and a full skirt with underslips to make it bouncy. The third was medium beige, floor length with side slits to midcalf. It had a square neckline with sleeves that ended just above the elbow; what made this dress stand out was it was covered in a white organdy with abstract leaves in the same medium beige as the dress. Layla asked to try the dress on and was ushered into a fitting room, the owner hovering as she slipped into the gown.

She stepped out into the viewing room, and Agnes gasped, "You look beautiful with your tan and sun-faded hair. The effect is amazing."

Layla went to the full-length mirror, studied herself, and smiled. "I feel right in this dress. What about my matron of honor?"

The owner brought out a book provided by the designer that displayed matching wedding party ensembles. She found the match to Layla's gown and showed them a medium brown dress, ankle length, with side slits to midcalf, also covered in white organdy with light brown abstract leaves.

"Agnes, don't you think, with Annie's coloring, this will look lovely on her?"

"Yes, but maybe we should let her decide." She turned and asked the owner if they could get a color copy of the page to send to Mrs. Boone via e-mail.

The copy was made, and Layla wrote a deposit check and profusely thanked the wedding planner. The planner said she would be meeting with Agnes on menu and decoration options. Layla told her she and Dewey would likely be leaving in the middle or end of next week and she would be available until then if needed, and she would get back to her as soon as she heard from Mrs. Boone.

On the way home, Layla was ecstatic about her dress. "Agnes, it is such a comfortable dress and yet so lovely. I felt beautiful just trying it on, and I know Dewey will like it. What do you think about wearing brushed gold sandal heels for Annie and me both, maybe two to two and a half inches? I want total comfort this time around."

"I like that idea, and let's hope we can have an early September wedding, much nicer weather."

"I'll call Fiona when we get home and see how things are coming along in Paia. I'm anxious to hear what all has been accomplished since we've been in Salt Lake City."

When they got back to Dewey's, Layla went into the den and scanned the photo of the matron-of-honor dress, then e-mailed it to Annie along with a description of her own dress. Next, she phoned Fiona. "Hi, Fiona, it's Layla. How are things coming along?"

"Faster than I anticipated. We had three days of very dry weather while Chris and Josie were doing the staining, and the floors dried almost instantly. They are beautiful. You will be astounded. Anyway, I've phoned the warehouse and told them to send the items they were storing. I'm meeting with the three brothers in about ten minutes to show them each room setup, then I'm taking them to lunch. Always an interesting event, we go to their favorite lunch truck and they get a Spam, rice, and gravy dish. A heart attack ready to happen just so the attacks hold off until all your furniture is delivered. I'm anticipating that within the next couple of weeks, the sale on Rebecca's estate will be finalized, and once that is done, we can have the items you selected also moved. When the furniture gets here from the mainland, I'll arrange to have the mattresses delivered and the oriental rugs. Marty is working, from his home, on the end table to go alongside your living room chair. I think that's all, at least all I can think of at the moment."

"Fiona, I'm amazed. I had no idea things would go this fast. You're doing a wonderful job. Where would I ever be without your knowledge and guidance?"

"Thank you, dear, I love doing this. I only wish the Visitors Center wasn't also coming to a grand opening date so soon. You know how it goes, everything at once!"

"They're getting close to finishing the Visitors Center too?"

"Yes, in fact, I'm meeting with my crafters this Sunday to set up their times and get their routine established. Annie and George are going to help me set up a schedule and presentation."

"I can tell you are very busy, and I don't want to take any more of your time. I've e-mailed Annie the details of my dress and asked her to be my matron of honor. I've also sent a color photo of the dress that matches my dress. See what you think. Enjoy your lunch with the brothers. Goodbye."

Once she had hung up from her conversation with Fiona, Layla found Agnes and relayed all the information to her and said how anxious she was to tell Dewey what all was happening. She thought it might be wise not to fly back to Maui until the end of next week because she wanted to stay out of Fiona's way, especially if the brothers were moving furniture.

When Annie and George got to Rebecca's, they found six boxes to be stored in the garage and three boxes to go to the Goodwill store. Rebecca and Annie worked two hours, then Rebecca announced they were free to leave. What she had left was mostly personal items she had to go through and felt she could do that quicker alone. Annie and George were happy to be on their way by one thirty. They stopped off at the Goodwill store before going home and made their deposit, much to the delight of the staff.

After receiving crushing hugs from each of the three brothers, Fiona took them inside, pointing out what would go where and how important it was to be very careful with the floors. As they were going through the house, Wade arrived and said he was planning on installing the shelves on Monday, if that met with Fiona's approval.

Fiona said that would be perfect. Wade and the brothers conferred on pieces of furniture from Rebecca's he was purchasing that they would bring down from her estate along with Layla's and deliver to his home.

After the brothers got their furniture instructions from Fiona, they all set off for the lunch truck, the brothers always knowing its position throughout the island. The brothers had their usual bowl of heart attack, and Fiona had a beef enchilada with beans and rice, enjoying every nonhealthy bite, including the triple order of nachos with avocado dip she and the brothers shared.

Back home, she noticed Annie and George were home and went over to enlist their help with her crafter scheduling and presentation. She relayed all her information on Layla's and how everything seemed to be happening at once and asked Annie about the e-mail photo of the dress. Annie said she hadn't looked at her e-mail, then went to the computer to see what Layla had sent.

Fiona asked George for his help in making a planning calendar for the crafters; he said it would be easy since he had the format already in the computer for the docents.

"Fiona, look at this photo," said Annie, rushing in with a copy of the gown Layla had sent along with the information on her gown.

Fiona looked at the gown and read the information from Layla. "This is very classy. Annie, you will look wonderful in this gown. You should think about wearing your hair up for the ceremony."

"Annie with her hair up drives me crazy," said George, grinning.

"For heaven's sakes, George, you shouldn't say such things with others around. What will Fiona think?"

"She'll think my sexy wife still has the ability to drive me crazy," George said, gently tapping Annie's backside.

Fiona smiled. "I love it when you two tease around like that. It makes our age group look good. Which we are, of course,"

"Of course," George and Annie said in unison.

"Annie, can you help me with my presentation? I wrote up some notes last night, but I want your opinion if I have covered everything I need to cover."

"Sure, let me see what you've got there." An hour later, Fiona was back home with a work sheet for her scheduling and typed-out notes for her presentation for the crafters. She found Ned setting at the counter and showed him what Annie and George helped her prepare.

Ned read through everything and thought it was excellent. He then asked, "Fiona, what's your schedule like for next week, specifically Wednesday?"

"Ned, is something wrong? I can tell by the tone of your voice something is up."

"Mr. Tomoko and I need your help. You offered to help, and now we are going to take you up on your offer."

"Let me see if I can surmise what is needed here. The producer's wife is flying in on Wednesday to see the estate, and you two gentlemen want me to be her guide. I assume by myself. Is that about the gist of what is going on here?"

"Yep, you're so clever. You caught on right away."

"Cut the bull, do you have any idea how bad next week is for me? I'll have the crafters to contend with working through their scheduling. Everything is coming to a head at Layla's house, and you and Mr. Tomoko want me to put on a dog-and-pony show?"

"That's about it, sugar," Ned said, smiling at his wife. "Honey, you know you can pull this off with greater success than either Mr. Tomoko or I could, and I have an idea for you to find out what type of lady she is. We'll have George call and talk to the producer, and once he's on the line, you ask him about his wife. You know, is she the plain type, the classy type so that you can play the appropriate guide. After all, besides the commission, we are doing this for Rebecca."

"Damn it, Ned, you know I'll do it. Quit pulling on my heartstrings. You get a hold of George and set up a call as soon as possible, hopefully by tomorrow."

"That's my gal," Ned said, hugging Fiona who rolled her eyes skyward.

CHAPTER 73

Layla walked into the kitchen to found Agnes conferring with the catering staff, making sure all was in order.

"Agnes, do I pass the DewMaster muster?" Layla said, laughing.

Agnes stepped from behind the counter and looked at Layla wearing a lightweight pale blue cardigan, ecru slacks, British tan loafers, and pearl earrings. "Just right, my dear, classy but not too chic, rather *Town & Country*. I like it."

"That would please Mother. She was so happy when I made an issue of *T&C*. I don't want to stand out but be perfect to stand beside Dewey."

"Did someone call my name?" asked Dewey, striding into the kitchen.

"Dewey, are you in Levi's?"

"Hey, these are very expensive Levi's. I got these on sale at Penny's for $29.99. I would harbor a guess that 75 percent or more of the guys will come in Levi's. It's sort of our dress code. You look lovely as usual. You're not nervous, are you?"

"No, I was for a bit, but after you assured me I wouldn't feel like a dunce among all you geniuses, I was fine. Remember my background, the family had me meeting and greeting when very young? It's all a part of what was expected," Layla said.

Within the half hour, guests began arriving. Dewey was right; most of the men arrived in Levi's and about half of the ladies too. One lady in her midthirties hugged Layla, saying in her ear, "I'm so glad you two are getting married. I've been worried about that boy. He never seemed truly happy. Now he beams."

Throughout the afternoon, people helped themselves at the buffet and gathered in groups to talk about the latest projects, the weather, and how happy Dewey and Layla seemed. One of the ladies, hearing that Layla was an artist, suggested, once she was settled, she could join a local artist group that included painters, sculptors, writers, and photographers. She told her they took trips to the mountains during the snow season and when the mountains were covered in lush greenery. She said it was very inspiring for the painters and photographers, which she was. She went on to say they sold their works at local craft fairs with some or all the proceeds going to charities. Layla got her name and phone number and assured her she would be in touch once she was settled.

After everyone left, Layla and Dewey went upstairs to relax.

"Well, honey, what did you think of my group of geniuses?"

"They were great. I never felt like the dumb one in the crowd, and I met some lovely people." She proceeded to tell him about the offer to join the artist group.

"That would be terrific. You are an excellent artist, and you should develop your talent even more."

"You're a bit prejudiced as an art critic, and I love you for it."

Ned picked up his cell and phoned the Boones. George answered, "Hi, George, it's Ned." Fiona took the phone from Ned.

"George, we once again have to ask a favor of you. Do you want us to come over there, or do you want to come over here?"

"I'll come over there. Annie is lying down, she has a headache. She's overthinking our Panama Canal trip, trying to fit everything in before the end of the year."

"Great, and, George, if you have two separate bills ready for you and Annie for work at Rebecca's, I'll write checks."

"Did that last night. I thought you might be needing them. When do you want me to come over?"

"Now is fine. Ned has a cold beer waiting for you."

"I'm on my way."

"Ned, get a beer opened for George. He's on his way. We should be able to get this over with quickly. I need to get our company checkbook. Do you have the producer's phone number?"

"Yes on the beer and yes on the phone number."

Within five minutes, George was enjoying a cold beer, and Fiona was writing checks for the work George and Annie had done for Rebecca. When she finished writing the checks and George had finished half his beer, she got to the favor. "George, would you please phone the producer and make sure he can talk privately, then I'll talk to him. I need to ascertain what type of woman his wife is. You see, I'm going to be her official guide this Wednesday when she flies over to tour Rebecca's estate. For me to do my best selling job, I need to know how to approach her."

"You folks are clever. I never realized so much went into selling a property."

"When talking property worth millions, we explore all options."

"Sure, I'll be glad to help. Do you have his phone number?"

Ned handed George the phone number, and Fiona supplied Ned's cell phone.

"Well, here goes," said George, dialing the producer's number.

After talking to someone other than the producer and announcing it was George Boone calling from Maui, he was put through to the producer. They exchanged pleasantries; George asked if he was alone. The producer said he was alone in his study, reading a script that might make a good next project. George nodded to Fiona, and she took the phone.

After explaining what she needed and why, the producer laughed and said, "I'll help you any way I can, I really want that property. My wife is a loving wife and mother and a killer businesswoman, but I already told you that. I'm guessing you want to know her likes and dislikes. You've heard of a safe room, I'm sure. We have two in our home. One for us if we ever need it, probably after a bad review, and the other is actually my wife's closet. She has some lovely jewelry and over a million dollars in Hermes shoes and purses and so many designer dresses, etc. I can't even begin to tell you everything. Is that what you needed?"

"Perfect!" exclaimed Fiona. "I know just how to approach her. Thank you for your time, and let's hope she and I can close this deal on Wednesday." Fiona said her goodbye and disconnected.

"How are you going to handle our Wednesday visitor?"

"It will be a designer meet. George, I need another favor. Can I borrow Pearl? There is nothing more chic than wearing designer clothes stepping out of an Escalade, ready to give someone a tour of an estate in a remote area."

"Sure, if that will help. The producer's wife won't have anything on you. I believe she has met her match."

"Probably, I'm older, wiser, and have been down this type of selling road before. Besides, I'm confident Rebecca's property will almost sell itself. I'll be sure and fill the tank when I'm finished with the tour. Now, I'll have to phone Rebecca and make sure she's dressed properly." Fiona walked into the living room to call Rebecca.

Ned shook his head. "She's something. I never underestimate her. I used to kid her that she could sell ice cubes to Eskimos and damned if I don't believe she could."

CHAPTER 74

George rinsed out his coffee cup, peered out the window, and noticed Fiona going toward Layla's.

"Fiona must be going to open up Layla's. She said Wade was coming today to install the living room shelving."

"I wonder how things went yesterday with her crafters' meeting. Here, George, I've got a deposit slip ready, and if you will run to the bank and deposit these three lovely checks, adding $1,900 to the Canal Fund. We're getting so close. Would you consider a cruise during the holidays? It's more money but very festive. We would end the cruise in Los Angeles, and we could visit the kids in the New Year."

"That would be fun. I'd enjoy just the two of us celebrating the holidays together with a couple of thousand others aboard ship."

"I'm going to check out those trips later today. Hopefully, Fiona will be successful in her assault on Wednesday."

"Perfect word. After being there when she talked with the producer, I'm confident in Fiona's take on the situation. I imagine Rebecca will be heading for Oahu in a couple of months."

"From the gist of the conversation I had with her earlier this morning, I think she's packed quite a few more boxes for the Goodwill. She plans to focus on the library next."

"I knew that room would be coming. I know I'm going to be checking out all the top shelves."

"I'm afraid so, darling. I don't think she plans to get rid of many books. Those she isn't taking with her, she's leaving with the house."

"That's good news. Packing all those books and toting them somewhere would be quite a task."

Fiona opened up the living room and dining room sliders so fresh air could circulate through Wade's working area. She noticed Wade driving into Layla's driveway and begin to unload his truck.

"Good morning, everything ready to install?"

"Yes, should have everything finished today. When does the furniture arrive?"

"My best guess is Thursday or Friday. I'm still waiting to hear from my Oahu shipper. If it gets here on Thursday, I can have it stored overnight and get the brothers to deliver on Friday. Otherwise, we will have to wait until next Monday."

"Don't take this the wrong way, Fiona, but you look a bit tired."

"Tired? I aged ten years overnight. Yesterday was my meeting with the crafters to tell them how the operation would work and to have them schedule their hours. Wade, I love artistic people, and with my degree in interior design, I consider myself an artist. But these folks drove me crazy. We spent three hours on the scheduling, and nothing is settled yet. We're having another meeting this coming Sunday afternoon to see if they have reached a decision once they have discussed things with their spouses, parents, grandparents, hairdressers, barbers, and God knows who else."

"Yikes, that sounds painful. I'll phone you when I'm finished so you can see how it looks and lock up. Go home and take a nap, you'll feel better."

"Excellent suggestion. I think I will. See you later this afternoon."

Fiona was waking up from her hour's nap when her cell phone rang. "Fiona Keller here."

"Mrs. Keller, hello, this is Gus Schwartz. Your shipment for Ms. Richfield will arrive in Maui on Thursday. Give my brother, Marvin, a call and let him know if you want to store it after it's unloaded or if your movers will be picking it up on Thursday. You have his number?"

"I do, Gus, thank you for calling. I'll phone your brother and let him know the brothers will pick up no earlier than Friday. Be sure and send me your bill. Gus, it's always a pleasure dealing with you and your brother."

"Thank you, Mrs. Keller, likewise and be sure and let Marvin know the brothers will be doing the pickup. He works with them frequently and knows how they, shall we say, operate. I put my bill in the mail this morning."

"I intend to. If they weren't the best movers on the island, I would use someone else, but those boys are so strong and so very careful, everyone puts up with their schedule," she said, laughing.

Fiona's next call was to the brothers; she didn't reach them but left a message. She thought it might be wise to call Marty to see how the end table was coming along. She used the landline to keep her cell open for the brothers' return call.

Marty answered on the third ring. "Hello, Marty, dear, it's Fiona. I was wondering how your work on the end table is coming along."

"I'll have it finished by Wednesday. This was so much easier than the larger one, and I had the luxury of working out of my own workshop. Would you like me to deliver it to your glass man for the top? I can just leave it there, and he can deliver it to Ms. Layla's when it's ready?"

"Marty, if you could do that, it would be wonderful. Layla's furniture is arriving this week, and I have to show an estate to a possible buyer from Los Angeles. My week is packed. Send me your bill, and I'll get a check out immediately."

"Thank you, Fiona. Anytime I can be of service, let me know. When you feel for an Italian meal again, give me a call, and we'll do another long lunch."

"I'm going to take you up on that offer in a couple of months. I can't do it too often, or I wouldn't be able to fit in any of my clothes."

Fiona's cell phone rang; she said goodbye to Marty and answered. It was the brothers. After discussing the arrival time, they agreed to do the pickup and delivery on Friday. Fiona did her best to get their assurance they would make it on Friday, but she knew it was always an iffy situation.

Next, she phoned Marvin Schwartz and let him know the arrival date and hopeful pickup the following day by the brothers. He understood the brothers' habits and said there would be no problem in holding the shipment over until their schedule permitted pickup. Fiona ended the conversation by thanking him for his understanding.

Her next call was to the mattress factory to arrange delivery on Tuesday of the following week. She called the cleaners and arranged to have the oriental rugs delivered on Wednesday of next week. Fiona phoned the glass shop, telling them to expect a table delivery from Marty and what she wanted for the top glass shelf. She checked her notes, deciding all her bases were covered, and then fixed lunch.

Fiona was almost finished with lunch when Ned walked in from his round of golf.

"Have you had lunch, honey? I'd be glad to fix you something."

Ned went to the counter and kissed Fiona on the cheek. "Thanks, sugar, but I ate at the club with the boys. Old Fred Kramer had a date this past weekend. His wife has been gone for almost two years, and he thought it would be proper to take a lady friend he met at the club out to dinner. He said she was too fast for him. When I asked him what that meant, he said she kissed him when he saw her to her door, and he believed she might have had even more in mind. Said it scared him right out of there."

"I can't believe that. When his wife was alive, he was always flirting with all the ladies, young and old. We gals called him Fast Freddie. I guess he was a figment of his own imagination," said Fiona, laughing. "How was your golf game?"

"I was so busy listening and laughing at Fred's tale, I missed half the greens and I'm not discussing my putting. How was your day?"

"I let Wade in so he could do the shelving, then I came home and took a nap. I needed to recover from yesterday. After I woke up, I was on the phone most of the time arranging pickup, deliveries, and I got an invitation from Marty for another Italian lunch. I would like to have him over for dinner one evening when I fix one of my Italian meals. I believe you would enjoy meeting him."

"Sounds great. I would enjoy hearing you two talk about Italy. What's your tomorrow like?"

"So far, it's blank. My week really picks up on Wednesday when I do my grand tour."

"How about we sleep in, go out for a late breakfast, then hang out together for the rest of the day?"

"Sounds terrific. I miss our quiet times together. Between Layla's, the Visitors Center, and Rebecca's, we've neglected each other."

The moment was interrupted by Fiona's cell phone ringing. "Fiona Keller here."

"Hi, Fiona, it's Layla. I'm calling because we were wondering how things are coming along and when we should plan on flying back to Maui."

"Plan on coming back a week from this Tuesday or Wednesday."

"Really? That long?"

"Yes, the brothers will pick up and deliver your furniture from Oahu on Friday, Tuesday the mattresses arrive, and Wednesday, the oriental rugs will be delivered. I would say fly in over this weekend, but I want to be sure the brothers get your furniture delivered on Friday, if not, it will be delivered on Monday."

"I'll tell Dewey and see which days work best for him and his crew. Things are really happening fast, just like you predicted. How did your crafters' meeting go?"

Fiona told her about the meeting and said how she wished she had never agreed to get in involved with the Visitors Center. It had turned into a real headache, literally.

"Fiona, you can pull it off, if anyone can. That's probably why Donnie tapped you for the job."

"You're right. I'm just not used to working with local craftspeople. Designer craftspeople are easier. They know what's expected."

"I'll let you go and speak with Dewey, then get back with you when we have an arrival date. Good luck with all your endeavors, and I miss all of you in Paia," said Layla softly.

Fiona relayed Layla's final words to Ned and wondered how she would do living in Salt Lake City full time. Her phone rang again, and it was Wade saying he had finished. Fiona said she would be right over. "Ned, why don't you come over with me and take a look at how things have progressed since your last visit? You will be amazed."

Ned and Fiona walked into Layla's and were greeted by Wade who was cleaning up his installation gear.

"Wade, this is something. Fiona explained to me what you were doing, but seeing the finished product really brings this wall to life. Excellent job!"

"This is better than I envisioned. These are truly floating shelves. Are you sure Layla's big-screen TV will be safe on that shelf?" asked Fiona.

"Yes, as you can see, that shelf is thicker than the others, and I have used extra bolts to hold the weight of the TV."

"I can't wait for Layla to see this wall. She will be thrilled. Be sure and send me a bill for all your work. Come to think of it, I need one from Herb too," said Fiona.

"I'm going to be working on those tomorrow. Herb is no good at paperwork, so we'll sit down at my computer, and I'll do the billing for both of us. I should have it in the mail by Wednesday."

"Thank you, Wade. You both have done outstanding work."

Fiona gave Ned a tour of Layla's house. He was stunned how the wood restoration and bathrooms had turned out. "Fiona, you put together an outstanding team of craftspeople and turned his place into a beautiful home. I bet Layla will want to live here full time. It will be hard to leave all this once the furniture has arrived and is placed."

"I believe they will spend more and more time here. With computers being what they are and Dewey's skills, I bet he finds he can be gone from the office more than he realized. They both love Paia and all of us. Hopefully, Salt Lake City will be their second home."

"I hope you're right, honey. I like having them around, and I know George, Annie, and Mr. Soo feel the same way."

CHAPTER 75

"George, I have eight boxes for you to load that go to the Goodwill. Then we can tackle the library," Rebecca said.

"I'll get these loaded now." Under his breath, George said, "While I still have the strength."

When the boxes were loaded, George joined Annie and Rebecca in the library. "Are we going to pack all these books?" George scanned the library, containing three walls of floor to ceiling books.

"Goodness, no. I'm only taking a few with me, and I've selected what I want and packed them. They are stored in the garage, along with everything else I'm taking. I just want you to go through the shelves and see if my husband stashed anything there. He was a good one at putting things down somewhere, then forgetting about it. If either of you see any books you would like, please take them. All the rest of these, I'll leave for the new owner. There are a lot of technical books on architecture, animal husbandry, management techniques, and historical biographies. I kept my books on the lower shelves so I wouldn't have to get on the ladder to get at them."

Rebecca pointed out where George should start, and he rolled the library ladder over to the first wall of shelves and began to search between the books while Annie and Rebecca worked on another section checking the lower shelves.

"Oh my gosh!" exclaimed Annie "I've found a pair of glasses."

"I knew it. He said he lost them in the kitchen and I must have thrown them out, but I knew he left them in the library," said Rebecca, laughing. "Thank you, dear, I'm so glad that mystery is solved."

They kept searching shelves, with George and Annie checking titles, making sure not to miss any they wanted. Annie and Rebecca finished their three bottom shelves and moved to the other side where George was working. They started work on the bottom three shelves where he had cleared the top. No more hidden items were found.

George finished one wall and moved onto the next. "Rebecca, did you say we could have any books we were interested in reading?"

"Yes, of course, help yourself."

"I've found a large book on Italian architecture, with emphasis on the older classical buildings. The pictures are terrific and is quite detailed on the building of these structures."

"George, I know my husband would be honored that an engineer would find pleasure in reading his books. Please take all you want."

George found five books he asked Annie to box up for him, then continued working through his second wall of shelves.

After lunch, they returned to the library. George found a book about Faberge eggs made for Nicholas and Alexandria of Russia that Annie was thrilled to have. Once all the shelves were checked, Annie and George went to make their drop-off at the Goodwill store. "I hope they don't turn us away. I fear we're overwhelming them with Rebecca's generosity."

"I'm sure they are grateful for everything we deliver. It will keep the volunteers busy. I'm glad we're finished at Rebecca's for the week. I've got to get back to my seniors. I'll phone when we get home and see if it's convenient I come by tomorrow. I love those dear folks, and I miss not seeing them weekly."

"I know you do, honey, and I'm sure they miss you too. Let's pick up something for dinner. I'm hungry and you must be too."

"That, my love, is an excellent idea. How about Chinese?"

"Perfect, order my usual and a side of egg rolls."

Annie pulled out her cell phone and placed the order. They dropped the boxes off at the Goodwill store and were greeted with forced smiles. After picking up their food order, they went home to enjoy dinner and browse through their newly acquired books.

*　　*　　*

Ned brought Fiona a cup of coffee as she sat at her dressing table, brushing through her hair. "Thank you, darling. I needed this."

"What would you like for breakfast? How about some oatmeal?"

"Are you crazy? I can't eat anything heavy. I'll want to curl up and go back to bed. Besides, if I wanted something that heavy, I would call Marty and tell him I'm coming over for breakfast," Fiona said.

"You need to eat something substantial, for energy to cope."

Fiona got up and put her arms around Ned's neck, pulling him to her. "You were wonderful last night, Mr. Keller."

"You were pretty wonderful yourself, Mrs. Keller."

"It's not as frequent as when we were younger, but I do believe it's gotten better. Although I can't figure out why, I always thought we were perfect together," Fiona said, smiling up to Ned.

"I think it's gotten better because we appreciate the intimacy of our lovemaking more. We're slower, gentler, and enjoy the pleasure we give to each other. Life's pleasures mean more as we age."

"How right you are, my darling. I married such a smart, sexy man. I'm a very lucky woman."

"How about french toast for breakfast, your favorite?"

"Perfect! Let me know when breakfast is ready."

After breakfast, Fiona dressed, grabbed her Hermes purse, and went to the kitchen for Ned's approval.

"Lovely as always. While you were dressing, George brought Pearl around. He dusted her off, and she's all ready to go."

"Bless that man. What good neighbors we've found in George and Annie. I believe we will enjoy many years of their company."

"I agree. Now get your cute little ass in the car and down to the airport. You don't want to keep our potential buyer waiting."

"No, I certainly don't. Wish me luck."

Ned kissed Fiona on the forehead and saw her to the Escalade.

When the producer's wife's plane arrived, Fiona drove up as far as she could, got out, and walked to greet her. Fiona was pleased to see a woman in her midfifties coming down the stairs dressed in designer jeans, expensive leather loafers, white blouse, carrying a huge Hermes tote and wearing a lot of gold jewelry.

They exchanged greetings, and Fiona escorted her to the Escalade. Fiona gave her a running commentary of the area, much like George had provided to her husband. Fiona maneuvered well over the road to Rebecca's and pulled under the porte cochere to find Rebecca outside ready to welcome them inside. After introductions, they walked into the foyer.

"My god!" exclaimed the producer's wife. "No wonder those two refused to tell me anything about this home, and it's truly something you have to see to believe."

From experience, Fiona and Rebecca knew not to say anything but to let the producer's wife explore, asking questions she may have.

She was very businesslike in her questioning, yet Fiona sensed an undertone of excitement. They took her on a tour of the home and the outside area.

Rebecca answered all questions with honesty and clarity and related her tale of years working on the big island cattle ranch. Finally, much to Fiona's relief, a phone call was placed to the pilots, and the producer's wife said she had to get back to the airport.

Returning to the airport, Fiona asked her what she thought of the estate and was thrilled to hear she would be negotiating the price with Mr. Tomoko tomorrow or the next day. She could not let this wonderful property fall to someone who might not appreciate it as much as her family would.

Fiona stood on the tarmac, waving as the plane departed. Once out of sight, she hurried into the car and phoned Ned.

"It's a done deal!"

"Honey, that's great news. Are you sure?"

"Yes, she said she would phone Mr. Tomoko in the next couple of days. As soon as I get home, I'll call Rebecca and tell her the good news. I've got to get going. I'm stopping to fill up Pearl, then I'm heading home. Have a drink ready for me. It's been a stressful day."

"You've got it, sugar."

Fiona pulled into George's driveway, honked the horn, and waited for him to come out and retrieve the keys. "I would have brought the keys up myself, but frankly, I'm drained. It was a trying experience but successful. She will be discussing the price with Mr. Tomoko in the next couple of days. And this sale is just as much your success as anyone's, George."

"Thank you, Fiona. I'm happy for everyone concerned. Does Rebecca know the good news yet?"

"No, I'm going to call her once I have a drink and ease down a little. Thank you again for Pearl. She did great, and I've filled her up for you," Fiona said, handing the keys to George.

Ned greeted Fiona with a martini; she took it and went to the bedroom to change. In shorts and a halter top, she found Ned in the kitchen and asked for a refill. He obliged, saying, "I think I should phone Rebecca, you look pooped. Besides, you downed that drink pretty quick."

"Fine with me, I've had enough of the real estate business for today. I'm going to go sit on the lanai."

Ned joined Fiona and phoned Rebecca putting the call on speaker so they both could her Rebecca's side of the conversation.

She was thrilled and asked Ned a number of questions. He told her to hang in there, and as soon as negations got underway, he would keep her updated on what was happening. After he hung up, they stayed on the lanai, enjoying the peace of the sunset.

Chapter 76

Ned and Fiona were on their way to the pier to be there when the shipment arrived. Fiona knew Marvin Schwartz would handle everything properly but felt it added to her creditability to show up whenever there was a large shipment coming in from either the mainland or Oahu.

"Ned, thank you for driving today. I'm enjoying being your passenger, just sitting here relaxing."

"After your great job yesterday, it's the least I could do." Ned touched his earphone and received a call from Mr. Tomoko. "She offered fifteen to start. That's amazing. I thought she would start around twelve."

Fiona picked up enough of the conversation to realize that Mr. Tomoko counter-offered at twenty and that Ned was standing firm at eighteen. Fiona had no doubt that figure would be reached in a couple of days. After Ned ended his conversation, Fiona said, "Do you want me to call Rebecca and tell her the latest?"

"Would you, darling? I really do not like driving and talking on the phone. I'm sure you were as delighted as I was that the producer's wife started off at fifteen million."

"Absolutely. That's a sure indicator how much pressure she must be getting from her husband and son to acquire that property. Besides, she liked it too."

Fiona phoned Rebecca and updated her on the call from Mr. Tomoko. She was semistunned at the amount of money being bantered around, still unreconciled to receiving such a large amount for her property.

"The brothers phoned this morning before we left. They are all set for pickup and delivery tomorrow. I told them I thought Rebecca's property would be sold soon, and they would be picking up there and delivering to both Layla's and Wade's in the next week or two. I wanted to prepare them in advance."

"That's smart. Those boys do not do well with last-minute requests," Ned said.

"Did you think that was a strange call we got last night from Layla?" Fiona asked Ned.

"No, why did you think it was strange?"

"Well, both she and Dewey wanted to come before Wednesday, but there were no rooms available at Mother's. The soonest they could get a room was next Wednesday, and that was at the Paia Inn. Why couldn't they have stayed with Mr. Soo? He would have enjoyed their company, and it's not like he doesn't understand they are young lovers and getting married soon."

"I'm sure it's out of respect for Mr. Soo. Both Layla and Dewey really care deeply for him, and they would have been uncomfortable sharing a room in his home, unless they were married."

"Perhaps you're right. It seems a little old-fashioned to me though."

"It might be, but remember, Mr. Soo is old-fashioned."

When they reached Marvin Schwartz's warehouse on the docks, things were being transferred as they arrived, and all was going smoothly. They stayed until everything was secured.

After lunch on the way back to Paia, Fiona received a call from Marty, letting her know he dropped off the end table and the glass people would deliver it to Layla's next Wednesday morning. Fiona thanked Marty and told him once the craziness from Layla's and the Visitors Center was over, she and Ned would have him over for one of her Italian dinners. Marty was thrilled.

Fiona turned to Ned, saying, "I'm sure tomorrow will go well, but I want to be there for the entire move, just to make sure everything is placed correctly. I've decided Saturday I'm going to target practice. That will relax me, and by then, I'll need to relax. I want to get ready for Sunday and my crafters' meeting. I'm not taking any more excuses from those people. If they aren't ready to post their own schedule, I'll post it for them or they're out. I'm not wasting any more of my time or of those that have made a sincere effort to cooperate."

"Honey, I have total faith that by the time you come home after your meeting, everyone will be scheduled and happy about their time slot. I'm anxious to meet with Donnie and the contractor at the Visitors Center tomorrow. Things are coming together nicely. Looks like the center and Layla's will both be ready about the same time, then we both can breathe a sigh of relief."

"Amen to that, and I refuse to take on any new projects for the remainder of the year!"

A little before ten Friday morning, Ned drove Fiona over to Layla's and helped her tote a cooler full of water and a bag of salty snacks inside. She wanted to keep the brothers watered and their salt level up. Fiona opened all the sliders, and Ned brought in the snacks.

The brother's large truck arrived from the warehouse fifteen minutes later. Fiona greeted them and asked if she could help. They said they were good until they started carrying things inside, then she could verify placement. They unloaded the items, carrying them up the back stairs to the rear lanai.

Two brothers donned CSI booties, as they called them, so they wouldn't scuff the newly refurbished floors. The largest brother stayed outside and got items through the back lanai screen door to the other brothers who placed them. It was a slow process, but the outcome was perfect and always pleased the customer. Fiona followed all items through the home, making sure of placement and angle. She made the brothers stop several times for water and chips. The brothers worked in such perfect coordination that things finished up a little before two that afternoon.

Fiona was closing up when Annie called from the back lanai.

"OK if I come in and see how things look?"

"Sure."

Fiona let Annie inside.

"My curiosity got the best of me."

Annie began walking through the kitchen, now full of new appliances, and into the still empty dining room. When she got to the living room, she stopped. "Holy cow, this is right out of a decorating magazine. It looks so chic and yet so livable. Believe me, Fiona, if we could afford it, I would have you redecorate our living room."

"Thank you, Annie. I would be happy to help you redecorate at no charge. We would have a ball shopping for everything."

"If I ever thought I could get George out of his big lounge chair, I would consider redecorating. It's the only chair that ever fits his height and he is so comfortable reading or watching television, I couldn't replace it. I'm anxious to see the rest of the furniture."

Fiona showed Annie throughout the house and enjoyed her many compliments. As they were closing up, Annie mentioned an idea she had regarding a housewarming gift for Layla.

"I thought, with her and Dewey going back and forth, a plant would be short-lived. I came up with the idea of filling a laundry basket full of things like salt, pepper, a few other spices, measuring spoons and cups, kitchen items. Then I thought maybe you would like to do one on paper items like paper towels, waxed paper, toilet paper, tissues, etc. What do you think? If we each spent about a hundred dollars, we could make a large dent in the things she will need, things she wouldn't have any idea she even needed."

"That's a splendid idea! I'm in. I'll let you know when she moves in officially, and we can get things before that. By the way,

I'm going shooting tomorrow to ease tension. I would be glad to have you and George join me. If you folks don't know how to shoot, I'm quite capable of giving lessons."

Annie looked wide-eyed at Fiona. "Thank you, that's a very generous offer, but George and I are both gun-shy. Neither of us have any problem with someone keeping a gun for their protection or that of their families, but it's just not for us. I hope you understand."

"Certainly, everyone reacts differently to the use of firearms. You know I never really liked the sheriff. He just hits me the wrong way. However, I agree with him that some drug crazies driving through town did not do the murders. I believe they were committed by someone local."

"I know. I've heard that from George more than once. That's why we are so diligent about keeping things locked up. Oh, before I forget, we want to invite you and Ned over tomorrow evening. We've invited Mr. Soo, and George is grilling some fresh salmon steaks we just received from our friends in Washington State. We hosted them a couple of years ago when they visited Maui, and he told us the next time he went salmon fishing, he would ice-ship us some. We got this shipment of salmon steaks yesterday afternoon and thought all of you would enjoy sharing them with us."

"Count us in. That sounds good. I've been dying for one of those fattening cheesecakes from the bakery. I'll bring one for dessert."

"I love those. Please do. I salivate every time I go by the bakery. Come over at five-ish for drinks before dinner. I'm looking forward to all of us being together again."

"Thanks, Annie. Wait until I tell Ned. He loves salmon."

*　　*　　*

Fiona was at the counter, enjoying an iced tea and sandwich, when Ned tapped on the lanai screen. She went to let him in. "Ned, I've accepted a dinner invitation for tomorrow from Annie. George is grilling fresh salmon steaks sent to them from Washington State. Mr. Soo is also invited."

"Great, I love fresh salmon. Did everything go OK at Layla's?"

"Yes, the brothers are terrific movers. For big men, they are so very careful. How did things go at the Visitors Center?"

"You are going to be amazed how much has been accomplished in the past week. The food people were there training staff and setting up utensils, and their inspection should be around the middle of next week. There are still a few items to finish up, but it will be done pretty soon now. Donnie asked me to be sure to have Layla see him when she and Dewey get back to Maui. I believe it has something to do with the opening of the center, but he didn't elaborate and I didn't ask."

"Heard any more from Mr. Tomoko?" Fiona asked.

"No, and I don't expect to until Monday."

"You're probably right. I hope that's settled soon. I would like to get everything moved into Layla's as soon as possible. The only thing missing is the dining room table and chairs coming from the mainland."

"Like you, honey, I'll be glad when everything is settled," said Ned with a sigh.

CHAPTER 77

Ned carried the cheesecake as he and Fiona went to George and Annie's for grilled salmon. Mr. Soo was already there, and everyone greeted one another warmly. Annie and Fiona went inside to place the cake in the refrigerator. Annie asked, "How was your day target shooting?"

"Wonderful. I feel much better. It relieves the stress in my shoulders. I'm in a better frame of mind to deal with the crafters tomorrow for our second scheduling meeting. Ned was at the Visitors Center yesterday and said things are going to wrap up there before too long. Your docents and my crafters will have to be ready to go soon. I don't know about you and George, but Ned and I will be glad when the center is opened and we will have that off our minds."

"George and I feel the same way. Although it has been a labor of love, we will be glad to see it come to fruition."

"Ladies, what are you drinking?" asked George, coming inside to fix drinks.

He prepared drinks, and soon everyone was sitting around outside, discussing a myriad of subjects. After dinner of rich salmon steaks, Annie's special coleslaw, and grilled asparagus spears, everyone said they were too full for cheesecake. Annie brought it out anyway, along with hot coffee, and half the cake managed to disappear.

Fiona and Annie carried things inside, and when they returned, Mr. Soo announced it was getting close to his bedtime and excused himself to go home. George and Ned said they needed the exercise and walked with him.

On the way, Mr. Soo said, "I sure miss Layla. Having her around has been a joy, and she makes wonderful casseroles. When she moves out, I might consider getting a dog. They are wonderful companions and could join me on my walks."

"You could go to the pound and get an older dog that is trained and needs a good home," suggested George.

"I never thought of training a dog. Your idea is a better plan for me than a puppy. An older dog for an older guy. Two bachelors," Mr. Soo said, laughing.

When George and Ned got back, they found Annie and Fiona making a list of items for Layla's housewarming gifts.

Sunday morning, Ned was having trouble getting Fiona out of bed. "Honey, you've got to get up and get ready to go to the Visitors Center."

"I don't want to go. I'll just sleep through the day."

"I was going to suggest that for breakfast, you have coffee and a piece of cheesecake that Annie sent home with us last night."

"Cheesecake? That does sound yummy. You sold me. I'll take a shower and eat before I get made-up and dressed. All that sugar should get me in fast gear."

Three hours later, they were up the hill to the center. Ned was going to a local deli to get sandwiches; they decided after their feast last night, sandwiches would do for dinner.

Fiona took a deep breath and went inside the center. All the crafters were sitting in a semicircle, having coffee and sweet rolls provided by Donnie.

"Good afternoon. Ready to get the time schedule worked out?"

"Not only are we ready, it's finished! We phoned each other and got it ironed out among ourselves. We all realized after our first meeting how silly we seemed, and we didn't want to put you through any more of that type of behavior, so we worked it out ourselves over the phone," reported one of the crafters.

Fiona sat down in an empty chair, a stunned look on her face. "I'm so very happy you have accomplished this on your own. It tells me you will be able to work through any obstacle that may come your way, and usually in an endeavor like this, something will. Thank you for your consideration and cooperation. It means a great deal to me personally."

Fiona went over procedures, thanked them again, and went back down the hill. When Ned let her in, he couldn't believe she had returned so swiftly.

"Honey, you're back so soon. Did it go horribly?"

"No, they worked everything out among themselves and handed me a complete schedule when I walked into the meeting. I reviewed procedures, and we were on our way. Do you believe it? All my worry and dreading for nothing, I'm so relieved."

Late Monday morning, Fiona was sitting at the counter, working on a crossword in the paper when George called from the lanai. "Fiona, Ned told me to come on up. He's puttering in the garage."

Fiona got up and let George in. "Welcome, neighbor."

"Here's our bill for helping Rebecca last week. We don't believe she will be needing our assistance any longer, so this is probably our last bill."

"Wait right here. I'll get our company checkbook."

Ned came in as Fiona was coming back with the checkbook. "Done deal, for eighteen million. Can't wait to tell Rebecca. There's only one possible problem. They want a forty-five-day escrow."

"That's a short escrow. Did they say why?"

"Seems our producer friend wants to shoot some scenes on the back acreage for a movie he's making."

"Wow, I bet Rebecca will be thrilled knowing how much she got for her estate. How much do you think she will actually see once commissions, fees, etc., are paid?" asked George.

"I'm not sure on the taxes," said Ned, "but I feel sure she will come out with a clean thirteen million. She should be able to purchase a nice piece of property on Oahu for about five million, and that will still leave her with a very nice legacy for her family."

"I believe the only problem might be to find something she likes in what is really a short period, plus obtain her own short escrow. What do you think, Ned?" asked Fiona.

"First, we talk to Rebecca, then we suggest she work with Mr. Tomoko. I've already discussed this with him, and he'll send the company plane and put her up in a hotel for a few days if necessary. He has a couple of listings that might work for her, and Mr. Tomoko feels he can get a quick escrow on them."

"Let's call Rebecca right away and get the ball rolling. I'll also need to schedule a furniture pickup for Layla and Wade. George, here's your check with our grateful appreciation. We could not have wrapped all this up as quickly without you and Annie."

"Thank you, Fiona. I can deposit this while I'm at the bank dropping off our final scheduling sheet to Donnie. Then Annie has me going on a grocery run," George said, grinning.

"George, can I ride along with you? I need to drop my crafters' scheduling off with Donnie, and I also need to pick up a few things at the market," asked Fiona.

"Sure, glad for the company. We'll scare the hell out of Donnie walking in together."

"You're right. He's become a nervous wreck. That man is actually getting skinny."

"Ned, while I'm gone, can you phone Rebecca, but before you hang up, tell her I'll be getting back with her sometime this week about a pickup date for the furniture."

"Sure, happy to break the good news to her."

Fiona and George walked into the bank and asked to speak with Donnie. He came out of his office, a worried look on his face.

"Donnie, don't look so glum. We come bearing good news," said Fiona, walking back to his office.

"Oh, I hope so. Every time I see somebody associated with the center, I fear something has gone wrong."

"Donnie, you've got to think more positive. You're going to waste away. You've lost a lot of weight," said George, caution in his voice.

"I've never been like this before. I worry about every little detail, and I have no appetite. Years of dieting and all I needed to do was become a nervous wreck," Donnie said with a weak smile.

George and Fiona presented their scheduling lists to Donnie, each containing names, work times, home addresses, phone numbers, and emergency contacts.

Leaving the bank and walking back to Pearl, they ran into Mr. Soo, who decided he would go along with them to the grocery store. All three neighbors set off to, as Fiona put it, "Storm the market."

CHAPTER 78

Fiona was at Layla's to receive the mattresses. The delivery people set up the bed in the master bedroom and main guest bedroom, then placed the two twin mattresses in Layla's spare room. Fiona would ask the brothers to place those when that pineapple furniture arrived from Rebecca's.

Back home, she phoned Wade, updating him on the sale of Rebecca's. They agreed to go to Rebecca's together; Wade wanted to pay Rebecca for the items he was taking, and Fiona wanted to get a detailed price list for Layla. She also wanted to determine a time to try and schedule the brothers for pickup and delivery. Fiona said she would call Rebecca to see if this coming Thursday would be a good day for them to come out, then get back to Wade.

After making her calls to both Rebecca and Wade, it was determined they would be at Rebecca's at ten on Thursday morning. Next, Fiona phoned the brothers. She told them about the situation at Rebecca's and asked what would be good for them. After checking their schedule, they opted for the next Tuesday morning, provided it was not raining. Fiona approved the date, then phoned Rebecca and Wade, verifying it with them.

Fiona phoned Annie. "We've got to get shopping for our housewarming gift baskets. Things are moving very rapidly, and I honestly expect Dewey and Layla might move in by this weekend."

"My gosh, things sure do happen all at once, don't they?"

"They sure do. How is Friday for you?"

"Friday is fine. I'll drive the Jeep because it can carry a ton of stuff. This is going to turn out to be fun."

"I agree. It will be a girls' day out. Plus, it's fun buying things we won't have to put away," said Fiona.

Wednesday morning, both Fiona and Ned were at Layla's. Fiona had asked Ned to help place the oriental rugs and move the coffee and end tables. Ned agreed, skeptical the two of them could handle the big coffee table.

The small end table arrived first, and even that was heavier than Fiona had anticipated. She and Ned put it where Fiona had envisioned and were waiting for the rugs to arrive when Fiona's cell rang. It was Layla saying she and Dewey had arrived in Maui and were on their way to Paia. It was a while before check-in, and she wondered if it would be a good time to see her home.

"Actually, it's a terrific time. We could use the extra manpower. Ned and I are here now, and the oriental rugs will be delivered shortly. The two of us will be unable to lift the coffee table onto the rug and could use Dewey's muscle."

"We'll be there shortly."

Fifteen minutes later, their car pulled into the drive, and they came up the stairs to the back lanai screen door. Fiona ushered them inside, and once hugs and handshakes were completed, Dewey and Layla began the tour of their Paia home.

Layla loved her kitchen, especially her large refrigerator. When they got to the living room entrance, they were stopped dead by the furniture and wall unit.

"This is so much more than I imagined. It looks perfect," said Layla.

"I'm not sure I want to bother returning to Salt Lake City," said Dewey. "This is like a dream home. Fiona, you do wondrous work."

"Thank you, Dewey, but Layla, with her sharp artistic eye, picked out a lot of the furniture. Wade's shelving adds a designer touch that sets the room off."

"It's wonderful, and the television fits just right. Plus, I have all these lovely shelves for added items, especially books. I am so happy with this room, and just think we have the rugs yet to lay."

"Layla, I have some very exciting news for you. This coming Tuesday, the brothers will be going to Rebecca's to pick up those items and deliver them. Once that is finished, all you will be missing is the dining room table and chairs."

"I can't believe this is all happening at once. This is so exciting."

There was a knock on the screen, and the cleaners that had stored the oriental rugs arrived. The rugs were rolled in brown wrapping paper and delivered in that manner. Ned and Dewey unwrapped the rugs and were directed where to place each rug. Dewey and Ned grunted and groaned but managed to get the coffee table in front of the sofa.

"Dewey, maybe we should just move in here and forget staying at the Paia Inn. All we have to do is make the bed up, and we're home!" Layla said happily.

"Actually, Layla, I've scheduled a cleaning crew in for Friday morning. As you can see, with all the furniture moving, there is quite a layer of dust around. I think your best bet would be to move in this weekend," encouraged Fiona.

"Honey, I'm sure Fiona knows what she's talking about. Besides, we'll have to get food and other supplies," Dewey said.

"You're right. I got excited about how great everything looks. Maybe we should shop on Saturday and get everything ready here, then move in on Sunday."

"Excellent. Call me Saturday morning, and I'll meet you here before you go shopping. That way, I can give you some advice on what you will need to get started," Fiona said, breathing a sigh of relief. She and Annie would surprise them Saturday morning with their baskets of housewarming gifts.

"Tomorrow, Wade and I are going to Rebecca's to get things priced. Layla, why don't you and Dewey join us? Dewey, I would like for you to see her home before it's sold."

"Thank you. Layla has told me so much about her home, but I still can't quite imagine it, and I'm pretty talented at imagining things."

Fiona turned to Layla. "Layla, stop by the bank and see Donnie. He asked that we make sure you see him. Also, while you're there, I'm going to need more money. Come back to the house with us. I've got a current balance sheet, and we're about down to zero. That doesn't take into account the bill for the items delivered today. We'll also need money for the items you are purchasing from Rebecca, the table from the mainland, paying the brothers for the Rebecca move, and my fee."

"How big of a check would you like?"

"Let's go and come up with a figure."

They all helped close up the house and walked back to the Kellers'. Ned asked Dewey if he would like to join him on his Friday tour of the Visitors Center, telling him they were close to opening day.

Dewey accepted eagerly. Layla asked Fiona if she was busy on Friday, and Fiona hurriedly said she was booked elsewhere the whole day. Layla said she would go sketch windsurfers for a final piece for their home, something she had never gotten around to doing, and would visit the bank in the morning.

Chapter 79

Wade pulled into Layla's driveway and noticed Fiona, Layla, and Dewey standing across at Mr. Soo's. "Hi, folks. I hope I'm not late."

"No, we were trying to figure out what car to take," said Fiona. "Wade, have you met Dewey?"

"We met when he was that windsurfer guy but never formally introduced as Dewey McMaster," said Wade, smiling.

Dewey strode across the street and shook hands. "Wade, it's a pleasure to meet the creator of the shelving in our living room and those terrific cabinets in the bathrooms."

"Thank you. Your home is a masterpiece. All that wonderful wood is priceless. I've told Layla if you folks decide to sell, I'll pay any price."

"Right now, Wade, I can't imagine us selling, but you never know what the future will bring, so we'll definitely keep your offer in mind, and I'll be sure and tell Fiona."

"If you don't mind, I'll drive my pickup. There are a couple of small things I can take with me. The larger items I'll let the brothers deliver."

"Fine with me. I'll tell the ladies," said Dewey. Dewey walked back and told Layla and Fiona that Wade would be taking his pickup and the reason why, and then he suggested he drive.

On the way, Dewey mentioned to Fiona the offer Wade made to purchase their home and asked if he actually had that kind of money.

"Goodness, yes," replied Fiona. "He's a trust-fund baby but enjoys working with his hands and being creative. He and Herb have a lovely bungalow just off the beach, a few miles up the coast. I don't know this for sure, but gossip has it he has a doctorate degree in finance from Harvard or Yale or one of those Ivy League schools. His dad is big on Wall Street."

"Why am I not surprised? The residents of this little rural community come from amazing backgrounds," said Dewey.

"You're a fine one to talk," said Fiona, giving her and Layla a good laugh.

When they pulled up to Rebecca's, she was outside to greet everyone. She was introduced to Dewey and seemed especially pleased to meet Layla's fiancé. She ushered them inside to the foyer.

"My god!" exclaimed Dewey and immediately took off toward the atrium. He peered through the glass and then made his way up one of the side staircases, commenting about the amazing sight before him. "Excuse me, I got carried away," Dewey said, making his way back down the stairs to rejoin the group.

"It's all right, dear," said Rebecca. "I think by now, we all have grown used to people's reaction. On behalf of my late husband and myself, thank you."

"I'm so happy I got to see this before it was sold. Would you mind if Layla snapped some photos with her cell phone? She's quite an artist in her own right, and this would make a fabulous charcoal."

"Why didn't I think of that?" said Layla, pulling out her cell phone.

"Please take as many photos as you like," said Rebecca.

"Rebecca, be sure and keep in touch with Fiona so that I can have your address in Oahu. When I get a completed charcoal, I'll send you one. I'll do two and keep one for myself."

"That would be a lovely remembrance, and I would cherish having it in my new home."

They went about reviewing the items selected, with Rebecca quoting prices from her notes. When they came to the pineapple bedroom set, Dewey was surprised Layla wanted it for their home. He looked at her with a slight frown, and she winked at him and mouthed, "Tell you later."

When they got to the dining room credenza, Dewey was amazed by the delicate look of the beveled glass piece and voiced his concern about a safe trip to their home. Everyone assured him the brothers would get it there safely. Dewey opened one of the doors and asked, "Rebecca, do you mean these candlesticks to go with the credenza?"

"I forgot all about those being in there. I meant to ask Layla or Fiona if they wanted them to go along with the credenza."

"Yes," both ladies said in unison.

"Those are perfect for that piece," said Fiona.

Final prices were agreed on by Layla and Wade, then Wade packed up the things he wanted into his pickup and headed back to Paia. Rebecca provided newspaper, and Fiona wrapped the candlesticks to take back with them in the station wagon.

On the way back to Paia, Dewey asked Layla, "Please explain the pineapple bedroom set. It's not what I thought you would want."

"First off, it's very authentic old Hawaiian and will fit right in with our home. I do have an ulterior motive," Layla said. "You see, I know we will host Kyle and Kim when they return to Paia for the opening of the Visitors Center, and that is where I plan on putting them."

Dewey turned toward Layla, a slow smile spreading across his face. "Well, this is a side of you I didn't know existed. I love it."

"Oh, that's priceless," said Fiona. "Every ounce of revenge is well placed."

Back at Mr. Soo's, Dewey said to Fiona, "Layla and I are taking Mr. Soo to dinner this evening. I was thinking it would be fun for you and Ned, George and Annie, all of us go to Bird's for dinner Friday night."

"Terrific, I can visit by little Bird. I'm sure he misses me. Layla, are you going to take the food orders?"

"Sure, you talk with Ned, and I'll call you later this evening. Dewey, let's walk over and see if Annie and George are home and ask them in person."

"OK, but let's get these candlesticks inside. They're so delicate."

Dewey and Layla went over to the Boones' and found them both at home. Dewey relayed his amazement about Rebecca's, and George explained, from and engineering point of view, the difficulties in building such an atrium. They agreed to meet at Bird's Friday evening at seven for dinner. Layla got their grill order, then she and Dewey set off to grab a sandwich and check into the Paia Inn.

Chapter 80

Layla got up, made a cup of courtesy coffee, dressed, gave sleeping Dewey a kiss on the forehead, and left for breakfast at a nearby café. After breakfast, she drove to Mr. Soo's, loaded her art supplies in the car, and went to meet with Donnie.

Although early, Donnie was in his office. "Layla, I hope I can impose upon you to do me a favor regarding the opening of the Visitors Center."

"Of course, Donnie, how may I help?"

"Would you mind contacting Kim and invite him and Kyle to the opening as soon as we have an exact date? If it's too difficult for you, I certainly understand, but I wanted to ask anyway."

"I had already planned to host them in our new home, provided it was ready when the center opened. Now I know for sure it will be, and I have no problem doing this, We parted amicably."

"Thank you, Layla. I was worried about being able to secure a short-notice reservation for them at either Mother's or the Paia Inn. I'm planning a meeting next week with the major people involved in the opening so we can set a date. I'll need to get publicity out, and we need to get all the docents, crafters, and restaurant workers in place. Will you and Dewey be available for that meeting?"

"We've not set a date to return to Salt Lake City. If need be, Dewey will return, and I'll stay here to finish up the house. As far as I know, we'll be here all of next week."

"Wonderful. I'll get back with you on a date. There are a lot of people to organize into one meeting, so it may take a couple of tries before we get it nailed down."

"While I'm here, I need to transfer some funds into Fiona's working account. Bills are coming in, and I want to be sure she has ample funds to pay everything promptly."

"Of course, how much would you like transferred?"

Layla told Donnie the amount agreed on, and he went to make the transfer. After completion, he returned to his office and gave the transfer slip to Layla. He thanked her for her assistance getting Kim to the opening and confirmed her cell phone number.

Layla left the bank and stopped at a deli for lunch and several bottles of water, putting everything in the cooler she brought with her. Then it was off to sketch the windsurfers. Sitting at her easel, she began working with various charcoals; hearing someone walking up behind her, she turned to find the sheriff coming her way.

"Good morning, Layla. I heard you and Dewey had returned. Glad to have you both back. Working on one of your lovely charcoals?"

"Hello, Sheriff. I'm glad to be back in Paia. I had always planned to do a charcoal of the windsurfers for us personally but never found the time. Today I'm making the time. Our home will be ready to move into soon, and I wanted this one in a particular place."

"I saw the one you did for George and Annie. It's special, Layla. You captured the colors so perfectly. You do excellent work, fitting right in with Paia's art community."

"Thank you, Sheriff. I enjoy doing landscape work, and the vistas available in this part of the world are endless. Isn't it exciting that the Visitors Center will be opening soon?"

"Yes, it is. I got a call a bit ago from Donnie to set up a meeting to determine an opening date. Getting down to the fun and festivities."

Layla thought "fun" was a strange term to use, considering the events that led to the creation of the Visitors Center but dismissed her thought, thinking it was because of his perception of the work involved by his department for the opening ceremonies.

"Dewey and I will be attending that meeting. I'll be coordinating the arrival of Kim for the event."

There was a crackle on the sheriff's radio, which he responded to. He bowed slightly and excused himself, saying there was a fender bender on the road to Hana, not an uncommon event.

Layla got back to her drawing while still feeling inspired.

Fiona walked to Annie's, bearing two travel mugs of latté. Handing one to Annie as she was greeted at the door, Fiona said, "Thought we might need an extra shot of the strong stuff this morning. I made these with a double shot of espresso. It'll give us a good jolt."

Annie took a sip from her mug. "Yummy, how I love strong coffee, and a latté is an extra special treat. Thank you."

"Where's George? I'm afraid I didn't make him a coffee."

"He was off early, doing some work with one of his volleyball groups. Those kids would have him out there every day if they could. Of course, he enjoys it as much as they do, and volleyball in the sand is excellent exercise."

"He certainly has more pep in the morning that I do," said Fiona, shaking her head.

Annie locked up; they got into the Jeep and went to do their shopping, lists in hand.

Their first stop was Costco, where they found large laundry baskets and plenty of paper supplies, Fiona almost completing her list. Annie didn't find too much from her list, as big-box items were not practical for Dewey and Layla's lifestyle. Their next stop was Kmart, where Annie found everything on her list, and Fiona completed her list, adding a couple more things she didn't think of. They stopped at a card store, and each bought an appropriate greeting card and very large bows for the baskets. Satisfied with their purchases, they stopped for lunch then back home.

They left the baskets on the dining room table at Annie's, adjusted the items in the baskets, adhered the bows, added the proper greetings to the inside of their cards, and placed them in their respective baskets.

George came in from the front lanai, eyeing the loaded baskets. "Well, ladies, did you leave anything in the stores for anyone else?"

"A few things, but we did real well, and I don't think we spent much over $100 each. This will give them a start on what they will need to set up their home," said Fiona.

"You ladies did a good job. They will be very grateful."

"I'm going home, take a shower, and maybe a nap. I want to be ready for a fun evening."

When Fiona got home, she found a note from Ned, saying he wasn't sure when he would get back, he and Dewey were at the Visitors Center.

Dewey was walking to the Visitors Center from the Paia Inn, giving himself plenty of time to stop and say hello to old friends along the way. As he was walking up the driveway, he noticed Ned walking up the hill and waited for him. Ned explained the latest exterior items, including George's plaque at the entryway. Dewey was amazed at the complete transformation of the Okamotos' market and living quarters into a modern and welcoming Visitors Center. The curved wood counter for the docents now had brochures displayed, along with maps of stores and sites of interest in Paia. They walked over to the crafter section; Ned explained the type of crafters Fiona had recruited. He pointed out on the back wall where the six charcoals that Layla had donated would be placed for sale.

Next, they toured the food area, where visitors placed their orders to take with them or if it was a grilled item, they would take a number. Everyone would go outside to eat, and if your order was served, it would be delivered to your table where a number was displayed on a small standard fitted into each table. Once you got into the food line and picked up your food, it would not be possible to get back into the Visitors Center. This plan would help ensure no food or drinks would be spilled on the wood floor of the center; at least that was the hope.

Ned opened the wide doors to the outside lanai that ran along the veranda. He explained to Dewey they had taken a large part of the Okamotos' living quarters, opened it up, and made it part of the lanai. This gave them plenty of outside eating tables, and being raised from the roadway, those driving by could see that food was available.

Donnie, the contractor, and Ned had worked on an outside sign that was in good taste, welcoming and encouraging travelers to come inside to shop and eat. The sign they had come up with would be ready for installation by next week. Ned said he had taken the inspector to the shop where the sign was being made to make sure everything stayed within the stringent island sign regulations.

The contractor joined them, and they returned to the inside of the center. Dewey had several questions for Ned or the contractor that were answered easily. Donnie came in, happy to see Dewey.

"Dewey, I hope you are pleased with what your money has accomplished. The contractor and Ned have done a wonderful job for our city, one that will forever honor the Okamotos."

"Donnie, you too are to be congratulated. You are the one that got the ball rolling, and you've outdone what I expected. This is so impressive."

"Thank you. I am proud of how it has turned out."

Dewey touched Donnie's elbow and directed him away from the others. "Donnie, I know you are working on a sign, and I know there will be quite elaborate opening ceremonies. Do you need any more money? Plus, you have all the utilities and start-up charges. I'm more than happy to write you another check."

"Frankly, the answer is yes. The project can use an infusion of funds for just the reasons you mentioned. I was beginning to get worried and thought I was going to have to put together a fund-raiser."

Dewey reached into his back pocket, withdrew his checkbook, walked to the docent's counter, and wrote a check for $75,000, handing it folded to Donnie. "Never hesitate to ask for more. Giving back to this town that was so good to me, not knowing who I was, makes me happy."

Donnie unfolded the check and said a soft "Whew, Dewey this is wonderful. I'll get a receipt to you before you leave. This will see us well beyond our opening. I'll heed your generous offer, and let you know if we are ever short funded."

Dewey clapped Donnie on the back, and both walked back to where Ned and the contractor were talking. They spent another half hour at the center, and then Ned and Dewey left, agreeing to meet at Bird's at seven that evening.

* * *

It was little before seven, and Ned sat at the bar, talking to Jessie. "Is Fiona the only person that comes to talk with him?"

"Yes, thank God. That bird has an attitude, and now that he and Fiona have some type of weird connection, I don't think we could handle any more admirers like that."

Dewey and Layla pulled into Bird's parking lot with Annie and George right behind them.

"I notice the Kellers' car is already here," said George. "Fiona is probably in conferring with her feathery Bird."

"No doubt," said Layla. "That's odd how they took to each other. Only Fiona."

Everyone went inside, greeting Fiona and Bird, then continued into the bar where Ned sat.

"Byrd has everyone set up outside for dinner, and I've reserved a booth for you folks inside after you've eaten. It's such a lovely evening, he thought you would enjoy being outside," said Jessie. "What would you like to drink, and I'll bring them to you?"

"That's so thoughtful," said Ned. "I'll corral Fiona, and we'll meet everyone out back. Come, Fiona, we're all going outside for dinner, and I gave Jessie a drink order for you," Ned said as he directed Fiona through the bar toward the outside.

"Isn't this lovely?" said Fiona as she gazed into the back area that Byrd had set up with tables and strung colored lights. Several other tables were taken by diners enjoying their meal.

"Just so peaceful," said Annie. "If you listen closely, you can hear the sound of waves and you can smell the ocean from here, but most of all, I enjoy the lovely scent of the tropical flowers."

"I think it's terribly romantic," said Layla.

"I have to agree with you," said Annie.

George drew Annie into his side and smiled down at her. "That's my wife, a wonderfully romantic woman."

"Yes, I am," said Annie, looking up at George, who bent down and kissed her lightly on the forehead.

Jessie brought drinks, and everyone sat down. There was light conversation, but everyone was immersed in the beauty of the evening until Byrd brought dinner. Large T-bone steaks for all the men and Fiona, and fish caught fresh that morning for Annie and Layla. Everyone had an active day and ate with abandon.

"Whew, I'm finally full," said George, pushing back from the table. "The kids ran me ragged today. I was starving."

"Dewey and I took the grand tour of the center this afternoon, and he walked to and from the Paia Inn. So we both had worked up a good appetite."

"I lugged my art supplies out to the bluff overlooking the windsurfers and painted for hours. Now, that may not sound like hard work, but I was so tired, I had to quit earlier than I planned."

Fiona and Annie glanced briefly at each other, hoping no one expected to hear about their day.

"I want dessert," said Fiona, breaking the train of conversation. "Does Byrd have any type of dessert?"

"I'll check for you, honey," offered Ned.

He walked over to where Byrd was finishing up his grilling and asked about dessert, then returned to the table. "He's going to fix us one big bowl of something special that we can share. Said he always has something ready when adults eat here with kids."

"Well, it probably isn't cheesecake," said Fiona.

Byrd brought a large salad bowl filled with scoops of chocolate, vanilla, and strawberry ice cream over bananas and topped with hot fudge then whipped cream, nuts, and cherries. He handed out six spoons and told them to enjoy their banana split.

"Oh my god," said Fiona, "this is terrific!"

The salad bowl was empty when Byrd brought out a large fresh pot of Kona coffee and six mugs. He came back with sugar and cream and whisked away the dessert bowl.

"Thank heavens for the coffee. This will help me settle all the food I've just eaten. We devoured that dessert," said Annie.

"It was so good. It's been years since I had a banana split. I had forgotten what a treat they can be," said Layla.

Everyone sat outside, having coffee and talking about the upcoming opening of the Visitors Center and the completion of Layla's house. When they felt they could move again, they went inside to their reserved table.

Sixties, seventies, and eighties rock music played, but no one had the energy to dance. A slow romantic ballad began, and all three couples decided they could handle dancing slowly. After that, a faster number was played, and Fiona convinced Dewey to stay on the dance floor with her while everyone else gladly went back to the booth.

"Has she always been a dancer?" asked Annie with a laugh.

"Lord yes, she used to have me on the dance floor all the time. I'm like you, George, I'm good with the slow stuff, but the fast ones I prefer to sit out. When we were younger, I never wanted her out there without me, now I let her go. Tonight, she should wear down quickly."

"Well, I'm worn down," said Annie, looking up at George, smiling.

"You had a busy day, why don't we call it a night?" said George.

"I think after that meal, we're all ready for home," said Layla, stifling a yawn.

Fiona and Dewey returned to the table. "That does it for me tonight," declared Dewey.

"I hate to admit it, me too," said Fiona. "What time shall we meet tomorrow?" she asked.

"Originally, I thought early, but after tonight, how about ten in the morning? That should give us time to recover," said Layla.

"Perfect," said Fiona.

"We're going to leave now," said George. "We certainly have a good time when we get together. Next time, I'll grill for us."

As they were leaving, Fiona whispered to Annie, "I'll call you in the morning, and we'll arrange everything."

Annie smiled and nodded.

Outside, George said to Annie, "You seemed anxious to leave. Anything wrong?"

"No, nothing's wrong. I just wanted to get home be kissed, hugged, and made love to."

"Well, in that case, let's get you in the car and get home right away," George said with a grin, ushering Annie swiftly into Pearl's passenger seat.

CHAPTER 81

George woke the next morning finding Annie looking at him. Startled, he asked, "Is something wrong? You're looking at me funny."

Annie reached her hand up and laid it on George's cheek. "No, sweetheart, I was just thinking how much I love you, and I couldn't imagine my life without you."

"I hate to ask, especially after last night, is something wrong?"

"I'm having a bout of anxiety over the opening of the Visitors Center. I know I've been to the center several times, but the opening ceremonies, with references to the Okamotos, is making me remember that horrible morning. I thought I had it pushed back in the recess of my mind, but it's managed to creep forward again."

"Oh, honey," said George, drawing her closer into him. "I'll be by your side, holding your hand. You can lean on me, and don't worry, you'll get through it—no, we'll get through it together."

A tear ran down Annie's cheek as her head lay on George's chest. She knew he would be there for her, but she was still worried about keeping her composure.

Fiona phoned Annie at eight thirty. "Good morning. I hope everyone slept well."

"After all that food, we slept quite well. What's the plan for this morning?"

"Ned and I were discussing things, and those baskets are so heavy. I'm sure Dewey and Layla wouldn't suspect anything if they saw my car in their driveway. So let's load the baskets into my SUV and drive over there. Then George and Ned can carry them inside to the counter. It took both of us to get one basket upstairs into your dining room. I think trying to carry them over there is silly. We'll be over at nine thirty, if that's OK with you folks?"

"George will be pleased he doesn't have to lug that heavy basket over to Layla's. We'll be ready when you get here."

Layla and Dewey walked up the stairs to the back lanai door; Fiona came to the screen and opened it for them.

"Goodness, everyone is here. What a surprise," said Layla.

Annie stepped forward from the group that was shielding the counter from view. "Kids, we seriously doubted that either of you has any experience setting up a house. Instead of the usual housewarming plant, we got something useful and practical."

With that said, everyone stepped away from the counter, revealing the two gift baskets.

"Dewey, look what they've done for us!"

"I don't know what to say. This is so thoughtful. Layla and I need all the help we can get in making this house a home."

"This will give you a good start," said Fiona. "Now look through things and start putting items away and crossing them off your list."

Ned and George were assigned to bathroom duty. They distributed toilet paper, soaps, and tissues to each of the bathrooms. Annie and Fiona helped Layla put the other items away where she would be able to find them. Dewey crossed items off the list he and Layla had made earlier.

Halfway through the distribution process, Ned's cell phone rang; it was Donnie calling. He wanted to know if Ned and Fiona would be available for a Tuesday evening meeting. Fiona shook her head no, reminding everyone that was the day the movers would be bringing Rebecca's items to Layla's. She doubted if she or Layla and Dewey would feel much like a meeting Tuesday evening.

Ned told Donnie that both George and Annie and Dewey and Layla were all present, and he was putting him on speakerphone to see if they could get them in agreement. After several minutes, Thursday at 7:00 p.m. was a good time for all those assembled. Donnie said he would continue making his calls and get back to everyone.

"I must place a call to Kim and let him know where things stand. I want to be sure he and probably Kyle will be able to attend in the near future."

"Why don't you do that now before Donnie calls back? You've been fretting about making that call," said Dewey.

"You're right, honey. I've been putting this off," Layla said, stepping outside; sitting on the back steps, she placed a call to Kim's number in Washington, DC. Kyle picked up the ringing phone.

"Layla, good to hear your voice."

Layla seriously doubted it, but she kept a light tone to her voice. "Kyle, I was calling to update Kim on the Visitors Center. We will be meeting one night this week to set a date for the opening ceremonies. Naturally, Kim should be at those ceremonies. I wanted to know if there is any date within the foreseeable future that wouldn't work. Also, our new home will be completed shortly, and Dewey and I insist that you both stay here."

"Really? Layla, that's is very kind of you and Dewey. I'll check with Kim. I'm pretty sure his schedule will allow him the freedom to attend the ceremonies. I would be honored to attend with him. Like you, I only met his parents briefly, but I know what a sacrifice they made for his education, and I would like to honor them on his behalf."

"If either you or Kim will get back to me as soon as possible, I can let Donnie know if there are any conflicting dates when Kim wouldn't be available."

"Will do. I want to congratulate you and Dewey on your upcoming wedding. My mother sent me the announcement your parents put in the local Hamptons paper. Naturally, their daughter marrying one of the world's richest men was a coup for them."

"I had no idea they did such a thing. They haven't even met Dewey," said Layla, laughing.

"You know your folks," said Kyle. "I'm sure after our breakup, they wanted to tell the world their daughter snared such a catch."

"Yes, that would be their attitude. Dewey and I are very much in love. This sounds like an old cliché, but we were truly meant for each other. We make each other complete."

"I can't tell you how glad I am for you. You deserve every happiness."

"Thank you. I have to be going. I'll be expecting a return call." Layla went back inside. "That's over and it went well. What a load off my mind. How's our list coming along, Dewey?"

"It's getting a lot shorter as more and more items are put away. We still have so much to purchase, especially fresh food items. We may not be able to move in as soon as we wanted. But when we do, it will be livable," said Dewey with determination.

When Fiona got to Rebecca's Tuesday morning, Wade came out, directing her to a side drive that led behind the home. She parked next to Wade's truck in a carport area.

"Fiona, I have coffee and homemade cinnamon rolls in the kitchen," said Rebecca.

"You do not want to miss these cinnamon rolls," Wade said, popping the last of one into his mouth, licking his fingers.

Fiona sat at the small kitchen table, soon to be at Layla's, eating the most delicious cinnamon roll she had ever had. Her praise did not go wasted on Rebecca, who beamed with pride. As Fiona was finishing, the brothers' truck pulled into the driveway. Rebecca directed them to the cinnamon rolls, each brother enjoying several.

After washing their sticky fingers, they got busy loading the van. Wade showed them his purchases, which would be loaded first, followed by those going to Layla's. When the van was almost loaded, Fiona called Layla, advising they would be on their way soon.

Great care had been given to the glass cabinet. The brothers wrapped it in padding, carried it carefully to the van, and added even more padding, then secured it by straps to the side and bottom of the truck. Everything was loaded with added padding, the brothers giving the care they were known for.

Wade and Fiona left first; Wade going home to wait for his delivery and Fiona going home to park her car and walk to Layla's.

Fiona was anxious to tell Layla and Dewey about the morning call she received from Georgia. "When I answered the phone there, was this lovely soft Southern drawl telling me that the semi carrying your table and chairs left Georgia yesterday and should be at the Port of Long Beach, at the latest in five days. They will be using a cargo ship coming into Oahu. She will get back to me on the container number and estimated date of arrival. When I have that information, I'll let Gus Schwartz know, and he will receive it, then ship it to Marvin here in Maui. We can then arrange to have the brothers deliver it, and this should take no more than four weeks. Isn't that wonderful?"

"It would be terrific if we had that before Kim and Kyle arrived. If not, we can live without it. I'm glad to know it's on the way."

"That will complete everything except your empty room," said Dewey.

"The empty room is still a work in progress in my mind."

"I'm going on the lanai and watch for the brothers," said Fiona.

"I'll keep you company," said Dewey. Outside, Dewey turned to Fiona, "Fiona, I need your help. Can we go shopping for furniture for both the front and back lanais? I realized this morning, when I went outside to have a cup of coffee, there was nothing to sit on. So I was hoping you could set up an account in my name, and we could shop for furniture soon. I would like to try and surprise Layla."

"Friday would be a good day for me. Do you think you can get away without telling Layla where you're going?"

"I'll use Mr. Soo as an excuse. He'll play along and enjoy it."

"I know just the place to find everything you'll need."

"We'll come over to your home, and we can go from there. Maybe Layla and Annie can go shopping. We'll plan something."

The furniture arrived and was unloaded without mishap.

That evening, Donnie called, confirming the meeting for 7:00 p.m. on Thursday. George contacted everyone, saying he would grill, and they could walk up the hill to the center after dinner.

CHAPTER 82

Donnie started the meeting promptly at seven. The mayor and city council members were present, the various restaurant operation managers, the contractor, the sheriff, and other major players. After nearly an hour of discussion, a Sunday afternoon at two was the designated day and time, but a specific date was needed. Enduring a litany of other Sunday events that were happening, a date of six weeks from the coming Sunday was scheduled. Donnie got assurances from the restaurant managers that all would be ready to go, from Fiona that her crafters would have their items ready for display and sale, and from the Boones that all the docents had their shirts and were scheduled.

The final discussion item was who would be speaking. Donnie would host the ceremonies and acknowledge the major donors and contributors to the building project. The mayor would welcome the addition to the city. Fiona would introduce her crafters and give a very brief summary of the items on display, George would explain the role of a docent, and the ceremonies would wrap up with Kim Okamoto thanking everyone for honoring his parents. Donnie ended the meeting, mentioning the sheriff and Danny Kimo would handle traffic and direct parking with the aid of two Boy Scout troops. Mercifully, three hours after the meeting began, it was over.

Fiona turned to Ned and said, "My bum is numb." Then she got up and began massaging her bum, much to the delight of several gentlemen sitting behind her. George leaned back and smiled, shaking his head.

Ned saw what she was doing and whispered, "Fiona, you're causing a scene."

"Well, how am I supposed to walk if I have a numb bum?"

Annie, sitting next to her, said, a slight distress in her voice, "I'm off to the ladies' room."

"I'm with you," said Layla.

"We'll be outside waiting for you, ladies," said Ned.

"I'm getting a piece of cheesecake to go. I need a treat for enduring that meeting."

Fiona came outside with a small plate of cheesecake covered with a napkin. Layla and Annie made it out shortly, Annie asking her what she had under the napkin. "I got a piece of cheesecake to go."

"I'm for that. I'm going back in and getting some."

"Me too," echoed Layla.

"Count me in," said Mr. Soo.

"We're going to make our way home and get a beer," said Ned. "I don't know about you guys, but I sure could use a cold Heineken.

"Amen," said Dewey. "George, I was a little surprised that you were going to be talking about the docents rather than Annie. I thought that was originally her idea."

"It was, but she told me this morning her anxiety was coming back. She'll never get over discovering those bodies, and she said being in the old market and hearing speeches about the Okamotos made her anxious about keeping her composure. I told her I would be by her side, holding her hand the whole time. I knew when Donnie mentioned a speech on the docents, she wouldn't be able to give one, and so I spoke up. While I'm there talking, I'm counting on one of you to watch over Annie."

"I'll do that, George. Annie and I shared those awful moments, something neither of us will ever get over."

When they got to Ned's, he brought cold beers for everyone. They settled on the lanai, waiting for the ladies and Mr. Soo to join them. "Thanks, Ned, I needed a cold one. I swear our city fathers can be long-winded. I thought Donnie did a good job, keeping them as brief as possible."

"The mayor is in one of my weekly golf groups. He's so different in person, quite a normal guy. When he gets a microphone in hand, his mouth takes over his mind." This statement elicited a hearty laugh from everyone.

The cheesecake brigade came up the stairs. "What's all the laughter about?"

"We were discussing how our mayor can be so long-winded behind a microphone."

"That ass," said Fiona. "I know he's one of your golf buddies, but he's so pompous."

Everyone ate their cheesecake, and the guys had a second beer, discussing the upcoming event at the Visitors Center.

Annie stood up. "George, we better be going. Tomorrow is our once every three month's trip to Sam's Club to buy the few big-box items we use. I like to browse and check out the books at discount prices."

"Layla, have you ever been to a Sam's Club?" asked Dewey.

"No, have you?"

"Sure, I went with my folks all the time. I checked out the video games and computer equipment."

"Well, since you and Mr. Soo are off together tomorrow, maybe I could hitch a ride with Annie and George."

"We'll be leaving at ten, so come on over," said George.

Fiona caught Dewey's eye and nodded.

Layla left with George and Annie, Ned was on the golf course, Dewey, Mr. Soo, and Fiona were off to purchase patio furniture. When they arrived at the store, Fiona ushered Dewey to the large section of outdoor furniture. She gave her pros and cons on several of the options available. There was one large ensemble of patio furniture that would take care of both lanais.

While the salesperson, Dewey, and Fiona were discussing the purchase, Mr. Soo wandered over to patio grills. He was in awe of a huge stainless grilling center with a triple-size grill, a small refrigerator, two stovetop burners, and plenty of workspace. He imagined all the fine meals one could prepare.

Mr. Soo returned to find Fiona, Dewey, and the salesperson busy on paperwork. He pulled Fiona aside and said, "I wish to purchase that large grill," nodding toward the largest grill in the store. "I want it to be a secret housewarming gift for Dewey and Layla. Can you arrange to have it delivered with Dewey's furniture without him knowing?"

"Sure, no problem. I'll work with the salesperson and explain your intent. You and Dewey go next door and get a coffee or cold drink and wait for me there."

"I like that coffee shop next door. I'm fond of their pastries."

After Dewey and Mr. Soo left, Fiona made the salesperson ecstatic with the addition of Mr. Soo's grill; they arranged to have all items delivered on Tuesday before noon.

Fiona joined the group at the coffee shop, giving a sly wink to Mr. Soo. She said everything would be delivered next Tuesday before noon. She asked Dewey to keep Layla away from their home until after noon Monday because she had phoned an electrician to come and inspect the wattage to make sure they could support the patio lights Dewey had selected. She didn't mention to either of the men, but she was more worried about the usage on the new grilling unit. The electrician, one of Fiona's key subcontractors, whom she had phoned while still in the store, said he would be able to check everything out in the morning and make any changes necessary.

Dewey told Fiona he and Layla planned to check out on Tuesday and begin living in their home. Fiona suggest Dewey stall until around one in the afternoon. Take her to lunch, go grocery shopping, so she could get everything set up with the patio furniture to surprise Layla.

Later in the day, Fiona called Mr. Soo and explained how the purchase would work and how thoughtful his gift was. She was going to call George and Annie and tell them, knowing Dewey would call on George for barbecue assistance.

After three hours in Sam's Club, Annie, George, and Layla made it through checkout. George was pushing one full cart and pulling another. Both Annie and Layla pushed well-laden shopping carts.

"We're going to have to work to get everything in Pearl. Annie, you're a good packer. I'm counting on your help here," George said, a bewildered tone to his voice.

"I might have gotten a bit carried away. The bargains were fabulous, and I saw so many things we needed, some we didn't even know we needed!"

"That happens to me every time I go to Sam's," said Annie.

It took almost thirty minutes to unload and situate the four shopping carts of items into Pearl. George got in the car and told the ladies he needed food or he wouldn't have the strength to unload. They stopped at a café, and George suggested Layla give Dewey a call to see if he would be home to assist in the unloading.

"Dewey, it's Layla. Are you home?"

"Got back about an hour ago. Where are you?"

"I got so many good bargains at Sam's Club, it took us forever to go through the store and we didn't even stop at the food section, probably a good thing. Anyway, we've stopped to eat, then we'll be home. We're going to need your help in unloading. There are quite a few large items. George was smart, he had me get a dolly, and you'll need that to take the trash cans out for weekly pickup. We also bought the three different types of trash cans needed."

"My god, you got all that in Pearl?"

"Yes, plus so much more. You simply won't believe all the items I found that we'll need. Got to go! Lunch is here. See you shortly."

Dewey was out on the back lanai, waiting for the shoppers to arrive. He saw them turn into the street and pull up to the stairs. He was astounded with the load of items he could see through the windows and wondered how they could possibly need so much.

"Hi, honey," said Layla, squeezing out the car door. "We have a lot to unload, and we owe George and Annie a big check. Since I don't have a Sam's card, they wrote a check for everything."

"I'll go over the bill and subtract all our items from the total, then let you know how much you folks owe," said Annie. "Right now, let's get started getting these things upstairs or in the garage."

George unloaded the dolly, and he and Dewey took the three trash cans into the garage. Next, they put a file cabinet on the dolly and hauled it upstairs where Layla sent them to the empty room.

"That's all we'll need the dolly for. I'll store it in the garage," said George.

"I bought us a large paper shredder, something important for every household to have."

"That's a good idea. I never thought about it. Those things are always taken care of for me," Dewey said with a weak smile.

Layla and Dewey toted three stacks of books to the living room for placement on the shelves.

Pearl was finally unloaded, except for the few items that George and Annie had originally gone for. "It was a lot easier unloading than loading. Glad you enjoyed your shopping trip, Layla. You ought to look into getting a Sam's card, but we're happy to have you join us."

"Thank you both. I had a grand time. I picked up an application for Sam's. I can't wait to get a card. Dewey and I will be doing a lot of shopping there. I imagine there is one in Salt Lake City. What do you think, Dewey?"

"Wouldn't surprise me. Come on, honey, let's get busy putting all these things away and let Annie and George go home. They're probably tired from all this shopping."

Early in the evening, Fiona phoned Annie. "I heard you and George got the pleasure of Layla's first experience at a big-box store."

"That girl bought over three carts full of items!"

"Dewey called and filled me in. I have to thank you both. Our shopping day turned out well too. Dewey bought enough patio furniture and light fixtures for both lanais as a surprise for Layla. Then, as a surprise housewarming gift for them, Mr. Soo bought the biggest grill unit in the store. It has everything except the kitchen sink!"

"George is going to have grill envy."

"I'm sure Dewey will seek his grilling expertise. It's a monster unit. Why I called is to discuss an idea I had with you and George about your docents and my crafters. I thought a week from this Sunday, we could get everyone together for a dry run. Your docents could use it as a dress rehearsal and look over the brochure setup. My crafters could get their items placed on the shelves. We could call Donnie and have him arrange to open up the center."

"Let me talk it over with George, but it sounds like a good idea. Will you call Donnie and let me know as soon as you can? We both have a lot of folks to round up."

"I'll call you back later this evening."

Annie spoke with George, who agreed it was a sound idea. Fiona phoned Annie, setting the date for a week from the coming Sunday.

CHAPTER 83

Annie arranged to visit the two resident facilities where the majority of her senior docents resided; George insisted on going with her to make sure she was coping. The docents were ready for a dry run, many eager to have something to take up their Sunday afternoon. Vans from the facilities would handle transport to and from the center. Before leaving for the afternoon, Annie had called her other docents, and all would be there, anxious to see the completed center.

Fiona had the same luck, although some of her crafters would have to arrange to have someone man their sales at local sites throughout the island, all agreed to be there. Most would bring their display items, but several did not want them there until opening day.

When Annie called Fiona that evening, both ladies were happy with the results. Fiona said Donnie thought it was a wise thing to do and would supply snacks and drinks for everyone.

Fiona told Annie her electrical contractor was out to check Dewey's lanais to verify he had adequate voltage for the lights and grill. He had to do some work but was finished and ready for delivery.

"I told George about the grill unit, and he made me promise if we had any money left over from our Panama Canal trip, he could have a new grill too."

"Wait until he see this one. It was the biggest unit in the store and was it ever expensive."

"That'll spoil him. I'm afraid."

Fiona waved to George who was standing by the rail on his back lanai, waiting for the furniture store delivery at Layla's.

"I bet you're waiting to see that grill."

"Sure am. As soon as the delivery folks leave, I'm coming over to check it out."

"Huge unit, George, you'll want one."

Twenty minutes later, the furniture truck pulled into Layla's, and the furniture began to be unloaded. George was using binoculars, not wanting to miss the coveted grill unit delivery.

"George, what are you doing with those binoculars?"

"Hi, honey, checking on the grill delivery. I told Fiona as soon as the movers were gone, we're going over. I've got to see that grill."

"Oh, for heaven's sakes, George. You're becoming a grill fanatic."

"Yep."

After the movers left, George and Annie went over to check out the new items, Mr. Soo closely behind them.

"My god, she's a beauty," George said admiringly.

"Good cooking will come from this grill. George, you'll have to teach Dewey your secrets."

"Fiona, is there anything I can help you with?" asked Annie.

"No, I think I've gotten everything set up properly. How do you think it looks?"

"Perfect, as your work always is." Annie whispered, "How much did that grill cost?"

Fiona whispered the cost to Annie who grabbed her throat and uttered, "My god!"

"Dewey, we'd better check out, no sense paying for another day."

"Be right there, honey. I'm starving. Let's eat before we go to the store. You wore me out this morning."

"I wore you out? Every time I started to get things ready to go, you had me back in bed, but I did enjoy it," Layla said with a smile.

At ten minutes to one, Dewey was at the front desk checking out and Layla was figuring out where they would eat lunch. "How about we eat at that nice café up the street?"

"You know what I'm dying for? Some fish and chips at one of the beach shacks."

"That will take us out of our way, but it sounds good. Let's go."

Dewey made sure they enjoyed a leisurely lunch, and he lingered at the grocery store. It was almost four in the afternoon before they drove into their driveway. Each carried grocery bags up the stairs.

"My god, Dewey, we have furniture on our lanai!"

"Surprise! My contribution to our home. There is also furniture on the front lanai. Do you like it? What the hell is this?" Dewey asked, walking toward the grill unit.

"Didn't you buy that too?"

"I did not. They made a delivery mistake. Let's get the groceries inside, and I'll phone Fiona."

After putting away groceries and bringing in their luggage, Dewey placed his call. "Fiona, the store made a terrible mistake. A huge grill unit was delivered with the furniture."

"I'll be right over."

Fiona called Mr. Soo, and both walked over to Layla and Dewey's.

They walked out to the lanai to greet them. "Some grill unit, isn't it, Mr. Soo?"

"Certainly is, Dewey. Do you like it?"

"Heck yes, but it was delivered in error. I didn't order it."

"No, you did not. I ordered it for you both as my housewarming gift. Imagine all the great meals you can prepare."

"This is ours?"

Layla hugged Mr. Soo, thanking him; Dewey stared at the grill like it was a foreign object.

"Dewey, I suggest you have George get you started on grilling. He's been over to check out the unit and is excited about your tutoring," said Fiona, trying to be serious.

"Definitely, we'll plan something for this coming Saturday evening. Layla, this will be the first event in our new home."

"Fiona, will Saturday evening be fine with you and Ned?"

"Sure, we have nothing planned."

"Mr. Soo?"

"I can't wait to partake of your first dinner party."

"I'll call George and Annie. Without them, this dinner is not happening," said Dewey.

Dewey called and George answered. He was elated they had planned a Saturday event, anxious to try out the new grill and asked if there was propane in the tanks. Dewey laughed. "I have no idea. You better come over and help me with that before Saturday."

George came right over and told Dewey they would get the twin tanks filled with propane before Saturday. Everyone headed back to his or her respective homes. George took the grill instructions with him to make sure he knew about all the features.

That evening, Layla and Dewey sat outside on their new patio furniture, under their new patio lighting, enjoying salad and sandwiches from the deli section of the market, Layla promising to fix a proper meal the next night.

The sheriff drove by slowly and pulled into their driveway. "Good evening. Are you folks officially living in your home?"

"We sure are, Sheriff, our first night and our first meal. Come on up and look at our housewarming gift from Mr. Soo."

"My goodness, I didn't know they made units this big."

"We're having a group over Saturday evening for its inauguration. Will you join us?"

"Thank you, Layla. I would be honored. Can I bring anything?"

"Yes, bring a big appetite. We're grilling steaks. George is giving me grilling lessons."

"You'll be learning from an expert, best steak griller I've ever met. I'll be here, what time?"

"Any time after five, but we won't eat until seven."

"Thanks for the invitation. I'll see you folks on Saturday. Your patio furniture looks terrific."

"See you on Saturday," Layla said as the sheriff descended the stairs, got in his car, and drove off.

"That was thoughtful of you to invite him," said Dewey.

"It's always good to be friendly to local law enforcement. We all formed some type of bond during the storm at George and Annie's. Which reminds me, are you looking after Annie when George gives his docent talk at the opening ceremonies? Annie is experiencing some anxiety about the day."

"Yes, Annie and I have a connection to that horrible morning, and I'll be there for her."

Before Saturday, George and Dewey filled the tanks with propane. Then they stopped at the market and bought top-quality steaks, a couple of cases of Heinekens, plus liquor to make the ladies fu-fu drinks as George called them.

When they returned and had the grill set up and the steaks in the refrigerator, Layla said she had received a call from Kim, and he and Kyle would arrive on the Friday afternoon flight to Maui and pick up a rental. Kim said they would leave for Oahu on Tuesday morning, as family members too elderly to travel to the ceremonies must hear of the honors to the Okamoto family.

"So we'll have them four nights. I hope they enjoy the pineapple room," said Dewey.

She also mentioned she had phoned Donnie with the news of Kim's arrival and that he was prepared to give a proper speech.

CHAPTER 84

Everyone was seated on new furniture at Layla and Dewey's back lanai, having drinks and enjoying chips, dips, and veggies. George brought his secret grilling spices and sprinkled both sides of the steaks, then put them back in the refrigerator. Dewey questioned him about the spices, and he admitted it was pepper, garlic, salt, and whatever else looked promising in Annie's spice cabinet. Dewey laughed, saying he hoped Layla was amassing a spice cabinet.

Layla had made two macaroni-and-cheese casseroles, Annie made her pineapple coleslaw, and Fiona brought her infamous Italian Bundt cake, a yellow cake filled with a white cream generously laced with Amaretto, drizzled with dark chocolate sauce, and topped with sifted powdered sugar.

George and Dewey huddled over the grill unit: George enjoying cooking on the massive unit while Dewey was trying to master when to remove the steaks from the grill to match the doneness order. George served up the massive steaks with Dewey delivering. In no time, talking had ceased, and everyone was in serious eating mode; they decided to defer dessert for a couple of hours.

The conversation drifted to the tourist invasion now in full swing and how the sheriff and Danny were trying to keep the illegal sale of marijuana out of Paia and how the windsurfers were trying to keep the amateurs out of the large waves. The visiting boogie boarders and surfers felt they could windsurf without a problem, causing endless water rescues. Posted warnings were ignored.

Layla told everyone that Kim and Kyle would be staying with her and Dewey for several days before going to Oahu. The sheriff seemed slightly shocked by the news and complimented Layla and Dewey on their open-mindedness, although it was obvious he was uncomfortable talking about the arrangement.

Layla, Fiona, and Annie brought coffee, dessert, and plates out to the lanai along with Fiona's cake. Everyone seemed tentative at the first bite, but once they tasted the sweetness with the liqueur flavor of the Amaretto, smiles were seen all around the table.

It was after eleven when the sheriff and Mr. Soo left, thanking Layla and Dewey for a delicious meal and lovely evening. Ned and Fiona soon followed. George explained to Dewey how to clean the grill, and then he and Annie went home.

Dewey turned out the lanai lights, and Layla took a tray of plates back into the kitchen. "I thought our first dinner party went well."

"It was perfect. The food, the company, the easy manner we all fit in makes me feel like I've always been a part of this community. Yet everyone is relatively new friends."

"I don't understand how Annie and George and Ned and Fiona could live across the street all those years and not become friends," commented Dewey.

"I asked Annie the same question, and she said it was because there was such an age difference in the age of their children that they didn't have too much in common. Plus, she and George were working all the time. For some years, Ned was occupied with the real estate market and Fiona focused on the design aspect. It wasn't until this past year they realized what a great friendship they had missed out on and began spending time together. Dewey, we're not going to make that mistake. We're going to have friends in Salt Lake City, right?"

"There were several couples from our gathering in Salt Lake City that you felt comfortable with, and I expect once you start working in the art community, we'll add more friends. However, we'll make our best friends when we start having children and meeting fellow school parents, dance class parents, you know that type of thing."

"This is when I realize I'm marrying someone with extraordinary brainpower. Your logic comes so easy, and it makes perfect sense. I, on the other hand, was worried about having friends. Silly me."

■■■

* * *

On Monday morning, Dewey was woke up with a call from the McMaster offices, detailing a problem they were having that needed his input. He told them he would contact the pilots and plan on flying back on Tuesday. He would phone back and verify his plans.

Dewey turned and gently began kissing Layla's neck.

"Goodness, is this an early morning romantic moment?"

"Well, I had planned on telling you something else, but that can wait till a bit later," Dewey said, continuing his caressing.

Later, Layla lay cuddled into Dewey's side. "What did you want to talk with me about?"

"I got a call from Salt Lake City this morning. There is a problem at the site that needs my attention. I'm going to call and see if the plane can be ready to leave tomorrow morning. Of course, I want you to join me, but I'll understand perfectly if you want to stay here."

"Don't even consider that. Get used to me being with you wherever you have to be. I always want us near to each other."

After checking with the pilots, Dewey and Layla would leave the next day around ten in the morning. Dewey phoned his office and told his secretary to inform everyone he would be there Wednesday morning. He then called Ted and Agnes and told them of their return.

Layla notified their neighbors and also Donnie and the sheriff. Not knowing how long they would be gone, she loaded up perishables in a couple of tote bags and took them over to Annie and George.

"Hate to see you two go so soon after you moved in. We'll miss you," said Annie.

"This is how our life will probably always be, and as long as we have this wonderful home and terrific neighbors to return to, we will be back as soon as possible."

The week flew by and Sunday afternoon brought the crafters and docents to the Visitors Center. The docents wore their shirts and blouses and those crafters bringing their merchandise sat up their display cases. The cases were secured, and Donnie held on to the keys, which would be locked in the restaurant safe nightly once the center was opened.

Donnie set out drinks and snacks, then spoke with Fiona about Layla's charcoals. They would be displayed on the wall behind the crafters' counter, and Donnie showed Fiona a sign that read: "Charcoals by Layla, $200 each." The sign was rimmed in ocean-blue waves with matching colored writing on a stark white background. Fiona thought it was done quite tastefully and gave her suggestion where the sign should be placed.

George and Annie worked with their docents, answering their questions and making sure they fully understood the photo blowups placed around the center. They also wanted to verify all the docents were comfortable with the information on the brochures and would be able to direct visitors to various sites.

The vans were called at five, and the groups broke up. Donnie closed and locked the center, and Annie, George, and Fiona walked back down the hill toward their homes.

"I'm certainly glad you had the idea for that meeting. It was definitely needed and took longer than I planned," said Annie.

"I agree. It was a good thing. My crafters were very precise in setting up their display areas. They are quite proud of being part of the Visitors Center. It seems to be quite a prestigious honor."

"That's the same impression I got from the docents," said George. "One of the seniors couldn't wait to get back to tell her friends about today. She was anxious to gloat about being a docent."

"George!" said Annie. "That's not nice but possibly true." Then Annie laughed at herself and asked Fiona to get Ned and come over for a drink.

"I like the sound of that. After a drink or two, let's all go out to dinner. I'm too worn out to cook, and I imagine you are too, Annie."

"Is that OK with you, George?"

"Yes, but I can't wait too long for dinner, I'm hungry."

Annie shook her head. "My husband has a wonderful appetite and never gains an ounce. I gain weight watching him eat."

George stopped, grabbed Annie, and pulled her into him, laughing. "You're perfect. I love you no matter what."

"Goodness, George, sometimes you're so dramatic," Annie said, loving every minute of his attention.

The two couples had their drinks, then continued out to dinner. The main topic of conversation was the opening of the Visitors Center. George told them Donnie said the sign would be going up very soon. Everyone was getting excited about the opening, except Annie, who only grew more anxious.

Chapter 85

Layla looked out the window of the DewMaster Gulfstream watching Maui slip away. She sighed and looked at Dewey sitting behind his onboard desk, already working on his computer. Dewey was worried this problem could be one of those that would take the team a concerted effort to solve. He had told her about one such programming problem that had taken their eight-man team three days of working straight through to figure out and repair. When someone got too tired to work, they went into a room where cots were set up and slept a few hours then back to work.

Layla decided to get a map and learn the area, then take one of the cars in the compound and drive around to make herself familiar with her surroundings. Expanding until she felt comfortable driving in Salt Lake City, she did not like Ted chauffeuring her around; she had enough of that growing up.

Layla got up, checked with Dewey and the pilots to see if they wanted anything to drink, got herself a cup of coffee, pulled a book from her tote, and settled in to do some reading.

Dewey came over and shook her gently. "Honey, wake up. We'll be landing shortly."

"I can't believe we're here already. Did I fall asleep?"

"You sure did about half an hour after you started reading. I was going to wake you for lunch, but you looked so peaceful, I let you sleep."

"Did you get any rest?"

"No, I've been working on our problem. Without any success, I might add. This little quirk has turned into a big problem," Dewey said, shaking his head.

"I'm sorry. If there is any way I can help, let me know."

"Having you here is a great help," Dewey said, sitting down next to her, strapping in for the landing.

Ted was waiting to help with the luggage and take them home. Layla admitted she had slept through lunch and was starving; Agnes fixed her a sandwich. Layla shared her driving ambitions with Agnes, who was a little surprised that she didn't want to be chauffeured, but once Layla explained, Agnes saw her logic.

At three on Friday afternoon, Dewey dragged himself through the door, found Layla, hugged her, saying he was off to bed, asking not be woke up unless it was an emergency.

At ten the next morning, Dewey strolled into the kitchen where Layla and Agnes were having coffee. He looked rested but disheveled. "I'm starving. I need one of your big breakfasts, Agnes."

"Of course, I'll get it started."

Dewey walked over and kissed Layla lightly on the lips. "God, I missed you. What a chore we had finding the problem, and it turned out to be such a simple programming error, in fact, so simple, it was continually overlooked by all of us supposedly geniuses."

"I missed you too, honey. You've lost weight. Didn't you eat anything?"

"Had slices of cold pizza, but once I get into something like this, I have trouble tearing myself away for anything. Get a bad case of tunnel vision."

"I'm glad you're home. I kept busy learning my way around the city. I got pretty far along these last few days."

"I knew you would catch on quickly. Anyone that can drive around Washington, DC, can drive anywhere."

Agnes served Dewey a large breakfast, which he devoured. Afterward, he and Layla retired to their rooms and made love, with Dewey falling fast asleep, a happy grin on his face. Layla smiled down at the man she was so in love with, tucked into his side, and laid next to him, awake and enjoying the closeness.

In Paia, the Kellers and Boones set about their normal routines. George and Annie had everyone over for fresh grilled fish topped off with Annie's mango salsa. Mr. Soo said it was the best fish he ever ate, a true compliment coming from a man who preferred red meat or fried foods. The Boones and Kellers had dinner one night at Bird's where Fiona conferred with her feathery Bird.

Everyone admitted they missed Layla and Dewey. The Kellers heard from their eldest son, saying he would be flying home to attend the opening of the Visitors Center and tribute to the Okamotos. He thought the world of Mrs. Okamoto, who always extended him credit when he ran out of his allowance. Fiona spent a couple of days getting things ready for his visit. George and Annie planned to have a barbecue for him, and Mr. Soo insisted he join him at Otis's for lunch one day after Fiona mentioned he loved Otis's malts.

Layla phoned her Paia group, as she lovingly called them, and let everyone know they would be returning in a couple of days and Dewey couldn't wait to fire up the grill. When Fiona mentioned her son was flying in to attend the opening of the Visitors Center, Layla said they would do a big cookout one night that also included Kim and Kyle.

Sunday, the sheriff arranged with the two Boy Scout troops to do a mock parking exercise, using their parents driving into the center as test subjects. After the third try, everything was down to a well-patterned drill. The sheriff, Danny, and Donnie were glad they had the dry run; at first, some of the scouts had been directionally challenged.

Donnie was taking pride in how everything was falling into place for opening day. The sign installation was a major triumph, receiving many compliments from members of the community. Donnie hoped he had planned for all contingencies; his list of to-dos and worries was becoming shorter and shorter.

Dewey, Layla, the Boones, and Kellers sat at Mama's, enjoying dinner together. It was their first night back in Paia; missing the company of the older couples, they invited them to dinner to catch up on the latest island news.

The ladies took the opportunity to confer on what they would be wearing to the opening ceremonies. Layla said she had a white gauze full skirt and matching top with strands of light blue ribbon running through it. Annie said she and George felt obligated to wear their docent shirts; she was going to pair it with a slim white skirt and George was going to wear an off-white pair of trousers. Fiona said she had a peach skirt and would pair it with a turquoise blouse, wanting an artsy appearance.

Fiona turned to Dewey, saying, "Dewey, make sure Mr. Soo dresses up for the ceremonies. I'm sure he has proper clothes. We can't have a major donor wearing cargo shorts."

"I'll take care of that, Fiona, but I know Mr. Soo will be respectful of the circumstances."

"I've been wondering if Otis is concerned about the loss of business with the Visitors Center opening right next door and offering meals," asked Layla.

"Mr. Soo told me Otis was thrilled. He said it will cut down on his tourist trade, and he can concentrate on the locals. He is not tourist friendly," said George.

"Good for him. We need someone who concentrates on us," declared Fiona.

"Fiona, I don't remember you ever eating at Otis's," said Ned.

"Well, I'm going to start."

The next morning Fiona received call from Gus Schultz, advising shipment from the mainland had arrived. He had already talked to Marvin, and it would be on its way to Maui the following day. Fiona immediately phoned the brothers, who were able to pick up and deliver to Layla the next day. Fiona was happy for Layla; now, her furnishings would be complete in time for the arrival of her guests.

Layla rushed out to the front lanai where Dewey was drinking coffee, enjoying the morning. "Dewey, Fiona just phoned, our dining room furniture should be here, at the latest in four days and possibly three. Isn't that wonderful!"

Dewey drew Layla onto his lap. "Except for your empty room, our home is complete. You and Fiona have done a wonderful job buying furniture and decorating. Our home looks fabulous."

"Thank you, darling. I'm so proud of this project. Our home has such a beautiful ring to it," Layla said as she gave Dewey a loving kiss.

The simplicity of the dining room table and chairs set off the dramatic effect of the glass cabinet. Layla ordered a simple arrangement of tropical green plants that sat low and long on the table. When Fiona and Annie came over to see the table, they shared Layla's sentiment that the room was perfect for the rest of the house. Layla placed a long oriental rug in front of the table between the living room and dining room with muted greens and gold that reflected well in the glass cabinet.

"Your home is ready to receive guests," declared Fiona.

"Can you believe the opening is almost here? Kyle and Kim will be here Thursday, and, Fiona, didn't you say your son is also arriving on Thursday?"

"Yes, he arrives on the afternoon flight to Maui. I believe you said Kyle and Kim arrive on the morning flight."

"George and I are planning on having everyone over for a cookout on Friday evening, and Dewey said he wants to cook on Saturday. We should all be fat and happy for the opening ceremonies," said Annie, laughing.

CHAPTER 86

Dewey and Layla sat on their back lanai, waiting for Kyle and Kim. Their plane arrived about an hour ago, and they thought their guests should be there any minute.

"Any concerns about our house guests?" asked Layla.

"None at all, honey. I'm fine with the situation. Just hope they like their authentic Hawaiian bedroom," Dewey said with a smile.

Layla grinned back at him. "I just couldn't resist, and I guess it's horrible of me, but a bit of innocent payback never hurt anyone."

"I think this is them coming down the hill now," Dewey said, nodding toward a car turning slowly onto their street.

"I guess we should pull into their driveway and unload our luggage. They can tell us where they want us to park the car," Kyle said, turning into the driveway.

Layla and Dewey came down the stairs as Kyle and Kim got out of their rental.

"Kyle, Kim, welcome. Hope you had a good trip, although a long one," Dewey said, extending his hand to both men.

"Thank you. We're glad to be here, and we appreciate your hospitality. It's a long trip from Washington, DC, to Maui," said Kyle.

"Thank you both. I only wish it were under different circumstances," said Kim.

Luggage was taken upstairs, and Layla opened the garage door for Kyle to park, then she and Dewey escorted Kyle and Kim inside.

"This is fabulous. I've been inside before, and you have refurbished it wonderfully. I can't believe it's the same place," said Kim.

"Most of it was the work of Fiona Keller and her various crews, although I did have an input on the furniture. Your room is down the hall. Right this way," said Layla.

Layla stepped inside the doorway, and Kyle and Kim walked into the room. "This furniture is authentic Hawaiian furniture, made many years ago on the island by Hawaiian craftsmen. Although a few things are modern-day, all the pieces of furniture are the real deal."

"I've never seen anything like this before," said Kyle.

"Nor have I and I've lived here all my life. This is really something," said Kim.

"Layla hoped you would be impressed with this room, so steeped in tradition," said Dewey, trying hard to keep a straight face.

"We'll leave you to get settled. I'm serving a light lunch on the lanai in an hour," said Layla as she and Dewey left and walked back down the hall.

In the kitchen, Dewey turned to Layla. "I think they were duly taken back by your Hawaiian Room."

"Me too. Did you see the look on Kyle's face? Priceless," said Layla, laughing softly.

Everyone sat on the back lanai having lunch. Kyle and Kim caught Layla up on people in Washington and the latest at the hospital. Layla and Dewey told them they planned a small wedding a couple months after the opening of the center.

They planned to spend a lot more time in Maui, Dewey saying he would be cutting back on his hands-on work at the DewMaster Corporation. "Time to enjoy the fruits of my labors and enjoy being married to this wonderful woman," Dewey said, smiling at Layla.

"We wish you both every happiness," said Kyle. "Layla is a wonderful woman and deserves all the best life has to offer."

"Thank you, Kyle. Dewey and I are very happy together."

"I can tell that by seeing you together. I'm very happy for you both," said Kim.

* * *

"Fredrico, my baby," chimed Fiona, arms extended to hug her son as he came to the luggage carousel.

"Mom, please, it's Fred," said the tall young man who had his mother's coloring and Italian nose and his father's build.

"You'll always be my Fredrico, my firstborn baby," Fiona said, hugging him fiercely.

Fred looked over his mother's shoulder at his father and rolled his eyes. Ned shook his head, holding up his hands in recognition of Fiona's exuberance.

"We are so happy you were able to come to the opening ceremonies. Mrs. Okamoto would be pleased to know you are honoring her."

"Mom, there is one bad thing I have to tell you that I know will be upsetting, but I'm leaving to go back to the mainland right after the ceremony. I'm catching the late-afternoon flight out of Maui. I have a big test on Tuesday, and I have to do some heavy studying."

"Oh, Fredrico, I was so hoping for a longer visit, but your father and I are happy you are here with us these few days," said Fiona, hugging him once again.

"Son, we are always glad to see you, no matter for how short a time. We wish your brother could have joined you, but we understand the demands of medical school," said Ned, giving his son a firm grip on the shoulder.

The three members of the Keller family left the airport for Paia. Fiona prepared a large Italian dinner for her family. After dinner, she insisted they go to Bird's so she could introduce her feathered friend to Fredrico. Fred asked his dad if his mom was getting weird as she got older. Ned told him she was the same as ever but that he was getting older and noticing her behavior more. Ned assured him it was part of her charm.

Dewey and Layla were Kyle and Kim's guests for dinner at Mama's.

Mr. Soo enjoyed a macaroni-and-cheese casserole Layla had brought over the day before.

Annie and George had a meal of leftovers from previous evenings.

CHAPTER 87

Mr. Soo and Fred were walking up the hill for lunch at Otis's. "The Visitors Center is a wonderful memorial to the Okamotos, don't you think?"

"Yes, sir, this is a terrific transformation, although I miss that old market. I spent many afternoons mopping the floor for Mrs. Okamoto, and she would make sure I left with soda, chips, and anything else I wanted. I always felt she missed Kim, who was away at college, and took me under her wing. I miss that lady."

"They were good people. This center continues their legacy of giving to the community."

"Mr. Soo, you have a wonderful way with words."

"Thank you, Fred, that is most kind of you. Right now, I need one of Otis's cheeseburgers, fries, and chocolate malt. How does that sound to you?"

"Make that onion rings instead of fries, and we're on the same page!"

Later that afternoon, Fred announced he didn't know how he was going to be able to eat any dinner tonight. "Old Otis sure can cook."

"Too much fried food is very bad for your health," warned Fiona.

"Mom, I just had lunch with Mr. Soo, who matched me bite for bite, and he must be pushing one hundred."

"Nonsense, I think he's only in his early nineties."

"Oh well, that makes all the difference," said Fred, laughing.

Fiona made sure she introduced Fredrico to everyone, and he made sure he asked everyone to call him Fred.

"Fiona, I didn't know your son was joining us for the opening," said the sheriff, visibly taken back at the sight of Fred.

"Yes, Sheriff, Fredrico wanted to pay tribute to the Okamotos. He practically lived there after school until one of us returned home. He and Mrs. Okamoto became quite close."

"When I went off to college, Mom latched on to Fred, and he became like a son to her," said Kim. "At first, I was jealous, but I realized Mom needed to fuss over someone, and I think Fred enjoyed being around Mom."

"I did. Both your parents told wonderful stories about their early lives in Japan and coming to Hawaii, meeting each other, and getting married. They were so proud of you, Kim. She would read me excerpts from every letter you wrote and tell me about every phone call you made to them. Your success reflected well on their years of hard work."

"Thank you, Fred, and I know they would be just as proud of your college success. Going for your MBA in business is very honorable. Ned tells me you plan on joining the Keller Real Estate firm on Oahu once you've graduated."

"The Keller name in real estate is well respected, and I want to see that legacy continued."

"We are very proud of Fred. With his business background and insight he's gained working summers in the Oahu office, he will do the name proud," beamed Ned.

"Both my babies will make us proud. Our youngest plans on being a GP and living in the Midwest although God only knows why," Fiona said.

"Mom, he grew up on the islands, is going to school in Los Angeles, and he's always dreamed of living where there are four seasons. He's told us that for years."

"I know, I just thought he was bluffing. Can you imagine wanting to live in snow?"

"Yes, I can, and it's quite beautiful," said the sheriff.

"That's right, I forgot you lived in Alaska. But the cold, brr. I remember skiing in the Italian Alps and I just couldn't get warm. No matter how many clothes I packed on or how close I sat to the fire. Here in Hawaii, I'm always warm and toasty," Fiona said, smiling.

"I admit, I did thaw out after I'd been here a couple of weeks," said the sheriff, laughing.

George grilled fish served with Annie's mango salsa; she also served white rice with peas, salad, and dessert of fresh berries with whipped cream. It was a light fare because Dewey was doing steaks tomorrow night and wanted everyone ready for a big meal.

Later, George was helping Annie clean up in the kitchen. "I still can't get over what a great kid Fred is."

"He has his mother's Italian looks but enjoys his father's gentle personality. I was amazed at how Fiona fussed over her Fredrico. I never thought she would be that type of mother. I believe I spent most of the evening suppressing a smile."

"She was a hoot, wasn't she? Ned said since becoming semiretired, Fiona has come to appreciate what great children they raised. They were never in any trouble, always good students, and both set high goals."

"Sounds like our kids, too. Except for our daughter, I worry how they're raising our grandchildren. They are way too lenient with them, not teaching them about consequences and responsibility."

"I agree. Do you think it would help if one of us talked to them?"

"I've already tried, only to hear how old-fashioned our thinking is."

"They actually said that to you?"

"Yes, and it hurt too."

George walked over to Annie as she slammed the dishwasher door and started the machine. He put his arms around her and drew her close, knowing a statement like that would hurt her deeply.

"You smell like mango salsa. That's sort of sexy."

"You find the smell of mango salsa sexy?"

"No, I find you sexy, and at the moment, you have a hint of mango salsa about you. Maybe it's here on your lips," George said as he kissed her lightly on the lips. "Maybe on the neck," he said, kissing her neck. "I think I'm going to have to do a lot more exploring to find out the exact location of that mango salsa."

*   *   *

As habit, the sheriff escorted Mr. Soo home.

"We are being blessed with some excellent meals, Sheriff."

"We are indeed, Mr. Soo."

"Are you ready for the opening day ceremonies?"

"As ready as can be. Hopefully, we have thought of every contingency. Sometimes things come up that no one ever planned. If that happens, we can only hope we do our best. I was surprised to meet Fiona's son. I didn't realize he would be flying in for the opening."

"He and Mrs. Okamoto were close. Like Kim said, she needed someone to fuss over when he went off to college."

"Looks like we will be enjoying another fine meal tomorrow evening. Some more of Dewey's big steaks. I'm looking forward to that."

"I believe steak is all he has learned to grill. He'll have to do more experimenting."

"I'll leave you off here, Mr. Soo. See you tomorrow evening."

The sheriff made sure Mr. Soo got safely into his home, then walked to the side of the Boones' home where he left his car and drove home.

*   *   *

"A fun evening," Layla said to Dewey as they lay in bed, "not to mention an excellent meal. They were smart to serve a light meal. We'll be doing steaks, grilling corn on the cob, and I'll do a salad and maybe a vegetable too. Still haven't figured out dessert yet."

"Let's do banana splits like Byrd made for us. Everyone love that."

"That's perfect and fun too."

"Speaking of fun, there's something about having your ex here that is very arousing," Dewey said, caressing Layla's hip.

"I don't think we need an excuse, but it does add a little excitement," Layla said, throwing her leg over Dewey and drawing his lips to hers.

CHAPTER 88

By the time their guests started arriving, Dewey had the corn on the grill and the steaks spiced and in the refrigerator. Chips, veggies, and several dips were on the table, and a pitcher of Mai Tais was ready along with a cooler of beer.

Kyle, Kim, and Mr. Soo sat at the table, discussing the Okamotos. When the Kellers got there, Fred joined them to add his memories to the conversation.

"A Mai Tai is a delightful idea, perfect for the evening. I'm so excited about tomorrow. It seems we've been working up to this day for such a long time. I'll be glad when it's here."

George and Annie were coming up the stairs when they heard Fiona's comment. "We agree with you, Fiona. Annie and I have enjoyed working with the docents and will continue our involvement, but once things are up and running, a great deal of tension will be gone."

"I hope Donnie starts eating again. I noticed the other day, he's getting way too thin," Ned said in a whisper so Kim wouldn't hear.

"I'm sure he will be relieved once everything gets going. He's done an outstanding job for the center and for Paia," said George.

"Evening, folks. I hope I'm not late," said the sheriff coming up the stairs.

"Sheriff, you are just in time for a cold one. There are goodies on the table. Help yourself."

"I can use a cold beer, thanks."

The conversation was lively, with memories being shared and discussed.

"It's time to grill the steaks. Layla, go ahead and begin roasting vegetables."

Dewey got everyone's steak order, and then he and George began grilling. Layla put two trays of vegetables in the oven for roasting and last-minute items in her salad, then tossed it with honey mustard dressing. She refreshed the pitcher of Mai Tais and refilled glasses. Ned handed out fresh beers.

Dewey placed the roasting ears of corn on a rack above the grill; when the steaks were about ready, he and George placed them on a large platter. The steaks began to come off the grill; the ladies brought out grilled vegetables and salad as everyone started eating.

*　　*　　*

"Dewey, Layla, thank you for an excellent meal. Since I've been back in Paia, I've eaten better than I've eaten for months. Makes it hard to leave and go back to school."

"I'm going to have to start back on my daily jogging routine," declared Fiona. "I know I've gained weight these last few days. My waistbands are tight, and my bra is killing me."

"Mom!"

Ned grinned. "No complaints from me."

"Like you, Fiona, I will have to get back to my regular jogging routine. George, I suppose you haven't gained an ounce?"

"Nope, I might have lost a few ounces doing all this chewing," he said, trying to be serious.

"I'm pleased to have been invited to all these wonderful meals. Makes me feel like you folks approve of my work," said the sheriff.

"Indeed, Sheriff," said Mr. Soo. "On my walks through the city, the merchants are so pleased your presence has rid the area of many of the hooligans that put a bad mark on Paia."

"I've always believed hooligans had no business in any city I was in charge of," the sheriff said, smiling fondly at Mr. Soo.

"I noticed a difference in the town, Sheriff," said Kim. "I don't see those gangs trying to sell illegally grown pot to the tourists. That had been a plague on our city for many years."

"With concentrated effort from Danny and me, it took us about three months for word to get out Paia would not tolerate the selling of illegal Maui Wowee anymore. We made arrests every day, and finally, the message was loud and clear. Glad to see it's still working."

Layla and Dewey took the dishes inside and brought a couple pots of coffee and cups. Dewey carried bananas, various toppings, whipped cream, and a tray with three types of ice cream.

"We had fun at Bird's making banana splits, so we thought we could try it again tonight."

"Cool," said Fred.

"Annie, we'll have to jog morning and evening. Pass the strawberry, please," said Fiona.

"This is such a lovely evening. Thanks to all of you for making it so memorable, and the food is the best. I haven't had a banana split in years," said Kyle.

"I must observe you, Fred, as you make your split. I've never had one of these before," admitted Mr. Soo.

"You are in for a real treat, Mr. Soo. Follow my lead. I guarantee it won't be your last."

After dessert, everyone had coffee, and several moans were heard around the table.

"I might have overeaten," said Fiona. "I have the beginnings of a stomachache."

"Undo the button on your shorts," suggested Ned.

Fiona followed Ned's suggestion. "Ah, much better. My god, I look pregnant. Look at my pouch, Ned. Why did you let me eat that much?"

"I always thought you looked exceptionally beautiful when you were pregnant, darling," Ned said, sliding over, hugging Fiona.

"Pregnant is one thing, downright fat is another," said Fiona, looking at her stomach.

"Monday morning, Fiona, we start a daily jogging regime until we get to our proper weight, agreed?"

"Agreed, Annie. It will help with two of us going together."

"Guess I'll have to play two games of golf a day for a while," said Ned, receiving a frown from Fiona.

"Our rounds at the hospital keep the weight off Kim and me," said Kyle. "We probably should exercise, but after the long days we put in, exercise is just more work."

"Mr. Soo and I run into each other walking through Paia. I believe that helps to keep our weight down," said the sheriff.

"Oh yes, walking throughout the city is a very pleasant way to keep one's weight off and to keep abreast of all that is going on in Paia. Right now, everyone is focused on the opening ceremonies for the Visitors Center. Once that has occurred, I wonder what everyone will be talking about."

"I'm sure something will replace it. Always does in a small community," said the sheriff. "Tomorrow is a big day, folks. Let me thank you, Dewey and Layla, for a memorable evening and a delicious meal, but I will be going now."

"Sheriff, I will let you escort me safely home, and I too will be retiring. Must let this lovely meal digest. Fred, thank you so much for the banana split instructions. I will be able to make them at home for myself. Thank you, all, for the wonderful evening. I'll see all of you tomorrow. Dewey, don't forget to come and get me. I'll walk up with everyone."

"I would never forget you, Mr. Soo. Sheriff, thank you for coming and good luck with your Scouts tomorrow."

The sheriff and Mr. Soo left. Fiona, Ned, and Fred also thanked everyone and said they would meet everyone at the center because Fiona was going early to make sure her crafters were properly set up.

"Do you and George have to get there early for the docents, Annie?"

"No, they have their assignments and are eager to get going. We'll leave them on their own. Let them know we have faith in them."

"We'll stop by and get you. We'll walk up together," said Layla.

"That will be nice. Kim, are you ready with your speech?"

"I'll say he is, Annie. He's practiced it on me for a couple of weeks now," said Kyle, smiling fondly at Kim.

"Good for you, Kim. I know how much it means to you to honor your parents," said George.

"This is will be a very important moment for me to tell all of Paia how much my wonderful parents sacrificed for me and how honored they would be to have the Visitors Center in their market and named after them."

Annie and George said their good nights and headed on home. Walking back, Annie said, "George, you're going to have to take another shower. You smell like charcoal."

"Yep, figured I would. The way the wind was whipping around, I kept being in the way of the smoke. Don't want my lovely wife sleeping next to Smoky the Bear all night. You doing OK, honey?"

"I'm trying to, but I'm anxious. I had a semi–panic attack this afternoon. I got that awful anxiety feeling I get before something bad happens. Probably just a case of nerves, worrying about tomorrow. I'm so grateful you're giving the speech instead of me."

"Glad to do it. Anything else I can do to make it easier for you?"

"No, sweetheart. I'll get through this. I'll be fine."

CHAPTER 89

He heard noise coming from the bathroom and knew one of the Boones was taking a shower, hoping it was George. Approaching the Boones' back lanai steps, he checked to make sure no lights were visible at the Kellers', and then he knocked softly on the screen, glad to see it was Annie in the kitchen.

"My goodness, surprised to see you this late. Come in." Annie opened the screen, stepping back to let him enter.

Reaching behind his back, he pulled one of the two Tasers he was carrying, the one powered with less voltage. He quickly aimed it at Annie's heart and released the button, sending voltage wires into her body. Her eyes widened in shock, and she slowly went down to her knees. Jumping in quickly, he grabbed her and maneuvered her into a recliner. Going back to the lanai, he turned the light off, closed the door, and pulled the drapes.

Opening the drapes and slider to the front lanai, he quietly pulled the recliner with Annie to the center of the window, sitting her upright and making sure she was still unconscious. He hurriedly pulled the other recliner in place beside her just as he heard the shower noise dissipate. He pulled the other Taser out and verified it was set for large voltage, wanting to make sure it brought the big man down. Standing at the hallway entrance, he waited; he heard the bathroom ceiling fan cease and saw the light go out. George stepped out into the hallway, pulling a T-shirt over his head.

"I feel better. I got all the charcoal smoke off me."

George looked up just as the Taser shot out the extreme voltage that coursed through his chest. For an instant, a look of shock and then sadness registered on George's face before he crumpled to the floor.

Quickly and with difficulty, his body was dragged, then lifted into the other recliner and posed in the same position as Annie's, their hands intertwined, their heads tilted toward each other.

The intruder then put on a plastic rain cape, surgical gloves, and paper booties. He rushed to the kitchen and got one of Annie's sharp knives. As he went back to the scene he had staged, a sorrowful look came on his face.

"This was not supposed to happen. It was supposed to be that bitch Fiona and her ever-so-proper husband, but their darling little Fredrico popped into town, and you can understand, you were my only other option."

That said, he first went to Annie and gently slit her throat. Walking over to George, once again giving his apologies, he slit his throat. He dropped the knife behind them, picked up his trophy, and going down the front lanai steps, he slipped off the booties and walked to the carport at Joe Wong's home, currently not being rented. He started his engine and went up the hill without his lights on and turned onto Baldwin, away from his home.

Never can be too careful, he thought. He had put the bloodstained gloves, booties, and rain cape in a large plastic bag to be burned once he was home.

Layla went to the front lanai where Kyle and Kim waited, shoes in hand, pants legs rolled up slightly, and grinning.

"Let's go over to the Boones' the front way. We looked at the beach and realized we had to feel the sand in our toes," said Kim.

"Sure, why not? I can shake it out of my sandals. Besides, I noticed their back lanai is still closed up. Dewey, we're going over to the Boones' the front way. Can you please lock up and get Mr. Soo?"

"No problem. We'll be right behind you."

The three laughed as Kyle and Kim scrunched their toes in the warm sand. Layla theorized that Kim was trying to relieve tension he was feeling about entering his former home and giving his speech. "Kim, did you bring your speech?"

"Are you kidding?" asked Kyle. "He's had that speech memorized for a couple of weeks. I think he rehearses it in his sleep. He does not need notes."

"Kyle, you are embarrassing me, but yes, I know my speech by heart. It's the least I could do."

Dewey locked up the house and went to collect Mr. Soo, who was waiting on his lanai. "Do I look proper for this occasion?"

"Mr. Soo, you look super. You are quite the natty dresser."

"Thank you. I've always been a fan of Armani suits. When I was doing business on Oahu, one or two days a week, it was important I presented myself as a well-off businessman, and I made sure I had the wardrobe to fulfill this image."

"You had better be careful. Those older ladies from the senior facilities will see you and go wild. You are definitely good material for husband hunting."

"I have no intention of finding another wife. I'm a happy bachelor, doing my own thing as you young people say."

"Fiona, your display is wonderful, and I can tell by the people already looking and picking out pieces, it will do quite well for the center," said Donnie.

"Thank you. This is a talented group of crafters, and their work displays a wide array of finer island products. I wonder where the rest of our neighbors are. They should be here by now."

"You know how that goes, getting a group of people somewhere all at once always finds someone running behind. Don't worry, everyone will be here for the opening ceremonies."

"You're right. I'm going to go sit with Ned and Fredrico."

Laughing, making their way in front of the Boones' lanai, Layla said, "What's that smell?"

"Maybe it's one of the algae odors the tide brings in occasionally," offered Kim.

"What's the buzzing sound? Sounds like a beehive or something?" questioned Kyle.

As Layla made her way up the stairs, she turned back and said to them, "It smells even worse up here."

Layla turned and took a couple of steps farther up onto the lanai. She saw the two bodies of her beloved friends sitting with blood congealed over them spilling onto the lanai and saw flies all around; dropping to her knees, she let out a bloodcurdling scream.

Kyle and Kim hurried up the stairs. Kim caught his breath; walking to the backside of the lanai, he dropped down, wide-eyed, mouth gaping. Kyle rushed to his side, trying to get his attention, without success.

Dewey heard Layla scream, "Something is wrong, Mr. Soo!" He rushed to the Boones', noticing the back lanai locked up and went around to the front. He hurried up the stairs and saw Layla kneeling, something red soaking into the bottom of her skirt. He looked up and saw the bodies of his friends. "My god, my god. Not these people. Come, Layla, let me get you out of here."

Dewey grabbed Layla, lifting her to her feet, then leading her down the stairs and around the outside of the Boone home. They reached the back lanai stairs where she sat down on a step. He pulled out his cell phone and dialed the sheriff's office.

"Charlene, this is Dewey McMaster, and this is an emergency. Get in touch with the sheriff and Danny immediately and get them to the Boones' home. I'll meet them here."

"What's the matter, Dewey?"

"Just get them here, Charlene," Dewey said and ended the call.

"Mr. Soo, do you have your cell phone?"

"Yes, right here."

"Call Fiona and tell her she and Ned need to get down here immediately. It's an emergency, and tell them not to say anything to anyone, just leave."

Mr. Soo did as he was asked. When Fiona questioned him, he didn't lie, saying he had no idea, but Layla was in bad shape; something was very wrong.

Danny came running down the hill with the sheriff closely following. Ned was a short way behind the sheriff, and Fiona was making her way down the stairs. Halfway down, she took off her high heels and continued on bare feet.

When they got to where Layla was sitting, Dewey directed them around to the front of the house. When Fiona arrived, Dewey asked her to stay with Layla while he followed the others to the front lanai.

Mr. Soo came to the stairs and softly asked Layla, "Can you help Fiona and me try to understand what is happening?"

Layla grabbed their hands, her eyes pleading, tears flowing. "They're gone. They're gone. How could they be gone?"

Fiona looked at Mr. Soo and shook her head. "Look at the bottom of Layla's skirt. I believe that's blood," she said in a whisper.

"Oh no, could this have happened again to our good friends?"

"Please, God, no," Fiona said, looking upward.

Danny came running up from the front lanai, phone in hand, calling for an ambulance. As directed by the sheriff, he was going back to the Visitors Center to tell Donnie there had been an accident at the Boones' and to take over for everyone that was missing and end the ceremonies as quickly as possible. After that, he was to put crime-scene tape up to the entrance to the side street and only let the ambulance, local police, CSI, the Five-O people, and the coroner into the crime scene, no exceptions.

Dewey and Ned came back to the stairs where everyone was assembled. Ned went over to Fiona, the color drained from his face and tears in his eyes. He grabbed Fiona and hugged her to him. "They're both gone, murdered just like the Okamotos."

"No!" wailed Fiona.

"Mom, what's the matter?" said Fred, making his way toward the crowd. "Mr. Soo, what's going on? Do you know?"

"No, not for sure, but I know it's bad."

Dewey walked over to both men and took a deep breath. "Someone has murdered George and Annie, just like the Okamotos were killed. It was horrible. Layla, Kim, and Kyle discovered the bodies. Kim is in bad shape. He's just sitting on the lanai, staring ahead, and Kyle doesn't seem to be able to get him to move. He'll need an ambulance. I'm not sure about Layla. She's also in shock but not like Kim. I can't believe they're gone." As Dewey said this, he broke down and began sobbing. Mr. Soo patted him on the arm, trying to soothe his friend.

"I wish I hadn't gone back there. I wish I had never seen what I saw," Ned said, visibly shaken.

The sheriff made his way to them, and he motioned Dewey aside. "Dewey, take Layla home and have her change her clothes. Her skirt and shoes need to be placed in a paper bag, and we'll need your shoes too. There may be trace evidence on those items."

"I understand, Sheriff, we'll do that right now. What's going to happen next?"

"The local detectives, CSI, and Five-O will come and ask questions. They will want to know what you saw and anything else you might be able to contribute. I'm going around to the front and into the house to open up the back to keep people off the front lanai. Ned, while I'm gone, if anyone comes, make them wait until I get the back opened. We don't need any more people tromping on the front lanai."

In a few moments, the sound of sirens could be heard as the sheriff opened up the back lanai. Dewey walked past Layla and up the stairs to speak with him. "Sheriff, when everyone is through with the questions, I would like to take Layla, Fiona,

Ned, and Mr. Soo over to the Four Seasons. I don't think anyone should stay here for a few days."

"That's an excellent idea, Dewey. I'll make it as easy for you as possible."

"Thank you, Sheriff." As Dewey was talking with the sheriff, his vision was directed inside to the Boones' home, and he noticed something but could not figure out what. He would come back to the notion when things settled down a little.

He still had the phone number to the Four Seasons on his cell phone and asked to speak directly to the hotel manager after identifying himself. After confirming they had a three-bedroom suite available, he told them he would be taking the suite for at least a week and would be arriving later this evening.

Returning to the group, he asked Fiona for assistance getting Layla changed, then he told them about staying at the hotel and how the sheriff would see to it that they would be free to leave as soon as possible. Ned and Fiona were happy to leave the area; Ned said he would take their car. He was also going to talk with the sheriff about letting Fred leave so he could catch his flight out of Maui.

Mr. Soo was eager to leave the area and went home to pack.

Dewey and Fiona helped Layla home and then removed her skirt and shoes as instructed by the sheriff. Dewey took his shoes off, bagged them, and took everything over to the sheriff while Fiona packed several bags for Layla. Dewey returned and began packing bags for himself. He threw the luggage in their car, along with Mr. Soo's who had joined them. They returned to the Boones' back lanai where the sheriff had everyone gathered.

Fiona packed for herself and Ned. They said sad goodbyes to Fred who arranged with a friend for a lift to the airport, the sheriff allowing him to walk up to Baldwin to meet his friend. Ned and Fiona joined everyone on the lanai.

Donnie and the mayor were there when the sheriff came to speak with everyone. The ambulance came and took Kim away, Kyle riding with him. The sheriff told Donnie and the mayor about the tragic situation and asked them to leave the area since they were not involved in the initial finding. It would save time when the official investigation began.

Within twenty minutes, the detectives and CSI techs arrived, and thirty minutes later, the Five-O group arrived. Once they all assessed the scene on the front lanai, the coroner was allowed to make his initial determinations.

Someone was kind enough to bring bottled water for those waiting on the back lanai; the group sat in silence, each deep in their own sorrow. Dewey sat with his arm protectively around Layla, who was still numb. She refused to go in an ambulance, saying she would be more comfortable with Dewey and surrounded by her friends.

In less than an hour, both groups of detectives began their questioning. After almost two hours of answering the same questions several times, the group was allowed to depart for the Four Seasons. The detectives made an appointment to meet with everyone the next afternoon.

*   *   *

Now on the periphery of the excitement, he enjoyed the chaos he had created. The opening of the Visitors Center paled compared to this, and to think, he really was responsible for both. What fun!

CHAPTER 90

When they got to their suite, the bellman, with a trolley loaded with luggage, had the lights on and the windows opened. A gentle evening tropical breeze drifted into the living and dining areas. Mr. Soo opted for the upstairs loft bedroom, saying he would enjoy walking up and down the stairs for exercise. Dewey decided he and Layla would take the master bedroom that offered a view of tropical gardens and a partial ocean view. Ned and Fiona had the master bedroom that had a full ocean view. When the luggage was sorted out, Dewey called room service and had sandwiches, salads, and dessert sent up; although the suite came with a chef, they decided not to use his services for the evening.

After making the call, Dewey and Fiona went to the well-appointed kitchen to make coffee and tea. Two coffee makers were sitting on the counter: one a drop-in with a tree of various selections and the other a brew pot with a canister of Kona coffee.

"Which type shall I use?" asked Fiona.

"How about a brew pot? It's easier to get refills,'" suggested Dewey.

Fiona was pouring water into the chamber and said, "Annie loved her coffee." She sat the water down, held on to the counter, and cried.

Ned, hearing Fiona, came into the kitchen and held on to her.

"Take her into the living room. I'll finish up here," said Dewey.

Mr. Soo entered the kitchen. "Don't worry about me. When I feel for tea, I'll put the kettle on. Is beer in the refrigerator?"

A surprised looked crossed Dewey's face, never knowing Mr. Soo to drink; he opened the refrigerator door. "There are several varieties, Mr. Soo, make a selection. I'll have one myself."

Dewey and Mr. Soo walked back through the dining area that opened to the living area.

"Would anyone like a beer or something else to drink?" asked Dewey.

"I would like a vodka on the rocks. A double, please," said Fiona.

"I'll get that for you, honey, and a beer for me," said Ned.

"Layla, you should drink something," said Dewey.

"I'll wait for the coffee," she said softly.

The massive living area had three large sofas in a U-shape pattern. The center sofa taking in the ocean view, the suite featured a wraparound lanai that covered the living area and both master bedrooms. The loft had a small balcony that opened to an ocean view. A full moon cast a silvery glow on the ocean, presenting a magnificent picture from their suite. No one noticed, grief was all consuming.

That night, when Layla and Dewey went to bed, Dewey found Layla curled up on her side, wearing a T-shirt and lightweight jogging shorts, a uniform she would continue to wear for some time to come.

The next morning their chef arrived and prepared breakfast. By then, the whole island had the news of yesterday's events, and some of the hotel staff realized the residents in the suite were directly involved. When the butler arrived, he told Dewey it would be wise for him to answer all phone calls then direct them, saying that as hard as the hotel tried to keep their suite number private, often, unthinking people managed to get the correct extension.

The first call was from the local police. The butler asked for a name and badge number before passing the call to Dewey. Dewey was told two detectives from the local police along with two from Five-O would come by at one that afternoon. He asked that all parties be available. Dewey thanked him and relayed the request to everyone.

The next call was from Donnie asking to speak with Fiona.

"Yes, Donnie, is something the matter with the crafters?"

"No, Fiona. However, a strange event happened this morning. Before the center opened, there was a line outside of about ten people. The restaurant manager phoned me at home and told me about it, saying he recognized the folks as local residents. I went to the center and opened up. They all rushed over to the craft counter. Within minutes, all of Layla's charcoals were sold. I wanted to tell you. I thought it was eerily interesting."

"Donnie, that is weird, but at least it's a good thing for the center. I'm not sure I'll tell Layla right now. She's not up for too much."

"How are you and Ned doing, Fiona?"

"This horrible tragedy is just beginning to become a reality for us. Ned and I talked last night. Too much bad has happened too close to home. We decided we are going to sell our home. We could not bear to look across and see Annie and George's home, knowing their fate."

"You're not going to leave Paia?"

"No, Paia is our home. We'll just find somewhere else to live. Please don't mention this to anyone else."

"You have my word, Fiona, it will stay between us. You take care and let everyone else know you all are in our prayers."

"Thank you, Donnie, for calling, and I'll pass on your regards."

After Donnie called, Fiona passed along his sentiments, then pulled Dewey aside to tell him about selling Layla's charcoals.

"My gosh, that's it! That's what was missing from the Boones', the charcoal Layla did for them on our trip together. I'll tell the detectives. I can't help but wonder if the murderer didn't take it as a souvenir."

"That's sick, Dewey."

"Whoever committed these murders is sick."

When the detectives arrived, they requestioned everyone. After several hours, Dewey suggested Layla go and lay down. Once she was in the bedroom with the door closed, Dewey explained to the detectives about the missing charcoal.

"I believe the murderer took it as a souvenir."

"Why do you think that, sir?"

"As Annie and I told the sheriff, after the Okamoto murders, someone took the overhead doorbell that rang each time someone opened the screen door to come into the market. It was there when I went in after the Okamotos came home, and it was gone when Annie discovered the bodies the next morning. I know Annie and I both mentioned it to the sheriff."

"We'll recheck our notes from the Okamoto file. It does appear you may be correct in your assumption about souvenir taking."

Everyone sat on the lanai after dinner and watched another perfect sunset.

"Fiona, Dewey and I talked about this earlier. Could you please call Wade and tell him the house is his? We can't live there anymore. I'm assuming he'll still want to buy it. If not, just put in on the market," said Layla.

"I'll do that, and since neither he nor Herb were close to the Boones, I don't think there will be a problem for them living there. Ned and I talked about the same subject, and we're going to sell also."

"If you and Ned are leaving and Dewey and Layla won't be back, I do not know how I could stay in my home either. There's too much sorrow on that street," said Mr. Soo. "I'll contact my sons and see if they want to keep my home for a retreat from Oahu or if they prefer for me to sell. I have no idea where I'll live. I hate the thought of going back to Oahu, too many people there. I am accustomed to the quiet life of Paia."

"Mr. Soo, our estate in Salt Lake City is huge. In fact, there is a wing that we don't even use. We could open that up, and you could live there for as long as you want. Agnes is an excellent cook, and there are a lot of fast-food restaurants nearby. I don't know if you would like the cold weather, but there is plenty of open space to walk."

"This is something interesting for me to consider. Where I grew up in China, winters were brutal. I am accustomed to cold and snow."

"Come with us, Mr. Soo. You are like family to both of us," pleaded Layla.

"Give me a day to ponder the idea, but it is very appealing."

"Ned, Fiona, my dad built a home about three-fourths a mile from the main estate. He and Mom were going to live there. It was finished and they were ready to move when Dad had a sudden heart attack and died. You folks are welcome to live there for as long as you like. It has three bedrooms, plenty of rooms for your sons to visit."

"Dewey, that's a generous offer, but Fiona could not live in cold weather, and I'm not sure I could either. Thank you. Your offer means so much to us both."

The next morning the sheriff phoned and spoke with Dewey. "I wanted to tell you the police tape has been removed from the area, except for around the Boones' home. Your home, the Kellers', and Mr. Soo's are accessible."

"Thank you for letting us know. However, we'll be staying here until we leave for Salt Lake City. Layla is simply not up to returning there. In fact, she has instructed Fiona to contact Wade as he had expressed interest in purchasing the home if we ever wanted to sell."

"I'm sure sorry to hear that, Dewey. Having you folks as part of our community was a good thing, and I personally enjoyed your company. You will be missed."

"Thank you, Sheriff, but although she seems pretty tough, Layla is too fragile to continue to live in Paia, even on a part-time basis."

"By the way, the Boones' son will be arriving tomorrow. Their lawyer informed me this morning their estate was in excellent order, leaving their son as executor. Donnie will speak with him. Because of their wide influence on so many people, he is going to suggest that funeral services be conducted in the high school gymnasium. Between George's and Annie's work, their interests after retiring, and their many friends in Paia, there will be hundreds wanting to attend."

"If approved by the family, I would like to say a few words at the service. Maybe you could give him my phone number here, and I'll speak with him at his convenience."

"I'll be glad to do that, and I'm sure your words will be welcome."

Later that morning, Kyle phoned and asked Dewey if he could meet him to could get their things. Kim was being transferred to a hospital in Oahu; he still had not come out of his catatonic state. After a few days, if there was no improvement, Kyle was going to charter a plane to take Kim back to Washington, DC. Dewey arranged to meet Kyle that afternoon.

Kyle was waiting on the back steps. "How's Layla doing?"

Dewey was shocked to see him; he looked as though he had aged ten years. "She's coping. Ned, Fiona, and Mr. Soo are with us. We have a huge suite at the Four Seasons. None of us wanted to stay in the area. Layla and I won't be coming back here at all. We're making arrangements to sell. Ned and Fiona will stay in Paia but will move to another location, and Mr. Soo is also leaving the area."

"So much sadness in such a small area."

While Kyle packed their luggage, Dewey began cleaning out the refrigerator. It was a way to kill the time without thinking too much.

Before Kyle left, he told Dewey he would let them know how Kim was doing and check on Layla. Dewey took the trash to the cans in the garage. He paused, remembering how George had managed to stuff all three cans and a dolly into the Escalade, along with a ton of other things Layla had bought for their home. Such a short time ago, now everyone's world had changed, and George and Annie were gone.

After dinner, everyone sat on the lanai. Mr. Soo said he had reached a decision, and he would take Dewey and Layla up on their offer to join them in Salt Lake City. Layla jumped up, ran over, and gave him a tearful hug.

Fiona told them she had phoned Wade, and he was thrilled Layla was offering him her home. He would accept, just name a price. Layla asked Fiona to come up with a fair price and figure in a commission. Fiona said she and Ned would handle everything; she also mentioned that Wade and Herb would be selling their current home. It was farther down the beach in a quieter area of Paia away from the center of town. It was a lovely home with many custom features added by both Wade and Herb. She and Ned were seriously considering purchasing that home for them to live in; it was actually larger than their current home. Fiona said that would work well, as she envisioned her sons marrying and bringing wives and grandchildren for visits.

Ned said he and Fiona discussed things, and they would be returning home the day after tomorrow. There were a lot of details to attend to, and they both wanted to get to work on the sale of Layla's home.

CHAPTER 91

Dewey sat alone on the lanai, having a second cup of coffee. The butler had fixed breakfast for everyone, and after that, Ned and Fiona, all packed, left to go back to their home. Mr. Soo was off to explore the lush tropical grounds. Late the previous afternoon, he had met an older couple from China and had arranged to have lunch with them at one of the outdoor restaurants. After lunch, they were taking a walking tour of the tropical plant life offered at the hotel.

He phoned his home in Salt Lake City and spoke with Ted. "Ted, I'm going to send a plane for you and Agnes, and I would like you to join us for Annie's and George's funeral services. You can assist in helping get Layla's things packed. We will not be coming back to Paia. Now I have some great news. Have Agnes get on the extension."

"She's already listening."

"Our dear friend, Mr. Soo—you've heard me talk fondly of him many times—will be coming to live with us. He is no longer comfortable living so close to where both the murders happened. Plus, he and Layla have developed a wonderful closeness. It will be good for both of them. I thought maybe we could open up the unused wing for him, and, Agnes, he's a connoisseur of fried foods, so you can ply him with all the fried foods you want."

"Is he in good health? Will he have any medical problems?"

"No, he's spry and walks miles each day. I was worried how he would adapt to the cold weather, but that is not a problem.

He grew up in an area of China that has intense winters. He's looking forward to going to different drive-through restaurants for lunch. We will have to hire another full-time employee to help with the upkeep, but I believe it's well worth it. Layla and I love this elderly gentleman."

"Good lord, are you kidding? He likes fast food. He and Ted should get along just fine. Dewey, he will be warmly welcomed by both of us. Ted and I always wanted this house full of people."

"Thank you, Agnes, and will you bring my lightweight medium gray suit, white shirt, proper dress shoes, and that black-and-white diagonal-striped tie. I will be speaking at the funeral service."

"Of course, do you know how long we'll be staying so I can determine how much to pack?"

"Not really but no more than two weeks. There is an empty master bedroom suite here in our suite of rooms, and you will be staying here. You'll get to know Mr. Soo. He's here too. Fiona and Ned just left to go back to their home. Agnes, we even have a chef and butler service. Think you can handle that?"

"You're going to spoil her, Dewey, with all that high-class help."

"Good, I deserve to be spoiled, now and then. Dewey, let us know the date you want us to leave, and we'll be on our way. Will you meet us in Maui?"

"Yes, I'll meet you at the airport. It will be a day before the pilots can be ready to go once I get in touch with them. They will have to wait a day before they can return to Maui, so three, four days at the most before you're here. Will that be OK?"

"We'll be ready. Just let us know the exact date and time."

"I'm going to pack that plane full on the return trip with as much of Layla's and Mr. Soo's things as we can get on board. I'll have them fly the big plane over. It will give us more space. You folks can use the bedroom to take a nap before you get to Maui."

"What a treat!" said Agnes.

"You two deserve it. You've spoiled me for years. I'll get back with you as soon as I know exact dates."

Dewey phoned his pilots and told them what he needed. They said they would call him back with the date of departure and return. Dewey went to the bedroom and sat on the edge of the bed. "Layla, are you awake?"

"Yes, is something wrong?"

"No, honey, just some news. I've phoned Agnes and Ted and arranged for them to join us here. They will help you and Mr. Soo pack, and they will also be attending the funeral. Layla, I want you to go with me to the airport to greet them when they arrive. Do you think you can do that? It would mean a great deal to me."

"Yes, I can manage that. I'll be glad to see them both, especially Agnes. Thank you for having them join us."

The next afternoon the butler announced a call from Mr. Charlie Boone.

Dewey took the phone. "Charlie, I hate having to get acquainted with you under these horrible circumstances, but I'm glad you've called. Any word yet on when the services will be held?"

"Dewey, our family is in your debt for handling things at the beginning. The sheriff told us what a good job you did in assisting him to get things in order until more police arrived. I know how difficult that must have been for you and poor Layla to have found our folks." Charlie's voice broke. "I'm sorry, I still have a hard time believing this has happened to Mom and Dad."

"Me too, Charlie, we loved those two and will miss them terribly."

"How is Layla holding up?"

"She's very quiet and what you might say closed in on herself. She needs time to heal. We'll be leaving after the funeral and selling our Paia home. We can't go back there now."

"The sheriff hasn't given us a date when the bodies will be released. I've spoken with Donnie Munson, and he has suggested that the services be held in the high school gymnasium because of the great number of people expected to attend. He also mentioned that you would like to say a few words at the services. We welcome your words, and I know Mom and Dad would be happy that you will be speaking on their behalf."

"Thank you, Charlie. Are all of you staying here in Paia?"

"I'm the only family member here currently. Since we didn't know when the funeral would be held, my sister and her family and my wife and kids are staying home until we have a specific date. Putting everyone in a hotel, with all those young children, would be hard to handle while still tending to the necessities of a funeral."

"That's probably a good idea. How are you doing? This has to be hard on you without anyone here."

"It's very hard. I miss my wife. We are very close. I had a good role model in Mom and Dad." Once again, Charlie's voice broke.

"Charlie, join us this Sunday for brunch here at the Four Seasons. It will give us a chance to meet, and I can share some of my thoughts with you about what I want to say at the services."

"Thank you, Dewey, I would like that."

Dewey gave Charlie their suite number and told him to come by any time after eleven Sunday morning. He told him they had their own chef and would eat brunch on their suite's lanai. "Nothing fancy, be comfortable."

"Thank you again. I look forward to meeting you and Layla."

"Mr. Soo is staying with us too. You know him, right?"

"Mr. Soo is with you? That's wonderful. He would let me tag along with him on his walks, and sometimes, when we knew Mom wouldn't catch us, we had a burger, fries, and malt at Otis's. I'm looking forward to seeing him again."

When Dewey finished his call, he told Layla about Charlie coming for brunch on Sunday. He stressed how important it would be for him to get away from Paia for a bit and how all alone he was. Layla cried for Charlie, feeling sorry for him being alone at this time.

Dewey and Layla stood outside their car, waving as Ted and Agnes deplaned. Dewey walked up and hugged both of them. Agnes had a garment bag slung over her arm. "Dewey, here are the clothes you requested."

"Thank you, Agnes. Ted, let's you I and get your luggage loaded. Agnes, Layla is waiting for you by the car."

Agnes walked to the car and embraced Layla. "Honey, I'm so sorry this had to happen to you. You simply do not deserve all this sorrow in your young life. You let me know if there is anything I can do to help you through this terrible ordeal."

"Agnes, having you here is a big help," Layla said.

When they entered the suite, both Ted and Agnes stopped abruptly, taking in the magnificent view, the plush furnishings, and the hugeness of the suite.

Dewey moved them along to their bedroom. He opened the double doors and ushered them into their suite.

"Holy cow, look at that view and the size of this room," said Ted, amazement in his voice.

"Ted, come see this bathroom. There is a steam shower and a Jacuzzi. Is this a sauna?"

"Yes, there is one in each of the master bedroom. They are terrific, really takes the kinks out. I'm spoiled. I'll be having one installed in our bath back in Salt Lake City. Let me know if you like using it. I'll put one in your bathroom too."

Agnes turned slowly and looked at Dewey. "Huh, will do," she said hesitantly.

"I guess you had lunch on the plane. Our chef is fixing fresh fish for dinner tonight, and as soon as Mr. Soo gets in from his afternoon hike, you'll meet him. I'll let you unpack. If there is anything you need, just ask. Oh, and there is a fully stocked fridge in the kitchen, beer, sodas, water. There is one of those coffee machines where you just drop a gizmo in and get a cup of coffee. Anything, just let us know."

"Thank you, Dewey. I think Ted and I are in semishock. We need to get unpacked."

"Agnes, come look. We have a huge patio off our bedroom with an ocean view."

"My god, Ted. I don't believe this!"

Dewey left the room and shut the door behind him. He smiled at the joy Ted and Agnes was experiencing.

An hour before dinner, Agnes and Ted emerged from their room. Agnes wore a peasant blouse and a bright print skirt; Ted was in cargo shorts and a Hawaiian shirt.

"It didn't take you two long to get into the spirit of the islands," said Layla, smiling.

"We had to do a bit of serious shopping in Salt Lake City, but we found a store that specialized in Hawaiian things."

Mr. Soo came down the stairs from his loft room.

"Agnes, Ted, let me introduce you to our Mr. Soo."

"It is with great pleasure I meet both of you," he said, extending his hand to them both.

"We've heard such wonderful things about you, Mr. Soo. It is our pleasure to meet you," said Agnes.

"I hear you like fried foods," said Ted, grinning. "Me too. You and I are going to have a great time exploring all the wonderful establishments offered in Salt Lake City. There is a drive-through that serves the most wonderful bacon double cheeseburger, simply heaven."

"Really? That is a delicacy I've missed. I am most anxious to try one of those."

"Oh brother," said Agnes in a whisper. "These two are going to get along just fine."

CHAPTER 92

On the way to Paia, Dewey stopped at an office supply store and picked up twenty flat cardboard boxes, masking tape, and two magic markers. Ted and Mr. Soo carried on a foodie conversation the entire trip, which made Agnes declare that just listening to all the fried-food talk had raised her cholesterol level. Dewey helped the ladies carry ten flats into their home, and Mr. Soo and Ted took ten with them.

"Dewey, you go work with Ted and Mr. Soo. Those two will be talking more than sorting and packing. Do you have any newspapers around?"

"Newspapers, why didn't I think of getting some? Let me call Fiona and see if she can suggest something."

Dewey dialed Fiona and explained where they were, who was with them, and what they were trying to accomplish. He asked where he could find newspapers for packing.

"I keep a supply here in our garage. Come over and help yourself. You take some to Mr. Soo's, and I'll take some over to Layla. I can see how she's doing and meet Agnes."

"You're terrific. I knew you would solve our dilemma. I'm heading out the door right now."

"I'll meet you in the garage."

In the garage, she directed him to a chest-high rack of newspapers.

"How many may I take?"

"Take all you need. I add to it daily. I imagine Mr. Soo will require more than Layla."

Layla saw Fiona coming her way with an armful of newspapers. She went out to take half the stack and walked back inside with her. She made the introduction and the three ladies went about assessing what was to go and what would be staying.

"Layla, do you intend to take all your charcoals with you or are you leaving some here?"

"Six are already hung, and another three are completed, which I intended to hang. Why do you ask?"

"If there are any you are not taking with you and feel Wade and Herb can live without, please donate them to the Visitors Center. Yours have already sold out."

"They're all sold?"

"They went right away, at $200 each. If you have any more to donate, we'll be asking $300 each. They are very popular and well worth the price."

"The set of four depicting windsurfers I plan to take and the one of the shops along Baldwin that includes the Visitors Center. All the rest can be donated."

"That will give the center another four to sell. No hurry, I'll take them when you're ready."

"Might as well take them today. We're trying to get everything packed and out of here as soon as possible."

"I'll call Donnie. He'll be very happy."

Donnie was so excited; he said he would be right over to pick up the charcoals.

Shortly, there was knock on the back screen. "Hello, ladies."

"Come in, Donnie," said Fiona, opening the screen door.

He went over to Layla and hugged her. "Layla, from the bottom of my heart, I'm so sorry you had to be the one to make that gruesome discovery. I am also personally sorry to see you and Dewey leave Paia, although I fully understand."

Layla pulled away, tears in her eyes. "Donnie, your friendship means so much to Dewey and me. I am grateful for your financial advice and handling all the things I fling at you. Donnie, this is Agnes. She and her husband look after Dewey and his home. They're like family. Ted is over with Mr. Soo, helping him pack."

Donnie shook hands with Agnes. "Agnes, I know you and your husband will take good care of our Layla. She and Dewey are special people to us. They have done so much to make the Visitors Center possible. And donating more of her artwork is a wonderful surprise."

After a bit more small talk, Fiona helped Donnie pack the charcoals and put them in his car, suggesting the new charcoals be sold at $300 each, to which he readily agreed

After clothes, personal toilet items, and art supplies were boxed, there wasn't much left to pack. Layla had just begun to set up housekeeping and she had lived at Mr. Soo's for so long, the things she had accumulated were few.

"Dewey, it's Layla. We're done."

"You're done? How many boxes do you have?"

"We have eight boxes, packed, taped, and labeled. How are you gentlemen doing?"

"Don't ask. Those two are spending more talking than doing. They are now replanting the backyard."

Layla had the phone on speaker, and when Agnes heard that, she said, "Oh lord, I'm on my way. I'll light a fire under Ted."

"I'll join you and help. Between the two of us, we'll get more accomplished," said Fiona.

"I'll come over and begin loading the cartons in the car, then take them to the hangar for storage. Hope they aren't too heavy."

"I'll call Ned and get him here to help. He's at the club chatting with the boys. Ned, we need you back here. I'm at Layla's, and you need to help Dewey load up his car with the cartons we've packed."

"On my way, honey."

When Ned arrived at Dewey's, he suggested they use his SUV because it held more and was easier to pack. He told Dewey he had an informal meeting with the man that owned the escrow company he would be using to sell their home. He explained what would be happening, and his friend promised to expedite the procedure.

"Thank you, Ned. I knew you would handle things very professionally for us. Well, let's get these loaded and off to the hangar."

Returning from the hangar, they spotted an empty parking spot near the sheriff's office and decided to park and see if there were any new developments.

"Hello, Charlene, is the sheriff in?"

"Hello, Dewey, how's Layla doing? How are you doing?"

"She's better each day. I'm good, keeping busy. Can't say how we'll be at the funeral."

"Don't think any of us will be handling it too well. George and Annie were so kind to me during the storm, letting me stay on the back lanai with the rest of you folks."

"I know what you mean. Remember back then, I was just more or less a surf bum. Didn't matter, I was welcomed."

"Let me tell the sheriff you're here before I start crying," Charlene said, blowing her nose.

The sheriff sat them down in his office. "I wish I had good news, but for all the high-tech forensics, nothing has been discovered. I can tell you that a Taser was used, which no doubt was how he was able to get George into a chair. According to the coroner, there was a substantial burn on George's chest, right above the heart, and two small entry wounds from the Taser. Annie had the same marks but not the burn. It would have taken a lesser jolt to take her down."

"My god, that's horrible," said Ned.

"I hope," said Dewey, "that neither of them were conscious when they lost their lives."

"I agree," said the sheriff.

As they were leaving the sheriff's office, Fiona called Ned on his cell. "Ned, we're starving. Mr. Soo suggested Otis's for lunch. Can you and Dewey meet us there?"

"Don't see why not, we'll be there."

"What's up?"

"Our packing group is hungry and want to meet at Otis's for lunch."

"I'm sure Mr. Soo had something to do with that decision, and Ted happily agreed. They've been talking about fried food ever since they met. It's driving Agnes crazy," Dewey said, chuckling. "Now they are talking about replanting our backyard, which is over an acre. Those two are going to be good buddies."

The group met at Otis's, startling the namesake owner seeing everyone walk into his restaurant. He put several tables together to accommodate the crowd.

"Fiona, I've never had the pleasure of serving you before," Otis said, smiling.

"No, I don't believe you have. Can I get something that isn't fried?"

"I recommend our tuna or chicken salad sandwich."

Layla and Fiona had tuna salad sandwiches; Mr. Soo, Dewey, Ted, and Ned settled on cheeseburgers; and Agnes ordered a hula burger, basically a hamburger with a piece of grilled pineapple. They ordered sides of onion rings and fries. When the food arrived, there wasn't any talk at the table; everyone was eating in earnest.

"All that packing made us hungrier than we realized. Everything tastes terrific," said Agnes.

"This is an excellent cheeseburger," said Ted.

"I'm so damned mad," declared Fiona. "I've lived so close to Otis's all these years and never ate here before. This is the best tuna salad I've ever eaten, certainly better than the one I make."

Otis returned to the table to refill the iced tea and coffee; he was delighted with all the praise he received on the meal, especially when Fiona raved about his tuna salad.

"How did the packing go at Mr. Soo's?" asked Dewey.

"We got three boxes packed, taped, and marked, but it was a struggle," said Agnes.

"Ms. Agnes, I thought Ted and I were doing a very thorough job."

"Discussing the providence of each item you're taking means we'll be at it for a long time."

Shaking his head, Mr. Soo agreed. "You make a very valid point. We will try and make better progress the next time we pack."

"We should come back on Monday. We want to be sure when the services are over and we are cleared to leave, the plane is packed and we can take off."

"Yes, you are correct, Dewey. We shall begin again on Monday."

Layla told the group about Charlie Boone coming for brunch on Sunday and how sad it was that he was all alone. Fiona said they would host him for an Italian meal next week.

"Dewey, was there any news from the sheriff?"

"Nothing." Dewey decided he would leave out the information on the Taser. "All the agencies are still investigating."

"That's not right. Two sets of horrible murders in this small town, and nobody saw or knows anything. That just doesn't seem possible," said Fiona.

"No, it certainly does not," said Mr. Soo.

CHAPTER 93

The butler answered the door and escorted Charlie through the living area to the lanai. Dewey came through the open lanai door, extending his hand and introducing himself.

"Thank you for inviting me. I'm just sorry it has to be under these circumstances," said Charlie.

"So am I. We're glad you were able to join us this afternoon. Come on out, and I'll introduce you to everyone. I'm being careful what I say around Layla. She still breaks down easily."

Dewey made the introductions, finishing with Mr. Soo, who gave Charlie a welcoming hug and expressed his deep sorrow for the loss of his parents. Charlie sat down at the table.

The butler came and asked everyone for his or her drink choice. He soon returned with drinks and canapés.

"Charlie, when will your wife be joining you?" asked Layla.

"She and the kids will be here on Wednesday. My folks will be released to the funeral home on Tuesday, and I need her advice on those matters. Our kids are old enough. They can hang out on the beach without getting into trouble. They understand the gravity of this visit. We will hold the services this Saturday at 10:00 a.m. in the high school gymnasium as Mr. Munson suggested. The interment will be private, just family."

"When will your sister be arriving?" asked Mr. Soo.

"She and her husband will arrive on Thursday. After a family discussion, they will leave their children at home. They are very young and, frankly, not well disciplined. None of us feel the funeral service would be a good place for them. They will stay with his parents. God help them," Charlie said, shaking his head.

"Annie was dismayed the way those children were being raised. She felt one day her daughter and son-in-law would regret the lack of teaching them boundaries," offered Layla.

"Mr. Munson phoned just before I was leaving and told me a group would like to plan a luau in honor of my folks. He said it would start at five Saturday evening with a special program at sunset. A group called the Brothers would roast several pigs, and there are many people ready to prepare food. What do you think of that idea?"

"A luau in their memory is an honor, Charlie. It's a wonderful Hawaiian tradition, one that your parents would be proud to know was held for them," said Mr. Soo.

"The Brothers are our friends. They are three Hawaiian gentlemen who move with expertise anything you need moved. I understand their pig roasting is the best," said Layla.

"I'll let Donnie know to go ahead and make plans. He said it would be on the bluff, wherever that is."

"Oh my," said Layla softly, "the memorial services for the Okamotos were held there. It's a large area looking out on the ocean, very peaceful. It will be lovely in the evening."

"After lunch, you and I can talk privately about what I have in mind to say at the services," Dewey said to Charlie.

The chef prepared a delicious brunch, which was served with quiet efficiency. Charlie told stories about his parents, his children, and his wife. After dessert and coffee, everyone drifted inside, leaving Dewey and Charlie on the lanai.

They spent an hour going over what Dewey thought he might say at the services. He specifically didn't want to be too maudlin nor did he want to appear too upbeat. Dewey made some rough notes, and finally, they finished their discussion and went back inside.

"Oh, I forgot to mention, I've received an invitation from Fiona and Ned Keller to an Italian dinner Tuesday evening. I didn't realize they were such good friends with Mom and Dad."

"Funny, they became good friends about six or seven months ago, and both couples realized what a mistake they made not getting to know each other sooner. Fiona and George were more outspoken and Annie and Ned more reserved. I guess there was such an age difference between you and your sister and their children, all the years when you were growing up, you two families didn't have much in common. They're going to handle the sale of our home here. They have an outstanding reputation in the real estate market."

"I'm sure we will sell Mom and Dad's home, Neither of our families could vacation there or live there. I guess they would be the ones to handle that for us."

"You can trust them completely."

"The sheriff has gotten a forensic cleanup team, and they start cleaning the house as soon as the police release it. My wife and sister will handle packing. I know the furniture, etc., will be sold with the home, but we have to take care of the personal items. So many years of accumulation, so many memories." Again, Charlie's voice broke.

Layla went over and touched Charlie on the shoulder. "Fiona will help too, and she'll be a good friend to your family. Charlie, I'm so glad you were able to join us today. Please excuse me. I have to lie down. I'm afraid I'm not back to my old self yet."

Charlie clasped Layla's hands in his. "Thank you, Layla, for all you've done today. You were special to my folks. Mom said she felt toward you like she would her own daughter. I'm so sorry you had to make the discovery."

Tears streaming down both Layla's and Charlie's cheeks, Layla smiled, said a weak thank you, and left the room.

"I'm sorry, folks. I guess I'm kind of a downer right now."

"No need to apologize, Charlie, you have every right to be sad and emotional. Losing both your parents in such a horrible manner is more than anyone should have to go through," said Mr. Soo.

Charlie left a few minutes later, leaving everyone feeling drained.

"That was rough, Dewey," said Ted.

"It sure was. He's a great guy, an excellent reflection on George and Annie. They did a good job raising him."

Monday morning, Dewey, Agnes, Ted, and Mr. Soo went to Paia and did more packing. Layla stayed in their suite, the emotion of yesterday had left her exhausted.

When they arrived, Fiona came over to help.

They kept packing until after one in the afternoon, when they broke for lunch, again at Otis's.

At lunch, Dewey mentioned his conversation with Charlie, regarding selling his parents' home and that he would be asking Fiona and Ned to handle the sale. She said they suspected that would be the case. She also mentioned she planned to offer her services helping them pack the personal things in the Boones' home.

On the way back to Mr. Soo's, Fiona said Ned was meeting with Wade today to start the paperwork. He would be at Mr. Soo's tomorrow and help Dewey load boxes to take to the hangar.

"I want him out of the house as much as possible while I'm cooking."

"You'll like Charlie. He has George's easy personality and gentle manner. He's a big guy like George but has Annie's coloring. I'm anxious to meet his sister," said Dewey.

"From what Annie told me, that girl did a complete turn from how she was raised after she married her husband. What can you do? Love is blind," said Fiona in her firm manner.

Mr. Soo kept Fiona out on the lanai as everyone else went inside. "I've talked with my sons. It is our decision to sell my home. Would you and Ned handle that transaction?"

"Why, of course, Mr. Soo. When do you want a For Sale sign in your yard and notice to go out to the market?"

"Not until I leave Paia. It is important that I say goodbye in person to all my friends. I do not want them to find out I'm leaving by seeing a sign or a notice in the paper."

"I understand. That will not be a problem. Do you have an idea of the price you will want?"

"I will leave that to you and Ned. Considering what has happened, it might reduce the selling price."

"That is a possibility, but we won't start out with that attitude."

"Thank you, Fiona. I feel confident you and Ned will handle things for me properly. I'll tell everyone tonight at dinner."

After lunch, Fiona went back to her home to begin cooking for the coming evening. The remainder of the group continued packing. When everything was completed, they sat all the boxes in the living room, ready to take to the hangar.

"Well, Mr. Soo, we finally got it all packed," declared Dewey.

"I'm sorry, Dewey, but this is not everything. We still have the garage."

"What? Is there a lot to pack in there?"

"Possibly, I will have to go through things. A lot of items of memory are kept there."

"In that case, let's leave for today and pick up more cartons on the way back to the hotel. That way, we'll be ready to start tomorrow morning."

"I have an announcement to make," declared Mr. Soo, when they were sitting on the lanai after dinner. "This afternoon, I spoke to Fiona about her and Ned selling my home. My sons are not interested in keeping it in the family," said Mr. Soo.

No one was surprised by the news, and shortly, everyone went to bed, except Layla and Dewey who stayed on the lanai.

"I'm going to start work on what I want to say at the services. Do you want to help?"

"I wouldn't be much help, I'm too emotional. You'll do a great job." Layla kissed Dewey on the cheek and went to bed.

Dewey spent several hours making a rough draft of his thoughts. He decided he would place them in more coherent order on the computer in the next couple of days.

CHAPTER 94

"Dewey, you aren't mad that I'm not joining everyone again today? Being on that street is difficult for me. The memories are too fresh."

"I understand completely. You stay here and rest. Hopefully, we'll be home early."

Dewey kissed Layla on the cheek, left their bedroom, and rounded up the remainder of the packing crew. He told the butler to make sure Layla ate lunch.

When he turned onto their street, Dewey saw Ned wave at them from his lanai. He got in his SUV and drove to Mr. Soo's. He and Dewey loaded up the boxes as the other three tackled the garage. Everything was nicely arranged in plastic storage boxes; however, there were quite a few, so sorting would take time. Dewey and Ned went to the hangar and began unloading the cartons, stacking them neatly in a corner. Dewey had arranged to meet one of the pilots to ascertain how much more weight they could get on board. After using a handheld weighing device, the pilot said they would be able to get another nine hundred pounds on board, at the maximum.

Dewey got in Ned's SUV that was parked in the shade of the hangar. Ned started to turn on the ignition, stopped, and turned to Dewey. "You're not looking too good. You have dark circles under your eyes, that's a couple of days' growth of beard, and when you walk, you look exhausted."

"Ned, I am exhausted. I'm trying to take care of Layla, and I worry about her, then getting everything packed in both houses and ready to ship. Having Agnes and Ted here was my idea, and things could never have been this far along without them. However, I still feel responsible for them while they're here. I worry about Mr. Soo selling everything and moving to a much colder climate. I'm not tending to company business. I know I have a wonderful staff, and things appear to be running smoothly. I've been away too long. I need to check on things firsthand. Maybe I shouldn't have added the extra burden of speaking at the services for George and Annie, but in my heart, I truly wanted to profess what a blessing they were to Layla and me. But what bothers me more than anything else is I can't get the scene on the Boones' front lanai out of my mind. That will haunt me the rest of my life. You saw what I saw. Will you ever forget?"

"When I'm in the shower and I know Fiona can't hear me for the sound of the water, I break down. Each day I think I'll make it through, but I keeping seeing them like that, and I lose it once again. Let's hope it will fade some from our minds, but I don't think we will ever be able to forget what we saw. I can imagine what Layla must be trying to process. She's had too much in her young life, with the tragic loss of her child, her marriage, and now this. She's strong, Dewey, or you would have lost her by now."

"I never thought of it that way, but you're right. She's very strong."

Ned started the SUV, and they drove back to Mr. Soo's. Ned dropped Dewey off and drove home. Inside, he was handed a small list of items to pick up at the grocery store. Fiona suggested he take everyone to lunch at one of the beach shacks to give Ted and Agnes another Maui experience.

When Ned returned from the grocery, he went to Mr. Soo's and offered to take everyone to lunch. The hungry group piled into his SUV. After they arrived and placed their orders, they sat at one of the picnic tables, enjoying the sights and sounds of the beach.

"This is the first time I've ever seen the ocean. Ted was in the navy and says he's had enough of the sea to last a lifetime. For me, this is an exciting new experience."

"Agnes, I didn't know you had never seen the ocean before. I feel bad. You and Ted could have come with me to Maui before this."

"Dewey, you were busy courting Layla, we would not have intruded for the world. We talked that when you two were married and settled, about bumming a ride when you came to Maui."

"This may not be the best of circumstances, but I'm pleased you finally got to see the ocean. It is a wonder. Growing up in Southern California, I've always been near the water. I enjoy the sound of the waves and the smell of the salt air."

"Spending six years in the navy, I enjoy the smell of the pines and the scent of mountain air," said Ted resolutely.

When they returned to Mr. Soo's, everyone thanked Ned for a wonderful lunch. He returned home to see if he could help Fiona.

"Folks, let's call it quits for today. Frankly, I'm pooped, and I need to spend more time with Layla. I also need to begin work on what I'm going to say at the services."

"Dewey, I was going to suggest that you stay at the hotel tomorrow, and Agnes, Mr. Soo, and I will come over and resume the sorting and packing. I've paid close attention to the route. This is, after all, a small island, and I know exactly how to get here."

"Ted, if you are sure that wouldn't be a problem, I would truly appreciate you handling the rest of the packing. When everything is ready to go, you and I can take it to the hangar. Layla will be pleased I will be able to spend more time with her."

When they were alone that evening, Dewey told Layla of the plan for tomorrow and possibly the following day. She cried softly and thanked him for being with her. "You are my reason for being. You are my strength."

"Honey, I'm sorry I've had to leave you alone. I had so much to attend to. Forgive me?"

"There is nothing to forgive. You are a wonder with all you've accomplished. I'm just glad I can have you all to myself tomorrow." With that, she hugged him to her.

When Dewey woke, he was astonished to find it was past ten in the morning. He showered and shaved, then found Layla on the lanai having coffee.

"Hi, you sure look better this morning. I tried to be quiet and not disturb you when I got up. I had breakfast with everyone before they left, and I'm on my third cup of coffee. Let's get you some breakfast."

"Good, I'm starved. I really needed the rest. I'm looking forward to a quiet day, just the two of us," he said, kissing her on the cheek.

Later that morning, the butler announced Mrs. Keller was calling. Dewey took the phone.

"Fiona, how did things go last night?"

"That's why I'm calling. What a lovely young man. You were right, he reminded us of George. I'm so glad his wife will be here today. I can tell he really misses his family. We enjoyed one of my outstanding Italian dinners, and he told us after conferring with his sister yesterday, he wanted Ned and me to sell the house once they have everything cleaned up and cleared out. I told him it would be our honor. I also told him I would be there for his wife and sister to help with cleaning out the house. How are you doing? Ned said you were looking terrible."

"I only got up about an hour ago. A long night's sleep has helped me considerably. Layla and I plan to spend the day together, just the two of us."

"Good, you both need that time together. I'll let you go. We'll be talking before Saturday. Love you both, goodbye."

Dewey relayed what Fiona had told him to Layla. They spent a couple of hours sitting together in one of the large chaise lounges. Dewey hugged Layla to him; a few words were said, the closeness was what they both needed.

When the others returned, they were pleased to report all was packed and ready to go to the hangar. Fiona arranged to have someone pick up other items for the local charity bank.

"Dewey, I'm going to drive back to Paia tomorrow. Mr. Soo and I are going to walk through the town so he can say goodbye to all his many friends. I'm really proud that he has asked me to join him," said Ted, beaming.

"Mr. Soo, this will be difficult for you, but you will make new friends in Salt Lake City. You're so charming, you will be on everyone's guest list," said Layla, smiling at her dear friend.

"Thank you, Layla. One should always look forward to new adventures and new friends."

The next morning after breakfast, Mr. Soo and Ted left for Paia. Agnes was finally free to explore the shops, select post cards, write notes, and have lunch on her own.

"Think you can stand another day with just me?"

"I'm looking forward to the rest of my life with you, and right now, any day is special to me. I know you need to work on your speech and I want you to spend some time doing that, but for right now, let's sit on the lanai again like we did yesterday."

Layla went in for a nap. Dewey took his laptop to the lanai and began to sort through the notes he previously made and composed them into something coherent. After a couple of hours, he went inside, got a beer, and checked on Layla.

"Honey, are you awake? How about lunch? I'm starving again."

"Give me a minute to freshen up, and tell someone we're hungry."

Sitting on the lanai waiting for lunch, Layla asked, "How is your speech coming?"

"I've got a rough draft and I'll have to shorten and refine it some, but I like what I've written. May I read it to you after lunch?"

"I should hear it first. If I hear it for the first time at the services, I may become too distraught. So after lunch, read to me what you've written."

As Dewey read his speech to Layla, she broke down several times. "It's beautiful. You have expressed how much both of us loved George and Annie. I'm so proud of you." Layla went over and kissed him on the cheek. "I'm going to lie down again. I get tired so easily, especially after an emotional outburst."

"You rest. I'm glad you like what I've written."

CHAPTER 95

Thursday afternoon, Ned phoned to speak with Dewey. "Dewey, if possible, we would like to meet with you, Layla, and Mr. Soo tomorrow regarding the sale of your homes, and you'll need to bring sets of keys. Afterward, I'll help you get the remainder of Mr. Soo's boxes to the hangar."

"Let me talk with Layla and Mr. Soo, and I'll get back with you." Dewey phoned Ned back fifteen minutes later. "Ned, we'll meet you at your house, say 10:00 a.m. Will that be satisfactory?"

"Perfect. Don't forget to bring the keys."

"No problem."

Friday morning, everyone sat in Fiona and Ned's living room as Ned discussed the papers needing to be signed. He told Layla how things were progressing with the sale to Wade and the price he offered. Layla agreed to the price and to anything Ned recommended to expedite the proceedings. He got Mr. Soo's signature on an agreement for his representation on the sale of his home, and they agreed on a tentative price. Ned told Mr. Soo if there was no interest at that price after a month, he would lower it to reflect the area where so much had happened. Mr. Soo said he had no problem with that approach.

Dewey and Ned loaded up the SUV and toted the remainder of Mr. Soo's boxes to the hangar. Once back, they all decided for a final lunch at Otis's.

Otis was pleased to see everyone come in for lunch. He told them his business had been cut in half, thanks to the Visitors Center opening, for which he was grateful. He enjoyed just serving the locals. He sat at their table and chatted while the cook prepared their lunch. When they were leaving, Otis hugged Mr. Soo, both men teary-eyed.

As they walked back down the hill, Fiona said, "Damn, that was a sad scene. Mr. Soo, you have so many friends that will miss you, which certainly include Ned and I."

"Thank you, Fiona, the people of Paia are good, honest, warm folks. I have enjoyed my time among all of you. I will enjoy Salt Lake City too. A place is as warm and friendly as you make it."

"Fiona, Layla and I have decided to leave her car to some organization in Annie or George's name. Do you or Ned know any group that could use her station wagon? It has some miles on it. Layla bought it from the rent-a-car agency because she got so used to driving it. It's still a darn good car."

"Annie was involved with two retirement homes. The large one caters to the more affluent retiree. The other is smaller, only has ten residents and much less costly. I don't believe they have their own vehicle and could use one for taking residents to appointments, picking items up for them, etc. Let me check on that for you, and if they could use the car, Ned and I can handle that for you through Donnie. How does that sound?"

"Fiona, that would be wonderful, thank you. I would like to see an organization like the retirement home get the car, especially in Annie's name," said Layla.

"I'll look into it and get back with you this evening."

When they were ready to go back to the Four Seasons, there was a lull in the conversation. Finally, Mr. Soo said, "The next time we see each other will be tomorrow at the funeral. It will be a sad and emotional time, but we need to be strong for Annie and George's children and grandchildren."

"I'm glad we're back home. I would hate to be in that hotel suite tonight. I'll get these papers over to the escrow company. Are you going to call the retirement home?" Ned asked once they were alone.

"Yes, I'll call them right away. I'm confident they will be pleased to get the station wagon and even more pleased it will be given in Annie's name. Hurry home, honey."

"I'll be back as soon as we finish with the paperwork. I want to call Wade and tell him the progress we've made. Everything will go easily from here on out. I'm going to suggest to Layla that she keep her account with Donnie until the sale is final. Then she can have her funds transferred to Salt Lake City."

"Do you think we should suggest the same thing to Mr. Soo?"

"Absolutely, hopefully, we can sell his home without too much difficulty."

Fiona phoned the retirement home and spoke with the director. He was thrilled to learn about the donation of a station wagon. Fiona said she would be in contact with Donnie Munson to finalize the procedure, which she said would take place sometime next week. She stressed the donation would be made in the name of Annie Boone.

Several hours later, Ned returned. When he came in from the garage, Fiona hugged him. "I'm so glad you're home safely. I've become paranoid about our safety lately. I guess that's silly, but when you're not here, I worry about losing you, my love."

"We'll be fine, honey. After all, I have my gun-toting wife to protect me, and I expect you to keep that little pistol handy at all times," Ned said in Fiona's ear.

"You can count on it. Ever since the Okamotos were murdered, I've kept it on me somewhere. Now I keep it on even in the house."

"Wow, should I be scared?"

"You, my love, should always be scared of me," Fiona said, giving Ned a very long and loving kiss.

Later that evening, Fiona called and told Dewey how happy the retirement home would be to get the station wagon. She and Ned would follow them to the airport, and one of them would drive the car to the bank where Donnie would finalize the necessary work. Dewey told her Layla would be very happy and thanked her.

Ned took the phone and asked Dewey to speak with Layla about leaving her account in Paia until the sale of her home was final. He also spoke with Mr. Soo and suggested the same thing to him. Mr. Soo saw the advantage and agreed to leave his account at the bank.

After speaking to Fiona and Ned, Dewey went into their bedroom and spoke with Layla, who was getting her clothes ready for tomorrow. "Honey, I just spoke with Fiona. The retirement center was thrilled to be the recipient of your station wagon in Annie's name. Donnie will handle the transaction. Ned and Fiona will follow us to the airport, and one of them will drive the wagon to the bank."

"I'm so pleased Fiona was able to get all this done so swiftly."

"I spoke with Ned, and he suggested you leave your account here in Paia until the sale of your house is finalized, saying it would make the transaction so much easier. Wade also banks with Donnie."

"I'll do that. Once all is settled, my trust fund manager can arrange for funds to be transferred."

"You're trust fund can sit and grow forever. We have more money than you or me and all our grandchildren will ever need. The royalties just keeping pouring in," Dewey said with a slight laugh.

"Dewey, did you think you would have so much money?"

"Seriously, I never cared too much about money. I just wanted to create things. However, I now realize all the good things money can buy and all the good work money can do for others."

"Once we've been married for a couple of years and settled, we should set up a foundation, like Bill and Melinda Gates have done."

"I actually have been thinking about that for some time now. We'll do it together."

"Are you going to lay out your things for tomorrow morning? We should leave here no later than nine."

"You're right. I'll go remind the others and tell our butler to have breakfast served at eight. Honey, it's going to be a very difficult morning. If for any reason you feel like you're in trouble, let me know. I don't want anything to happen to you."

"I'll be fine. I've been telling myself how important it is to be respectful to Annie and George. I don't want to cause any type of scene that will distract from their moment when we express our sorrow in losing them."

Dewey went over and hugged Layla to him, whispering in her ear, "I love you so much."

He left their bedroom and went to speak with the others.

CHAPTER 96

He stood on the periphery as the crowd made their way into the high school auditorium. Everyone was dressed in their Sunday best; everyone was so solemn. *As it should be,* he thought.

He followed a group inside and stood to the side of some bleachers, observing and nodding at those who he recognized or that recognized him. The first two rows were roped off, probably for family and pallbearers. Both caskets were closed and covered in massive floral blankets of tropical flowers. The whole front of the auditorium was a sea of flower baskets or stands with floral offerings, making the place smell sickening sweet. Slight overkill in his opinion; local florists were making a sweet penny off this funeral, thank you very much.

He saw Dewey enter with Layla hanging on his arm. Damn, she looked ghastly. Her light gray dress washed her out until she looked like a shadow. Dewey was dressed in a dark suit, white shirt, and an expensive-looking tie. Didn't he look smart. Following on their heels were his help. He was in a Western-looking dark suit, and she was wearing a dowdy dark dress, probably just the thing for funerals in Salt Lake City. Walking with them down the center aisle was Mr. Soo. He looked splendid in an expensive suit with all the right trimmings; rich folks knew how to dress up. Most of the locals were in light-colored clothes, suitable for island funerals. They took their place in one of the front rows.

Next came Donnie Munson and family. Donnie was also wearing a dark suit. Well, of course, they were the pallbearers.

How come no one asked me? They took seats behind Dewey's entourage. Guess he had better take a seat. As he started to move forward, he stopped short. Well, here they were. La-di-da, wasn't she making an entrance in a tight black dress with a big batch of pearls around her neck and Ned in his perfectly fitting dark suit. *Bitch, bitch, bitch,* he thought as Fiona and Ned made their way to sit next to Dewey and Layla. *Because you two were out late is why we're here today having a funeral for my good friends, George and Annie. You're next!*

The services started ten minutes late, which, considering the huge crowd, was amazing. First to the podium was a couple dressed in choir robes. Their voices rose throughout the auditorium in a haunting rendition of "Amazing Grace." Some fools even started to clap until they were duly chastened.

Next, the Boones' minister came to the podium and droned on for way too long a time, blah, blah, blah. Next, one of the men from the local volleyball teams that George mentored spoke how George gave so much of his experience and knowledge to the kids and how much both he and the kids enjoyed their time together. It was a short and well-received tribute.

The principal from the school that Annie retired from spoke next. He did fine for a minute or two, and then he seemed to take a cue from the minister and blah, blah, blah. Next came George's boss from the airlines. He told of George's contributions to the airport and also some cute stories about George's height that affected how he perceived many things that ultimately affected the whole industry, a nice, light speech. Then came the director of one of the retirement homes where Annie volunteered. He told how much she meant to the residents and what a blessing it was that a donation of a station wagon in her name was being made to the home.

Finally, Dewey got up to speak. Well, this was a surprise. He told everyone how even as Dewey, the surf bum, George saw through him and knew he was more than he let on. He told how a group had spent several days on the Boones' back lanai, how kind both Annie and George had been, and how it was the first time he saw Layla and fell in love with her instantly. He went on briefly, thank God, to tell of the developing bond between the two couples and the impact they had on both their lives. How deeply they would be missed and how much they were loved.

After his speech, the minister came back and asked everyone to refer to the handout of the song "Softly and Tenderly" that they received when entering the auditorium. He explained this was the Boones' favorite hymn and asked that everyone sing it in their honor. *We all stood, and I can tell you, I sang loud and with feeling. I'll miss those folks.*

After the throng had passed by the caskets, the pallbearers assembled in a back room while the immediate family said their farewells. There were six pallbearers for George's casket, it being extra long and weighty to accommodate his height and four for the much smaller Annie. Ned was with the group tending to George and Dewey with Annie.

After the caskets were placed in the hearse, it slowly began Annie and George's final trip through their beloved Paia. Once at the cemetery, the family took their place above the gravesite under a canopy. The pallbearers began carrying the caskets toward the site. Layla and Mr. Soo got out of their car, with Fiona joining them.

"Layla, are you sure you are going to be able to hold up at the gravesite?"

"Yes, I must see George and Annie safely placed."

Fiona gently hooked Layla's arm into hers and proceeded to the graveside ceremony. It was very brief, lasting less than ten minutes. Dewey came to Layla's side and drew into him so she was leaning on his shoulder. Ned held Fiona closely too. No one spoke after the service as they made their way to the cars. When they arrived, Dewey turned toward Ned and Fiona, saying, "We'll see you at the luau tonight. Take care going home."

Layla huddled next to Dewey in the back seat along with Mr. Soo. Ted drove them back to the hotel. They had a light lunch, then everyone went to their rooms to rest, the emotions of the past few hours casting weariness over all of them.

Mr. Soo and Ted sat on the lanai, gazing out onto the ocean. Mr. Soo was dressed in his usual long cargo shorts, tropical shirt, and tennis shoes. Ted was in faded dark denim Levi's, short-sleeved Western shirt, and cowboy boots, and Agnes joined them in white Capri pants, a Hawaiian blouse, and sandals.

Dewey walked to the lanai and said, "Well, folks, looks like we're ready to go. Ted, I'll drive since I know a back way to the bluff."

Dewey wore white denim pants and a pastel Hawaiian shirt. Layla joined the group and wore a halter dress that fell to just about her knees in greens and blues. The middle was all-elastic, which still fit even though she had lost weight.

They drove silently to the bluff, Dewey circling around the back way to avoid the large crowd going to the luau. Luckily, they found a parking place not too far from the bluff.

They were surprised to find Charlie Boone, his wife, and family greeting everyone as they entered. He introduced his wife and children, then introduced them to his sister, Jennie, and her family.

Jennie embraced both Dewey and Layla. "I want you both to know how much you meant to my parents. Every time we talked, they told us about something one or both of you were doing and how excited they were that your Paia home was next to theirs. I cannot begin to imagine the devastation you must be feeling about making the discovery. If there is ever anything my husband or I can do, please let us know."

"Thank you, Jennie, that is very kind of you to offer. Please accept our deepest sympathy on the loss of your parents."

They spoke awhile, then went over to the bar where they got a cold beer. As they were walking away, Fiona and Ned joined them.

"Did you meet Jennie and her husband?"

"Yes, and she was quite nice to both of us."

"I was surprised myself," said Fiona, "how charming she and her husband were. Of course, that doesn't reflect their parenting skills, which was what irked Annie and George."

Mrs. Steinmetz came up to Fiona and Ned, tears in her eyes. "This is the last thing I ever thought I would be returning to Paia for, the funeral of those lovely people. What a horrible thing to have happened. I wish you two were moving out of that area."

Ned and Fiona both hugged her, then Fiona said quietly, "We will be. Don't tell anyone. We are trying to keep it quiet for the time being. The gentleman that purchased Layla's home is selling his beach cottage, and we are moving there. It's in Paia but more out of town."

"Please don't dawdle, my dears. I don't like you two living so close to where the murders of both of those couples occurred."

"We won't, Mrs. Steinmetz, but we have so much to pack and now we have Mr. Soo's home to sell and will no doubt be asked to sell the Boones' home. We'll be fine. Please don't worry," said Ned.

After chatting for a while, Fiona and Ned drifted over to a table where Layla, Dewey, Mr. Soo, Agnes, and Ted sat.

"So far, this is turning into a tearful event," said Fiona. "They need to bring the food out or something. This is supposed to be a celebration of their lives."

"Honey, people are still streaming in. They will probably bring the food out shortly."

"We went over to the pit where those three big men were roasting the pigs. My, it was quite a sight, all covered in big palm leaves and steaming," said Agnes.

"They should be taking them out and pulling the pork," said Ned.

"Hope it's tender. Pork needs to be cooked well," said Ted.

"Don't worry about that. The brothers are the best pig roasters in Hawaii. Their roasted pigs are always done perfectly and tender."

"Mind if I join you?" asked the sheriff, pulling out a chair.

"Please do. We're glad to have your company," said Dewey.

"Smart of Donnie to have the foresight to have people park at the high school and bus them over. The street is really crowded with parked cars, clogging the town up. God forbid there's a fire. This bluff is getting packed. I noticed a bus coming over that was only half full, so maybe the crowd is letting up. This is all new to me. They don't do things like this where I'm from."

"It should be a lovely tribute to the Boones," said Mr. Soo.

"I wanted to speak with you folks to let you know that you are cleared to leave Maui as of Tuesday. We have your contact information in Salt Lake City, and if there are any more inquiries, we trust we can reach you there."

"No problem, Sheriff," said Layla. "We're glad to help."

"There is one interesting development. The other agencies have finally come around to my way of thinking that these crimes have been committed by a local."

"That's so troubling," said Mr. Soo.

"I agree with you, Mr. Soo, but it doesn't mean they have to live in Paia. It could mean they live in any one of the small neighboring towns or outlying areas."

"I like that scenario better," said Fiona.

"If you'll excuse me, I'm going to get something to eat. I want to be able to keep an eye on traffic once the ceremony is over. Should be quite a traffic tie-up," said the sheriff, shaking his head. "If I don't see you again before you leave, I want you to know I'll miss your visits, Mr. Soo. Layla, you added beautiful art to our community. And, Dewey, you were an excellent host. It's been my pleasure to know all of you." The sheriff shook hands with everyone and left to join the food line.

"I'm going find a quiet area, phone my pilot, and tell him we'll leave Tuesday morning," Dewey said, getting up from the table.

"I'm both happy and sad we're leaving," said Layla. "I can't stay here anymore. Too many painful memories, but I'm going to miss my home, the Visitors Center, and most of all, I'm going to miss you and Ned," Layla said, grabbing Fiona's hand.

"We'll come and visit, and there's a wedding in the near future."

"Yes, but it won't be as large as planned. Somehow, with Annie and George gone, the idea of a big wedding is gone. Something very small is all I want now but definitely with you and Ned attending."

"We'll be there. Just let us know the date."

"Maybe we should follow the sheriff's lead and get in the food line. Something is smelling mighty good," said Ted.

The group made their way to the food line, making room for Dewey when he returned.

"The pilot said leaving Tuesday morning would be fine. He's hiring a crew from the airport to load the boxes. It will be crowded, but we'll still have plenty of room in the main cabin. He will also see we have food brought on board. He's going to file a flight plan to leave at 10:00 a.m. Tuesday. We'll want to be sure we have an early breakfast, check out, and get to the airfield in plenty of time to get us and our luggage loaded on time. Gosh, this spread looks good. All contributed by the locals, what a lovely thing to do."

Ted pushed back from his plate, which he had loaded with pulled pork. "Man, that was the best pork I've ever eaten."

A group of Hawaiian musicians began playing. The program celebrated life and the Hawaiian tradition of giving back to others. George and Annie's life was briefly reviewed, focusing on their community outreach. The program lasted for almost an hour, and true to the sheriff's concern, a massive traffic jam occurred.

Dewey used the back roads to return to the hotel.

CHAPTER 97

The DewMaster jet soared away from Maui as Dewey looked out a window and saw the island drop from view. Layla sat in a lounge chair next to him, crying softly. Mr. Soo sat across on a sofa, his head bowed, hands clasped in his lap. Agnes and Ted sat side by side, each deep in their own thoughts.

When the pilot announced seat belts were no longer necessary, Dewey lifted the armrest between them and drew Layla to him.

"I'm going to make us something to drink," said Agnes, going forward to the galley.

She brought Mr. Soo a cup of hot tea, sat a tray a sweet rolls on a side table, and served coffee to the crew and everyone else in the cabin. Three hours out of Maui, Agnes readied the pre-prepared lunch the crew had brought on board. Everyone ate, then Mr. Soo, Agnes, and Ted played a card game to pass the time. Layla and Dewey sat holding on to each other.

When they landed in Salt Lake City, Ted went to the hangar and retrieved their SUV, helped to load luggage, then drove to the compound. Dewey had the pilots arrange to have the other items stored in the hangar where he would have Ted work with movers to bring them to his home.

Prior to arriving, Agnes had arranged to have the wing Mr. Soo would occupy opened, cleaned, and aired out. Ted and Dewey escorted him to his new home.

"My goodness, this is so big. This is like a home within a home."

"That's exactly what it was intended to be. I had this built for my parents, but my mom didn't like it, so Dad and I built the other house down the road. Unfortunately, we lost Dad before they could move in. It just sits empty. If you're not comfortable here, you are welcome to move into that house."

"I believe I will be very happy here," said Mr. Soo as he walked through the rooms. There was a large master bedroom with an en suite bath and a balcony that looked out over the backyard. There was a nice-sized kitchenette, another bedroom with bath, and a large living room with a walkout balcony.

"Ted will arrange to have everything you packed delivered tomorrow or the next day, if that is all right with you."

"That will be fine. I am very appreciative of your efforts to make me feel welcome. This is a lovely home and that backyard, I will enjoy working with Ted on it."

Ted had things delivered the following day, keeping both Layla and Mr. Soo busy sorting and putting things away. Dewey went to his office on the second day back and was relieved to find things in good shape, only several things needing his attention.

By the end of the first week, Agnes had hired two full-time ladies to help her with the cleaning and some of the cooking. Ted and Mr. Soo were busy making drawings of what the backyard's first acre would look like once they began their remodeling. Dewey suggested they go to Ted's favorite nursery and hire a landscape architect to make sure they didn't dig into underground pipes and verify anything done was up to code. Ted and Mr. Soo interviewed five different landscape architects and decided on a young lady originally from Japan who loved the outline Mr. Soo and Ted had drawn.

Layla kept busy fussing with all her things in her and Dewey's rooms. She finally began to eat a little more and help Agnes with the cooking. Toward the end of the week, she opened the carton with her drawing supplies and set them up on the sun porch, saying they would be ready when she decided to sketch again.

On his fourth day back at work, there was a slight problem in manufacturing that kept Dewey at the plant well into the night. Close to midnight, he arrived home, showered, and crawled into bed.

"I'm glad you're home. I was worried," Layla said, kissing him.

Dewey returned the kiss, and as his arm went around her, he realized she was without her usual nightshirt. "Honey, please tell me this is an invitation to make love to you."

"Oh yes!"

Dewey shot out of bed, throwing off his T-shirt and boxer shorts. They made love well into the morning, craving the closeness. Layla would swear this was the exact night she became pregnant.

Fiona and Ned arranged with Wade and Herb to purchase their home, and Fiona was wading through years of items, sorting and tossing. She and Ned would pack at night what she sorted, but during the day, she sent him to the golf course. One afternoon, she had to have one of Otis's tuna salad sandwiches and walked up the hill.

Otis saw her come in and sit at the counter. He motioned her to one of the empty booths. After her order was taken, he returned and said, "Fiona, I'm interested in buying Mr. Soo's home if it isn't way over what I could afford."

"You are? I thought you had a large lovely home several miles from here."

"I do, but you know I lost my wife a couple of years ago, the kids are married and live on the mainland, and I just rattle around in that big house. Besides, I spend more time here than at home. It would be nice to just walk up the hill to work. I believe my current home should sell for a good price, hopefully enough to afford Mr. Soo's."

"Let me call Ned, and we'll get right on this."

Otis went to bring Fiona her lunch, and she phoned Ned. "Ned, can you talk?"

"Sure can. I'm sitting here on the nineteenth hole, having a drink, waiting for you to call and tell me I can come home."

"You need to come over to Otis's right now and meet me here. You won't believe this, but he wants to buy Mr. Soo's home. You need to appraise his home to see how much he would realize to apply on the purchase of Mr. Soo's."

"Honey, do you know where Otis lives?"

"I have no idea, except Mr. Soo once said it was quite large and not too far from here."

"He lives in that beautiful Hawaiian-style home that sits off the road, you know the one you've always admired."

"I had no idea that was Otis's. That will sell for a very large sum. He'll have no problem affording Mr. Soo's."

"Stay there. I'm on my way."

Fiona caught Otis's eye and motioned him over. "I got Ned on the phone, and he's on his way here. He will give you an appraisal on your home, and considering where you live, I can almost guarantee you that you will be able to afford Mr. Soo's home."

"Great. I'll give Ned the key, and he can go over this afternoon. I would like to get things started right away."

When Ned returned home, he found Fiona preparing dinner. "He's going to get a bundle for that property. Besides the home, he also owns the five surrounding acres. That's enough to build several more elegant homes. I might know just the person to buy his home."

"I had no idea all that land was his. Ned, you've got to call and tell Mr. Soo. He will be thrilled his friend will be buying his home."

"You're right. It's rather early in the proceedings, but I think I will call him. I can also tell Layla her sale will be finalized next week."

Ned phoned Salt Lake City; Agnes answered. She called Layla to the phone and went to find Mr. Soo.

Ned told Layla the good news on the closing and told her Donnie would contact her when she could transfer her funds. When Mr. Soo got on the line, he was thrilled to hear about Otis buying his home. When all the business talk was concluded, Layla spoke with Fiona for a while and heard all about her packing woes.

Mr. Soo announced at dinner that Otis was buying his home.

About a month later, Layla's funds were transferred, and the sale of Mr. Soo's home was being finalized. Ted and Fiona were still packing but had taken possession of their new home, and Fiona was beginning to put her things away and decorate. She said she wanted everything move-in ready.

Mr. Soo, Ted, and their landscape architect had installed three fire pits around the patio and were laying a flagstone walkway that would lead to a gazebo, completing phase 1. Phase 2 was being put off until the spring.

Layla walked into the kitchen late one morning. "Agnes, I guess you'll have to make an appointment for me with a doctor. I've been sick for about a week now, and I even think I'm losing weight. I can't keep anything down. In fact, just smelling that coffee is making me, excuse me," she said, rushing off to the bathroom.

When she returned, she found crackers, a bottle of soda water, and a white sack on the counter for her. "What's in the sack, Agnes?"

"Something I believe you need, dear."

Layla opened the sack and peered in. "Oh my god," she said and rushed back to the bathroom.

Shortly, Agnes heard a loud yes coming from Layla.

Layla came out of the bathroom and asked Agnes for a baggie. "I want to show this to Dewey when he gets home. I believe we're going to have a quickie wedding," she said, laughing.

"I'll still need to see a doctor. Let's find me a good one. I guess we should call the wedding planner and see if she can put something together in a hurry, but I insist that Fiona and Ned be here."

"After you tell Dewey and see what he says about the wedding, we can call her tomorrow and see what she can put together in a hurry. Layla, I'm so happy for you both," Agnes said, hugging Layla.

That evening Dewey came home early, and Layla said she needed to speak with him privately. They went into his office and closed the door. Layla had her little white sack with her containing the baggie. She set it on Dewey's desk and told him to open it; there was a surprise in it for him.

He opened it and pulled out the baggie. He looked puzzled and asked, "What the heck is this?"

"You have no idea?"

"No, I never saw anything like it before."

"Oh, Dewey, I sometimes forget you computer folk can be a bit sheltered. This is a stick that I peed on, and the color it turned tells me that we're going to be parents."

Dewey held the baggie up and studied the stick. "This little thing told you that?"

"Yes, dear."

"Holy cow, you mean we're going to have a baby?"

"Yes, dear."

"How did this happen?"

"What? Surely you know how this happened."

"Yes, yes, of course. This is wonderful." He got up and gently hugged and kissed Layla, asking if she was feeling all right.

"Except for the dreadful morning sickness I've had for the last week or so, I feel great. I'm so happy, Dewey. You know how I've longed for a family. I was expecting to be married first, but this way is fine with me. We should get married before too long though."

"Want to fly to Vegas tomorrow? We can do that."

"No way, I want Fiona and Ned here. We can do something very simple. I'll call the wedding planner tomorrow and see what she can put together on short notice. Are you OK with that?"

"Anything you want," Dewey said with a goofy smile. "I'm so damned happy. The woman of my dreams is having my baby. Wow!"

CHAPTER 98

The next morning at breakfast, Dewey, Layla, and Agnes sat down for a chat; Dewey said he wanted to find the best baby doctor in the city for Layla. Agnes said she had already made an appointment for Layla. Next, they discussed their wedding plans. Dewey would invite his mom, but Layla said she would pass on inviting her parents. Not fancy enough for their tastes. She would e-mail them photos after the fact. Agnes shook her head, unable to comprehend such parents. They decided to be somewhat frank with the wedding planner and tell her that because of the past events in Paia, they wanted a simple ceremony with only a few close friends and family.

Layla decided to ask Fiona to stand with her, and Dewey would ask Mr. Soo. Layla asked Agnes to contact the wedding planner and make an appointment for her to come out and meet with them.

"When are you going to tell everyone about the baby?" asked Agnes.

"I'll wait until I see the doctor. Right now, it's just between the three of us."

Two weeks later, Layla had seen her doctor, who assured her everything was progressing nicely. Layla had Kyle forward her medical files to her new doctor, which necessitated telling him the news. He said he was very happy for both her and Dewey. Layla could tell by the tone of his voice it was meant in all sincerity. He told her Kim was doing slightly better; he was home with a live-in attendant. Layla said to pass on their good wishes and ended the call, sensing what their future lives would entail.

That night at dinner, Dewey made the announcement about the upcoming addition to the household and the soon-to-be wedding.

"Agnes, you didn't tell me," said Ted, looking surprised.

"It wasn't my place and you know now, so stop complaining."

"I'm so happy for all of us," said Mr. Soo, smiling broadly.

Later in the evening, Dewey got Mr. Soo alone and asked him to be his best man at the wedding. Mr. Soo was astonished and considered it an honor.

The following afternoon, Layla phoned Fiona who was still sorting. She first told her about the baby, causing twenty minutes of baby-related chatter. Next, she told her about the upcoming wedding plans and asked if her to be her matron of honor. Fiona was happy to be asked. Layla said Dewey would send a plane for her and Ned several days before the wedding, and they could stay with her and Dewey if that was fine with them.

Fiona said there shouldn't be a problem but would call her back after confirming the date with Ned, then asked what she should wear.

"Well, I really don't care. Remember, we had a special dress made for Annie, but there's not enough time for anything special, so whatever you have in your closet will be fine. I know with your good taste, you'll find something."

"I hope you don't think this is insensitive, but I would like to wear Annie's dress. I could e-mail you my measurements, and there should be enough time for alterations. I have a deep feeling of standing in for Annie. She would like that."

"Fiona, that's a beautiful thought. Yes, I believe Annie would like that. I'll contact the bridal shop, and when you call back after talking with Ned, I'll let you know."

When Fiona called back, she told her the date was fine with Ned. Layla said to e-mail her measurements direct to the shop so they would make the alterations, then gave her their e-mail address. They talked another hour, and finally, Layla said it was past her bedtime and she would be talking with her soon.

Upstairs, she told Dewey that Fiona and Ned had no trouble with the scheduling, then told him Fiona wanted to wear Annie's dress.

"Are you all right with that?"

"Very much so. Annie would approve, I know it."

Dewey walked over and placed his hand on Layla's stomach. "Speaking of feeling, how's our baby doing?"

"He's doing fine, growing bigger each day," Layla said, smiling.

"What's this he thing?"

"It's a boy."

"How do you know it's a boy?"

"Mother's intuition. I just know you will have a son. You better think of some names."

"I already have a name, figured that out right away. He'll be Jeffery George McMaster. Jeffery after my dad and George after George Boone."

"Honey, that's beautiful. I love it."

The next morning Dewey phoned his mother and told her about the wedding date and that it was to be a simple affair. He said he would send a plane for her, but he did not tell her about the baby, putting that off until she arrived and met Layla.

His mother was glad everything was moving forward; she had been worried after the disaster in Paia.

Dewey invited his two vice presidents and their spouses and his secretary and her husband; he asked Layla if she wanted to invite anyone else. She said no, she was happy with those invited.

Two weeks before the ceremony, the wedding planner arrived to go over the details. She informed Agnes that she and Ted were wedding guests and therefore would not be involved in food preparations, setup, or decorations. She would handle everything. There would be a sit-down dinner following the sunset wedding. The menu was reviewed, guests would receive a memento of the wedding, and a harpist would play at the ceremony.

On Monday before the Saturday ceremony, Dewey and Layla went to greet Fiona and Ned as they arrived from Maui.

Fiona rushed down the stairs, gently hugged Layla, placing her hand on Layla's tummy and asking how our baby was doing.

"He's doing great. I felt a small kick yesterday morning when I got out of bed."

"Definitely a boy," said Fiona.

Dewey backed the SUV up to load the luggage. When the pilots began unloading, Dewey turned to Ned, shaking his head in amazement.

"Dewey, it's Fiona," Ned said, making a helpless gesture. "She has to plan for any event."

"No problem. We have plenty of room in the SUV and at home," Dewey said, laughing.

"How are you folks doing?" asked Ned.

"The news about the baby brought us out of the sadness that had imbedded itself in our hearts. That and the excitement about the wedding, and next, we'll be putting a nursery together. Mr. Soo and Ted have about finished phase 1 of remodeling the backyard, only some odds and ends of planting to be done. Looks great too. I've been busy at work on some added refinements to our digital film processing, and like Mr. Soo says, life goes on."

"Fiona and I have been going like crazy. All of a sudden, I'm back in the real estate business almost full time, and Fiona has been getting our new home ready so that it's totally complete when we move in. When she says something has to be totally complete, we are talking down to the pictures on the wall and everything put away in the cabinets and closets. I'm thrilled to be here. First real rest I've had in ages," said Ned, laughing. "I have Otis's home sold. He also had the five surrounding acres. It's worth a fortune. He should get around twenty million clear when we're all done."

"My gosh, I bet he was surprised. Is he going to keep the diner?"

"He was thrilled and has no plans to get rid of the diner. That's his link to people. He's a happy man now, living so close and just serving the locals."

"Mr. Soo will be glad to hear that. Let's get you guys back to the house and unloaded."

When they drove up, Dewey was grateful Ted was there to help with the unloading. When he looked in and saw the mass of luggage, he decided to get a dolly and wheel everything in through the back door. He went off, shaking his head.

"This is amazing," said Fiona. "Here I pictured you living in some woody place with lots of logs. This is a mansion. Look at that view!" she exclaimed, walking into the living room and looking out the panorama of windows that took in the neighboring mountains.

"Ned, Fiona," said Mr. Soo, coming in from the kitchen, "I'm so happy you are here."

"Layla, where are you holding the ceremony?" asked Fiona.

"Here let me show you," Layla said as she walked out to the sunroom that encompassed a wide portion of the back section of the house. "Uncertain what the weather would be like, our wedding planner decided we would be safer having it in here at sunset. With the forest and mountains as a backdrop, it should be lovely."

"Definitely, the perfect place."

"Let me take you to your rooms so you can settle in before dinner."

Ned and Fiona followed Layla to their rooms consisting of a large sitting room, master bedroom, and lavish bathroom.

"This is better than a five-star hotel. Ned, look at this bathroom."

"Layla, this is lovely. I know we are going to enjoy our stay. I can already tell I'm going to sleep like a baby tonight," said Ned.

"Honey, you sleep like a baby every night."

The next morning Layla and Fiona went to the bridal shop. Fiona tried on her dress, and except for a hem adjustment, it fit perfectly. Both dresses would be delivered the next day.

That afternoon Dewey and Layla went to meet Dewey's mother at the airstrip. "I hope she likes me. I guess we'll know the right time to tell her about our baby."

"Don't worry, honey. She'll love you, and we'll know when to tell her about the baby."

Dewey's mother, Elizabeth McMaster, strode down the stairway toward Dewey; a tall shapely woman, tanned, with white-gray hair worn clipped short to her head. She hugged him and then stepped back to be introduced to Layla.

"Mom, this is the love of my life, Layla."

"Layla, I can't tell you how pleased I am to meet you. I know what you been through in your young life, and I believe you are a strong woman, which I might add, you will need to be to put up with this genius." Elizabeth then gave Layla a warm hug.

"I'm so happy we found each other. I'm very much in love with your son," Layla said, smiling up at Dewey.

"Mom, guess what? We're pregnant!"

Layla looked at Dewey, shock registering on her face.

"What?" exclaimed Elizabeth.

"You're going to be a grandma."

"That's wonderful. I couldn't be happier. Are you feeling all right, dear?"

"Yes, I'm doing fine, except for morning sickness, but my doctor assured me that will dissipate soon. He better be right because I'm a mess in the mornings."

"I'm sure that will be over shortly. You certainly look good and healthy. Dewey, you must look after her and make sure she takes good care of herself. Don't overdo things even if you feel you have a ton of energy."

"Don't worry, Mom. Agnes is hovering when I'm not there."

"Good," said Elizabeth, walking between Dewey and Layla, holding each of their hands as they made their way to the SUV.

When Layla and Dewey were alone, Layla turned to Dewey. "I thought we were going to wait until the right time to tell your mom about the baby. You blurted it right out."

"Sorry, sugar. Guess I got a case of fatherly pride. It just flew out of my mouth. Are you mad at me?"

"No, I was shocked but grateful she took it all so well."

"You and me both. Sometimes Mom can be a bit judgmental."

CHAPTER 99

Early Friday evening, the wedding planner and all the participants were having a rehearsal. The wedding planner asked Layla who was going to walk her down the aisle. A short trip though it may be, she felt Layla should be escorted.

Layla looked wide-eyed, then scanned the room. "There he is." Layla walked over to Ned. "I know you have two sons, and you probably never expected to walk a bride-to-be down the aisle, but would you be so kind as to escort me to Dewey?"

Ned beamed at Layla. He stood up and locked her arm through his. "My dear lady, it would be my pleasure."

"This is so lovely," said Fiona softly.

The rehearsal went well, and afterward, Dewey took everyone out to dinner.

As the harpist played a soft rendition of "Here Comes the Bride," a smiling Ned brought Layla down the aisle to Dewey. Vows and rings were exchanged. The reception dinner was lovely; when all the guests had departed, everyone else moved to the living room and began talking about a variety of subjects.

Fiona asked, "Are you two going on a honeymoon?"

"We've talked about that, but we both agreed we would be happiest staying home and getting settled into married life. Plus, we have a nursery to put together."

"I'm still plagued by morning sickness, and a honeymoon while being sick each morning doesn't sound like fun. I'll be happy here, and let's face it, the holidays aren't too far away."

"Don't mention that. The boys will be home for the holidays, and we haven't moved into our new home yet," said Fiona.

"Honey, if everything didn't need to be perfect, we would have moved several weeks ago."

"I've spent my whole career making other people's homes ready for them to move into, I can at least do that for us. Anyway, I figure, at the most, three weeks by the time we get back, we should be moved. Then I'll stage our old place and you can put it on the market."

"How many homes will that leave you to sell?"

"Mr. Soo's and Otis's homes are in escrow. The sale of your home and Layla's is complete. That leaves the Boones' and ours, once I get it on the market. Then hopefully, I can retire again and get back to my golf, which, I might add, has begun to suffer."

"Have you had any interest in Annie's and George's home?" asked Layla.

"No, it's a great property and the price is extremely low, but because of the publicity, it may take a year or so to sell. I hope it can be sold without having to tear it down, then I would sell a beachfront lot. That's the last consideration if it doesn't sell after a couple of years," said Ned.

"I hope that can be avoided," said Layla.

Early Tuesday afternoon, Ned and Fiona left for Maui. Fiona made Layla a promise that she and Ned would be out of their old home in three weeks.

Dewey's mom left the next day for California after getting a promise from Layla that she would call her if she needed her help when the baby came. Otherwise, she would visit about a month after the birth.

"We flew home in the luxury of a private jet, and I still feel drained," said Fiona, dropping down on the sofa. "Just leave the luggage in the bedroom, I'll put things away tomorrow."

"Tomorrow I meet with the buyers for Otis's property to get that finalized. That's a huge undertaking with a consortium and lots of money changing hands."

"Tomorrow I'm going to take Annie's dress to the dry cleaners, have it cleaned, and put in a storage bag. I enjoyed wearing it for Annie, and I thought it went well with my coloring."

"You looked absolutely beautiful. I was very proud of you."

"I'm anxious to get a set of the proofs from the wedding. I want to make sure we have a picture of you walking Layla down the aisle, one of me in Annie's dress, and one of the entire wedding party. I thought it was a lovely simple wedding in a beautiful setting. I certainly never imagined Dewey having such a magnificent home."

"He's a very rich man, surely you had to assume he lived in something other than a log cabin," Ned said, laughing.

"I imagine it's my perception of Salt Lake City and perhaps Utah in general. All I ever knew about it was the Grand Canyon, wilderness, and rock formations, and the photos Annie, George, and Layla showed us were of the trailer and the outdoors. After briefly seeing Salt Lake City, I'll have to adjust my thinking."

"You should call Gus Schwartz tomorrow and see if there are any furniture pieces ready to ship. If not, call your outlets and have them get a move on. I really do want to be out of here within three weeks. I want to get this home on the market."

"I had already planned to phone Gus and, if necessary, light a fire under some furniture salespeople. I don't like living as a minimalist. I keep looking for things that we've already taken to our new home. I want to get in our new home as much as you do. I've got to start working on our Christmas card list. I was hoping to reduce our current list of over two hundred, but since we seem to have gotten back into the real estate business, I'm going to have to enlarge the list. That, plus holiday shopping usually takes me several months. I'm wearing myself out just thinking of everything."

The last week at their old home was going by quickly.

"Honey, is the last box to go out tonight?"

"That's the last big box. I have a few kitchen items I want to drop off. It won't take us long to get these things put away, then over to Bird's. I can't wait for one of his big steaks. These piecemeal dinners in order to clean out the fridge has left me hungry for a hearty meal."

"Me too. I feel like celebrating the close of Otis's property. What a load off my mind."

"Sweetheart, you're going to make a huge commission on Otis's property. When we get settled, maybe we should think of going on a luxury vacation."

"Fiona, I would like nothing more, but let's at least get our home sold first. I don't believe the Boones' home is going to move for about a year. Not until people forget and only see a great beachfront property at a great price."

"When are you going to put the sign out for our home?"

"Since the brothers are moving the few items we are taking with us on Monday, I'll put the sign up on Tuesday and have ads in the papers this coming weekend. Just think, sugar, our last weekend in our old home. Any regrets?"

"No, because every time I look across the street, my heart sinks. Annie and George are gone. Dewey and Layla are in Salt Lake City and won't be back along with our dear Mr. Soo. I feel like we are stuck here all by ourselves. We, too, need to move on."

"That's exactly how I feel. I'll put this box in the car, and you can hand me the last box."

"Be careful taking that box. It is heavier than you think."

Just as Fiona warned Ned, he bumped into the screen, knocking it off track.

"Don't worry, I'll put it back on after I get this box in the car."

"I warned you," Fiona said, following Ned downstairs with her small box of items.

Ned came back upstairs and worked on the screen, trying to get it placed correctly on the track. "This damned thing is obstinate, but I think I've got it now."

Ned slid the screen close, emitting a high-pitched screech.

"My god, Ned, fix that. It sounds like nails scraping on a blackboard."

"It closes so we can lock up. Let's leave it for tonight and I'll fix it tomorrow. I think the track need to be cleaned out or something. I can see it better in the morning light, and besides, I'm really getting hungry."

"I guess that will be fine as long as the few neighbors remaining can live with a screech when we get home tonight."

"Well, they'll have to. I'll fix it tomorrow morning for sure."

Ned and Fiona left their home after locking up. They drove to their new home, put the items in the boxes away, and went to Bird's to enjoy dinner.

EPILOGUE

The Killer

On the way home, he stopped at a three-way stoplight. He sat in the right lane, window down, arm resting out the open window. A car pulled next to him in the left-turn lane. He glanced over and noticed Fiona Keller sitting in the passenger's seat. She looked over at the same time, noticing him.

"Good evening, Ms. Fiona."

"Good evening."

"I expect you folks will be moving soon?"

"This is our last weekend. We move on Monday. We've just taken some boxes over to our new home and are headed to Bird's for a steak dinner."

"Well, I'm glad you folks are moving on. I imagine it's been difficult for you to live across the street from the Boone home. There goes our light. You be careful now," he said and drove forward as the Kellers made their left turn.

"This is the night. That bitch has eluded me for the last time. I'll give myself two hours to get everything set and tuck myself into Joe Wong's carport. The murders at the Boone house slowed his rentals for this season. Good for me. It's working out perfectly," he mused out loud.

Once home, he checked the Tasers in his duffel bag to make sure they were charged, then made sure his action gear was packed. He left his place and went around to Baldwin, turned down the side street with his lights off, and quietly backed into the Wong's carport. He unloaded the Tasers from the duffel and put them on the back of his belt. He had his duffel at hand so he could grab it easily.

They were gone longer than he had anticipated, but when he saw them turn down the street and into their driveway, he slowly moved forward. He saw Ned put the car in the garage and Fiona wait for him to close the garage door. They walked upstairs together; he unlocked the screen door and pushed it open.

"My god, the noise, sounds like two male cats fighting over a female in heat," he mumbled.

Fiona said something to Ned, and then they both went inside, and Ned locked the screen door but left the slider open, letting fresh air into the house. He checked to make sure no cars were coming, no one was out walking a dog or generally being on foot, then he made his way across the street and up the stairs to the Kellers. He could hear the shower running. He saw Ned and rapped on the screen.

Ned walked toward the screen and opened it. "Is there a problem?"

"Yes, and I could use your help. May I come in?"

"Sure," he said, stepping back into the room.

Quickly, he brought the Taser out, and before Ned could make a move, he was hit in the chest with the charge. His body slumped to the floor but was caught and sat in the love seat to be arranged later.

The Kellers

When Ned and Fiona arrived home and unlocked the front screen, they both jumped at the screech.

"I'm going to take a shower. I got overheated with all that dancing. You go ahead and lock up," Fiona said, going into the bedroom.

She took off her dress and shoes, then walked into the bathroom and turned on the shower. Reaching into her bra, she unhooked her Beretta holster hidden between her underarm and breast. She laid it on the cabinet top and placed a towel over it to keep out any moisture. As she was ready to step out of her panties, she heard the screech of the screen. She wasn't sure with the shower running but thought she better check with Ned; that was too much noise for this time of night. Because she was in the habit of always having her Beretta with her, she unconsciously grabbed the towel and gun. She left the bathroom through the bedroom and into the hallway to the living room.

"You! What the hell have you done to my Ned?" Fiona said, her eyes wide at the sight of Ned slumped in the love seat with Taser wires still embedded in his chest.

"Now, Fiona, don't get excited," he said, reaching behind his back to find the second Taser.

"Hold it right there," Fiona said and took her shooting stance.

"You look mighty sexy in those skimpy undies," he said, smiling, hoping to distract her.

"I said stop right there."

He didn't stop. He drew the Taser out and took aim at Fiona.

Fiona dropped the towel, aimed quickly, and fired.

Her shot hit him directly between the eyes; he dropped the Taser, fell to his knees, then backward onto the floor.

Fiona stepped over the sheriff and rushed to Ned. "Oh, Ned, honey, stay with me. Look at me, please, Ned."

Fiona felt for a pulse and found one. She got up and dialed 911, saying, "This is Fiona Keller." She gave her address. "I've shot and killed the Paia murderer after he Tasered my husband Ned. You need to send the police and an ambulance immediately."

She hung up to go back to Ned's side.

Five minutes later, Danny came rushing up the stairs and into the house. "My god, Fiona, that's the sheriff lying on your floor. You shot him between the eyes."

"Damn right I did, after he Tasered Ned and had that other Taser out and was ready to hit me. That son of a bitch is our murderer."

"Oh lord, how could this be?" said Danny. "I've got to call the main office. The ambulance is coming. Fiona, I suggest you put some clothes on. You don't want to be seen in your panties and bra."

"Thank you, Danny. I forgot that's all I had on. I'll do that right now. I'm going in the ambulance with Ned, and don't even think of stopping me."

"Yes, ma'am."

The EMTs arrived and began working on Ned. They decided to leave the wires on and have them removed in the emergency room. They gave him some oxygen, and he started to come around.

Fiona dressed, came back into the room, and rushed to Ned's side. "Honey, you're awake. Thank God, I was so scared."

"Mrs. Keller, we need to get him to the hospital. You can come along in the ambulance."

Before they left, Danny gave the EMTs and the Kellers strict instructions not to divulge anything they had seen. The scene and circumstances must be kept under wraps for the time being.

At the hospital, Fiona was asked to wait outside the emergency room and was joined by two detectives from Five-O. They asked her questions until the emergency room doctor came out to speak with her. He said Ned was coming around nicely and that she could take him home; however, he would have burn marks on his chest that would need to be attended to by using a salve and dressing twice a day. Fiona said she could do that without a problem. The detectives told her it was impossible for her to return home for several days. That was fine, she had no intentions of going home but planned to phone Four Seasons and get a suite. First, she had to go home and pack clothes and toiletries and would not take no for an answer.

She called the hotel, securing a one-bedroom suite, then told the detectives they could drive her and Ned back to their home to pack. At this point, they realized they might just as well let her pack. She was a very determined lady.

When they arrived back at their street, it was roped off; bright lights had been placed around her home and that of Joe Wong's with the coroner's van parked in their driveway.

Fiona told the detectives the van would have to be moved so she could use their car to drive to the hotel. She packed quickly, loaded the car, then Ned was helped into the car.

When Ned was securely in bed, Fiona went out to their patio, surprised to see the sun slowly rising. She got out her cell phone and made the only call she would make for now.

When Agnes answered, she asked to speak with Dewey. "Dewey, I'm glad it's Saturday, and you're home. I have some unbelievable news to tell you, but I must warn you, I've been told I'm not to say a word to anyone. You must keep this between you folks. You'll understand once I tell you what's happened."

After relating the entire story to Dewey, he said, "Fiona, you're amazing. You saved both Ned and yourself. And you've killed a monster. I simply can't believe that he could have done such terrible things. He must have snapped somewhere along the line. This is hard for me to comprehend."

"Me too, Dewey. I'm going to hang up now, I'm exhausted. I just thank God my Ned is alive."

It took four weeks for the Kellers to get settled in their new home. Both their sons had rushed home to be with them during the days after Ned's injury. Fiona no longer felt the need to wear a concealed weapon.

The Investigation

There was no doubt the about sheriff's guilt. Upon inspection of his trailer, the charcoal from the Boones' and the bell that hung over the Okamotos' door was found. The head of the Maui Sheriff's Office deferred to Five-O because investigating one of their own, even thought he was not officially on the payroll but paid by the local citizens, was not allowed.

Five-O tried to keep a news blackout on events, but a reporter from a network news channel got someone to tell them it was the local sheriff who was the Paia murderer. Then all hell broke loose. There were newspeople coming over from the mainland. Because the news did not break until the evening, Hawaii time, it didn't make network stations until the following morning.

It did, however, make the early edition of the Fox Cable News Channel. They flashed a photo of the sheriff with a brief story and promised more news would follow as soon as their reporter from Oahu got to Maui.

Cyrus Blackfeather sat in his recliner, watching that news channel from Sitka, Alaska. He was in his late seventies, lived alone, and found his need for sleep dwindling. He saw the photo of the murdering sheriff, identified as former hero officer, Lester Phillips.

He sat forward quickly in his recliner and said out loud, "No damned way!"

He got up and called information, asking to be connected to the head Five-O investigator in Maui, regarding those murders. He had information on Lester Phillips.

"Sergeant Lee speaking, may I help you?"

"Sergeant, are you in charge of the murder investigation where you've named Lester Phillips as the killer?"

"No, sir, that's my boss, but he's on another call right now. Perhaps you can tell me what you needed."

"Well, I needed to tell you that is not Lester Phillips. I buried Lester and his wife over two years ago. I went to the funeral

630

myself and saw him in the coffin. I tend the local cemetery here, and I can tell you he has not left his grave."

"What is your name, sir, and where are you calling from?"

"My name is Cyrus Blackfeather, and I'm calling from Sitka, Alaska."

"My boss just hung up. He will want to speak with you. Just a second, I'll connect you."

Sergeant Lee rushed in and told his boss about the call and thought he should talk to Mr. Blackfeather; he agreed and answered the phone.

Cyrus repeated everything and told him he had better do more checking because he had made a bad identification.

The detective asked if he knew the name and phone number of the dentist Lester Phillips dealt with to send for copies of his dental records. Cyrus Blackfeather chuckled softly. "Can't help you there. No one can. Lester Phillips wore dentures for years."

"Oh lord," said the detective. Before hanging up, he got Cyrus Blackfeather's phone number and the name of the cemetery where Lester Phillips and his wife were buried.

Sergeant Lee phoned Lester Phillips's former boss in Reno, Chief Michael Burton. After speaking with him for several minutes, Sergeant Lee said he was e-mailing a photo from the coroner's office, and he would stay on the line while Chief Burton received the e-mail.

"Jesus, god!" Chief Burton exclaimed when he saw the photo. "That's not Lester Phillips. That's Bailey Frye, the serial killer everyone thought was killed in the blast and fire at the prison for the criminally insane where he was housed."

"Thank you, Chief Burton. We'll be getting back with you shortly, and please keep this quiet until you hear further from us."

Sergeant Lee went in to the detective's office and told him what Chief Burton said. "I don't understand, Sergeant. The fingerprints on file match those of Lester Phillips. How did things get so fucked up?"

"I'm calling the FBI. There are too many state lines being crossed here. We need to find out how Lester Phillips's fingerprints got replaced with those of Bailey Frye. That involves federal databases, out of our jurisdiction. Besides, there may be others involved who will need to be identified. This is a can of worms. Let them wiggle through."

After talking with the head of the Hawaii FBI, the detective was informed they would take over the case, and not a word should leak out about Bailey Frye. They would personally contact Mr. Blackfeather and Chief Burton to assure their cooperation on the news blackout.

Three weeks after the FBI case takeover, they assembled the Five-O detectives, the head of the Maui Sheriff's Office, and Danny Keno to give them the official findings. While Bailey Frye was institutionalized, his closest friend was a paranoid young man guilty of hacking into the Pentagon's computer, the European Union's monetary funds computer, and the president's personal iPad; he was a genius. He replaced Lester Phillip's photo and fingerprints with those of Bailey Frye. He, along with the deliveryman that brought the canister of gas into the prison, were killed in the blast, and because of the extreme heat, it was assumed Bailey Frye was incinerated; all that was found that identified him was a single molar.

Upon close microscopic inspection by the FBI lab, it was determined that the molar was extracted before the fire. This left Bailey Frye free to start a new life as Lester Phillips. The FBI believed that he somehow caused the avalanche that killed the Phillipses then waited until the right time to assume Lester's identify. That time came with the advertisement for a sheriff in Paia.

The FBI would be holding a press conference the following morning about the findings.

Donnie Munson

Danny Keno asked permission to tell Donnie Munson about the findings before he heard it on television. He felt since it was Donnie's initial plan to bring in a special sheriff to Paia, he deserved to hear the news from an official source. They all agreed it would be proper; however, he would need to keep the information to himself until after the news conference.

Danny got to the bank an hour before closing. He went into Donnie's office and closed the door. Donnie's appearance had not improved; he still looked thin and drawn. Finding out the sheriff had murdered four beloved people of the Paia community had taken a toll on Donnie in addition to the building of the Visitors Center.

Danny told him the whole story of Bailey Frye and his identity switch with Lester Phillips. Donnie sat at his desk in a state of shock. He finally got up and came around to the side of his desk. "I brought that monster into this town. I'm just as responsible for the murders as he is."

After saying that, he fell to his knees, grabbed his chest, and died immediately of a massive heart attack.

As far as Danny was concerned, Bailey Frye had committed another murder.

The McMasters

The news about the true identity of the sheriff had been a shock to everyone and, accompanied with the death of Donnie Munson, had left the household upset for days. But they had a nursery to put together, final plantings to get in, and Dewey was involved in his next video game. Layla finally got over her morning sickness, and she and Agnes were enjoying shopping trips for baby items.

Layla gave birth to six-pound, dive-ounce Jeffery George McMaster. It was a quick delivery, and all went well except for Dewey having to be taken out of the delivery room right before he fainted. He later admitted he got queasy at the sight of blood but promised to do better next time. Agnes replaced him and was with Layla when she delivered.

Mr. Soo and Ted were already planning a large playground area for the baby when he got older and had his friends over; it would be better than going to a park.

The Producer

When the FBI gave their news conference identifying Bailey Frye, the notorious serial killer, as the person who assumed the identity of the late Lester Phillips, the producer was immediately on the phone and called two of the top screenwriters in Hollywood. He flew them to Paia a couple of days later, assembled all the information he had, and told them to get busy on a script. The screenwriters would interview the locals.

The producer personally contacted Ned Keller and asked if he and Fiona would allow themselves to be interviewed for a movie script he was working on. After a discussion, they felt obligated because they had sold the Steinmetz property to the producer and had made a hefty commission. They were interviewed for two days.

The producer made several attempts to get interviews with Layla, Dewey, or Mr. Soo, but none of his calls were returned.

He spoke with MayLee, Donnie Munson's wife, who agreed to be interviewed because she wanted Donnie's memory to be in a favorable light.

Film crews were busy filming exterior shorts. Associate producers were getting a slew of permits required by the State of Hawaii, the Island of Maui, and the City of Paia.

Eight weeks after the screenwriters arrived, filming began on the motion picture, featuring big-name stars in an ensemble-type cast.

Homes for Sale

After the filming ended, a couple from the Midwest were on the Maui stop of a cruise. They rented a car for the drive to Hana and stopped at Paia to see the place where the murders occurred and where the film had just finished being made. They were enchanted by the town; it was charming, and the people were friendly and folksy. At the Visitors Center, a docent told them where the murders happened, and they drove to look at the homes. They liked the looks of the Kellers' home and phoned the number on the For Sale sign.

Ned Keller answered the phone and felt it was probably lookie lous but told them he would be there in about ten minutes to show the home. They introduced themselves to Ned and told him they were retired after selling their large farm to a co-op and wanted to move to a warmer climate. They wanted a friendly town and to be near the center of town. They said their former home was fifty miles from the nearest town, and in the harsh winter months, they might be marooned for two or three weeks without being able to make it into town. They found the home charming and just right for them. Ned was obligated to tell them about what had happened across the street and at his home. They told him they already knew, and since the murderer was no longer alive, they had no worry.

Ned wasn't optimistic when they told him they had to get back to their cruise ship but would be in contact and was surprised to hear from them several days later. They had ended their cruise, changed their flight back home, and were flying over from Oahu to Maui the next day. They met again with Ned, settled on a price, telling him they would pay cash. Ned was amazed, and six weeks later, the couple moved into the Kellers' former home.

Three months later, he received a call from a lady wanting to see the Boone home. Ned was met by a couple in their midthirties; he was a financial advisor who worked from his computer at home and she, a stay-at-home mom raising two young sons.

They toured the home, and Ned was again obligated to relate the history of the area. The woman told Ned they knew of the past, but when she saw the home, she had to see the inside and feel the home. She said she would contact the local Catholic priest and have him bless each room and each deck of the home if they wanted to purchase the property.

She told Ned she was very intuitive and felt their family would be happy there. When Ned told them the price included a Cadillac Escalade, they agreed that very day. Nine weeks later, the family moved into the Boones' former home.

Three months later, Ned and Fiona left on a luxury European holiday.

Paia

After the murders and the naming of Bailey Frye as the perpetrator, Paia was on everyone's must-see list. Business was brisk and only became brisker when the movie cast and crew took over. The Visitors Center was packed; the food court always had a line. The crafters were overwhelmed with sales bringing in more money than anyone anticipated. The two main hotels were always booked. An independent film was being made on windsurfing. Paia was bustling.

The only person unhappy with all the business was Otis, who once again lamented he was back to serving "Those pesky tourists!"

Printed in the United States
By Bookmasters